Heroes in the Wind: From Kull to Conan

Robert Ervin Howard (1906–36) ranks among the greatest writers of action and adventure stories. The creator of Conan the Cimmerian, Kull of Atlantis, Solomon Kane, Bran Mak Morn, El Borak, and many other memorable characters, Howard wrote well over a hundred stories for the pulp magazines of his day, in a career that spanned barely twelve years. He shot himself on 11 June 1936 and died without ever regaining consciousness. His mother died the following day.

John Clute has been writing criticism and encyclopedias in the field of the fantastic for many years. His latest book is *Canary Fever: Reviews* (2009). Scholarly recognitions include the Pilgrim Award and the ICFA Distinguished Guest Scholar Award. Forthcoming are a new collection of reviews and essays, *Pardon This Intrusion: Fantastika in the World Storm*, and the third edition of *The Encyclopedia of Science Fiction*.

CU00951909

Heroes in the Wind:
From Kull to Conan
The Best of Robert E. Howard

Selected with an Introduction by John Clute

PENGUIN BOOKS

PENGUIN CLASSICS

Published by the Penguin Group
Penguin Books Ltd, 80 Strand, London WC2R ORL, England
Penguin Group (USA) Inc., 375 Hudson Street, New York, New York 10014, USA
Penguin Group (Canada), 90 Eglinton Avenue East, Suite 700, Toronto, Ontario, Canada M4P 2Y3
(a division of Pearson Penguin Canada Inc.)
Penguin Ireland, 25 St Stephen's Green, Dublin 2, Ireland
(a division of Penguin Books Ltd)
Penguin Group (Australia), 250 Camberwell Road, Camberwell, Victoria 3124, Australia
(a division of Pearson Australia Group Pty Ltd)
Penguin Books India Pvt Ltd, 11 Community Centre, Panchsheel Park, New Delhi – 110 017, India
Penguin Group (NZ), 67 Apollo Drive, Rosedale, North Shore 0632, New Zealand
(a division of Pearson New Zealand Ltd)
Penguin Books (South Africa) (Pty) Ltd, 24 Sturdee Avenue, Rosebank, Johannesburg 2196, South Africa

Penguin Books Ltd, Registered Offices: 80 Strand, London WC2R ORL, England

www.penguin.com

This edition first published in Penguin Modern Classics 2009
1

Selection and introduction copyright © John Clute, 2009
All rights reserved

The moral right of the author and editor has been asserted

Set in 11.25 / 14pt Monotype Dante
Typeset by Palimpsest Book Production Limited, Grangemouth, Stirlingshire
Printed in England by Clays Ltd, St Ives plc

ISBN: 978-0-141-18943-7

www.greenpenguin.co.uk

Penguin Books is committed to a sustainable future
for our business, our readers and our planet.
The book in your hands is made from paper
certified by the Forest Stewardship Council.

Contents

Contents

Acknowledgements

I would like to thank Rusty Burke of the Howard Foundation, and Leo Grin, editor of *The Cimmerian*, for information and good advice; Lorna Toolis, Mary Canning and Annette Mocek of the Merril Collection in Toronto, Canada, for supplying scans of material from *Weird Tales*; and Rob Roehm and Paul Herman for scans of additional material. I would also like to thank Mariateresa Boffo and Jill Foulston of Penguin Books.

'Recompense' is taken from *Weird Tales*, November 1938; 'The Shadow Kingdom' from *Weird Tales*, August 1929; 'The Mirrors of Tuzun Thune' from *Weird Tales*, September 1929; 'Kings of the Night' from *Weird Tales*, November 1930; 'Worms of the Earth' from *Weird Tales*, November 1932; 'The Dark Man' from *Weird Tales*, December 1931; 'The Footfalls Within' from *Weird Tales*, September 1931; 'Pigeons from Hell' from *Weird Tales*, May 1938 (written 1934); 'Graveyard Rats' from *Thrilling Mystery*, February 1936; 'Vultures of Wahpeton' from *Smashing Novels*, December 1936; 'The Tower of the Elephant' from *Weird Tales*, March 1933; 'Queen of the Black Coast' from *Weird Tales*, May 1934; 'A Witch Shall Be Born' from *Weird Tales*, December 1934; and 'Red Nails' from *Weird Tales*, July / October 1936.

Introduction

In the end it may boil down to a question of trust. How could anyone in this seared and wary day and age ever trust Robert E. Howard enough to read him? He was ignorant: a Texas boy who hadn't seen much more of the world than the hardscrabble plains surrounding the early twentieth-century small towns he lived in all his life. He didn't really have time to grow up: having more or less stopped writing before his thirtieth birthday, he was dead in months, hardly weaned, unmarried. He was a hack who published hundreds of stories in a wide range of 1920s and 1930s American pulp magazines with atrocious illustrations between the acne ads; and he would write anything for a buck, or so it seemed, as long as he could give his protagonists mighty thews: boxing stories, Westerns, horror, sword and sorcery (which it is true he more or less invented). But even within this world he was not particularly prominent: no book by Robert E. Howard was ever published in his lifetime, though three or four novels had already been released in serial form. So Robert E. Howard was an ignorant, coarse-grained, cynical bottom-feeder hack barely out of his teens before he began to peak. True? Is this a portrait of someone we could ever trust to marshal our dreams? Is there the slightest chance that Howard himself thought his life and work worthy of such trust?

There is every chance.

When it addresses the complex fuzzy contract between writer and reader, literary criticism (after Wayne C. Booth) normally

and rightly now makes reference to the 'figure' of the Implied
Author, a kind of ghost artefact with legs who negotiates
aspects between the written and the read. Normally and rightly,
authors are assumed to create an embodied voice which readers
identify (naively or sophisticatedly) as the speaker of the tale;
but I think there is more to the Implied Author than this, as far
as the actual reader in action is concerned. In our hearts, most
of us incorporate the Implied Author more deeply into the
dreamwork of the act of reading than simply understanding
that it is not the 'real' author, in his or her existential entirety,
who speaks to us. Most of us also draw on deeper structures
when we read, thinking of Implied Authors as ferrymen of a
sort: hypnopomps who guide us through the night inside the
head, across the river of the mind, into the chamber where stories sound. I think that when we are in the act of reading we
retain some primitive sense of being *carried*, and that some form
of creative collaboration with this ferryman is intrinsic to the
suspension of disbelief. Why look, there's our own Marcel
Proust, in his sealed chamber, tracing memory particles in the
charged air over the Paris that has left him; there's Henry James,
decanting interminable velleities to his stenographer/typist,
passages which even now come astonishingly alive when we
read them aloud; there's James Joyce, peering nearsightedly at
each syllable, like Richard Dadd touching up the eye of a fairy;
there's Anthony Trollope, setting his clock by the number of
words he'd written that a.m.; there's Georges Simenon, writing
a chapter a day in a closet for a week till the completed novel is
ready for cutting.

And here is a young man in rural Texas, late at night in his
bedroom, typing a story. So caught up is he in the thrust of creation that (as his neighbours have attested) he is shouting the
tale aloud into the night as he works. Every word he types is
being sung to every reader he will ever have. If I had never read
a word he had written, this would have been enough for me to

start. I would have loved him already, because he was a teller. Having read Robert E. Howard before learning that he sang Conan in the night, I love him all the more. Who could ask more of the Implied Author you allow inside, than that he be a hypnopomp so embedded in the tale he wants to tell you that he seems beside himself? If you cannot take the gamble of listening to a man who so desperately wants to carry you with him, who can you trust?

Howard is a writer who composes in a passion, and so inevitably there are burdens he wants to convey to us. Whether or not he succeeds will depend on the stories themselves, of course. He did not emerge full-grown upon the scene, and quite a few of the tales he shouted into the night were clearly apprentice-work. But his output increased as he gained competence and markets, and most of the 160 or more stories he sold to the magazines were written during his short-lived prime, from about 1928 to 1935. Even some of these are of relatively little interest. (I for one find his boxing stories, for all their bellowing exuberance, fatally undercut by the viciousness and pathos of the subject matter.) Some promising tales simply don't quite come off (as though Howard had an attack of laryngitis). But that leaves dozens upon dozens of tales in which he can be heard: like some dawn magus with electrifying news to impart. There is an icy Weltschmerz to even his early sword and sorcery tales – those featuring Bran Mak Morn or King Kull – that colours every passage of blood and thunder, and illuminates storylines which sound cartoonlike in synopsis. (It is central to any understanding of Howard to realize that his stories read hugely better than synopsis can convey.)

As for the late work, no one could possibly read the novellas from 1935, from just before he stopped writing – the two finest, 'Vultures of Wahpeton' and 'Red Nails', are reprinted here – without sensing that the ferryman had more on his mind than simply transporting us into dreamlands of tooth and claw, where a man had to be a man with a Big Stick, or die. It may have been as simple and crude as an intuition that to be a whole man in Texas was to wear a Cloak of Nessus; it may have been a somewhat crudely expressed but ultimately haunting suspicion that the twentieth century was not going to work out. I think it is pretty clearly both; some intimation of this dual doom shapes *The Whole Wide World*, Dan Ireland's fine 1996 film about Howard, which he based on *One Who Walked Alone: Robert E. Howard, the Final Years* (1986), a memoir by Novalyne Price Ellis (1908–99), the only woman Howard ever dated seriously. I think he was a claustrophobe caught in the claws of the world; that Conan may have been his last attempt to imagine cleaner air. In the end, though, he could not breathe, and stopped himself from trying.

Robert Ervin Howard was born 22 January 1906 in Peaster, Texas, somewhere west of Fort Worth; his father was an itinerant doctor, his mother was sick. There was tuberculosis in her family; there were mood attacks; for the whole of her son's life she remained ill. Mother and son were very close, but it is a cheap shot to assume that this closeness – and the threat that her death would terminate it – defined Howard's life and his own death. Certainly there were moments of family-romance intensity; but there is a growing consensus in Howard studies that a clearly unhealthy familial intimacy may have contributed to, but comes very short of explaining, the exorbitant intensity of his emotional and creative life; the Tourette's-like exaggerations of his behaviour with friends and relations, an anguished ill-fittedness Vincent D'Onofrio captures superbly in the film; the deep cultural pessimism that surges through the work; or the frequent, calm, clearly articulated statements that fairly soon he would end his own life.

After years of nomadic drift – probably due to his father's need to gain some financial security to pay for his wife's illnesses – in 1919 the small family finally landed in Cross Plains, where

Howard would spend the rest of his days. He had already begun to write stories and poems; it is not recorded whether or not he wrote them aloud. As a teenager he thought of himself primarily as a poet; he was never a very good one, though 'Recompense' – written towards the end of his life, and reprinted here – is a strikingly accurate self-portrayal: 'I have not died as men may die, nor sinned as men have sinned, / But I have reached a misty sky upon a granite wind.' In general he wrote the kind of poetry one might expect from a person whose list of favourite poets included not only Walter de la Mare and Rudyard Kipling and Siegried Sassoon, but also Bret Harte and Alfred Noyes and Robert W. Service. It is perhaps lucky that at the age of eighteen he made his first professional sale of a story, and concentrated mostly on fiction for the rest of his life. He never left the family home. In 1930 he began an extensive, hugely illuminating correspondence with H. P. Lovecraft, another man whose personal life had the skewed intensity of the outsider artist, but whose work also spoke eloquently and professionally to a contemporary audience. The correspondents shared a disgust with twentieth-century America (and a gloom about the future of the world as a whole) which might have seemed grotesquely avid then, even at the heart of the Great Depression, but which eighty years later seems far less eccentric. In 1933 Howard met Novalyne; the relationship had foundered by 1935. He gave up on Conan the Barbarian. His mother sank into a terminal coma in June 1936. He had already made it clear he was staying alive because of his financial responsibility to her; this reason had now expired. On Thursday, 11 June 1936, in Cross Plains, Robert E. Howard shot himself through the head. The ferryman is all this person. I think he wants to speak to us.

Some cobwebs must be swept away, however, before we find the pure quill of the man. The stories assembled in this collection are (it's hoped) among the best of those Howard completed: thirteen stories and one poem out of more than 160 publications, a little less than 10 per cent of his primary output. Nothing published after 1938 – which is to say nothing that Howard had not himself signed off on and sold to *Weird Tales* or some other contemporary magazine before his death – is reprinted here. In all cases, the primary copy text has been the original magazine version. In his first years as a professional writer, Howard could be careless about presenting his work to editors in a form they could accept without feeling they needed to intervene; but, for almost all of the stories printed here, the first of them published in 1929 and the bulk of them written late in his career, the first magazine publication matches very closely indeed to surviving manuscripts. By 1929 or 1930, Howard had become an extremely professional worker who meant exactly what he said; and what he meant to say got printed. No subsequent readings or edits of Howard's work have therefore been accepted.

The story of Howard's posthumous career – from the decade of obscurity immediately following his death through to the extraordinary popularity of various versions and extensions of his work in recent decades – falls outside the central remit of this collection, which is to present a shaped sample of his best work in texts he would recognize. High points in the recovery and re-creation of the man and his oeuvre include Arkham House's well-selected *Skull-Face and Others* (1946), though it focuses perhaps too heavily on early work, before Howard had begun to find out how far he could go with Conan, how far he could shout Conan aloud through the nightmare of Texas. Real problems began in 1950, when Gnome Press started to release its six-volume set of Conan tales, as these volumes, which incorporate a large number of editorial interventions on the part of L. Sprague de Camp, mark the beginning of the Conan industry. By the end of the twentieth century, a vast mountain of work was in print: original stories, of course, though often modified; plus recensions and renamings and revisions and rewritings and wirings-together of material Howard had never himself signed off on: drafts from his bottom drawer, fragments, rejected passages, orts. More recently the tide has ebbed. The most conspicuous evidence of this happy retreat to basics is a two-volume assembly, *The Best of Robert E. Howard*, published by Ballantine Books in 2007, which is restricted to words Howard himself wrote. Our own decision to take magazine versions as copy text was influenced by a similar use of magazine texts by Ballantine's text editor, Rusty Burke. Spelling inconsistencies and typographical errors in the current selection have been corrected; and I am more willing than Burke to close line spaces within the text – some of them imposed by the original magazine editors to shape their own double-column pages – where they impede the narrative flow. But there is a consensus about the basic texts.

The Ballantine edition does include a number of posthumous works – stories and poems that Howard had not himself sold – and some fragments. Some of this material is extremely worthwhile, but it remains clear to me that to a remarkable extent Howard shaped his own oeuvre; and that there is some chance that when he stopped doing serious work, by the end of 1935, he had in fact finished it. After 'Recompense', which feels to me like a statement of principle and an epitaph before the fact, the selection presented here is divided into three parts.

Part I: Black Dawn includes five tales, none of them over about 10,000 words. (Howard was never comfortable with the novel, perhaps through lack of time; his most powerful and shapely stories seem to hover around 25,000 words.) 'The Shadow Kingdom' (1929) features Kull, king of Valusia, a usurper from fabled Atlantis, a man whose gaze is like iron, a brooder. There is some fustian in the tale, as Howard only slowly mastered the pulp habit of petticoating dark thoughts in florid adjectives; but the cosmic terror of the climax, the ontological insecurity generated by the shapechanging Secret Master aliens, comes across with near absolute conviction. Kull's later existential crisis – in

'The Mirrors of Tuzun Thune' (1929) – neatly grafts a sickly chinoiserie on to the Nordic chiaroscuro of the first tale. Kull appears once more, as a once and future king figure, in 'Kings of the Night' (1930), whose main protagonist is Bran Mak Morn, Howard's second starter hero, leader of the Picts in their ultimately doomed refusal to knuckle down to Rome. The contours of a crude but powerfully affecting contrast between the kinetic hero caught like Laocoon or Gulliver in the coils of the mundane world, and the debilitating allure of civilization, here takes preliminary shape. As a philosophical argument, one articulated in the correspondence with Lovecraft, this is dangerous nonsense; as a spinal cord giving nerve to the longing to escape from prison, Howard's binary is very highly charged indeed, and shapes the savage horror of 'Worms of the Earth' (1932). 'The Dark Man' (1931) carries Bran Mak Morn out of his torn time to a point dangerously adjacent to the claustrophobia of mundane history, the world closing in: no brilliant thrust of axe and parry (by now Howard had become perhaps the most word-perfect, consistent, unrelenting, irresistibly succinct narrator of violent action ever to write in English) can save the hero from the night.

Part II: Dark Interlude reduces the pressure, for a moment. In 'The Footfalls Within' (1931), Solomon Kane, a haunted Puritan devourer of evil, survives a blasphemous invasion of the past in desert sands; 'Pigeons from Hell' (1934) is a horror tale haunted by the energy of its telling; 'Graveyard Rats' (1936) superbly translates trite grand guignol and melodramatic encounters into an oneiric vision of how the world claws its victims into obedience or death; but 'Vultures of Wahpeton' (1936) is something altogether harsher and more incandescent than the shorter works presented here. Ostensibly, it is a Western tale, with good guys and bad guys, a heroine no better than she should be but sporting a heart of gold, and loot, and gangs, and shootouts. Finally, however, we are left with a sense of the profound entrapping starkness of the world: like an ideogram of some Jacobean tragedy, the tale systematically strips every character (except the protagonist) of any pretence that their 'civilization' is anything but a sham, then kills them off. To read the story is like watching a train wreck, but a train wreck in a magic realist dream: every detail of the disaster fixes in the eye like poison.

In Part III: High Noon we reach Conan at last, and it is possible to relax, because we sense that Howard has come home. In Conan – a black-maned, blue-eyed, lithe but massive, rumbustious, highly sexed, unstoppable warrior renegade and buccaneer and ruler – he had a figure he could ride, a semblance he could shape himself around. It is now possible to think of Howard singing in Texas, as though to break free of a modern, secular, reduced world, a world that the closing of the American Frontier has evacuated. The first of the Conan tales, 'The Tower of the Elephant' (1933), is pure joy, an escapade in a Land of Fable with death all around but Rescue at the heart of things. 'Queen of the Black Coast' (1934) may be the most perfect tale Howard ever wrote: not a word too long; not a moment without a ripple of something moving within; panther dense. Eros is unsweetened for once, entirely naked and without stint. The ending is grim, but without melodrama. The hero continues. He can do so. He is unbound. 'A Witch Shall Be Born' (1934) is, on the other hand, a superb tale of bondage: the princess whose life has been eaten by her double; Conan himself crucified, nails driven through his wrists and ankles; enemies whose motives for encumbering the world are sophisticated beyond reason. It is all a nightmare (though it ends with Conan in the ascendent, as it must); and in hindsight it reads like an intimation of the closing of the prison doors upon its author.

We end with the great 'Red Nails' (1936), almost the length of a short novel, the culmination of Howard's career. As in 'A Witch Shall Be Born', the world is in a state of bondage, of claustrophobia. Conan and his woman arrive at a vast city in a ruined landscape. Once inside they find it is not a city but a preternaturally huge and airless edifice, various quarters of which have been occupied for centuries by dwindling tribes, each tiny devolved culture built around hatred of its neighbours. Nothing happens inside this Lost World dystopia but death and more death. Villains and demons caper in the shadows. A succubus longs for the blood of the heroine. There are whippings and torture. In the end, Conan cleans the stable like some figure of myth.

But just as in 'Vultures of Wahpeton', the world of 'Red Nails' is an evacuated waste land. Conan's sword may sing in the night; Howard's readers may long for the unkillable hero to make another astonishing somersault out of penury and bondage; the editors of *Weird Tales* may beg for more. But this time it really is the end. We read and reread 'Red Nails' because it is direr and has more storytelling energy than we can quite imagine. But every reading tells us what is truly happening here. Robert E. Howard is singing us across the Styx.

Prelude

Recompense

I have not heard lutes beckon me, nor the brazen bugles call,
But once in the dim of a haunted lea I heard the silence fall.
I have not heard the regal drum, nor seen the flags unfurled,
But I have watched the dragons come, fire-eyed, across the
 world.

I have not seen the horsemen fall before the hurtling host,
But I have paced a silent hall where each step waked a ghost.
I have not kissed the tiger-feet of a strange-eyed golden god,
But I have walked a city's street where no man else had trod.

I have not raised the canopies that shelter revelling kings,
But I have fled from crimson eyes and black unearthly wings.
I have not knelt outside the door to kiss a pallid queen,
But I have seen a ghostly shore that no man else has seen.

I have not seen the standards sweep from keep and castle wall,
But I have seen a woman leap from a dragon's crimson stall,
And I have heard strange surges boom that no man heard
 before,
And seen a strange black city loom on a mystic night-black
 shore.

And I have felt the sudden blow of a nameless wind's cold
  breath,
And watched the grisly pilgrims go that walk the roads of
  Death,
And I have seen black valleys gape, abysses in the gloom,
And I have fought the deathless Ape that guards the Doors of
  Doom.

I have not seen the face of Pan, nor mocked the dryad's haste,
But I have trailed a dark-eyed Man across a windy waste.
I have not died as men may die, nor sinned as men have sinned,
But I have reached a misty sky upon a granite wind.

I

Black Dawn

The Shadow Kingdom

1   A King Comes Riding

The blare of the trumpets grew louder, like a deep golden tide surge, like the soft booming of the evening tides against the silver beaches of Valusia. The throng shouted, women flung roses from the roofs as the rhythmic chiming of silver hoofs came clearer and the first of the mighty array swung into view in the broad white street that curved round the golden-spired Tower of Splendor.

First came the trumpeters, slim youths, clad in scarlet, riding with a flourish of long, slender golden trumpets; next the bowmen, tall men from the mountains; and behind these the heavily armed footmen, their broad shields clashing in unison, their long spears swaying in perfect rhythm to their stride. Behind them came the mightiest soldiery in all the world, the Red Slayers, horsemen, splendidly mounted, armed in red from helmet to spur. Proudly they sat their steeds, looking neither to right nor to left, but aware of the shouting for all that. Like bronze statues they were, and there was never a waver in the forest of spears that reared above them.

Behind those proud and terrible ranks came the motley files of the mercenaries, fierce, wild-looking warriors, men of Mu and of Kaa-u and of the hills of the east and the isles of the west. They bore spears and heavy swords, and a compact group that marched somewhat apart were the bowmen of Lemuria.

Then came the light foot of the nation, and more trumpeters brought up the rear.

A brave sight, and a sight which aroused a fierce thrill in the soul of Kull, king of Valusia. Not on the Topaz Throne at the front of the regal Tower of Splendor sat Kull, but in the saddle, mounted on a great stallion, a true warrior king. His mighty arm swung up in reply to the salutes as the hosts passed. His fierce eyes passed the gorgeous trumpeters with a casual glance, rested longer on the following soldiery; they blazed with a ferocious light as the Red Slayers halted in front of him with a clang of arms and a rearing of steeds, and tendered him the crown salute. They narrowed slightly as the mercenaries strode by. They saluted no one, the mercenaries. They walked with shoulders flung back, eyeing Kull boldly and straightly, albeit with a certain appreciation; fierce eyes, unblinking; savage eyes, staring from beneath shaggy manes and heavy brows.

And Kull gave back a like stare. He granted much to brave men, and there were no braver in all the world, not even among the wild tribesmen who now disowned him. But Kull was too much the savage to have any great love for these. There were too many feuds. Many were age-old enemies of Kull's nation, and though the name of Kull was now a word accursed among the mountains and valleys of his people, and though Kull had put them from his mind, yet the old hates, the ancient passions still lingered. For Kull was no Valusian but an Atlantean.

The armies swung out of sight around the gem-blazing shoulders of the Tower of Splendor and Kull reined his stallion about and started toward the palace at an easy gait, discussing the review with the commanders that rode with him, using not many words, but saying much.

'The army is like a sword,' said Kull, 'and must not be allowed to rust.' So down the street they rode, and Kull gave no heed to any of the whispers that reached his hearing from the throngs that still swarmed the streets.

'That is Kull, see! Valka! But what a king! And what a man! Look at his arms! His shoulders!'

And an undertone of more sinister whisperings: 'Kull! Ha, accursed usurper from the pagan isles' – 'Aye, shame to Valusia that a barbarian sits on the Throne of Kings.' . . .

Little did Kull heed. Heavy-handed had he seized the decaying throne of ancient Valusia and with a heavier hand did he hold it, a man against a nation.

After the council chamber, the social palace where Kull replied to the formal and laudatory phrases of the lords and ladies, with carefully hidden, grim amusement at such frivolities; then the lords and ladies took their formal departure and Kull leaned back upon the ermine throne and contemplated matters of state until an attendant requested permission from the great king to speak, and announced an emissary from the Pictish embassy.

Kull brought his mind back from the dim mazes of Valusian statecraft where it had been wandering, and gazed upon the Pict with little favor. The man gave back the gaze of the king without flinching. He was a lean-hipped, massive-chested warrior of middle height, dark, like all his race, and strongly built. From strong, immobile features gazed dauntless and inscrutable eyes.

'The chief of the Councilors, Ka-nu of the tribe, right hand of the king of Pictdom, sends greetings and says: "There is a throne at the feast of the rising moon for Kull, king of kings, lord of lords, emperor of Valusia."'

'Good,' answered Kull. 'Say to Ka-nu the Ancient, ambassador of the western isles, that the king of Valusia will quaff wine with him when the moon floats over the hills of Zalgara.'

Still the Pict lingered. 'I have a word for the king, not' – with a contemptuous flirt of his hand – 'for these slaves.'

Kull dismissed the attendants with a word, watching the Pict warily.

The man stepped nearer, and lowered his voice: 'Come alone to feast tonight, lord king. Such was the word of my chief.'

The king's eyes narrowed, gleaming like gray sword steel, coldly.

'Alone?'

'Aye.'

They eyed each other silently, their mutual tribal enmity seething beneath their cloak of formality. Their mouths spoke the cultured speech, the conventional court phrases of a highly polished race, a race not their own, but from their eyes gleamed the primal traditions of the elemental savage. Kull might be the king of Valusia and the Pict might be an emissary to her courts, but there in the throne hall of kings, two tribesmen glowered at each other, fierce and wary, while ghosts of wild wars and world-ancient feuds whispered to each.

To the king was the advantage and he enjoyed it to its fullest extent. Jaw resting on hand, he eyed the Pict, who stood like an image of bronze, head flung back, eyes unflinching.

Across Kull's lips stole a smile that was more a sneer.

'And so I am to come – alone?' Civilization had taught him to speak by innuendo and the Pict's dark eyes glittered, though he made no reply. 'How am I to know that you come from Ka-nu?'

'I have spoken,' was the sullen response.

'And when did a Pict speak truth?' sneered Kull, fully aware that the Picts never lied, but using this means to enrage the man.

'I see your plan, king,' the Pict answered imperturbably. 'You wish to anger me. By Valka, you need go no further! I am angry enough. And I challenge you to meet me in single battle, spear, sword or dagger, mounted or afoot. Are you king or man?'

Kull's eyes glinted with the grudging admiration a warrior must needs give a bold foeman, but he did not fail to use the chance of further annoying his antagonist.

'A king does not accept the challenge of a nameless savage,' he sneered, 'nor does the emperor of Valusia break the Truce of Ambassadors. You have leave to go. Say to Ka-nu I will come alone.'

The Pict's eyes flashed murderously. He fairly shook in the grasp of the primitive blood-lust; then, turning his back squarely upon the king of Valusia, he strode across the Hall of Society and vanished through the great door.

Again Kull leaned back upon the ermine throne and meditated.

So the chief of the Council of Picts wished him to come alone? But for what reason? Treachery? Grimly Kull touched the hilt of his great sword. But scarcely. The Picts valued too greatly the alliance with Valusia to break it for any feudal reason. Kull might be a warrior of Atlantis and hereditary enemy of all Picts, but too, he was king of Valusia, the most potent ally of the Men of the West.

Kull reflected long upon the strange state of affairs that made him ally of ancient foes and foe of ancient friends. He rose and paced restlessly across the hall, with the quick, noiseless tread of a lion. Chains of friendship, tribe and tradition had he broken to satisfy his ambition. And, by Valka, god of the sea and the land, he had realized that ambition! He was king of Valusia – a fading, degenerate Valusia, a Valusia living mostly in dreams of bygone glory, but still a mighty land and the greatest of the Seven Empires. Valusia – Land of Dreams, the tribesmen named it, and sometimes it seemed to Kull that he moved in a dream. Strange to him were the intrigues of court and palace, army and people. All was like a masquerade, where men and women hid their real thoughts with a smooth mask. Yet the seizing of the throne had been easy – a bold snatching of opportunity, the swift whirl of swords, the slaying of a tyrant of whom men had wearied unto death, short, crafty plotting with ambitious statesmen out of favor at court – and Kull, wandering adventurer, Atlantean exile, had swept up to the dizzy heights of his dreams:

he was lord of Valusia, king of kings. Yet now it seemed that the seizing was far easier than the keeping. The sight of the Pict had brought back youthful associations to his mind, the free, wild savagery of his boyhood. And now a strange feeling of dim unrest, of unreality, stole over him as of late it had been doing. Who was he, a straightforward man of the seas and the mountain, to rule a race strangely and terribly wise with the mysticisms of antiquity? An ancient race –

'I am Kull!' said he, flinging back his head as a lion flings back his mane. 'I am Kull!'

His falcon gaze swept the ancient hall. His self-confidence flowed back . . . And in a dim nook of the hall a tapestry moved – slightly.

2   Thus Spake the Silent Halls of Valusia

The moon had not risen, and the garden was lighted with torches aglow in silver cressets when Kull sat down in the throne before the table of Ka-nu, ambassador of the western isles. At his right hand sat the ancient Pict, as much unlike an emissary of that fierce race as a man could be. Ancient was Ka-nu and wise in statecraft, grown old in the game. There was no elemental hatred in the eyes that looked at Kull appraisingly; no tribal traditions hindered his judgments. Long associations with the statesmen of the civilized nations had swept away such cobwebs. Not: who and what is this man? was the question ever foremost in Ka-nu's mind, but: can I use this man, and how? Tribal prejudices he used only to further his own schemes.

And Kull watched Ka-nu, answering his conversation briefly, wondering if civilization would make of him a thing like the Pict. For Ka-nu was soft and paunchy. Many years had stridden across the sky-rim since Ka-nu had wielded a sword. True, he was old, but Kull had seen men older than he in the forefront of battle. The Picts were a long-lived race. A beautiful girl stood at Ka-nu's elbow, refilling his goblet, and she was kept busy. Meanwhile Ka-nu kept up a running fire of jests and comments, and Kull, secretly contemptuous of his garrulity, nevertheless missed none of his shrewd humor.

At the banquet were Pictish chiefs and statesmen, the latter jovial and easy in their manner, the warriors formally courteous, but plainly hampered by their tribal affinities. Yet Kull, with a tinge of envy, was cognizant of the freedom and ease of the affair as contrasted with like affairs of the Valusian court. Such freedom prevailed in the rude camps of Atlantis – Kull shrugged his shoulders. After all, doubtless Ka-nu, who had seemed to have forgotten he was a Pict as far as time-hoary custom and prejudice went, was right and he, Kull, would better become a Valusian in mind as in name.

At last when the moon had reached her zenith, Ka-nu, having eaten and drunk as much as any three men there, leaned back upon his divan with a comfortable sigh and said, 'Now, get you gone, friends, for the king and I would converse on such matters as concern not children. Yes, you too, my pretty; yet first let me kiss those ruby lips – so; now dance away, my rose-bloom.'

Ka-nu's eyes twinkled above his white beard as he surveyed Kull, who sat erect, grim and uncompromising.

'You are thinking, Kull,' said the old statesman, suddenly, 'that Ka-nu is a useless old reprobate, fit for nothing except to guzzle wine and kiss wenches!'

In fact, this remark was so much in line with his actual thoughts, and so plainly put, that Kull was rather startled, though he gave no sign.

Ka-nu gurgled and his paunch shook with his mirth. 'Wine is red and women are soft,' he remarked tolerantly. 'But – ha! ha! – think not old Ka-nu allows either to interfere with business.'

Again he laughed, and Kull moved restlessly. This seemed

much like being made sport of, and the king's scintillant eyes began to glow with a feline light.

Ka-nu reached for the wine-pitcher, filled his beaker and glanced questioningly at Kull, who shook his head irritably.

'Aye,' said Ka-nu equably, 'it takes an old head to stand strong drink. I am growing old, Kull, so why should you young men begrudge me such pleasures as we oldsters must find? Ah me, I grow ancient and withered, friendless and cheerless.'

But his looks and expressions failed far of bearing out his words. His rubicund countenance fairly glowed, and his eyes sparkled, so that his white beard seemed incongruous. Indeed, he looked remarkably elfin, reflected Kull, who felt vaguely resentful. The old scoundrel had lost all of the primitive virtues of his race and of Kull's race, yet he seemed more pleased in his aged days than otherwise.

'Hark ye, Kull,' said Ka-nu, raising an admonitory finger, ''tis a chancy thing to laud a young man, yet I must speak my true thoughts to gain your confidence.'

'If you think to gain it by flattery –'

'Tush. Who spake of flattery? I flatter only to disguard.'

There was a keen sparkle in Ka-nu's eyes, a cold glimmer that did not match his lazy smile. He knew men, and he knew that to gain his end he must smite straight with this tigerish barbarian, who, like a wolf scenting a snare, would scent out unerringly any falseness in the skein of his word-web.

'You have power, Kull,' said he, choosing his words with more care than he did in the council rooms of the nation, 'to make yourself mightiest of all kings, and restore some of the lost glories of Valusia. So. I care little for Valusia – though the women and wine be excellent – save for the fact that the stronger Valusia is, the stronger is the Pict nation. More, with an Atlantean on the throne, eventually Atlantis will become united –'

Kull laughed in harsh mockery. Ka-nu had touched an old wound.

'Atlantis made my name accursed when I went to seek fame and fortune among the cities of the world. We – they – are age-old foes of the Seven Empires, greater foes of the allies of the Empires, as you should know.'

Ka-nu tugged his beard and smiled enigmatically.

'Nay, nay. Let it pass. But I know whereof I speak. And then warfare will cease, wherein there is no gain; I see a world of peace and prosperity – man loving his fellow man – the good supreme. All this can you accomplish – *if you live!*'

'Ha!' Kull's lean hand closed on his hilt and he half rose, with a sudden movement of such dynamic speed that Ka-nu, who fancied men as some men fancy blooded horses, felt his old blood leap with a sudden thrill. Valka, what a warrior! Nerves and sinews of steel and fire, bound together with the perfect co-ordination, the fighting instinct, that makes the terrible warrior.

But none of Ka-nu's enthusiasm showed in his mildly sarcastic tone.

'Tush. Be seated. Look about you. The gardens are deserted, the seats empty save for ourselves. You fear not *me?*'

Kull sank back, gazing about him warily.

'There speaks the savage,' mused Ka-nu. 'Think you if I planned treachery I would enact it here where suspicion would be sure to fall upon me? Tut. You young tribesmen have much to learn. There were my chiefs who were not at ease because you were born among the hills of Atlantis, and you despise me in your secret mind because I am a Pict. Tush. I see you as Kull, king of Valusia, not as Kull, the reckless Atlantean, leader of the raiders who harried the western isles. So you should see in me, not a Pict but an international man, a figure of the world. Now to that figure, hark! If you were slain tomorrow who would be king?'

'Kaanuub, baron of Blaal.'

'Even so. I object to Kaanuub for many reasons, yet most of all for the fact that he is but a figurehead.'

'How so? He was my greatest opponent, but I did not know that he championed any cause but his own.'

'The night can hear,' answered Ka-nu obliquely. 'There are worlds within worlds. But you may trust me and you may trust Brule, the Spear-slayer. Look!' He drew from his robes a bracelet of gold representing a winged dragon coiled thrice, with three horns of ruby on the head.

'Examine it closely. Brule will wear it on his arm when he comes to you tomorrow night so that you may know him. Trust Brule as you trust yourself, and do what he tells you to. And in proof of trust, look ye!'

And with the speed of a striking hawk, the ancient snatched something from his robes, something that flung a weird green light over them, and which he replaced in an instant.

'The stolen gem!' exclaimed Kull recoiling. 'The green jewel from the Temple of the Serpent! Valka! You! And why do you show it to me?'

'To save your life. To prove my trust. If I betray your trust, deal with me likewise. You hold my life in your hand. Now I could not be false to you if I would, for a word from you would be my doom.'

Yet for all his words the old scoundrel beamed merrily and seemed vastly pleased with himself.

'But why do you give me this hold over you?' asked Kull, becoming more bewildered each second.

'As I told you. Now, you see that I do not intend to deal you false, and tomorrow night when Brule comes to you, you will follow his advice without fear of treachery. Enough. An escort waits outside to ride to the palace with you, lord.'

Kull rose. 'But you have told me nothing.'

'Tush. How impatient are youths!' Ka-nu looked more like a mischievous elf than ever. 'Go you and dream of thrones and power and kingdoms, while I dream of wine and soft women and roses. And fortune ride with you, King Kull.'

As he left the garden, Kull glanced back to see Ka-nu still reclining lazily in his seat, a merry ancient, beaming on all the world with jovial fellowship.

A mounted warrior waited for the king just without the garden and Kull was slightly surprised to see that it was the same that had brought Ka-nu's invitation. No word was spoken as Kull swung into the saddle nor as they clattered along the empty streets.

The color and the gayety of the day had given away to the eery stillness of night. The city's antiquity was more than ever apparent beneath the bent, silver moon. The huge pillars of the mansions and palaces towered up into the stars. The broad stairways, silent and deserted, seemed to climb endlessly until they vanished in the shadowy darkness of the upper realms. Stairs to the stars, thought Kull, his imaginative mind inspired by the weird grandeur of the scene.

Clang! clang! clang! sounded the silver hoofs on the broad, moon-flooded streets, but otherwise there was no sound. The age of the city, its incredible antiquity, was almost oppressive to the king; it was as if the great silent buildings laughed at him, noiselessly, with unguessable mockery. And what secrets did they hold?

'You are young,' said the palaces and the temples and the shrines, 'but we are old. The world was wild with youth when we were reared. You and your tribe shall pass, but we are invincible, indestructible. We towered above a strange world, ere Atlantis and Lemuria rose from the sea; we still shall reign when the green waters sigh for many a restless fathom above the spires of Lemuria and the hills of Atlantis and when the isles of the Western Men are the mountains of a strange land.

'How many kings have we watched ride down these streets before Kull of Atlantis was even a dream in the mind of Ka, bird of Creation? Ride on, Kull of Atlantis; greater shall follow you;

greater came before you. They are dust; they are forgotten; we stand; we know; we are. Ride, ride on, Kull of Atlantis; Kull the king, Kull the fool!'

And it seemed to Kull that the clashing hoofs took up the silent refrain to beat it into the night with hollow re-echoing mockery:

'Kull – the – king! Kull – the – fool!'

Glow, moon; you light a king's way! Gleam, stars; you are torches in the train of an emperor! And clang, silver-shod hoofs; you herald that Kull rides through Valusia.

Ho! Awake, Valusia! It is Kull that rides, Kull the king!

'We have known many kings,' said the silent halls of Valusia.

And so in a brooding mood Kull came to the palace, where his bodyguard, men of the Red Slayers, came to take the rein of the great stallion and escort Kull to his rest. There the Pict, still sullenly speechless, wheeled his steed with a savage wrench of the rein and fled away in the dark like a phantom; Kull's heightened imagination pictured him speeding through the silent streets like a goblin out of the Elder World.

There was no sleep for Kull that night, for it was nearly dawn and he spent the rest of the night hours pacing the throneroom, and pondering over what had passed. Ka-nu had told him nothing, yet he had put himself in Kull's complete power. At what had he hinted when he had said the baron of Blaal was naught but a figurehead? And who was this Brule who was to come to him by night, wearing the mystic armlet of the dragon? And why? Above all, why had Ka-nu shown him the green gem of terror, stolen long ago from the Temple of the Serpent, for which the world would rock in wars were it known to the weird and terrible keepers of that temple, and from whose vengeance not even Ka-nu's ferocious tribesmen might be able to save him? But Ka-nu knew he was safe, reflected Kull, for the statesman was too shrewd to expose himself to risk without profit. But was it to throw the king off his guard and pave the way to treachery? Would Ka-nu dare let him live now? Kull shrugged his shoulders.

3   They That Walk the Night

The moon had not risen when Kull, hand to hilt, stepped to a window. The windows opened upon the great inner gardens of the royal palace, and the breezes of the night, bearing the scents of spice trees, blew the filmy curtains about. The king looked out. The walks and groves were deserted; carefully trimmed trees were bulky shadows; fountains near by flung their slender sheen of silver in the starlight and distant fountains rippled steadily. No guards walked those gardens, for so closely were the outer walls guarded that it seemed impossible for any invader to gain access to them.

Vines curled up the walls of the palace, and even as Kull mused upon the ease with which they might be climbed, a segment of shadow detached itself from the darkness below the window and a bare, brown arm curved up over the sill. Kull's great sword hissed half-way from the sheath; then the king halted. Upon the muscular forearm gleamed the dragon armlet shown him by Ka-nu the night before.

The possessor of the arm pulled himself up over the sill and into the room with the swift, easy motion of a climbing leopard.

'You are Brule?' asked Kull, and then stopped in surprize not unmingled with annoyance and suspicion; for the man was he whom Kull had taunted in the hall of Society; the same who had escorted him from the Pictish embassy.

'I am Brule, the Spear-slayer,' answered the Pict in a guarded voice; then swiftly, gazing closely in Kull's face, he said, barely above a whisper:

'*Ka nama kaa lajerama!*'

Kull started. 'Ha! What mean you?'

'Know you not?'

'Nay, the words are unfamiliar; they are of no language I ever heard – and yet, by Valka! – somewhere – I have heard –'

'Aye,' was the Pict's only comment. His eyes swept the room, the study room of the palace. Except for a few tables, a divan or two and great shelves of books of parchment, the room was barren compared to the grandeur of the rest of the palace.

'Tell me, king, who guards the door?'

'Eighteen of the Red Slayers. But how come you, stealing through the gardens by night and scaling the walls of the palace?'

Brule sneered. 'The guards of Valusia are blind buffaloes. I could steal their girls from under their noses. I stole amid them and they saw me not nor heard me. And the walls – I could scale them without the aid of vines. I have hunted tigers on the foggy beaches when the sharp east breezes blew the mist in from seaward and I have climbed the steeps of the western sea mountain. But come – nay, touch this armlet.'

He held out his arm and, as Kull complied wonderingly, gave an apparent sigh of relief.

'So. Now throw off those kingly robes; for there are ahead of you this night such deeds as no Atlantean ever dreamed of.'

Brule himself was clad only in a scanty loin-cloth through which was thrust a short, curved sword.

'And who are you to give me orders?' asked Kull, slightly resentful.

'Did not Ka-nu bid you follow me in all things?' asked the Pict irritably, his eyes flashing momentarily. 'I have no love for you, lord, but for the moment I have put the thought of feuds from my mind. Do you likewise. But come.'

Walking noiselessly, he led the way across the room to the door. A slide in the door allowed a view of the outer corridor, unseen from without, and the Pict bade Kull look.

'What see you?'

'Naught but the eighteen guardsmen.'

The Pict nodded, motioned Kull to follow him across the room. At a panel in the opposite wall Brule stopped and fumbled there a moment. Then with a light movement he stepped back, drawing his sword as he did so. Kull gave an exclamation as the panel swung silently open, revealing a dimly lighted passageway.

'A secret passage!' swore Kull softly. 'And I knew nothing of it! By Valka, someone shall dance for this!'

'Silence!' hissed the Pict.

Brule was standing like a bronze statue as if straining every nerve for the slightest sound; something about his attitude made Kull's hair prickle slightly, not from fear but from some eery anticipation. Then beckoning, Brule stepped through the secret doorway which stood open behind them. The passage was bare, but not dust-covered as should have been the case with an unused secret corridor. A vague, gray light filtered through somewhere, but the source of it was not apparent. Every few feet Kull saw doors, invisible, as he knew, from the outside, but easily apparent from within.

'The palace is a very honeycomb,' he muttered.

'Aye. Night and day you are watched, king, by many eyes.'

The king was impressed by Brule's manner. The Pict went forward slowly, warily, half crouching, blade held low and thrust forward. When he spoke it was in a whisper and he continually flung glances from side to side.

The corridor turned sharply and Brule warily gazed past the turn.

'Look!' he whispered. 'But remember! No word! No sound – on your life!'

Kull cautiously gazed past him. The corridor changed just at the bend to a flight of steps. And then Kull recoiled. At the foot of those stairs lay the eighteen Red Slayers who were that night stationed to watch the king's study room. Brule's grip upon his mighty arm and Brule's fierce whisper at his shoulder alone kept Kull from leaping down those stairs.

'Silent, Kull! Silent, in Valka's name!' hissed the Pict. 'These corridors are empty now, but I risked much in showing you, that you might then believe what I had to say. Back now to the room of study.' And he retraced his steps, Kull following; his mind in a turmoil of bewilderment.

'This is treachery,' muttered the king, his steel-gray eyes a-smolder, 'foul and swift! Mere minutes have passed since those men stood at guard.'

Again in the room of study Brule carefully closed the secret panel and motioned Kull to look again through the slit of the outer door. Kull gasped audibly. *For without stood the eighteen guardsmen!*

'This is sorcery!' he whispered, half-drawing his sword. 'Do dead men guard the king?'

'*Aye!*' came Brule's scarcely audible reply; there was a strange expression in the Pict's scintillant eyes. They looked squarely into each other's eyes for an instant, Kull's brow wrinkled in a puzzled scowl as he strove to read the Pict's inscrutable face. Then Brule's lips, barely moving, formed the words:

'*The – snake – that – speaks!*'

'Silent!' whispered Kull, laying his hand over Brule's mouth. 'That is death to speak! That is a name accursed!'

The Pict's fearless eyes regarded him steadily.

'Look again, King Kull. Perchance the guard was changed.'

'Nay, those are the same men. In Valka's name, this is sorcery – this is insanity! I saw with my own eyes the bodies of those men, not eight minutes agone. Yet there they stand.'

Brule stepped back, away from the door, Kull mechanically following.

'Kull, what know ye of the traditions of this race ye rule?'

'Much – and yet, little. Valusia is so old –'

'Aye,' Brule's eyes lighted strangely, 'we are but barbarians – infants compared to the Seven Empires. Not even they themselves know how old they are. Neither the memory of man nor the annals of the historians reach back far enough to tell us when the first men came up from the sea and built cities on the shore. But Kull, *men were not always ruled by men!'*

The king started. Their eyes met.

'Aye, there is a legend of my people –'

'And mine!' broke in Brule. 'That was before we of the isles were allied with Valusia. Aye, in the reign of Lion-fang, seventh war chief of the Picts, so many years ago no man remembers how many. Across the sea we came, from the isles of the sunset, skirting the shores of Atlantis, and falling upon the beaches of Valusia with fire and sword. Aye, the long white beaches resounded with the clash of spears, and the night was like day from the flame of the burning castles. And the king, the king of Valusia, who died on the red sea sands that dim day –' His voice trailed off; the two stared at each other, neither speaking; then each nodded.

'Ancient is Valusia!' whispered Kull. 'The hills of Atlantis and Mu were isles of the sea when Valusia was young.'

The night breeze whispered through the open window. Not the free, crisp sea air such as Brule and Kull knew and reveled in, in their land, but a breath like a whisper from the past, laden with musk, scents of forgotten things, breathing secrets that were hoary when the world was young.

The tapestries rustled, and suddenly Kull felt like a naked child before the inscrutable wisdom of the mystic past. Again the sense of unreality swept upon him. At the back of his soul stole dim, gigantic phantoms, whispering monstrous things. He sensed that Brule experienced similar thoughts. The Pict's eyes were fixed upon his face with a fierce intensity. Their glances met. Kull felt warmly a sense of comradeship with this member of an enemy tribe. Like rival leopards turning at bay against hunters, these two savages made common cause against the inhuman powers of antiquity.

*

Brule again led the way back to the secret door. Silently they entered and silently they proceeded down the dim corridor, taking the opposite direction from that in which they had previously traversed it. After a while the Pict stopped and pressed close to one of the secret doors, bidding Kull look with him through the hidden slot.

'This opens upon a little-used stair which leads to a corridor running past the study-room door.'

They gazed, and presently, mounting the stair silently, came a silent shape.

'Tu! Chief councilor!' exclaimed Kull. 'By night and with bared dagger! How, what means this, Brule?'

'Murder! And foulest treachery!' hissed Brule. 'Nay' – as Kull would have flung the door aside and leaped forth – 'we are lost if you meet him here, for more lurk at the foot of those stairs. Come!'

Half running, they darted back along the passage. Back through the secret door Brule led, shutting it carefully behind them, then across the chamber to an opening into a room seldom used. There he swept aside some tapestries in a dim corner nook and, drawing Kull with him, stepped behind them. Minutes dragged. Kull could hear the breeze in the other room blowing the window curtains about, and it seemed to him like the murmur of ghosts. Then through the door, stealthily, came Tu, chief councilor of the king. Evidently he had come through the study room and, finding it empty, sought his victim where he was most likely to be.

He came with upraised dagger, walking silently. A moment he halted, gazing about the apparently empty room, which was lighted dimly by a single candle. Then he advanced cautiously, apparently at a loss to understand the absence of the king. He stood before the hiding place – and –

'Slay!' hissed the Pict.

Kull with a single mighty leap hurled himself into the room.

Tu spun, but the blinding, tigerish speed of the attack gave him no chance for defense or counter-attack. Sword steel flashed in the dim light and grated on bone as Tu toppled backward, Kull's sword standing out between his shoulders.

Kull leaned above him, teeth bared in the killer's snarl, heavy brows ascowl above eyes that were like the gray ice of the cold sea. Then he released the hilt and recoiled, shaken, dizzy, the hand of death at his spine.

For as he watched, Tu's face became strangely dim and unreal; the features mingled and merged in a seemingly impossible manner. Then, like a fading mask of fog, the face suddenly vanished and in its stead gaped and leered *a monstrous serpent's head*!

'Valka!' gasped Kull, sweat beading his forehead, and again: 'Valka!'

Brule leaned forward, face immobile. Yet his glittering eyes mirrored something of Kull's horror.

'Regain your sword, lord king,' said he. 'There are yet deeds to be done.'

Hesitantly Kull set his hand to the hilt. His flesh crawled as he set his foot upon the terror which lay at their feet, and as some jerk of muscular reaction caused the frightful mouth to gape suddenly, he recoiled, weak with nausea. Then, wrathful at himself, he plucked forth his sword and gazed more closely at the nameless thing that had been known as Tu, chief councilor. Save for the reptilian head, the thing was the exact counterpart of a man.

'A man with the head of a snake!' Kull murmured. 'This, then, is a priest of the serpent god?'

'Aye. Tu sleeps unknowing. These fiends can take any form they will. That is, they can, by a magic charm or the like, fling a web of sorcery about their faces, as an actor dons a mask, so that they resemble anyone they wish to.'

'Then the old legends were true,' mused the king; 'the grim

old tales few dare even whisper, lest they die as blasphemers, are no fantasies. By Valka, I had thought – I had guessed – but it seems beyond the bounds of reality. Ha! The guardsmen outside the door –'

'They too are snake-men. Hold! What would you do?'

'Slay them!' said Kull between his teeth.

'Strike at the skull if at all,' said Brule. 'Eighteen wait without the door and perhaps a score more in the corridors. Hark ye, king, Ka-nu learned of this plot. His spies have pierced the inmost fastnesses of the snake priests and they brought hints of a plot. Long ago he discovered the secret passageways of the palace, and at his command I studied the map thereof and came here by night to aid you, lest you die as other kings of Valusia have died. I came alone for the reason that to send more would have roused suspicion. Many could not steal into the palace as I did. Some of the foul conspiracy you have seen. Snake-men guard your door, and that one, as Tu, could pass anywhere else in the palace; in the morning, if the priests failed, the real guards would be holding their places again, nothing knowing, nothing remembering; there to take the blame if the priests succeeded. But stay you here while I dispose of this carrion.'

So saying, the Pict shouldered the frightful thing stolidly and vanished with it through another secret panel. Kull stood alone, his mind a-whirl. Neophytes of the mighty serpent, how many lurked among his cities? How might he tell the false from the true? Aye, how many of his trusted councilors, his generals, were men? He could be certain – of whom?

The secret panel swung inward and Brule entered.

'You were swift.'

'Aye!' The warrior stepped forward, eyeing the floor. 'There is gore upon the rug. See?'

Kull bent forward; from the corner of his eye he saw a blur of movement, a glint of steel. Like a loosened bow he whipped erect, thrusting upward. The warrior sagged upon the sword, his own clattering to the floor. Even at that instant Kull reflected grimly that it was appropriate that the traitor should meet his death upon the sliding, upward thrust used so much by his race. Then, as Brule slid from the sword to sprawl motionless on the floor, the face began to merge and fade, and as Kull caught his breath, his hair a-prickle, the human features vanished and there the jaws of a great snake gaped hideously, the terrible beady eyes venomous even in death.

'He was a snake priest all the time!' gasped the king. 'Valka! what an elaborate plan to throw me off my guard! Ka-nu there, is he a man? Was it Ka-nu to whom I talked in the gardens? Almighty Valka!' as his flesh crawled with a horrid thought; 'are the people of Valusia men or are they *all* serpents?'

Undecided he stood, idly seeing that the thing named Brule no longer wore the dragon armlet. A sound made him wheel.

Brule was coming through the secret door.

'Hold!' upon the arm upthrown to halt the king's hovering sword gleamed the dragon armlet. 'Valka!' The Pict stopped short. Then a grim smile curled his lips.

'By the gods of the seas! These demons are crafty past reckoning. For it must be that that one lurked in the corridors, and seeing me go carrying the carcass of that other, took my appearance. So. I have another to do away with.'

'Hold!' there was the menace of death in Kull's voice; 'I have seen two men turn to serpents before my eyes. How may I know if you are a true man?'

Brule laughed. 'For two reasons, King Kull. No snake-man wears this' – he indicated the dragon armlet – 'nor can any say these words,' and again Kull heard the strange phrase: '*Ka nama kaa lajerama.*'

'*Ka nama kaa lajerama,*' Kull repeated mechanically. 'Now where, in Valka's name, have I heard that? I have not! And yet – and yet –'

'Aye, you remember, Kull,' said Brule. 'Through the dim

corridors of memory those words lurk; though you never heard them in this life, yet in the bygone ages they were so terribly impressed upon the soul mind that never dies, that they will always strike dim chords in your memory, though you be reincarnated for a million years to come. For that phrase has come secretly down the grim and bloody eons, since when, uncounted centuries ago, those words were watchwords for the race of men who battled with the grisly beings of the Elder Universe. For none but a real man of men may speak them, whose jaws and mouth are shaped different from any other creature. Their meaning has been forgotten but not the words themselves.'

'True,' said Kull. 'I remember the legends – Valka!' He stopped short, staring, for suddenly, like the silent swinging wide of a mystic door, misty, unfathomed reaches opened in the recesses of his consciousness and for an instant he seemed to gaze back through the vastnesses that spanned life and life; seeing through the vague and ghostly fogs dim shapes reliving dead centuries – men in combat with hideous monsters, vanquishing a planet of frightful terrors. Against a gray, ever-shifting background moved strange nightmare forms, fantasies of lunacy and fear; and man, the jest of the gods, the blind, wisdomless striver from dust to dust, following the long bloody trail of his destiny, knowing not why, bestial, blundering, like a great murderous child, yet feeling somewhere a spark of divine fire . . . Kull drew a hand across his brow, shaken; these sudden glimpses into the abysses of memory always startled him.

'They are gone,' said Brule, as if scanning his secret mind; 'the bird-women, the harpies, the bat-men, the flying fiends, the wolf-people, the demons, the goblins – all save such as this being that lies at our feet, and a few of the wolf-men. Long and terrible was the war, lasting through the bloody centuries, since first the first men, risen from the mire of apedom, turned upon those who then ruled the world. And at last mankind conquered,

so long ago that naught but dim legends come to us through the ages. The snake-people were the last to go, yet at last men conquered even them and drove them forth into the waste lands of the world, there to mate with true snakes until some day, say the sages, the horrid breed shall vanish utterly. Yet the Things returned in crafty guise as men grew soft and degenerate, forgetting ancient wars. Ah, that was a grim and secret war! Among the men of the Younger Earth stole the frightful monsters of the Elder Planet, safeguarded by their horrid wisdom and mysticisms, taking all forms and shapes, doing deeds of horror secretly. No man knew who was true man and who false. No man could trust any man. Yet by means of their own craft they formed ways by which the false might be known from the true. Men took for a sign and a standard the figure of the flying dragon, the winged dinosaur, a monster of past ages, which was the greatest foe of the serpent. And men used those words which I spoke to you as a sign and symbol, for as I said, none but a true man can repeat them. So mankind triumphed. Yet again the fiends came after the years of forgetfulness had gone by – for man is still an ape in that he forgets what is not ever before his eyes. As priests they came; and for that men in their luxury and might had by then lost faith in the old religions and worships, the snakemen, in the guise of teachers of a new and truer cult, built a monstrous religion about the worship of the serpent god. Such is their power that it is now death to repeat the old legends of the snake-people, and people bow again to the serpent god in new form; and blind fools that they are, the great hosts of men see no connection between this power and the power men overthrew eons ago. As priests the snake-men are content to rule – and yet –' He stopped.

'Go on.' Kull felt an unaccountable stirring of the short hair at the base of his scalp.

'Kings have reigned as true men in Valusia,' the Pict whispered, 'and yet, slain in battle, have died serpents – as died he who fell beneath the spear of Lion-fang on the red beaches when we of the isles harried the Seven Empires. And how can this be, Lord Kull? These kings were born of women and lived as men! This – the true kings died in secret – as you would have died tonight – and priests of the Serpent reigned in their stead, no man knowing.'

Kull cursed between his teeth. 'Aye, it must be. No one has ever seen a priest of the Serpent and lived, that is known. They live in utmost secrecy.'

'The statecraft of the Seven Empires is a mazy, monstrous thing,' said Brule. 'There the true men know that among them glide the spies of the serpent, and the men who are the Serpent's allies – such as Kaanuub, baron of Blaal – yet no man dares seek to unmask a suspect lest vengeance befall him. No man trusts his fellow and the true statesmen dare not speak to each other what is in the minds of all. Could they be sure, could a snake-man or plot be unmasked before them all, then would the power of the Serpent be more than half broken; for all would then ally and make common cause, sifting out the traitors. Ka-nu alone is of sufficient shrewdness and courage to cope with them, and even Ka-nu learned only enough of their plot to tell me what would happen – what has happened up to this time. Thus far I was prepared; from now on we must trust to our luck and our craft. Here and now I think we are safe; those snake-men without the door dare not leave their post lest true men come here unexpectedly. But tomorrow they will try something else, you may be sure. Just what they will do, none can say, not even Ka-nu; but we must stay at each other's sides, King Kull, until we conquer or both be dead. Now come with me while I take this carcass to the hiding-place where I took the other being.'

Kull followed the Pict with his grisly burden through the secret panel and down the dim corridor. Their feet, trained to the

silence of the wilderness, made no noise. Like phantoms they glided through the ghostly light, Kull wondering that the corridors should be deserted; at every turn he expected to run full upon some frightful apparition. Suspicion surged back upon him; was this Pict leading him into ambush? He fell back a pace or two behind Brule, his ready sword hovering at the Pict's unheeding back. Brule should die first if he meant treachery. But if the Pict was aware of the king's suspicion, he showed no sign. Stolidly he tramped along, until they came to a room, dusty and long unused, where moldy tapestries hung heavy. Brule drew aside some of these and concealed the corpse behind them.

Then they turned to retrace their steps, when suddenly Brule halted with such abruptness that he was closer to death than he knew; for Kull's nerves were on edge.

'Something moving in the corridor,' hissed the Pict. 'Ka-nu said these ways would be empty, yet –'

He drew his sword and stole into the corridor, Kull following warily.

A short way down the corridor a strange, vague glow appeared that came toward them. Nerves a-leap, they waited, backs to the corridor wall; for what they knew not, but Kull heard Brule's breath hiss through his teeth and was reassured as to Brule's loyalty.

The glow merged into a shadowy form. A shape vaguely like a man it was, but misty and illusive, like a wisp of fog, that grew more tangible as it approached, but never fully material. A face looked at them, a pair of luminous great eyes, that seemed to hold all the tortures of a million centuries. There was no menace in that face, with its dim, worn features, but only a great pity – and that face – that face –

'Almighty gods!' breathed Kull, an icy hand at his soul: 'Eallal, king of Valusia, who died a thousand years ago!'

Brule shrank back as far as he could, his narrow eyes widened in a blaze of pure horror, the sword shaking in his grip, unnerved for the first time that weird night. Erect and defiant stood Kull, instinctively holding his useless sword at the ready; flesh a-crawl, hair a-prickle, yet still a king of kings, as ready to challenge the powers of the unknown dead as the powers of the living.

The phantom came straight on, giving them no heed; Kull shrank back as it passed them, feeling an icy breath like a breeze from the arctic snow. Straight on went the shape with slow, silent footsteps, as if the chains of all the ages were upon those vague feet; vanishing about a bend of the corridor.

'Valka!' muttered the Pict, wiping the cold beads from his brow; 'that was no man! That was a ghost!'

'Aye!' Kull shook his head wonderingly. 'Did you not recognize the face? That was Eallal, who reigned in Valusia a thousand years ago and who was found hideously murdered in his throneroom – the room now known as the Accursed Room. Have you not seen his statue in the Fame Room of Kings?'

'Yes, I remember the tale now. Gods, Kull! that is another sign of the frightful and foul power of the snake priests – that king was slain by snake-people and thus his soul became their slave, to do their bidding throughout eternity! For the sages have ever maintained that if a man is slain by a snake-man his ghost becomes their slave.'

A shudder shook Kull's gigantic frame. 'Valka! But what a fate! Hark ye' – his fingers closed upon Brule's sinewy arm like steel – 'hark ye! If I am wounded unto death by these foul monsters, swear that ye will smite your sword through my breast lest my soul be enslaved.'

'I swear,' answered Brule, his fierce eyes lighting. 'And do ye the same by me, Kull.'

Their strong right hands met in a silent sealing of their bloody bargain.

4 Masks

Kull sat upon his throne and gazed broodingly out upon the sea of faces turned toward him. A courtier was speaking in evenly modulated tones, but the king scarcely heard him. Close by, Tu, chief councilor, stood ready at Kull's command, and each time the king looked at him, Kull shuddered inwardly. The surface of court life was as the unrippled surface of the sea between tide and tide. To the musing king the affairs of the night before seemed as a dream, until his eyes dropped to the arm of his throne. A brown, sinewy hand rested there, upon the wrist of which gleamed a dragon armlet; Brule stood beside his throne and ever the Pict's fierce secret whisper brought him back from the realm of unreality in which he moved.

No, that was no dream, that monstrous interlude. As he sat upon his throne in the Hall of Society and gazed upon the courtiers, the ladies, the lords, the statesmen, he seemed to see their faces as things of illusion, things unreal, existent only as shadows and mockeries of substance. Always he had seen their faces as masks, but before he had looked on them with contemptuous tolerance, thinking to see beneath the masks shallow, puny souls, avaricious, lustful, deceitful; now there was a grim undertone, a sinister meaning, a vague horror that lurked beneath the smooth masks. While he exchanged courtesies with some nobleman or councilor he seemed to see the smiling face fade like smoke and the frightful jaws of a serpent gaping there. How many of those he looked upon were horrid, inhuman monsters, plotting his death, beneath the smooth mesmeric illusion of a human face?

Valusia – land of dreams and nightmares – a kingdom of the shadows, ruled by phantoms who glided back and forth behind the painted curtains, mocking the futile king who sat upon the throne – himself a shadow.

And like a comrade shadow Brule stood by his side, dark eyes glittering from immobile face. A real man, Brule! And Kull felt his friendship for the savage become a thing of reality and sensed that Brule felt a friendship for him beyond the mere necessity of statecraft.

And what, mused Kull, were the realities of life? Ambition, power, pride? The friendship of man, the love of women – which Kull had never known – battle, plunder, what? Was it the real Kull who sat upon the throne or was it the real Kull who had scaled the hills of Atlantis, harried the far isles of the sunset, and laughed upon the green roaring tides of the Atlantean sea? How could a man be so many different men in a lifetime? For Kull knew that there were many Kulls and he wondered which was the real Kull. After all, the priests of the Serpent merely went a step further in their magic, for all men wore masks, and many a different mask with each different man or woman; and Kull wondered if a serpent did not lurk under every mask.

So he sat and brooded in strange, mazy thought ways, and the courtiers came and went and the minor affairs of the day were completed, until at last the king and Brule sat alone in the Hall of Society save for the drowsy attendants.

Kull felt a weariness. Neither he nor Brule had slept the night before, nor had Kull slept the night before that, when in the gardens of Ka-nu he had had his first hint of the weird things to be. Last night nothing further had occurred after they had returned to the study room from the secret corridors, but they had neither dared nor cared to sleep. Kull, with the incredible vitality of a wolf, had aforetime gone for days upon days without sleep, in his wild savage days, but now his mind was edged from constant thinking and from the nervebreaking eeriness of the past night. He needed sleep, but sleep was furthest from his mind.

And he would not have dared sleep if he had thought of it. Another thing that had shaken him was the fact that though he and Brule had kept a close watch to see if, or when, the study-room guard was changed, yet it was changed without their knowledge; for the next morning those who stood on guard were able to repeat the magic words of Brule, but they remembered nothing out of the ordinary. They thought that they had stood at guard all night, as usual, and Kull said nothing to the contrary. He believed them true men, but Brule had advised absolute secrecy, and Kull also thought it best.

Now Brule leaned over the throne, lowering his voice so not even a lazy attendant could hear: 'They will strike soon, I think, Kull. A while ago Ka-nu gave me a secret sign. The priests know that we know of their plot, of course, but they know not how much we know. We must be ready for any sort of action. Ka-nu and the Pictish chiefs will remain within hailing distance now until this is settled one way or another. Ha, Kull, if it comes to a pitched battle, the streets and the castles of Valusia will run red!'

Kull smiled grimly. He would greet any sort of action with a ferocious joy. This wandering in a labyrinth of illusion and magic was extremely irksome to his nature. He longed for the leap and clang of swords, for the joyous freedom of battle.

Then into the Hall of Society came Tu again, and the rest of the councilors.

'Lord king, the hour of the council is at hand and we stand ready to escort you to the council room.'

Kull rose, and the councilors bent the knee as he passed through the way opened by them for his passage, rising behind him and following. Eyebrows were raised as the Pict strode defiantly behind the king, but no one dissented. Brule's challenging gaze swept the smooth faces of the councilors with the defiance of an intruding savage.

The group passed through the halls and came at last to the council chamber. The door was closed, as usual, and the councilors arranged themselves in the order of their rank before the dais upon which stood the king. Like a bronze statue Brule took up his stand behind Kull.

Kull swept the room with a swift stare. Surely no chance of treachery here. Seventeen councilors there were, all known to him; all of them had espoused his cause when he ascended the throne.

'Men of Valusia –' he began in the conventional manner, then halted, perplexed. The councilors had risen as a man and were moving toward him. There was no hostility in their looks, but their actions were strange for a council room. The foremost was close to him when Brule sprang forward, crouched like a leopard.

'*Ka nama kaa lajerama!*' his voice crackled through the sinister silence of the room and the foremost councilor recoiled, hand flashing to his robes; and like a spring released Brule moved and the man pitched headlong to the glint of his sword – headlong he pitched and lay still while his face faded and became the head of a mighty snake.

'Slay, Kull!' rasped the Pict's voice. 'They be all serpent men!'

The rest was a scarlet maze. Kull saw the familiar faces dim like fading fog and in their places gaped horrid reptilian visages as the whole band rushed forward. His mind was dazed but his giant body faltered not.

The singing of his sword filled the room, and the onrushing flood broke in a red wave. But they surged forward again, seemingly willing to fling their lives away in order to drag down the king. Hideous jaws gaped at him; terrible eyes blazed into his unblinkingly; a frightful fetid scent pervaded the atmosphere – the serpent scent that Kull had known in southern jungles. Swords and daggers leaped at him and he was dimly aware that they wounded him. But Kull was in his element; never before had he faced such grim foes but it mattered little; they lived, their veins held blood that could be spilt and they died when his great sword cleft their skulls or drove through their bodies. Slash, thrust, thrust and swing. Yet had Kull died there but for the man who crouched at his side, parrying and thrusting. For the king was clear berserk, fighting in the terrible Atlantean way, that seeks death to deal death; he made no effort to avoid thrusts and slashes, standing straight up and ever plunging forward, no thought in his frenzied mind but to slay. Not often did Kull forget his fighting craft in his primitive fury, but now some chain had broken in his soul, flooding his mind with a red wave of slaughter-lust. He slew a foe at each blow, but they surged about him, and time and again Brule turned a thrust that would have slain, as he crouched beside Kull, parrying and warding with cold skill, slaying not as Kull slew with long slashes and plunges, but with short overhand blows and upward thrusts.

Kull laughed, a laugh of insanity. The frightful faces swirled about him in a scarlet blaze. He felt steel sink into his arm and dropped his sword in a flashing arc that cleft his foe to the breastbone. Then the mists faded and the king saw that he and Brule stood alone above a sprawl of hideous crimson figures who lay still upon the floor.

'Valka! what a killing!' said Brule, shaking the blood from his eyes. 'Kull, had these been warriors who knew how to use the steel, we had died here. These serpent priests know naught of swordcraft and die easier than any men I ever slew. Yet had there been a few more, I think the matter had ended otherwise.'

Kull nodded. The wild berserker blaze had passed, leaving a mazed feeling of great weariness. Blood seeped from wounds on breast, shoulder, arm and leg. Brule, himself bleeding from a score of flesh wounds, glanced at him in some concern.

'Lord Kull, let us hasten to have your wounds dressed by the women.'

Kull thrust him aside with a drunken sweep of his mighty arm.

'Nay, we'll see this through ere we cease. Go you, though, and have your wounds seen to – I command it.'

The Pict laughed grimly. 'Your wounds are more than mine, lord king –' he began, then stopped as a sudden thought struck him. 'By Valka, Kull, this is not the council room!'

Kull looked about and suddenly other fogs seemed to fade. 'Nay, this is the room where Eallal died a thousand years ago – since unused and named "Accursed".'

'Then by the gods, they tricked us after all!' exclaimed Brule in a fury, kicking the corpses at their feet. 'They caused us to walk like fools into their ambush! By their magic they changed the appearance of all –'

'Then there is further deviltry afoot,' said Kull, 'for if there be true men in the councils of Valusia they should be in the real council room now. Come swiftly.'

And leaving the room with its ghastly keepers they hastened through halls that seemed deserted until they came to the real council room. Then Kull halted with a ghastly shudder. *From the council room sounded a voice speaking, and the voice was his!*

With a hand that shook he parted the tapestries and gazed into the room. There sat the councilors, counterparts of the men he and Brule had just slain, and upon the dais stood Kull, king of Valusia.

He stepped back, his mind reeling.

'This is insanity!' he whispered. 'Am I Kull? Do I stand here or is that Kull yonder in very truth and am I but a shadow, a figment of thought?'

Brule's hand clutching his shoulder, shaking him fiercely, brought him to his senses.

'Valka's name, be not a fool! Can you yet be astounded after all we have seen? See you not that those are true men bewitched by a snake-man who has taken your form, as those others took their forms? By now you should have been slain and yon monster reigning in your stead, unknown by those who bowed to you. Leap and slay swiftly or else we are undone. The Red Slayers, true men, stand close on each hand and none but you can reach and slay him. Be swift!'

Kull shook off the onrushing dizziness, flung back his head in the old, defiant gesture. He took a long, deep breath as does a strong swimmer before diving into the sea; then, sweeping back the tapestries, made the dais in a single lionlike bound. Brule had spoken truly. There stood men of the Red Slayers, guardsmen trained to move quick as the striking leopard; any but Kull had died ere he could reach the usurper. But the sight of Kull, identical with the man upon the dais, held them in their tracks, their minds stunned for an instant, and that was long enough. He upon the dais snatched for his sword, but even as his fingers closed upon the hilt, Kull's sword stood out behind his shoulders and the thing that men had thought the king pitched forward from the dais to lie silent upon the floor.

'Hold!' Kull's lifted hand and kingly voice stopped the rush that had started, and while they stood astounded he pointed to the thing which lay before them – whose face was fading into that of a snake. They recoiled, and from one door came Brule and from another came Ka-nu.

These grasped the king's bloody hand and Ka-nu spoke: 'Men of Valusia, you have seen with your own eyes. This is the true Kull, the mightiest king to whom Valusia has ever bowed. The power of the Serpent is broken and ye be all true men. King Kull, have you commands?'

'Lift that carrion,' said Kull, and men of the guard took up the thing.

'Now follow me,' said the king, and he made his way to the Accursed Room. Brule, with a look of concern, offered the support of his arm but Kull shook him off.

The distance seemed endless to the bleeding king, but at last he stood at the door and laughed fiercely and grimly when he heard the horrified ejaculations of the councilors.

At his orders the guardsmen flung the corpse they carried beside the others, and motioning all from the room Kull stepped out last and closed the door.

A wave of dizziness left him shaken. The faces turned to him, pallid and wonderingly, swirled and mingled in a ghostly fog. He felt the blood from his wound trickling down his limbs and he knew that what he was to do, he must do quickly or not at all.

His sword rasped from its sheath.

'Brule, are you there?'

'Aye!' Brule's face looked at him through the mist, close to his shoulder, but Brule's voice sounded leagues and eons away.

'Remember our vow, Brule. And now, bid them stand back.'

His left arm cleared a space as he flung up his sword. Then with all his waning power he drove it through the door into the jamb, driving the great sword to the hilt and sealing the room forever.

Legs braced wide, he swayed drunkenly, facing the horrified councilors. 'Let this room be doubly accursed. And let those rotting skeletons lie there forever as a sign of the dying might of the serpent. Here I swear that I shall hunt the serpent-men from land to land, from sea to sea, giving no rest until all be slain, that good triumph and the power of Hell be broken. This thing I swear – I – Kull – king – of – Valusia.'

His knees buckled as the faces swayed and swirled. The councilors leaped forward, but ere they could reach him, Kull slumped to the floor, and lay still, face upward.

The councilors surged about the fallen king, chattering and shrieking. Ka-nu beat them back with his clenched fists, cursing savagely.

'Back, you fools! Would you stifle the little life that is yet in him? How, Brule, is he dead or will he live?' – to the warrior who bent above the prostrate Kull.

'Dead?' sneered Brule irritably. 'Such a man as this is not so easily killed. Lack of sleep and loss of blood have weakened him – by Valka, he has a score of deep wounds, but none of them mortal. Yet have those gibbering fools bring the court women here at once.'

Brule's eyes lighted with a fierce, proud light.

'Valka, Ka-nu, but here is such a man as I knew not existed in these degenerate days. He will be in the saddle in a few scant days and then may the serpent-men of the world beware of Kull of Valusia. Valka! but that will be a rare hunt! Ah, I see long years of prosperity for the world with such a king upon the throne of Valusia.'

The Mirrors of Tuzun Thune

'A wild, weird clime that lieth sublime
Out of Space, out of Time.'

Poe

There comes, even to kings, the time of great weariness. Then the gold of the throne is brass, the silk of the palace becomes drab. The gems in the diadem and upon the fingers of the women sparkle drearily like the ice of the white seas; the speech of men is as the empty rattle of a jester's bell and the feel comes of things unreal; even the sun is copper in the sky and the breath of the green ocean is no longer fresh.

Kull sat upon the throne of Valusia and the hour of weariness was upon him. They moved before him in an endless, meaningless panorama, men, women, priests, events and shadows of events; things seen and things to be attained. But like shadows they came and went, leaving no trace upon his consciousness, save that of a great mental fatigue. Yet Kull was not tired. There was a longing in him for things beyond himself and beyond the Valusian court. An unrest stirred in him and strange, luminous dreams roamed his soul. At his bidding there came to him Brule the Spear-slayer, warrior of Pictland, from the islands beyond the West.

'Lord king, you are tired of the life of the court. Come with me upon my galley and let us roam the tides for a space.'

'Nay.' Kull rested his chin moodily upon his mighty hand. 'I am weary beyond all these things. The cities hold no lure for me

– and the borders are quiet. I hear no more the sea-songs I heard when I lay as a boy on the booming crags of Atlantis, and the night was alive with blazing stars. No more do the green woodlands beckon me as of old. There is a strangeness upon me and a longing beyond life's longings. Go!'

Brule went forth in a doubtful mood, leaving the king brooding upon his throne. Then to Kull stole a girl of the court and whispered:

'Great king, seek Tuzun Thune, the wizard. The secrets of life and death are his, and the stars in the sky and the lands beneath the seas.'

Kull looked at the girl. Fine gold was her hair and her violet eyes were slanted strangely; she was beautiful, but her beauty meant little to Kull.

'Tuzun Thune,' he repeated. 'Who is he?'

'A wizard of the Elder Race. He lives here, in Valusia, by the Lake of Visions in the House of a Thousand Mirrors. All things are known to him, lord king; he speaks with the dead and holds converse with the demons of the Lost Lands.'

Kull arose.

'I will seek out this mummer; but no word of my going, do you hear?'

'I am your slave, my lord.' And she sank to her knees meekly, but the smile of her scarlet mouth was cunning behind Kull's back and the gleam of her narrow eyes was crafty.

Kull came to the house of Tuzun Thune, beside the Lake of Visions. Wide and blue stretched the waters of the lake and many a fine palace rose upon its banks; many swan-winged pleasure boats drifted lazily upon its hazy surface and evermore there came the sound of soft music.

Tall and spacious, but unpretentious, rose the House of a Thousand Mirrors. The great doors stood open and Kull ascended the broad stair and entered, unannounced. There in a great chamber, whose walls were of mirrors, he came upon Tuzun Thune, the wizard. The man was ancient as the hills of Zalgara; like wrinkled leather was his skin, but his cold gray eyes were like sparks of sword steel.

'Kull of Valusia, my house is yours,' said he, bowing with old-time courtliness and motioning Kull to a throne-like chair.

'You are a wizard, I have heard,' said Kull bluntly, resting his chin upon his hand and fixing his somber eyes upon the man's face. 'Can you do wonders?'

The wizard stretched forth his hand; his fingers opened and closed like a bird's claws.

'Is that not a wonder – that this blind flesh obeys the thoughts of my mind? I walk, I breathe, I speak – are they all not wonders?'

Kull meditated a while, then spoke. 'Can you summon up demons?'

'Aye. I can summon up a demon more savage than any in ghostland – by smiting you in the face.'

Kull started, then nodded. 'But the dead, can you talk to the dead?'

'I talk with the dead always – as I am talking now. Death begins with birth and each man begins to die when he is born; even now you are dead, King Kull, because you were born.'

'But you, you are older than men become; do wizards never die?'

'Men die when their time comes. No later, no sooner. Mine has not come.'

Kull turned these answers over in his mind.

'Then it would seem that the greatest wizard of Valusia is no more than an ordinary man, and I have been duped in coming here.'

Tuzun Thune shook his head. 'Men are but men, and the greatest men are they who soonest learn the simpler things. Nay, look into my mirrors, Kull.'

The ceiling was a great many mirrors, and the walls were mirrors, perfectly jointed, yet many mirrors of many sizes and shapes.

'Mirrors are the world, Kull,' droned the wizard. 'Gaze into my mirrors and be wise.'

Kull chose one at random and looked into it intently. The mirrors upon the opposite wall were reflected there, reflecting others, so that he seemed to be gazing down a long, luminous corridor, formed by mirror behind mirror; and far down this corridor moved a tiny figure. Kull looked long ere he saw that the figure was the reflection of himself. He gazed and a queer feeling of pettiness came over him; it seemed that that tiny figure was the true Kull, representing the real proportions of himself. So he moved away and stood before another.

'Look closely, Kull. That is the mirror of the past,' he heard the wizard say.

Gray fogs obscured the vision, great billows of mist, ever heaving and changing like the ghost of a great river; through these fogs Kull caught swift fleeting visions of horror and strangeness; beasts and men moved there and shapes neither men nor beasts; great exotic blossoms glowed through the grayness; tall tropic trees towered high over reeking swamps, where reptilian monsters wallowed and bellowed; the sky was ghastly with flying dragons and the restless seas rocked and roared and beat endlessly along the muddy beaches. Man was not, yet man was the dream of the gods and strange were the nightmare forms that glided through the noisome jungles. Battle and onslaught were there, and frightful love. Death was there, for Life and Death go hand in hand. Across the slimy beaches of the world sounded the bellowing of the monsters, and incredible shapes loomed through the steaming curtain of the incessant rain.

'This is of the future.'

Kull looked in silence.

'See you – what?'

'A strange world,' said Kull heavily. 'The Seven Empires are crumbled to dust and are forgotten. The restless green waves roar for many a fathom above the eternal hills of Atlantis; the mountains of Lemuria of the West are the islands of an unknown sea. Strange savages roam the elder lands and new lands flung strangely from the deeps, defiling the elder shrines. Valusia is vanished and all the nations of today; they of tomorrow are strangers. They know us not.'

'Time strides onward,' said Tuzun Thune calmly. 'We live today; what care we for tomorrow – or yesterday? The Wheel turns and nations rise and fall; the world changes, and times return to savagery to rise again through the long ages. Ere Atlantis was, Valusia was, and ere Valusia was, the Elder Nations were. Aye, we, too, trampled the shoulders of lost tribes in our advance. You, who have come from the green sea hills of Atlantis to seize the ancient crown of Valusia, you think my tribe is old, we who held these lands ere the Valusians came out of the East, in the days before there were men in the sea lands. But men were here when the Elder Tribes rode out of the waste lands, and men before men, tribe before tribe. The nations pass and are forgotten, for that is the destiny of man.'

'Yes,' said Kull. 'Yet is it not a pity that the beauty and glory of men should fade like smoke on a summer sea?'

'For what reason, since that is their destiny? I brood not over the lost glories of my race, nor do I labor for races to come. Live now, Kull, live now. The dead are dead; the unborn are not. What matters men's forgetfulness of you when you have forgotten yourself in the silent worlds of death? Gaze in my mirrors and be wise.'

Kull chose another mirror and gazed into it.

'That is the mirror of the deepest magic; what see ye, Kull?'

'Naught but myself.'

'Look closely, Kull; is it in truth you?'

Kull stared into the great mirror, and the image that was his reflection returned his gaze.

'I come before this mirror,' mused Kull, chin on fist, 'and I bring this man to life. This is beyond my understanding, since first I saw him in the still waters of the lakes of Atlantis, till I saw him again in the gold-rimmed mirrors of Valusia. He is I, a shadow of myself, part of myself – I can bring him into being or slay him at my will; yet' – he halted, strange thoughts whispering through the vast dim recesses of his mind like shadowy bats flying through a great cavern – 'yet where is he when I stand not in front of a mirror? May it be in man's power thus lightly to form and destroy a shadow of life and existence? How do I know that when I step back from the mirror he vanishes into the void of Naught?

'Nay, by Valka, am I the man or is he? Which of us is the ghost of the other? Mayhap these mirrors are but windows through which we look into another world. Does he think the same of me? Am I no more than a shadow, a reflection of himself – to him, as he to me? And if I am the ghost, what sort of a world lives upon the other side of this mirror? What armies ride there and what kings rule? This world is all I know. Knowing naught of any other, how can I judge? Surely there are green hills there and booming seas and wide plains where men ride to battle. Tell me, wizard who are wiser than most men, tell me, are there worlds beyond our worlds?'

'A man has eyes, let him see,' answered the wizard. 'Who would see must first believe.'

The hours drifted by and Kull still sat before the mirrors of Tuzun Thune, gazing into that which depicted himself. Sometimes it seemed that he gazed upon hard shallowness; at other times gigantic depths seemed to loom before him. Like the surface of the sea was the mirror of Tuzun Thune; hard as the sea in the sun's slanting beams, in the darkness of the stars, when no eye can pierce her deeps; vast and mystic as the sea when the sun smites her in such way that the watcher's breath is caught at the glimpse of tremendous abysses. So was the mirror in which Kull gazed.

At last the king rose with a sigh and took his departure still wondering. And Kull came again to the House of a Thousand Mirrors; day after day he came and sat for hours before the mirror. The eyes looked out at him, identical with his, yet Kull seemed to sense a difference – a reality that was not of him. Hour upon hour he would stare with strange intensity into the mirror; hour after hour the image gave back his gaze.

The business of the palace and of the council went neglected. The people murmured; Kull's stallion stamped restlessly in his stable and Kull's warriors diced and argued aimlessly with one another. Kull heeded not. At times he seemed on the point of discovering some vast, unthinkable secret. He no longer thought of the image in the mirror as a shadow of himself; the thing, to him, was an entity, similar in outer appearance, yet basically as far from Kull himself as the poles are far apart. The image, it seemed to Kull, had an individuality apart from Kull's; he was no more dependent on Kull than Kull was dependent on him. And day by day Kull doubted in which world he really lived; was he the shadow, summoned at will by the other? Did he instead of the other live in a world of delusion, the shadow of the real world?

Kull began to wish that he might enter the personality beyond the mirror for a space, to see what might be seen; yet should he manage to go beyond that door could he ever return? Would he find a world identical with the one in which he moved? A world, of which his was but a ghostly reflection? Which was reality and which illusion?

At times Kull halted to wonder how such thoughts and dreams had come to enter his mind and at times he wondered if they came of his own volition or – here his thoughts would become mazed. His meditations were his own; no man ruled his thoughts and he would summon them at his pleasure; yet could he? Were they not as bats, coming and going, not at his pleasure but at the bidding or ruling of – of whom? The gods? The Women who wove the webs of Fate? Kull could come to no conclusion, for at each mental step he became more and more bewildered in a hazy gray fog of illusory assertions and refutations. This much he knew: that strange visions entered his mind, like bats flying unbidden from the whispering void of nonexistence; never had he thought these thoughts, but now they ruled his mind, sleeping and waking, so that he seemed to walk in a daze at times; and his sleep was fraught with strange, monstrous dreams.

'Tell me, wizard,' he said, sitting before the mirror, eyes fixed intently upon his image, 'how can I pass yon door? For of a truth, I am not sure that that is the real world and this the shadow; at least, that which I see must exist in some form.'

'See and believe,' droned the wizard. 'Man must believe to accomplish. Form is shadow, substance is illusion, materiality is dream; man is because he believes he is; what is man but a dream of the gods? Yet man can be that which he wishes to be; form and substance, they are but shadows. The mind, the ego, the essence of the god-dream – that is real, that is immortal. See and believe, if you would accomplish, Kull.'

The king did not fully understand; he never fully understood the enigmatical utterances of the wizard, yet they struck somewhere in his being a dim responsive chord. So day after day he sat before the mirrors of Tuzun Thune. Ever the wizard lurked behind him like a shadow.

Then came a day when Kull seemed to catch glimpses of strange lands; there flitted across his consciousness dim thoughts and recognitions. Day by day he had seemed to lose touch with the world; all things had seemed each succeeding day more ghostly and unreal; only the man in the mirror seemed like reality. Now Kull seemed to be close to the doors of some mightier worlds; giant vistas gleamed fleetingly; the fogs of unreality thinned, 'form is shadow, substance is illusion; they are but shadows' sounded as if from some far country of his consciousness. He remembered the wizard's words and it seemed to him that now he almost understood – form and substance, could not he change himself at will, if he knew the master key that opened this door? What worlds within what worlds awaited the bold explorer?

The man in the mirror seemed smiling at him – closer, closer – a fog enwrapped all and the reflection dimmed suddenly – Kull knew a sensation of fading, of change, of merging –

'Kull!' The yell split the silence into a million vibratory fragments!

Mountains crashed and worlds tottered as Kull, hurled back by that frantic shout, made a superhuman effort, how or why he did not know.

A crash, and Kull stood in the room of Tuzun Thune before a shattered mirror, mazed and half blind with bewilderment. There before him lay the body of Tuzun Thune, whose time had come at last, and above him stood Brule the Spear-slayer, sword dripping red and eyes wide with a kind of horror.

'Valka!' swore the warrior. 'Kull, it was time I came!'

'Aye, yet what happened?' The king groped for words.

'Ask this traitress,' answered the Spear-slayer, indicating a girl who crouched in terror before the king; Kull saw that it was she who first sent him to Tuzun Thune. 'As I came in I saw you fading into yon mirror as smoke fades into the sky, by Valka! Had I not seen I would not have believed – you had almost vanished when my shout brought you back.'

'Aye,' muttered Kull, 'I had almost gone beyond the door that time.'

'This fiend wrought most craftily,' said Brule. 'Kull, do you not now see how he spun and flung over you a web of magic? Kaannub of Blaal plotted with this wizard to do away with you, and this wench, a girl of Elder Race, put the thought in your mind so that you would come here. Kananu of the council learned of the plot today; I know not what you saw in that mirror, but with it Tuzun Thune enthralled your soul and almost by his witchery he changed your body to mist –'

'Aye.' Kull was still mazed. 'But being a wizard, having knowledge of all the ages and despising gold, glory and position, what could Kaanuub offer Tuzun Thune that would make of him a foul traitor?'

'Gold, power and position,' grunted Brule. 'The sooner you learn that men are men whether wizard, king or thrall, the better you will rule, Kull. Now what of her?'

'Naught, Brule,' as the girl whimpered and groveled at Kull's feet. 'She was but a tool. Rise, child, and go your ways; none shall harm you.'

Alone with Brule, Kull looked for the last time on the mirrors of Tuzun Thune.

'Mayhap he plotted and conjured, Brule; nay, I doubt you not, yet – was it his witchery that was changing me to thin mist, or had I stumbled on a secret? Had you not brought me back, had I faded in dissolution or had I found worlds beyond this!'

Brule stole a glance at the mirrors, and twitched his shoulders as if he shuddered. 'Aye. Tuzun Thune stored the wisdom of all the hells here. Let us begone, Kull, ere they bewitch me, too.'

'Let us go, then,' answered Kull, and side by side they went forth from the House of a Thousand Mirrors – where, mayhap, are prisoned the souls of men.

None look now in the mirrors of Tuzun Thune. The pleasure boats shun the shore where stands the wizard's house and no one goes in the house or to the room where Tuzun Thune's dried and withered carcass lies before the mirrors of illusion. The place is shunned as a place accursed, and though it stands for a thousand years to come, no footsteps shall echo there. Yet Kull upon his throne meditates often upon the strange wisdom and untold secrets hidden there and wonders . . .

For there are worlds beyond worlds, as Kull knows, and whether the wizard bewitched him by words or by mesmerism, vistas did open to the king's gaze beyond that strange door, and Kull is less sure of reality since he gazed into the mirrors of Tuzun Thune.

Kings of the Night

The Cæsar lolled on his ivory throne –
His iron legions came
To break a king in a land unknown,
And a race without a name.

The Song of Bran

The dagger flashed downward. A sharp cry broke in a gasp. The form on the rough altar twitched convulsively and lay still. The jagged flint edge sawed at the crimsoned breast, and thin bony fingers, ghastly dyed, tore out the still twitching heart. Under matted white brows, sharp eyes gleamed with a ferocious intensity.

Besides the slayer, four men stood about the crude pile of stones that formed the altar of the God of Shadows. One was of medium height, lithely built, scantily clad, whose black hair was confined by a narrow iron band in the center of which gleamed a single red jewel. Of the others, two were dark like the first. But where he was lithe, they were stocky and misshapen, with knotted limbs, and tangled hair falling over sloping brows. His face denoted intelligence and implacable will; theirs merely a beast-like ferocity. The fourth man had little in common with the rest. Nearly a head taller, though his hair was black as theirs, his skin was comparatively light and he was gray-eyed. He eyed the proceedings with little favor.

And, in truth, Cormac of Connacht was little at ease. The

Druids of his own isle of Erin had strange dark rites of worship, but nothing like this. Dark trees shut in this grim scene, lit by a single torch. Through the branches moaned an eery night-wind. Cormac was alone among men of a strange race and he had just seen the heart of a man ripped from his still pulsing body. Now the ancient priest, who looked scarcely human, was glaring at the throbbing thing. Cormac shuddered, glancing at him who wore the jewel. Did Bran Mak Morn, king of the Picts, believe that this white-bearded old butcher could foretell events by scanning a bleeding human heart? The dark eyes of the king were inscrutable. There were strange depths to the man that Cormac could not fathom, nor any other man.

'The portents are good!' exclaimed the priest wildly, speaking more to the two chieftains than to Bran. 'Here from the pulsing heart of a captive Roman I read – defeat for the arms of Rome! Triumph for the sons of the heather!'

The two savages murmured beneath their breath, their fierce eyes smoldering.

'Go and prepare your clans for battle,' said the king, and they lumbered away with the ape-like gait assumed by such stunted giants. Paying no more heed to the priest who was examining the ghastly ruin on the altar, Bran beckoned to Cormac. The Gael followed him with alacrity. Once out of that grim grove, under the starlight, he breathed more freely. They stood on an eminence, looking out over long swelling undulations of gently waving heather. Near at hand a few fires twinkled, their fewness giving scant evidence of the hordes of tribesmen who lay close by. Beyond these were more fires and beyond these still more, which last marked the camp of Cormac's own men, hard-riding, hard-fighting Gaels, who were of that band which was just beginning to get a foothold on the western coast of Caledonia – the nucleus of what was later to become the kingdom of Dalriadia. To the left of these, other fires gleamed.

And far away to the south were more fires – mere pinpoints

of light. But even at that distance the Pictish king and his Celtic ally could see that these fires were laid out in regular order.

'The fires of the legions,' muttered Bran. 'The fires that have lit a path around the world. The men who light those fires have trampled the races under their iron heels. And now – we of the heather have our backs at the wall. What will fall on the morrow?'

'Victory for us, says the priest,' answered Cormac.

Bran made an impatient gesture. 'Moonlight on the ocean. Wind in the fir tops. Do you think that I put faith in such mummery? Or that I enjoyed the butchery of a captive legionary? I must hearten my people; it was for Gron and Bocah that I let old Gonar read the portents. The warriors will fight better.'

'And Gonar?'

Bran laughed. 'Gonar is too old to believe – anything. He was high priest of the Shadows a score of years before I was born. He claims direct descent from that Gonar who was a wizard in the days of Brule, the Spear-slayer who was the first of my line. No man knows how old he is – sometimes I think he is the original Gonar himself!'

'At least,' said a mocking voice, and Cormac started as a dim shape appeared at his side, 'at least I have learned that in order to keep the faith and trust of the people, a wise man must appear to be a fool. I know secrets that would blast even your brain, Bran, should I speak them. But in order that the people may believe in me, I must descend to such things as they think proper magic – and prance and yell and rattle snakeskins, and dabble about in human blood and chicken livers.'

Cormac looked at the ancient with new interest. The semi-madness of his appearance had vanished. He was no longer the charlatan, the spell-mumbling shaman. The starlight lent him a dignity which seemed to increase his very height, so that he stood like a white-bearded patriarch.

'Bran, your doubt lies there.' The lean arm pointed to the fourth ring of fires.

'Aye,' the king nodded gloomily. 'Cormac – you know as well as I. Tomorrow's battle hinges upon that circle of fires. With the chariots of the Britons and your own Western horsemen, our success would be certain, but – surely the devil himself is in the heart of every Northman! You know how I trapped that band – how they swore to fight for me against Rome! And now that their chief, Rognar, is dead, they swear that they will be led only by a king of their own race! Else they will break their vow and go over to the Romans. Without them we are doomed, for we can not change our former plan.'

'Take heart, Bran,' said Gonar. 'Touch the jewel in your iron crown. Mayhap it will bring you aid.'

Bran laughed bitterly. 'Now you talk as the people think. I am no fool to twist with empty words. What of the gem? It is a strange one, truth, and has brought me luck ere now. But I need now, no jewels, but the allegiance of three hundred fickle Northmen who are the only warriors among us who may stand the charge of the legions on foot.'

'But the jewel, Bran, the jewel!' persisted Gonar.

'Well, the jewel!' cried Bran impatiently. 'It is older than this world. It was old when Atlantis and Lemuria sank into the sea. It was given to Brule, the Spear-slayer, first of my line, by the Atlantean Kull, king of Valusia, in the days when the world was young. But shall that profit us now?'

'Who knows?' asked the wizard obliquely. 'Time and space exist not. There was no past, and there shall be no future. NOW is all. All things that ever were, are, or ever will be, transpire *now*. Man is forever at the center of what we call time and space. I have gone into yesterday and tomorrow and both were as real as today – which is like the dreams of ghosts! But let me sleep and talk with Gonar. Mayhap he shall aid us.'

'What means he?' asked Cormac, with a slight twitching of his shoulders, as the priest strode away in the shadows.

'He has ever said that the first Gonar comes to him in his

dreams and talks with him,' answered Bran. 'I have seen him perform deeds that seemed beyond human ken. I know not. I am but an unknown king with an iron crown, trying to lift a race of savages out of the slime into which they have sunk. Let us look to the camps.'

As they walked Cormac wondered. By what strange freak of fate had such a man risen among this race of savages, survivors of a darker, grimmer age? Surely he was an atavism, an original type of the days when the Picts ruled all Europe, before their primitive empire fell before the bronze swords of the Gauls. Cormac knew how Bran, rising by his own efforts from the negligent position of the son of a Wolf clan chief, had to an extent united the tribes of the heather and now claimed kingship over all Caledon. But his rule was loose and much remained before the Pictish clans would forget their feuds and present a solid front to foreign foes. On the battle of the morrow, the first pitched battle between the Picts under their king and the Romans, hinged the future of the rising Pictish kingdom.

Bran and his ally walked through the Pictish camp where the swart warriors lay sprawled about their small fires, sleeping or gnawing half-cooked food. Cormac was impressed by their silence. A thousand men camped here, yet the only sounds were occasional low guttural intonations. The silence of the Stone Age rested in the souls of these men.

They were all short – most of them crooked of limb. Giant dwarfs; Bran Mak Morn was a tall man among them. Only the older men were bearded and they scantily, but their black hair fell about their eyes so that they peered fiercely from under the tangle. They were barefoot and clad scantily in wolfskins. Their arms consisted in short barbed swords of iron, heavy black bows, arrows tipped with flint, iron and copper, and stone-headed mallets. Defensive armor they had none, save for a crude shield of hide-covered wood; many had worked bits of metal into their tangled manes as a slight protection against sword-cuts. Some few, sons of long lines of chiefs, were smooth-limbed and lithe like Bran, but in the eyes of all gleamed the unquench-able savagery of the primeval.

These men are fully savages, thought Cormac, worse than the Gauls, Britons and Germans. Can the old legends be true – that they reigned in a day when strange cities rose where now the sea rolls? And that they survived the flood that washed those gleaming empires under, sinking again into that savagery from which they once had risen?

Close to the encampment of the tribesmen were the fires of a group of Britons – members of fierce tribes who lived south of the Roman Wall but who dwelt in the hills and forests to the west and defied the power of Rome. Powerfully built men they were, with blazing blue eyes and shocks of tousled yellow hair, such men as had thronged the Ceanntish beaches when Cæsar brought the Eagles into the Isles. These men, like the Picts, wore no armor, and were clad scantily in coarse-worked cloth and deerskin san-dals. They bore small round bucklers of hard wood, braced with bronze, to be worn on the left arm, and long heavy bronze swords with blunt points. Some had bows, though the Britons were indif-ferent archers. Their bows were shorter than the Picts' and effect-ive only at close range. But ranged close by their fires were the weapons that had made the name Briton a word of terror to Pict, Roman and Norse raider alike. Within the circle of firelight stood fifty bronze chariots with long cruel blades curving out from the sides. One of these blades could dismember half a dozen men at once. Tethered close by under the vigilant eyes of their guards grazed the chariot horses – big, rangy steeds, swift and powerful.

'Would that we had more of them!' mused Bran. 'With a thousand chariots and my bowmen I could drive the legions into the sea.'

'The free British tribes must eventually fall before Rome,' said Cormac. 'It would seem they would rush to join you in your war.'

Bran made a helpless gesture. 'The fickleness of the Celt. They can not forget old feuds. Our ancient men have told us how they would not even unite against Cæsar when the Romans first came. They will not make head against a common foe together. These men came to me because of some dispute with their chief, but I can not depend on them when they are not actually fighting.'

Cormac nodded. 'I know; Cæsar conquered Gaul by playing one tribe against another. My own people shift and change with the waxing and waning of the tides. But of all Celts, the Cymry are the most changeable, the least stable. Not many centuries ago my own Gaelic ancestors wrested Erin from the Cymric Danaans, because though they outnumbered us, they opposed us as separate tribes, rather than as a nation.'

'And so these Cymric Britons face Rome,' said Bran. 'These will aid us on the morrow. Further I can not say. But how shall I expect loyalty from alien tribes, who am not sure of my own people? Thousands lurk in the hills, holding aloof. I am king in name only. Let me win tomorrow and they will flock to my standard; if I lose, they will scatter like birds before a cold wind.'

A chorus of rough welcome greeted the two leaders as they entered the camp of Cormac's Gaels. Five hundred in number they were, tall rangy men, black-haired and gray-eyed mainly, with the bearing of men who lived by war alone. While there was nothing like close discipline among them, there was an air of more system and practical order than existed in the lines of the Picts and Britons. These men were of the last Celtic race to invade the Isles and their barbaric civilization was of much higher order than that of their Cymric kin. The ancestors of the Gaels had learned the arts of war on the vast plains of Scythia and at the courts of the Pharaohs where they had fought as mercenaries of Egypt, and much of what they learned they brought into Ireland with them. Excelling in metal work, they were armed, not with clumsy bronze swords, but with high-grade weapons of iron.

They were clad in well-woven kilts and leathern sandals. Each wore a light shirt of chain mail and a vizorless helmet, but this was all of their defensive armor. Celts, Gaelic or Brythonic, were prone to judge a man's valor by the amount of armor he wore. The Britons who faced Cæsar deemed the Romans cowards because they cased themselves in metal, and many centuries later the Irish clans thought the same of the mail-clad Norman knights of Strongbow.

Cormac's warriors were horsemen. They neither knew nor esteemed the use of the bow. They bore the inevitable round, metal-braced buckler, dirks, long straight swords and light single-handed axes. Their tethered horses grazed not far away – big-boned animals, not so ponderous as those raised by the Britons, but swifter.

Bran's eyes lighted as the two strode through the camp. 'These men are keen-beaked birds of war! See how they whet their axes and jest of the morrow! Would that the raiders in yon camp were as staunch as your men, Cormac! Then would I greet the legions with a laugh when they come up from the south tomorrow.'

They were entering the circle of the Northmen fires. Three hundred men sat about gambling, whetting their weapons and drinking deep of the heather ale furnished them by their Pictish allies. These gazed upon Bran and Cormac with no great friendliness. It was striking to note the difference between them and the Picts and Celts – the difference in their cold eyes, their strong moody faces, their very bearing. Here was ferocity, and savagery, but not of the wild, upbursting fury of the Celt. Here was fierceness backed by grim determination and stolid stubbornness. The charge of the British clans was terrible, overwhelming. But they had no patience; let them be balked of immediate victory and they were likely to lose heart and scatter or fall to bickering among themselves. There was the patience of the cold blue North in these seafarers – a lasting determination that would keep them stedfast to the bitter end, once their face was set toward a definite goal.

As to personal stature, they were giants; massive yet rangy. That they did not share the ideas of the Celts regarding armor was shown by the fact that they were clad in heavy scale mail shirts that reached below mid-thigh, heavy horned helmets and hardened hide leggings, reinforced, as were their shoes, with plates of iron. Their shields were huge oval affairs of hard wood, hide and brass. As to weapons, they had long iron-headed spears, heavy iron axes, and daggers. Some had long wide-bladed swords.

Cormac scarcely felt at ease with the cold magnetic eyes of these flaxen-haired men fixed upon him. He and they were hereditary foes, even though they did chance to be fighting on the same side at present – but were they?

A man came forward, a tall gaunt warrior on whose scarred, wolfish face the flickering firelight reflected deep shadows. With his wolfskin mantle flung carelessly about his wide shoulders, and the great horns on his helmet adding to his height, he stood there in the swaying shadows, like some half-human thing, a brooding shape of the dark barbarism that was soon to engulf the world.

'Well, Wulfhere,' said the Pictish king, 'you have drunk the mead of council and have spoken about the fires – what is your decision?'

The Northman's eyes flashed in the gloom. 'Give us a king of our own race to follow if you wish us to fight for you.'

Bran flung out his hands. 'Ask me to drag down the stars to gem your helmets! Will not your comrades follow you?'

'Not against the legions,' answered Wulfhere sullenly. 'A king led us on the viking path – a king must lead us against the Romans. And Rognar is dead.'

'I am a king,' said Bran. 'Will you fight for me if I stand at the tip of your fight wedge?'

'A king of our own race,' said Wulfhere doggedly. 'We are all picked men of the North. We fight for none but a king, and a king must lead us – against the legions.'

Cormac sensed a subtle threat in this repeated phrase.

'Here is a prince of Erin,' said Bran. 'Will you fight for the Westerner?'

'We fight under no Celt, West or East,' growled the viking, and a low rumble of approval rose from the onlookers. 'It is enough to fight by their side.'

The hot Gaelic blood rose in Cormac's brain and he pushed past Bran, his hand on his sword. 'How mean you that, pirate?'

Before Wulfhere could reply Bran interposed: 'Have done! Will you fools throw away the battle before it is fought, by your madness? What of your oath, Wulfhere?'

'We swore it under Rognar; when he died from a Roman arrow we were absolved of it. We will follow only a king – against the legions.'

'But your comrades will follow you – against the heather people!' snapped Bran.

'Aye,' the Northman's eyes met his brazenly. 'Send us a king or we join the Romans tomorrow.'

Bran snarled. In his rage he dominated the scene, dwarfing the huge men who towered over him.

'Traitors! Liars! I hold your lives in my hand! Aye, draw your swords if you will – Cormac, keep your blade in its sheath. These wolves will not bite a king! Wulfhere – I spared your lives when I could have taken them.

'You came to raid the countries of the South, sweeping down from the northern sea in your galleys. You ravaged the coasts and the smoke of burning villages hung like a cloud over the shores of Caledon. I trapped you all when you were pillaging and burning – with the blood of my people on your hands. I burned your long ships and ambushed you when you followed. With thrice your number of bowmen who burned for your lives hidden in the heathered hills about you, I spared you when we could have shot you down like trapped wolves. Because I spared you, you swore to come and fight for me.'

'And shall we die because the Picts fight Rome?' rumbled a bearded raider.

'Your lives are forfeit to me; you came to ravage the South. I did not promise to send you all back to your homes in the North unharmed and loaded with loot. Your vow was to fight one battle against Rome under my standard. Then I will aid your survivors to build ships and you may go where you will, with a goodly share of the plunder we take from the legions. Rognar had kept his oath. But Rognar died in a skirmish with Roman scouts and now you, Wulfhere the Dissension-breeder, you stir up your comrades to dishonor themselves by that which a Northman hates – the breaking of the sworn word.'

'We break no oath,' snarled the viking, and the king sensed the basic Germanic stubbornness, far harder to combat than the fickleness of the fiery Celts. 'Give us a king, neither Pict, Gael nor Briton, and we will die for you. If not – then we will fight tomorrow for the greatest of all kings – the emperor of Rome!'

For a moment Cormac thought that the Pictish king, in his black rage, would draw and strike the Northman dead. The concentrated fury that blazed in Bran's dark eyes caused Wulfhere to recoil and drop a hand to his belt.

'Fool!' said Mak Morn in a low voice that vibrated with passion. 'I could sweep you from the earth before the Romans are near enough to hear your death howls. Choose – fight for me on the morrow – or die tonight under a black cloud of arrows, a red storm of swords, a dark wave of chariots!'

At the mention of the chariots, the only arm of war that had ever broken the Norse shield-wall, Wulfhere changed expression, but he held his ground.

'War be it,' he said doggedly. 'Or a king to lead us!'

The Northmen responded with a short deep roar and a clash

of swords on shields. Bran, eyes blazing, was about to speak again when a white shape glided silently into the ring of firelight.

'Soft words, soft words,' said old Gonar tranquilly. 'King, say no more. Wulfhere, you and your fellows will fight for us if you have a king to lead you?'

'We have sworn.'

'Then be at ease,' quoth the wizard; 'for ere battle joins on the morrow I will send you such a king as no man on earth has followed for a hundred thousand years! A king neither Pict, Gael not Briton, but one to whom the emperor of Rome is as but a village headman!'

While they stood undecided, Gonar took the arms of Cormac and Bran. 'Come. And you, Northmen, remember your vow, and my promise which I have never broken. Sleep now, nor think to steal away in the darkness to the Roman camp, for if you escaped our shafts you would not escape either my curse or the suspicions of the legionaries.'

So the three walked away and Cormac, looking back, saw Wulfhere standing by the fire, fingering his golden beard, with a look of puzzled anger on his lean evil face.

The three walked silently through the waving heather under the far-away stars while the weird night wind whispered ghostly secrets about them.

'Ages ago,' said the wizard suddenly, 'in the days when the world was young, great lands rose where now the ocean roars. On these lands thronged mighty nations and kingdoms. Greatest of all these was Valusia – Land of Enchantment. Rome is as a village compared to the splendor of the cities of Valusia. And the greatest king was Kull, who came from the land of Atlantis to wrest the crown of Valusia from a degenerate dynasty. The Picts who dwelt in the isles which now form the mountain peaks of a strange land upon the Western Ocean, were allies of Valusia, and the greatest of all the Pictish war-chiefs was Brule the Spear-slayer, first of the line men call Mak Morn.

'Kull gave to Brule the jewel which you now wear in your iron crown, oh king, after a strange battle in a dim land, and down the long ages it has come to us, ever a sign of the Mak Morn, a symbol of former greatness. When at last the sea rose and swallowed Valusia, Atlantis and Lemuria, only the Picts survived and they were scattered and few. Yet they began again the slow climb upward, and though many of the arts of civilization were lost in the great flood, yet they progressed. The art of metal-working was lost, so they excelled in the working of flint. And they ruled all the new lands flung up by the sea and now called Europe, until down from the north came younger tribes who had scarce risen from the ape when Valusia reigned in her glory, and who, dwelling in the icy lands about the Pole, knew naught of the lost splendor of the Seven Empires and little of the flood that had swept away half a world.

'And still they have come – Aryans, Celts, Germans, swarming down from the great cradle of their race which lies near the Pole. So again was the growth of the Pictish nation checked and the race hurled into savagery. Erased from the earth, on the fringe of the world with our backs to the wall we fight. Here in Caledon is the last stand of a once mighty race. And we change. Our people have mixed with the savages of an elder age which we drove into the North when we came into the Isles, and now, save for their chieftains, such as thou, Bran, a Pict is strange and abhorrent to look upon.'

'True, true,' said the king impatiently, 'but what has that to do –'

'Kull, king of Valusia,' said the wizard imperturbably, 'was a barbarian in his age as thou art in thine, though he ruled a mighty empire by the weight of his sword. Gonar, friend of Brule, your first ancestor, has been dead a hundred thousand years as we reckon time. Yet I talked with him a scant hour agone.'

'You talked with his ghost –'

'Or he with mine? Did I go back a hundred thousand years, or did he come forward? If he came to me out of the past, it is not I who talked with a dead man, but he who talked with a man unborn. Past, present and future are one to a wise man. I talked to Gonar while he was alive; likewise was I alive. In a timeless, spaceless land we met and he told me many things.'

The land was growing light with the birth of dawn. The heather waved and bent in long rows before the dawn wind as bowing in worship of the rising sun.

'The jewel in your crown is a magnet that draws down the eons,' said Gonar. 'The sun is rising – and who comes out of the sunrise?'

Cormac and the king started. The sun was just lifting a red orb above the eastern hills. And full in the glow, etched boldly against the golden rim, a man suddenly appeared. They had not seen him come. Against the golden birth of day he loomed colossal; a gigantic god from the dawn of creation. Now as he strode toward them the waking hosts saw him and sent up a sudden shout of wonder.

'Who – or what is it?' exclaimed Bran.

'Let us go to meet him, Bran,' answered the wizard. 'He is the king Gonar has sent to save the people of Brule.'

2

'I have reached these lands but newly
From an ultimate dim Thule;
From a wild weird clime that lieth sublime
Out of Space – out of Time.'

Poe

The army fell silent as Bran, Cormac and Gonar went toward the stranger who approached in long swinging strides. As they neared him the illusion of monstrous size vanished, but they

saw he was a man of great stature. At first Cormac thought him
to be a Northman but a second glance told him that nowhere
before had he seen such a man. He was built much like the
vikings, at once massive and lithe – tigerish. But his features
were not as theirs, and his square-cut, lion-like mane of hair was
as black as Bran's own. Under heavy brows glittered eyes gray as
steel and cold as ice. His bronzed face, strong and inscrutable,
was clean-shaven, and the broad forehead betokened a high
intelligence, just as the firm jaw and thin lips showed will-power
and courage. But more than all, the bearing of him, the unconscious lion-like stateliness, marked him as a natural king, a ruler
of men.

Sandals of curious make were on his feet and he wore a pliant
coat of strangely meshed mail which came almost to his knees. A
broad belt with a great golden buckle encircled his waist, supporting a long straight sword in a heavy leather scabbard. His hair was
confined by a wide, heavy golden band about his head.

Such was the man who paused before the silent group. He
seemed slightly puzzled, slightly amused. Recognition flickered
in his eyes. He spoke in a strange archaic Pictish which Cormac
scarcely understood. His voice was deep and resonant.

'Ha, Brule, Gonar did not tell me I would dream of you!'

For the first time in his life Cormac saw the Pictish king completely thrown off his balance. He gaped, speechless. The
stranger continued:

'And wearing the gem I gave you, in a circlet on your head!
Last night you wore it in a ring on your finger.'

'Last night?' gasped Bran.

'Last night or a hundred thousand years ago – all one!' murmured Gonar in evident enjoyment of the situation.

'I am not Brule,' said Bran. 'Are you mad to thus speak of a
man dead a hundred thousand years? He was first of my line.'

The stranger laughed unexpectedly. 'Well, now I know I am
dreaming! This will be a tale to tell Brule when I waken on the

morrow! That I went into the future and saw men claiming descent from the Spear-slayer who is, as yet, not even married. No, you are not Brule, I see now, though you have his eyes and his bearing. But he is taller and broader in the shoulders. Yet you have his jewel – oh, well – anything can happen in a dream, so I will not quarrel with you. For a time I thought I had been transported to some other land in my sleep, and was in reality awake in a strange country, for this is the clearest dream I ever dreamed. Who are you?'

'I am Bran Mak Morn, king of the Caledonian Picts. And this ancient is Gonar, a wizard, of the line of Gonar. And this warrior is Cormac na Connacht, a prince of the isle of Erin.'

The stranger slowly shook his lion-like head. 'These words sound strangely to me, save Gonar – and that one is not Gonar, though he too is old. What land is this?'

'Caledon, or Alba, as the Gaels call it.'

'And who are those squat ape-like warriors who watch us yonder, all agape?'

'They are the Picts who own my rule.'

'How strangely distorted folk are in dreams!' muttered the stranger. 'And who are those shock-headed men about the chariots?'

'They are Britons – Cymry from south of the Wall.'

'What Wall?'

'The Wall built by Rome to keep the people of the heather out of Britain.'

'Britain?' the tone was curious. 'I never heard of that land – and what is Rome?'

'What!' cried Bran. 'You never heard of Rome, the empire that rules the world?'

'No empire rules the world,' answered the other haughtily. 'The mightiest kingdom on earth is that wherein I reign.'

'And who are you?'

'Kull of Atlantis, king of Valusia!'

Cormac felt a coldness trickle down his spine. The cold gray eyes were unswerving – but this was incredible – monstrous – unnatural.

'Valusia!' cried Bran. 'Why, man, the sea waves have rolled above the spires of Valusia for untold centuries!'

Kull laughed outright. 'What a mad nightmare this is! When Gonar put on me the spell of deep sleep last night – or this night! – in the secret room of the inner palace, he told me I would dream strange things, but this is more fantastic than I reckoned. And the strangest thing is, I know I am dreaming!'

Gonar interposed as Bran would have spoken. 'Question not the acts of the gods,' muttered the wizard. 'You are king because in the past you have seen and seized opportunities. The gods or the first Gonar have sent you this man. Let me deal with him.'

Bran nodded, and while the silent army gaped in speechless wonder, just within ear-shot, Gonar spoke: 'Oh great king, you dream, but is not all life a dream? How reckon you but that your former life is but a dream from which you have just awakened? Now we dream-folk have our wars and our peace, and just now a great host comes up from the south to destroy the people of Brule. Will you aid us?'

Kull grinned with pure zest. 'Aye! I have fought battles in dreams ere now, have slain and been slain and was amazed when I woke from my visions. And at times, as now, dreaming I have known I dreamed. See, I pinch myself and feel it, but I know I dream for I have felt the pain of fierce wounds, in dreams. Yes, people of my dream, I will fight for you against the other dream-folk. Where are they?'

'And that you enjoy the dream more,' said the wizard subtly, 'forget that it is a dream and pretend that by the magic of the first Gonar, and the quality of the jewel you gave Brule, that now gleams on the crown of the Morni, you have in truth been transported forward into another, wilder age where the people of Brule fight for their life against a stronger foe.'

For a moment the man who called himself king of Valusia seemed startled; a strange look of doubt, almost of fear, clouded his eyes. Then he laughed.

'Good! Lead on, wizard.'

But now Bran took charge. He had recovered himself and was at ease. Whether he thought, like Cormac, that this was all a gigantic hoax arranged by Gonar, he showed no sign.

'King Kull, see you those men yonder who lean on their long-shafted axes as they gaze upon you?'

'The tall men with the golden hair and beards?'

'Aye – our success in the coming battle hinges on them. They swear to go over to the enemy if we give them not a king to lead them – their own having been slain. Will you lead them to battle?'

Kull's eyes glowed with appreciation. 'They are men such as my own Red Slayers, my picked regiment. I will lead them.'

'Come then.'

The small group made their way down the slope, through throngs of warriors who pushed forward eagerly to get a better view of the stranger, then pressed back as he approached. An undercurrent of tense whispering ran through the horde.

The Northmen stood apart in a compact group. Their cold eyes took in Kull and he gave back their stares, taking in every detail of their appearance.

'Wulfhere,' said Bran, 'we have brought you a king. I hold you to your oath.'

'Let him speak to us,' said the viking harshly.

'He can not speak your tongue,' answered Bran, knowing that the Northmen knew nothing of the legends of his race. 'He is a great king of the South –'

'He comes out of the past,' broke in the wizard calmly. 'He was the greatest of all kings, long ago.'

'A dead man!' The vikings moved uneasily and the rest of the horde pressed forward, drinking in every word. But Wulfhere scowled: 'Shall a ghost lead living men? You bring us a man you say is dead. We will not follow a corpse.'

'Wulfhere,' said Bran in still passion, 'you are a liar and a traitor. You set us this task, thinking it impossible. You yearn to fight under the Eagles of Rome. We have brought you a king neither Pict, Gael nor Briton and you deny your vow!'

'Let him fight me, then!' howled Wulfhere in uncontrollable wrath, swinging his ax about his head in a glittering arc. 'If your dead man overcomes me – then my people will follow you. If I overcome him, you shall let us depart in peace to the camp of the legions!'

'Good!' said the wizard. 'Do you agree, wolves of the North?'

A fierce yell and a brandishing of swords was the answer. Bran turned to Kull, who had stood silent, understanding nothing of what was said. But the Atlantean's eyes gleamed. Cormac felt that those cold eyes had looked on too many such scenes not to understand something of what had passed.

'This warrior says you must fight him for the leadership,' said Bran, and Kull, eyes glittering with growing battle-joy, nodded: 'I guessed as much. Give us space.'

'A shield and a helmet!' shouted Bran, but Kull shook his head.

'I need none,' he growled. 'Back and give us room to swing our steel!'

Men pressed back on each side, forming a solid ring about the two men, who now approached each other warily. Kull had drawn his sword and the great blade shimmered like a live thing in his hand. Wulfhere, scarred by a hundred savage fights, flung aside his wolfskin mantle and came in cautiously, fierce eyes peering over the the top of his out-thrust shield, ax half lifted in his right hand.

Suddenly when the warriors were still many feet apart Kull sprang. His attack brought a gasp from men used to deeds of prowess; for like a leaping tiger he shot through the air and his sword crashed on the quickly lifted shield. Sparks flew and Wulfhere's ax hacked in, but Kull was under its sweep and as it swished viciously above his head he thrust upward and sprang out again, cat-like. His motions had been too quick for the eye to follow. The upper edge of Wulfhere's shield showed a deep cut, and there was a long rent in his mail shirt where Kull's sword had barely missed the flesh beneath.

Cormac, trembling with the terrible thrill of the fight, wondered at this sword that could thus slice through scale-mail. And the blow that gashed the shield should have shattered the blade. Yet not a notch showed in the Valusian steel! Surely this blade was forged by another people in another age!

Now the two giants leaped again to the attack and like double strokes of lightning their weapons crashed. Wulfhere's shield fell from his arm in two pieces as the Atlantean's sword sheared clear through it, and Kull staggered as the Northman's ax, driven with all the force of his great body, descended on the golden circlet about his head. That blow should have sheared through the gold like butter to split the skull beneath, but the ax rebounded, showing a great notch in the edge. The next instant the Northman was overwhelmed by a whirlwind of steel – a storm of strokes delivered with such swiftness and power that he was borne back as on the crest of a wave, unable to launch an attack of his own. With all his tried skill he sought to parry the singing steel with his ax. But he could only avert his doom for a few seconds; could only for an instant turn the whistling blade that hewed off bits of his mail, so close fell the blows. One of the horns flew from his helmet; then the ax-head itself fell away, and the same blow that severed the handle, bit through the viking's helmet into the scalp beneath. Wulfhere was dashed to his knees, a trickle of blood starting down his face.

Kull checked his second stroke, and tossing his sword to

Cormac, faced the dazed Northman weaponless. The Atlantean's eyes were blazing with ferocious joy and he roared something in a strange tongue. Wulfhere gathered his legs under him and bounded up, snarling like a wolf, a dagger flashing into his hand. The watching horde gave tongue in a yell that ripped the skies as the two bodies clashed. Kull's clutching hand missed the Northman's wrist but the desperately lunging dagger snapped on the Atlantean's mail, and dropping the useless hilt, Wulfhere locked his arms about his foe in a bear-like grip that would have crushed the ribs of a lesser man. Kull grinned tigerishly and returned the grapple, and for a moment the two swayed on their feet. Slowly the black-haired warrior bent his foe backward until it seemed his spine would snap. With a howl that had nothing of the human in it, Wulfhere clawed frantically at Kull's face, trying to tear out his eyes, then turned his head and snapped his fang-like teeth into the Atlantean's arm. A yell went up as a trickle of blood started: 'He bleeds! He bleeds! He is no ghost, after all, but a mortal man!'

Angered, Kull shifted his grip, shoving the frothing Wulfhere away from him, and smote him terrifically under the ear with his right hand. The viking landed on his back a dozen feet away. Then, howling like a wild man, he leaped up with a stone in his hand and flung it. Only Kull's incredible quickness saved his face; as it was, the rough edge of the missile tore his cheek and inflamed him to madness. With a lion-like roar he bounded upon his foe, enveloped him in an irresistible blast of sheer fury, whirled him high above his head as if he were a child and cast him a dozen feet away. Wulfhere pitched on his head and lay still – broken and dead.

Dazed silence reigned for an instant; then from the Gaels went up a thundering roar, and the Britons and Picts took it up, howling like wolves, until the echoes of the shouts and the clangor of sword on shield reached the ears of the marching legionaries, miles to the south.

'Men of the gray North,' shouted Bran, 'will you hold by your oath *now*?'

The fierce souls of the Northmen were in their eyes as their spokesman answered. Primitive, superstitious, steeped in tribal lore of fighting gods and mythical heroes, they did not doubt that the black-haired fighting man was some supernatural being sent by the fierce gods of battle.

'Aye! Such a man as this we have never seen! Dead man, ghost or devil, we will follow him, whether the trail lead to Rome or Valhalla!'

Kull understood the meaning, if not the words. Taking his sword from Cormac with a word of thanks, he turned to the waiting Northmen and silently held the blade toward them high above his head, in both hands, before he returned it to its scabbard. Without understanding, they appreciated the action. Blood-stained and disheveled, he was an impressive picture of stately, magnificent barbarism.

'Come,' said Bran, touching the Atlantean's arm; 'a host is marching on us and we have much to do. There is scant time to arrange our forces before they will be upon us. Come to the top of yonder slope.'

There the Pict pointed. They were looking down into a valley which ran north and south, widening from a narrow gorge in the north until it debouched upon a plain to the south. The whole valley was less than a mile in length.

'Up this valley will our foes come,' said the Pict, 'because they have wagons loaded with supplies and on all sides of this vale the ground is too rough for such travel. Here we plan an ambush.'

'I would have thought you would have had your men lying in wait long before now,' said Kull. 'What of the scouts the enemy is sure to send out?'

'The savages I lead would never have waited in ambush so long,' said Bran with a touch of bitterness. 'I could not post them until I was sure of the Northmen. Even so I had not dared to post them ere now – even yet they may take panic from the drifting of a cloud or the blowing of a leaf, and scatter like birds before a cold wind. King Kull – the fate of the Pictish nation is at stake. I am called king of the Picts, but my rule as yet is but a hollow mockery. The hills are full of wild clans who refuse to fight for me. Of the thousand bowmen now at my command, more than half are of my own clan.

'Some eighteen hundred Romans are marching against us. It is not a real invasion, but much hinges upon it. It is the beginning of an attempt to extend their boundaries. They plan to build a fortress a day's march to the north of this valley. If they do, they will build other forts, drawing bands of steel about the heart of the free people. If I win this battle and wipe out this army, I will win a double victory. Then the tribes will flock to me and the next invasion will meet a solid wall of resistance. If I lose, the clans will scatter, fleeing into the north until they can no longer flee, fighting as separate clans rather than as one strong nation.

'I have a thousand archers, five hundred horsemen, fifty chariots with their drivers and swordsmen – one hundred fifty men in all – and, thanks to you, three hundred heavily armed Northern pirates. How would you arrange your battle lines?'

'Well,' said Kull, 'I would have barricaded the north end of the valley – no! That would suggest a trap. But I would block it with a band of desperate men, like those you have given me to lead. Three hundred could hold the gorge for a time against any number. Then, when the enemy was engaged with these men to the narrow part of the valley, I would have my archers shoot down into them until their ranks are broken, from both sides of the vale. Then, having my horsemen concealed behind one ridge and my chariots behind the other, I would charge with both simultaneously and sweep the foe into a red ruin.'

Bran's eyes glowed. 'Exactly, king of Valusia. Such was my exact plan –'

'But what of the scouts?'

'My warriors are like panthers; they hide under the noses of the Romans. Those who ride into the valley will see only what we wish them to see. Those who ride over the ridge will not come back to report. An arrow is swift and silent.

'You see that the pivot of the whole thing depends on the men that hold the gorge. They must be men who can fight on foot and resist the charges of the heavy legionaries long enough for the trap to close. Outside these Northmen I had no such force of men. My naked warriors with their short swords could never stand such a charge for an instant. Nor is the armor of the Celts made for such work; moreover, they are not foot-fighters, and I need them elsewhere.

'So you see why I had such desperate need of the Northmen. Now will you stand in the gorge with them and hold back the Romans until I can spring the trap? Remember, most of you will die.'

Kull smiled. 'I have taken chances all my life, though Tu, chief councilor, would say my life belongs to Valusia and I have no right to so risk it –' His voice trailed off and a strange look flitted across his face. 'By Valka,' said he, laughing uncertainly, 'sometimes I forget this is a dream! All seems so real. But it is – of course it is! Well, then, if I die I will but awaken as I have done in times past. Lead on, king of Caledon!'

Cormac, going to his warriors, wondered. Surely it was all a hoax; yet – he heard the arguments of the warriors all about him as they armed themselves and prepared to take their posts. The black-haired king was Neid himself, the Celtic war-god; he was an antediluvian king brought out of the past by Gonar; he was a mythical fighting man out of Valhalla. He was no man at all but a ghost! No, he was mortal, for he had bled. But the gods themselves bled, though they did not die. So the controversies raged. At least, thought Cormac, if it was all a hoax to inspire the warriors with the feeling of supernatural aid, it had succeeded. The belief that Kull was more than a mortal man had fired Celt, Pict and viking alike into a sort of inspired madness. And Cormac asked himself – what did he himself believe? This man was surely one from some far land – yet in his every look and action there was a vague hint of a greater difference than mere distance of space – a hint of alien Time, of misty abysses and gigantic gulfs of eons lying between the black-haired stranger and the men with whom he walked and talked. Clouds of bewilderment mazed Cormac's brain and he laughed in whimsical self-mockery.

3

'And the two wild peoples of the north
Stood fronting in the gloom,
And heard and knew each in his mind
A third great sound upon the wind,
The living walls that hedge mankind,
The walking walls of Rome.'

Chesterton

The sun slanted westward. Silence lay like an invisible mist over the valley. Cormac gathered the reins in his hand and glanced up at the ridges on both sides. The waving heather which grew rank on those steep slopes gave no evidence of the hundreds of savage warriors who lurked there. Here in the narrow gorge which widened gradually southward was the only sign of life. Between the steep walls three hundred Northmen were massed solidly in their wedge-shaped shield-wall, blocking the pass. At the tip, like the point of a spear, stood the man who called himself Kull, king of Valusia. He wore no helmet, only the great, strangely worked head-band of hard gold, but he bore on his left arm the great shield borne by the dead Rognar; and in his right hand he held the heavy iron mace wielded by the sea-king. The vikings eyed him in wonder and savage admiration. They could not understand his language, or he theirs. But no further orders were necessary. At Bran's directions they had bunched themselves in the gorge, and their only order was – hold the pass!

Bran Mak Morn stood just in front of Kull. So they faced each other, he whose kingdom was yet unborn, and he whose kingdom had been lost in the mists of Time for unguessed ages. Kings of darkness, thought Cormac, nameless kings of the night, whose realms are gulfs and shadows.

The hand of the Pictish king went out. 'King Kull, you are more than king – you are a man. Both of us may fall within the next hour – but if we both live, ask what you will of me.'

Kull smiled, returning the firm grip. 'You too are a man after my own heart, king of the shadows. Surely you are more than a figment of my sleeping imagination. Mayhap we will meet in waking life some day.'

Bran shook his head in puzzlement, swung into the saddle and rode away, climbing the eastern slope and vanishing over the ridge. Cormac hesitated: 'Strange man, are you in truth of flesh and blood, or are you a ghost?'

'When we dream, we are all flesh and blood – so long as we are dreaming,' Kull answered. 'This is the strangest nightmare I have ever known – but you, who will soon fade into sheer nothingness as I awaken, seem as real to me *now*, as Brule, or Kananu, or Tu, or Kelkor.'

Cormac shook his head as Bran had done, and with a last salute, which Kull returned with barbaric stateliness, he turned and trotted away. At the top of the western ridge he paused. Away to the south a light cloud of dust rose and the head of the marching column was in sight. Already he believed he could feel the earth vibrate slightly to the measured tread of a thousand mailed feet beating in perfect unison. He dismounted, and one of his chieftains, Domnail, took his steed and led it down the slope away from the valley, where trees grew thickly. Only an occasional vague movement among them gave evidence of the five hundred men who stood there, each at his horse's head with a ready hand to check a chance nicker.

Oh, thought Cormac, the gods themselves made this valley for Bran's ambush! The floor of the valley was treeless and the inner slopes were bare save for the waist-high heather. But at the foot of each ridge on the side facing away from the vale, where the soil long washed from the rocky slopes had accumulated, there grew enough trees to hide five hundred horsemen or fifty chariots.

At the northern end of the valley stood Kull and his three hundred vikings, in open view, flanked on each side by fifty Pictish bowmen. Hidden on the western side of the western ridge were the Gaels. Along the top of the slopes, concealed in the tall heather, lay a hundred Picts with their shafts on string. The rest of the Picts were hidden on the eastern slopes beyond which lay the Britons with their chariots in full readiness. Neither they nor the Gaels to the west could see what went on in the vale, but signals had been arranged.

Now the long column was entering the wide mouth of the valley and their scouts, light-armed men on swift horses, were spreading out between the slopes. They galloped almost within bowshot of the silent host that blocked the pass, then halted. Some whirled and raced back to the main force, while the others deployed and cantered up the slopes, seeking to see what lay beyond. This was the crucial moment. If they got any hint of the ambush, all was lost. Cormac, shrinking down into the heather, marveled at the ability of the Picts to efface themselves from view so completely. He saw a horseman pass within three feet of where he knew a bowman lay, yet the Roman saw nothing.

The scouts topped the ridges, gazed about; then most of them turned and trotted back down the slopes. Cormac wondered at their desultory manner of scouting. He had never fought Romans before, knew nothing of their arrogant self-confidence, of their incredible shrewdness in some ways, their incredible stupidity in others. These men were over-confident; a feeling radiating from their officers. It had been years since a force of Caledonians had stood before the legions. And most of these men were but newly come to Britain; part of a legion which had been quartered in Egypt. They despised their foes and suspected nothing.

But stay – three riders on the opposite ridge had turned and vanished on the other side. And now one, sitting his steed at the crest of the western ridge, not a hundred yards from where Cormac lay, looked long and narrowly down into the mass of trees at the foot of the slope. Cormac saw suspicion grow on his brown, hawk-like face. He half turned as though to call to his comrades, then instead reined his steed down the slope, leaning forward in his saddle. Cormac's heart pounded. Each moment he expected to see the man wheel and gallop back to raise the alarm. He resisted a mad impulse to leap up and charge the Roman on foot. Surely the man could feel the tenseness in the air – the hundreds of fierce eyes upon him. Now he was half-way down the slope, out of sight of the men in the valley. And now the twang of an unseen bow broke the painful stillness. With a strangled gasp the Roman flung his hands high, and as the steed reared, he pitched headlong, transfixed by a long black arrow that had flashed from the heather. A stocky dwarf sprang out of nowhere, seemingly, and seized the bridle, quieting the snorting horse, and leading it down the slope. At the fall of the Roman, short crooked men rose like a sudden flight of birds from the grass and Cormac saw the flash of a knife. Then with unreal suddenness all had subsided. Slayers and slain were unseen and only the still waving heather marked the grim deed.

The Gael looked back into the valley. The three who had ridden over the eastern ridge had not come back and Cormac knew they never would. Evidently the other scouts had borne word that only a small band of warriors were ready to dispute the passage of the legionaries. Now the head of the column was almost below him and he thrilled at the sight of these men who were doomed, swinging along with their superb arrogance. And the sight of their splendid armor, their hawk-like faces and perfect discipline awed him as much as it is possible for a Gael to be awed.

Twelve hundred men in heavy armor who marched as one so that the ground shook to their tread! Most of them were of middle height, with powerful chests and shoulders and bronzed faces – hard-bitten veterans of a hundred campaigns. Cormac noted their javelins, short keen swords and heavy shields; their gleaming armor and crested helmets, the eagles on the standards. These were the men beneath whose tread the world had shaken and empires crumbled! Not all were Latins; there were Romanized Britons among them and one century or hundred was composed of huge yellow-haired men – Gauls and Germans, who fought for Rome as fiercely as did the native-born, and hated their wilder kinsmen more savagely.

On each side was a swarm of cavalry, outriders, and the column was flanked by archers and slingers. A number of lumbering wagons carried the supplies of the army. Cormac saw the commander riding in his place – a tall man with a lean, imperious face, evident even at that distance. Marcus Sulius – the Gael knew him by repute.

A deep-throated roar rose from the legionaries as they approached their foes. Evidently they intended to slice their way through and continue without a pause, for the column moved implacably on. Whom the gods destroy they first make mad – Cormac had never heard the phrase but it came to him that the great Sulius was a fool. Roman arrogance! Marcus was used to lashing the cringing peoples of a decadent East; little he guessed of the iron in these western races.

A group of cavalry detached itself and raced into the mouth of the gorge, but it was only a gesture. With loud jeering shouts they wheeled three spears length away and cast their javelins, which rattled harmlessly on the overlapping shields of the silent Northmen. But their leader dared too much; swinging in, he leaned from his saddle and thrust at Kull's face. The great shield turned the lance and Kull struck back as a snake strikes; the ponderous mace crushed helmet and head like an eggshell, and the very steed went to its knees from the shock of that terrible blow. From the Northmen went up a short fierce roar, and the Picts beside them howled exultantly and loosed their arrows among the retreating horsemen. First blood for the people of the heather! The oncoming Romans shouted vengefully and quickened their pace as the frightened horse raced by, a ghastly travesty of a man, foot caught in the stirrup, trailing beneath the pounding hoofs.

Now the first line of the legionaries, compressed because of the narrowness of the gorge, crashed against the solid wall of shields – crashed and recoiled upon itself. The shield-wall had not shaken an inch. This was the first time the Roman legions had met with that unbreakable formation – that oldest of all Aryan battle-lines – the ancestor of the Spartan regiment – the Theban phalanx – the Macedonian formation – the English square.

Shield crashed on shield and the short Roman sword sought for an opening in that iron wall. Viking spears bristling in solid ranks above, thrust and reddened; heavy axes chopped down, shearing through iron, flesh and bone. Cormac saw Kull, looming above the stocky Romans in the forefront of the fray, dealing blows like thunderbolts. A burly centurion rushed in, shield held high, stabbing upward. The iron mace crashed terribly, shivering the sword, rending the shield apart, shattering the helmet, crushing the skull down between the shoulders – in a single blow.

The front line of the Romans bent like a steel bar about the wedge, as the legionaries sought to struggle through the gorge on each side and surround their opposers. But the pass was too narrow; crouching close against the steep walls the Picts drove their black arrows in a hail of death. At this range the heavy shafts tore through shield and corselet, transfixing the armored men. The front line of battle rolled back, red and broken, and the Northmen trod their few dead under foot to close the gaps their fall had made. Stretched the full width of their front lay a thin line of shattered forms – the red spray of the tide which had broken upon them in vain.

Cormac had leaped to his feet, waving his arms. Domnail and his men broke cover at the signal and came galloping up the slope, lining the ridge. Cormac mounted the horse brought him and glanced impatiently across the narrow vale. No sign of life appeared on the eastern ridge. Where was Bran – and the Britons?

Down in the valley, the legions, angered at the unexpected opposition of the paltry force in front of them, but not suspicious, were forming in more compact body. The wagons which had halted were lumbering on again and the whole column was once more in motion as if it intended to crash through by sheer weight. With the Gaulish century in the forefront, the legionaries were advancing again in the attack. This time, with the full force of twelve hundred men behind, the charge would batter down the resistance of Kull's warriors like a heavy ram; would stamp them down, sweep over their red ruins. Cormac's men trembled in impatience. Suddenly Marcus Sulius turned and gazed westward, where the line of horsemen was etched against the sky. Even at that distance Cormac saw his face pale. The Roman at last realized the metal of the men he faced, and that he had walked into a trap. Surely in that moment there flashed a chaotic picture through his brain – defeat – disgrace – red ruin!

It was too late to retreat – too late to form into a defensive square with the wagons for barricade. There was but one way possible out, and Marcus, crafty general in spite of his recent blunder, took it. Cormac heard his voice cut like a clarion through the din, and though he did not understand the words, he knew that the Roman was shouting for his men to smite that knot of Northmen like a blast – to hack their way through and out of the trap before it could close!

Now the legionaries, aware of their desperate plight, flung themselves headlong and terribly on their foes. The shield-wall rocked, but it gave not an inch. The wild faces of the Gauls and the hard brown Italian faces glared over locked shields into the blazing eyes of the North. Shields touching, they smote and slew and died in a red storm of slaughter, where crimsoned axes rose and fell and dripping spears broke on notched swords.

Where in God's name was Bran with his chariots? A few minutes more would spell the doom of every man who held that pass. Already they were falling fast, though they locked their ranks closer and held like iron. Those wild men of the North were dying in their tracks; and looming among their golden heads the black lion-mane of Kull shone like a symbol of slaughter, and his reddened mace showered a ghastly rain as it splashed brains and blood like water.

Something snapped in Cormac's brain.

'These men will die while we wait for Bran's signal!' he shouted. 'On! Follow me into Hell, sons of Gael!'

A wild roar answered him, and loosing rein he shot down the slope with five hundred yelling riders plunging headlong after him. And even at that moment a storm of arrows swept the valley from either side like a dark cloud and the terrible clamor of the Picts split the skies. And over the eastern ridge, like a sudden burst of rolling thunder on Judgment Day, rushed the war-chariots. Headlong down the slope they roared, foam flying from the horses' distended nostrils, frantic feet scarcely seeming to touch the ground, making naught of the tall heather. In the foremost chariot, with his dark eyes blazing, crouched Bran Mak Morn, and in all of them the naked Britons were screaming and lashing as if possessed by demons. Behind the flying chariots came the Picts, howling like wolves and loosing their arrows as they ran. The heather belched them forth from all sides in a dark wave.

So much Cormac saw in chaotic glimpses during that wild ride down the slopes. A wave of cavalry swept between him and the main line of the column. Three long leaps ahead of his men, the Gaelic prince met the spears of the Roman riders. The first lance turned on his buckler, and rising in his stirrups he smote downward, cleaving his man from shoulder to breastbone. The next Roman flung a javelin that killed Domnail, but at that instant Cormac's steed crashed into his, breast to breast, and the lighter horse rolled headlong under the shock, flinging his rider beneath the pounding hoofs.

Then the whole blast of the Gaelic charge smote the Roman cavalry, shattering it, crashing and rolling it down and under. Over its red ruins Cormac's yelling demons struck the heavy Roman infantry, and the whole line reeled at the shock. Swords and axes flashed up and down and the force of their rush carried them deep into the massed ranks. Here, checked, they swayed and strove. Javelins thrust, swords flashed upward, bringing down horse and rider, and greatly outnumbered, leaguered on every side, the Gaels had perished among their foes, but at that instant, from the other side the crashing chariots smote the Roman ranks. In one long line they struck almost simultaneously, and at the moment of impact the charioteers wheeled their horses side-long and raced parallel down the ranks, shearing men down like the mowing of wheat. Hundreds died on those curving blades in that moment, and leaping from the chariots, screaming like blood-mad wildcats, the British swordsmen flung themselves upon the spears of the legionaries, hacking madly with their two-handed swords. Crouching, the Picts drove their arrows point-blank and then sprang in to slash and thrust. Maddened with the sight of victory, these wild peoples were like wounded tigers, feeling no wounds, and dying on their feet with their last gasp a snarl of fury.

But the battle was not over yet. Dazed, shattered, their formation broken and nearly half their number down already, the Romans fought back with desperate fury. Hemmed in on all sides they slashed and smote singly, or in small clumps, fought back to back, archers, slingers, horsemen and heavy legionaries mingled into a chaotic mass. The confusion was complete, but not the victory. Those bottled in the gorge still hurled themselves upon the red axes that barred their way, while the massed and serried battle thundered behind them. From one side Cormac's Gaels raged and slashed; from the other chariots swept back and forth, retiring and returning like iron whirlwinds. There was no retreat, for the Picts had flung a cordon across the way they had come, and having cut the throats of the camp followers and possessed themselves of the wagon, they sent their shafts in a storm of death into the rear of the shattered column. Those long black arrows pierced armor and bone, nailing men together. Yet the slaughter was not all on one side. Picts died beneath the lightning thrust of javelin and shortsword, Gaels pinned beneath their falling horses were hewed to pieces, and chariots, cut loose from their horses, were deluged with the blood of the charioteers.

And at the narrow head of the valley still the battle surged and eddied. Great gods – thought Cormac, glancing between lightning-like blows – do these men still hold the gorge? Aye! They held it! A tenth of their original number, dying on their feet, they still held back the frantic charges of the dwindling legionaries.

Over all the field went up the roar and the clash of arms, and birds of prey, swift-flying out of the sunset, circled above. Cormac, striving to reach Marcus Sulius through the press, saw the Roman's horse sink under him, and the rider rise alone in a waste of foes. He saw the Roman sword flash thrice, dealing a death at each blow; then from the thickest of the fray bounded a terrible figure. It was Bran Mak Morn, stained from head to foot. He cast away his broken sword as he ran, drawing a dirk. The Roman struck, but the Pictish king was under the thrust, and gripping the sword-wrist, he drove the dirk again and again through the gleaming armor.

A mighty roar went up as Marcus died, and Cormac, with a shout, rallied the remnants of his force about him and, striking in the spurs, burst through the shattered lines and rode full speed for the other end of the valley.

But as he approached he saw that he was too late. As they had lived, so had they died, those fierce sea-wolves, with their faces to the foe and their broken weapons red in their hands. In a grim and silent band they lay, even in death preserving some of the shield-wall formation. Among them, in front of them and all about them lay high-heaped the bodies of those who had sought to break them, in vain. *They had not given back a foot!* To the last man, they had died in their tracks. Nor were there any left to stride over their torn shapes; those Romans who had escaped the viking axes had been struck down by the shafts of the Picts and swords of the Gaels from behind.

Yet this part of the battle was not over. High up on the steep western slope Cormac saw the ending of that drama. A group of Gauls in the armor of Rome pressed upon a single man – a black-haired giant on whose head gleamed a golden crown. There was iron in these men, as well as in the man who had held them to their fate. They were doomed – their comrades were being slaughtered behind them – but before their turn came they would at least have the life of the black-haired chief who had led the golden-haired men of the North.

Pressing upon him from three sides they had forced him

slowly back up the steep gorge wall, and the crumpled bodies that stretched along his retreat showed how fiercely every foot of the way had been contested. Here on this steep it was task enough to keep one's footing alone; yet these men at once climbed and fought. Kull's shield and the huge mace were gone, and the great sword in his right hand was dyed crimson. His mail, wrought with a forgotten art, now hung in shreds, and blood streamed from a hundred wounds on limbs, head and body. But his eyes still blazed with the battle-joy and his wearied arm still drove the mighty blade in strokes of death.

But Cormac saw that the end would come before they could reach him. Now at the very crest of the steep, a hedge of points menaced the strange king's life, and even his iron strength was ebbing. Now he split the skull of a huge warrior and the back-stroke shore through the neck-cords of another; reeling under a very rain of swords he struck again and his victim dropped at his feet, cleft to the breast-bone. Then, even as a dozen swords rose above the staggering Atlantean for the death stroke, a strange thing happened. The sun was sinking into the western sea; all the heather swam red like an ocean of blood. Etched in the dying sun, as he had first appeared, Kull stood, and then, like a mist lifting, a mighty vista opened behind the reeling king. Cormac's astounded eyes caught a fleeting gigantic glimpse of other climes and spheres – as if mirrored in summer clouds he saw, instead of the heather hills stretching away to the sea, a dim and mighty land of blue mountains and gleaming quiet lakes – the golden, purple and sapphirean spires and towering walls of a mighty city such as the earth has not known for many a drifting age.

Then like the fading of a mirage it was gone, but the Gauls on the high slope had dropped their weapons and stared like men dazed – *For the man called Kull had vanished and there was no trace of his going!*

*

As in a daze Cormac turned his steed and rode back across the trampled field. His horse's hoofs splashed in lakes of blood and clanged against the helmets of dead men. Across the valley the shout of victory was thundering. Yet all seemed shadowy and strange. A shape was striding across the torn corpses and Cormac was dully aware that it was Bran. The Gael swung from his horse and fronted the king. Bran was weaponless and gory; blood trickled from gashes on brow, breast and limb; what armor he had worn was clean hacked away and a cut had shorn half-way through his iron crown. But the red jewel still gleamed unblemished like a star of slaughter.

'It is in my mind to slay you,' said the Gael heavily and like a man speaking in a daze, 'for the blood of brave men is on your head. Had you given the signal to charge sooner, some would have lived.'

Bran folded his arms; his eyes were haunted. 'Strike if you will; I am sick of slaughter. It is a cold mead, this kinging it. A king must gamble with men's lives and naked swords. The lives of all my people were at stake; I sacrificed the Northmen – yes; and my heart is sore within me, for they were men! But had I given the order when you would have desired, all might have gone awry. The Romans were not yet massed in the narrow mouth of the gorge, and might have had time and space to form their ranks again and beat us off. I waited until the last moment – and the rovers died. A king belongs to his people, and can not let either his own feelings or the lives of men influence him. Now my people are saved; but my heart is cold in my breast.'

Cormac wearily dropped his sword-point to the ground.

'You are a born king of men, Bran,' said the Gaelic prince.

Bran's eyes roved the field. A mist of blood hovered over all, where the victorious barbarians were looting the dead, while those Romans who had escaped slaughter by throwing down their swords and now stood under guard, looked on with hot smoldering eyes.

'My kingdom – my people – are saved,' said Bran wearily. 'They will come from the heather by the thousands and when Rome moves against us again, she will meet a solid nation. But I am weary. What of Kull?'

'My eyes and brain were mazed with battle,' answered Cormac. 'I thought to see him vanish like a ghost into the sunset. I will seek his body.'

'Seek not for him,' said Bran. 'Out of the sunrise he came – into the sunset he has gone. Out of the mists of the ages he came to us, and back into the mists of the eons has he returned – to his own kingdom.'

Cormac turned away; night was gathering. Gonar stood like a white specter before him.

'To his own kingdom,' echoed the wizard. 'Time and Space are naught. Kull has returned to his own kingdom – his own crown – his own age.'

'Then he was a ghost?'

'Did you not feel the grip of his solid hand? Did you not hear his voice – see him eat and drink, laugh and slay and bleed?'

Still Cormac stood like one in a trance.

'Then if it be possible for a man to pass from one age into one yet unborn, or come forth from a century dead and forgotten, whichever you will, with his flesh-and-blood body and his arms – then he is as mortal as he was in his own day. Is Kull dead, then?'

'He died a hundred thousand years ago, as men reckon time,' answered the wizard, 'but in his own age. He died not from the swords of the Gauls of this age. Have we not heard in legends how the king of Valusia traveled into a strange, timeless land of the misty future ages, and there fought in a great battle? Why, so he did! A hundred thousand years ago, or today!

'And a hundred thousand years ago – or a moment agone! – Kull, king of Valusia, roused himself on the silken couch in his secret chamber and laughing, spoke to the first Gonar, saying:

"Ha, wizard, I have in truth dreamed strangely, for I went into a far clime and a far time in my visions, and fought for the king of a strange shadow-people!" And the great sorcerer smiled and pointed silently at the red, notched sword, and the torn mail and the many wounds that the king carried. And Kull, fully woken from his 'vision' and feeling the sting and the weakness of these yet bleeding wounds, fell silent and mazed, and all life and time and space seemed like a dream of ghosts to him, and he wondered thereat all the rest of his life. For the wisdom of the Eternities is denied even unto princes and Kull could no more understand what Gonar told him than you can understand my words.'

'And then Kull lived despite his many wounds,' said Cormac, 'and has returned to the mists of silence and the centuries. Well – he thought us a dream; we thought him a ghost. And sure, life is but a web spun of ghosts and dreams and illusion, and it is in my mind that the kingdom which has this day been born of swords and slaughter in this howling valley is a thing no more solid than the foam of the bright sea.'

Worms of the Earth

'Strike in the nails, soldiers, and let our guest see the reality of
our good Roman justice!'

The speaker wrapped his purple cloak closer about his powerful frame and settled back into his official chair, much as he might
have settled back in his seat at the Circus Maximus to enjoy the
clash of gladiatorial swords. Realization of power colored his
every move. Whetted pride was necessary to Roman satisfaction,
and Titus Sulla was justly proud; for he was military governor of
Ebbracum and answerable only to the emperor of Rome. He was
a strongly built man of medium height, with the hawk-like features of the pure-bred Roman. Now a mocking smile curved his
full lips, increasing the arrogance of his haughty aspect. Distinctly
military in appearance, he wore the golden-scaled corselet and
chased breastplate of his rank, with the short stabbing sword at
his belt, and he held on his knee the silvered helmet with its
plumed crest. Behind him stood a clump of impassive soldiers
with shield and spear – blond titans from the Rhineland.

Before him was taking place the scene which apparently gave
him so much real gratification – a scene common enough wherever stretched the far-flung boundaries of Rome. A rude cross
lay flat upon the barren earth and on it was bound a man – half
naked, wild of aspect with his corded limbs, glaring eyes and
shock of tangled hair. His executioners were Roman soldiers,
and with heavy hammers they prepared to pin the victim's hands
and feet to the wood with iron spikes.

Only a small group of men watched this ghastly scene, in the dread place of execution beyond the city walls: the governor and his watchful guards; a few young Roman officers; the man to whom Sulla had referred as 'guest' and who stood like a bronze image, unspeaking. Beside the gleaming splendor of the Roman, the quiet garb of this man seemed drab, almost somber.

He was dark, but he did not resemble the Latins around him. There was about him none of the warm, almost Oriental sensuality of the Mediterranean which colored their features. The blond barbarians behind Sulla's chair were less unlike the man in facial outline than were the Romans. Not his were the full curving red lips, nor the rich waving locks suggestive of the Greek. Nor was his dark complexion the rich olive of the south; rather it was the bleak darkness of the north. The whole aspect of the man vaguely suggested the shadowed mists, the gloom, the cold and the icy winds of the naked northern lands. Even his black eyes were savagely cold, like black fires burning through fathoms of ice.

His height was only medium but there was something about him which transcended mere physical bulk – a certain fierce innate vitality, comparable only to that of a wolf or a panther. In every line of his supple, compact body, as well as in his coarse straight hair and thin lips, this was evident – in the hawk-like set of the head on the corded neck, in the broad square shoulders, in the deep chest, the lean loins, the narrow feet. Built with the savage economy of a panther, he was an image of dynamic potentialities, pent in with iron self-control.

At his feet crouched one like him in complexion – but there the resemblance ended. This other was a stunted giant, with gnarly limbs, thick body, a low sloping brow and an expression of dull ferocity, now clearly mixed with fear. If the man on the cross resembled, in a tribal way, the man Titus Sulla called guest, he far more resembled the stunted crouching giant.

'Well, Partha Mac Othna,' said the governor with studied

effrontery, 'when you return to your tribe, you will have a tale to tell of the justice of Rome, who rules the south.'

'I will have a tale,' answered the other in a voice which betrayed no emotion, just as his dark face, schooled to immobility, showed no evidence of the maelstrom in his soul.

'Justice to all under the rule of Rome,' said Sulla. 'Pax Romana! Reward for virtue, punishment for wrong!' He laughed inwardly at his own black hypocrisy, then continued: 'You see, emissary of Pictland, how swiftly Rome punishes the transgressor.'

'I see,' answered the Pict in a voice which strongly-curbed anger made deep with menace, 'that the subject of a foreign king is dealt with as though he were a Roman slave.'

'He has been tried and condemned in an unbiased court,' retorted Sulla.

'Aye! and the accuser was a Roman, the witnesses Roman, the judge Roman! He committed murder? In a moment of fury he struck down a Roman merchant who cheated, tricked and robbed him, and to injury added insult – aye, and a blow! Is his king but a dog, that Rome crucifies his subjects at will, condemned by Roman courts? Is his king too weak or foolish to do justice, were he informed and formal charges brought against the offender?'

'Well,' said Sulla cynically, 'you may inform Bran Mak Morn yourself. Rome, my friend, makes no account of her actions to barbarian kings. When savages come among us, let them act with discretion or suffer the consequences.'

The Pict shut his iron jaws with a snap that told Sulla further badgering would elicit no reply. The Roman made a gesture to the executioners. One of them seized a spike and placing it against the thick wrist of the victim, smote heavily. The iron point sank deep through the flesh, crunching against the bones. The lips of the man on the cross writhed, though no moan escaped him. As a trapped wolf fights against his cage, the bound victim instinctively wrenched and struggled. The veins swelled in his temples, sweat beaded his low forehead, the muscles in arms and legs writhed and knotted. The hammers fell in inexorable strokes, driving the cruel points deeper and deeper, through wrists and ankles; blood flowed in a black river over the hands that held the spikes, staining the wood of the cross, and the splintering of bones was distinctly heard. Yet the sufferer made no outcry, though his blackened lips writhed back until the gums were visible, and his shaggy head jerked involuntarily from side to side.

The man called Partha Mac Othna stood like an iron image, eyes burning from an inscrutable face, his whole body hard as iron from the tension of his control. At his feet crouched his misshapen servant, hiding his face from the grim sight, his arms locked about his master's knees. Those arms gripped like steel and under his breath the fellow mumbled ceaselessly as if in invocation.

The last stroke fell; the cords were cut from arm and leg, so that the man would hang supported by the nails alone. He had ceased his struggling that only twisted the spikes in his agonizing wounds. His bright black eyes, unglazed, had not left the face of the man called Partha Mac Othna; in them lingered a desperate shadow of hope. Now the soldiers lifted the cross and set the end of it in the hole prepared, stamped the dirt about it to hold it erect. The Pict hung in midair, suspended by the nails in his flesh, but still no sound escaped his lips. His eyes still hung on the somber face of the emissary, but the shadow of hope was fading.

'He'll live for days!' said Sulla cheerfully. 'These Picts are harder than cats to kill! I'll keep a guard of ten soldiers watching night and day to see that no one takes him down before he dies. Ho, there, Valerius, in honor of our esteemed neighbor, King Bran Mak Morn, give him a cup of wine!'

With a laugh the young officer came forward, holding a brimming wine-cup, and rising on his toes, lifted it to the parched lips of the sufferer. In the black eyes flared a red wave of unquenchable hatred; writhing his head aside to avoid even touching the cup, he spat full into the young Roman's eyes. With a curse Valerius dashed the cup to the ground, and before any could halt him, wrenched out his sword and sheathed it in the man's body.

Sulla rose with an imperious exclamation of anger; the man called Partha Mac Othna had started violently, but he bit his lip and said nothing. Valerius seemed somewhat surprized at him, as he sullenly cleansed his sword. The act had been instinctive, following the insult to Roman pride, the one thing unbearable.

'Give up your sword, young sir!' exclaimed Sulla. 'Centurion Publius, place him under arrest. A few days in a cell with stale bread and water will teach you to curb your patrician pride, in matters dealing with the will of the empire. What, you young fool, do you not realize that you could not have made the dog a more kindly gift? Who would not rather desire a quick death on the sword than the slow agony on the cross? Take him away. And you, centurion, see that guards remain at the cross so that the body is not cut down until the ravens pick bare the bones. Partha Mac Othna, I go to a banquet at the house of Demetrius – will you not accompany me?'

The emissary shook his head, his eyes fixed on the limp form which sagged on the black-stained cross. He made no reply. Sulla smiled sardonically, then rose and strode away, followed by his secretary who bore the gilded chair ceremoniously, and by the stolid soldiers, with whom walked Valerius, head sunken.

The man called Partha Mac Othna flung a wide fold of his cloak about his shoulder, halted a moment to gaze at the grim cross with its burden, darkly etched against the crimson sky, where the clouds of night were gathering. Then he stalked away, followed by his silent servant.

2

In an inner chamber of Ebbracum, the man called Partha Mac Othna paced tigerishly to and fro. His sandalled feet made no sound on the marble tiles.

'Grom!' he turned to the gnarled servant, 'well I know why you held my knees so tightly – why you muttered aid of the Moon-Woman – you feared I would lose my self-control and make a mad attempt to succor that poor wretch. By the gods, I believe that was what the dog Roman wished – his iron-cased watch-dogs watched me narrowly, I know, and his baiting was harder to bear than ordinarily.

'Gods black and white, dark and light!' he shook his clenched fists above his head in the black gust of his passion. 'That I should stand by and see a man of mine butchered on a Roman cross – without justice and with no more trial than that farce! Black gods of R'lyeh, even you would I invoke to the ruin and destruction of those butchers! I swear by the Nameless Ones, men shall die howling for that deed, and Rome shall cry out as a woman in the dark who treads upon an adder!'

'He knew you, master,' said Grom.

The other dropped his head and covered his eyes with a gesture of savage pain.

'His eyes will haunt me when I lie dying. Aye, he knew me, and almost until the last, I read in his eyes the hope that I might aid him. Gods and devils, is Rome to butcher my people beneath my very eyes? Then I am not king but dog!'

'Not so loud, in the name of all the gods!' exclaimed Grom in affright. 'Did these Romans suspect you were Bran Mak Morn, they would nail you on a cross beside that other.'

'They will know it ere long,' grimly answered the king. 'Too long I have lingered here in the guise of an emissary, spying upon mine enemies. They have thought to play with me, these

Romans, masking their contempt and scorn only under polished satire. Rome is courteous to barbarian ambassadors, they give us fine houses to live in, offer us slaves, pander to our lusts with women and gold and wine and games, but all the while they laugh at us; their very courtesy is an insult, and sometimes – as today – their contempt discards all veneer. Bah! I've seen through their baitings – have remained imperturbably serene and swallowed their studied insults. But this – by the fiends of Hell, this is beyond human endurance! My people look to me; if I fail them – if I fail even one – even the lowest of my people, who will aid them? To whom shall they turn? By the gods, I'll answer the gibes of these Roman dogs with black shaft and trenchant steel!'

'And the chief with the plumes?' Grom meant the governor and his gutturals thrummed with the blood-lust. 'He dies?' He flicked out a length of steel.

Bran scowled. 'Easier said than done. He dies – but how may I reach him? By day his German guards keep at his back; by night they stand at door and window. He has many enemies, Romans as well as barbarians. Many a Briton would gladly slit his throat.'

Grom seized Bran's garment, stammering as fierce eagerness broke the bonds of his inarticulate nature.

'Let me go, master! My life is worth nothing. I will cut him down in the midst of his warriors!'

Bran smiled fiercely and clapped his hand on the stunted giant's shoulder with a force that would have felled a lesser man.

'Nay, old war-dog, I have too much need of thee! You shall not throw your life away uselessly. Sulla would read the intent in your eyes, besides, and the javelins of his Teutons would be through you ere you could reach him. Not by the dagger in the dark will we strike this Roman, not by the venom in the cup nor the shaft from the ambush.'

The king turned and paced the floor a moment, his head bent in thought. Slowly his eyes grew murky with a thought so fearful he did not speak it aloud to the waiting warrior.

'I have become somewhat familiar with the maze of Roman politics during my stay in this accursed waste of mud and marble,' said he. 'During a war on the Wall, Titus Sulla, as governor of this province, is supposed to hasten thither with his centuries. But this Sulla does not do; he is no coward, but the bravest avoid certain things – to each man, however bold, his own particular fear. So he sends in his place Caius Camillus, who in times of peace patrols the fens of the west, lest the Britons break over the border. And Sulla takes his place in the Tower of Trajan. Ha!'

He whirled and gripped Grom with steely fingers.

'Grom, take the red stallion and ride north! Let no grass grow under the stallion's hoofs! Ride to Cormac na Connacht and tell him to sweep the frontier with sword and torch! Let his wild Gaels feast their fill of slaughter. After a time I will be with him. But for a time I have affairs in the west.'

Grom's black eyes gleamed and he made a passionate gesture with his crooked hand – an instinctive move of savagery.

Bran drew a heavy bronze seal from beneath his tunic.

'This is my safe-conduct as an emissary to Roman courts,' he said grimly. 'It will open all gates between this house and Baaldor. If any official questions you too closely – here!'

Lifting the lid of an iron-bound chest, Bran took out a small, heavy leather bag which he gave into the hands of the warrior.

'When all keys fail at a gate,' said he, 'try a golden key. Go now!'

There were no ceremonious farewells between the barbarian king and his barbarian vassal. Grom flung up his arm in a gesture of salute; then turning, he hurried out.

Bran stepped to a barred window and gazed out into the moonlit streets.

'Wait until the moon sets,' he muttered grimly. 'Then I'll take the road to – Hell! But before I go I have a debt to pay.'

The stealthy clink of a hoof on the flags reached him.

'With the safe-conduct and gold, not even Rome can hold a Pictish reaver,' muttered the king. 'Now I'll sleep until the moon sets.'

With a snarl at the marble frieze-work and fluted columns, as symbols of Rome, he flung himself down on a couch, from which he had long since impatiently torn the cushions and silk stuffs, as too soft for his hard body. Hate and the black passion of vengeance seethed in him, yet he went instantly to sleep. The first lesson he had learned in his bitter hard life was to snatch sleep any time he could, like a wolf that snatches sleep on the hunting trail. Generally his slumber was as light and dreamless as a panther's, but tonight it was otherwise.

He sank into fleecy gray fathoms of slumber and in a time-less, misty realm of shadows he met the tall, lean, white-bearded figure of old Gonar, the priest of the Moon, high councilor to the king. And Bran stood aghast, for Gonar's face was white as driven snow and he shook as with ague. Well might Bran stand appalled, for in all the years of his life he had never before seen Gonar the Wise show any sign of fear.

'What now, old one?' asked the king. 'Goes all well in Baal-dor?'

'All is well in Baal-dor where my body lies sleeping,' answered old Gonar. 'Across the void I have come to battle with you for your soul. King, are you mad, this thought you have thought in your brain?'

'Gonar,' answered Bran somberly, 'this day I stood still and watched a man of mine die on the cross of Rome. What his name or his rank, I do not know. I do not care. He might have been a faithful unknown warrior of mine, he might have been an outlaw. I only know that he was mine; the first scents he knew were the scents of the heather; the first light he saw was the sunrise on the Pictish hills. He belonged to me, not to Rome. If punishment was just, then none but me should have dealt it. If he were to be tried, none but me should have been his judge. The same blood flowed in our veins; the same fire maddened our brains; in infancy we listened to the same old tales, and in youth we sang the same old songs. He was bound to my heart-strings, as every man and every woman and every child of Pictland is bound. It was mine to protect him; now it is mine to avenge him.'

'But in the name of the gods, Bran,' expostulated the wizard, 'take your vengeance in another way! Return to the heather – mass your warriors – join with Cormac and his Gaels, and spread a sea of blood and flame the length of the great Wall!'

'All that I will do,' grimly answered Bran. 'But now – *now* – I will have a vengeance such as no Roman ever dreamed of! Ha, what do they know of the mysteries of this ancient isle, which sheltered strange life long before Rome rose from the marshes of the Tiber?'

'Bran, there are weapons too foul to use, even against Rome!'

Bran barked short and sharp as a jackal.

'Ha! There are no weapons I would not use against Rome! My back is at the wall. By the blood of the fiends, has Rome fought me fair? Bah! I am a barbarian king with a wolfskin mantle and an iron crown, fighting with my handful of bows and broken pikes against the queen of the world. What have I? The heather hills, the wattle huts, the spears of my shock-headed tribesmen! And I fight Rome – with her armored legions, her broad fertile plains and rich seas – her mountains and her rivers and her gleaming cities – her wealth, her steel, her gold, her mastery and her wrath. By steel and fire I will fight her – and by subtlety and treachery – by the thorn in the foot, the adder in the path, the venom in the cup, the dagger in the dark; aye,' his voice sank somberly, 'and by the worms of the earth!'

'But it is madness!' cried Gonar. 'You will perish in the attempt you plan – you will go down to Hell and you will not return! What of your people then?'

'If I can not serve them I had better die,' growled the king.

'But you can not even reach the beings you seek,' cried Gonar. 'For untold centuries they have dwelt *apart*. There is no door by which you can come to them. Long ago they severed the bonds that bound them to the world we know.'

'Long ago,' answered Bran somberly 'you told me that nothing in the universe was separated from the stream of Life – a saying the truth of which I have often seen evident. No race, no form of life but is close-knit somehow, by some manner, to the rest of Life and the world. Somewhere there is a thin link connecting *those* I seek to the world I know. Somewhere there is a Door. And somewhere among the bleak fens of the west I will find it.'

Stark horror flooded Gonar's eyes and he gave back crying, 'Wo! Wo! Wo! to Pictdom! Wo to the unborn kingdom! Wo, black wo to the sons of men! Wo, wo, wo, wo!'

Bran awoke to a shadowed room and the starlight on the window-bars. The moon had sunk from sight though its glow was still faint above the house tops. Memory of his dream shook him and he swore beneath his breath.

Rising, he flung off cloak and mantle, donning a light shirt of black mesh-mail, and girding on sword and dirk. Going again to the iron-bound chest he lifted several compact bags and emptied the clinking contents into the leathern pouch at his girdle. Then wrapping his wide cloak about him, he silently left the house. No servants there were to spy on him – he had impatiently refused the offer of slaves which it was Rome's policy to furnish her barbarian emissaries. Gnarled Grom had attended to all Bran's simple needs.

The stables fronted on the courtyard. A moment's groping in

the dark and he placed his hand over a great stallion's nose, checking the nicker of recognition. Working without a light he swiftly bridled and saddled the great brute, and went through the courtyard into a shadowy side-street, leading him. The moon was setting, the border of floating shadows widening along the western wall. Silence lay on the marble palaces and mud hovels of Ebbracum under the cold stars.

Bran touched the pouch at his girdle, which was heavy with minted gold that bore the stamp of Rome. He had come to Ebbracum posing as an emissary of Pictdom, to act the spy. But being a barbarian, he had not been able to play his part in aloof formality and sedate dignity. He retained a crowded memory of wild feasts where wine flowed in fountains; of white-bosomed Roman women, who, sated with civilized lovers, looked with something more than favor on a virile barbarian; of gladiatorial games; and of other games where dice clicked and spun and tall stacks of gold changed hands. He had drunk deeply and gambled recklessly, after the manner of barbarians, and he had had a remarkable run of luck, due possibly to the indifference with which he won or lost. Gold to the Pict was so much dust, flowing through his fingers. In his land there was no need of it. But he had learned its power in the boundaries of civilization.

Almost under the shadow of the northwestern wall he saw ahead of him loom the great watch-tower which was connected with and reared above the outer wall. One corner of the castle-like fortress, farthest from the wall, served as a dungeon. Bran left his horse standing in a dark alley, with the reins hanging on the ground, and stole like a prowling wolf into the shadows of the fortress.

The young officer Valerius was awakened from a light, unquiet sleep by a stealthy sound at the barred window. He sat up, cursing softly under his breath as the faint starlight which etched the window-bars fell across the bare stone floor and reminded him of his disgrace. Well, in a few days, he ruminated, he'd be well out of it; Sulla would not be too harsh on a man with such high connections; then let any man or woman gibe at him! Damn that insolent Pict! But wait, he thought suddenly, remembering: what of the sound which had roused him?

'Hsssst!' it was a voice from the window.

Why so much secrecy? It could hardly be a foe – yet, why should it be a friend? Valerius rose and crossed his cell, coming close to the window. Outside all was dim in the starlight and he made out but a shadowy form close to the window.

'Who are you?' he leaned close against the bars, straining his eyes into the gloom.

His answer was a snarl of wolfish laughter, a long flicker of steel in the starlight. Valerius reeled away from the window and crashed to the floor, clutching his throat, gurgling horribly as he tried to scream. Blood gushed through his fingers, forming about his twitching body a pool that reflected the dim starlight dully and redly.

Outside Bran glided away like a shadow, without pausing to peer into the cell. In another minute the guards would round the corner on their regular routine. Even now he heard the measured tramp of their iron-clad feet. Before they came in sight he had vanished and they clumped stolidly by the cell-windows with no intimation of the corpse that lay on the floor within.

Bran rode to the small gate in the western wall, unchallenged by the sleepy watch. What fear of foreign invasion in Ebbracum? – and certain well-organized thieves and women-stealers made it profitable for the watchmen not to be too vigilant. But the single guardsman at the western gate – his fellows lay drunk in a near-by brothel – lifted his spear and bawled for Bran to halt and give an account of himself. Silently the Pict reined closer. Masked in the dark cloak, he seemed dim and indistinct to the Roman, who was only aware of the glitter of his cold eyes in the gloom. But Bran held up his hand against the starlight and the soldier caught the gleam of gold; in the other hand he saw a long sheen of steel. The soldier understood, and he did not hesitate between the choice of a golden bribe or a battle to the death with this unknown rider who was apparently a barbarian of some sort. With a grunt he lowered his spear and swung the gate open. Bran rode through, casting a handful of coins to the Roman. They fell about his feet in a golden shower, clinking against the flags. He bent in greedy haste to retrieve them and Bran Mak Morn rode westward like a flying ghost in the night.

3

Into the dim fens of the west came Bran Mak Morn. A cold wind breathed across the gloomy waste and against the gray sky a few herons flapped heavily. The long reeds and marsh-grass waved in broken undulations and out across the desolation of the wastes a few still meres reflected the dull light. Here and there rose curiously regular hillocks above the general levels, and gaunt against the somber sky Bran saw a marching line of upright monoliths – menhirs, reared by what nameless hands?

A faint blue line to the west lay the foothills that beyond the horizon grew to the wild mountains of Wales where dwelt still wild Celtic tribes – fierce blue-eyed men that knew not the yoke of Rome. A row of well-garrisoned watch-towers held them in check. Even now, far away across the moors, Bran glimpsed the unassailable keep men called the Tower of Trajan.

These barren wastes seemed the dreary accomplishment of desolation, yet human life was not utterly lacking. Bran met the silent men of the fen, reticent, dark of eye and hair, speaking a strange mixed tongue whose long-blended elements had forgotten their pristine separate sources. Bran recognized a certain kinship in these people to himself, but he looked on them with the scorn of a pure-blooded patrician for men of mixed strains.

Not that the common people of Caledonia were altogether

pure-blooded; they got their stocky bodies and massive limbs from a primitive Teutonic race which had found its way into the northern tip of the isle even before the Celtic conquest of Britain was completed, and had been absorbed by the Picts. But the chiefs of Bran's folk had kept their blood from foreign taint since the beginnings of time, and he himself was a pure-bred Pict of the Old Race. But these fenmen, overrun repeatedly by British, Gaelic and Roman conquerors, had assimilated blood of each, and in the process almost forgotten their original language and lineage.

For Bran came of a race that was very old, which had spread over western Europe in one vast Dark Empire before the coming of the Aryans, when the ancestors of the Celts, the Hellenes and the Germans were one primal people, before the days of tribal splitting-off and westward drift.

Only in Caledonia, Bran brooded, had his people resisted the flood of Aryan conquest. He had heard of a Pictish people called Basques, who in the crags of the Pyrenees called themselves an unconquered race; but he knew that they had paid tribute for centuries to the ancestors of the Gaels, before these Celtic conquerors abandoned their mountain-realm and set sail for Ireland. Only the Picts of Caledonia had remained free, and they had been scattered into small feuding tribes – he was the first acknowledged king in five hundred years – the beginning of a new dynasty – no, a revival of an ancient dynasty under a new name. In the very teeth of Rome he dreamed his dreams of empire.

He wandered through the fens, seeking a Door. Of his quest he said nothing to the dark-eyed fenmen. They told him news that drifted from mouth to mouth – a tale of war in the north, the skirl of war-pipes along the winding Wall, of gathering-fires in the heather, of flame and smoke and rapine and the glutting of Gaelic swords in the crimson sea of slaughter. The eagles of the legions were moving northward and the ancient road resounded to the measured tramp of the iron-clad feet. And Bran, in the fens of the west, laughed, well pleased.

In Ebbracum Titus Sulla gave secret word to seek out the Pictish emissary with the Gaelic name who had been under suspicion, and who had vanished the night young Valerius was found dead in his cell with his throat ripped out. Sulla felt that this sudden bursting flame of war on the Wall was connected closely with his execution of a condemned Pictish criminal, and he set his spy system to work, though he felt sure that Partha Mac Othna was by this time far beyond his reach. He prepared to march from Ebbracum, but he did not accompany the considerable force of legionaries which he sent north. Sulla was a brave man, but each man has his own dread, and Sulla's was Cormac na Connacht, the black-haired prince of the Gaels, who had sworn to cut out the governor's heart and eat it raw. So Sulla rode with his ever-present bodyguard, westward, where lay the Tower of Trajan with its war-like commander, Caius Camillus, who enjoyed nothing more than taking his superior's place when the red waves of war washed at the foot of the Wall. Devious politics, but the legate of Rome seldom visited this far isle, and what of his wealth and intrigues, Titus Sulla was the highest power in Britain.

And Bran, knowing all this, patiently waited his coming, in the deserted hut in which he had taken up his abode.

One gray evening he strode on foot across the moors, a stark figure, blackly etched against the dim crimson fire of the sunset. He felt the incredible antiquity of the slumbering land, as he walked like the last man on the day after the end of the world. Yet at last he saw a token of human life – a drab hut of wattle and mud, set in the reedy breast of the fen.

A woman greeted him from the open door and Bran's somber eyes narrowed with a dark suspicion. The woman was not old, yet the evil wisdom of ages was in her eyes; her garments were ragged and scanty, her black locks tangled and unkempt, lending her an aspect of wildness well in keeping with her grim surroundings. Her red lips laughed but there was no mirth in her laughter, only a hint of mockery, and under the lips her teeth showed sharp and pointed like fangs.

'Enter, master,' said she, 'if you do not fear to share the roof of the witch-woman of Dagon-moor!'

Bran entered silently and sat him down on a broken bench while the woman busied herself with the scanty meal cooking over an open fire on the squalid hearth. He studied her lithe, almost serpentine motions, the ears which were almost pointed, the yellow eyes which slanted curiously.

'What do you seek in the fens, my lord?' she asked, turning toward him with a supple twist of her whole body.

'I seek a Door,' he answered, chin resting on his fist. 'I have a song to sing to the worms of the earth!'

She started upright, a jar falling from her hands to shatter on the hearth.

'This is an ill saying, even spoken in chance,' she stammered.

'I speak not by chance but by intent,' he answered.

She shook her head. 'I know not what you mean.'

'Well you know,' he returned. 'Aye, you know well! My race is very old – they reigned in Britain before the nations of the Celts and the Hellenes were born out of the womb of peoples. But my people were not first in Britain. By the mottles on your skin, by the slanting of your eyes, by the taint in your veins, I speak with full knowledge and meaning.'

Awhile she stood silent, her lips smiling but her face inscrutable.

'Man, are you mad?' she asked, 'that in your madness you come seeking that from which strong men fled screaming in old times?'

'I seek a vengeance,' he answered, 'that can be accomplished only by Them I seek.'

She shook her head.

'You have listened to a bird singing; you have dreamed empty dreams.'

'I have heard a viper hiss,' he growled, 'and I do not dream.

Enough of this weaving of words. I came seeking a link between two worlds; I have found it.'

'I need lie to you no more, man of the North,' answered the woman. 'They you seek still dwell beneath the sleeping hills. They have drawn *apart*, farther and farther from the world you know.'

'But they still steal forth in the night to grip women straying on the moors,' said he, his gaze on her slanted eyes. She laughed wickedly.

'What would you of me?'

'That you bring me to Them.'

She flung back her head with a scornful laugh. His left hand locked like iron in the breast of her scanty garment and his right closed on his hilt. She laughed in his face.

'Strike and be damned, my northern wolf! Do you think that such life as mine is so sweet that I would cling to it as a babe to the breast?'

His hand fell away.

'You are right. Threats are foolish. I will buy your aid.'

'How?' the laugh voice hummed with mockery.

Bran opened his pouch and poured into his cupped palm a stream of gold.

'More wealth than the men of the fen ever dreamed of.'

Again she laughed. 'What is this rusty metal to me? Save it for some white-breasted Roman woman who will play the traitor for you!'

'Name me a price!' he urged. 'The head of an enemy –'

'By the blood in my veins, with its heritage of ancient hate, who is mine enemy but thee?' she laughed and springing, struck cat-like. But her dagger splintered on the mail beneath his cloak and he flung her off with a loathsome flirt of his wrist which tossed her sprawling across her grass-strewn bunk. Lying there she laughed up at him.

'I will name you a price, then, my wolf, and it may be in days to come you will curse the armor that broke Atla's dagger!' She rose and came close to him, her disquietingly long hands fastened fiercely into his cloak. 'I will tell you, Black Bran, king of Caledon! Oh, I knew you when you came into my hut with your black hair and your cold eyes! I will lead you to the doors of Hell if you wish – and the price shall be the kisses of a king!

'What of my blasted and bitter life, I, whom mortal men loathe and fear? I have not known the love of men, the clasp of a strong arm, the sting of human kisses, I, Atla, the were-woman of the moors! What have I known but the lone winds of the fens, the dreary fire of cold sunsets, the whispering of the marsh grasses? – the faces that blink up at me in the waters of the meres, the foot-pad of night – things in the gloom, the glimmer of red eyes, the grisly murmur of nameless beings in the night!

'I am half-human, at least! Have I not known sorrow and yearning and crying wistfulness, and the drear ache of loneliness? Give to me, king – give me your fierce kisses and your hurtful barbarian's embrace. Then in the long drear years to come I shall not utterly eat out my heart in vain envy of the white-bosomed women of men; for I shall have a memory few of them can boast – the kisses of a king! One night of love, oh king, and I will guide you to the gates of Hell!'

Bran eyed her somberly; he reached forth and gripped her arm in his iron fingers. An involuntary shudder shook him at the feel of her sleek skin. He nodded slowly and drawing her close to him, forced his head down to meet her lifted lips.

4

The cold gray mists of dawn wrapped King Bran like a clammy cloak. He turned to the woman whose slanted eyes gleamed in the gray gloom.

'Make good your part of the contract,' he said roughly. 'I

sought a link between worlds, and in you I found it. I seek the one thing sacred to Them. It shall be the Key opening the Door that lies unseen between me and Them. Tell me how I can reach it.'

'I will,' the red lips smiled terribly. 'Go to the mound men call Dagon's Barrow. Draw aside the stone that blocks the entrance and go under the dome of the mound. The floor of the chamber is made of seven great stones, six grouped about the seventh. Lift out the center stone – and you will see!'

'Will I find the Black Stone?' he asked.

'Dagon's Barrow is the Door to the Black Stone,' she answered, 'if you dare follow the Road.'

'Will the symbol be well guarded?' He unconsciously loosened his blade in its sheath. The red lips curled mockingly.

'If you meet any on the Road you will die as no mortal man has died for long centuries. The Stone is not guarded, as men guard their treasures. Why should They guard what man has never sought? Perhaps They will be near, perhaps not. It is a chance you must take, if you wish the Stone. Beware, king of Pictdom! Remember it was your folk who, so long ago, cut the thread that bound Them to human life. They were almost human then – they overspread the land and knew the sunlight. Now they have drawn *apart*. They know not the sunlight and they shun the light of the moon. Even the starlight they hate. Far, far apart have they drawn, who might have been men in time, but for the spears of your ancestors.'

The sky was overcast with misty gray, through which the sun shone coldly yellow when Bran came to Dagon's Barrow, a round hillock overgrown with rank grass of a curious fungoid appearance. On the eastern side of the mound showed the entrance of a crudely built stone tunnel which evidently penetrated the barrow. One great stone blocked the entrance to the tomb. Bran laid hold of the sharp edges and exerted all his strength. It held fast. He drew his sword and worked the blade between the blocking stone and the sill. Using the sword as a lever, he worked carefully, and managed to loosen the great stone and wrench it out. A foul charnel-house scent flowed out of the aperture and the dim sunlight seemed less to illuminate the cavern-like opening than to be fouled by the rank darkness which clung there.

Sword in hand, ready for he knew not what, Bran groped his way into the tunnel, which was long and narrow, built up of heavy joined stones, and was too low for him to stand erect. Either his eyes became somewhat accustomed to the gloom, or the darkness was, after all, somewhat lightened by the sunlight filtering in through the entrance. At any rate he came into a round low chamber and was able to make out its general dome-like outline. Here, no doubt, in old times, had reposed the bones of him for whom the stones of the tomb had been joined and the earth heaped high above them; but now of those bones no vestige remained on the stone floor. And bending close and straining his eyes, Bran made out the strange, startlingly regular pattern of that floor: six well-cut slabs clustered about a seventh, six-sided stone.

He drove his sword-point into a crack and pried carefully. The edge of the central stone tilted slightly upward. A little work and he lifted it out and leaned it against the curving wall. Straining his eyes downward he saw only the gaping blackness of a dark well, with small, worn steps that led downward and out of sight. He did not hesitate. Though the skin between his shoulders crawled curiously he swung himself into the abyss and felt the clinging blackness swallow him.

Groping downward, he felt his feet slip and stumble on steps too small for human feet. With one hand pressed hard against the side of the well he steadied himself, fearing a fall into unknown and unlighted depths. The steps were cut into solid rock, yet they were greatly worn away. The farther he progressed, the less like steps they became, mere bumps of worn stone. Then the direction of the shaft changed sharply. It still led down, but at a shallow slant down which he could walk, elbows braced against the hollowed sides, head bent low beneath the curved roof. The steps had ceased altogether and the stone felt slimy to the touch, like a serpent's lair. What beings, Bran wondered, had slithered up and down this slanting shaft, for how many centuries?

The tunnel narrowed until Bran found it rather difficult to shove through. He lay on his back and pushed himself along with his hands, feet first. Still he knew he was sinking deeper and deeper into the very guts of the earth; how far below the surface he was, he dared not contemplate. Then ahead a faint witch-fire gleam tinged the abysmal blackness. He grinned savagely and without mirth. If They he sought came suddenly upon him, how could he fight in that narrow shaft? But he had put the thought of personal fear behind him when he began this hellish quest. He crawled on, thoughtless of all else but his goal.

And he came at last into a vast space where he could stand upright. He could not see the roof of the place, but he got an impression of dizzying vastness. The blackness pressed in on all sides and behind him he could see the entrance to the shaft from which he had just emerged – a black well in the darkness. But in front of him a strange grisly radiance glowed about a grim altar built of human skulls. The source of that light he could not determine, but on the altar lay a sullen night-black object – the Black Stone!

Bran wasted no time in giving thanks that the guardians of the grim relic were nowhere near. He caught up the Stone, and gripping it under his left arm, crawled into the shaft. When a man turns his back on peril its clammy menace looms more grisly than when he advances upon it. So Bran, crawling back up the nighted shaft with his grisly prize, felt the darkness turn on him and slink behind him, grinning with dripping fangs. Clammy sweat beaded his flesh and he hastened to the best of his ability, ears strained for some stealthy sound to betray that fell shapes were at his heels. Strong shudders shook him, despite himself, and the short hair on his neck prickled as if a cold wind blew at his back.

When he reached the first of the tiny steps he felt as if he had attained to the outer boundaries of the mortal world. Up them he went, stumbling and slipping, and with a deep gasp of relief, came out into the tomb, whose spectral grayness seemed like the blaze of noon in comparison to the stygian depths he had just traversed. He replaced the central stone and strode into the light of the outer day, and never was the cold yellow light of the sun more grateful, as it dispelled the shadows of black-winged nightmares of fear and madness that seemed to have ridden him up out of the black deeps. He shoved the great blocking stone back into place, and picking up the cloak he had left at the mouth of the tomb, he wrapped it about the Black Stone and hurried away, a strong revulsion and loathing shaking his soul and lending wings to his strides.

A gray silence brooded over the land. It was desolate as the blind side of the moon, yet Bran felt the potentialities of life – under his feet, in the brown earth – sleeping, but how soon to waken, and in what horrific fashion?

He came through the tall masking reeds to the still deep men called Dagon's Mere. No slightest ripple ruffled the cold blue water to give evidence of the grisly monster legend said dwelt beneath. Bran closely scanned the breathless landscape. He saw no hint of life, human or unhuman. He sought the instincts of his savage soul to know if any unseen eyes fixed their lethal gaze upon him, and found no response. He was alone as if he were the last man alive on earth.

Swiftly he unwrapped the Black Stone, and as it lay in his hands like a solid sullen block of darkness, he did not seek to learn the secret of its material nor scan the cryptic characters carved thereon. Weighing it in his hands and calculating the distance, he flung it far out, so that it fell almost exactly in the middle of the lake. A sullen splash and the waters closed over it. There was a moment of shimmering flashes on the bosom of the lake; then the blue surface stretched placid and unrippled again.

5

The were-woman turned swiftly as Bran approached her door. Her slant eyes widened.

'You! And alive! And sane!'

'I have been into Hell and I have returned,' he growled. 'What is more, I have that which I sought.'

'The Black Stone?' she cried. 'You really dared steal it? Where is it?'

'No matter; but last night my stallion screamed in his stall and I heard something crunch beneath his thundering hoofs which was not the wall of the stable – and there was blood on his hoofs when I came to see, and blood on the floor of the stall. And I have heard stealthy sounds in the night, and noises beneath my dirt floor, as if worms burrowed deep in the earth. They know I have stolen their Stone. Have you betrayed me?'

She shook her head.

'I keep your secret; they do not need my word to know you. The farther they have retreated from the world of men, the greater have grown their powers in other uncanny ways. Some dawn your hut will stand empty and if men dare investigate they will find nothing – except crumbling bits of earth on the dirt floor.'

Bran smiled terribly.

'I have not planned and toiled thus far to fall prey to the talons of vermin. If They strike me down in the night, They will never know what became of their idol – or whatever it be to Them. I would speak with Them.'

'Dare you come with me and meet them in the night?' she asked.

'Thunder of all gods!' he snarled. 'Who are you to ask me if I dare? Lead me to Them and let me bargain for a vengeance this night. The hour of retribution draws nigh. This day I saw silvered helmets and bright shields gleam across the fens – the new commander has arrived at the Tower of Trajan and Caius Camillus has marched to the Wall.'

That night the king went across the dark desolation of the moors with the silent were-woman. The night was thick and still as if the land lay in ancient slumber. The stars blinked vaguely, mere points of red struggling through the unbreathing gloom. Their gleam was dimmer than the glitter in the eyes of the woman who glided beside the king. Strange thoughts shook Bran, vague, titanic, primeval. Tonight ancestral linkings with these slumbering fens stirred in his soul and troubled him with the fantasmal, eon-veiled shapes of monstrous dreams. The vast age of his race was borne upon him; where now he walked an outlaw and an alien, dark-eyed kings in whose mold he was cast, had reigned in old times. The Celtic and Roman invaders were as strangers to this ancient isle beside his people. Yet his race likewise had been invaders, and there was an older race than his – a race whose beginnings lay lost and hidden back beyond the dark oblivion of antiquity.

Ahead of them loomed a low range of hills, which formed the easternmost extremity of those straying chains which far away climbed at last to the mountains of Wales. The woman led the way up what might have been a sheep-path, and halted before a wide black gaping cave.

'A door to those you seek, oh king!' her laughter rang hateful in the gloom. 'Dare ye enter?'

His fingers closed in her tangled locks and he shook her viciously.

'Ask me but once more if I dare,' he grated, 'and your head and shoulders part company! Lead on.'

Her laughter was like sweet deadly venom. They passed into the cave and Bran struck flint and steel. The flicker of the tinder showed him a wide dusty cavern, on the roof of which hung clusters of bats. Lighting a torch, he lifted it and scanned the shadowy recesses, seeing nothing but dust and emptiness.

'Where are They?' he growled.

She beckoned him to the back of the cave and leaned against the rough wall, as if casually. But the king's keen eyes caught the motion of her hand pressing hard against a projecting ledge. He recoiled as a round black well gaped suddenly at his feet. Again her laughter slashed him like a keen silver knife. He held the torch to the opening and again saw small worn steps leading down.

'They do not need those steps,' said Atla. 'Once they did, before your people drove them into the darkness. But you will need them.'

She thrust the torch into a niche above the well; it shed a faint red light into the darkness below. She gestured into the well and Bran loosened his sword and stepped into the shaft. As he went down into the mystery of the darkness, the light was blotted out above him, and he thought for an instant Atla had covered the opening again. Then he realized that she was descending after him.

The descent was not a long one. Abruptly Bran felt his feet on a solid floor. Atla swung down beside him and stood in the dim circle of light that drifted down the shaft. Bran could not see the limits of the place into which he had come.

'Many caves in these hills,' said Atla, her voice sounding small and strangely brittle in the vastness, 'are but doors to greater caves which lie beneath, even as a man's words and deeds are but small indications of the dark caverns of murky thought lying behind and beneath.'

And now Bran was aware of movement in the gloom. The darkness was filled with stealthy noises not like those made by any human foot. Abruptly sparks began to flash and float in the blackness, like flickering fireflies. Closer they came until they girdled him in a wide half-moon. And beyond the ring gleamed other sparks, a solid sea of them, fading away in the gloom until the farthest were mere tiny pin-points of light. And Bran knew they were the slanted eyes of the beings who had come upon him in such numbers that his brain reeled at the contemplation – and at the vastness of the cavern.

Now that he faced his ancient foes, Bran knew no fear. He felt the waves of terrible menace emanating from them, the grisly hate, the inhuman threat to body, mind and soul. More than a member of a less ancient race, he realized the horror of his position, but he did not fear, though he confronted the ultimate Horror of the dreams and legends of his race. His blood raced fiercely but it was with the hot excitement of the hazard, not the drive of terror.

'They know you have the Stone, oh king,' said Atla, and though he knew she feared, though he felt her physical efforts to control her trembling limbs, there was no quiver of fright in her voice. 'You are in deadly peril; they know your breed of old – oh, they remember the days when their ancestors were men! I can not save you; both of us will die as no human has died for ten centuries. Speak to them, if you will; they can understand your speech, though you may not understand theirs. But it will avail not – you are human – and a Pict.'

Bran laughed and the closing ring of fire shrank back at the savagery in his laughter. Drawing his sword with a soul-chilling rasp of steel, he set his back against what he hoped was a solid stone wall. Facing the glittering eyes with his sword gripped in his right hand and his dirk in his left, he laughed as a blood-hungry wolf snarls.

'Aye,' he growled, 'I am a Pict, a son of those warriors who drove your brutish ancestors before them like chaff before the storm! – who flooded the land with your blood and heaped high your skulls for a sacrifice to the Moon-Woman! You who fled of old before my race, dare ye now snarl at your master? Roll on me like a flood, now, if ye dare! Before your viper fangs drink my life I will reap your multitudes like ripened barley – of your severed heads will I build a tower and of your mangled corpses will I rear up a wall! Dogs of the dark, vermin of Hell, worms of the earth, rush in and try my steel! When Death finds me in this dark cavern, your living will howl for the scores of your dead and your Black Stone will be lost to you for ever – for only I know where it is hidden and not all the tortures of all the Hells can wring the secret from my lips!'

Then followed a tense silence; Bran faced the fire-lit darkness, tensed like a wolf at bay, waiting the charge; at his side the woman cowered, her eyes ablaze. Then from the silent ring that hovered beyond the dim torchlight rose a vague abhorrent murmur. Bran, prepared as he was for anything, started. Gods, was *that* the speech of creatures which had once been called men?

Atla straightened, listening intently. From her lips came the same hideous soft sibilances, and Bran, though he had already known the grisly secret of her being, knew that never again could he touch her save with soul-shaken loathing.

She turned to him, a strange smile curving her red lips dimly in the ghostly light.

'They fear you, oh king! By the black secrets of R'lyeh, who are you that Hell itself quails before you? Not your steel, but the stark ferocity of your soul has driven unused fear into their strange minds. They will buy back the Black Stone at any price.'

'Good,' Bran sheathed his weapons. 'They shall promise not to molest you because of your aid of me. And,' his voice hummed like the purr of a hunting tiger, 'They shall deliver into my hands Titus Sulla, governor of Ebbracum, now commanding the Tower of Trajan. This They can do – how, I know not. But I know that in the old days, when my people warred with these Children of the Night, babes disappeared from guarded huts and none saw the stealers come or go. Do They understand?'

Again rose the low frightful sounds and Bran, who feared not their wrath, shuddered at their voices.

'They understand,' said Atla, 'Bring the Black Stone to Dagon's Ring tomorrow night when the earth is veiled with the blackness that foreruns the dawn. Lay the Stone on the altar. There They will bring Titus Sulla to you. Trust Them; They have not interfered in human affairs for many centuries, but They will keep their word.'

Bran nodded and turning, climbed the stair with Atla close behind him. At the top he turned and looked down once more. As far as he could see floated a glittering ocean of slanted yellow eyes upturned. But the owners of those eyes kept carefully beyond the dim circle of torchlight and of their bodies he could see nothing. Their low hissing speech floated up to him and he shuddered as his imagination visualized, not a throng of biped creatures, but a swarming, swaying myriad of serpents, gazing up at him with their glittering unwinking eyes.

He swung into the upper cave and Atla thrust the blocking stone back in place. It fitted into the entrance of the well with uncanny precision; Bran was unable to discern any crack in the apparently solid floor of the cavern. Atla made a motion to extinguish the torch, but the king stayed her.

'Keep it so until we are out of the cave,' he grunted. 'We might tread on an adder in the dark.'

Atla's sweetly hateful laughter rose maddeningly in the flickering gloom.

6

It was not long before sunset when Bran came again to the reed-grown marge of Dagon's Mere. Casting cloak and sword-belt on the ground, he stripped himself of his short leathern breeches. Then gripping his naked dirk in his teeth, he went into the water with the smooth ease of a diving seal. Swimming strongly, he gained the center of the small lake, and turning, drove himself downward.

The mere was deeper than he had thought. It seemed he would never reach the bottom, and when he did, his groping hands failed to find what he sought. A roaring in his ears warned him and he swam to the surface.

Gulping deep of the refreshing air, he dived again, and again his quest was fruitless. A third time he sought the depth, and this time his groping hands met a familiar object in the silt of the bottom. Grasping it, he swam up to the surface.

The Stone was not particularly bulky, but it was heavy. He swam leisurely, and suddenly was aware of a curious stir in the waters about him which was not caused by his own exertions. Thrusting his face below the surface, he tried to pierce the blue depths with his eyes and thought to see a dim gigantic shadow hovering there.

He swam faster, not frightened, but wary. His feet struck the shallows and he waded up on the shelving shore. Looking back he saw the waters swirl and subside. He shook his head, swearing. He had discounted the ancient legend which made Dagon's Mere the lair of a nameless water-monster, but now he had a feeling as if his escape had been narrow. The time-worn myths of the ancient land were taking form and coming to life before his eyes. What primeval shape lurked below the surface of that treacherous mere, Bran could not guess, but he felt that the fen-men had good reason for shunning the spot, after all.

Bran donned his garments, mounted the black stallion and rode across the fens in the desolate crimson of the sunset's afterglow, with the Black Stone wrapped in his cloak. He rode, not to his hut, but to the west, in the direction of the Tower of Trajan and the Ring of Dagon. As he covered the miles that lay between, the red stars winked out. Midnight passed him in the moonless night and still Bran rode on. His heart was hot for his meeting with Titus Sulla. Atla had gloated over the anticipation of watching the Roman writhe under torture, but no such thought was in the Pict's mind. The governor should have his chance with weapons – with Bran's own sword he should face the Pictish king's dirk, and live or die according to his prowess. And though Sulla was famed throughout the provinces as a swordsman, Bran felt no doubt as to the outcome.

Dagon's Ring lay some distance from the Tower – a sullen circle of tall gaunt stones planted upright, with a rough-hewn stone altar in the center. The Romans looked on these menhirs with aversion; they thought the Druids had reared them; but the Celts supposed Bran's people, the Picts, had planted them – and Bran well knew what hands reared those grim monoliths in lost ages, though for what reasons, he but dimly guessed.

The king did not ride straight to the Ring. He was consumed with curiosity as to how his grim allies intended carrying out their promise. That They could snatch Titus Sulla from the very midst of his men, he felt sure, and he believed he knew how They would do it. He felt the gnawings of a strange misgiving, as if he had tampered with powers of unknown breadth and depth, and had loosed forces which he could not control. Each time he remembered that reptilian murmur, those slanted eyes of the night before, a cold breath passed over him. They had been abhorrent enough when his people drove Them into the caverns under the hills, ages ago; what had long centuries of retrogression made of them? In their nighted, subterranean life, had They retained any of the attributes of humanity at all?

Some instinct prompted him to ride toward the Tower. He knew he was near; but for the thick darkness he could have plainly seen its stark outline tusking the horizon. Even now he should be able to make it out dimly. An obscure, shuddersome premonition shook him and he spurred the stallion into swift canter.

And suddenly Bran staggered in his saddle as from a physical impact, so stunning was the surprize of what met his gaze. The impregnable Tower of Trajan was no more! Bran's astounded gaze rested on a gigantic pile of ruins – of shattered stone and crumbled granite, from which jutted the jagged and splintered ends of broken beams. At one corner of the tumbled heap one tower rose out of the waste of crumpled masonry, and it leaned drunkenly as if its foundations had been half cut away.

Bran dismounted and walked forward, dazed by bewilderment. The moat was filled in places by fallen stones and broken pieces of mortared wall. He crossed over and came among the ruins. Where, he knew, only a few hours before the flags had resounded to the martial tramp of iron-clad feet, and the walls had echoed to the clang of shields and the blast of the loud-throated trumpets, a horrific silence reigned.

Almost under Bran's feet, a broken shape writhed and groaned. The king bent down to the legionary who lay in a sticky red pool of his own blood. A single glance showed the Pict that the man, horribly crushed and shattered, was dying.

Lifting the bloody head, Bran placed his flask to the pulped lips and the Roman instinctively drank deep, gulping through splintered teeth. In the dim starlight Bran saw his glazed eyes roll.

'The walls fell,' muttered the dying man. 'They crashed down like the skies falling on the day of doom. Ah Jove, the skies rained shards of granite and hailstones of marble!'

'I have felt no earthquake shock,' Bran scowled, puzzled.

'It was no earthquake,' muttered the Roman. 'Before last

dawn it began, the faint dim scratching and clawing far below the earth. We of the guard heard it – like rats burrowing, or like worms hollowing out the earth. Titus laughed at us, but all day long we heard it. Then at midnight the Tower quivered and seemed to settle – as if the foundations were being dug away –'

A shudder shook Bran Mak Morn. The worms of the earth! Thousands of vermin digging like moles far below the castle, burrowing away the foundations – gods, the land must be honeycombed with tunnels and caverns – these creatures were even less human than he had thought – what ghastly shapes of darkness had he invoked to his aid?

'What of Titus Sulla?' he asked, again holding the flask to the legionary's lips; in that moment the dying Roman seemed to him almost like a brother.

'Even as the Tower shuddered we heard a fearful scream from the governor's chamber,' muttered the soldier. 'We rushed there – as we broke down the door we heard his shrieks – they seemed to recede – *into the bowels of the earth!* We rushed in; the chamber was empty. His blood-stained sword lay on the floor, in the stone flags of the floor a black hole gaped. Then – the – towers – reeled – the – roof – broke; – through – a – storm – of – crashing – walls – I – crawled –'

A strong convulsion shook the broken figure.

'Lay me down, friend,' whispered the Roman. 'I die.'

He had ceased to breathe before Bran could comply. The Pict rose, mechanically cleansing his hands. He hastened from the spot, and as he galloped over the darkened fens, the weight of the accursed Black Stone under his cloak was as the weight of a foul nightmare on a mortal breast.

As he approached the Ring, he saw an eery glow within, so that the gaunt stones stood etched like the ribs of a skeleton in which a witch-fire burns. The stallion snorted and reared as Bran tied him to one of the menhirs. Carrying the Stone he strode into the grisly circle and saw Atla standing beside the altar, one hand on her hip, her sinuous body swaying in a serpentine manner. The altar glowed all over with ghastly light and Bran knew some one, probably Atla, had rubbed it with phosphorus from some dank swamp or quagmire.

He strode forward and whipping his cloak from about the Stone, flung the accursed thing on to the altar.

'I have fulfilled my part of the contract,' he growled.

'And They, theirs,' she retorted. 'Look! – they come!'

He wheeled, his hand instinctively dropping to his sword. Outside the Ring the great stallion screamed savagely and reared against his tether. The night wind moaned through the waving grass and an abhorrent soft hissing mingled with it. Between the menhirs flowed a dark tide of shadows, unstable and chaotic. The Ring filled with glittering eyes which hovered beyond the dim illusive circle of illumination cast by the phosphorescent altar. Somewhere in the darkness a human voice tittered and gibbered idiotically. Bran stiffened, the shadows of a horror clawing at his soul.

He strained his eyes, trying to make out the shapes of those who ringed him. But he glimpsed only billowing masses of shadow which heaved and writhed and squirmed with almost fluid consistency.

'Let them make good their bargain!' he exclaimed angrily.

'Then see, oh king!' cried Atla in a voice of piercing mockery.

There was a stir, a seething in the writhing shadows, and from the darkness crept, like a four-legged animal, a human shape that fell down and groveled at Bran's feet and writhed and mowed, and lifting a death's-head, howled like a dying dog. In the ghastly light, Bran, soul-shaken, saw the blank glassy eyes, the bloodless features, the loose, writhing, froth-covered lips of sheer lunacy – gods, was this Titus Sulla, the proud lord of life and death in Ebbracum's proud city?

Bran bared his sword.

'I had thought to give this stroke in vengeance,' he said somberly. 'I give it in mercy – *Vale Cæsar!*'

The steel flashed in the eery light and Sulla's head rolled to the foot of the glowing altar, where it lay staring up at the shadowed sky.

'They harmed him not!' Atla's hateful laugh slashed the sick silence. 'It was what he saw and came to know that broke his brain! Like all his heavy-footed race, he knew nothing of the secrets of this ancient land. This night he has been dragged through the deepest pits of Hell, where even you might have blenched!'

'Well for the Romans that they know not the secrets of this accursed land!' Bran roared, maddened, 'with its monster-haunted meres, its foul witch-women, and its lost caverns and subterranean realms where spawn in the darkness shapes of Hell!'

'Are they more foul than a mortal who seeks their aid?' cried Atla with a shriek of fearful mirth. 'Give them their Black Stone!'

A cataclysmic loathing shook Bran's soul with red fury.

'Aye, take your cursed Stone!' he roared, snatching it from the altar and dashing it among the shadows with such savagery that bones snapped under its impact. A hurried babel of grisly tongues rose and the shadows heaved in turmoil. One segment of the mass detached itself for an instant and Bran cried out in fierce revulsion, though he caught only a fleeting glimpse of the thing, had only a brief impression of a broad strangely flattened head, pendulous writhing lips that bared curved pointed fangs, and a hideously misshapen, dwarfish body that seemed *mottled* – all set off by those unwinking reptilian eyes. Gods! – the myths had prepared him for horror in human aspect, horror induced by bestial visage and stunted deformity – but this was the horror of nightmare and the night.

'Go back to Hell and take your idol with you!' he yelled, brandishing his clenched fists to the skies, as the thick shadows receded, flowing back and away from him like the foul waters of some black flood. 'Your ancestors were men, though strange and monstrous – but gods, ye have become in ghastly fact what my people called ye in scorn! Worms of the earth, back into your holes and burrows! Ye foul the air and leave on the clean earth the slime of the serpents ye have become! Gonar was right – there are shapes too foul to use even against Rome!'

He sprang from the Ring as a man flees the touch of a coiling snake, and tore the stallion free. At his elbow Atla was shrieking with fearful laughter, all human attributes dropped from her like a cloak in the night.

'King of Pictland!' she cried. 'King of fools! Do you blench at so small a thing? Stay and let me show you real fruits of the pits! Ha! ha! ha! Run, fool, run! But you are stained with the taint – you have called them forth and they will remember! And in their own time they will come to you again!'

He yelled a wordless curse and struck her savagely in the mouth with his open hand. She staggered, blood starting from her lips, but her fiendish laughter only rose higher.

Bran leaped into the saddle, wild for the clean heather and the cold blue hills of the north where he could plunge his sword into clean slaughter and his sickened soul into the red maelstrom of battle, and forget the horror which lurked below the fens of the west. He gave the frantic stallion the rein, and rode through the night like a hunted ghost, until the hellish laughter of the howling were-woman died out in the darkness behind.

The Dark Man

'For this is the night of the drawing of swords,
And the painted tower of the heathen hordes
Leans to our hammers, fires and cords,
Leans a little and falls.'

                                        Chesterton

A biting wind drifted the snow as it fell. The surf snarled along
the rugged shore and farther out the long leaden combers
moaned ceaselessly. Through the gray dawn that was stealing
over the coast of Connacht a fisherman came trudging, a man
rugged as the land that bore him. His feet were wrapped in
rough cured leather; a single garment of deerskin scantily sheltered his body. He wore no other clothing. As he strode stolidly
along the shore, as heedless of the bitter cold as if he were the
shaggy beast he appeared at first glance, he halted. Another man
loomed up out of the veil of falling snow and drifting sea-mist.
Turlogh Dubh stood before him.

This man was nearly a head taller than the stocky fisherman,
and he had the bearing of a fighting man. No single glance
would suffice, but any man or woman whose eyes fell on Turlogh Dubh would look long. Six feet and one inch he stood, and
the first impression of slimness faded on closer inspection. He
was big but trimly molded; a magnificent sweep of shoulder and
depth of chest. Rangy he was, but compact, combining the
strength of a bull with the lithe quickness of a panther. The

slightest movement he made showed that steel trap co-ordination that makes the super-fighter. Turlogh Dubh – Black Turlogh, once of the Clan na O'Brien.* And black he was as to hair, and dark of complexion. From under heavy black brows gleamed eyes of a hot volcanic blue. And in his clean-shaven face there was something of the somberness of dark mountains, of the ocean at midnight. Like the fisherman, he was a part of this fierce western land.

On his head he wore a plain vizorless helmet without crest or symbol. From neck to mid-thigh he was protected by a close-fitting shirt of black chain mail. The kilt he wore below his armor and which reached to his knees, was of plain drab material. His legs were wrapped with hard leather that might turn a sword edge, and the shoes on his feet were worn with much traveling.

A broad belt encircled his lean waist, holding a long dirk in a leather sheath. On his left arm he carried a small round shield of hide-covered wood, hard as iron, braced and reinforced with steel, and having a short, heavy spike in the center. An ax hung from his right wrist, and it was to this feature that the fisherman's eyes wandered. The weapon with its three-foot handle and graceful lines looked slim and light when the fisherman mentally compared it to the great axes carried by the Norsemen. Yet scarcely three years had passed, as the fisherman knew, since such axes as these had shattered the northern hosts into red defeat and broken the pagan power forever.

There was individuality about the ax as about its owner. It was not like any other the fisherman had ever seen. Single-edged it was, with a short three-edged spike on the back and another on the top of the head. Like the wielder, it was heavier than it looked. With its slightly curved shaft and the graceful artistry of

---

*To avoid confusion I have used the modern terms for places and clans. – AUTHOR.

the blade, it looked the weapon of an expert – swift, lethal, deadly, cobra-like. The head was of finest Irish workmanship, which meant, at that day, the finest in the world. The handle, cut from the heart of a century-old oak, specially fire-hardened and braced with steel, was as unbreakable as an iron bar.

'Who are you?' asked the fisherman with the bluntness of the west.

'Who are you to ask?' answered the other.

The fisherman's eyes roved to the single ornament the warrior wore – a heavy golden armlet on his left arm.

'Clean-shaven and close-cropped in the Norman fashion,' he muttered. 'And dark – you'd be Black Turlogh, the outlaw of Clan na O'Brien. You range far; I heard of you last in the Wicklow hills preying off the O'Reillys and the Oastmen alike.'

'A man must eat, outcast or not,' growled the Dalcassian.

The fisherman shrugged his shoulders. A masterless man – it was a hard road. In those days of clans, when a man's own kin cast him out he became a son of Ishmael with a vengeance. All men's hands were against him. The fisherman had heard of Turlogh Dubh – a strange, bitter man, a terrible warrior and a crafty strategist, but one whom sudden bursts of strange madness made a marked man even in that land and age of madmen.

'It's a bitter day,' said the fisherman apropos of nothing.

Turlogh stared somberly at his tangled beard and wild matted hair. 'Have you a boat?'

The other nodded toward a small sheltered cove where lay snugly anchored a trim craft built with the skill of a hundred generations of men who had torn their livelihood from the stubborn sea.

'It scarce looks seaworthy,' said Turlogh.

'Seaworthy? You who were born and bred on the western coast should know better. I've sailed her alone to Drumcliff Bay and back, and all the devils in the wind ripping at her.'

'You can't take fish in such a sea.'

'Do ye think it's only you chiefs that take sport in risking their hides? By the saints, I've sailed to Ballinskellings in a storm – and back too – just for the fun of the thing.'

'Good enough,' said Turlogh. 'I'll take your boat.'

'Ye'll take the devil! What kind of talk is this? If you want to leave Erin, go to Dublin and take ship with your Dane friends.'

A black scowl made Turlogh's face a mask of menace. 'Men have died for less than that.'

'Did you not intrigue with the Danes? – and is that not why your clan drove you out to starve in the heather?'

'The jealousy of a cousin and the spite of a woman,' growled Turlogh. 'Lies – all lies. But enough. Have you seen a long serpent beating up from the south in the last few days?'

'Aye – three days ago we sighted a dragon-beaked galley before the scud. But she didn't put in – faith, the pirates get naught from the western fishers but hard blows.'

'That would be Thorfel the Fair,' muttered Turlogh, swaying his ax by its wrist-strap. 'I knew it.'

'There has been a ship-harrying in the south?'

'A band of reavers fell by night on the castle on Kilbaha. There was a sword-quenching – and the pirates took Moira, daughter of Murtagh, a chief of the Dalcassians.'

'I've heard of her,' muttered the fisherman. 'There'll be a whetting of swords in the south – a red sea-plowing, eh, my black jewel?'

'Her brother Dermod lies helpless from a sword-cut in the foot. The lands of her clan are harried by the MacMurroughs in the east and the O'Connors from the north. Not many men can be spared from the defense of the tribe, even to seek for Moira – the clan is fighting for its life. All Erin is rocking under the Dalcassian throne since great Brian fell. Even so, Cormac O'Brien has taken ship to hunt down her ravishers – but he follows the trail of a wild goose, for it is thought the raiders were Danes from Coningbeg. Well – we outcasts have ways of knowledge – it was Thorfel the Fair who holds the isle of Slyne, that the Norse call Helni, in the Hebrides. There he has taken her – there I follow him. Lend me your boat.'

'You are mad!' cried the fisherman sharply. 'What are you saying? From Connacht to the Hebrides in an open boat? In this weather? I say you are mad.'

'I will essay it,' answered Turlogh absently. 'Will you lend me your boat?'

'No.'

'I might slay you and take it,' said Turlogh.

'You might,' returned the fisherman stolidly.

'You crawling swine,' snarled the outlaw in swift passion, 'a princess of Erin languishes in grip of a red-bearded reaver of the north and you haggle like a Saxon.'

'Man, I must live!' cried the fisherman as passionately. 'Take my boat and I shall starve! Where can I get another like it? It is the cream of its kind!'

Turlogh reached for the armlet on his left arm. 'I will pay you. Here is a torc that Brian Boru put on my arm with his own hand before Clontarf. Take it; it would buy a hundred boats. I have starved with it on my arm, but now the need is desperate.'

But the fisherman shook his head, the strange illogic of the Gael burning in his eyes. 'No! My hut is no place for a torc that King Brian's hands have touched. Keep it – and take the boat, in the name of the saints, if it means that much to you.'

'You shall have it back when I return,' promised Turlogh, 'and mayhap a golden chain that now decks the bull neck of some northern rover.'

The day was sad and leaden. The wind moaned and the everlasting monotone of the sea was like the sorrow that is born in the heart of man. The fisherman stood on the rocks and watched the frail craft glide and twist serpent-like among the rocks until the blast of the open sea smote it and tossed it like a feather. The wind caught the sail and the slim boat leaped and staggered, then righted herself and raced before the gale, dwindling until it was but a dancing speck in the eyes of the watcher. And then a flurry of snow hid it from his sight.

Turlogh realized something of the madness of his pilgrimage. But he was bred to hardships and peril. Cold and ice and driving sleet that would have frozen a weaker man, only spurred him to greater efforts. He was as hard and supple as a wolf. Among a race of men whose hardiness astounded even the toughest Norseman, Turlogh Dubh stood out alone. At birth he had been tossed into a snow-drift to test his right to survive. His childhood and boyhood had been spent on the mountains, coast and moors of the west. Until manhood he had never worn woven cloth upon his body; a wolfskin had formed the apparel of this son of a Dalcassian chief. Before his outlawry he could out-tire a horse, running all day long beside it. He had never wearied at swimming. Now, since the intrigues of jealous clansmen had driven him into the wastelands and the life of the wolf, his ruggedness was such as can not be conceived by a civilized man.

The snow ceased, the weather cleared, the wind held. Turlogh necessarily hugged the coast line, avoiding the reefs against which it seemed again and again that his craft would be dashed. With tiller, sail and oar he worked tirelessly. Not one man out of a thousand of seafarers could have accomplished it, but Turlogh did. He needed no sleep; as he steered he ate from the rude provisions the fisherman had provided him. By the time he sighted Malin Head the weather had calmed wonderfully. There was still a heavy sea, but the gale had slackened to a sharp breeze that sent the little boat skipping along. Days and nights merged into each other; Turlogh drove eastward. Once he put into shore for fresh water and to snatch a few hours' sleep.

As he steered he thought of the fisherman's last words: 'Why should you risk your life for a clan that's put a price on your head?'

Turlogh shrugged his shoulders. Blood was thicker than water. The mere fact that his people had booted him out to die like a hunted wolf on the moors did not alter the fact that they *were* his people. Little Moira, daughter of Murtagh na Kilbaha, had nothing to do with it. He remembered her – he had played with her when he was a boy and she a babe – he remembered the deep grayness of her eyes and the burnished sheen of her black hair, the fairness of her skin. Even as a child she had been remarkably beautiful – why, she was only a child now, for he, Turlogh, was young and he was many years her senior. Now she was speeding north to become the unwilling bride of a Norse reaver. Thorfel the Fair – the Handsome – Turlogh swore by gods that knew not the Cross. A red mist waved across his eyes so that the rolling sea swam crimson all about him. An Irish girl a captive in the skalli of a Norse pirate – with a vicious wrench Turlogh turned his bows straight for the open sea. There was a tinge of madness in his eyes.

It is a long slant from Malin Head to Helni straight out across the foaming billows, as Turlogh took it. He was aiming for a small island that lay, with many other small islands, between Mull and the Hebrides. A modern seaman with charts and compass might have difficulty in finding it. Turlogh had neither. He sailed by instinct and through knowledge. He knew these seas as a man knows his house. He had sailed them as a raider and an avenger, and once he had sailed them as a captive lashed to the deck of a Danish dragon ship. And he followed a red trail. Smoke drifting from headlands, floating pieces of wreckage, charred timbers showed that Thorfel was ravaging as he went. Turlogh growled in savage satisfaction; he was close behind the viking, in spite of the long lead. For Thorfel was burning and pillaging the shores as he went, and Turlogh's course was like an arrow's.

He was still a long way from Helni when he sighted a small island slightly off his course. He knew it of old as one uninhabited, but there he could get fresh water. So he steered for it. The

Isle of Swords it was called, no man knew why. And as he neared the beach he saw a sight which he rightly interpreted. Two boats were drawn up on the shelving shore. One was a crude affair, something like the one Turlogh had, but considerably larger. The other was a long low craft – undeniably viking. Both were deserted. Turlogh listened for the clash of arms, the cry of battle, but silence reigned. Fishers, he thought, from the Scotch isles; they had been sighted by some band of rovers on ship or on some other island, and had been pursued in the long rowboat. But it had been a longer chase than they had anticipated, he was sure; else they would not have started out in an open boat. But inflamed with the murder lust, the reavers would have followed their prey across a hundred miles of rough water, in an open boat, if necessary.

Turlogh drew inshore, tossed over the stone that served for anchor and leaped upon the beach, ax ready. Then up the shore a short distance he saw a strange red huddle of forms. A few swift strides brought him face to face with mystery. Fifteen red-bearded Danes lay in their own gore in a rough circle. Not one breathed. Within this circle, mingling with the bodies of their slayers, lay other men, such as Turlogh had never seen. Short of stature they were, and very dark; their staring dead eyes were the blackest Turlogh had ever seen. They were scantily armored, and their stiff hands still gripped broken swords and daggers. Here and there lay arrows that had shattered on the corselets of the Danes, and Turlogh observed with surprize that many of them were tipped with flint.

'This was a grim fight,' he muttered. 'Aye, this was a rare sword-quenching. Who are these people? In all the isles I have never seen their like before. Seven – is that all? Where are their comrades who helped them slay these Danes?'

No tracks led away from the bloody spot. Turlogh's brow darkened.

'These were all – seven against fifteen – yet the slayers died with the slain. What manner of men are these who slay twice their number of vikings? They are small men – their armor is mean. Yet –'

Another thought struck him. Why did not the strangers scatter and flee, hide themselves in the woods? He believed he knew the answer. There, at the very center of the silent circle, lay a strange thing. A statue it was of some dark substance and it was in the form of a man. Some five feet long – or high – it was, carved in a semblance of life that made Turlogh start. Half over it lay the corpse of an ancient man, hacked almost beyond human semblance. One lean arm was locked about the figure; the other was outstretched, the hand gripping a flint dagger which was sheathed to the hilt in the breast of a Dane. Turlogh noted the fearful wounds that disfigured all the dark men. They had been hard to kill – they had fought until literally hacked to pieces, and dying, they had dealt death to their slayers. So much Turlogh's eyes showed him. In the dead faces of the dark strangers was a terrible desperation. He noted how their dead hands were still locked in the beards of their foes. One lay beneath the body of a huge Dane, and on this Dane Turlogh could see no wound; until he looked closer and saw the dark man's teeth were sunk, beast-like, into the bull throat of the other.

He bent and dragged the figure from among the bodies. The ancient's arm was locked about it, and he was forced to tear it away with all his strength. It was as if, even in death, the old one clung to his treasure; for Turlogh felt that it was for this image that the small dark men had died. They might have scattered and eluded their foes, but that would have meant giving up their image. They chose to die beside it. Turlogh shook his head; his hatred of the Norse, a heritage of wrongs and outrages, was a burning, living thing, almost an obsession that at times drove him to the point of insanity. There was, in his fierce heart, no room for mercy; the sight of these Danes, lying dead at his feet, filled him with savage satisfaction. Yet he sensed here, in these silent dead men, a passion stronger than his. Here was some driving impulse deeper than his hate. Aye – and older. These little men seemed very ancient to him, not old as individuals are old, but old as a race is old. Even their corpses exuded an intangible aura of the primeval. And the image –

The Gael bent and grasped it, to lift it. He expected to encounter great weight and was astonished. It was no heavier than if it had been made of light wood. He tapped it, and the sound was solid. At first he thought it was of iron; then he decided it was of stone, but such stone as he had never seen; and he felt that no such stone was to be found in the British Isles or anywhere in the world he knew. For like the little dead men it looked *old*. It was as smooth and free from corrosion as if carved yesterday, but for all that, it was a symbol of antiquity, Turlogh knew. It was the figure of a man who much resembled the small dark men who lay about it. But it differed subtly. Turlogh felt somehow that this was the image of a man who had lived long ago, for surely the unknown sculptor had had a living model. And he had contrived to breathe a touch of life into his work. There was the sweep of the shoulders, the depth of the chest, the powerfully molded arms; the strength of the features was evident. The firm jaw, the regular nose, the high forehead, all indicated a powerful intellect, a high courage, an inflexible will. Surely, thought Turlogh, this man was a king – or a god. Yet he wore no crown; his only garment was a sort of loin-cloth, wrought so cunningly that every wrinkle and fold was carved as in reality.

'This was their god,' mused Turlogh, looking about him. 'They fled before the Danes – but died for their god at last. Who are these people? Whence come they? Whither were they bound?'

He stood, leaning on his ax, and a strange tide rose in his soul. A sense of mighty abysses of time and space opened before; of the strange, endless tides of mankind that drift for ever; of the waves of humanity that wax and wane with the waxing and waning of the sea-tides. Life was a door opening upon two black, unknown worlds – and how many races of men with their hopes and fears, their loves and their hates, had passed through that door – on their pilgrimage from the dark to the dark? Turlogh sighed. Deep in his soul stirred the mystic sadness of the Gael.

'You were a king, once, Dark Man,' he said to the silent image. 'Mayhap you were a god and reigned over all the world. Your people passed – as mine are passing. Surely you were a king of the Flint People, the race whom my Celtic ancestors destroyed. Well – we have had our day and we, too, are passing. These Danes who lie at your feet – they are the conquerors now. They must have their day – but they too will pass. But you shall go with me, Dark Man, king, god or devil though you be. Aye, for it is in my mind that you will bring me luck, and luck is what I shall need when I sight Helni, Dark Man.'

Turlogh bound the image securely in the bows. Again he set out for his sea-plowing. Now the skies grew gray and the snow fell in driving lances that stung and cut. The waves were gray-grained with ice and the winds bellowed and beat on the open boat. But Turlogh feared not. And his boat rode as it had never ridden before. Through the roaring gale and the driving snow it sped, and to the mind of the Dalcassian it seemed that the Dark Man lent him aid. Surely he had been lost a hundred times without supernatural assistance. With all his skill at boat-handling he wrought, and it seemed to him that there was an unseen hand on the tiller, and at the oar; that more than human skill aided him when he trimmed his sail.

And when all the world was a driving white veil in which even the Gael's sense of direction was lost, it seemed to him that he was steering in compliance with a silent voice that spoke in the dim reaches of his consciousness. Nor was he surprized when at last, when the snow had ceased and the clouds had rolled away beneath a cold silvery moon, he saw land loom up ahead and recognized it as the isle of Helni. More, he knew that just around a point of land was the bay where Thorfel's dragon ship was moored when not ranging the seas, and a hundred yards back from the bay lay Thorfel's skalli. He grinned fiercely. All the skill in the world could not have brought him to this exact spot – it was pure luck – no, it was more than luck. Here was the best place possible for him to make an approach – within half a mile of his foe's hold, yet hidden from sight of any watchers by this jutting promontory. He glanced at the Dark Man in the bows – brooding, inscrutable as the sphinx. A strange feeling stole over the Gael – that all this was his work; that he, Turlogh, was only a pawn in the game. What was this fetish? What grim secret did those carven eyes hold? Why did the dark little men fight so terribly for him?

Turlogh ran his boat inshore, into a small creek. A few yards up this he anchored and stepped out on shore. A last glance at the brooding Dark Man in the bows, and he turned and went hurriedly up the slope of the promontory, keeping to cover as much as possible. At the top of the slope he gazed down on the other side. Less than half a mile away Thorfel's dragon ship lay at anchor. And there lay Thorfel's skalli, also the long low building of rough-hewn log emitting the gleams that betokened the roaring fires within. Shouts of wassail came clearly to the listener through the sharp still air. He ground his teeth. Wassail! Aye, they were celebrating the ruin and destruction they had committed – the homes left in smoking embers – the slain men – the ravished girls. They were lords of the world, these vikings – all the southland lay helpless beneath their swords. The southland folk lived only to furnish them sport – and slaves – Turlogh shuddered violently and shook as if in a chill. The blood-sickness was on him like a physical pain, but he fought back the mists of passion that clouded his brain. He was here, not to fight but to steal away the girl they had stolen.

He took careful note of the ground, like a general going over the plan of his campaign. He noted that the trees grew thick close behind the skalli; that the smaller houses, the storehouses and servants' huts were between the main building and the bay. A huge fire was blazing down by the shore and a few carles were roaring and drinking about it, but the fierce cold had driven most of them into the drinking-hall of the main building.

Turlogh crept down the thickly wooded slope, entering the forest which swept about in a wide curve away from the shore. He kept to the fringe of its shadows, approaching the skalli in a rather indirect route, but afraid to strike out boldly in the open lest he be seen by the watchers that Thorfel surely had out. Gods, if he only had the warriors of Clare at his back as he had of old! Then there would be no skulking like a wolf among the trees! His hand locked like iron on his ax-haft as he visualized the scene – the charge, the shouting, the blood-letting, the play of the Dalcassian axes – he sighed. He was a lone outcast; never again would he lead the swordsmen of his clan to battle.

He dropped suddenly in the snow behind a low shrub and lay still. Men were approaching from the same direction in which he had come – men who grumbled loudly and walked heavily. They came into sight – two of them, huge Norse warriors, their silver-scaled armor flashing in the moonlight. They were carrying something between them with difficulty and to Turlogh's amazement he saw it was the Dark Man. His consternation at the realization that they had found his boat was gulfed in a greater astonishment. These men were giants; their arms bulged with iron muscles. Yet they were staggering under what seemed a stupendous weight. In their hands the Dark Man seemed to weigh hundreds of pounds; yet Turlogh had lifted it lightly as a feather! He almost swore in his amazement. Surely these men were drunk. One of them spoke, and Turlogh's short neck hairs bristled at the sound of the guttural accents, as a dog will bristle at the sight of a foe.

'Let it down; Thor's death, the thing weighs a ton. Let's rest.'

The other grunted a reply and they began to ease the image to the earth. Then one of them lost his hold on it; his hand slipped and the Dark Man crashed heavily into the snow. The first speaker howled.

'You clumsy fool, you dropped it on my foot! Curse you, my ankle's broken!'

'It twisted out of my hand!' cried the other. 'The thing's alive, I tell you!'

'Then I'll slay it,' snarled the lamed viking, and drawing his sword, he struck savagely at the prostrate figure. Fire flashed as the blade shivered into a hundred pieces, and the other Norseman howled as a flying sliver of steel gashed his cheek.

'The devil's in it!' shouted the other, throwing his hilt away. 'I've not even scratched it! Here, take hold – let's get it into the ale-hall and let Thorfel deal with it.'

'Let it lie,' growled the second man, wiping the blood from his face. 'I'm bleeding like a butchered hog. Let's go back and tell Thorfel that there's no ship stealing on the island. That's what he sent us to the point to see.'

'What of the boat where we found this?' snapped the other. 'Some Scotch fisher driven out of his course by the storm and hiding like a rat in the woods now, I guess. Here, bear a hand; idol or devil, we'll carry this to Thorfel.'

Grunting with the effort, they lifted the image once more and went on slowly, one groaning and cursing as he limped along, the other shaking his head from time to time as the blood got into his eyes.

Turlogh rose stealthily and watched them. A touch of chilliness traveled up and down his spine. Either of these men was as strong as he, yet it was taxing their powers to the utmost to carry what he had handled easily. He shook his head and took up his way again.

At last he reached a point in the woods nearest the skalli. Now was the crucial test. Somehow he must reach that building and hide himself, unperceived. Clouds were gathering. He waited until one obscured the moon, and in the gloom that followed, ran swiftly and silently across the snow, crouching. A shadow out of the shadows he seemed. The shouts and songs from within the long building were deafening. Now he was close to its side, flattening himself against the rough-hewn logs. Vigilance was most certainly relaxed now – yet what foe should Thorfel expect, when he was friends with all northern reavers, and none else could be expected to fare forth on a night such as this had been?

A shadow among the shadows, Turlogh stole about the house. He noted a side door and slid cautiously to it. Then he drew back close against the wall. Someone within was fumbling at the latch. Then the door was flung open and a big warrior lurched out, slamming the door to behind him. Then he saw Turlogh. His bearded lips parted, but in that instant the Gael's hands shot to his throat and locked there like a wolf-trap. The threatened yell died in a gasp. One hand flew to Turlogh's wrist, the other drew a dagger and stabbed upward. But already the man was senseless; the dagger rattled feebly against the outlaw's corselet and dropped into the snow. The Norseman sagged in his slayer's grasp, his throat literally crushed by that iron grip. Turlogh flung him contemptuously into the snow and spat in his dead face before he turned again to the door.

The latch had not fastened within. The door sagged a trifle. Turlogh peered in and saw an empty room, piled with ale barrels. He entered noiselessly, shutting the door but not latching it. He thought of hiding his victim's body, but he did not know how he could do it. He must trust to luck that no one saw it in the deep snow where it lay. He crossed the room and found it let into another parallel with the outer wall. This was also a storeroom, and was empty. From this a doorway, without a door but furnished with a curtain of skins, let into the main hall, as

Turlogh could tell from the sounds on the other side. He peered out cautiously.

He was looking into the drinking-hall – the great hall which served as banquet, council and living-hall of the master of the skalli. This hall, with its smoke-blackened rafters, great roaring fireplaces, and heavily laden boards, was a scene of terrific revelry tonight. Huge warriors with golden beards and savage eyes sat or lounged on the rude benches, strode about the hall or sprawled full length on the floor. They drank mightily from foaming horns and leathern jacks, and gorged themselves on great pieces of rye bread, and huge chunks of meat they cut with their daggers from whole roasted joints. It was a scene of strange incongruity, for in contrast with these barbaric men and their rough songs and shouts, the walls were hung with rare spoils that betokened civilized workmanship. Fine tapestries that Norman women had worked; richly chased weapons that princes of France and Spain had wielded; armor and silken garments from Byzantium and the Orient – for the dragon ships ranged far. With these were placed the spoils of the hunt, to show the viking's mastery of beasts as well as men.

The modern man can scarcely conceive of Turlogh O'Brien's feeling toward these men. To him they were devils – ogres who dwelt in the north only to descend on the peaceful people of the south. All the world was their prey to pick and choose, to take and spare as it pleased their barbaric whims. His brain throbbed and burned as he gazed. As only the Gael can hate, he hated them – their magnificent arrogance, their pride and their power, their contempt for all other races, their stern, forbidding eyes – above all else he hated the eyes that looked scorn and menace on the world. The Gaels were cruel but they had strange moments of sentiment and kindness. There was no sentiment in the Norse make-up.

The sight of this revelry was like a slap in Black Turlogh's face, and only one thing was needed to make his madness complete.

This was furnished. At the head of the board sat Thorfel the Fair, young, handsome, arrogant, flushed with wine and pride. He *was* handsome, was young Thorfel. In build he much resembled Turlogh himself, except that he was larger in every way, but there the resemblance ceased. As Turlogh was exceptionally dark among a dark people, Thorfel was exceptionally blond among a people essentially fair. His hair and mustache were like fine-spun gold and his light gray eyes flashed scintillant lights. By his side – Turlogh's nails bit into his palms. Moira of the O'Briens seemed greatly out of place among these huge blond men and strapping yellow-haired women. She was small, almost frail, and her hair was black with glossy bronze tints. But her skin was fair as theirs, with a delicate rose tint their most beautiful women could not boast. Her full lips were white now with fear and she shrank from the clamor and uproar. Turlogh saw her tremble as Thorfel insolently put his arm about her. The hall waved redly before Turlogh's eyes and he fought doggedly for control.

'Thorfel's brother, Osric, to his right,' he muttered to himself; 'on the other side Tosting, the Dane, who can cleave an ox in half with that great sword of his – they say. And there is Halfgar, and Sweyn, and Oswick, and Athelstane, the Saxon – the one *man* of a pack of sea-wolves. And name of the devil – what is this? A priest?'

A priest it was, sitting white and still in the rout, silently counting his beads, while his eyes wandered pityingly toward the slender Irish girl at the head of the board. Then Turlogh saw something else. On a smaller table to one side, a table of mahogany whose rich scrollwork showed that it was loot from the south-land, stood the Dark Man. The two crippled Norsemen had brought it to the hall, after all. The sight of it brought a strange shock to Turlogh and cooled his seething brain. Only five feet tall? It seemed much larger now, somehow. It loomed above the revelry, as a god that broods on deep dark matters beyond the ken of the human insects who howl at his feet. As always when looking at the Dark Man, Turlogh felt as if a door had suddenly opened on outer space and the wind that blows among the stars. Waiting – waiting – for whom? Perhaps the carven eyes of the Dark Man looked through the skalli walls, across the snowy waste, and over the promontory. Perhaps those sightless eyes saw the five boats that even now slid silently with muffled oars, through the calm dark waters. But of this Turlogh Dubh knew nothing; nothing of the boats or their silent rowers; small, dark men with inscrutable eyes.

Thorfel's voice cut through the din: 'Ho, friends!' They fell silent and turned as the young sea-king rose to his feet. 'Tonight,' he thundered, 'I am taking a bride!'

A thunder of applause shook the smoky rafters. Turlogh cursed with sick fury.

Thorfel caught up the girl with rough gentleness and set her on the board.

'Is she not a fit bride for a viking?' he shouted. 'True, she's a bit shy, but that's only natural.'

'All Irish are cowards!' shouted Oswick.

'As proved by Clontarf and the scar on your jaw!' rumbled Athelstane, which gentle thrust made Oswick wince and brought a roar of rough mirth from the throng.

''Ware her temper, Thorfel,' called a bold-eyed young Juno who sat with the warriors; 'Irish girls have claws like cats.'

Thorfel laughed with the confidence of a man used to mastery. 'I'll teach her her lessons with a stout birch switch. But enough. It grows late. Priest, marry us.'

'Daughter,' said the priest, unsteadily, rising, 'these pagan men have brought me here by violence to perform Christian nuptials in an ungodly house. Do you marry this man willingly?'

'No! No! Oh God, no!' Moira screamed with a wild despair that brought the sweat to Turlogh's forehead. 'Oh most holy master, save me from this fate! They tore me from my home – struck down the brother that would have saved me! This man bore me off as if I were a chattel – a soulless beast!'

'Be silent!' thundered Thorfel, slapping her across the mouth, lightly but with enough force to bring a trickle of blood from her delicate lips. 'By Thor, you grow independent. I am determined to have a wife, and all the squeals of a puling little wench will not stop me. Why, you graceless hussy, am I not wedding you in the Christian manner, simply because of your foolish superstitions? Take care that I do not dispense with the nuptials, and take you as slave, not wife!'

'Daughter,' quavered the priest, afraid, not for himself, but for her, 'bethink you! This man offers you more than many a man would offer. It is at least an honorable married state.'

'Aye,' rumbled Athelstane, 'marry him like a good wench and make the best of it. There's more than one south-land woman on the cross benches of the north.'

What can I do? The question tore through Turlogh's brain. There was but one thing to do – wait until the ceremony was over and Thorfel had retired with his bride. Then steal her away as best he could. After that – but he dared not look ahead. He had done and would do his best. What he did, he of necessity did alone; a masterless man had no friends, even among masterless men. There was no way to reach Moira to tell her of his presence. She must go through with the wedding without even the slim hope of deliverance that knowledge of his presence might have lent. Instinctively his eyes flashed to the Dark Man standing somber and aloof from the rout. At his feet the old quarreled with the new – the pagan with the Christian – and Turlogh even in that moment felt that the old and new were alike young to the Dark Man.

Did the carven ears of the Dark Man hear strange prows grating on the beach, the stroke of a stealthy knife in the night, the gurgle that marks the severed throat? Those in the skalli heard only their own noise and those who revelled by the fires outside sang on, unaware of the silent coils of death closing about them.

'Enough!' shouted Thorfel. 'Count your beads and mutter your mummery, priest! Come here, wench, and marry!' He jerked the girl off the board and plumped her down on her feet before him. She tore loose from him with flaming eyes. All the hot Gaelic blood was roused in her.

'You yellow-haired swine!' she cried. 'Do you think that a princess of Clare, with Brian Boru's blood in her veins, would sit at the cross bench of a barbarian and bear the tow-headed cubs of a northern thief? No – I'll never marry you!'

'Then I'll take you as a slave!' he roared, snatching at her wrist.

'Nor that way, either, swine!' she exclaimed, her fear forgotten in fierce triumph. With the speed of light she snatched a dagger from his girdle, and before he could seize her she drove the keen blade under her heart. The priest cried out as though he had received the wound, and springing forward, caught her in his arms as she fell.

'The curse of Almighty God on you, Thorfel!' he cried, with a voice that rang like a clarion, as he bore her to a couch near by.

Thorfel stood nonplussed. Silence reigned for an instant, and in that instant Turlogh O'Brien went mad.

'*Lamh Laidir Abu!*' the war-cry of the O'Briens ripped through the stillness like the scream of a wounded panther, and as men whirled toward the shriek, the frenzied Gael came through the doorway like the blast of a wind from hell. He was in the grip of the Celtic black fury beside which the berserk rage of the viking pales. Eyes glaring and a tinge of froth on his writhing lips, he crashed among the men who sprawled, off guard, in his path. Those terrible eyes were fixed on Thorfel at the other end of the hall, but as Turlogh rushed he smote to the right and left. His charge was the rush of a whirlwind that left a litter of dead and dying men in his wake.

Benches crashed to the floor, men yelled, ale flooded from upset casks. Swift as was the Celt's attack, two men blocked his way with drawn swords before he could reach Thorfel – Halfgar and Oswick. The scarred-faced viking went down with a cleft skull before he could lift his weapon, and Turlogh, catching Halfgar's blade on his shield, struck again like lightning and the keen ax sheared through hauberk, ribs and spine.

The hall was in a terrific uproar. Men were seizing weapons and pressing forward from all sides, and in the midst the lone Gael raged silently and terribly. Like a wounded tiger was Turlogh Dubh in his madness. His eery movement was a blur of speed, an explosion of dynamic force. Scarce had Halfgar fallen before the Gael leaped across his crumpling form at Thorfel, who had drawn his sword and stood as if bewildered. But a rush of carles swept between them. Swords rose and fell and the Dalcassian ax flashed among them like the play of summer lightning. On either hand and from before and behind a warrior drove at him. From one side Osric rushed, swinging a two-handed sword; from the other a house-carle drove in with a spear. Turlogh stooped beneath the swing of the sword and struck a double blow, forehand and back. Thorfel's brother dropped, hewed through the knee, and the carle died on his feet as the back-lash return drove the ax's back-spike through his skull. Turlogh straightened, dashing his shield into the face of the swordsman who rushed him from the front. The spike in the center of the shield made a ghastly ruin of his features; then even as the Gael wheeled cat-like to guard his rear, he felt the shadow of Death loom over him. From the corner of his eye he saw the Dane Tostig swinging his great two-handed sword, and jammed against the table, off balance, he knew that even his superhuman quickness could not save him. Then the whistling sword struck the Dark Man on the table and with a clash like thunder, shivered to a thousand blue sparks. Tostig staggered, dazedly, still holding the useless hilt, and Turlogh thrust as with a sword; the upper spike of his ax struck the Dane over the eye and crashed through to the brain.

And even at that instant, the air was filled with a strange singing and men howled. A huge carle, ax still lifted, pitched forward clumsily against the Gael, who split his skull before he saw that a flint-pointed arrow transfixed his throat. The hall seemed full of glancing beams of light that hummed like bees and carried quick death in their humming. Turlogh risked his life for a glance toward the great doorway at the other end of the hall. Through it was pouring a strange horde. Small, dark men they were, with beady black eyes and immobile faces. They were scantily armored, but they bore swords, spears and bows. Now at close range they drove their long black arrows point-blank and the carles went down in windrows.

Now a red wave of combat swept the skalli hall, a storm of strife that shattered tables, smashed the benches, tore the hangings and the trophies from the walls, and stained the floors with a red lake. There had been less of the dark strangers than vikings, but in the surprize of the attack, the first flight of arrows had evened the odds, and now at hand-grips the strange warriors showed themselves in no way inferior to their huge foes. Dazed by surprise and the ale they had drunken, with no time to arm themselves fully, the Norsemen yet fought back with all the reckless ferocity of their race. But the primitive fury of their attackers matched their own valor, and at the head of the hall, where a white-faced priest shielded a dying girl, Black Turlogh tore and ripped with a frenzy that made valor and fury alike futile.

And over all towered the Dark Man. To Turlogh's shifting glances, caught between the flash of sword and ax, it seemed that the image had grown – expanded – heightened; that it loomed giant-like over the battle; that its head rose into the smoke-filled rafters of the great hall; that it brooded like a dark cloud of death over these insects who cut each other's throats at its feet. Turlogh sensed in the lightning sword-play and the slaughter that this was the proper element of the Dark Man. Violence and fury were exuded by him. The raw scent of fresh-spilled blood was good to his nostrils and these yellow-haired corpses that rattled at his feet were as sacrifices to him.

The storm of battle rocked the mighty hall. The skalli became a shambles where men slipped in pools of blood, and slipping, died. Heads spun grinning from slumping shoulders. Barbed spears tore the heart, still beating, from the gory breast. Brains splashed and clotted the madly driving axes. Daggers lunged upward, ripping bellies and spilling entrails upon the floor. The clash and clangor of steel rose deafeningly. No quarter was asked or given. A wounded Norseman had dragged down one of the dark men, and doggedly strangled him regardless of the dagger his victim plunged again and again into his body.

One of the dark men seized a child who ran howling from an inner room, and dashed its brains out against the wall. Another gripped a Norse woman by her golden hair and hurling her to her knees, cut her throat, while she spat in his face. One listening for cries of fear or pleas for mercy would have heard none; men, women or children, they died slashing and clawing, their last gasp a sob of fury, or a snarl of quenchless hatred.

And about the table where stood the Dark Man, immovable as a mountain, washed the red waves of slaughter. Norseman and tribesman died at his feet. How many red infernos of slaughter and madness have your strange carved eyes gazed upon, Dark Man?

Shoulder to shoulder Sweyn and Thorfel fought. The Saxon Athelstane, his golden beard a-bristle with the battle-joy, had placed his back against the wall and a man fell at each sweep of his two-handed ax. Now Turlogh came in like a wave, avoiding, with a lithe twist of his upper body, the first ponderous stroke. Now the superiority of the light Irish ax was proved, for before the Saxon could shift his heavy weapon, the Dalcassian ax licked out like a striking cobra and Athelstane reeled as the edge bit through the corselet into the ribs beneath. Another stroke and he crumpled, blood gushing from his temple.

Now none barred Turlogh's way to Thorfel except Sweyn, and even as the Gael leaped like a panther toward the slashing pair, one was ahead of him. The chief of the dark men glided like a shadow under the slash of Sweyn's sword, and his own short blade thrust upward under the shirt of mail. Thorfel faced Turlogh alone. Thorfel was no coward; he even laughed with pure battle-joy as he thrust, but there was no mirth in Black Turlogh's face, only a frantic rage that writhed his lips and made his eyes coals of blue fire.

In the first whirl of steel Thorfel's sword broke. The young sea-king leaped like a tiger at his foe, thrusting with the shards of the blade. Turlogh laughed fiercely as the jagged remnant gashed his cheek, and at the same instant he cut Thorfel's left foot from under him. The Norseman fell with a heavy crash, then struggled to his knees, clawing for his dagger. His eyes were clouded.

'Make an end, curse you!' he snarled.

Turlogh laughed. 'Where is your power and your glory, now?' he taunted. 'You who would have for unwilling wife an Irish princess – you –'

Suddenly his hate strangled him, and with a howl like a maddened panther he swung his ax in a whistling arc that cleft the Norseman from shoulder to breastbone. Another stroke severed the head, and with the grisly trophy in his hand he approached the couch where lay Moira O'Brien. The priest had lifted her head and held a goblet of wine to her pale lips. Her cloudy gray eyes rested with slight recognition on Turlogh – but it seemed at last she knew him and she tried to smile.

'Moira, blood of my heart,' said the outlaw heavily, 'you die in a strange land. But the birds in the Cullane hills will weep for you, and the heather will sigh in vain for the tread of your little feet. But you shall not be forgotten; axes shall drip for you and for you shall galleys crash and walled cities go up in flames. And that your ghost go not unassuaged into the realms of Tir-na-n-Oge, behold this token of vengeance!'

And he held forth the dripping head of Thorfel.

'In God's name, my son,' said the priest, his voice husky with horror, 'have done – have done. Will you do your ghastly deeds in the very presence of – see, she is dead. May God in His infinite justice have mercy on her soul, for though she took her own life, yet she died as she lived, in innocence and purity.'

Turlogh dropped his ax-head to the floor and his head was bowed. All the fire of his madness had left him and there remained only a dark sadness, a deep sense of futility and weariness. Over all the hall there was no sound. No groans of the wounded were raised, for the knives of the little dark men had been at work, and save their own, there were no wounded. Turlogh sensed that the survivors had gathered about the statue on the table and now stood looking at him with inscrutable eyes. The priest mumbled over the corpse of the girl, telling his beads. Flame ate at the farther wall of the building, but none heeded it. Then from among the dead on the floor a huge form heaved up unsteadily. Athelstane the Saxon, overlooked by the killers, leaned against the wall and stared about dazedly. Blood flowed from a wound in his ribs and another in his scalp where Turlogh's ax had struck glancingly.

The Gael walked over to him. 'I have no hatred for you, Saxon,' said he, heavily, 'but blood calls for blood and you must die.'

Athelstane looked at him without an answer. His large gray eyes were serious but without fear. He too was a barbarian – more pagan than Christian; he too realized the rights of the blood-feud. But as Turlogh raised his ax, the priest sprang between, his thin hands outstretched, his eyes haggard.

'Have done! In God's name I command you! Almighty Powers, has not enough blood been shed this fearful night? In the name of the Most High, I claim this man.'

Turlogh dropped his ax. 'He is yours; not for your oath or your curse, not for your creed but for that you too are a man and did your best for Moira.'

A touch on his arm made Turlogh turn. The chief of the strangers stood regarding him with inscrutable eyes.

'Who are you?' asked the Gael idly. He did not care; he felt only weariness.

'I am Brogar, chief of the Picts, Friend of the Dark Man.'

'Why do you call me that?' asked Turlogh.

'He rode in the bows of your boat and guided you to Helni through wind and snow. He saved your life when he broke the great sword of the Dane.'

Turlogh glanced at the brooding Dark One. It seemed there must be a human or superhuman intelligence behind those strange stone eyes. Was it chance alone that caused Tostig's sword to strike the image as he swung it in a death blow?

'What is this thing?' asked the Gael.

'It is the only god we have left,' answered the other somberly. 'It is the image of our greatest king, Bran Mak Morn, he who gathered the broken lines of the Pictish tribes into a single mighty nation, he who drove forth the Norseman and Briton and shattered the legions of Rome, centuries ago. A wizard made this statue while the great Morni yet lived and reigned, and when he died in the last great battle, his spirit entered into it. It is our god.

'Ages ago we ruled. Before the Dane, before the Gael, before the Briton, before the Roman, we reigned in the western isles. Our stone circles rose to the sun. We worked in flint and hides and were happy. Then came the Celts and drove us into the wildernesses. They held the south-land. But we throve in the north and were strong. Rome broke the Britons and came against us. But there rose among us Bran Mak Morn, of the blood of Brule the Spear-slayer, the friend of King Kull of Valusia who reigned thousands of years ago before Atlantis sank. Bran became king of all Caledon. He broke the iron ranks of Rome and sent the legions cowering south behind their Wall.

'Bran Mak Morn fell in battle; the nation fell apart. Civil wars rocked it. The Gaels came and reared the kingdom of Dalriadia above the ruins of the Cruithni. When the Scot Kenneth Mac-Alpine broke the kingdom of Galloway, the last remnant of the Pictish empire faded like snow on the mountains. Like wolves we live now among the scattered islands, among the crags of the highlands and the dim hills of Galloway. We are a fading people. We pass. But the Dark Man remains – the Dark One, the great king, Bran Mak Morn, whose ghost dwells forever in the stone likeness of his living self.'

As in a dream Turlogh saw an ancient Pict who looked much like the one in whose dead arms he had found the Dark Man, lift the image from the table. The old man's arms were thin as withered branches and his skin clung to his skull like a mummy's, but he handled with ease the image that two strong vikings had had trouble in carrying.

As if reading his thoughts Brogar spoke softly: 'Only a friend may with safety touch the Dark One. We knew you to be a friend, for he rode in your boat and did you no harm.'

'How know you this?'

'The Old One,' pointing to the white-bearded ancient, 'Gonar, high priest of the Dark One – the ghost of Bran comes to him in dreams. It was Grok, the lesser priest and his people who stole the image and took to sea in a long boat. In dreams Gonar followed; aye, as he slept he sent his spirit with the ghost of the Morni, and he saw the pursuit by the Danes, the battle and slaughter on the Isle of Swords. He saw you come and find the

Dark One, and he saw that the ghost of the great king was pleased with you. Wo to the foes of the Mak Morn! But good luck shall fare the friends of him.'

Turlogh came to himself as from a trance. The heat of the burning hall was in his face and the flickering flames lit and shadowed the carven face of the Dark Man as his worshippers bore him from the building, lending it a strange life. Was it, in truth, that the spirit of a long-dead king lived in that cold stone? Bran Mak Morn loved his people with a savage love; he hated their foes with a terrible hate. Was it possible to breathe into inanimate blind stone a pulsating love and hate that should outlast the centuries?

Turlogh lifted the still, slight form of the dead girl and bore her out of the flaming hall. Five long open boats lay at anchor, and scattered about the embers of the fires the carles had lit, lay the reddened corpses of the revelers who had died silently.

'How stole ye upon these undiscovered?' asked Turlogh. 'And whence came you in those open boats?'

'The stealth of the panther is theirs who live by stealth,' answered the Pict. 'And these were drunken. We followed the path of the Dark One and we came hither from the Isle of the Altar, near the Scottish mainland, from whence Grok stole the Dark Man.'

Turlogh knew no island of that name but he did realize the courage of these men in daring the seas in boats such as these. He thought of his own boat and requested Brogar to send some of his men for it. The Pict did so. While he waited for them to bring it around the point, he watched the priest bandaging the wounds of the survivors. Silent, immobile, they spoke no word either of complaint or thanks.

The fisherman's boat came scudding around the point just as the first hint of sunrise reddened the waters. The Picts were getting into their boats, lifting in the dead and wounded. Turlogh stepped into his boat and gently eased his pitiful burden down.

'She shall sleep in her own land,' he said somberly. 'She shall not lie in this cold foreign isle. Brogar, whither go you?'

'We take the Dark One back to his isle and his altar,' said the Pict. 'Through the mouth of his people he thanks you. The tie of blood is between us, Gael, and mayhap we shall come to you again in your need, as Bran Mak Morn, great king of Pictdom, shall come again to his people some day in the days to come.'

'And you, good Jerome? You will come with me?'

The priest shook his head and pointed to Athelstane. The wounded Saxon reposed on a rude couch made of skins piled in the snow.

'I stay here to attend to this man. He is sorely wounded.'

Turlogh looked about. The walls of the skalli had crashed into a mass of glowing embers. Brogar's men had set fire to the storehouses and the long galley, and the smoke and flame vied luridly with the growing morning light.

'You will freeze or starve. Come with me.'

'I will find sustenance for us both. Persuade me not, my son.'

'He is a pagan and a reaver.'

'No matter. He is a human – a living creature. I will not leave him to die.'

'So be it.'

Turlogh prepared to cast off. The boats of the Picts were already rounding the point. The rhythmic clack of their oarlocks came clearly to him. They looked not back, bending stolidly to their work.

He glanced at the stiff corpses about the beach, at the charred embers of the skalli and the glowing timbers of the galley. In the glare the priest seemed unearthly in his thinness and whiteness, like a saint from some old illuminated manuscript. In his worn pallid face was a more than human sadness, a greater than human weariness.

'Look!' he cried suddenly, pointing seaward. 'The ocean is of blood! See how it swims red in the rising sun! Oh, my people, my people, the blood you have spilt in anger turns the very seas to scarlet! How can you win through?'

'I came in the snow and sleet,' said Turlogh, not understanding at first. 'I go as I came.'

The priest shook his head. 'It is more than a mortal sea. Your hands are red with blood and you follow a red sea-path, yet the fault is not wholly with you. Almighty God, when will the reign of blood cease?'

Turlogh shook his head. 'Not so long as the race lasts.'

The morning wind caught and filled his sail. Into the west he raced like a shadow fleeing the dawn. And so passed Turlogh Dubh O'Brien from the sight of the priest Jerome, who stood watching, shading his weary brow with his thin hand, until the boat was but a tiny speck far out on the tossing wastes of the blue ocean.

II

Dark Interlude

The Footfalls Within

Solomon Kane gazed somberly at the black woman who lay dead at his feet. Little more than a girl she was, but her wasted limbs and staring eyes showed that she had suffered much before death brought her merciful relief. Kane noted the chain galls on her limbs, the deep crisscrossed scars on her back, the mark of the yoke on her neck. His cold eyes deepened strangely, showing chill glints and lights like clouds passing across depths of ice.

'Even into this lonesome land they come,' he muttered. 'I had not thought –'

He raised his head and gazed eastward. Black dots against the blue wheeled and circled.

'The kites mark their trail,' muttered the tall Englishman. 'Destruction goeth before them and death followeth after. Wo unto ye, sons of iniquity, for the wrath of God is upon ye. The cords be loosed on the iron necks of the hounds of hate and the bow of vengeance is strung. Ye are proud-stomached and strong, and the people cry out beneath your feet, but retribution cometh in the blackness of midnight and the redness of dawn.'

He shifted the belt that held his heavy pistols and the keen dirk, instinctively touched the long rapier at his hip, and went stealthily but swiftly eastward. A cruel anger burned in his deep eyes like blue volcanic fires burning beneath leagues of ice, and the hand that gripped his long, cat-headed stave hardened into iron.

After some hours of steady striding, he came within hearing of the slave train that wound its laborious way through the jungle. The piteous cries of the slaves, the shouts and curses of the drivers, and the cracking of the whips came plainly to his ears. Another hour brought him even with them, and gliding along through the jungle parallel to the trail taken by the slavers, he spied upon them safely. Kane had fought Indians in Darien and had learned much of their woodcraft.

More than a hundred blacks, young men and women, staggered along the trail, stark naked and made fast together by cruel yoke-like affairs of wood. These yokes, rough and heavy, fitted over their necks and linked them together, two by two. The yokes were in turn fettered together, making one long chain. Of the drivers there were fifteen Arabs and some seventy black warriors, whose weapons and fantastic apparel showed them to be of some eastern tribe – one of those tribes subjugated and made Moslems and allies by the conquering Arabs.

Five Arabs walked ahead of the train with some thirty of their warriors, and five brought up the rear with the rest of the black Moslems. The rest marched beside the staggering slaves, urging them along with shouts and curses and with long, cruel whips which brought spurts of blood at almost every blow. These slavers were fools as well as rogues, reflected Kane – not more than half of the slaves would survive the hardships of that trek to the coast. He wondered at the presence of these raiders, for this country lay far to the south of the districts usually frequented by the Moslems. But avarice can drive men far, as the Englishman knew. He had dealt with these gentry of old. Even as he watched, old scars burned in his back – scars made by Moslem whips in a Turkish galley. And deeper still burned Kane's unquenchable hate.

He followed, shadowing his foes like a ghost, and as he stole through the jungle, he racked his brain for a plan. How might he prevail against that horde? All the Arabs and many of the blacks were armed with guns – long, clumsy firelock affairs, it is true, but guns just the same, enough to awe any tribe of natives who might oppose them. Some carried in their wide girdles long, silver-chased pistols of more effective pattern – flintlocks of Moorish and Turkish make.

Kane followed like a brooding ghost and his rage and hatred ate into his soul like a canker. Each crack of the whips was like a blow on his own shoulders. The heat and cruelty of the tropics play queer tricks with white men. Ordinary passions become monstrous things; irritation turns to a berserker rage; anger flames into unexpected madness and men kill in a red mist of passion, and wonder, aghast, afterward.

The fury Solomon Kane felt would have been enough at any time and in any place to shake a man to his foundation; now it assumed monstrous proportions, so that Kane shivered as if with a chill, iron claws scratched at his brain and he saw the slaves and the slavers through a crimson mist. Yet he might not have put his hate-born insanity into action had it not been for a mishap.

One of the slaves, a slim young girl, suddenly faltered and slipped to the earth, dragging her yoke-mate with her. A tall, hook-nosed Arab yelled savagely and lashed her viciously. Her yoke-mate staggered partly up, but the girl remained prone, writhing weakly beneath the lash, but evidently unable to rise. She whimpered pitifully between her parched lips, and the other slavers came about, their whips descending on her quivering flesh in slashes of red agony.

A half-hour of rest and a little water would have revived her, but the Arabs had no time to spare. Solomon, biting his arm until his teeth met in the flesh as he fought for control, thanked God that the lashing had ceased and steeled himself for the swift flash of the dagger that would put the child beyond torment, But the Arabs were in a mood for sport. Since the girl would fetch them no profit on the market block, they would utilize her for their pleasure – and the humor of their breed is such as to turn men's blood to icy water.

A shout from the first whipper brought the rest crowding around, their bearded faces split in grins of delighted anticipation, while the black warriors edged nearer, their brutish eyes gleaming. The wretched slaves realized their masters' intentions and a chorus of pitiful cries rose from them.

Kane, sick with horror, realized, too, that the girl's was to be no easy death. He knew what the tall Moslem intended to do, as he stooped over her with a keen dagger such as the Arabs used for skinning game. Madness overcame the Englishman. He valued his own life little; he had risked it without thought for the sake of a negro baby or a small animal. Yet he would not have premeditatedly thrown away his one hope of succoring the wretches in the train. But he acted without conscious thought. A pistol was smoking in his hand and the tall butcher was down in the dust of the trail with his brains oozing out, before Kane realized what he had done.

He was almost as astonished as the Arabs, who stood frozen for a moment and then burst into a medley of yells. Several threw up their clumsy firelocks and sent their heavy balls crashing through the trees, and the rest, thinking no doubt that they were ambushed, led a reckless charge into the jungle. The bold suddenness of that move was Kane's undoing. Had they hesitated a moment longer he might have faded away unobserved, but as it was he saw no choice but to meet them openly and sell his life as highly as he could.

And indeed it was with a certain ferocious satisfaction that he faced his howling attackers. They halted in sudden amazement as the tall, grim Englishman stepped from behind his tree, and in that instant one of them died with a bullet from Kane's remaining pistol in his heart. Then with yells of savage rage they flung themselves on their lone defier. Kane placed his back against a huge tree and his long rapier played a shining wheel about him. Three blacks and an Arab were hacking at him with their heavy curved blades while the rest milled about, snarling like wolves, as they sought to drive in blade or ball without maiming one of their own number.

The flickering rapier parried the whistling simitars and the Arab died on its point, which seemed to hesitate in his heart only an instant before it pierced the brain of a black swordsman. Another ebon warrior, dropping his sword and leaping in to grapple at close quarters, was disemboweled by the dirk in Kane's left hand, and the others gave back in sudden fear. A heavy ball smashed against the tree close to Kane's head and he tensed himself to spring and die in the thick of them. Then their sheikh lashed them on with his long whip and Kane heard him shouting fiercely for his warriors to take the infidel alive. Kane answered the command with a sudden cast of his dirk, which hummed so close to the sheikh's head that it slit his turban and sank deep in the shoulder of one behind him.

The sheikh drew his silver-chased pistols, threatening his own men with death if they did not take the white man, and they charged in again desperately. One of the black men ran full upon Kane's sword and an Arab behind the fellow, with the craft of his race, thrust the screaming wretch suddenly forward on the weapon, driving it hilt-deep in his writhing body, fouling the blade. Before Kane could wrench it clear, with a yell of triumph the pack rushed in on him and bore him down by sheer weight of numbers. As they grappled him from all sides, the Puritan wished in vain for the dirk he had thrown away. But even so, his taking was none too easy.

Blood spattered and faces caved in beneath his iron-hard fists that splintered teeth and shattered bone. A black warrior reeled away disabled from a vicious drive of knee to groin. Even when they had him stretched out and piled man-weight on him until he could no longer strike with fists or foot, his long lean fingers sank fiercely through a black beard to lock about a corded throat in a grip that took the power of three strong men to break and left the victim gasping and green-faced.

At last, panting from the terrific struggle, they had him bound hand and foot and the sheikh, thrusting his pistols back into his silken sash, came striding to stand and look down at his captive. Kane glared up at the tall, lean frame, at the hawk-like face with its black curled beard and arrogant brown eyes.

'I am the sheikh Hassim ben Said,' said the Arab. 'Who are you?'

'My name is Solomon Kane,' growled the Puritan in the sheikh's own language. 'I am an Englishman, you heathen jackal.'

The dark eyes of the Arab flickered with interest.

'Sulieman Kahani,' said he, giving the Arabesque equivalent of the English name, 'I have heard of you – you have fought the Turks betimes and the Barbary corsairs have licked their wounds because of you.'

Kane deigned no reply. Hassim shrugged his shoulders.

'You will bring a fine price,' said he, 'Mayhap I will take you to Stamboul, where there are shas who would desire such a man among their slaves. And I mind me now of one Kemal Bey, a man of ships, who wears a deep scar across his face of your making and who curses the name of Englishman. He will pay me a high price for you. And behold, oh Frank, I do you the honor of appointing you a separate guard. You shall not walk in the yoke-chain but free save for your hands.'

Kane made no answer, and at a sign from the sheikh, he was hauled to his feet and his bonds loosened except for his hands, which they left bound firmly behind him. A stout cord was looped about his neck and the other end of this was given into the hand of a huge black warrior who bore in his free hand a great curved simitar.

'And now what think ye of my favor to you, Frank?' queried the sheikh.

'I am thinking,' answered Kane in a slow, deep voice of menace, 'that I would trade my soul's salvation to face you and your sword, alone and unarmed, and to tear the heart from your breast with my naked fingers.'

Such was the concentrated hate in his deep resounding voice, and such primal, unconquerable fury blazed from his terrible eyes, that the hardened and fearless chieftain blanched and involuntarily recoiled as if from a maddened beast.

Then Hassim recovered his poise and with a short word to his followers, strode to the head of the cavalcade. Kane noted, with thankfulness, that the respite occasioned by his capture had given the girl who had fallen a chance to rest and revive. The skinning knife had not had time to more than touch her; she was able to reel along. Night was not far away. Soon the slavers would be forced to halt and camp.

The Englishman perforce took up the trek, his black guard remaining a few paces behind with his huge blade ever ready. Kane also noted with a touch of grim vanity, that three more blacks marched close behind, muskets ready and matches burning. They had tasted his prowess and they were taking no chances. His weapons had been recovered and Hassim had promptly appropriated all except the cat-headed ju-ju staff. This had been contemptuously cast aside by him and taken up by one of the blacks.

The Englishman was presently aware that a lean, gray-bearded Arab was walking along at his side. This Arab seemed desirous of speaking but strangely timid, and the source of his timidity seemed, curiously enough, the ju-ju stave which he had taken from the black man who had picked it up, and which he now turned uncertainly in his hands.

'I am Yussef the Hadji,' said this Arab suddenly. 'I have naught against you. I had no hand in attacking you and would be your friend if you would let me. Tell me, Frank, whence comes this staff and how comes it into your hands?'

Kane's first inclination was to consign his questioner to the infernal regions, but a certain sincerity of manner in the old man made him change his mind and he answered: 'It was given me by my blood-brother – a black magician of the Slave Coast, named N'Longa.'

The old Arab nodded and muttered in his beard and presently sent a black running forward to bid Hassim return. The tall sheikh presently came striding back along the slow-moving column, with a clank and jingle of daggers and sabers, with Kane's dirk and pistols thrust into his wide sash.

'Look, Hassim,' the old Arab thrust forward the stave, 'you cast it away without knowing what you did!'

'And what of it?' growled the sheikh. 'I see naught but a staff – sharp-pointed and with the head of a cat on the other end – a staff with strange infidel carvings upon it.'

The older man shook it at him in excitement: 'This staff is older than the world! It holds mighty magic! I have read of it in the old iron-bound books and Mohammed – on whom peace! – himself hath spoken of it by allegory and parable! See the cat-head upon it? It is the head of a goddess of ancient Egypt! Ages ago, before Mohammed taught, before Jerusalem was, the priests of Bast bore this rod before the bowing, chanting worshippers! With it Musa did wonders before Pharaoh and when the Yahudi fled from Egypt they bore it with them. And for centuries it was the scepter of Israel and Judah and with it Sulieman ben Daoud drove forth the conjurers and magicians and prisoned the efreets and the evil genii! Look! Again in the hands of a Sulieman we find the ancient rod!'

Old Yussef had worked himself into a pitch of almost fanatic fervor but Hassim merely shrugged his shoulders.

'It did not save the Jews from bondage nor this Sulieman from our captivity,' said he; 'so I value it not as much as I esteem the long thin blade with which he loosed the souls of three of my best swordsmen.'

Yussef shook his head. 'Your mockery will bring you to no good end, Hassim. Some day you will meet a power that will not divide before your sword or fall to your bullets. I will keep the staff, and I warn you – abuse not the Frank. He has borne the holy and terrible staff of Sulieman and Musa and the Pharaohs, and who knows what magic he has drawn therefrom? For it is older than the world and has known the terrible hands of strange, dark pre-Adamite priests in the silent cities beneath the seas, and has drawn from an Elder World mystery and magic unguessed by humankind. There were strange kings and stranger priests when the dawns were young, and evil was, even in their day. And with this staff they fought the evil which was ancient when their strange world was young, so many millions of years ago that a man would shudder to count them.'

Hassim answered impatiently and strode away with old Yussef following him persistently and chattering away in a querulous tone. Kane shrugged his mighty shoulders. With what he knew of the strange powers of that strange staff, he was not one to question the old man's assertions, fantastic as they seemed. This much he knew – that it was made of a wood that existed nowhere on earth today. It needed but the proof of sight and touch to realize that its material had grown in some world apart. The exquisite workmanship of the head, of a pre-pyramidal age, and the hieroglyphics, symbols of a language that was forgotten when Rome was young – these, Kane sensed, were additions as modern to the antiquity of the staff itself, as would be English words carved on the stone monoliths of Stonehenge.

As for the cat-head – looking at it sometimes Kane had a peculiar feeling of alteration; a faint sensing that once the pommel of the staff was carved with a different design. The dust-ancient Egyptian who had carved the head of Bast had merely altered the original figure, and what that figure had been, Kane had never tried to guess. A close scrutiny of the staff always aroused a disquieting and almost dizzy suggestion of abysses of eons, unprovocative to further speculation.

The day wore on. The sun beat down mercilessly, then screened itself in the great trees as it slanted toward the horizon. The slaves suffered fiercely for water and a continual whimpering rose from their ranks as they staggered blindly on. Some fell and half crawled, and were half dragged by their reeling yoke-mates. When all were buckling from exhaustion, the sun dipped, night rushed on, and a halt was called. Camp was pitched, guards thrown out, and the slaves were fed scantily and given enough water to keep life in them – but only just enough. Their fetters were not loosened but they were allowed to sprawl about as they might. Their fearful thirst and hunger having been some-what eased, they bore the discomforts of their shackles with characteristic stoicism.

Kane was fed without his hands being untied and he was given all the water he wished. The patient eyes of the slaves watched him drink, silently, and he was sorely ashamed to guzzle what others suffered for; he ceased before his thirst was fully quenched. A wide clearing had been selected, on all sides of which rose gigantic trees. After the Arabs had eaten and while the black Moslems were still cooking their food, old Yussef came to Kane and began to talk about the staff again. Kane answered his questions with admirable patience, considering the hatred he bore the whole race to which the Hadji belonged, and during their conversation, Hassim came striding up and looked down in contempt. Hassim, Kane ruminated, was the very symbol of militant Islam – bold, reckless, materialistic, sparing nothing, fearing nothing, as sure of his own destiny and as contemptuous of the rights of others as the most powerful Western king.

'Are you maundering about that stick again?' he gibed. 'Hadji, you grow childish in your old age.'

Yussef's beard quivered in anger. He shook the staff at his sheikh like a threat of evil.

'Your mockery little befits your rank, Hassim,' he snapped. 'We are in the heart of a dark and demon-haunted land, to which long ago were banished the devils from Arabia. If this staff, which any but a fool can tell is no rod of any world we know, has existed down to our day, who knows what other things, tangible or intangible, may have existed through the ages? This very trail we follow – know you how old it is? Men followed it before the Seljuk came out of the East or the Roman came out of the West. Over this very trail, legends say, the great Sulieman came when he drove the demons westward out of Asia and prisoned them in strange prisons. And will you say –'

A wild shout interrupted him. Out of the shadows of the jungle a black came flying as if from the hounds of Doom. With arms flinging wildly, eyes rolling to display the whites and mouth wide open so that all his gleaming teeth were visible, he made an image of stark terror not soon forgotten. The Moslem horde leaped up, snatching their weapons, and Hassim swore: 'That's Ali, whom I sent to scout for meat – perchance a lion –'

But no lion followed the black man who fell at Hassim's feet, mouthing gibberish, and pointing wildly back at the black jungle whence the nerve-strung watchers expected some brain-shattering horror to burst.

'He says he found a strange mausoleum back in the jungle,' said Hassim with a scowl, 'but he cannot tell what frightened him. He only knows a great horror overwhelmed him and sent him flying. Ali, you are a fool and a rogue.'

He kicked the groveling black viciously, but the other Arabs drew about him in some uncertainty. The panic was spreading among the black warriors.

'They will bolt in spite of us,' muttered a bearded Arab, uneasily watching the blacks who milled together, jabbered excitedly and flung fearsome glances over the shoulders. 'Hassim, 'twere better to march on a few miles. This is an evil place after all, and though 'tis likely the fool Ali was frighted by his own shadow – still –'

'Still,' jeered the sheikh, 'you will all feel better when we have left it behind. Good enough; to still your fears I will move camp – but first I will have a look at this thing. Lash up the slaves; we'll swing into the jungle and pass by this mausoleum; perhaps some great king lies there. The blacks will not be afraid if we all go in a body with guns.'

So the weary slaves were whipped into wakefulness and stumbled along beneath the whips again. The black warriors went silently and nervously, reluctantly obeying Hassim's implacable will but huddling close to their white masters. The moon had risen, huge, red and sullen, and the jungle was bathed in a sinister silver glow that etched the brooding trees in black shadow. The trembling Ali pointed out the way, somewhat reassured by his savage master's presence.

And so they passed through the jungle until they came to a strange clearing among the giant trees – strange because nothing grew there. The trees ringed it in a disquieting symmetrical manner and no lichen or moss grew on the earth, which seemed to have been blasted and blighted in a strange fashion. And in the midst of the glade stood the mausoleum. A great brooding mass of stone it was, pregnant with ancient evil. Dead with the death of a hundred centuries it seemed, yet Kane was aware that the air *pulsed* about it, as with the slow, unhuman breathing of some gigantic, invisible monster.

The black Moslems drew back, muttering, assailed by the evil atmosphere of the place. The slaves stood in a patient, silent group beneath the trees. The Arabs went forward to the frowning black mass, and Yussef, taking Kane's cord from his ebon guard, led the Englishman with him like a surly mastiff, as if for protection against the unknown.

'Some mighty sultan doubtless lies here,' said Hassim, tapping the stone with his scabbard-end.

'Whence come these stones?' muttered Yussef uneasily. 'They are of dark and forbidding aspect. Why should a great sultan lie in state so far from any habitation of man? If there were ruins of an old city hereabouts it would be different –'

He bent to examine the heavy metal door with its huge lock, curiously sealed and fused. He shook his head forebodingly as he made out the ancient Hebraic characters carved on the door.

'I can not read them,' he quavered, 'and belike it is well for me I can not. What ancient kings sealed up, is not good for men to disturb. Hassim, let us hence. This place is pregnant with evil for the sons of men.'

But Hassim gave him no heed. 'He who lies within is no son of Islam,' said he, 'and why should we not despoil him of the gems and riches that undoubtedly were laid to rest with him? Let us break open this door.'

Some of the Arabs shook their heads doubtfully but Hassim's word was law. Calling to him a huge black who bore a heavy hammer, he ordered him to break open the door.

As the black swung up his sledge, Kane gave a sharp exclamation. Was he mad? The apparent antiquity of this brooding mass of stone was proof that it had stood undisturbed for thousands of years. *Yet he could have sworn that he heard the sound of footfalls within.* Back and forth they padded, as if something paced the narrow confines of that grisly prison in a never-ending monotony of movement. A cold hand touched the spine of Solomon Kane. Whether the sounds registered on his conscious ear or on some unsounded deep of soul or sub-feeling, he could not tell, but he *knew* that somewhere within his consciousness there re-echoed the tramp of monstrous feet from within that ghastly mausoleum.

'Stop!' he exclaimed. 'Hassim, I may be mad, but I hear the tread of some fiend within that pile of stone.'

Hassim raised his hand and checked the hovering hammer. He listened intently, and the others strained their ears in a silence that had suddenly become tense.

'I hear nothing,' grunted a bearded giant.

'Nor I,' came a quick chorus. 'The Frank is mad!'

'Hear ye anything, Yussef?' asked Hassim sardonically.

The old Hadji shifted nervously. His face was uneasy.

'No, Hassim, no, yet –'

Kane decided he must be mad. Yet in his heart he knew he was never saner, and he knew somehow that this occult keenness of the deeper senses that set him apart from the Arabs came from long association with the ju-ju staff that old Yussef now held in his shaking hands.

Hassim laughed harshly and made a gesture to the black. The hammer fell with a crash that re-echoed deafeningly and shivered off through the black jungle in a strangely altered cachinnation. Again – again – and again the hammer fell, driven with all the power of the rippling black muscles and the mighty ebon body. And between the blows Kane still heard that lumbering tread, and he who had never known fear as men know it, felt the cold hand of terror clutching at his heart.

This fear was apart from earthly or mortal fear, as the sound of the footfalls was apart from mortal tread. Kane's fright was like a cold wind blowing on him from outer realms of unguessed Darkness, bearing him the evil and decay of an outlived epoch and an unutterably ancient period. Kane was not sure whether he heard those footfalls or by some dim instinct sensed them. But he was sure of their reality. They were not the tramp of man or beast; but inside that black, hideously ancient mausoleum some nameless *thing* moved with soul-shaking and elephantine tread.

The great black sweated and panted with the difficulty of his task. But at last, beneath the heavy blows the ancient lock shattered; the hinges snapped; the door burst inward. And Yussef screamed. From that black gaping entrance no tiger-fanged beast or demon of solid flesh and blood leaped forth. But a fearful stench flowed out in billowing, almost tangible waves and in one brain-shattering, ravening rush, whereby the gaping door seemed to gush *blood*, the Horror was upon them. It enveloped Hassim, and the fearless chieftain, hewing vainly at the almost intangible terror, screamed with sudden, unaccustomed fright as his lashing simitar whistled only through stuff as yielding and unharmable as air, and he felt himself lapped by coils of death and destruction.

Yussef shrieked like a lost soul, dropped the ju-ju stave and joined his fellows who streamed out into the jungle in mad flight, preceded by the howling black warriors. Only the black slaves fled not, but stood shackled to their doom, wailing their terror. As in a nightmare of delirium Kane saw Hassim swayed like a reed in the wind, lapped about by a gigantic pulsing red Thing that had neither shape nor earthly substance. Then as the crack of splintering bones came to him, and the sheikh's body buckled like a straw beneath a stamping hoof, the Englishman burst his bonds with one volcanic effort and caught up the ju-ju stave.

Hassim was down, crushed and dead, sprawled like a broken toy with shattered limbs awry, and the red pulsing Thing was lurching toward Kane like a thick cloud of blood in the air, that continually changed its shape and form, and yet somehow *trod* lumberingly as if on monstrous legs!

Kane felt the cold fingers of fear claw at his brain but he braced himself, and lifting the ancient staff, struck with all his power into the center of the Horror. And he felt an unnamable, immaterial substance meet and give way before the falling staff. Then he was almost strangled by the nauseous burst of unholy stench that flooded the air, and somewhere down the dim vistas of his soul's consciousness re-echoed unbearably a hideous formless cataclysm that he knew was the death-screaming of the monster. For it was down and dying at his feet, its crimson paling in slow surges like the rise and receding of red waves on some foul coast. And as it paled, the soundless screaming dwindled away into cosmic distances as though it faded into some sphere apart and aloof beyond human ken.

Kane, dazed and incredulous, looked down on a shapeless, colorless, all but invisible mass at his feet which he knew was the corpse of the Horror, dashed back into the black realms from whence it had come, by a single blow of the staff of Solomon. Aye, the same staff, Kane knew, that in the hands of a mighty king and magician had ages ago driven the monster into that strange prison, to bide until ignorant hands loosed it again upon the world.

The old tales were true then, and King Solomon had in truth driven the demons westward and sealed them in strange places. Why had he let them live? Was human magic too weak in those dim days to more than subdue the devils? Kane shrugged his shoulders in wonderment. He knew nothing of magic, yet he had slain where that other Solomon had but imprisoned.

And Solomon Kane shuddered, for he had looked on Life that was not Life as he knew it, and had dealt and witnessed Death that was not Death as he knew it. Again the realization swept over him, as it had in the dust-haunted halls of Atlantean Negari, as it had in the abhorrent Hills of the Dead, as it had in Akaana – that human life was but one of a myriad forms of existence, that worlds existed within worlds, and that there was more than one plane of existence. The planet men call the earth spun on through the untold ages, Kane realized, and as it spun it spawned Life, and living things which wriggled about it as maggots are spawned in rot and corruption. Man was the dominant maggot now – why should he in his pride suppose that he and his adjuncts were the first maggots – or the last to rule a planet quick with unguessed life?

He shook his head, gazing in new wonder at the ancient gift of N'Longa, seeing in it at last, not merely a tool of black magic, but a sword of good and light against the powers of inhuman evil forever. And he was shaken with a strange reverence for it that was almost fear. Then he bent to the Thing at his feet, shuddering to feel its strange mass slip through his fingers like wisps of heavy fog. He thrust the staff beneath it and somehow lifted and levered the mass back into the mausoleum and shut the door.

Then he stood gazing down at the strangely mutilated body of Hassim, noting how it was smeared with foul slime and how it had already begun to decompose. He shuddered again, and suddenly a low timid voice aroused him from his somber cogitations. The slaves knelt beneath the trees and watched with great patient eyes. With a start he shook off his strange mood. He took from the moldering corpse his own pistols, dirk and rapier, making shift to wipe off the clinging foulness that was already flecking the steel with rust. He also took up a quantity of powder and shot dropped by the Arabs in their frantic flight. He knew they would return no more. They might die in their flight, or they might gain through the interminable leagues of jungle to the coast; but they would not turn back to dare the terror of that grisly glade.

Kane came to the black slaves and after some difficulty released them.

'Take up these weapons which the warriors dropped in their haste,' said he, 'and get you home. This is an evil place. Get ye back to your villages and when the next Arabs come, die in the ruins of your huts rather than be slaves.'

Then they would have knelt and kissed his feet, but he, in much confusion, forbade them roughly. Then as they made preparations to go, one said to him: 'Master, what of thee? Wilt thou not return with us? Thou shalt be our king!'

But Kane shook his head.

'I go eastward,' said he. And so the tribespeople bowed to him and turned back on the long trail to their own homeland. And Kane shouldered the staff that had been the rod of the Pharaohs and of Moses and of Solomon and of nameless Atlantean kings behind them, and turned his face eastward, halting only for a single backward glance at the great mausoleum that other Solomon had built with strange arts so long ago, and which now loomed dark and forever silent against the stars.

Pigeons from Hell

1   The Whistler in the Dark

Griswell awoke suddenly, every nerve tingling with a premonition of imminent peril. He stared about wildly, unable at first to remember where he was, or what he was doing there. Moonlight filtered in through the dusty windows, and the great empty room with its lofty ceiling and gaping black fireplace was spectral and unfamiliar. Then as he emerged from the clinging cobwebs of his recent sleep, he remembered where he was and how he came to be there. He twisted his head and stared at his companion, sleeping on the floor near him. John Branner was but a vaguely bulking shape in the darkness that the moon scarcely grayed.

Griswell tried to remember what had awakened him. There was no sound in the house, no sound outside except the mournful hoot of an owl, far away in the piny woods. Now he had captured the illusive memory. It was a dream, a nightmare so filled with dim terror that it had frightened him awake. Recollection flooded back, vividly etching the abominable vision.

Or was it a dream? Certainly it must have been, but it had blended so curiously with recent actual events that it was difficult to know where reality left off and fantasy began.

Dreaming, he had seemed to relive his past few waking hours, in accurate detail. The dream had begun, abruptly, as he and John Branner came in sight of the house where they now lay.

They had come rattling and bouncing over the stumpy, uneven old road that led through the pinelands, he and John Branner, wandering far afield from their New England home, in search of vacation pleasure. They had sighted the old house with its balustraded galleries rising amidst a wilderness of weeds and bushes, just as the sun was setting behind it. It dominated their fancy, rearing black and stark and gaunt against the low lurid rampart of sunset, barred by the black pines.

They were tired, sick of bumping and pounding all day over woodland roads. The old deserted house stimulated their imagination with its suggestion of antebellum splendor and ultimate decay. They left the automobile beside the rutty road, and as they went up the winding walk of crumbling bricks, almost lost in the tangle of rank growth, pigeons rose from the balustrades in a fluttering, feathery crowd and swept away with a low thunder of beating wings.

The oaken door sagged on broken hinges. Dust lay thick on the floor of the wide, dim hallway, on the broad steps of the stair that mounted up from the hall. They turned into a door opposite the landing, and entered a large room, empty, dusty, with cobwebs shining thickly in the corners. Dust lay thick over the ashes in the great fireplace.

They discussed gathering wood and building a fire, but decided against it. As the sun sank, darkness came quickly, the thick, black, absolute darkness of the pinelands. They knew that rattlesnakes and copperheads haunted Southern forests, and they did not care to go groping for firewood in the dark. They ate frugally from tins, then rolled in their blankets fully clad before the empty fireplace, and went instantly to sleep.

This, in part, was what Griswell had dreamed. He saw again the gaunt house looming stark against the crimson sunset; saw the flight of the pigeons as he and Branner came up the shattered walk. He saw the dim room in which they presently lay, and he saw the two forms that were himself and his companion, lying wrapped in their blankets on the dusty floor. Then from that point his dream altered subtly, passed out of the realm of the commonplace and became tinged with fear. He was looking into a vague, shadowy chamber, lit by the gray light of the moon which streamed in from some obscure source. For there was no window in that room. But in the gray light he saw three silent shapes that hung suspended in a row, and their stillness and their outlines woke chill horror in his soul. There was no sound, no word, but he sensed a Presence of fear and lunacy crouching in a dark corner . . . Abruptly he was back in the dusty, high-ceilinged room, before the great fireplace.

He was lying in his blankets, staring tensely through the dim door and across the shadowy hall, to where a beam of moonlight fell across the balustraded stair, some seven steps up from the landing. And there was something on the stair, a bent, misshapen, shadowy thing that never moved fully into the beam of light. But a dim yellow blur that might have been a face was turned toward him, as if *something* crouched on the stair, regarding him and his companion. Fright crept chilly through his veins, and it was then that he awoke – if indeed he had been asleep.

He blinked his eyes. The beam of moonlight fell across the stair just as he had dreamed it did; but no figure lurked there. Yet his flesh still crawled from the fear the dream or vision had roused in him; his legs felt as if they had been plunged in ice-water. He made an involuntary movement to awaken his companion, when a sudden sound paralyzed him.

It was the sound of whistling on the floor above. Eery and sweet it rose, not carrying any tune, but piping shrill and melodious. Such a sound in a supposedly deserted house was alarming enough; but it was more than the fear of a physical invader that held Griswell frozen. He could not himself have defined the horror that gripped him. But Branner's blankets rustled, and Griswell saw he was sitting upright. His figure bulked dimly in the soft darkness, the head turned toward the stair as if the man were listening intently. More sweetly and more subtly evil rose that weird whistling.

'John!' whispered Griswell from dry lips. He had meant to shout – to tell Branner that there was somebody upstairs, somebody who could mean them no good; that they must leave the house at once. But his voice died dryly in his throat.

Branner had risen. His boots clumped on the floor as he moved toward the door. He stalked leisurely into the hall and made for the lower landing, merging with the shadows that clustered black about the stair.

Griswell lay incapable of movement, his mind a whirl of bewilderment. Who was that whistling upstairs? Why was Branner going up those stairs? Griswell saw him pass the spot where the moonlight rested, saw his head tilted back as if he were looking at something Griswell could not see, above and beyond the stair. But his face was like that of a sleepwalker. He moved across the bar of moonlight and vanished from Griswell's view, even as the latter tried to shout to him to come back. A ghastly whisper was the only result of his effort.

The whistling sank to a lower note, died out. Griswell heard the stairs creaking under Branner's measured tread. Now he had reached the hallway above, for Griswell heard the clump of his feet moving along it. Suddenly the footfalls halted, and the whole night seemed to hold its breath. Then an awful scream split the stillness, and Griswell started up, echoing the cry.

The strange paralysis that had held him was broken. He took a step toward the door, then checked himself. The footfalls were resumed. Branner was coming back. He was not running. The tread was even more deliberate and measured than before. Now the stairs began to creak again. A groping hand, moving along the balustrade, came into the bar of moonlight; then another, and a ghastly thrill went through Griswell as he saw that the other hand gripped a hatchet – a hatchet which dripped blackly. *Was* that Branner who was coming down that stair?

Yes! The figure had moved into the bar of moonlight now, and Griswell recognized it. Then he saw Branner's face, and a shriek burst from Griswell's lips. Branner's face was bloodless, corpse-like; gouts of blood dripped darkly down it; his eyes were glassy and set, and blood oozed from the great gash *which cleft the crown of his head!*

Griswell never remembered exactly how he got out of that accursed house. Afterward he retained a mad, confused impression of smashing his way through a dusty cobwebbed window, of stumbling blindly across the weed-choked lawn, gibbering his frantic horror. He saw the black wall of the pines, and the moon floating in a blood-red mist in which there was neither sanity nor reason.

Some shred of sanity returned to him as he saw the automobile beside the road. In a world gone suddenly mad, that was an object reflecting prosaic reality; but even as he reached for the door, a dry chilling whir sounded in his ears, and he recoiled from the swaying undulating shape that arched up from its scaly coils on the driver's seat and hissed sibilantly at him, darting a forked tongue in the moonlight.

With a sob of horror he turned and fled down the road, as a man runs in a nightmare. He ran without purpose or reason. His numbed brain was incapable of conscious thought. He merely obeyed the blind primitive urge to run – run – run until he fell exhausted.

The black walls of the pines flowed endlessly past him; so he was seized with the illusion that he was getting nowhere. But presently a sound penetrated the fog of his terror – the steady, inexorable patter of feet behind him. Turning his head, he saw *something* loping after him – wolf or dog, he could not tell which, but its eyes glowed like balls of green fire. With a gasp he increased his speed, reeled around a bend in the road, and heard a horse snort; saw it rear and heard its rider curse; saw the gleam of blue steel in the man's lifted hand.

He staggered and fell, catching at the rider's stirrup.

'For God's sake, help me!' he panted 'The thing! It killed Branner – it's coming after me! *Look!*'

Twin balls of fire gleamed in the fringe of bushes at the turn of the road. The rider swore again, and on the heels of his profanity came the smashing report of his six-shooter – again and yet again. The fire-sparks vanished, and the rider, jerking his stirrup free from Griswell's grasp, spurred his horse at the bend. Griswell staggered up, shaking in every limb. The rider was out of sight only a moment; then he came galloping back.

'Took to the brush. Timber wolf, I reckon, though I never heard of one chasin' a man before. Do you know what it was?'

Griswell could only shake his head weakly.

The rider, etched in the moonlight, looked down at him, smoking pistol still lifted in his right hand. He was a compactly-built man of medium height, and his broad-brimmed planter's hat and his boots marked him as a native of the country as definitely as Griswell's garb stamped him as a stranger.

'What's all this about, anyway?'

'I don't know,' Griswell answered helplessly. 'My name's Griswell. John Branner – my friend who was traveling with me – we stopped at a deserted house back down the road to spend the night. Something –' at the memory he was choked by a rush of horror. 'My God!' he screamed. 'I must be mad! *Something* came and looked over the balustrade of the stair – something with a yellow face! I thought I dreamed it, but it must have been real. Then somebody began whistling upstairs, and Branner rose and went up the stairs walking like a man in his sleep, or hypnotized. I heard him scream – or someone screamed; then he came down the stair again with a bloody hatchet in his hand – and my God, sir, he was *dead*! His head had been split open. I saw brains and clotted blood oozing down his face, and his face was that of a dead man. *But he came down the stair!* As God is my witness, John Branner was murdered in that dark upper hallway, and then his dead body came stalking down the stairs with a hatchet in its hand – to kill me!'

The rider made no reply; he sat his horse like a statue, outlined against the stars, and Griswell could not read his expression, his face shadowed by his hat-brim.

'You think I'm mad,' he said hopelessly. 'Perhaps I am.'

'I don't know what to think,' answered the rider. 'If it was any house but the old Blassenville Manor – well, we'll see. My name's Buckner. I'm sheriff of this country. Took a nigger over to the county seat in the next county and was ridin' back late.'

He swung off his horse and stood beside Griswell, shorter than the lanky New Englander, but much harder knit. There was a natural manner of decision and certainty about him, and it was easy to believe that he would be a dangerous man in any sort of a fight.

'Are you afraid to go back to the house?' he asked, and Griswell shuddered, but shook his head, the dogged tenacity of Puritan ancestors asserting itself.

'The thought of facing that horror again turns me sick. But poor Branner –' he choked again. 'We must find his body. My God!' he cried, unmanned by the abysmal horror of the thing; '*what* will we find? If a dead man walks, what –'

'We'll see.' The sheriff caught the reins in the crook of his left elbow and began filling the empty chambers of his big blue pistol as they walked along.

As they made the turn Griswell's blood was ice at the thought of what they might see lumbering up the road with bloody, grinning death-mask, but they saw only the house looming spectrally among the pines, down the road. A strong shudder shook Griswell.

'God, how *evil* that house looks, against those black pines! It looked sinister from the very first – when we went up the broken walk and saw those pigeons fly up from the porch –'

'Pigeons?' Buckner cast him a quick glance. 'You saw the pigeons?'

'Why, yes! Scores of them perching on the porch railing.'

They strode on for a moment in silence, before Buckner said abruptly: 'I've lived in this country all my life. I've passed the old Blassenville place a thousand times, I reckon, at all hours of the day and night. But I never saw a pigeon anywhere around it, or anywhere else in these woods.'

'There were scores of them,' repeated Griswell, bewildered.

'I've seen men who swore they'd seen a flock of pigeons perched along the balusters just at sundown,' said Buckner slowly. 'Niggers, all of them except one man. A tramp. He was buildin' a fire in the yard, aimin' to camp there that night. I passed along there about dark, and he told me about the pigeons. I came back by there the next mornin'. The ashes of his fire were there, and his tin cup, and skillet where he'd fried pork, and his blankets looked like they'd been slept in. Nobody ever saw him again. That was twelve years ago. The niggers say they can see the pigeons, but no nigger would pass along this road between sundown and sun-up. They say the pigeons are the souls of the Blassenvilles, let out of hell at sunset. The niggers say the red glare in the west is the light from hell, because then the gates of hell are open, and the Blassenvilles fly out.'

'Who were the Blassenvilles?' asked Griswell, shivering.

'They owned all this land here. French-English family. Came here from the West Indies before the Louisiana Purchase. The Civil War ruined them, like it did so many. Some were killed in the War; most of the others died out. Nobody's lived in the Manor since 1890 when Miss Elizabeth Blassenville, the last of the line, fled from the old house one night like it was a plague spot, and never came back to it – this your auto?'

They halted beside the car, and Griswell stared morbidly at the grim house. Its dusty panes were empty and blank; but they did not seem blind to him. It seemed to him that ghastly eyes were fixed hungrily on him through those darkened panes. Buckner repeated his question.

'Yes. Be careful. There's a snake on the seat – or there was.'

'Not there now,' grunted Buckner, tying his horse and pulling an electric torch out of the saddle-bag. 'Well, let's have a look.'

He strode up the broken brick-walk as matter-of-factly as if he were paying a social call on friends. Griswell followed close at his heels, his heart pounding suffocatingly. A scent of decay and moldering vegetation blew on the faint wind, and Griswell grew faint with nausea, that rose from a frantic abhorrence of these black woods, these ancient plantation houses that hid forgotten secrets of slavery and bloody pride and mysterious intrigues. He had thought of the South as a sunny, lazy land washed by soft breezes laden with spice and warm blossoms, where life ran tranquilly to the rhythm of black folk singing in sun-bathed cottonfields. But now he had discovered another, unsuspected side – a dark, brooding, fear-haunted side, and the discovery repelled him.

The oaken door sagged as it had before. The blackness of the interior was intensified by the beam of Buckner's light playing on the sill. That beam sliced through the darkness of the hallway and roved up the stair, and Griswell held his breath, clenching his fists. But no shape of lunacy leered down at them. Buckner went in, walking light as a cat, torch in one hand, gun in the other.

As he swung his light into the room across from the stairway, Griswell cried out – and cried out again, almost fainting with the intolerable sickness at what he saw. A trail of blood drops led across the floor, crossing the blankets Branner had occupied, which lay between the door and those in which Griswell had lain. And Griswell's blankets had a terrible occupant.

John Branner lay there, face down, his cleft head revealed in merciless clarity in the steady light. His outstretched hand still gripped the haft of a hatchet, and the blade was imbedded deep in the blanket and the floor beneath, just where Griswell's head had lain when he slept there.

A momentary rush of blackness engulfed Griswell. He was not aware that he staggered, or that Buckner caught him. When he could see and hear again, he was violently sick and hung his head against the mantel, retching miserably.

Buckner turned the light full on him, making him blink. Buckner's voice came from behind the blinding radiance, the man himself unseen.

'Griswell, you've told me a yarn that's hard to believe. I saw something chasin' you, but it might have been a timber wolf, or a mad dog.

'If you're holdin' back anything, you better spill it. What you told me won't hold up in any court. You're bound to be accused of killin' your partner. I'll have to arrest you. If you'll give me the straight goods now, it'll make it easier. Now, didn't you kill this fellow, Branner?

'Wasn't it something like this: you quarreled, he grabbed a hatchet and swung at you, but you dodged and then let *him* have it?'

Griswell sank down and hid his face in his hands, his head swimming.

'Great God, man, I didn't murder John! Why, we've been friends ever since we were children in school together. I've told you the truth. I don't blame you for not believing me. But God help me, it is the truth!'

The light swung back to the gory head again, and Griswell closed his eyes.

He heard Buckner grunt.

'I believe this hatchet in his hand is the one he was killed with. Blood and brains plastered on the blade, and hairs stickin' to it – hairs exactly the same color as his. This makes it tough for you, Griswell.'

'How so?' the New Englander asked dully.

'Knocks any plea of self-defense in the head. Branner couldn't have swung at you with this hatchet after you split his skull with it. You must have pulled the ax out of his head, stuck it into the floor and clamped his fingers on it to make it look like he'd attacked you. And it would have been damned clever – if you'd used another hatchet.'

'But I didn't kill him,' groaned Griswell. 'I have no intention of pleading self-defense.'

'That's what puzzles me,' Buckner admitted frankly, straightening. 'What murderer would rig up such a crazy story as you've told me, to prove his innocence? Average killer would have told a logical yarn, at least. Hmmm! Blood drops leadin' from the door. The body was dragged – no, couldn't have been dragged. The floor isn't smeared. You must have carried it here, after killin' him in some other place. But in that case, why isn't there any blood on your clothes? Of course you could have changed clothes and washed your hands. But the fellow hasn't been dead long.'

'He walked downstairs and across the room,' said Griswell hopelessly. 'He came to kill me. I knew he was coming to kill me when I saw him lurching down the stair. He struck where I would have been, if I hadn't awakened. That window – I burst out at it. You see it's broken.'

'I see. But if he walked then, why isn't he walkin' now?'

'I don't know! I'm too sick to think straight. I've been fearing that he'd rise up from the floor where he lies and come at me again. When I heard that wolf running up the road after me, I thought it was John chasing me – John, running through the night with his bloody ax and his bloody head, and his death-grin!'

His teeth chattered as he lived that horror over again.

Buckner let his light play across the floor.

'The blood drops lead into the hall. Come on. We'll follow them.'

Griswell cringed. 'They lead upstairs.'

Buckner's eyes were fixed hard on him.

'Are you afraid to go upstairs, with me?'

Griswell's face was gray.

'Yes. But I'm going, with you or without you. The thing that killed poor John may still be hiding up there.'

'Stay behind me,' ordered Buckner. 'If anything jumps us, I'll take care of it. But for your own sake, I warn you that I shoot quicker than a cat jumps, and I don't often miss. If you've got any ideas of layin' me out from behind, forget them.'

'Don't be a fool!' Resentment got the better of his apprehension, and this outburst seemed to reassure Buckner more than any of his protestations of innocence.

'I want to be fair,' he said quietly. 'I haven't indicted and condemned you in my mind already. If only half of what you're tellin' me is the truth, you've been through a hell of an experience, and I don't want to be too hard on you. But you can see how hard it is for me to believe all you've told me.'

Griswell wearily motioned for him to lead the way, unspeaking. They went out into the hall, paused at the landing. A thin string of crimson drops, distinct in the thick dust, led up the steps.

'Man's tracks in the dust,' grunted Buckner. 'Go slow. I've got to be sure of what I see, because we're obliteratin' them as we go up. Hmmm! One set goin' up, one comin' down. Same man. Not your tracks. Branner was a bigger man than you are. Blood drops all the way – blood on the bannisters like a man had laid his bloody hand there – a smear of stuff that looks – *brains*. Now what –'

'He walked down the stair, a dead man,' shuddered Griswell. 'Groping with one hand – the other gripping the hatchet that killed him.'

'Or was carried,' muttered the sheriff. 'But if somebody carried him – *where are the tracks?*'

They came out into the upper hallway, a vast, empty space of dust and shadows where time-crusted windows repelled the moonlight and the ring of Buckner's torch seemed inadequate. Griswell trembled like a leaf. Here, in darkness and horror, John Branner had died.

'Somebody whistled up here,' he muttered. 'John came, as if he were being called.'

Buckner's eyes were blazing strangely in the light.

'The footprints lead down the hall,' he muttered. 'Same as on the stair – one set going, one coming. Same prints – *Judas!*'

Behind him Griswell stifled a cry, for he had seen what prompted Buckner's exclamation. A few feet from the head of the stair Branner's footprints stopped abruptly, then returned, treading almost in the other tracks. And where the trail halted there was a great splash of blood on the dusty floor – and other tracks met it – tracks of bare feet, narrow but with splayed toes. They too receded in a second line from the spot.

Buckner bent over them, swearing.

'The tracks meet! And where they meet there's blood and brains on the floor! Branner must have been killed on that spot – with a blow from a hatchet. Bare feet coming out of the darkness to meet shod feet – then both turned away again; the shod feet went downstairs, the bare feet went back down the hall.' He directed his light down the hall. The footprints faded into darkness, beyond the reach of the beam. On either hand the closed doors of chambers were cryptic portals of mystery.

'Suppose your crazy tale *was* true,' Buckner muttered, half to himself. 'These aren't your tracks. They look like a woman's. Suppose somebody did whistle, and Branner went upstairs to investigate. Suppose somebody met him here in the dark and split his head. The signs and tracks would have been, in that case, just as they really are. But if that's so, why isn't Branner lyin' here where he was killed? Could he have lived long enough to take the hatchet away from whoever killed him, and stagger downstairs with it?'

'No, no!' Recollection gagged Griswell. 'I *saw* him on the stair. He was dead. No man could live a minute after receiving such a wound.'

'I believe it,' muttered Buckner. 'But – it's madness! Or else it's *too* clever – yet, what sane man would think up and work out such an elaborate and utterly insane plan to escape punishment for murder, when a simple plea of self-defense would have been so much more effective? No court would recognize that story. Well, let's follow these other tracks. They lead down the hall – here, what's this?'

With an icy clutch at his soul, Griswell saw the light was beginning to grow dim.

'This battery is new,' muttered Buckner, and for the first time Griswell caught an edge of fear in his voice. 'Come on – out of here quick!'

The light had faded to a faint red glow. The darkness seemed straining into them, creeping with black cat-feet. Buckner retreated, pushing Griswell stumbling behind him as he walked backward, pistol cocked and lifted, down the dark hall. In the growing darkness Griswell heard what sounded like the stealthy opening of a door. And suddenly the blackness about them was vibrant with menace. Griswell knew Buckner sensed it as well as he, for the sheriff's hard body was tense and taut as a stalking panther's.

But without haste he worked his way to the stair and backed down it, Griswell preceding him, and fighting the panic that urged him to scream and burst into mad flight. A ghastly thought brought icy sweat out on his flesh. *Suppose the dead man were creeping up the stair behind them in the dark, face frozen in the death-grin, blood-caked hatchet lifted to strike?*

This possibility so overpowered him that he was scarcely aware when his feet struck the level of the lower hallway, and he was only then aware that the light had grown brighter as they descended, until it now gleamed with its full power – but when Buckner turned it back up the stairway, it failed to illuminate the darkness that hung like a tangible fog at the head of the stair.

'The damn thing was conjured,' muttered Buckner. 'Nothin' else. It couldn't act like that naturally.'

'Turn the light into the room,' begged Griswell. 'See if John – if John is –'

He could not put the ghastly thought into words, but Buckner understood.

He swung the beam around, and Griswell had never dreamed that the sight of the gory body of a murdered man could bring such relief.

'He's still there,' grunted Buckner. 'If he walked after he was killed, he hasn't walked since. But that thing –'

Again he turned the light up the stair, and stood chewing his lip and scowling. Three times he half lifted his gun. Griswell read his mind. The sheriff was tempted to plunge back up that stair, take his chance with the unknown. But common sense held him back.

'I wouldn't have a chance in the dark,' he muttered. 'And I've got a hunch the light would go out again.'

He turned and faced Griswell squarely.

'There's no use dodgin' the question. There's somethin' hellish in this house, and I believe I have an inklin' of what it is. I don't believe you killed Branner. Whatever killed him is up there – now. There's a lot about your yarn that don't sound sane; but there's nothin' sane about a flashlight goin' out like this one did. I don't believe that thing upstairs is human. I never met anything I was afraid to tackle in the dark before, but I'm not goin' up there until daylight. It's not long until dawn. We'll wait for it out there on that gallery.'

The stars were already paling when they came out on the broad porch. Buckner seated himself on the balustrade, facing the door, his pistol dangling in his fingers. Griswell sat down near him and leaned back against a crumbling pillar. He shut his eyes, grateful for the faint breeze that seemed to cool his throbbing brain. He experienced a dull sense of unreality. He was a stranger in a strange land, a land that had become suddenly imbued with black horror. The shadow of the noose hovered above him, and in that dark house lay John Branner, with his butchered head – like the figments of a dream these facts spun and eddied in his brain until all merged in a gray twilight as sleep came uninvited to his weary soul.

He awoke to a cold white dawn and full memory of the horrors of the night. Mists curled about the stems of the pines, crawled in smoky wisps up the broken walk. Buckner was shaking him.

'Wake up! It's daylight.'

Griswell rose, wincing at the stiffness of his limbs. His face was gray and old.

'I'm ready. Let's go upstairs.'

'I've already been!' Buckner's eyes burned in the early dawn. 'I didn't wake you up. I went as soon as it was light. I found nothin'.'

'The tracks of the bare feet –'

'Gone!'

'*Gone?*'

'Yes, gone! The dust had been disturbed all over the hall, from the point where Branner's tracks ended; swept into corners. No chance of trackin' anything there now. Something obliterated those tracks while we sat here, and I didn't hear a sound. I've gone through the whole house. Not a sign of anything.'

Griswell shuddered at the thought of himself sleeping alone on the porch while Buckner conducted his exploration.

'What shall we do?' he asked listlessly. 'With those tracks gone, there goes my only chance of proving my story.'

'We'll take Branner's body into the county seat,' answered Buckner. 'Let me do the talkin'. If the authorities knew the facts as they appear, they'd insist on you being confined and indicted. I don't believe you killed Branner – but neither a district attorney, judge nor jury would believe what you told me, or what happened to us last night. I'm handlin' this thing my own way. I'm not goin' to arrest you until I've exhausted every other possibility.

'Say nothin' about what's happened here, when we get to town. I'll simply tell the district attorney that John Branner was killed by a party or parties unknown, and that I'm workin' on the case.

'Are you game to come back with me to this house and spend the night here, sleepin' in that room as you and Branner slept last night?'

Griswell went white, but answered as stoutly as his ancestors might have expressed their determination to hold their cabins in the teeth of the Pequots: 'I'll do it.'

'Let's go then; help me pack the body out to your auto.'

Griswell's soul revolted at the sight of John Branner's blood-less face in the chill white dawn, and the feel of his clammy flesh. The gray fog wrapped wispy tentacles about their feet as they carried their grisly burden across the lawn.

2   The Snake's Brother

Again the shadows were lengthening over the pinelands, and again two men came bumping along the old road in a car with a New England license plate.

Buckner was driving. Griswell's nerves were too shattered for him to trust himself at the wheel. He looked gaunt and haggard, and his face was still pallid. The strain of the day spent at the county seat was added to the horror that still rode his soul like the shadow of a black-winged vulture. He had not slept, had not tasted what he had eaten.

'I told you I'd tell you about the Blassenvilles,' said Buckner. 'They were proud folks, haughty, and pretty damn ruthless when they wanted their way. They didn't treat their niggers as well as the other planters did – got their ideas in the West Indies, I reckon. There was a streak of cruelty in them – especially Miss Celia, the last one of the family to come to these parts. That was long after the slaves had been freed, but she used to whip her mulatto maid just like she was a slave, the old folks say . . . The niggers said when a Blassenville died, the devil was always waitin' for him out in the black pines.

'Well, after the Civil War they died off pretty fast, livin' in poverty on the plantation which was allowed to go to ruin. Finally only four girls were left, sisters, livin' in the old house and ekin' out a bare livin', with a few niggers livin' in the old slave huts and workin' the fields on the share. They kept to themselves, bein' proud, and ashamed of their poverty. Folks wouldn't see them for months at a time. When they needed supplies they sent a nigger to town after them.

'But folks knew about it when Miss Celia came to live with them. She came from somewhere in the West Indies, where the whole family originally had its roots – a fine, handsome woman, they say, in the early thirties. But she didn't mix with folks any more than the girls did. She brought a mulatto maid with her, and the Blassenville cruelty cropped out in her treatment of this maid. I knew an old nigger, years ago, who swore he saw Miss Celia tie this girl up to a tree, stark naked, and whip her with a horsewhip. Nobody was surprized when she disappeared. Everybody figured she'd run away, of course.

'Well, one day in the spring of 1890 Miss Elizabeth, the youngest girl, came in to town for the first time in maybe a year. She came after supplies. Said the niggers had all left the place. Talked a little more, too, a bit wild. Said Miss Celia had gone, without leaving any word. Said her sisters thought she'd gone back to the West Indies, but she believed her aunt *was still in the house*. She didn't say what she meant. Just got her supplies and pulled out for the Manor.

'A month went past, and a nigger came into town and said that Miss Elizabeth was livin' at the Manor alone. Said her three sisters weren't there any more, that they'd left one by one without givin' any word or explanation. She didn't know where they'd gone, and was afraid to stay there alone, but didn't know where else to go. She'd never known anything but the Manor, and had neither relatives nor friends. But she was in mortal terror of *something*. The nigger said she locked herself in her room at night and kept candles burnin' all night . . .

'It was a stormy spring night when Miss Elizabeth came tearin' into town on the one horse she owned, nearly dead from fright. She fell from her horse in the square; when she could talk she said she'd found a secret room in the Manor that had been forgotten for a hundred years. And she said that there she found her three sisters, dead, and hangin' by their necks from the ceilin'. She said *something* chased her and nearly brained her with an ax as she ran out the front door, but somehow she got to the horse and got away. She was nearly crazy with fear, and didn't know what it was that chased her – said it looked like a woman with a yellow face.

'About a hundred men rode out there, right away. They searched the house from top to bottom, but they didn't find any secret room, or the remains of the sisters. But they did find a hatchet stickin' in the doorjamb downstairs, with some of Miss Elizabeth's hairs stuck on it, just as she'd said. She wouldn't go back there and show them how to find the secret door; almost went crazy when they suggested it.

'When she was able to travel, the people made up some money and loaned it to her – she was still too proud to accept charity – and she went to California. She never came back, but later it was learned, when she sent back to repay the money they'd loaned her, that she'd married out there.

'Nobody ever bought the house. It stood there just as she'd left it, and as the years passed folks stole all the furnishings out of it, poor white trash, I reckon. A nigger wouldn't go about it. But they came after sun-up and left long before sundown.'

'What did the people think about Miss Elizabeth's story?' asked Griswell.

'Well, most folks thought she'd gone a little crazy, livin' in that old house alone. But some people believed that mulatto girl, Joan, didn't run away, after all. They believed she'd hidden in the woods, and glutted her hatred of the Blassenvilles by murderin' Miss Celia and the three girls. They beat up the woods with bloodhounds, but never found a trace of her. If there was a secret room in the house, she might have been hidin' there – if there was anything to that theory.'

'She couldn't have been hiding there all these years,' muttered Griswell. 'Anyway, the thing in the house now isn't human.'

Buckner wrenched the wheel around and turned into a dim trace that left the main road and meandered off through the pines.

'Where are you going?'

'There's an old nigger that lives off this way a few miles. I want to talk to him. We're up against something that takes more than white man's sense. The black people know more than we do about some things. This old man is nearly a hundred years old. His master educated him when he was a boy, and after he was freed he traveled more extensively than most white men do. They say he's a voodoo man.'

Griswell shivered at the phrase, staring uneasily at the green forest walls that shut them in. The scent of the pines was mingled with the odors of unfamiliar plants and blossoms. But underlying all was a reek of rot and decay. Again a sick abhorrence of these dark mysterious woodlands almost overpowered him.

'Voodoo!' he muttered. 'I'd forgotten about that – I never could think of black magic in connection with the South. To me witchcraft was always associated with old crooked streets in waterfront towns, overhung by gabled roofs that were old when they were hanging witches in Salem; dark musty alleys where black cats and other things might steal at night. Witchcraft always meant the old towns of New England, to me – but all this is more terrible than any New England legend – these somber pines, old deserted houses, lost plantations, mysterious black people, old tales of madness and horror – God, what frightful, ancient terrors there are on this continent fools call "young"!'

'Here's old Jacob's hut,' announced Buckner, bringing the automobile to a halt.

Griswell saw a clearing and a small cabin squatting under the shadows of the huge trees. There pines gave way to oaks and cypresses, bearded with gray trailing moss, and behind the cabin lay the edge of a swamp that ran away under the dimness of the trees, choked with rank vegetation. A thin wisp of blue smoke curled up from the stick-and-mud chimney.

He followed Buckner to the tiny stoop, where the sheriff pushed open the leather-hinged door and strode in. Griswell blinked in the comparative dimness of the interior. A single small window let in a little daylight. An old negro crouched beside the hearth, watching a pot stew over the open fire. He looked up as they entered, but did not rise. He seemed incredibly old. His face was a mass of wrinkles, and his eyes, dark and vital, were filmed momentarily at times as if his mind wandered.

Buckner motioned Griswell to sit down in a string-bottomed chair, and himself took a rudely-made bench near the hearth, facing the old man.

'Jacob,' he said bluntly, 'the time's come for you to talk. I know you know the secret of Blassenville Manor. I've never questioned you about it, because it wasn't in my line. But a man was murdered there last night, and this man here may hang for it, unless you tell me what haunts that old house of the Blassenvilles.'

The old man's eyes gleamed, then grew misty as if clouds of extreme age drifted across his brittle mind.

'The Blassenvilles,' he murmured, and his voice was mellow and rich, his speech not the patois of the piny woods darky. 'They were proud people, sirs – proud and cruel. Some died in the war, some were killed in duels – the menfolks, sirs. Some died in the Manor – the old Manor –' His voice trailed off into unintelligible mumblings.

'What of the Manor?' asked Buckner patiently.

'Miss Celia was the proudest of them all,' the old man muttered. 'The proudest and the cruelest. The black people hated her; Joan most of all. Joan had white blood in her, and she was proud, too. Miss Celia whipped her like a slave.'

'What is the secret of Blassenville Manor?' persisted Buckner.

The film faded from the old man's eyes; they were dark as moonlit wells.

'What secret, sir? I do not understand.'

'Yes, you do. For years that old house has stood there with its mystery. You know the key to its riddle.'

The old man stirred the stew. He seemed perfectly rational now.

'Sir, life is sweet, even to an old black man.'

'You mean somebody would kill you if you told me?'

But the old man was mumbling again, his eyes clouded.

'Not somebody. No human. No human being. The black gods of the swamps. My secret is inviolate, guarded by the Big Serpent, the god above all gods. He would send a little brother to kiss me with his cold lips – a little brother with a white crescent moon on his head. I sold my soul to the Big Serpent when he made me maker of *zuvembies* –'

Buckner stiffened.

'I heard that word once before,' he said softly, 'from the lips of a dying black man, when I was a child. What does it mean?'

Fear filled the eyes of old Jacob.

'What have I said? No – no! I said nothing.'

'*Zuvembies*,' prompted Buckner.

'*Zuvembies*,' mechanically repeated the old man, his eyes vacant. 'A *zuvembie* was once a woman – on the Slave Coast they know of them. The drums that whisper by night in the hills of Haiti tell of them. The makers of *zuvembies* are honored of the people of Damballah. It is death to speak of it to a white man – it is one of the Snake God's forbidden secrets.'

'You speak of the *zuvembies*,' said Buckner softly.

'I must not speak of it,' mumbled the old man, and Griswell realized that he was thinking aloud, too far gone in his dotage to be aware that he was speaking at all. 'No white man must know that I danced in the Black Ceremony of the voodoo, and was made a maker of *zombies* and *zuvembies*. The Big Snake punishes loose tongues with death.'

'A *zuvembie* is a woman?' prompted Buckner.

'*Was* a woman,' the old negro muttered. '*She* knew I was a maker of *zuvembies* – she came and stood in my hut and asked for the awful brew – the brew of ground snake-bones, and the blood of vampire bats, and the dew from a night-hawk's wings, and other elements unnamable. She had danced in the Black Ceremony – she was ripe to become a *zuvembie* – the Black Brew was all that was needed – the other was beautiful – I could not refuse her.'

'Who?' demanded Buckner tensely, but the old man's head was sunk on his withered breast, and he did not reply. He seemed to slumber as he sat. Buckner shook him. 'You gave a brew to make a woman a *zuvembie* – what is a *zuvembie*?'

The old man stirred resentfully and muttered drowsily.

'A *zuvembie* is no longer human. It knows neither relatives nor friends. It is one with the people of the Black World. It commands the natural demons – owls, bats, snakes and were-wolves, and can fetch darkness to blot out a little light. It can be slain by lead or steel, but unless it is slain thus, it lives for ever, and it eats no such food as humans eat. It dwells like a bat in a cave or an old house. Time means naught to the *zuvembie*; an hour, a day, a year, all is one. It cannot speak human words, nor think as a human thinks, but it can hypnotize the living by the sound of its voice, and when it slays a man, it can command his lifeless body until the flesh is cold. As long as the blood flows, the corpse is its slave. Its pleasure lies in the slaughter of human beings.'

'And why should one become a *zuvembie?*' asked Buckner softly.

'Hate,' whispered the old man. 'Hate! Revenge!'

'Was her name Joan?' murmured Buckner.

It was as if the name penetrated the fogs of senility that clouded the voodoo-man's mind. He shook himself and the film faded from his eyes, leaving them hard and gleaming as wet black marble.

'Joan?' he said slowly. 'I have not heard that name for the span of a generation. I seem to have been sleeping, gentlemen; I do not remember – I ask your pardon. Old men fall asleep before the fire, like old dogs. You asked me of Blassenville Manor? Sir, if I were to tell you why I cannot answer you, you would deem it mere superstition. Yet the white man's God be my witness –'

As he spoke he was reaching across the hearth for a piece of firewood, groping among the heaps of sticks there. And his voice broke in a scream, as he jerked back his arm convulsively. And a horrible, thrashing, trailing *thing* came with it. Around the voodoo-man's arm a mottled length of that shape was wrapped, and a wicked wedge-shaped head struck again in silent fury.

The old man fell on the hearth, screaming, upsetting the simmering pot and scattering the embers, and then Buckner caught up a billet of firewood and crushed that flat head. Cursing, he kicked aside the knotting, twisting trunk, glaring briefly at the mangled head. Old Jacob had ceased screaming and writhing; he lay still, staring glassily upward.

'Dead?' whispered Griswell.

'Dead as Judas Iscariot,' snapped Buckner, frowning at the twitching reptile. 'That infernal snake crammed enough poison into his veins to kill a dozen men his age. But I think it was the shock and fright that killed him.'

'What shall we do?' asked Griswell, shivering.

'Leave the body on that bunk. Nothin' can hurt it, if we bolt the door so the wild hogs can't get in, or any cat. We'll carry it into town tomorrow. We've got work to do tonight. Let's get goin'.'

Griswell shrank from touching the corpse, but he helped Buckner lift it on the rude bunk, and then stumbled hastily out of the hut. The sun was hovering above the horizon, visible in dazzling red flame through the black stems of the trees.

They climbed into the car in silence, and went bumping back along the stumpy trail.

'He said the Big Snake would send one of his brothers,' muttered Griswell.

'Nonsense!' snorted Buckner. 'Snakes like warmth, and that swamp is full of them. It crawled in and coiled up among that firewood. Old Jacob disturbed it, and it bit him. Nothin' supernatural about that.' After a short silence he said, in a different voice, 'That was the first time I ever saw a rattler strike without singin'; and the first time I ever saw a snake *with a white crescent moon on its head*.'

They were turning in to the main road before either spoke again.

'You think that the mulatto Joan has skulked in the house all these years?' Griswell asked.

'You heard what old Jacob said,' answered Buckner grimly. 'Time means nothin' to a *zuvembie*.'

As they made the last turn in the road, Griswell braced himself against the sight of Blassenville Manor looming black against the red sunset. When it came into view he bit his lip to keep from shrieking. The suggestion of cryptic horror came back in all its power.

'Look!' he whispered from dry lips as they came to a halt beside the road. Buckner grunted.

From the balustrades of the gallery rose a whirling cloud of pigeons that swept away into the sunset, black against the lurid glare . . .

3   The Call of Zuvembie

Both men sat rigid for a few moments after the pigeons had flown.

'Well, I've seen them at last,' muttered Buckner.

'Only the doomed see them, perhaps,' whispered Griswell. 'That tramp saw them –'

'Well, we'll see,' returned the Southerner tranquilly, as he climbed out of the car, but Griswell noticed him unconsciously hitch forward his scabbarded gun.

The oaken door sagged on broken hinges. Their feet echoed on the broken brick walk. The blind windows reflected the sunset in sheets of flame. As they came into the broad hall Griswell saw the string of black marks that ran across the floor and into the chamber, marking the path of a dead man.

Buckner had brought blankets out of the automobile. He spread them before the fireplace.

'I'll lie next to the door,' he said. 'You lie where you did last night.'

'Shall we light a fire in the grate?' asked Griswell, dreading the thought of the blackness that would cloak the woods when the brief twilight had died.

'No. You've got a flashlight and so have I. We'll lie here in the dark and see what happens. Can you use that gun I gave you?'

'I suppose so. I never fired a revolver, but I know how it's done.'

'Well, leave the shootin' to me, if possible.' The sheriff seated himself cross-legged on his blankets and emptied the cylinder of his big blue Colt, inspecting each cartridge with a critical eye before he replaced it.

Griswell prowled nervously back and forth, begrudging the slow fading of the light as a miser begrudges the waning of his gold. He leaned with one hand against the mantelpiece, staring down into the dust-covered ashes. The fire that produced those ashes must have been builded by Elizabeth Blassenville, more than forty years before. The thought was depressing. Idly he stirred the dusty ashes with his toe. Something came to view among the charred debris – a bit of paper, stained and yellowed. Still idly he bent and drew it out of the ashes. It was a note-book with moldering cardboard backs.

'What have you found?' asked Buckner, squinting down the gleaming barrel of his gun.

'Nothing but an old note-book. Looks like a diary. The pages are covered with writing – but the ink is so faded, and the paper is in such a state of decay that I can't tell much about it. How do you suppose it came in the fireplace, without being burned up?'

'Thrown in long after the fire was out,' surmised Buckner. 'Probably found and tossed in the fireplace by somebody who was in here stealin' furniture. Likely somebody who couldn't read.'

Griswell fluttered the crumbling leaves listlessly, straining his eyes in the fading light over the yellowed scrawls. Then he stiffened.

'Here's an entry that's legible! Listen!' He read:

'"I know someone is in the house besides myself. I can hear someone prowling about at night when the sun has set and the pines are black outside. Often in the night I hear *it* fumbling at my door. *Who* is it? Is it one of my sisters? Is it Aunt Celia? If it is either of these, why does she steal so subtly about the house? Why does she tug at my door, and glide away when I call to her? Shall I open the door and go out to her? No, no! I dare not! I am afraid. Oh God, what shall I do? I dare not stay here – but where am I to go?"'

'By God!' ejaculated Buckner. 'That must be Elizabeth Blassenville's diary! Go on!'

'I can't make out the rest of the page,' answered Griswell. 'But a few pages further on I can make out some lines.' He read:

'"Why did the negroes all run away when Aunt Celia disappeared? My sisters are dead. I know they are dead. I seem to sense that they died horribly, in fear and agony. But why? *Why?* If someone murdered Aunt Celia, why should that person murder my poor sisters? They were always kind to the black people. Joan –"' He paused, scowling futilely.

'A piece of the page is torn out. Here's another entry under another date – at least I judge it's a date; I can't make it out for sure.

'"– the awful thing that the old negress hinted at? She named Jacob Blount, and Joan, but she would not speak plainly; perhaps she feared to –" Part of it gone here; then: "No, no! How can it be? *She* is dead – or gone away. Yet – she was born and raised in the West Indies, and from hints she let fall in the past, I know she delved into the mysteries of the voodoo. I believe she even danced in one of their horrible ceremonies – how could she have been such a beast? And this – this horror. God, can such things be? I know not what to think. If it is *she* who roams the house at night, who fumbles at my door, who *whistles* so weirdly and sweetly – no, no, I must be going mad. If I stay here alone I shall die as hideously as my sisters must have died. Of that I am convinced."'

The incoherent chronicle ended as abruptly as it had begun. Griswell was so engrossed in deciphering the scraps that he was not aware that darkness had stolen upon them, hardly aware that Buckner was holding his electric torch for him to read by. Waking from his abstraction he started and darted a quick glance at the black hallway.

'What do you make of it?'

'What I've suspected all the time,' answered Buckner. 'That mulatto maid Joan turned *zuvembie* to avenge herself on Miss Celia. Probably hated the whole family as much as she did her mistress. She'd taken part in voodoo ceremonies on her native island until she was "ripe," as old Jacob said. All she needed was the Black Brew – he supplied that. She killed Miss Celia and the three older girls, and would have gotten Elizabeth but for chance. She's been lurkin' in this old house all these years, like a snake in a ruin.'

'But why should she murder a stranger?'

'You heard what old Jacob said,' reminded Buckner. 'A *zuvembie* finds satisfaction in the slaughter of humans. She called Branner up the stair and split his head and stuck the hatchet in his hand, and sent him downstairs to murder you. No court will ever believe that, but if we can produce her body, that will be evidence enough to prove your innocence. My word will be taken, that she murdered Branner. Jacob said a *zuvembie* could be killed ... in reporting this affair I don't have to be too accurate in detail.'

'She came and peered over the balustrade of the stair at us,' muttered Griswell. 'But why didn't we find her tracks on the stair?'

'Maybe you dreamed it. Maybe a *zuvembie* can project her spirit – hell! why try to rationalize something that's outside the bounds of rationality? Let's begin our watch.'

'Don't turn out the light!' exclaimed Griswell involuntarily. Then he added: 'Of course. Turn it out. We must be in the dark as' – he gagged a bit – 'as Branner and I were.'

But fear like a physical sickness assailed him when the room was plunged in darkness. He lay trembling and his heart beat so heavily he felt as if he would suffocate.

'The West Indies must be the plague spot of the world,' muttered Buckner, a blur on his blankets. 'I've heard of *zombies*. Never knew before what a *zuvembie* was. Evidently some drug concocted by the voodoo-men to induce madness in women. That doesn't explain the other things, though: the hypnotic powers, the abnormal longevity, the ability to control corpses – no, a *zuvembie* can't be merely a madwoman. It's a monster, something more and less than a human being, created by the magic that spawns in black swamps and jungles – well, we'll see.'

His voice ceased, and in the silence Griswell heard the pounding of his own heart. Outside in the black woods a wolf howled eerily, and owls hooted. Then silence fell again like a black fog.

Griswell forced himself to lie still on his blankets. Time seemed at a standstill. He felt as if he were choking. The suspense was growing unendurable; the effort he made to control his crumbling nerves bathed his limbs in sweat. He clenched his teeth until his jaws ached and almost locked, and the nails of his fingers bit deeply into his palms.

He did not know what he was expecting. The fiend would strike again – but how? Would it be a horrible, sweet whistling, bare feet stealing down the creaking steps, or a sudden hatchet-stroke in the dark? Would it choose him or Buckner? *Was Buckner already dead?* He could see nothing in the blackness, but he heard the man's steady breathing. The Southerner must have nerves of steel. Or was that Buckner breathing beside him, separated by a narrow strip of darkness? Had the fiend already struck in silence, and taken the sheriff's place, there to lie in ghoulish glee until it was ready to strike? – a thousand hideous fancies assailed Griswell tooth and claw.

He began to feel that he would go mad if he did not leap to his feet, screaming, and burst frenziedly out of that accursed house – not even the fear of the gallows could keep him lying there in the darkness any longer – the rhythm of Buckner's breathing was suddenly broken, and Griswell felt as if a bucket of ice-water had been poured over him. From somewhere above them rose a sound of weird, sweet whistling . . .

Griswell's control snapped, plunging his brain into darkness deeper than the physical blackness which engulfed him. There was a period of absolute blankness, in which a realization of *motion* was his first sensation of awakening consciousness. He was running, madly, stumbling over an incredibly rough road. All was darkness about him, and he ran blindly. Vaguely he realized that he must have bolted from the house, and fled for perhaps miles before his overwrought brain began to function. He did not care; dying on the gallows for a murder he never committed did not terrify him half as much as the thought of returning to that house of horror. He was overpowered by the urge to run – run – run as he was running now, blindly, until he reached the end of his endurance. The mist had not yet fully lifted from his brain, but he was aware of a dull wonder that he could not see the stars through the black branches. He wished vaguely that he could see where he was going. He believed he must be climbing a hill, and that was strange, for he knew there were no hills within miles of the Manor. Then above and ahead of him a dim glow began.

He scrambled toward it, over ledge-like projections that were more and more taking on a disquieting symmetry. Then he was horror-stricken to realize that a sound was impacting on his ears

– *a weird mocking whistle*. The sound swept the mists away. Why, what was this? *Where was he?* Awakening and realization came like the stunning stroke of a butcher's maul. He was not fleeing along a road, or climbing a hill; he was mounting a stair. He was still in Blassenville Manor! *And he was climbing the stair!*

An inhuman scream burst from his lips. Above it the mad whistling rose in a ghoulish piping of demoniac triumph. He tried to stop – to turn back – even to fling himself over the balustrade. His shrieking rang unbearably in his own ears. But his will-power was shattered to bits. It did not exist. He had no will. He had dropped his flashlight, and he had forgotten the gun in his pocket. He could not command his own body. His legs, moving stiffly, worked like pieces of mechanism detached from his brain, obeying an outside will. Clumping methodically they carried him shrieking up the stair toward the witch-fire glow shimmering above him.

'Buckner!' he screamed. 'Buckner! Help, for God's sake!'

His voice strangled in his throat. He had reached the upper landing. He was tottering down the hallway. The whistling sank and ceased, but its impulsion still drove him on. He could not see from what source the dim glow came. It seemed to emanate from no central focus. But he saw a vague figure shambling toward him. It looked like a woman, but no human woman ever walked with that skulking gait, and no human woman ever had that face of horror, that leering yellow blur of lunacy – he tried to scream at the sight of that face, at the glint of keen steel in the uplifted claw-like hand – but his tongue was frozen.

Then something crashed deafeningly behind him; the shadows were split by a tongue of flame which lit a hideous figure falling backward. Hard on the heels of the report rang an inhuman squawk.

In the darkness that followed the flash Griswell fell to his knees and covered his face with his hands. He did not hear

Buckner's voice. The Southerner's hand on his shoulder shook him out of his swoon.

A light in his eyes blinded him. He blinked, shaded his eyes, looked up into Buckner's face, bending at the rim of the circle of light. The sheriff was pale.

'Are you hurt? God, man, are you hurt? There's a butcher knife there on the floor –'

'I'm not hurt,' mumbled Griswell. 'You fired just in time – the fiend! Where is it? Where did it go?'

'Listen!'

Somewhere in the house there sounded a sickening flopping and flapping as of something that thrashed and struggled in its death convulsions.

'Jacob was right,' said Buckner grimly. 'Lead can kill them. I hit her, all right. Didn't dare use my flashlight, but there was enough light. When that whistlin' started you almost walked over me gettin' out. I knew you were hypnotized, or whatever it is. I followed you up the stairs. I was right behind you, but crouchin' low so she wouldn't see me, and maybe get away again. I almost waited too long before I fired – but the sight of her almost paralyzed me. Look!'

He flashed his light down the hall, and now it shone bright and clear. And it shone on an aperture gaping in the wall where no door had showed before.

'The secret panel Miss Elizabeth found!' Buckner snapped. 'Come on!'

He ran across the hallway and Griswell followed him dazedly. The flopping and thrashing came from beyond that mysterious door, and now the sounds had ceased.

The light revealed a narrow, tunnel-like corridor that evidently led through one of the thick walls. Buckner plunged into it without hesitation.

'Maybe it couldn't think like a human,' he muttered, shining his light ahead of him. 'But it had sense enough to erase its tracks last night so we couldn't trail it to that point in the wall and maybe find the secret panel. There's a room ahead – the secret room of the Blassenvilles!'

And Griswell cried out: 'My God! It's the windowless chamber I saw in my dream, with the three bodies hanging – ahhhhh!'

Buckner's light playing about the circular chamber became suddenly motionless. In that wide ring of light three figures appeared, three dried, shriveled, mummy-like shapes, still clad in the moldering garments of the last century. Their slippers were clear of the floor as they hung by their withered necks from chains suspended from the ceiling.

'The three Blassenville sisters!' muttered Buckner. 'Miss Elizabeth wasn't crazy, after all.'

'Look!' Griswell could barely make his voice intelligible. 'There – over there in the corner!'

The light moved, halted.

'Was that thing a woman once?' whispered Griswell. 'God, look at that face, even in death. Look at those claw-like hands, with black talons like those of a beast. Yes, it was human, though – even the rags of an old ballroom gown. Why should a mulatto maid wear such a dress, I wonder?'

'This has been her lair for over forty years,' muttered Buckner, brooding over the grinning grisly thing sprawling in the corner. 'This clears you, Griswell – a crazy woman with a hatchet – that's all the authorities need to know. God, what a revenge! – what a foul revenge! Yet what a bestial nature she must have had, in the beginnin', to delve into voodoo as she must have done –'

'The mulatto woman?' whispered Griswell, dimly sensing a horror that overshadowed all the rest of the terror.

Buckner shook his head. 'We misunderstood old Jacob's maunderin's, and the things Miss Elizabeth wrote – *she* must have known, but family pride sealed her lips. Griswell, I understand now; the mulatto woman had her revenge, but not as we'd supposed. She didn't drink the Black Brew old Jacob fixed for her. It was for somebody else, to be given secretly in her food, or coffee, no doubt. Then Joan ran away, leavin' the seeds of the hell she'd sowed to grow.'

'That – that's not the mulatto woman?' whispered Griswell.

'When I saw her out there in the hallway I knew she was no mulatto. And those distorted features still reflect a family likeness. I've seen her portrait, and I can't be mistaken. There lies the creature that was once Celia Blassenville.'

Graveyard Rats

I   The Head from the Grave

Saul Wilkinson awoke suddenly, and lay in the darkness with beads of cold sweat on his hands and face. He shuddered at the memory of the dream from which he had awakened.

But horrible dreams were nothing uncommon. Grisly nightmares had haunted his sleep since early childhood. It was another fear that clutched his heart with icy fingers – fear of the sound that had roused him. It had been a furtive step – hands fumbling in the dark.

And now a small scurrying sounded in the room – a rat running back and forth across the floor.

He groped under his pillow with trembling fingers. The house was still, but imagination peopled its darkness with shapes of horror. But it was not all imagination. A faint stir of air told him the door that gave on the broad hallway was open. He knew he had closed that door before he went to bed. And he knew it was not one of his brothers who had come so subtly to his room.

In that fear-tense, hate-haunted household, no man came by night to his brother's room without first making himself known.

This was especially the case since an old feud had claimed the eldest brother four days since – John Wilkinson, shot down in the streets of the little hill-country town by Joel Middleton, who had escaped into the post-oak grown hills, swearing still greater vengeance against the Wilkinsons.

All this flashed through Saul's mind as he drew the revolver from under his pillow.

As he slid out of bed, the creak of the springs brought his heart into his throat, and he crouched there for a moment, holding his breath and straining his eyes into the darkness.

Richard was sleeping upstairs, and so was Harrison, the city detective Peter had brought out to hunt down Joel Middleton. Peter's room was on the ground floor, but in another wing. A yell for help might awaken all three, but it would also bring a hail of lead at him, if Joel Middleton were crouching over there in the blackness.

Saul knew this was his fight, and must be fought out alone, in the darkness he had always feared and hated. And all the time sounded that light, scampering patter of tiny feet, racing up and down, up and down . . .

Crouching against the wall, cursing the pounding of his heart, Saul fought to steady his quivering nerves. He was backed against the wall which formed the partition between his room and the hall.

The windows were faint grey squares in the blackness, and he could dimly make out objects of furniture in all except one side of the room. Joel Middleton must be over there, crouching by the old fireplace, which was invisible in the darkness.

But why was he waiting? And why was that accursed rat racing up and down before the fireplace, as if in a frenzy of fear and greed? Just so Saul had seen rats race up and down the floor of the meat-house, frantic to get at flesh suspended out of reach.

Noiselessly, Saul moved along the wall toward the door. If a man was in the room, he would presently be lined between himself and a window. But as he glided along the wall like a night-shirted ghost, no ominous bulk grew out of the darkness.

He reached the door and closed it soundlessly, wincing at his nearness to the unrelieved blackness of the hall outside.

But nothing happened. The only sounds were the wild beating of his heart, the loud ticking of the old clock on the mantelpiece – the maddening patter of the unseen rat. Saul clenched his teeth against the shrieking of his tortured nerves. Even in his growing terror he found time to wonder frantically why that rat ran up and down before the fireplace.

The tension became unbearable. The open door proved that Middleton, or someone – or *something* – had come into that room. Why would Middleton come save to kill? But why in God's name had he not struck already? What was he waiting for?

Saul's nerve snapped suddenly. The darkness was strangling him and those pattering rat-feet were red-hot hammers on his crumbling brain. He must have light, even though that light brought hot lead ripping through him.

In stumbling haste he groped to the mantelpiece, fumbling for the lamp. And he cried out – a choked, horrible croak that could not have carried beyond his room. For his hand, groping in the dark on the mantel, had touched the hair on a human scalp!

A furious squeal sounded in the darkness at his feet and a sharp pain pierced his ankle as the rat attacked him, as if he were an intruder seeking to rob it of some coveted object.

But Saul was hardly aware of the rodent as he kicked it away and reeled back, his brain a whirling turmoil. Matches and candles were on the table, and to it he lurched, his hands sweeping the dark and finding what he wanted.

He lighted a candle and turned, gun lifted in a shaking hand. There was no living man in the room except himself. But his distended eyes focused themselves on the mantelpiece – and the object on it.

He stood frozen, his brain at first refusing to register what his eyes revealed. Then he croaked inhumanly and the gun crashed on the hearth as it slipped through his numb fingers.

John Wilkinson was dead, with a bullet through his heart. It had been three days since Saul had seen his body nailed into the crude coffin and lowered into the grave in the old Wilkinson family graveyard. For three days the hard clay soil had baked in the hot sun above the coffined form of John Wilkinson.

Yet from the mantel John Wilkinson's face leered at him – white and cold and dead.

It was no nightmare, no dream of madness. There on the mantelpiece rested John Wilkinson's severed head.

And before the fireplace, up and down, up and down, scampered a creature with red eyes, that squeaked and squealed – a great grey rat, maddened by its failure to reach the flesh its ghoulish hunger craved.

Saul Wilkinson began to laugh – horrible, soul-shaking shrieks that mingled with the squealing of the grey ghoul. Saul's body rocked to and fro, and the laughter turned to insane weeping, that gave way in turn to hideous screams that echoed through the old house and brought the sleepers out of their sleep.

They were the screams of a madman. The horror of what he had seen had blasted Saul Wilkinson's reason like a blown-out candle flame.

2   Madman's Hate

It was those screams which roused Steve Harrison, sleeping in an upstairs chamber. Before he was fully awake he was on his way down the unlighted stairs, pistol in one hand and flashlight in the other.

Down in the hallway he saw light streaming from under a closed door, and made for it. But another was before him. Just as

Harrison reached the landing, he saw a figure rushing across the hall, and flashed his beam on it.

It was Peter Wilkinson, tall and gaunt, with a poker in his hand. He yelled something incoherent, threw open the door and rushed in.

Harrison heard him exclaim: 'Saul! What's the matter? What are you looking at –' Then a terrible cry: '*My God!*'

The poker clanged on the floor, and then the screams of the maniac rose to a crescendo of fury.

It was at this instant that Harrison reached the door and took in the scene with one startled glance. He saw two men in night-shirts grappling in the candlelight, while from the mantel a cold, dead, white face looked blindly down on them, and a grey rat ran in mad circles about their feet.

Into that scene of horror and madness Harrison propelled his powerful, thick-set body. Peter Wilkinson was in sore straits. He had dropped his poker and now, with blood streaming from a wound in his head, he was vainly striving to tear Saul's lean fingers from his throat.

The glare in Saul's eyes told Harrison the man was mad. Crooking one massive arm about the maniac's neck, he tore him loose from his victim with an exertion of sheer strength that not even the abnormal energy of insanity could resist.

The madman's stringy muscles were like steel wires under the detective's hands, and Saul twisted about in his grasp, his teeth snapping, beastlike, for Harrison's bull-throat. The detective shoved the clawing, frothing fury away from him and smashed a fist to the madman's jaw. Saul crashed to the floor and lay still, eyes glazed and limbs quivering.

Peter reeled back against a table, purple-faced and gagging. 'Get cords, quick!' snapped Harrison, heaving the limp figure off the floor and letting it slump into a great arm-chair. 'Tear that sheet in strips. We've got to tie him up before he comes to. Hell's fire!'

The rat had made a ravening attack on the senseless man's bare feet. Harrison kicked it away, but it squeaked furiously and came charging back with ghoulish persistence. Harrison crushed it under his foot, cutting short its maddened squeal.

Peter, gasping convulsively, thrust into the detective's hands the strips he had torn from the sheet, and Harrison bound the limp limbs with professional efficiency. In the midst of his task he looked up to see Richard, the youngest brother, standing in the doorway, his face like chalk.

'Richard!' choked Peter. 'Look! My God! John's head!'

'I see!' Richard licked his lips. 'But why are you tying up Saul?'

'He's crazy,' snapped Harrison. 'Get me some whisky, will you?'

As Richard reached for a bottle on a curtained shelf, booted feet hit the porch outside, and a voice yelled: 'Hey, there! Dick! What's wrong?'

'That's our neighbor, Jim Allison,' muttered Peter.

He stepped to the door opposite the one that opened into the hall and turned the key in the ancient lock. That door opened upon a side porch, A tousle-headed man with his pants pulled on over his nightshirt came blundering in.

'What's the matter?' he demanded. 'I heard somebody hollerin', and run over quick as I could. What you doin' to Saul – good God Almighty!'

He had seen the head on the mantel, and his face went ashen.

'Go get the marshal, Jim!' croaked Peter. 'This is Joel Middleton's work!'

Allison hurried out, stumbling as he peered back over his shoulder in morbid fascination.

Harrison had managed to spill some liquor between Saul's livid lips. He handed the bottle to Peter and stepped to the mantel. He touched the grisly object, shivering slightly as he did so. His eyes narrowed suddenly.

'You think Middleton dug up your brother's grave and cut off his head?' he asked.

'Who else?' Peter stared blankly at him.

'Saul's mad. Madmen do strange things. Maybe Saul did this.'

'No! No!' exclaimed Peter, shuddering. 'Saul hasn't left the house all day. John's grave was undisturbed this morning, when I stopped by the old graveyard on my way to the farm. Saul was sane when he went to bed. It was seeing John's head that drove him mad. Joel Middleton has been here, to take this horrible revenge!' He sprang up suddenly, shrilling, 'My God, he may still be hiding in the house somewhere!'

'We'll search it,' snapped Harrison. 'Richard, you stay here with Saul. You might come with me, Peter.'

In the hall outside the detective directed a beam of light on the heavy front door. The key was turned in the massive lock. He turned and strode down the hall, asking: 'Which door is farthest from any sleeping-chamber?'

'The back kitchen door!' Peter answered, and led the way. A few moments later they were standing before it. It stood partly open, framing a crack of starlit sky.

'He must have come and gone this way,' muttered Harrison. 'You're sure this door was locked?'

'I locked all outer doors myself,' asserted Peter. 'Look at those scratches on the outer side! And there's the key lying on the floor inside.'

'Old-fashioned lock,' grunted Harrison. 'A man could work the key out with a wire from the outer side and force the lock easily. And this is the logical lock to force, because the noise of breaking it wouldn't likely be heard by anybody in the house.'

He stepped out onto the deep back porch. The broad back yard was without trees or bushes, separated by a barbed-wire fence from a pasture lot, which ran to a wood-lot thickly grown with post-oaks, part of the woods which hemmed in the village of Lost Knob on all sides.

Peter stared toward that woodland, a low, black rampart in the faint starlight, and he shivered.

'He's out there, somewhere!' he whispered. 'I never suspected he'd dare strike at us in our own house. I brought you here to hunt him down. I never thought we'd need you to protect us!'

Without replying, Harrison stepped down into the yard. Peter cringed back from the starlight, and remained crouching at the edge of the porch.

Harrison crossed the narrow pasture and paused at the ancient rail fence which separated it from the woods. They were black as only post-oak thickets can be.

No rustle of leaves, no scrape of branches betrayed a lurking presence. If Joel Middleton had been there, he must have already sought refuge in the rugged hills that surrounded Lost Knob.

Harrison turned back toward the house. He had arrived at Lost Knob late the preceding evening. It was now somewhat past midnight. But the grisly news was spreading, even in the dead of night.

The Wilkinson house stood at the western edge of the town, and the Allison house was the only one within a hundred yards of it. But Harrison saw lights springing up in distant windows.

Peter stood on the porch, head out-thrust on his long, buzzard-like neck.

'Find anything?' he called anxiously.

'Tracks wouldn't show on this hard-baked ground,' grunted the detective. 'Just what did you see when you ran into Saul's room?'

'Saul standing before the mantelboard, screaming with his mouth wide open,' answered Peter. 'When I saw – what he saw, I must have cried out and dropped the poker. Then Saul leaped on me like a wild beast.'

'Was his door locked?'

'Closed, but not locked. The lock got broken accidentally a few days ago.'

'One more question: has Middleton ever been in this house before?'

'Not to my knowledge,' replied Peter grimly. 'Our families have hated each other for twenty-five years. Joel's the last of his name.'

Harrison re-entered the house. Allison had returned with the marshal, McVey, a tall, taciturn man who plainly resented the detective's presence. Men were gathering on the side porch and in the yard. They talked in low mutters, except for Jim Allison, who was vociferous in his indignation.

'This finishes Joel Middleton!' he proclaimed loudly. 'Some folks sided with him when he killed John. I wonder what they think now? Diggin' up a dead man and cuttin' his head off! That's Injun work! I reckon folks won't wait for no jury to tell 'em what to do with Joel Middleton!'

'Better catch him before you start lynchin' him,' grunted McVey. 'Peter, I'm takin' Saul to the county seat.'

Peter nodded mutely. Saul was recovering consciousness, but the mad glaze of his eyes was unaltered. Harrison spoke:

'Suppose we go to the Wilkinson graveyard and see what we can find? We might be able to track Middleton from there.'

'They brought you in here to do the job they didn't think I was good enough to do,' snarled McVey. 'All right. Go ahead and do it – alone. I'm takin' Saul to the county seat.'

With the aid of his deputies he lifted the bound maniac and strode out. Neither Peter nor Richard offered to accompany him. A tall, gangling man stepped from among his fellows and awkwardly addressed Harrison:

'What the marshal does is his own business, but all of us here are ready to help all we can, if you want to git a posse together and comb the country.'

'Thanks, no.' Harrison was unintentionally abrupt. 'You can help me by all clearing out, right now. I'll work this thing out alone, in my own way, as the marshall suggested.'

The men moved off at once, silent and resentful, and Jim Allison followed them, after a moment's hesitation. When all had gone Harrison closed the door and turned to Peter.

'Will you take me to the graveyard?'

Peter shuddered. 'Isn't it a terrible risk? Middleton has shown he'll stop at nothing.'

'Why should he?' Richard laughed savagely. His mouth was bitter, his eyes alive with harsh mockery, and lines of suffering were carven deep in his face.

'We never stopped hounding him,' said he. 'John cheated him out of his last bit of land – that's why Middleton killed him. For which you were devoutly thankful!'

'You're talking wild!' exclaimed Peter.

Richard laughed bitterly. 'You old hypocrite! We're all beasts of prey, we Wilkinsons – like this thing!' He kicked the dead rat viciously. 'We all hated each other. You're glad Saul's crazy! You're glad John's dead. Only me left now, and I have a heart disease. Oh, stare if you like! I'm no fool. I've seen you poring over Aaron's lines in "Titus Andronicus":

> '"Oft have I digg'd up dead men
> 　 from their graves,
> And set them upright at their
> 　 dear friends' doors!"'

'You're mad yourself!' Peter sprang up, livid.

'Oh, am I?' Richard had lashed himself almost into a frenzy. 'What proof have we that you didn't cut off John's head? You knew Saul was a neurotic, that a shock like that might drive him mad! And you visited the graveyard yesterday!'

Peter's contorted face was a mask of fury. Then with an effort of iron control he relaxed and said quietly: 'You are over-wrought, Richard.'

'Saul and John hated you,' snarled Richard. 'I know why. It was because you wouldn't agree to leasing our farm on Wild River to that oil company. But for your stubbornness we might all be wealthy.'

'You know why I wouldn't lease,' snapped Peter. 'Drilling there would ruin the agricultural value of the land – certain profit, not a risky gamble like oil.'

'So you say,' sneered Richard. 'But suppose that's just a smoke screen? Suppose you dream of being the sole, surviving heir, and becoming an oil millionaire all by yourself, with no brothers to share –'

Harrison broke in: 'Are we going to chew the rag all night?'

'No!' Peter turned his back on his brother. 'I'll take you to the graveyard. I'd rather face Joel Middleton in the night than listen to the ravings of this lunatic any longer.'

'I'm not going,' snarled Richard. 'Out there in the black night there's too many chances for you to remove the remaining heir. I'll go and stay the rest of the night with Jim Allison.'

He opened the door and vanished in the darkness.

Peter picked up the head and wrapped it in a cloth, shivering slightly as he did so.

'Did you notice how well preserved the face is?' he muttered. 'One would think that after three days – Come on. I'll take it and put it back in the grave where it belongs.'

'I'll kick this dead rat outdoors,' Harrison began, turning – and then stopped short. 'The damned thing's gone!'

Peter Wilkinson paled as his eyes swept the empty floor.

'It was there!' he whispered. 'It was dead. You smashed it! It couldn't come to life and run away.'

'Well, what about it?' Harrison did not mean to waste time on this minor mystery.

Peter's eyes gleamed wearily in the candlelight.

'It was a graveyard rat!' he whispered. 'I never saw one in an inhabited house, in town, before! The Indians used to tell strange tales about them! They said they were not beasts at all, but evil, cannibal demons, into which entered the spirits of wicked, dead men at whose corpses they gnawed!'

'Hell's fire!' Harrison snorted, blowing out the candle. But his flesh crawled. After all, a dead rat could not crawl away of itself.

3   The Feathered Shadow

Clouds had rolled across the stars. The air was hot and stifling. The narrow, rutty road that wound westward into the hills was atrocious. But Peter Wilkinson piloted his ancient Model T Ford skillfully, and the village was quickly lost to sight behind them. They passed no more houses. On each side the dense post-oak thickets crowded close to the barbed-wire fences.

Peter broke the silence suddenly:

'How did that rat come into our house? They overrun the woods along the creeks, and swarm in every country graveyard in the hills. But I never saw one in the village before. It must have followed Joel Middleton when he brought the head –'

A lurch and a monotonous bumping brought a curse from Harrison. The car came to a stop with a grind of brakes.

'Flat,' muttered Peter. 'Won't take me long to change tires. You watch the woods. Joel Middleton might be hiding anywhere.'

That seemed good advice. While Peter wrestled with rusty metal and stubborn rubber, Harrison stood between him and the nearest clump of trees, with his hand on his revolver. The night wind blew fitfully through the leaves, and once he thought he caught the gleam of tiny eyes among the stems.

'That's got it,' announced Peter at last, turning to let down the jack. 'We've wasted enough time.'

'*Listen!*' Harrison started, tensed. Off to the west had sounded a sudden scream of pain or fear. Then there came the impact of racing feet on the hard ground, the crackling of brush, as if someone fled blindly through the bushes within a few hundred yards of the road. In an instant Harrison was over the fence and running toward the sounds.

'Help! Help!' It was the voice of dire terror. 'Almighty God! Help!'

'This way!' yelled Harrison, bursting into an open flat. The unseen fugitive evidently altered his course in response, for the heavy footfalls grew louder, and then there rang out a terrible shriek, and a figure staggered from the bushes on the opposite side of the glade and fell headlong.

The dim starlight showed a vague writhing shape, with a darker figure on its back. Harrison caught the glint of steel, heard the sound of a blow. He threw up his gun and fired at a venture. At the crack of the shot the darker figure rolled free, leaped up and vanished in the bushes. Harrison ran on, a queer chill crawling along his spine because of what he had seen in the flash of the shot.

He crouched at the edge of the bushes and peered into them. The shadowy figure had come and gone, leaving no trace except the man who lay groaning in the glade.

Harrison bent over him, snapping on his flashlight. He was an old man, a wild, unkempt figure with matted white hair and beard. That beard was stained with red now, and blood oozed from a deep stab in his back.

'Who did this?' demanded Harrison, seeing that it was useless to try to stanch the flow of blood. The old man was dying. 'Joel Middleton?'

'It couldn't have been!' Peter had followed the detective. 'That's old Joash Sullivan, a friend of Joel's. He's half crazy, but I've suspected that he's been keeping in touch with Joel and giving him tips –'

'Joel Middleton,' muttered the old man. 'I'd been to find him, to tell the news about John's head –'

'Where's Joel hiding?' demanded the detective.

Sullivan choked on a flow of blood, spat and shook his head.

'You'll never learn from me!' He directed his eyes on Peter with the eery glare of the dying. 'Are you taking your brother's head back to his grave, Peter Wilkinson? Be careful you don't find your own grave before this night's done! Evil on all your name! The devil owns your souls and the graveyard rats'll eat your flesh! The ghost of the dead walks the night!'

'What do you mean?' demanded Harrison. 'Who stabbed you?'

'A dead man!' Sullivan was going fast. 'As I come back from meetin' Joel Middleton I met him. Wolf Hunter, the Tonkawa chief your grandpap murdered so long ago, Peter Wilkinson! He chased me and knifed me. I saw him plain, in the starlight – naked in his loin-clout and feathers and paint, just as I saw him when I was a child, before your grandpap killed him!

'Wolf Hunter took your brother's head from the grave!' Sullivan's voice was a ghastly whisper. 'He's come back from hell to fulfill the curse he laid onto your grandpap when your grandpap shot him in the back, to get the land his tribe claimed. Beware! His ghost walks the night! The graveyard rats are his servants. The graveyard rats –'

Blood burst from his white-bearded lips and he sank back, dead.

Harrison rose somberly.

'Let him lie. We'll pick up his body as we go back to town. We're going on to the graveyard.'

'Dare we?' Peter's face was white. 'A human I do not fear, not even Joel Middleton, but a ghost –'

'Don't be a fool!' snorted Harrison. 'Didn't you say the old man was half crazy?'

'But what if Joel Middleton is hiding somewhere near –'

'I'll take care of him!' Harrison had an invincible confidence in his own fighting ability. What he did not tell Peter, as they returned to the car, was that he had had a glimpse of the slayer in the flash of his shot. The memory of that glimpse still had the short hair prickling at the base of his skull.

That figure had been naked but for a loin-cloth and moccasins and a headdress of feathers.

'Who was Wolf Hunter?' he demanded as they drove on.

'A Tonkawa chief,' muttered Peter. 'He befriended my grandfather and was later murdered by him, just as Joash said. They say his bones lie in the old graveyard to this day.'

Peter lapsed into silence, seemingly a prey of morbid broodings.

Some four miles from town the road wound past a dim clearing. That was the Wilkinson graveyard. A rusty barbed-wire fence surrounded a cluster of graves whose white headstones leaned at crazy angles. Weeds grew thick, straggling over the low mounds.

The post oaks crowded close on all sides, and the road wound through them, past the sagging gate. Across the tops of the trees, nearly half a mile to the west, there was visible a shapeless bulk which Harrison knew was the roof of a house.

'The old Wilkinson farmhouse,' Peter answered in reply to his question. 'I was born there, and so were my brothers. Nobody's lived in it since we moved to town, ten years ago.'

Peter's nerves were taut. He glanced fearfully at the black woods around him, and his hands trembled as he lighted a lantern he took from the car. He winced as he picked up the round cloth-wrapped object that lay on the back seat; perhaps he was visualizing the cold, white, stony face that cloth concealed.

As he climbed over the low gate and led the way between the weed-grown mounds he muttered: 'We're fools. If Joel Middleton's laying out there in the woods he could pick us both off easy as shooting rabbits.'

Harrison did not reply, and a moment later Peter halted and

shone the light on a mound which was bare of weeds. The surface was tumbled and disturbed, and Peter exclaimed: 'Look! I expected to find an open grave. Why do you suppose he took the trouble of filling it again?'

'We'll see,' grunted Harrison. 'Are you game to open that grave?'

'I've seen my brother's head,' answered Peter grimly. 'I think I'm man enough to look on his headless body without fainting. There are tools in the tool-shed in the corner of the fence. I'll get them.'

Returning presently with pick and shovel, he set the lighted lantern on the ground, and the cloth-wrapped head near it. Peter was pale, and sweat stood on his brow in thick drops. The lantern cast their shadows, grotesquely distorted, across the weed-grown graves. The air was oppressive. There was an occasional dull flicker of lightning along the dusky horizons.

'What's that?' Harrison paused, pick lifted. All about them sounded rustlings and scurryings among the weeds. Beyond the circle of lantern light clusters of tiny red beads glittered at him.

'Rats!' Peter hurled a stone and the beads vanished, though the rustlings grew louder. 'They swarm in this graveyard. I believe they'd devour a living man, if they caught him helpless. Begone, you servants of Satan!'

Harrison took the shovel and began scooping out mounds of loose dirt.

'Ought not to be hard work,' he grunted. 'If he dug it out today or early tonight, it'll be loose all the way down –'

He stopped short, with his shovel jammed hard against the dirt, and a prickling in the short hairs at the nape of his neck. In the tense silence he heard the graveyard rats running through the grass.

'What's the matter?' A new pallor grayed Peter's face.

'I've hit solid ground,' said Harrison slowly. 'In three days this clayey soil bakes hard as a rick. But if Middleton or anybody else had opened this grave and refilled it today, the soil would be loose all the way down. It's not. Below the first few inches it's packed and baked hard! The top has been scratched, but the grave has never been opened since it was first filled, three days ago!'

Peter staggered with an inhuman cry.

'Then it's true!' he screamed. 'Wolf Hunter *has* come back! He reached up from hell and took John's head without opening the grave! He sent his familiar devil into our house in the form of a rat! A ghost-rat that could not be killed! Hands off, curse you!'

For Harrison caught at him, growling: 'Pull yourself together, Peter!'

But Peter struck his arm aside and tore free. He turned and ran – not toward the car parked outside the graveyard, but toward the opposite fence. He scrambled across the rusty wires with a ripping of cloth and vanished in the woods, heedless of Harrison's shouts.

'Hell!' Harrison pulled up, and swore fervently. Where but in the black-hill country could such things happen? Angrily he picked up the tools and tore into the close-packed clay, baked by a blazing sun into almost iron hardness.

Sweat rolled from him in streams, and he grunted and swore, but persevered with all the power of his massive muscles. He meant to prove or disprove a suspicion growing in his mind – a suspicion that the body of John Wilkinson had never been placed in that grave.

The lightning flashed oftener and closer, and a low mutter of thunder began in the west. An occasional gust of wind made the lantern flicker, and as the mound beside the grave grew higher, and the man digging there sank lower and lower in the earth, the rustling in the grass grew louder and the red beads began to glint in the weeds. Harrison heard the eery gnashings of tiny teeth all about him, and swore at the memory of grisly legends, whispered by the Negroes of his boyhood region about the graveyard rats.

The grave was not deep. No Wilkinson would waste much labor on the dead. At last the rude coffin lay uncovered before him. With the point of the pick he pried up one corner of the lid, and held the lantern close. A startled oath escaped his lips. The coffin was not empty. It held a huddled, headless figure.

Harrison climbed out of the grave, his mind racing, fitting together pieces of the puzzle. The stray bits snapped into place, forming a pattern, dim and yet uncomplete, but taking shape. He looked for the cloth-wrapped head, and got a frightful shock.

The head was gone!

For an instant Harrison felt cold sweat clammy on his hands. Then he heard a clamorous squeaking, the gnashing of tiny fangs.

He caught up the lantern and shone the light about. In its reflection he saw a white blotch on the grass near a straggling clump of bushes that had invaded the clearing. It was the cloth in which the head had been wrapped. Beyond that a black, squirming mound heaved and tumbled with nauseous life.

With an oath of horror he leaped forward, striking and kicking. The graveyard rats abandoned the head with rasping squeaks, scattering before him like darting black shadows. And Harrison shuddered. It was no face that stared up at him in the lantern light, but a white, grinning skull, to which clung only shreds of gnawed flesh.

While the detective burrowed into John Wilkinson's grave, the graveyard rats had torn the flesh from John Wilkinson's head.

Harrison stooped and picked up the hideous thing, now triply hideous. He wrapped it in the cloth, and as he straightened, something like fright took hold of him.

He was ringed in on all sides by a solid circle of gleaming red sparks that shone from the grass. Held back by their fear, the graveyard rats surrounded him, squealing their hate.

Demons, the Negroes called them, and in that moment Harrison was ready to agree.

They gave back before him as he turned toward the grave, and he did not see the dark figure that slunk from the bushes behind him. The thunder boomed out, drowning even the squeaking of the rats, but he heard the swift footfall behind him an instant before the blow was struck.

He whirled, drawing his gun, dropping the head, but just as he whirled, something like a louder clap of thunder exploded in his head, with a shower of sparks before his eyes.

As he reeled backward he fired blindly, and cried out as the flash showed him a horrific, half-naked, painted, feathered figure, crouching with a tomahawk uplifted – the open grave was behind Harrison as he fell.

Down into the grave he toppled, and his head struck the edge of the coffin with a sickening impact. His powerful body went limp; and like darting shadows, from every side raced the graveyard rats, hurling themselves into the grave in a frenzy of hunger and blood-lust.

4   Rats in Hell

It seemed to Harrison's stunned brain that he lay in blackness on the darkened floors of hell, a blackness lit by darts of flame from the eternal fires. The triumphant shrieking of demons was in his ears as they stabbed him with red-hot skewers.

He saw them, now – dancing monstrosities with pointed noses, twitching ears, red eyes and gleaming teeth – a sharp pain knifed through his flesh.

And suddenly the mists cleared. He lay, not on the floor of

hell, but on a coffin in the bottom of a grave; the fires were lightning flashes from the black sky; and the demons were rats that swarmed over him, slashing with razor-sharp teeth.

Harrison yelled and heaved convulsively, and at his movement the rats gave back in alarm. But they did not leave the grave; they massed solidly along the walls, their eyes glittering redly.

Harrison knew he could have been senseless only a few seconds. Otherwise these gray ghouls would have already stripped the living flesh from his bones – as they had ripped the dead flesh from the head of the man on whose coffin he lay.

Already his body was stinging in a score of places, and his clothing was damp with his own blood.

Cursing, he started to rise – and a chill of panic shot through him! Falling, his left arm had been jammed into the partly-open coffin, and the weight of his body on the lid clamped his hand fast. Harrison fought down a mad wave of terror.

He would not withdraw his hand unless he could lift his body from the coffin lid – and the imprisonment of his hand held him prostrate there.

Trapped!

In a murdered man's grave, his hand locked in the coffin of a headless corpse, with a thousand gray ghoul-rats ready to tear the flesh from his living frame!

As if sensing his helplessness, the rats swarmed upon him. Harrison fought for his life, like a man in a nightmare. He kicked, he yelled, he cursed, he smote them with the heavy six-shooter he still clutched in his hand.

Their fangs tore at him, ripping cloth and flesh, their acrid scent nauseated him; they almost covered him with their squirming, writhing bodies. He beat them back, smashed and crushed them with blows of his six-shooter barrel.

The living cannibals fell on their dead brothers. In desperation he twisted half over and jammed the muzzle of his gun against the coffin lid.

At the flash of fire and the deafening report, the rats scurried in all directions.

Again and again he pulled the trigger until the gun was empty. The heavy slugs crashed through the lid, splitting off a great sliver from the edge. Harrison drew his bruised hand from the aperture.

Gagging and shaking, he clambered out of the grave and rose groggily to his feet. Blood was clotted in his hair from the gash the ghostly hatchet had made in his scalp, and blood trickled from a score of tooth-wounds in his flesh. Lightning played constantly, but the lantern was still shining. But it was not on the ground.

It seemed to be suspended in midair – and then he was aware that it was held in the hand of a man – a tall man in a black slicker, whose eyes burned dangerously under his broad hat-brim. In his other hand a black pistol muzzle menaced the detective's midriff.

'You must be that damn' low-country law Pete Wilkinson brung up here to run me down!' growled this man.

'Then you're Joel Middleton!' grunted Harrison.

'Sure I am!' snarled the outlaw. 'Where's Pete, the old devil?'

'He got scared and ran off.'

'Crazy, like Saul, maybe,' sneered Middleton. 'Well, you tell him I been savin' a slug for his ugly mug a long time. And one for Dick, too.'

'Why did you come here?' demanded Harrison.

'I heard shootin'. I got here just as you was climbin' out of the grave. What's the matter with you? Who was it that broke your head?'

'I don't know his name,' answered Harrison, caressing his aching head.

'Well, it don't make no difference to me. But I want to tell you that I didn't cut John's head off. I killed him because he needed it.' The outlaw swore and spat. 'But I didn't do that other!'

'I know you didn't,' Harrison answered.

'Eh?' The outlaw was obviously startled.

'Do you know which rooms the Wilkinsons sleep in, in their house in town?'

'Naw,' snorted Middleton. 'Never was in their house in my life.'

'I thought not. Whoever put John's head on Saul's mantel knew. The back kitchen door was the only one where the lock could have been forced without waking somebody up. The lock on Saul's door was broken. You couldn't have known those things. It looked like an inside job from the start. The lock was forced to make it look like an outside job.

'Richard spilled some stuff that cinched my belief that it was Peter. I decided to bring him out to the graveyard and see if his nerve would stand up under an accusation across his brother's open coffin. But I hit hard-packed soil and knew the grave hadn't been opened. It gave me a turn and I blurted out what I'd found. But it's simple, after all.

'Peter wanted to get rid of his brothers. When you killed John, that suggested a way to dispose of Saul. John's body stood in its coffin in the Wilkinsons' parlor until it was placed in the grave the next day. No death watch was kept. It was easy for Peter to go into the parlor while his brothers slept, pry up the coffin lid and cut off John's head. He put it on ice somewhere to preserve it. When I touched it I found it was nearly frozen.

'No one knew what had happened, because the coffin was not opened again. John was an atheist, and there was the briefest sort of ceremony. The coffin was not opened for his friends to take a last look, as is the usual custom. Then tonight the head was placed in Saul's room. It drove him raving mad.

'I don't know why Peter waited until tonight, or why he called me into the case. He must be partly insane himself. I don't think he meant to kill me when we drove out here tonight. But when he discovered I knew the grave hadn't been opened tonight, he saw the game was up. I ought to have been smart enough to keep my mouth shut, but I was so sure that Peter had opened the grave to get the head, that when I found it *hadn't* been opened, I spoke involuntarily, without stopping to think of the other alternative. Peter pretended a panic and ran off. Later he sent back his partner to kill me.'

'Who's he?' demanded Middleton.

'How should I know? Some fellow who looks like an Indian!'

'That old yarn about a Tonkawa ghost has went to your brain!' scoffed Middleton.

'I didn't say it was a ghost,' said Harrison, nettled. 'It was real enough to kill your friend Joash Sullivan!'

'What?' yelled Middleton. 'Joash killed? Who done it?'

'The Tonkawa ghost, whoever he is. The body is lying about a mile back, beside the road, amongst the thickets, if you don't believe me.'

Middleton ripped out a terrible oath.

'By God, I'll kill somebody for that! Stay where you are! I ain't goin' to shoot no unarmed man, but if you try to run me down I'll kill you sure as hell. So keep off my trail I'm goin', and don't you try to follow me!'

The next instant Middleton had dashed the lantern to the ground where it went out with a clatter of breaking glass.

Harrison blinked in the sudden darkness that followed, and the next lightning flash showed him standing alone in the ancient graveyard.

The outlaw was gone.

5 The Rats Eat

Cursing, Harrison groped on the ground, lit by the lightning flashes. He found the broken lantern, and he found something else.

Rain drops splashed against his face as he started toward the gate. One instant he stumbled in velvet blackness, the next the tombstones shone white in the dazzling glare. Harrison's head ached frightfully. Only chance and a tough skull had saved his life. The would-be killer must have thought the blow was fatal and fled, taking John Wilkinson's head for what grisly purpose there was no knowing. But the head was gone.

Harrison winced at the thought of the rain filling the open grave, but he had neither the strength nor the inclination to shovel the dirt back in it. To remain in that dark graveyard might well be death. The slayer might return.

Harrison looked back as he climbed the fence. The rain had disturbed the rats; the weeds were alive with scampering, flame-eyed shadows. With a shudder Harrison made his way to the flivver. He climbed in, found his flashlight and reloaded his revolver.

The rain grew in volume. Soon the rutty road to Lost Knob would be a welter of mud. In his condition he did not feel able to the task of driving back through the storm over that abominable road. But it could not be long until dawn. The old farmhouse would afford him a refuge until daylight.

The rain came down in sheets, soaking him, dimming the already uncertain lights as he drove along the road, splashing noisily through the mud-puddles. Wind ripped through the post-oaks. Once he grunted and batted his eyes. He could have sworn that a flash of lightning had fleetingly revealed a painted, naked, feathered figure gliding among the trees!

The road wound up a thickly wooded eminence, rising close to the bank of a muddy creek. On the summit the old house squatted. Weeds and low bushes straggled from the surrounding woods up to the sagging porch. He parked the car as close to the house as he could get it, and climbed out, struggling with the wind and rain.

He expected to have to blow the lock off the door with his

gun, but it opened under his fingers. He stumbled into a musty-smelling room, weirdly lit by the flickering of the lightning through the cracks of the shutters.

His flashlight revealed a rude bunk built against a side wall, a heavy hand-hewn table, a heap of rags in a corner. From this pile of rags black furtive shadows darted in all directions.

Rats! Rats again!

Could he never escape them?

He closed the door and lit the lantern, placing it on the table. The broken chimney caused the flame to dance and flicker, but not enough wind found its way into the room to blow it out. Three doors, leading into the interior of the house, were closed. The floor and walls were pitted with holes gnawed by the rats.

Tiny red eyes glared at him from the apertures.

Harrison sat down on the bunk, flashlight and pistol on his lap. He expected to fight for his life before day broke. Peter Wilkinson was out there in the storm somewhere, with a heart full of murder, and either allied to him or working separately – in either case an enemy to the detective – was that mysterious painted figure.

And that figure was Death, whether living masquerader or Indian ghost. In any event, the shutters would protect him from a shot from the dark, and to get at him his enemies would have to come into the lighted room where he would have an even chance – which was all the big detective had ever asked.

To get his mind off the ghoulish red eyes glaring at him from the floor, Harrison brought out the object he had found lying near the broken lantern, where the slayer must have dropped it.

It was a smooth oval of flint, made fast to a handle with rawhide thongs – the Indian tomahawk of an elder generation. And Harrison's eyes narrowed suddenly; there was blood on the flint, and some of it was his own. But on the other point of the oval there was more blood, dark and crusted, with strands of hair lighter than his, clinging to the clotted point.

Joash Sullivan's blood? No. The old man had been knifed. But some one else had died that night. The darkness had hidden another grim deed . . .

Black shadows were stealing across the floor. The rats were coming back – ghoulish shapes, creeping from their holes, converging on the heap of rags in the far corner – a tattered carpet, Harrison now saw, rolled in a long compact heap. Why should the rats leap upon that rag? Why should they race up and down along it, squealing and biting at the fabric?

There was something hideously suggestive about its contour – a shape that grew more definite and ghastly as he looked.

The rats scattered, squeaking, as Harrison sprang across the room. He tore away the carpet – and looked down on the corpse of Peter Wilkinson.

The back of the head had been crushed. The white face was twisted in a leer of awful terror.

For an instant Harrison's brain reeled with the ghastly possibilities his discovery summoned up. Then he took a firm grasp on himself, fought off the whispering potency of the dark, howling night, the thrashing wet black woods and the abysmal aura of the ancient hills, and recognized the only sane solution of the riddle.

Somberly he looked down on the dead man. Peter Wilkinson's fright had been genuine, after all. In his blind panic he had reverted to the habits of his boyhood and fled toward his old home – and met death instead of security.

Harrison started convulsively as a weird sound smote his ears above the roar of the storm – the wailing horror of an Indian war-whoop. The killer was upon him!

Harrison sprang to a shuttered window, peered through a crack, waiting for a flash of lightning. When it came he fired through the window at a feathered head he saw peering around a tree close to the car.

In the darkness that followed the flash he crouched, waiting

– there came another white glare – he grunted explosively but did not fire. The head was still there, and he got a better look at it. The lightning shone weirdly white upon it.

It was John Wilkinson's fleshless skull, clad in a feathered headdress and bound in place – and it was the bait of a trap.

Harrison wheeled and sprang toward the lantern on the table. That grisly ruse had been to draw his attention to the front of the house while the killer slunk upon him through the rear of the building! The rats squealed and scattered. Even as Harrison whirled an inner door began to open. He smashed a heavy slug through the panels, heard a groan and the sound of a falling body, and then, just as he reached a hand to extinguish the lantern, the world crashed over his head.

A blinding burst of lightning, a deafening clap of thunder, and the ancient house staggered from gables to foundations! Blue fire crackled from the ceiling and ran down the walls and over the floor. One livid tongue just flicked the detective's shin in passing.

It was like the impact of a sledge-hammer. There was an instant of blindness and numb agony, and Harrison found himself sprawling, half-stunned on the floor. The lantern lay extinguished beside the over-turned table, but the room was filled with a lurid light.

He realized that a bolt of lightning had struck the house, and that the upper story was ablaze. He hauled himself to his feet, looking for his gun. It lay half-way across the room, and as he started toward it, the bullet-split door swung open. Harrison stopped dead in his tracks.

Through the door limped a man naked but for a loin-clout and moccasins on his feet. A revolver in his hand menaced the detective. Blood oozing from a wound in his thigh mingled with the paint with which he had smeared himself.

'So it was you who wanted to be the oil millionaire, Richard!' said Harrison.

The other laughed savagely. 'Aye, and I will be! And no cursed brothers to share with – brothers I always hated, damn them! Don't move! You nearly got me when you shot through the door. I'm taking no chances with you! Before I send you to hell I'll tell you everything.

'As soon as you and Peter started for the graveyard, I realized my mistake in merely scratching the top of the grave – knew you'd hit hard clay and know the grave hadn't been opened. I knew then I'd have to kill you, as well as Peter. I took the rat you mashed when neither of you were looking, so its disappearance would play on Peter's superstitions.

'I rode to the graveyard through the woods, on a fast horse. The Indian disguise was one I thought up long ago. What with that rotten road, and the flat that delayed you, I got to the grave-yard before you and Peter did. On the way, though, I dismounted and stopped to kill that old fool Joash Sullivan. I was afraid he might see and recognize me.

'I was watching when you dug into the grave. When Peter got panicky and ran through the woods I chased him, killed him, and brought his body here to the old house. Then I went back after you. I intended bringing your body here, or rather your bones, after the rats finished you, as I thought they would. Then I heard Joel Middleton coming and had to run for it – I don't care to meet that gun-fighting devil anywhere!

'I was going to burn this house with both your bodies in it. People would think, when they found the bones in the ashes, that Middleton killed you both and burnt the house! And now you play right into my hands by coming here! Lightning has struck the house and it's burning! Oh, the gods fight for me tonight!'

A light of unholy madness played in Richard's eyes, but the pistol muzzle was steady, as Harrison stood clenching his great fists helplessly.

'You'll lie here with that fool Peter!' raved Richard. 'With a bullet through your head, until your bones are burnt to such a crisp that nobody can tell how you died! Joel Middleton will be shot down by some posse without a chance to talk. Saul will rave out his days in a madhouse! And I, who will be safely sleeping in my house in town before sun-up, will live out my allotted years in wealth and honor, never suspected – never –'

He was sighting along the black barrel, eyes blazing, teeth bared like the fangs of a wolf between painted lips – his finger was curling on the trigger.

Harrison crouched tensely, desperately, poising to hurl himself with bare hands at the killer and try to pit his naked strength against hot lead spitting from that black muzzle – then –

The door crashed inward behind him and the lurid glare framed a tall figure in a dripping slicker.

An incoherent yell rang to the roof and the gun in the outlaw's hand roared. Again, and again, and yet again it crashed, filling the room with smoke and thunder, and the painted figure jerked to the impact of the tearing lead.

Through the smoke Harrison saw Richard Wilkinson toppling – but he too was firing as he fell. Flames burst through the ceiling, and by their brighter glare Harrison saw a painted figure writhing on the floor, a taller figure wavering in the doorway. Richard was screaming in agony.

Middleton threw his empty gun at Harrison's feet.

'Heard the shootin' and come,' he croaked. 'Reckon that settles the feud for good!' He toppled, and Harrison caught him in his arms, a lifeless weight.

Richard's screams rose to an unbearable pitch. The rats were swarming from their holes. Blood streaming across the floor had dripped into their holes, maddening them. Now they burst forth in a ravening horde that heeded not cries, or movement, or the devouring flames, but only their own fiendish hunger.

In a gray-black wave they swept over the dead man and the dying man. Peter's white face vanished under that wave. Richard's screaming grew thick and muffled. He writhed, half covered by gray, tearing figures who sucked at his gushing blood, tore at his flesh.

Harrison retreated through the door, carrying the dead outlaw. Joel Middleton, outlaw and killer, yet deserved a better fate than was befalling his slayer.

To save that ghoul, Harrison would not have lifted a finger, had it been in his power.

It was not. The graveyard rats had claimed their own. Out in the yard, Harrison let his burden fall limply. Above the roar of the flames still rose those awful, smothered cries.

Through the blazing doorway he had a glimpse of a horror, a gory figure rearing upright, swaying, enveloped by a hundred clinging, tearing shapes. He glimpsed a face that was not a face at all, but a blind, bloody skull-mask. Then the awful scene was blotted out as the flaming roof fell with a thundering, ear-rending crash.

Sparks showered against the sky, the flames rose as the walls fell in, and Harrison staggered away, dragging the dead man, as a storm-wrapped dawn came haggardly over the oak-clad ridges.

Vultures of Wahpeton

1 Guns in the Dark

The bare plank walls of the Golden Eagle Saloon seemed still to vibrate with the crashing echoes of the guns which had split the sudden darkness with spurts of red. But only a nervous shuffling of booted feet sounded in the tense silence that followed the shots. Then somewhere a match rasped on leather and a yellow flicker sprang up, etching a shaky hand and a pallid face. An instant later an oil lamp with a broken chimney illuminated the saloon, throwing tense bearded faces into bold relief. The big lamp that hung from the ceiling was a smashed ruin; kerosene dripped from it to the floor, making an oily puddle beside a grimmer, darker pool.

Two figures held the center of the room, under the broken lamp. One lay face-down, motionless arms outstretching empty hands. The other was crawling to his feet, blinking and gaping stupidly, like a man whose wits are still muddled by drink. His right arm hung limply by his side, a long-barreled pistol sagging from his fingers.

The rigid line of figures along the bar melted into movement. Men came forward, stooping to stare down at the limp shape. A confused babble of conversation rose. Hurried steps sounded outside, and the crowd divided as a man pushed his way abruptly through. Instantly he dominated the scene. His broad-shouldered, trim-hipped figure was above medium height, and his broad-brimmed white hat, neat boots and cravat contrasted with the rough garb of the others, just as his keen, dark face with its narrow black mustache contrasted with the bearded countenances about him. He held an ivory-butted gun in his right hand, muzzle tilted upward.

'What devil's work is this?' he harshly demanded; and then his gaze fell on the man on the floor. His eyes widened.

'Grimes!' he ejaculated. 'Jim Grimes, my deputy! Who did this?' There was something tigerish about him as he wheeled toward the uneasy crowd. 'Who did this?' he demanded, half crouching, his gun still lifted, but seeming to hover like a live thing ready to swoop.

Feet shuffled as men backed away, but one man spoke up: 'We don't know, Middleton. Jackson there was havin' a little fun, shootin' at the ceilin', and the rest of us was at the bar, watchin' him, when Grimes come in and started to arrest him –'

'So Jackson shot him!' snarled Middleton, his gun covering the befuddled one in a baffling blur of motion. Jackson yelped in fear and threw up his hands, and the man who had first spoken interposed.

'No, Sheriff, it couldn't have been Jackson. His gun was empty when the lights went out. I know he slung six bullets into the ceilin' while he was playin' the fool, and I heard him snap the gun three times afterwards, so I know it was empty. But when Grimes went up to him, somebody shot the light out, and a gun banged in the dark, and when we got a light on again, there Grimes was on the floor, and Jackson was just gettin' up.'

'I didn't shoot him,' muttered Jackson. 'I was just havin' a little fun. I was drunk, but I ain't now. I wouldn't have resisted arrest. When the light went out I didn't know what had happened. I heard the gun bang, and Grimes dragged me down with him as he fell. I didn't shoot him. I dunno who did.'

'None of us knows,' added a bearded miner. 'Somebody shot in the dark –'

'More'n one,' muttered another, 'I heard at least three or four guns speakin'.'

Silence followed, in which each man looked sidewise at his neighbor. The men had drawn back to the bar, leaving the middle of the big room clear, where the sheriff stood. Suspicion and fear galvanized the crowd, leaping like an electric spark from man to man. Each man knew that a murderer stood near him, possibly at his elbow. Men refused to look directly into the eyes of their neighbors, fearing to surprise guilty knowledge there – and die for the discovery. They stared at the sheriff who stood facing them, as if expecting to see him fall suddenly before a blast from the same unknown guns that had mowed down his deputy.

Middleton's steely eyes ranged along the silent line of men. Their eyes avoided or gave back his stare. In some he read fear; some were inscrutable; in others flickered a sinister mockery.

'The men who killed Jim Grimes are in this saloon,' he said finally. 'Some of you are the murderers.' He was careful not to let his eyes single out anyone when he spoke; they swept the whole assemblage.

'I've been expecting this. Things have been getting a little too hot for the robbers and murderers who have been terrorizing this camp, so they've started shooting my deputies in the back. I suppose you'll try to kill me, next. Well, I want to tell you sneaking rats, whoever you are, that I'm ready for you, any time.'

He fell silent, his rangy frame tense, his eyes burning with watchful alertness. None moved. The men along the bar might have been figures cut from stone.

He relaxed and shoved his gun into its scabbard; a sneer twisted his lips.

'I know your breed. You won't shoot a man unless his back is toward you. Forty men have been murdered in the vicinity of this camp within the last year, and not one had a chance to defend himself.

'Maybe this killing is an ultimatum to me. All right; I've got an answer ready: I've got a new deputy, and you won't find him so easy as Grimes. I'm fighting fire with fire from here on. I'm riding out of the Gulch early in the morning, and when I come back, I'll have a man with me. A gunfighter from Texas!'

He paused to let this information sink in, and laughed grimly at the furtive glances that darted from man to man.

'You'll find him no lamb,' he predicted vindictively. 'He was too wild for the country where gun-throwing was invented. What he did down there is none of my business. What he'll do here is what counts. And all I ask is that the men who murdered Grimes here, try that same trick on this Texan.

'Another thing, on my own account. I'm meeting this man at Ogalala Spring tomorrow morning. I'll be riding out alone, at dawn. If anybody wants to try to waylay me, let him make his plans now! I'll follow the open trail, and anyone who has any business with me will find me ready.'

And turning his trimly-tailored back scornfully on the throng at the bar, the sheriff of Wahpeton strode from the saloon.

Ten miles east of Wahpeton a man squatted on his heels, frying strips of deer meat over a tiny fire. The sun was just coming up. A short distance away a rangy mustang nibbled at the wiry grass that grew sparsely between broken rocks. The man had camped there that night, but his saddle and blanket were hidden back in the bushes. That fact showed him to be a man of wary nature. No one following the trail that led past Ogalala Spring could have seen him as he slept among the bushes. Now, in full daylight, he was making no attempt to conceal his presence.

The man was tall, broad-shouldered, deep-chested, lean-hipped, like one who had spent his life in the saddle. His unruly black hair matched a face burned dark by the sun, but his eyes were a burning blue. Low on either hip the black butt of a heavy Colt jutted from a worn black leather scabbard. These guns seemed as much part of the man as his eyes or his hands. He had worn them so constantly and so long that their association was as natural as the use of his limbs.

As he fried his meat and watched his coffee boiling in a battered old pot, his gaze darted continually eastward where the trail crossed a wide open space before it vanished among the thickets of a broken hill country. Westward the trail mounted a gentle slope and quickly disappeared among trees and bushes that crowded up within a few yards of the spring. But it was always eastward that the man looked.

When a rider emerged from the thickets to the east, the man at the spring set aside the skillet with its sizzling meat strips, and picked up his rifle – a long range Sharps .50. His eyes narrowed with satisfaction. He did not rise, but remained on one knee, the rifle resting negligently in his hands, the muzzle tilted upward, not aimed.

The rider came straight on, and the man at the spring watched him from under the brim of his hat. Only when the stranger pulled up a few yards away did the first man lift his head and give the other a full view of his face.

The horseman was a supple youth of medium height, and his hat did not conceal the fact that his hair was yellow and curly. His wide eyes were ingenuous, and an infectious smile curved his lips. There was no rifle under his knee, but an ivory-butted .45 hung low at his right hip.

His expression as he saw the other man's face gave no hint to his reaction, except for a slight, momentary contraction of the muscles that control the eyes – a movement involuntary and all but uncontrollable. Then he grinned broadly, and hailed:

'That meat smells prime, stranger!'

'Light and help me with it,' invited the other instantly. 'Coffee, too, if you don't mind drinkin' out of the pot.'

He laid aside the rifle as the other swung from his saddle. The blond youngster threw his reins over the horse's head, fumbled in his blanket roll and drew out a battered tin cup. Holding this

in his right hand he approached the fire with the rolling gait of
a man born to a horse.

'I ain't et my breakfast,' he admitted. 'Camped down the trail
a piece last night, and come on up here early to meet a man.
Thought you was the *hombre* till you looked up. Kinda startled
me,' he added frankly. He sat down opposite the taller man,
who shoved the skillet and coffee pot toward him. The tall man
moved both these utensils with his left hand. His right rested
lightly and apparently casually on his right thigh.

The youth filled his tin cup, drank the black, unsweetened
coffee with evident enjoyment, and filled the cup again. He
picked out pieces of the cooling meat with his fingers – and he
was careful to use only his left hand for that part of the breakfast
that would leave grease on his fingers. But he used his right hand
for pouring coffee and holding the cup to his lips. He did not
seem to notice the position of the other's right hand.

'Name's Glanton,' he confided. 'Billy Glanton. Texas. Guadalupe country. Went up the trail with a herd of mossy horns,
went broke buckin' faro in Hayes City, and headed west lookin'
for gold. Hell of a prospector I turned out to be! Now I'm lookin'
for a job, and the man I was goin' to meet here said he had one
for me. If I read your marks right you're a Texan, too?'

The last sentence was more a statement than a question.

'That's my brand,' grunted the other. 'Name's O'Donnell.
Pecos River country, originally.'

His statement, like that of Glanton's, was indefinite. Both the
Pecos and the Guadalupe cover considerable areas of territory.
But Glanton grinned boyishly and stuck out his hand.

'Shake!' he cried. 'I'm glad to meet an *hombre* from my home
state, even if our stampin' grounds down there are a right smart
piece apart!'

Their hands met and locked briefly – brown, sinewy hands
that had never worn gloves, and that gripped with the abrupt
tension of steel springs.

The hand-shake seemed to relax O'Donnell. When he poured out another cup of coffee he held the cup in one hand and the pot in the other, instead of setting the cup on the ground beside him and pouring with his left hand.

'I've been in California,' he volunteered. 'Drifted back on this side of the mountains a month ago. Been in Wahpeton for the last few weeks, but gold huntin' ain't my style. I'm a *vaquero*. Never should have tried to be anything else. I'm headin' back for Texas.'

'Why don't you try Kansas?' asked Glanton. 'It's fillin' up with Texas men, bringin' cattle up the trail to stock the ranges. Within a year they'll be drivin' 'em into Wyoming and Montana.'

'Maybe I might.' O'Donnell lifted the coffee cup absently. He held it in his left hand, and his right lay in his lap, almost touching the big black pistol butt. But the tension was gone out of his frame. He seemed relaxed, absorbed in what Glanton was saying. The use of his left hand and the position of his right seemed mechanical, merely an unconscious habit.

'It's a great country,' declared Glanton, lowering his head to conceal the momentary and uncontrollable flicker of triumph in his eyes. 'Fine ranges. Towns springin' up wherever the railroad touches.

'Everybody gettin' rich on Texas beef. Talkin' about "cattle kings"! Wish I could have knowed this beef boom was comin' when I was a kid! I'd have rounded up about fifty thousand of them maverick steers that was roamin' loose all over lower Texas, and put me a brand on 'em, and saved 'em for the market!' He laughed at his own conceit.

'They wasn't worth six-bits a head then,' he added, as men in making small talk will state a fact well known to everyone. 'Now twenty dollars a head ain't the top price.'

He emptied his cup and set it on the ground near his right hip. His easy flow of speech flowed on – but the natural movement of his hand away from the cup turned into a blur of speed that flicked the heavy gun from its scabbard.

Two shots roared like one long stuttering detonation.

The blond newcomer slumped sidewise, his smoking gun falling from his fingers, a widening spot of crimson suddenly dyeing his shirt, his wide eyes fixed in sardonic self-mockery on the gun in O'Donnell's right hand.

'Corcoran!' he muttered. 'I thought I had you fooled – you –'

Self-mocking laughter bubbled to his lips, cynical to the last; he was laughing as he died.

The man whose real name was Corcoran rose and looked down at his victim unemotionally. There was a hole in the side of his shirt, and a seared spot on the skin of his ribs burned like fire. Even with his aim spoiled by ripping lead, Glanton's bullet had passed close.

Reloading the empty chamber of his Colt, Cocoran started toward the horse the dead man had ridden up to the spring. He had taken but one step when a sound brought him around, the heavy Colt jumping back into his hand.

He scowled at the man who stood before him: a tall man, trimly built, and clad in frontier elegance.

'Don't shoot,' this man said imperturbably. 'I'm John Middleton, sheriff of Wahpeton Gulch.'

The warning attitude of the other did not relax.

'This was a private matter,' he said.

'I guessed as much. Anyway, it's none of my business. I saw two men at the spring as I rode over a rise in the trail some distance back. I was only expecting one. I can't afford to take any chance. I left my horse a short distance back and came on afoot. I was watching from the bushes and saw the whole thing. He reached for his gun first, but you already had your hand almost on your gun. Your shot was first by a flicker. He fooled me. His move came as an absolute surprise to me.'

'He thought it would to me,' said Corcoran. 'Billy Glanton

always wanted the drop on his man. He always tried to get some advantage before he pulled his gun.

'He knew me as soon as he saw me; knew that I knew him. But he thought he was making me think that he didn't know me. I made him think that. He could take chances because he knew I wouldn't shoot him down without warnin' – which is just what he figured on doin' to me. Finally he thought he had me off my guard, and went for his gun. I was foolin' him all along.'

Middleton looked at Corcoran with much interest. He was familiar with the two opposite breeds of gunmen. One kind was like Glanton; utterly cynical, courageous enough when courage was necessary, but always preferring to gain an advantage by treachery whenever possible. Corcoran typified the opposite breed; men too direct by nature, or too proud of their skill to resort to trickery when it was possible to meet their enemies in the open and rely on sheer speed and nerve and accuracy. But that Corcoran was a strategist was proved by his tricking Glanton into drawing.

Middleton looked down at Glanton; in death the yellow curls and boyish features gave the youthful gunman an appearance of innocence. But Middleton knew that that mask had covered the heart of a merciless grey wolf.

'A bad man!' he muttered, staring at the rows of niches on the ivory stock of Glanton's Colt.

'Plenty bad,' agreed Corcoran. 'My folks and his had a feud between 'em down in Texas. He came back from Kansas and killed an uncle of mine – shot him down in cold blood. I was in California when it happened. Got a letter a year after the feud was over. I was headin' for Kansas, where I figured he'd gone back to, when I met a man who told me he was in this part of the country, and was ridin' towards Wahpeton. I cut his trail and camped here last night waitin' for him.

'It'd been years since we'd seen each other, but he knew me

– didn't know I knew he knew me, though. That gave me the edge. You're the man he was goin' to meet here?'

'Yes. I need a gun-fighting deputy bad. I'd heard of him. Sent him word.'

Middleton's gaze wandered over Corcoran's hard frame, lingering on the guns at his hips.

'You pack two irons,' remarked the sheriff. 'I know what you can do with your right. But what about the left? I've seen plenty of men who wore two guns, but those who could use both I can count on my fingers.'

'Well?'

'Well,' smiled the sheriff, 'I thought maybe you'd like to show what you can do with your left.'

'Why do you think it makes any difference to me whether you believe I can handle both guns or not?' retorted Corcoran without heat.

Middleton seemed to like the reply.

'A tin-horn would be anxious to make me believe he could. You don't have to prove anything to me. I've seen enough to show me that you're the man I need. Corcoran, I came out here to hire Glanton as my deputy. I'll make the same proposition to you. What you were down in Texas, or out in California, makes no difference to me. I know your breed, and I know that you'll shoot square with a man who trusts you, regardless of what you may have been in other parts, or will be again, somewhere else.

'I'm up against a situation in Wahpeton that I can't cope with alone, or with the forces I have.

'For a year the town and the camps up and down the gulch have been terrorized by a gang of outlaws who call themselves the Vultures.

'That describes them perfectly. No man's life or property is safe. Forty or fifty men have been murdered, hundreds robbed. It's next to impossible for a man to pack out any dust, or for a big shipment of gold to get through on the stage. So many men have been shot trying to protect shipments that the stage com-pany has trouble hiring guards any more.

'Nobody knows who are the leaders of the gang. There are a number of ruffians who are suspected of being members of the Vultures, but we have no proof that would stand up, even in a miners' court. Nobody dares give evidence against any of them. When a man recognizes the men who rob him he doesn't dare reveal his knowledge. I can't get anyone to identify a criminal, though I know that robbers and murderers are walking the streets, and rubbing elbows with me along the bars. It's mad-dening! And yet I can't blame the poor devils. Any man who dared testify against one of them would be murdered.

'People blame me some, but I can't give adequate protection to the camp with the resources allowed me. You know how a gold camp is; everybody so greedy-blind they don't want to do anything but grab for the yellow dust. My deputies are brave men, but they can't be everywhere, and they're not gun-fighters. If I arrest a man there are a dozen to stand up in a miners' court and swear enough lies to acquit him. Only last night they mur-dered one of my deputies, Jim Grimes, in cold blood.

'I sent for Billy Glanton when I heard he was in this country, because I need a man of more than usual skill. I need a man who can handle a gun like a streak of forked lightning, and knows all the tricks of trapping and killing a man. I'm tired of arresting criminals to be turned loose! Wild Bill Hickok has the right idea – kill the badmen and save the jails for the petty offenders!'

.   The Texan scowled slightly at the mention of Hickok, who was not loved by the riders who came up the cattle trails, but he nodded agreement with the sentiment expressed. The fact that he, himself, would fall into Hickok's category of those to be exterminated did not prejudice his viewpoint.

'You're a better man than Glanton,' said Middleton abruptly. 'The proof is that Glanton lies there dead, and here you stand very much alive. I'll offer you the same terms I meant to offer him.'

He named a monthly salary considerably larger than that drawn by the average Eastern city marshal. Gold was the most plentiful commodity in Wahpeton.

'And a monthly bonus,' added Middleton. 'When I hire talent I expect to pay for it; so do the merchants and miners who look to me for protection.'

Corcoran meditated a moment.

'No use in me goin' on to Kansas now,' he said finally. 'None of my folks in Texas are havin' any feud that I know of. I'd like to see this Wahpeton. I'll take you up.'

'Good!' Middleton extended his hand and as Corcoran took it he noticed that it was much browner than the left. No glove had covered that hand for many years.

'Let's get it started right away! But first we'll have to dispose of Glanton's body.'

'I'll take along his gun and horse and send 'em to Texas to his folks,' said Corcoran.

'But the body?'

'Hell, the buzzards'll 'tend to it.'

'No, no!' protested Middleton. 'Let's cover it with bushes and rocks, at least.'

Corcoran shrugged his shoulders. It was not vindictiveness which prompted his seeming callousness. His hatred of the blond youth did not extend to the lifeless body of the man. It was simply that he saw no use in going to what seemed to him an unnecessary task. He had hated Glanton with the merciless hate of his race, which is more enduring and more relentless than the hate of an Indian or a Spaniard. But toward the body that was no longer animated by the personality he had hated, he was simply indifferent. He expected some day to leave his own corpse stretched on the ground, and the thought of buzzards tearing at his dead flesh moved him no more than the sight of his dead enemy. His creed was pagan and nakedly elemental.

A man's body, once life had left it, was no more than any other carcass, moldering back into the soil which once produced it.

But he helped Middleton drag the body into an opening among the bushes, and build a rude cairn above it. And he waited patiently while Middleton carved the dead youth's name on a rude cross fashioned from broken branches, and thrust upright among the stones.

Then they rode for Wahpeton, Corcoran leading the riderless roan; over the horn of the empty saddle hung the belt supporting the dead man's gun, the ivory stock of which bore eleven notches, each of which represented a man's life.

2   Golden Madness

The mining town of Wahpeton sprawled in a wide gulch that wandered between sheer rock walls and steep hillsides. Cabins, saloons and dance-halls backed against the cliffs on the south side of the gulch. The houses facing them were almost on the bank of Wahpeton Creek, which wandered down the gulch, keeping mostly to the center. On both sides of the creek cabins and tents straggled for a mile and a half each way from the main body of the town. Men were washing gold dust out of the creek, and out of its smaller tributaries which meandered into the canyon along tortuous ravines. Some of these ravines opened into the gulch between the houses built against the wall, and the cabins and tents which straggled up them gave the impression that the town had overflowed the main gulch and spilled into its tributaries.

Buildings were of logs, or of bare planks laboriously freighted over the mountains. Squalor and draggled or gaudy elegance rubbed elbows. An intense virility surged through the scene. What other qualities it might have lacked, it overflowed with a superabundance of vitality. Color, action, movement – growth and power! The atmosphere was alive with these elements, stinging and tingling. Here there were no delicate shadings or subtle contrasts. Life painted here in broad, raw colors, in bold, vivid strokes. Men who came here left behind them the delicate nuances, the cultured tranquillities of life. An empire was being built on muscle and guts and audacity, and men dreamed gigantically and wrought terrifically. No dream was too mad, no enterprise too tremendous to be accomplished.

Passions ran raw and turbulent. Boot heels stamped on bare plank floors, in the eddying dust of the street. Voices boomed, tempers exploded in sudden outbursts of primitive violence. Shrill voices of painted harpies mingled with the clank of gold on gambling tables, gusty mirth and vociferous altercation along the bars where raw liquor hissed in a steady stream down hairy, dust-caked throats. It was one of a thousand similar panoramas of the day, when a giant empire was bellowing in lusty infancy.

But a sinister undercurrent was apparent. Corcoran, riding by the sheriff, was aware of this, his senses and intuitions whetted to razor keenness by the life he led. The instincts of a gunfighter were developed to an abnormal alertness, else he had never lived out his first year of gunmanship. But it took no abnormally developed instinct to tell Corcoran that hidden currents ran here, darkly and strongly.

As they threaded their way among trains of pack-mules, rumbling wagons and swarms of men on foot which thronged the straggling street, Corcoran was aware of many eyes following them. Talk ceased suddenly among gesticulating groups as they recognized the sheriff, then the eyes swung to Corcoran, searching and appraising. He did not seem to be aware of their scrutiny.

Middleton murmured: 'They know I'm bringing back a gun-fighting deputy. Some of those fellows are Vultures, though I can't prove it. Look out for yourself.'

Corcoran considered this advice too unnecessary to merit a reply. They were riding past the King of Diamonds gambling hall at the moment, and a group of men clustered in the door-way turned to stare at them. One lifted a hand in greeting to the sheriff.

'Ace Brent, the biggest gambler in the gulch,' murmured Middleton as he returned the salute. Corcoran got a glimpse of a slim figure in elegant broadcloth, a keen, inscrutable counten-ance, and a pair of piercing black eyes.

Middleton did not enlarge upon his description of the man, but rode on in silence.

They traversed the body of the town – the clusters of stores and saloons – and passed on, halting at a cabin apart from the rest. Between it and the town the creek swung out in a wide loop that carried it some distance from the south wall of the gulch, and the cabins and tents straggled after the creek. That left this particular cabin isolated, for it was built with its back wall squarely against the sheer cliff. There was a corral on one side, a clump of trees on the other. Beyond the trees a narrow ravine opened into the gulch, dry and unoccupied.

'This is my cabin,' said Middleton. 'That cabin back there' – he pointed to one which they had passed, a few hundred yards back up the road – 'I use for a sheriff's office. I need only one room. You can bunk in the back room. You can keep your horse in my corral, if you want to. I always keep several there for my deputies. It pays to have a fresh supply of horse-flesh always on hand.'

As Corcoran dismounted he glanced back at the cabin he was to occupy. It stood close to a clump of trees, perhaps a hundred yards from the steep wall of the gulch.

There were four men at the sheriff's cabin, one of which

Middleton introduced to Corcoran as Colonel Hopkins, formerly of Tennessee. He was a tall, portly man with an iron gray mustache and goatee, as well dressed as Middleton himself.

'Colonel Hopkins owns the rich Elinor A. claim, in partnership with Dick Bisley,' said Middleton; 'in addition to being one of the most prominent merchants in the Gulch.'

'A great deal of good either occupation does me, when I can't get my money out of town,' retorted the colonel. 'Three times my partner and I have lost big shipments of gold on the stage. Once we sent out a load concealed in wagons loaded with supplies supposed to be intended for the miners at Teton Gulch. Once clear of Wahpeton the drivers were to swing back east through the mountains. But somehow the Vultures learned of our plan; they caught the wagons fifteen miles south of Wahpeton, looted them and murdered the guards and drivers.'

'The town's honeycombed with their spies,' muttered Middleton.

'Of course. One doesn't know who to trust. It was being whispered in the streets that my men had been killed and robbed, before their bodies had been found. We know that the Vultures knew all about our plan, that they rode straight out from Wahpeton, committed that crime and rode straight back with the gold dust. But we could do nothing. We can't prove anything, or convict anybody.'

Middleton introduced Corcoran to the three deputies, Bill McNab, Richardson, and Stark. McNab was as tall as Corcoran and more heavily built, hairy and muscular, with restless eyes that reflected a violent temper. Richardson was more slender, with cold, unblinking eyes, and Corcoran instantly classified him as the most dangerous of the three. Stark was a burly, bearded fellow, not differing in type from hundreds of miners. Corcoran found the appearances of these men incongruous with their protestations of helplessness in the face of the odds against them. They looked like hard men, well able to take care of themselves in any situation.

Middleton, as if sensing his thoughts, said: 'These men are not afraid of the devil, and they can throw a gun as quick as the average man, or quicker. But it's hard for a stranger to appreciate just what we're up against here in Wahpeton. If it was a matter of an open fight, it would be different. I wouldn't need any more help. But it's blind going, working in the dark, not knowing who to trust. I don't dare to deputize a man unless I'm sure of his honesty. And who can be sure of who? We know the town is full of spies. We don't know who they are; we don't know who the leader of the Vultures is.'

Hopkins' bearded chin jutted stubbornly as he said: 'I still believe that gambler, Ace Brent, is mixed up with the gang. Gamblers have been murdered and robbed, but Brent's never been molested. What becomes of all the dust he wins? Many of the miners, despairing of ever getting out of the gulch with their gold, blow it all in the saloons and gambling halls. Brent's won thousands of dollars in dust and nuggets. So have several others. What becomes of it? It doesn't all go back into circulation. I believe they get it out, over the mountains. And if they do, when no one else can, that proves to my mind that they're members of the Vultures.'

'Maybe they cache it, like you and the other merchants are doing,' suggested Middleton. 'I don't know. Brent's intelligent enough to be the chief of the Vultures. But I've never been able to get anything on him.'

'You've never been able to get anything definite on anybody, except petty offenders,' said Colonel Hopkins bluntly, as he took up his hat. 'No offense intended, John. We know what you're up against, and we can't blame you. But it looks like, for the good of the camp, we're going to have to take direct action.'

Middleton stared after the broadcloth-clad back as it receded from the cabin.

'"We,"' he murmured. 'That means the vigilantes – or rather the men who have been agitating a vigilante movement. I can understand their feelings, but I consider it an unwise move. In the first place, such an organization is itself outside the law, and would be playing into the hands of the lawless element. Then, what's to prevent outlaws from joining the vigilantes, and diverting it to suit their own ends?'

'Not a damned thing!' broke in McNab heatedly. 'Colonel Hopkins and his friends are hot-headed. They expect too much from us. Hell, we're just ordinary workin' men. We do the best we can, but we ain't gun-slingers like this man Corcoran here.'

Corcoran found himself mentally questioning the whole truth of this statement; Richardson had all the earmarks of a gunman, if he had ever seen one, and the Texan's experience in such matters ranged from the Pacific to the Gulf.

Middleton picked up his hat. 'You boys scatter out through the camp. I'm going to take Corcoran around, when I've sworn him in and given him his badge, and introduce him to the leading men of the camp.

'I don't want any mistake, or any chance of mistake, about his standing. I've put you in a tight spot, Corcoran, I'll admit – boasting about the gun-fighting deputy I was going to get. But I'm confident that you can take care of yourself.'

The eyes that had followed their ride down the street focused on the sheriff and his companion as they made their way on foot along the straggling street with its teeming saloons and gambling halls. Gamblers and bartenders were swamped with business, and merchants were getting rich with all commodities selling at unheard-of prices. Wages for day-labor matched prices for groceries, for few men could be found to toil for a prosaic, set salary when their eyes were dazzled by visions of creeks fat with yellow dust and gorges crammed with nuggets. Some of those dreams were not disappointed; millions of dollars in virgin gold was being taken out of the claims up and down the gulch. But the finders frequently found it a golden weight hung to their necks to drag them down to a bloody death. Unseen, unknown, on furtive feet the human wolves stole among them unerringly marking their prey and striking in the dark.

From saloon to saloon, dance hall to dance hall, where weary girls in tawdry finery allowed themselves to be tussled and hauled about by bear-like males who emptied sacks of gold-dust down the low necks of their dresses, Middleton piloted Corcoran, talking rapidly and incessantly. He pointed out men in the crowd and gave their names and status in the community, and introduced the Texan to the more important citizens of the camp.

All eyes followed Corcoran curiously. The day was still in the future when the northern ranges would be flooded by Texas cattle, driven by wiry Texas riders; but Texans were not unknown, even then, in the mining camps of the Northwest. In the first days of the gold rushes they had drifted in from the camps of California, to which, at a still earlier date, the South-west had sent some of her staunchest and some of her most turbulent sons. And of late others had drifted in from the Kansas cattle towns along whose streets the lean riders were swaggering and fighting out feuds brought up from the far south country. Many in Wahpeton were familiar with the characteristics of the Texas breed, and all had heard tales of the fighting men bred among the live oaks and mesquites of that hot, turbulent country where racial traits met and clashed, and the traditions of the Old South mingled with those of the untamed West.

Here, then, was a lean gray wolf from that southern pack; some of the men looked their scowling animosity; but most merely looked, in the rôle of spectators, eager to witness the drama all felt imminent.

'You're, primarily, to fight the Vultures, of course,' Middleton told Corcoran as they walked together down the street. 'But that doesn't mean you're to overlook petty offenders. A lot of small-time crooks and bullies are so emboldened by the success of the big robbers that they think they can get away with things, too. If you see a man shooting up a saloon, take his gun away and throw him into jail to sober up. That's the jail, up yonder at the other end of town. Don't let men fight on the street or in saloons. Innocent bystanders get hurt.'

'All right.' Corcoran saw no harm in shooting up saloons or fighting in public places. In Texas few innocent bystanders were ever hurt, for there men sent their bullets straight to the mark intended. But he was ready to follow instructions.

'So much for the smaller fry. You know what to do with the really bad men. We're not bringing any more murderers into court to be acquitted through their friends' lies!'

3 Gunman's Trap

Night had fallen over the roaring madness that was Wahpeton Gulch. Light streamed from the open doors of saloons and honky-tonks, and the gusts of noise that rushed out into the street smote the passers-by like the impact of a physical blow.

Corcoran traversed the street with the smooth, easy stride of perfectly poised muscles. He seemed to be looking straight ahead, but his eyes missed nothing on either side of him. As he passed each building in turn he analyzed the sounds that issued from the open door, and knew just how much was rough merriment and horse-play, recognized the elements of anger and menace when they edged some of the voices, and accurately appraised the extent and intensity of those emotions. A real gun-fighter was not merely a man whose eye was truer, whose muscles were quicker than other men; he was a practical psychologist, a student of human nature, whose life depended on the correctness of his conclusions.

It was the Golden Garter dance hall that gave him his first job as a defender of law and order.

As he passed a startling clamor burst forth inside – strident feminine shrieks piercing a din of coarse masculine hilarity. Instantly he was through the door and elbowing a way through the crowd which was clustered about the center of the room. Men cursed and turned belligerently as they felt his elbows in their ribs, twisted their heads to threaten him, and then gave back as they recognized the new deputy.

Corcoran broke through into the open space the crowd ringed, and saw two women fighting like furies. One, a tall, fine blond girl, had bent a shrieking, biting, clawing Mexican girl back over a billiard table, and the crowd was yelling joyful encouragement to one or the other: 'Give it to her, Glory!' 'Slug her, gal!' 'Hell, Conchita, bite her!'

The brown girl heeded this last bit of advice and followed it so energetically that Glory cried out sharply and jerked away her wrist, which dripped blood. In the grip of the hysterical frenzy which seizes women in such moments, she caught up a billiard ball and lifted it to crash it down on the head of her screaming captive.

Corcoran caught that uplifted wrist, and deftly flicked the ivory sphere from her fingers. Instantly she whirled on him like a tigress, her yellow hair falling in disorder over her shoulders, bared by the violence of the struggle, her eyes blazing. She lifted her hands toward his face, her fingers working spasmodically, at which some drunk bawled, with a shout of laughter: 'Scratch his eyes out, Glory!'

Corcoran made no move to defend his features; he did not seem to see the white fingers twitching so near his face. He was staring into her furious face, and the candid admiration of his gaze seemed to confuse her, even in her anger. She dropped her hands but fell back on woman's traditional weapon – her tongue.

'You're Middleton's new deputy! I might have expected you to butt in! Where are McNab and the rest? Drunk in some gutter? Is this the way you catch murderers? You lawmen are all alike – better at bullying girls than at catching outlaws!'

Corcoran stepped past her and picked up the hysterical Mexican girl. Conchita seeing that she was more frightened than hurt, scurried toward the back rooms, sobbing in rage and humiliation, and clutching about her the shreds of garments her enemy's tigerish attack had left her.

Corcoran looked again at Glory, who stood clenching and unclenching her white fists. She was still fermenting with anger, and furious at his intervention. No one in the crowd about them spoke; no one laughed, but all seemed to hold their breaths as she launched into another tirade. They knew Corcoran was a dangerous man, but they did not know the code by which he had been reared; did not know that Glory, or any other woman, was safe from violence at his hands, whatever her offense.

'Why don't you call McNab?' she sneered. 'Judging from the way Middleton's deputies have been working, it will probably take three or four of you to drag one helpless girl to jail!'

'Who said anything about takin' you to jail?' Corcoran's gaze dwelt in fascination on her ruddy cheeks, the crimson of her full lips in startling contrast against the whiteness of her teeth. She shook her yellow hair back impatiently, as a spirited young animal might shake back its flowing mane.

'You're not arresting me?' She seemed startled, thrown into confusion by this unexpected statement.

'No. I just kept you from killin' that girl. If you'd brained her with that billiard ball I'd have had to arrest you.'

'She lied about me!' Her wide eyes flashed, and her breast heaved again.

'That wasn't no excuse for makin' a public show of yourself,' he answered without heat. 'If ladies have got to fight, they ought to do it in private.'

And so saying he turned away. A gusty exhalation of breath seemed to escape the crowd, and the tension vanished, as they turned to the bar. The incident was forgotten, merely a trifling episode in an existence crowded with violent incidents. Jovial masculine voices mingled with the shriller laughter of women, as glasses began to clink along the bar.

Glory hesitated, drawing her torn dress together over her bosom, then darted after Corcoran, who was moving toward the door. When she touched his arm he whipped about as quick as a cat, a hand flashing to a gun. She glimpsed a momentary gleam in his eyes as menacing and predatory as the threat that leaps in a panther's eyes. Then it was gone as he saw whose hand had touched him.

'She lied about me,' Glory said, as if defending herself from a charge of misconduct. 'She's a dirty little cat.'

Corcoran looked her over from head to foot, as if he had not heard her; his blue eyes burned her like a physical fire.

She stammered in confusion. Direct and unveiled admiration was commonplace, but there was an elemental candor about the Texan such as she had never before encountered.

He broke in on her stammerings in a way that showed he had paid no attention to what she was saying.

'Let me buy you a drink. There's a table over there where we can sit down.'

'No. I must go and put on another dress. I just wanted to say that I'm glad you kept me from killing Conchita. She's a slut, but I don't want her blood on my hands.'

'All right.'

She found it hard to make conversation with him, and could not have said why she wished to make conversation.

'McNab arrested me once,' she said, irrelevantly, her eyes dilating as if at the memory of an injustice. 'I slapped him for something he said. He was going to put me in jail for resisting an officer of the law! Middleton made him turn me loose.'

'McNab must be a fool,' said Corcoran slowly.

'He's mean; he's got a nasty temper, and he – what's that?'

Down the street sounded a fusillade of shots, a blurry voice yelling gleefully.

'Some fool shooting up a saloon,' she murmured, and darted a strange glance at her companion, as if a drunk shooting into the air was an unusual occurrence in that wild mining camp.

'Middleton said that's against the law,' he grunted, turning away.

'Wait!' she cried sharply, catching at him. But he was already moving through the door, and Glory stopped short as a hand fell lightly on her shoulder from behind. Turning her head she paled to see the keenly-chiselled face of Ace Brent. His hand lay gently on her shoulder, but there was a command and a blood-chilling threat in its touch. She shivered and stood still as a statue, as Corcoran, unaware of the drama being played behind him, disappeared into the street.

The racket was coming from the Blackfoot Chief Saloon, a few doors down, and on the same side of the street as the Golden Garter. With a few long strides Corcoran reached the door. But he did not rush in. He halted and swept his cool gaze deliberately over the interior. In the center of the saloon a roughly dressed man was reeling about, whooping and discharging a pistol into the ceiling, perilously close to the big oil lamp which hung there. The bar was lined with men, all bearded and uncouthly garbed, so it was impossible to tell which were ruffians and which were honest miners. All the men in the room were at the bar, with the exception of the drunken man.

Corcoran paid little heed to him as he came through the door, though he moved straight toward him, and to the tense watchers it seemed the Texan was looking at no one else. In reality, from the corner of his eye he was watching the men at the bar; and as he moved deliberately from the door, across the room, he distinguished the pose of honest curiosity from the tension of intended murder. He saw the three hands that gripped gun butts.

And as he, apparently ignorant of what was going on at the bar, stepped toward the man reeling in the center of the room, a gun jumped from its scabbard and pointed toward the lamp. And even as it moved, Corcoran moved quicker. His turn was a blur of motion too quick for the eye to follow and even as he turned his gun was burning red.

The man who had drawn died on his feet with his gun still pointed toward the ceiling, unfired. Another stood gaping, stunned, a pistol dangling in his fingers, for that fleeting tick of time; then as he woke and whipped the gun up, hot lead ripped through his brain. A third gun spoke once as the owner fired wildly, and then he went to his knees under the blast of ripping lead, slumped over on the floor and lay twitching.

It was over in a flash, action so blurred with speed that not one of the watchers could ever tell just exactly what had happened. One instant Corcoran had been moving toward the man in the center of the room, the next both guns were blazing and three men were falling from the bar, crashing dead on the floor.

For an instant the scene held, Corcoran half crouching, guns held at his hips, facing the men who stood stunned along the bar. Wisps of blue smoke drifted from the muzzles of his guns, forming a misty veil through which his grim face looked, implacable and passionless as that of an image carved from granite. But his eyes blazed.

Shakily, moving like puppets on a string, the men at the bar lifted their hands clear of their waistline. Death hung on the crook of a finger for a shuddering tick of time. Then with a choking gasp the man who had played drunk made a stumbling rush toward the door. With a catlike wheel and stroke Corcoran crashed a gun barrel over his head and stretched him stunned and bleeding on the floor.

The Texan was facing the men at the bar again before any of them could have moved. He had not looked at the men on the floor since they had fallen.

'Well, *amigos!*' His voice was soft, but it was thick with killer's lust. 'Why don't you-all keep the *baile* goin'? Ain't these *hombres* got no friends?'

Apparently they had not. No one made a move.

Realizing that the crisis had passed, that there was no more killing to be done just then, Corcoran straightened, shoving his guns back in his scabbards.

'Purty crude,' he criticized. 'I don't see how anybody could fall for a trick that stale. Man plays drunk and starts shootin' at the roof. Officer comes in to arrest him. When the officer's back's turned, somebody shoots out the light, and the drunk falls on the floor to get out of the line of fire. Three or four men planted along the bar start blazin' away in the dark at the place where they know the law's standin', and out of eighteen or twenty-four shots, some's bound to connect.'

With a harsh laugh he stooped, grabbed the 'drunk' by the collar and hauled him upright. The man staggered and stared wildly about him, blood dripping from the gash in his scalp.

'You got to come along to jail,' said Corcoran unemotionally. 'Sheriff says it's against the law to shoot up saloons. I ought to shoot you, but I ain't in the habit of pluggin' men with empty guns. Reckon you'll be more value to the sheriff alive than dead, anyway.'

And propelling his dizzy charge, he strode out into the street. A crowd had gathered about the door, and they gave back suddenly. He saw a supple, feminine figure dart into the circle of light, which illumined the white face and golden hair of the girl Glory.

'Oh!' she exclaimed sharply. 'Oh!' Her exclamation was almost drowned in a sudden clamor of voices as the men in the street realized what had happened in the Blackfoot Chief.

Corcoran felt her pluck at his sleeve as he passed her, heard her tense whisper.

'I was afraid – I tried to warn you – I'm glad they didn't –'

A shadow of a smile touched his hard lips as he glanced down at her. Then he was gone, striding down the street toward the jail, half pushing, half dragging his bewildered prisoner.

4   The Madness That Blinds Men

Corcoran locked the door on the man who seemed utterly unable to realize just what had happened, and turned away, heading for the sheriff's office at the other end of town. He kicked on the door of the jailer's shack, a few yards from the jail, and roused that individual out of a slumber he believed was alcoholic and informed him he had a prisoner in his care. The jailer seemed as surprised as the victim was.

No one had followed Corcoran to the jail and the street was almost deserted, as the people jammed morbidly into the Blackfoot Chief to stare at the bodies and listen to conflicting stories as to just what had happened.

Colonel Hopkins came running up breathlessly, to grab Corcoran's hand and pump it vigorously.

'By gad, sir, you have the real spirit! Guts! Speed! They tell me the loafers at the bar didn't even have time to dive for cover before it was over! I'll admit I'd ceased to expect much of John's deputies, but you've shown your metal! These fellows were undoubtedly Vultures. That Tom Deal, you've got in jail, I've suspected him for some time. We'll question him – make him tell us who the rest are, and who their leader is. Come in and have a drink, sir!'

'Thanks, but not just now. I'm goin' to find Middleton and report this business. His office ought to be closer to the jail. I don't think much of his jailer. When I get through reportin' I'm goin' back and guard that fellow myself.'

Hopkins emitted more laudations, and then clapped the Texan on the back and darted away to take part in whatever informal inquest was being made, and Corcoran strode on through the emptying street. The fact that so much uproar was being made over the killing of three would-be murderers showed him how rare was a successful resistance to the Vultures. He shrugged his shoulders as he remembered feuds and range wars in his native Southwest: men falling like flies under the unerring drive of bullets on the open range and in the streets of Texas towns. But there all men were frontiersmen, sons and grandsons of frontiersmen; here, in the mining camps, the frontier element was only one of several elements, many drawn from sections where men had forgotten how to defend themselves through generations of law and order.

He saw a light spring up in the sheriff's cabin just before he reached it, and, with his mind on possible gunmen lurking in ambush – for they must have known he would go directly to the cabin from the jail – he swung about and approached the building by a route that would not take him across the bar of light pouring from the window. So it was that the man who came running noisily down the road passed him without seeing the Texan as he kept in the shadows of the cliff. The man was McNab; Corcoran knew him by his powerful build, his slouching carriage. And as he burst through the door, his face was illuminated and Corcoran was amazed to see it contorted in a grimace of passion.

Voices rose inside the cabin, McNab's bull-like roar, thick with fury, and the calmer tones of Middleton. Corcoran hurried forward, and as he approached he heard McNab roar: 'Damn you, Middleton, you've got a lot of explainin' to do! Why didn't you warn the boys he was a killer?'

At that moment Corcoran stepped into the cabin and demanded: 'What's the trouble, McNab?'

The big deputy whirled with a feline snarl of rage, his eyes glaring with murderous madness as they recognized Corcoran.

'You damned –' A string of filthy expletives gushed from his thick lips as he ripped out his gun. Its muzzle had scarcely cleared leather when a Colt banged in Corcoran's right hand. McNab's gun clattered to the floor and he staggered back, grasping his right arm with his left hand, and cursing like a madman.

'What's the matter with you, you fool?' demanded Corcoran harshly. 'Shut up! I did you a favor by not killin' you. If you wasn't a deputy I'd have drilled you through the head. But I will anyway, if you don't shut your dirty trap.'

'You killed Breckman, Red Bill and Curly!' raved McNab; he looked like a wounded grizzly as he swayed there, blood trickling down his wrist and dripping off his fingers.

'Was that their names? Well, what about it?'

'Bill's drunk, Corcoran,' interposed Middleton. 'He goes crazy when he's full of liquor.'

McNab's roar of fury shook the cabin. His eyes turned red and he swayed on his feet as if about to plunge at Middleton's throat.

'Drunk?' he bellowed. 'You lie, Middleton! Damn you, what's your game? You sent your own men to death! Without warnin'!'

'His own men?' Corcoran's eyes were suddenly glittering slits. He stepped back and made a half turn so that he was facing both men; his hands became claws hovering over his gun-butts.

'Yes, his men!' snarled McNab. 'You fool, *he's* the chief of the Vultures!'

An electric silence gripped the cabin. Middleton stood rigid, his empty hands hanging limp, knowing that his life hung on a thread no more substantial than a filament of morning dew. If he moved, if, when he spoke, his tone jarred on Corcoran's suspicious ears, guns would be roaring before a man could snap his fingers.

'Is that so?' Corcoran shot at him.

'Yes,' Middleton said calmly, with no inflection in his voice that could be taken as a threat. 'I'm chief of the Vultures.'

Corcoran glared at him puzzled. 'What's your game?' he demanded, his tone thick with the deadly instinct of his breed.

'That's what I want to know!' bawled McNab. 'We killed Grimes for you, because he was catchin' on to things. And we set the same trap for this devil. He knew! He must have known! You warned him – told him all about it!'

'He told me nothin',' grated Corcoran. 'He didn't have to. Nobody but a fool would have been caught in a trap like that. Middleton, before I blow you to hell, I want to know one thing: what good was it goin' to do you to bring me into Wahpeton, and have me killed the first night I was here?'

'I didn't bring you here for that,' answered Middleton.

'Then what'd you bring him here for?' yelled McNab. 'You told us –'

'I told you I was bringing a new deputy here, that was a gun-slinging fool,' broke in Middleton. 'That was the truth. That should have been warning enough.'

'But we thought that was just talk, to fool the people,' protested McNab bewilderedly. He sensed that he was beginning to be wound in a web he could not break.

'Did I tell you it was just talk?'

'No, but we thought –'

'I gave you no reason to think anything. The night when Grimes was killed I told everyone in the Golden Eagle that I was bringing in a Texas gunfighter as my deputy. I spoke the truth.'

'But you wanted him killed, and –'

'I didn't. I didn't say a word about having him killed.'

'But –'

'Did I?' Middleton pursued relentlessly. 'Did I give you a definite order to kill Corcoran, to molest him in any way?'

Corcoran's eyes were molten steel, burning into McNab's soul. The befuddled giant scowled and floundered, vaguely

realizing that he was being put in the wrong, but not understanding how, or why.

'No, you didn't tell us to kill him in so many words; but you
didn't tell us to let him alone.'

'Do I have to tell you to let people alone to keep you from
killing them? There are about three thousand people in this
camp I've never given any definite orders about. Are you going
out and kill them, and say you thought I meant you to do it,
because I didn't tell you not to?'

'Well, I –' McNab began apologetically, then burst out in
righteous though bewildered wrath: 'Damn it, it was the under-
standin' that we'd get rid of deputies like that, who wasn't on
the inside. We thought you were bringin' in an honest deputy to
fool the folks, just like you hired Jim Grimes to fool 'em. We
thought you was just makin' a talk to the fools in the Golden
Eagle. We thought you'd want him out of the way as quick as
possible –'

'You drew your own conclusions and acted without my
orders,' snapped Middleton. 'That's all that it amounts to. Naturally Corcoran defended himself. If I'd had any idea that you
fools would try to murder him, I'd have passed the word to let
him alone. I thought you understood my motives. I brought
Corcoran in here to fool the people; yes. But he's not a man like
Jim Grimes. Corcoran is with us. He'll clean out the thieves that
are working outside our gang, and we'll accomplish two things
with one stroke: get rid of competition and make the miners
think we're on the level.'

McNab stood glaring at Middleton; three times he opened his
mouth, and each time he shut it without speaking. He knew
that an injustice had been done him; that a responsibility that
was not rightfully his had been dumped on his brawny shoulders. But the subtle play of Middleton's wits was beyond him;
he did not know how to defend himself or make a countercharge.

'All right,' he snarled. 'We'll forget it. But the boys ain't goin' to forget how Corcoran shot down their pards. I'll talk to 'em, though. Tom Deal's got to be out of that jail before daylight. Hopkins is aimin' to question him about the gang. I'll stage a fake jail-break for him. But first I've got to get this arm dressed.' And he slouched out of the cabin and away through the darkness, a baffled giant, burning with murderous rage, but too tangled in a net of subtlety to know where or how or who to smite.

Back in the cabin Middleton faced Corcoran who still stood with his thumbs hooked in his belt, his fingers near his gun butts. A whimsical smile played on Middleton's thin lips, and Corcoran smiled back; but it was the mirthless grin of a crouching panther.

'You can't tangle me up with words like you did that big ox,' Corcoran said. 'You let me walk into that trap. You knew your men were ribbin' it up. You let 'em go ahead, when a word from you would have stopped it. You knew they'd think you wanted me killed, like Grimes, if you didn't say nothin'. You let 'em think that, but you played safe by not givin' any definite orders, so if anything went wrong, you could step out from under and shift the blame onto McNab.'

Middleton smiled appreciatively, and nodded coolly.

'That's right. All of it. You're no fool, Corcoran.'

Corcoran ripped out an oath, and this glimpse of the passionate nature that lurked under his inscrutable exterior was like a momentary glimpse of an enraged cougar, eyes blazing, spitting and snarling.

'Why?' he exclaimed. 'Why did you plot all this for me? If you had a grudge against Glanton, I can understand why you'd rib up a trap for him, though you wouldn't have had no more luck with him than you have with me. But you ain't got no feud against me. I never saw you before this mornin'!'

'I have no feud with you; I had none with Glanton. But if Fate hadn't thrown you into my path, it would have been Glanton who would have been ambushed in the Blackfoot Chief. Don't you see, Corcoran? It was a test. I had to be sure you were the man I wanted.'

Corcoran scowled, puzzled himself now.

'What do you mean?'

'Sit down!' Middleton himself sat down on a near-by chair, unbuckled his gun-belt and threw it, with the heavy, holstered gun, onto a table, out of easy reach. Corcoran seated himself, but his vigilance did not relax, and his gaze rested on Middleton's left arm pit, where a second gun might be hidden.

'In the first place,' said Middleton, his voice flowing tranquilly, but pitched too low to be heard outside the cabin, 'I'm chief of the Vultures, as that fool said. I organized them, even before I was made sheriff. Killing a robber and murderer, who was working outside my gang, made the people of Wahpeton think I'd make a good sheriff. When they gave me the office, I saw what an advantage it would be to me and my gang.

'Our organization is air-tight. There are about fifty men in the gang. They are scattered throughout these mountains. Some pose as miners; some are gamblers – Ace Brent, for instance. He's my right-hand man. Some work in saloons, some clerk in stores. One of the regular drivers of the stage-line company is a Vulture, and so is a clerk of the company, and one of the men who works in the company's stables, tending the horses.

'With spies scattered all over the camp, I know who's trying to take out gold, and when. It's a cinch. We can't lose.'

'I don't see how the camp stands for it,' grunted Corcoran.

'Men are too crazy after gold to think about anything else. As long as a man isn't molested himself, he doesn't care much what happens to his neighbors. We are organized; they are not. We know who to trust; they don't. It can't last forever. Sooner or later the more intelligent citizens will organize themselves into a vigilante committee and sweep the gulch clean. But when that happens, I intend to be far away – with one man I can trust.'

Corcoran nodded, comprehension beginning to gleam in his eyes.

'Already some men are talking vigilante. Colonel Hopkins, for instance. I encourage him as subtly as I can.'

'Why, in the name of Satan?'

'To avert suspicion; and for another reason. The vigilantes will serve my purpose at the end.'

'And your purpose is to skip out and leave the gang holdin' the sack!'

'Exactly! Look here!'

Taking the candle from the table, he led the way through a back room, where heavy shutters covered the one window. Shutting the door, he turned to the back wall and drew aside some skins which were hung over it. Setting the candle on a roughly hewed table, he fumbled at the logs, and a section swung outward, revealing a heavy plank door set in the solid rock against which the back wall of the cabin was built. It was braced with iron and showed a ponderous lock. Middleton produced a key, and turned it in the lock, and pushed the door inward. He lifted the candle and revealed a small cave, lined and heaped with canvas and buckskin sacks. One of these sacks had burst open, and a golden stream caught the glints of the candle.

'Gold! Sacks and sacks of it!'

Corcoran caught his breath, and his eyes glittered like a wolf's in the candlelight. No man could visualize the contents of those bags unmoved. And the gold-madness had long ago entered Corcoran's veins, more powerfully than he had dreamed, even though he had followed the lure to California and back over the mountains again. The sight of that glittering heap, of those bulging sacks, sent his pulses pounding in his temples, and his hand unconsciously locked on the butt of a gun.

'There must be a million there!'

'Enough to require a good-sized mule-train to pack it out,' answered Middleton. 'You see why I have to have a man to help me the night I pull out. And I need a man like you. You're an outdoor man, hardened by wilderness-travel. You're a frontiersman, a *vaquero*, a trail-driver. These men I lead are mostly rats that grew up in border towns – gamblers, thieves, barroom gladiators, saloon-bred gunmen; a few miners gone wrong. You can stand things that would kill any of them.

'The flight we'll have to make will be hard traveling. We'll have to leave the beaten trails and strike out through the mountains. They'll be sure to follow us, and we'll probably have to fight them off. Then there are Indians – Blackfeet and Crows; we may run into a war-party of them. I knew I had to have a fighting man of the keenest type; not only a fighting man, but a man bred on the frontier. That's why I sent for Glanton. But you're a better man than he was.'

Corcoran frowned his suspicion.

'Why didn't you tell me all this at first?'

'Because I wanted to try you out. I wanted to be sure you were the right man. I had to be sure. If you were stupid enough, and slow enough to be caught in such a trap as McNab and the rest would set for you, you weren't the man I wanted.'

'You're takin' a lot for granted,' snapped Corcoran. 'How do you know I'll fall in with you and help you loot the camp and then double-cross your gang? What's to prevent me from blowin' your head off for the trick you played on me? Or spillin' the beans to Hopkins, or to McNab?'

'Half a million in gold!' answered Middleton. 'If you do any of those things, you'll miss your chance to share that cache with me.'

He shut the door, locked it, pushed the other door to and hung the skins over it. Taking the candle he led the way back into the outer room.

He seated himself at the table and poured whisky from a jug into two glasses.

'Well, what about it?'

Corcoran did not at once reply. His brain was still filled with blinding golden visions. His countenance darkened, became sinister as he meditated, staring into his whisky-glass.

The men of the West lived by their own code. The line between the outlaw and the honest cattleman or *vaquero* was sometimes a hair line, too vague to always be traced with accuracy. Men's personal codes were frequently inconsistent, but rigid as iron. Corcoran would not have stolen one cow, or three cows from a squatter, but he had swept across the border to loot Mexican *rancherios* of hundreds of head. He would not hold up a man and take his money, nor would he murder a man in cold blood; but he felt no compunctions about killing a thief and taking the money the thief had stolen. The gold in that cache was blood-stained, the fruit of crimes to which he would have scorned to stoop. But his code of honesty did not prevent him from looting it from the thieves who had looted it in turn from honest men.

'What's my part in the game?' Corcoran asked abruptly.

Middleton grinned zestfully.

'Good! I thought you'd see it my way. No man could look at that gold and refuse a share of it! They trust me more than they do any other member of the gang. That's why I keep it here. They know – or think they know – that I couldn't slip out with it. But that's where we'll fool them.

'Your job will be just what I told McNab: you'll uphold law and order. I'll tell the boys not to pull any more hold-ups inside the town itself, and that'll give you a reputation. People will think you've got the gang too scared to work in close. You'll enforce laws like those against shooting up saloons, fighting on the street, and the like. And you'll catch the thieves that are still working alone. When you kill one we'll make it appear that he was a Vulture. You've put yourself solid with the people tonight, by killing those fools in the Blackfoot Chief. We'll keep up the deception.

'I don't trust Ace Brent. I believe he's secretly trying to usurp my place as chief of the gang. He's too damned smart. But I don't want you to kill him. He has too many friends in the gang. Even if they didn't suspect I put you up to it, even if it looked like a private quarrel, they'd want your scalp. I'll frame him – get somebody outside the gang to kill him, when the time comes.

'When we get ready to skip, I'll set the vigilantes and the Vultures to battling each other – how, I don't know, but I'll find a way – and we'll sneak while they're at it. Then for California – South America and the sharing of the gold!'

'The sharin' of the gold!' echoed Corcoran, his eyes lit with grim laughter.

Their hard hands met across the rough table, and the same enigmatic smile played on the lips of both men.

5   The Wheel Begins to Turn

Corcoran stalked through the milling crowd that swarmed in the street, and headed toward the Golden Garter Dance Hall and Saloon. A man lurching through the door with the wide swing of hilarious intoxication stumbled into him and clutched at him to keep from falling to the floor.

Corcoran righted him, smiling faintly into the bearded, rubicund countenance that peered into his.

'Steve Corcoran, by thunder!' whooped the inebriated one gleefully. 'Besh damn' deputy in the Territory! 'S a honor to get picked up by Steve Corcoran! Come in and have a drink.'

'You've had too many now,' returned Corcoran.

'Right!' agreed the other. 'I'm goin' home now, 'f I can get there. Lasht time I was a little full, I didn't make it, by a quarter of a mile! I went to sleep in a ditch across from your shack. I'd 'a' come in and slept on the floor, only I was 'fraid you'd shoot me for one of them derned Vultures!'

Men about them laughed. The intoxicated man was Joe Willoughby, a prominent merchant in Wahpeton, and extremely popular for his free-hearted and open-handed ways.

'Just knock on the door next time and tell me who it is,' grinned Corcoran. 'You're welcome to a blanket in the sheriff's office, or a bunk in my room, any time you need it.'

'Soul of gener – generoshity!' proclaimed Willoughby boisterously. 'Goin' home now before the licker gets down in my legs. S'long, old pasd!'

He weaved away down the street, amidst the jovial joshings of the miners, to which he retorted with bibulous good nature.

Corcoran turned again into the dance hall and brushed against another man, at whom he glanced sharply, noting the set jaw, the haggard countenance and the bloodshot eyes. This man, a young miner well known to Corcoran, pushed his way through the crowd and hurried up the street with the manner of a man who goes with a definite purpose. Corcoran hesitated, as though to follow him, then decided against it and entered the dance hall. Half the reason for a gunfighter's continued existence lay in his ability to read and analyze the expressions men wore, to correctly interpret the jut of jaw, the glitter of eye. He knew this young miner was determined on some course of action that might result in violence. But the man was not a criminal, and Corcoran never interfered in private quarrels so long as they did not threaten the public safety.

A girl was singing, in a clear, melodious voice, to the accompaniment of a jangling, banging piano. As Corcoran seated himself at a table, with his back to the wall and a clear view of the whole hall before him, she concluded her number amid a boisterous clamor of applause. Her face lit as she saw him. Coming lightly across the hall, she sat down at his table. She rested her elbows on the table, cupped her chin in her hands, and fixed her wide clear gaze on his brown face.

'Shot any Vultures today, Steve?'

He made no answer as he lifted the glass of beer brought him by a waiter.

'They must be scared of you,' she continued, and something of youthful hero-worship glowed in her eyes. 'There hasn't been a murder or hold-up in town for the past month, since you've been here. Of course you can't be everywhere. They still kill men and rob them in the camps up the ravines, but they keep out of town.

'And that time you took the stage through to Yankton! It wasn't your fault that they held it up and got the gold on the other side of Yankton. You weren't in it, then. I wish I'd been there and seen the fight, when you fought off the men who tried to hold you up, half-way between here and Yankton.'

'There wasn't any fight to it,' he said impatiently, restless under praise he knew he did not deserve.

'I know; they were afraid of you. You shot at them and they ran.'

Very true; it had been Middleton's idea for Corcoran to take the stage through to the next town east, and beat off a fake attempt at hold-up. Corcoran had never relished the memory; whatever his faults, he had the pride of his profession; a fake gunfight was as repugnant to him as a business hoax to an honest business man.

'Everybody knows that the stage company tried to hire you away from Middleton, as a regular shotgun-guard. But you told them that your business was to protect life and property here in Wahpeton.'

She meditated a moment and then laughed reminiscently.

'You know, when you pulled me off of Conchita that night, I thought you were just another blustering bully like McNab. I was beginning to believe that Middleton was taking pay from the Vultures, and that his deputies were crooked. I know things that some people don't.' Her eyes became shadowed as if by an unpleasant memory in which, though her companion could not know it, was limned the handsome, sinister face of Ace Brent. 'Or maybe people do. Maybe they guess things, but are afraid to say anything.

'But I was mistaken about you, and since you're square, then Middleton must be, too. I guess it was just too big a job for him and his other deputies. None of them could have wiped out that gang in the Blackfoot Chief that night like you did. It wasn't your fault that Tom Deal got away that night, before he could be questioned. If he hadn't though, maybe you could have made him tell who the other Vultures were.'

'I met Jack McBride comin' out of here,' said Corcoran abruptly. 'He looked like he was about ready to start gunnin' for somebody. Did he drink much in here?'

'Not much. I know what's the matter with him. He's been gambling too much down at the King of Diamonds. Ace Brent has been winning his money for a week. McBride's nearly broke, and I believe he thinks Brent is crooked. He came in here, drank some whisky, and let fall a remark about having a show-down with Brent.'

Corcoran rose abruptly. 'Reckon I better drift down towards the King of Diamonds. Somethin' may bust loose there. McBride's quick with a gun and high-tempered. Brent's deadly. Their private business is none of my affair. But if they want to fight it out, they'll have to get out where innocent people won't get hit by stray slugs.'

Glory Bland watched him as his tall, erect figure swung out of the door, and there was a glow in her eyes that had never been awakened there by any other man.

Corcoran had almost reached the King of Diamonds gambling hall, when the ordinary noises of the street were split by the crash of a heavy gun. Simultaneously men came headlong out of the doors, shouting, shoving, plunging in their haste.

'McBride's killed!' bawled a hairy miner.

'No, it's Brent!' yelped another. The crowd surged and milled, craning their necks to see through the windows, yet crowding back from the door in fear of stray bullets. As Corcoran made for the door he heard a man bawl in answer to an eager question: 'McBride accused Brent of usin' marked cards, and offered to prove it to the crowd. Brent said he'd kill him and pulled his gun to do it. But it snapped. I heard the hammer click. Then McBride drilled him before he could try again.'

Men gave way as Corcoran pushed through the crowd. Somebody yelped: 'Look out, Steve! McBride's on the warpath!'

Corcoran stepped into the gambling hall, which was deserted except for the gambler who lay dead on the floor, with a bullet-hole over his heart, and the killer who half-crouched with his back to the bar, and a smoking gun lifted in his hand.

McBride's lips were twisted hard in a snarl, and he looked like a wolf at bay.

'Get back, Corcoran,' he warned. 'I ain't got nothin' against you, but I ain't goin' to be murdered like a sheep.'

'Who said anything about murderin' you?' demanded Corcoran impatiently.

'Oh, I know you wouldn't. But Brent's got friends. They'll never let me get away with killin' him. I believe he was a Vulture. I believe the Vultures will be after me for this. But if they get me, they've got to get me fightin'.'

'Nobody's goin' to hurt you,' said Corcoran tranquilly. 'You better give me your gun and come along. I'll have to arrest you, but it won't amount to nothin', and you ought to know it. As soon as a miner's court can be got together, you'll be tried and acquitted. It was a plain case of self-defense. I reckon no honest folks will do any grievin' for Ace Brent.'

'But if I give up my gun and go to jail,' objected McBride, wavering, 'I'm afraid the toughs will take me out and lynch me.'

'I'm givin' you my word you won't be harmed while you're under arrest,' answered Corcoran.

'That's enough for me,' said McBride promptly, extending his pistol.

Corcoran took it and thrust it into his waist-band. 'It's damned foolishness, takin' an honest man's gun,' he grunted. 'But accordin' to Middleton that's the law. Give me your word that you won't skip, till you've been properly acquitted, and I won't lock you up.'

'I'd rather go to jail,' said McBride. 'I wouldn't skip. But I'll be safer in jail, with you guardin' me, than I would be walkin' around loose for some of Brent's friends to shoot me in the back. After I've been cleared by due process of law, they won't dare to lynch me, and I ain't afraid of 'em when it comes to gun-fightin', in the open.'

'All right.' Corcoran stooped and picked up the dead gambler's gun, and thrust it into his belt. The crowd surging about the door gave way as he led his prisoner out.

'There the skunk is!' bawled a rough voice. 'He murdered Ace Brent!'

McBride turned pale with anger and glared into the crowd, but Corcoran urged him along, and the miner grinned as other voices rose: 'A damned good thing, too!' 'Brent was crooked!' 'He was a Vulture!' bawled somebody, and for a space a tense silence held. That charge was too sinister to bring openly against even a dead man. Frightened by his own indiscretion the man who had shouted slunk away, hoping none had identified his voice.

'I've been gamblin' too much,' growled McBride, as he strode along beside Corcoran. 'Afraid to try to take my gold out, though, and didn't know what else to do with it. Brent won thousands of dollars' worth of dust from me; poker, mostly.

'This mornin' I was talkin' to Middleton, and he showed a card he said a gambler dropped in his cabin last night. He showed me it was marked, in a way I'd never have suspected. I recognized it as one of the same brand Brent always uses, though Middleton wouldn't tell me who the gambler was. But later I learned that Brent slept off a drunk in Middleton's cabin. Damned poor business for a gambler to get drunk.

'I went to the King of Diamonds awhile ago, and started playin' poker with Brent and a couple of miners. As soon as he raked in the first pot, I called him – flashed the card I got from Middleton and started to show the boys where it was marked. Then Brent pulled his gun; it snapped, and I killed him before he could cock it again. He knew I had the goods on him. He didn't even give me time to tell where I'd gotten the card.'

Corcoran made no reply. He locked McBride in the jail, called the jailer from his near-by shack and told him to furnish the prisoner with food, liquor and anything else he needed, and then hurried to his own cabin. Sitting on his bunk in the room behind the sheriff's office, he ejected the cartridge on which Brent's pistol had snapped. The cap was dented, but had not detonated the powder. Looking closely he saw faint abrasions on both the bullet and brass case. They were such as might have been made by the jaws of iron pinchers and a vise.

Securing a wire-cutter with pincher jaws, he began to work at the bullet. It slipped out with unusual ease, and the contents of the case spilled into his hand. He did not need to use a match to prove that it was not powder. He knew what the stuff was at first glance – iron filings, to give the proper weight to the cartridge from which the powder had been removed.

At that moment he heard someone enter the outer room, and recognized the firm, easy tread of Sheriff Middleton. Corcoran went into the office and Middleton turned, hung his white hat on a nail.

'McNab tells me McBride killed Ace Brent!'

'You ought to know!' Corcoran grinned. He tossed the bullet

and empty case on the table, dumped the tiny pile of iron dust beside them.

'Brent spent the night with you. You got him drunk, and stole one of his cards to show to McBride. You knew how his cards were marked. You took a cartridge out of Brent's gun and put that one in place. One would be enough. You knew there'd be gunplay between him and McBride, when you showed McBride that marked card, and you wanted to be sure it was Brent who stopped lead.'

'That's right,' agreed Middleton. 'I haven't seen you since early yesterday morning. I was going to tell you about the frame I'd ribbed, as soon as I saw you. I didn't know McBride would go after Brent as quickly as he did.

'Brent got too ambitious. He acted as if he were suspicious of us both, lately. Maybe, though, it was just jealousy as far as you were concerned. He liked Glory Bland, and she could never see him. It gouged him to see her falling for you.

'And he wanted my place as leader of the Vultures. If there was one man in the gang that could have kept us from skipping with the loot, it was Ace Brent.

'But I think I've worked it neatly. No one can accuse me of having him murdered, because McBride isn't in the gang. I have no control over him. But Brent's friends will want revenge.'

'A miners' court will acquit McBride on the first ballot.'

'That's true. Maybe we'd better let him get shot, trying to escape!'

'We will like hell!' rapped Corcoran. 'I swore he wouldn't be harmed while he was under arrest. His part of the deal was on the level. He didn't know Brent had a blank in his gun, any more than Brent did. If Brent's friends want his scalp, let 'em go after McBride, like white men ought to, when he's in a position to defend himself.'

'But after he's acquitted,' argued Middleton, 'they won't dare gang up on him in the street, and he'll be too sharp to give them a chance at him in the hills.'

'What the hell do I care?' snarled Corcoran. 'What difference does it make to me whether Brent's friends get even or not? Far as I'm concerned, he got what was comin' to him. If they ain't got the guts to give McBride an even break, I sure ain't goin' to fix it so they can murder him without riskin' their own hides. If I catch 'em sneakin' around the jail for a shot at him, I'll fill 'em full of hot lead.

'If I'd thought the miners would be crazy enough to do anything to him for killin' Brent, I'd never arrested him. They won't. They'll acquit him. Until they do, I'm responsible for him, and I've give my word. And anybody that tries to lynch him while he's in my charge better be damned sure they're quicker with a gun than I am.'

'There's nobody of that nature in Wahpeton,' admitted Middleton with a wry smile. 'All right, if you feel your personal honor is involved. But I'll have to find a way to placate Brent's friends, or they'll be accusing me of being indifferent about what happened to him.'

6   Vultures' Court

Next morning Corcoran was awakened by a wild shouting in the street.

He had slept in the jail that night, not trusting Brent's friends, but there had been no attempt at violence. He jerked on his boots, and went out into the street, followed by McBride, to learn what the shouting was about.

Men milled about in the street, even at that early hour – for the sun was not yet up – surging about a man in the garb of a miner. This man was astride a horse whose coat was dark with sweat; the man was wild-eyed, bare-headed, and he held his hat in his hands, holding it down for the shouting, cursing throng to see.

'Look at 'em!' he yelled. 'Nuggets as big as hen eggs! I took 'em out in an hour, with a pick, diggin' in the wet sand by the creek! And there's plenty more! It's the richest strike these hills ever seen!'

'Where?' roared a hundred voices.

'Well, I got my claim staked out, all I need,' said the man, 'so I don't mind tellin' you. It ain't twenty miles from here, in a little canyon everybody's overlooked and passed over – Jackrabbit Gorge! The creek's buttered with dust, and the banks are crammed with pockets of nuggets!'

An exuberant whoop greeted this information, and the crowd broke up suddenly as men raced for their shacks.

'New strike,' sighed McBride enviously. 'The whole town will be surgin' down Jack-rabbit Gorge. Wish I could go.'

'Gimme your word you'll come back and stand trial, and you can go,' promptly offered Corcoran. McBride stubbornly shook his head.

'No, not till I've been cleared legally. Anyway, only a handful of men will get anything. The rest will be pullin' back in to their claims in Wahpeton Gulch tomorrow. Hell, I've been in plenty of them rushes. Only a few ever get anything.'

Colonel Hopkins and his partner Dick Bisley hurried past. Hopkins shouted: 'We'll have to postpone your trial until this rush is over, Jack! We were going to hold it today, but in an hour there won't be enough men in Wahpeton to impanel a jury! Sorry you can't make the rush. If we can, Dick and I will stake out a claim for you!'

'Thanks, Colonel!'

'No thanks! The camp owes you something for ridding it of that scoundrel Brent. Corcoran, we'll do the same for you, if you like.'

'No, thanks,' drawled Corcoran. 'Minin's too hard work. I've got a gold mine right here in Wahpeton that don't take so much labor!'

The men burst into laughter at this conceit, and Bisley shouted back as they hurried on: 'That's right! Your salary looks like an assay from the Comstock lode! But you earn it, all right!'

Joe Willoughby came rolling by, leading a seedy-looking burro on which illy-hung pick and shovel banged against skillet and kettle. Willoughby grasped a jug in one hand, and that he had already been sampling it was proved by his wide-legged gait.

'H'ray for the new diggin's!' he whooped, brandishing the jug at Corcoran and McBride. 'Git along, jackass! I'll be scoopin' out nuggets bigger'n this jug before night – if the licker don't git in my legs before I git there!'

'And if it does, he'll fall into a ravine and wake up in the mornin' with a fifty pound nugget in each hand,' said McBride. 'He's the luckiest son of a gun in the camp; and the best natured.'

'I'm goin' and get some ham-and-eggs,' said Corcoran. 'You want to come and eat with me, or let Pete Daley fix your breakfast here?'

'I'll eat in the jail,' decided McBride. 'I want to stay in jail till I'm acquitted. Then nobody can accuse me of tryin' to beat the law in any way.'

'All right.' With a shout to the jailer, Corcoran swung across the road and headed for the camp's most pretentious restaurant, whose proprietor was growing rich, in spite of the terrific prices he had to pay for vegetables and food of all kinds – prices he passed on to his customers.

While Corcoran was eating, Middleton entered hurriedly, and bending over him, with a hand on his shoulder, spoke softly in his ear.

'I've just got wind that that old miner, Joe Brockman, is trying to sneak his gold out on a pack mule, under the pretense of making this rush. I don't know whether it's so or not, but some of the boys up in the hills think it is, and are planning to waylay him and kill him. If he intends getting away, he'll leave the trail to Jack-rabbit Gorge a few miles out of town, and swing back toward Yankton, taking the trail over Grizzly Ridge – you know where the thickets are so close. The boys will be laying for him either on the ridge or just beyond.

'He hasn't enough dust to make it worth our while to take it. If they hold him up they'll have to kill him, and we want as few murders as possible. Vigilante sentiment is growing, in spite of the people's trust in you and me. Get on your horse and ride to Grizzly Ridge and see that the old man gets away safe. Tell the boys Middleton said to lay off. If they won't listen – but they will. They wouldn't buck you, even without my word to back you. I'll follow the old man, and try to catch up with him before he leaves the Jack-rabbit Gorge road.

'I've sent McNab up to watch the jail, just as a formality. I know McBride won't try to escape, but we mustn't be accused of carelessness.'

'Let McNab be mighty careful with his shootin' irons,' warned Corcoran. 'No "shot while attemptin' to escape", Middleton. I don't trust McNab. If he lays a hand on McBride, I'll kill him as sure as I'm sittin' here.'

'Don't worry. McNab hated Brent. Better get going. Take the short cut through the hills to Grizzly Ridge.'

'Sure.' Corcoran rose and hurried out in the street which was all but deserted. Far down toward the other end of the gulch rose the dust of the rearguard of the army which was surging toward the new strike. Wahpeton looked almost like a deserted town in the early morning light, foreshadowing its ultimate destiny.

Corcoran went to the corral beside the sheriff's cabin and saddled a fast horse, glancing cryptically at the powerful pack mules whose numbers were steadily increasing. He smiled grimly as he remembered Middleton telling Colonel Hopkins that pack mules were a good investment. As he led his horse out of the corral his gaze fell on a man sprawling under the trees across the road, lazily whittling. Day and night, in one way or another, the gang kept an eye on the cabin which hid the cache of their gold. Corcoran doubted if they actually suspected Middleton's intentions. But they wanted to be sure that no stranger did any snooping about.

Corcoran rode into a ravine that straggled away from the gulch, and a few minutes later he followed a narrow path to its rim, and headed through the mountains toward the spot, miles away, where a trail crossed Grizzly Ridge, a long, steep backbone, thickly timbered.

He had not left the ravine far behind him when a quick rattle of hoofs brought him around, in time to see a horse slide recklessly down a low bluff amid a shower of shale. He swore at the sight of its rider.

'Glory! What the hell?'

'Steve!' She reined up breathlessly beside him. 'Go back! It's a trick! I heard Buck Gorman talking to Conchita; he's sweet on her. He's a friend of Brent's – a Vulture! She twists all his secrets out of him. Her room is next to mine, she thought I was out. I overheard them talking. Gorman said a trick had been played on you to get you out of town. He didn't say how. Said you'd go to Grizzly Ridge on a wild-goose chase. While you're gone they're going to assemble a "miner's court," out of the riff-raff left in town. They're going to appoint a "judge" and "jury," take McBride out of jail, try him for killing Ace Brent – and hang him!'

A lurid oath ripped through Steve Corcoran's lips, and for an instant the tiger flashed into view, eyes blazing, fangs bared. Then his dark face was an inscrutable mask again. He wrenched his horse around.

'Much obliged, Glory. I'll be dustin' back into town. You circle around and come in another way. I don't want folks to know you told me.'

'Neither do I!' she shuddered. 'I knew Ace Brent was a Vulture. He boasted of it to me, once when he was drunk. But I never dared tell anyone. He told me what he'd do to me if I did. I'm glad he's dead. I didn't know Gorman was a Vulture, but I might have guessed it. He was Brent's closest friend. If they ever find out I told you –'

'They won't,' Corcoran assured her. It was natural for a girl to fear such black-hearted rogues as the Vultures, but the thought of them actually harming her never entered his mind. He came from a country where not even the worst of scoundrels would ever dream of hurting a woman.

He drove his horse at a reckless gallop back the way he had come, but not all the way. Before he reached the Gulch he swung wide of the ravine he had followed out, and plunged into another, that would bring him into the Gulch at the end of town where the jail stood. As he rode down it he heard a deep, awesome roar he recognized – the roar of the man-pack, hunting its own kind.

A band of men surged up the dusty street, roaring, cursing. One man waved a rope. Pale faces of bartenders, store-clerks and dance-hall girls peered timidly out of doorways as the unsavory mob roared past. Corcoran knew them, by sight or reputation: plug-uglies, barroom loafers, skulkers – many were Vultures, as he knew; others were riff-raff, ready for any sort of deviltry that required neither courage nor intelligence – the scum that gathers in any mining camp.

Dismounting, Corcoran glided through the straggling trees that grew behind the jail, and heard McNab challenge the mob.

'What do you want?'

'We aim to try your prisoner!' shouted the leader. 'We come in the due process of law. We've app'inted a jedge and panelled a jury, and we demands that you hand over the prisoner to be tried in miners' court, accordin' to legal precedent!'

'How do I know you're representative of the camp?' parried McNab.

''Cause we're the only body of men in camp right now!' yelled someone, and this was greeted by a roar of laughter.

'We come empowered with the proper authority –' began the leader, and broke off suddenly: 'Grab him, boys!'

There was the sound of a brief scuffle, McNab swore vigorously, and the leader's voice rose triumphantly: 'Let go of him, boys, but don't give him his gun. McNab, you ought to know better'n to try to oppose legal procedure, and you a upholder of law and order!'

Again a roar of sardonic laughter, and McNab growled: 'All right; go ahead with the trial. But you do it over my protests. I don't believe this is a representative assembly.'

'Yes, it is,' averred the leader, and then his voice thickened with blood-lust. 'Now, Daley, gimme that key and bring out the prisoner.'

The mob surged toward the door of the jail, and at that instant Corcoran stepped around the corner of the cabin and leaped up on the low porch it boasted. There was a hissing intake of breath. Men halted suddenly, digging their heels against the pressure behind them. The surging line wavered backward, leaving two figures isolated – McNab, scowling, disarmed, and a hairy giant whose huge belly was girt with a broad belt bristling with gun butts and knife hilts. He held a noose in one hand, and his bearded lips gaped as he glared at the unexpected apparition.

For a breathless instant Corcoran did not speak. He did not look at McBride's pallid countenance peering through the barred door behind him. He stood facing the mob, his head slightly bent, a somber, immobile figure, sinister with menace.

'Well,' he said finally, softly, 'what's holdin' up the *baile*?'

The leader blustered feebly.

'We come here to try a murderer!'

Corcoran lifted his head and the man involuntarily recoiled at the lethal glitter of his eyes.

'Who's your judge?' the Texan inquired softly.

'We appointed Jake Bissett, there,' spoke up a man, pointing at the uncomfortable giant on the porch.

'So you're goin' to hold a miners' court,' murmured Corcoran. 'With a judge and jury picked out of the dives and honky-tonks – scum and dirt of the gutter!' And suddenly uncontrollable fury flamed in his eyes. Bissett, sensing his intention, bellowed in ox-like alarm and grabbed frantically at a gun. His fingers had scarcely touched the checkered butt when smoke and flame roared from Corcoran's right hip. Bissett pitched backward off the porch as if he had been struck by a hammer; the rope tangled about his limbs as he fell, and he lay in the dust that slowly turned crimson, his hairy fingers twitching spasmodically.

Corcoran faced the mob, livid under his sun-burnt bronze. His eyes were coals of blue hell's-fire. There was a gun in each hand, and from the right-hand muzzle a wisp of blue smoke drifted lazily upward.

'I declare this court adjourned!' he roared. 'The judge is done impeached, and the jury's discharged! I'll give you thirty seconds to clear the court-room!'

He was one man against nearly a hundred, but he was a gray wolf facing a pack of yapping jackals. Each man knew that if the mob surged on him, they would drag him down at last; but each man knew what an awful toll would first be paid, and each man feared that he himself would be one of those to pay that toll.

They hesitated, stumbled back – gave way suddenly and scattered in all directions. Some backed away, some shamelessly turned their backs and fled. With a snarl Corcoran thrust his guns back in their scabbards and turned toward the door where McBride stood, grasping the bars.

'I thought I was a goner that time, Corcoran,' he gasped. The

Texan pulled the door open, and pushed McBride's pistol into his hand.

'There's a horse tied behind the jail,' said Corcoran. 'Get on it and dust out of here. I'll take the full responsibility. If you stay here they'll burn down the jail, or shoot you through the window. You can make it out of town while they're scattered. I'll explain to Middleton and Hopkins. In a month or so, if you want to, come back and stand trial, as a matter of formality. Things will be cleaned up around here by then.'

McBride needed no urging. The grisly fate he had just escaped had shaken his nerve. Shaking Corcoran's hand passionately, he ran stumblingly through the trees to the horse Corcoran had left there. A few moments later he was fogging it out of the Gulch.

McNab came up, scowling and grumbling.

'You had no authority to let him go. I tried to stop the mob –'

Corcoran wheeled and faced him, making no attempt to conceal his hatred.

'You did like hell! Don't pull that stuff with me, McNab. You was in on this, and so was Middleton. You put up a bluff of talk, so afterwards you could tell Colonel Hopkins and the others that you tried to stop the lynchin' and was overpowered. I saw the scrap you put up when they grabbed you! Hell! You're a rotten actor.'

'You can't talk to me like that!' roared McNab.

The old tigerish light flickered in the blue eyes. Corcoran did not exactly move, yet he seemed to sink into a half crouch, as a cougar does for the killing spring.

'If you don't like my style, McNab,' he said softly, thickly, 'you're more'n welcome to open the *baile* whenever you get ready!'

For an instant they faced each other, McNab black-browed and scowling, Corcoran's thin lips almost smiling, but blue fire lighting his eyes. Then with a grunt McNab turned and slouched away, his shaggy head swaying from side to side like that of a surly bull.

7   A Vulture's Wings Are Clipped

Middleton pulled up his horse suddenly as Corcoran reined out of the bushes. One glance showed the sheriff that Corcoran's mood was far from placid. They were amidst a grove of alders, perhaps a mile from the Gulch.

'Why, hello, Corcoran,' began Middleton, concealing his surprize. 'I caught up with Brockman. It was just a wild rumor. He didn't have any gold. That –'

'Drop it!' snapped Corcoran. 'I know why you sent me off on that wild-goose chase – same reason you pulled out of town. To give Brent's friends a chance to get even with McBride. If I hadn't turned around and dusted back into Wahpeton, McBride would be kickin' his life out at the end of a rope, right now.'

'You came back – ?'

'Yeah! And now Jake Bissett's in hell instead of Jack McBride, and McBride's dusted out – on a horse I gave him. I told you I gave him my word he wouldn't be lynched.'

'You killed Bissett?'

'Deader'n hell!'

'He was a Vulture,' muttered Middleton, but he did not seem displeased. 'Brent, Bissett – the more Vultures die, the easier it will be for us to get away when we go. That's one reason I had Brent killed. But you should have let them hang McBride. Of course I framed this affair; I had to do something to satisfy Brent's friends. Otherwise they might have gotten suspicious.

'If they suspicioned I had anything to do with having him killed, or thought I wasn't anxious to punish the man who killed him, they'd make trouble for me. I can't have a split in the gang now. And even I can't protect you from Brent's friends, after this.'

'Have I ever asked you, or any man, for protection?' The quick jealous pride of the gunfighter vibrated in his voice.

'Breckman, Red Bill, Curly, and now Bissett. You've killed too many Vultures. I made them think the killing of the first three was a mistake, all around. Bissett wasn't very popular. But they won't forgive you for stopping them from hanging the man who killed Ace Brent. They won't attack you openly, of course. But you'll have to watch every step you make. They'll kill you if they can, and I won't be able to prevent them.'

'If I'd tell 'em just how Ace Brent died, you'd be in the same boat,' said Corcoran bitingly. 'Of course, I won't. Our final get-away depends on you keepin' their confidence – as well as the confidence of the honest folks. This last killin' ought to put me, and therefore you, ace-high with Hopkins and his crowd.'

'They're still talking vigilante. I encourage it. It's coming anyway. Murders in the outlying camps are driving men to a frenzy of fear and rage, even though such crimes have ceased in Wahpeton. Better to fall in line with the inevitable and twist it to a man's own ends, than to try to oppose it. If you can keep Brent's friends from killing you for a few more weeks, we'll be ready to jump. Look out for Buck Gorman. He's the most dangerous man in the gang. He was Brent's friend, and he has his own friends – all dangerous men. Don't kill him unless you have to.'

'I'll take care of myself,' answered Corcoran somberly. 'I looked for Gorman in the mob, but he wasn't there. Too smart. But he's the man behind the mob. Bissett was just a stupid ox; Gorman planned it – or rather, I reckon he helped you plan it.'

'I'm wondering how you found out about it,' said Middleton. 'You wouldn't have come back unless somebody told you. Who was it?'

'None of your business,' growled Corcoran. It did not occur

to him that Glory Bland would be in any danger from Middleton, even if the sheriff knew about her part in the affair, but he did not relish being questioned, and did not feel obliged to answer anybody's queries.

'That new gold strike sure came in mighty handy for you and Gorman,' he said. 'Did you frame that, too?'

Middleton nodded.

'Of course. That was one of my men who poses as a miner. He had a hatful of nuggets from the cache. He served his purpose and joined the men who hide up there in the hills. The mob of miners will be back tomorrow, tired and mad and disgusted, and when they hear about what happened, they'll recognize the handiwork of the Vultures; at least some of them will. But they won't connect me with it in any way. Now we'll ride back to town. Things are breaking our way, in spite of your foolish interference with the mob. But let Gorman alone. You can't afford to make any more enemies in the gang.'

Buck Gorman leaned on the bar in the Golden Eagle and expressed his opinion of Steve Corcoran in no uncertain terms. The crowd listened sympathetically, for, almost to a man, they were the ruffians and riff-raff of the camp.

'The dog pretends to be a deputy!' roared Gorman, whose blood-shot eyes and damp tangled hair attested to the amount of liquor he had drunk. 'But he kills an appointed judge, breaks up a court and drives away the jury – yes, and releases the prisoner, a man charged with murder!'

It was the day after the fake gold strike, and the disillusioned miners were drowning their chagrin in the saloons. But few honest miners were in the Golden Eagle.

'Colonel Hopkins and other prominent citizens held an investigation,' said some one. 'They declared that evidence showed Corcoran to have been justified – denounced the court as a mob, acquitted Corcoran of killing Bissett, and then went ahead and acquitted McBride for killing Brent, even though he wasn't there.'

Gorman snarled like a cat, and reached for his whisky glass. His hand did not twitch or quiver, his movements were more catlike than ever. The whisky had inflamed his mind, illumined his brain with a white-hot certainty that was akin to insanity, but it had not affected his nerves or any part of his muscular system. He was more deadly drunk than sober.

'I was Brent's best friend!' he roared. 'I was Bissett's friend.'

'They say Bissett was a Vulture,' whispered a voice. Gorman lifted his tawny head and glared about the room as a lion might glare.

'Who says he was a Vulture? Why don't these slanderers accuse a living man? It's always a dead man they accuse! Well, what if he was? He was my friend! Maybe that makes *me* a Vulture!'

No one laughed or spoke as his flaming gaze swept the room, but each man, as those blazing eyes rested on him in turn, felt the chill breath of Death blowing upon him.

'Bissett a Vulture!' he said, wild enough with drink and fury to commit any folly, as well as any atrocity. He did not heed the eyes fixed on him, some in fear, a few in intense interest. 'Who knows who the Vultures are? Who knows who, or what any-body really is? Who really knows anything about this man Corcoran, for instance? I could tell –'

A light step on the threshold brought him about as Corcoran loomed in the door. Gorman froze, snarling, lips writhed back, a tawny-maned incarnation of hate and menace.

'I heard you was makin' a talk about me down here, Gor-man,' said Corcoran. His face was bleak and emotionless as that of a stone image, but his eyes burned with murderous purpose.

Gorman snarled wordlessly.

'I looked for you in the mob,' said Corcoran, tonelessly, his voice as soft and without emphasis as the even strokes of a feather. It seemed almost as if his voice were a thing apart from him; his lips murmuring while all the rest of his being was tense with concentration on the man before him.

'You wasn't there. You sent your coyotes, but you didn't have the guts to come yourself, and –'

The dart of Gorman's hand to his gun was like the blurring stroke of a snake's head, but no eye could follow Corcoran's hand. His gun smashed before anyone knew he had reached for it. Like an echo came the roar of Gorman's shot. But the bullet ploughed splinteringly into the floor, from a hand that was already death-stricken and falling. Gorman pitched over and lay still, the swinging lamp glinting on his upturned spurs and the blue steel of the smoking gun which lay by his hand.

8   The Coming of the Vigilantes

Colonel Hopkins looked absently at the liquor in his glass, stirred restlessly, and said abruptly: 'Middleton, I might as well come to the point. My friends and I have organized a vigilante committee, just as we should have done months ago. Now, wait a minute. Don't take this as a criticism of your methods. You've done wonders in the last month, ever since you brought Steve Corcoran in here. Not a hold-up in the town, not a killing – that is, not a murder, and only a few shootings among the honest citizens.

'Added to that the ridding of the camp of such scoundrels as Jake Bissett and Buck Gorman. They were both undoubtedly members of the Vultures. I wish Corcoran hadn't killed Gorman just when he did, though. The man was drunk, and about to make some reckless disclosures about the gang. At least that's what a friend of mine thinks, who was in the Golden Eagle that night. But anyway it couldn't be helped.

'No, we're not criticizing you at all. But obviously you can't stop the murders and robberies that are going on up and down the Gulch, all the time. And you can't stop the outlaws from holding up the stage regularly.

'So that's where we come in. We have sifted the camp, carefully, over a period of months, until we have fifty men we can trust absolutely. It's taken a long time, because we've had to be sure of our men. We didn't want to take in a man who might be a spy for the Vultures. But at last we know where we stand. We're not sure just who *is* a Vulture, but we know who *isn't*, in as far as our organization is concerned.

'We can work together, John. We have no intention of interfering within your jurisdiction, or trying to take the law out of your hands. We demand a free hand outside the camp; inside the limits of Wahpeton we are willing to act under your orders, or at least according to your advice. Of course we will work in absolute secrecy until we have proof enough to strike.'

'You must remember, Colonel,' reminded Middleton, 'that all along I've admitted the impossibility of my breaking up the Vultures with the limited means at my disposal. I've never opposed a vigilante committee. All I've demanded was that when it was formed, it should be composed of honest men, and be free of any element which might seek to twist its purpose into the wrong channels.'

'That's true. I didn't expect any opposition from you, and I can assure you that we'll always work hand-in-hand with you and your deputies.' He hesitated, as if over something unpleasant, and then said: 'John, are you sure of *all* your deputies?'

Middleton's head jerked up and he shot a startled glance at the Colonel, as if the latter had surprised him by putting into words a thought that had already occurred to him.

'Why do you ask?' he parried.

'Well,' Hopkins was embarrassed. 'I don't know – maybe I'm

prejudiced – but – well, damn it, to put it bluntly, I've sometimes wondered about Bill McNab!'

Middleton filled the glasses again before he answered.

'Colonel, I never accuse a man without iron-clad evidence. I'm not always satisfied with McNab's actions, but it may merely be the man's nature. He's a surly brute. But he has his virtues. I'll tell you frankly, the reason I haven't discharged him is that I'm not sure of him. That probably sounds ambiguous.'

'Not at all. I appreciate your position. You have as much as said you suspect him of double-dealing, and are keeping him on your force so you can watch him. Your wits are not dull, John. Frankly – and this will probably surprise you – until a month ago some of the men were beginning to whisper some queer things about you – queer suspicions, that is. But your bringing Corcoran in showed us that you were on the level. You'd have never brought him in if you'd been taking pay from the Vultures!'

Middleton halted with his glass at his lips.

'Great heavens!' he ejaculated. 'Did they suspect me of *that*?'

'Just a fool idea some of the men had,' Hopkins assured him. 'Of course I never gave it a thought. The men who thought it are ashamed now. The killing of Bissett, of Gorman, of the men in the Blackfoot Chief, show that Corcoran's on the level. And of course, he's merely taking his orders from you. All those men were Vultures, of course. It's a pity Tom Deal got away before we could question him.' He rose to go.

'McNab was guarding Deal,' said Middleton, and his tone implied more than his words said.

Hopkins shot him a startled glance.

'By heaven, so he was! But he was really wounded – I saw the bullet hole in his arm, where Deal shot him in making his get-away.'

'That's true.' Middleton rose and reached for his hat. 'I'll walk along with you. I want to find Corcoran and tell him what you've just told me.'

'It's been a week since he killed Gorman,' mused Hopkins. 'I've been expecting Gorman's Vulture friends to try to get him, any time.'

'So have I!' answered Middleton, with a grimness which his companion missed.

9   The Vultures Swoop

Down the gulch lights blazed; the windows of cabins were yellow squares in the night, and beyond them the velvet sky reflected the lurid heart of the camp. The intermittent breeze brought faint strains of music and the other noises of hilarity. But up the gulch, where a clump of trees straggled near an unlighted cabin, the darkness of the moonless night was a mask that the faint stars did not illuminate.

Figures moved in the deep shadows of the trees, voices whispered, their furtive tones mingling with the rustling of the wind through the leaves.

'We ain't close enough. We ought to lay alongside his cabin and blast him as he goes in.'

A second voice joined the first, muttering like a bodyless voice in a conclave of ghosts.

'We've gone all over that. I tell you this is the best way. Get him off guard. You're sure Middleton was playin' cards at the King of Diamonds?'

Another voice answered: 'He'll be there till daylight, likely.'

'He'll be awful mad,' whispered the first speaker.

'Let him. He can't afford to do anything about it. *Listen!* Somebody's comin' up the road!'

They crouched down in the bushes, merging with the blacker shadows. They were so far from the cabin, and it was so dark, that the approaching figure was only a dim blur in the gloom.

'It's him!' a voice hissed fiercely, as the blur merged with the bulkier shadow that was the cabin.

In the stillness a door rasped across a sill. A yellow light sprang up, streaming through the door, blocking out a small window high up in the wall. The man inside did not cross the lighted doorway, and the window was too high to see through into the cabin.

The light went out after a few minutes.

'Come on!' The three men rose and went stealthily toward the cabin. Their bare feet made no sound, for they had discarded their boots. Coats too had been discarded, any garment that might swing loosely and rustle, or catch on projections. Cocked guns were in their hands, they could have been no more wary had they been approaching the lair of a lion. And each man's heart pounded suffocatingly, for the prey they stalked was far more dangerous than any lion.

When one spoke it was so low that his companions hardly heard him with their ears a matter of inches from his bearded lips.

'We'll take our places like we planned, Joel. You'll go to the door and call him; like we told you. He knows Middleton trusts you. He don't know you'd be helpin' Gorman's friends. He'll recognize your voice, and he won't suspect nothin'. When he comes to the door and opens it, step back into the shadows and fall flat. We'll do the rest from where we'll be layin'.'

His voice shook slightly as he spoke, and the other man shuddered; his face was a pallid oval in the darkness.

'I'll do it, but I bet he kills some of us. I bet he kills me, anyway. I must have been crazy when I said I'd help you fellows.'

'You can't back out now!' hissed the other. They stole forward, their guns advanced, their hearts in their mouths. Then the foremost man caught at the arms of his companions.

'Wait! Look there! He's left the door open!'

The open doorway was a blacker shadow in the shadow of the wall.

'He knows we're after him!' There was a catch of hysteria in the babbling whisper. 'It's a trap!'

'Don't be a fool! How could he know? He's asleep. I hear him snorin'. We won't wake him. We'll step into the cabin and let him have it! We'll have enough light from the window to locate the bunk, and we'll rake it with lead before he can move. He'll wake up in hell. Come on, and for God's sake, don't make no noise!'

The last advice was unnecessary. Each man, as he set his bare foot down, felt as if he were setting it into the lair of a diamond-backed rattler.

As they glided, one after another, across the threshold, they made less noise than the wind blowing through the black branches. They crouched by the door, straining their eyes across the room, whence came the rhythmic snoring. Enough light sifted through the small window to show them a vague outline that was a bunk, with a shapeless mass upon it.

A man caught his breath in a short, uncontrollable gasp. Then the cabin was shaken by a thunderous volley, three guns roaring together. Lead swept the bunk in a devastating storm, thudding into flesh and bone, smacking into wood. A wild cry broke in a gagging gasp. Limbs thrashed wildly and a heavy body tumbled to the floor. From the darkness on the floor beside the bunk welled up hideous sounds, choking gurgles and a convulsive flopping and thumping. The men crouching near the door poured lead blindly at the sounds. There was fear and panic in the haste and number of their shots. They did not cease jerking their triggers until their guns were empty, and the noises on the floor had ceased.

'Out of here, quick!' gasped one.

'No! Here's the table, and a candle on it. I felt it in the dark. I've got to *know* that he's dead before I leave this cabin. I've got to see him lyin' dead if I'm goin' to sleep easy. We've got plenty of time to get away. Folks down the gulch must have heard the shots, but it'll take time for them to get here. No danger. I'm goin' to light the candle –'

There was a rasping sound, and a yellow light sprang up, etching three staring, bearded faces. Wisps of blue smoke blurred the light as the candle-wick ignited from the fumbling match, but the men saw a huddled shape crumpled near the bunk, from which streams of dark crimson radiated in every direction.

'Ahhh!'

They whirled at the sound of running footsteps.

'Oh, God!' shrieked one of the men, falling to his knees, his hands lifted to shut out a terrible sight. The other ruffians staggered with the shock of what they saw. They stood gaping, livid, helpless, empty guns sagging in their hands.

For in the doorway, glaring in dangerous amazement, with a gun in each hand, stood the man whose lifeless body they thought lay over there by the splintered bunk!

'Drop them guns!' Corcoran rasped. They clattered on the floor as the hands of their owner mechanically reached skyward. The man on the floor staggered up, his hands empty; he retched, shaken by the nausea of fear.

'Joel Miller!' said Corcoran evenly; his surprise was passed, as he realized what had happened. 'Didn't know you run with Gorman's crowd. Reckon Middleton'll be some surprised, too.'

'You're a devil!' gasped Miller. 'You can't be killed! We killed you – heard you roll off your bunk and die on the floor, in the dark. We kept shooting after we knew you were dead. But you're alive!'

'You didn't shoot me,' grunted Corcoran. 'You shot a man you thought was me. I was comin' up the road when I heard the shots. You killed Joe Willoughby! He was drunk and I reckon he staggered in here and fell in my bunk, like he's done before.'

The men went whiter yet under their bushy beards, with rage and chagrin and fear.

'Willoughby!' babbled Miller. 'The camp will never stand for this! Let us go, Corcoran! Hopkins and his crowd will hang us! It'll mean the end of the Vultures! Your end, too, Corcoran! If they hang us, we'll talk first! They'll find out that you're one of us!'

'In that case,' muttered Corcoran, his eyes narrowing, 'I'd better kill the three of you. That's the sensible solution. You killed Willoughby, tryin' to get me; I kill you, in self-defense.'

'Don't do it, Corcoran!' screamed Miller, frantic with terror.

'Shut up, you dog,' growled one of the other men, glaring balefully at their captor. 'Corcoran wouldn't shoot down unarmed men.'

'No, I wouldn't,' said Corcoran. 'Not unless you made some kind of a break. I'm peculiar that way, which I see is a handicap in this country. But it's the way I was raised, and I can't get over it. No, I ain't goin' to beef you cold, though you've just tried to get me that way.

'But I'll be damned if I'm goin' to let you sneak off, to come back here and try it again the minute you get your nerve bucked up. I'd about as soon be hanged by the vigilantes as shot in the back by a passle of rats like you-all. Vultures, hell! You ain't even got the guts to be good buzzards.

'I'm goin' to take you down the gulch and throw you in jail. It'll be up to Middleton to decide what to do with you. He'll probably work out some scheme that'll swindle everybody except himself; but I warn you – one yap about the Vultures to anybody, and I'll forget my raisin' and send you to hell with your belts empty and your boots on.'

The noise in the King of Diamonds was hushed suddenly as a man rushed in and bawled: 'The Vultures have murdered Joe Willoughby! Steve Corcoran caught three of 'em, and has just locked 'em up! This time we've got some live Vultures to work on!'

A roar answered him and the gambling hall emptied itself as

men rushed yelling into the street. John Middleton laid down his hand of cards, donned his white hat with a hand that was steady as a rock, and strode after them.

Already a crowd was surging and roaring around the jail. The miners were lashed into a murderous frenzy and were restrained from shattering the door and dragging forth the cowering prisoners only by the presence of Corcoran, who faced them on the jail-porch. McNab, Richardson and Stark were there, also. McNab was pale under his whiskers, and Stark seemed nervous and ill at ease, but Richardson, as always, was cold as ice.

'Hang 'em!' roared the mob. 'Let us have 'em, Steve! You've done your part! This camp's put up with enough! Let us have 'em!'

Middleton climbed up on the porch, and was greeted by loud cheers but his efforts to quiet the throng proved futile. Somebody brandished a rope with a noose in it. Resentment, long smoldering, was bursting into flame, fanned by hysterical fear and hate. The mob had no wish to harm either Corcoran or Middleton – did not intend to harm them. But they were determined to drag out the prisoners and string them up.

Colonel Hopkins forced his way through the crowd, mounted the step, and waved his hands until he obtained a certain amount of silence.

'Listen, men!' he roared, 'this is the beginning of a new era for Wahpeton! This camp has been terrorized long enough. We're beginning a rule of law and order, right now! But don't spoil it at the very beginning! These men shall hang – I swear it! But let's do it legally, and with the sanction of law. Another thing: if you hang them out of hand, we'll never learn who their companions and leaders are.

'Tomorrow, I promise you, a court of inquiry will sit on their case. They'll be questioned and forced to reveal the men above and behind them. This camp is going to be cleaned up! Let's clean it up lawfully and in order!'

'Colonel's right!' bawled a bearded giant. 'Ain't no use to hang the little rats till we find out who's the big 'uns!'

A roar of approbation rose as the temper of the mob changed. It began to break up, as the men scattered to hasten back to the bars and indulge in their passion to discuss the new development.

Hopkins shook Corcoran's hand heartily.

'Congratulations, sir! I've seen poor Joe's body. A terrible sight. The fiends fairly shot the poor fellow to ribbons. Middleton, I told you the vigilantes wouldn't usurp your authority in Wahpeton. I keep my word. We'll leave these murderers in your jail, guarded by your deputies. Tomorrow the vigilante court will sit in session, and I hope we'll come to the bottom of this filthy mess.'

And so saying he strode off, followed by a dozen or so steely-eyed men whom Middleton knew formed the nucleus of the Colonel's organization.

When they were out of hearing, Middleton stepped to the door and spoke quickly to the prisoners: 'Keep your mouths shut. You fools have gotten us all in a jam, but I'll snake you out of it, somehow.' To McNab he spoke: 'Watch the jail. Don't let anybody come near it. Corcoran and I have got to talk this over.' Lowering his voice so the prisoners could not hear, he added: 'If anybody does come, that you can't order off, and these fools start shooting off their heads, close their mouths with lead.'

Corcoran followed Middleton into the shadow of the gulch-wall. Out of earshot of the nearest cabin, Middleton turned. 'Just what happened?'

'Gorman's friends tried to get me. They killed Joe Willoughby by mistake. I hauled them in. That's all.'

'That's not all,' muttered Middleton. 'There'll be hell to pay if they come to trial. Miller's yellow. He'll talk, sure. I've been afraid Gorman's friends would try to kill you – wondering how it would work out. It's worked out just about the worst way it possibly could. You should either have killed them or let them go. Yet I appreciate your attitude. You have scruples against cold-blooded murder; and if you'd turned them loose, they'd have been back potting at you the next night.'

'I couldn't have turned them loose if I'd wanted to. Men had heard the shots; they came runnin'; found me there holdin' a gun on those devils, and Joe Willoughby's body layin' on the floor, shot to pieces.'

'I know. But we can't keep members of our own gang in jail, and we can't hand them over to the vigilantes. I've got to delay that trial, somehow. If I were ready, we'd jump tonight, and to hell with it. But I'm not ready. After all, perhaps it's as well this happened. It may give us our chance to skip. We're one jump ahead of the vigilantes and the gang, too. We know the vigilantes have formed and are ready to strike, and the rest of the gang don't. I've told no one but you what Hopkins told me early in the evening.

'Listen, Corcoran, we've got to move tomorrow night! I wanted to pull one last job, the biggest of all – the looting of Hopkins and Bisley's private cache. I believe I could have done it, in spite of all their guards and precautions. But we'll have to let that slide. I'll persuade Hopkins to put off the trial another day. I think I know how. Tomorrow night I'll have the vigilantes and the Vultures at each other's throats! We'll load the mules and pull out while they're fighting. Once let us get a good start, and they're welcome to chase us if they want to.

'I'm going to find Hopkins now. You get back to the jail. If McNab talks to Miller or the others, be sure you listen to what's said.'

Middleton found Hopkins in the Golden Eagle Saloon.

'I've come to ask a favor of you, Colonel,' he began directly. 'I want you, if it's possible, to put off the investigating trial until day after tomorrow. I've been talking to Joel Miller. He's cracking. If I can get him away from Barlow and Letcher, and talk to him, I believe he'll tell me everything I want to know. It'll be better to get his confession, signed and sworn to, before we bring the matter into court. Before a judge, with all eyes on him, and his friends in the crowd, he might stiffen and refuse to incriminate anyone. I don't believe the others will talk. But talking to me, alone, I believe Miller will spill the whole works. But it's going to take time to wear him down. I believe that by tomorrow night I'll have a full confession from him.'

'That would make our work a great deal easier,' admitted Hopkins.

'And another thing: these men ought to be represented by proper counsel. You'll prosecute them, of course; and the only other lawyer within reach is Judge Bixby, at Yankton. We're doing this thing in as close accordance to regular legal procedure as possible. Therefore we can't refuse the prisoner the right to be defended by an attorney. I've sent a man after Bixby. It will be late tomorrow evening before he can get back with the Judge, even if he has no trouble in locating him.

'Considering all these things, I feel it would be better to postpone the trial until we can get Bixby here, and until I can get Miller's confession.'

'What will the camp think?'

'Most of them are men of reason. The few hotheads who might want to take matters into their own hands can't do any harm.'

'All right,' agreed Hopkins. 'After all, they're your prisoners, since your deputy captured them, and the attempted murder of an officer of the law is one of the charges for which they'll have to stand trial. We'll set the trial for day after tomorrow. Meanwhile, work on Joel Miller. If we have his signed confession, naming the leaders of the gang, it will expedite matters a great deal at the trial.'

10   The Blood on the Gold

Wahpeton learned of the postponement of the trial and reacted in various ways. The air was surcharged with tension. Little work was done that day. Men gathering in heated, gesticulating groups, crowded in at the bars. Voices rose in hot altercation, fists pounded on the bars. Unfamiliar faces were observed, men who were seldom seen in the gulch – miners from claims in distant canyons, or more sinister figures from the hills, whose business was less obvious.

Lines of cleavage were noticed. Here and there clumps of men gathered, keeping to themselves and talking in low tones. In certain dives the ruffian element of the camp gathered, and these saloons were shunned by honest men. But still the great mass of the people milled about, suspicious and uncertain. The status of too many men was still in doubt. Certain men were known to be above suspicion, certain others were known to be ruffians and criminals; but between these two extremes there were possibilities for all shades of distrust and suspicion.

So most men wandered aimlessly to and fro, with their weapons ready to their hands, glancing at their fellows out of the corners of their eyes.

To the surprise of all, Steve Corcoran was noticed at several bars, drinking heavily, though the liquor did not seem to affect him in any way.

The men in the jail were suffering from nerves. Somehow the word had gotten out that the vigilante organization was a reality, and that they were to be tried before a vigilante court. Joel Miller, hysterical, accused Middleton of double-crossing his men.

'Shut up, you fool!' snarled the sheriff, showing the strain under which he was laboring merely by the irascible edge on his voice. 'Haven't you seen your friends drifting by the jail? I've

gathered the men in from the hills. They're all here. Forty-odd
men, every Vulture in the gang, is here in Wahpeton.

'Now, get this: and McNab, listen closely: we'll stage the
break just before daylight, when everybody is asleep. Just before
dawn is the best time, because that's about the only time in the
whole twenty-four hours that the camp isn't going full blast.

'Some of the boys, with masks on, will swoop down and
overpower you deputies. There'll be no shots fired until they've
gotten the prisoners and started off. Then start yelling and
shooting after them – in the air, of course. That'll bring everybody on the run to hear how you were overpowered by a gang
of masked riders.

'Miller, you and Letcher and Barlow will put up a fight –'

'Why?'

'Why, you fool, to make it look like it's a mob that's capturing
you, instead of friends rescuing you. That'll explain why none
of the deputies are hurt. Men wanting to lynch you wouldn't
want to hurt the officers. You'll yell and scream blue murder,
and the men in the masks will drag you out, tie you and throw
you across horses and ride off. Somebody is bound to see them
riding away. It'll look like a capture, not a rescue.'

Bearded lips gaped in admiring grins at the strategy.

'All right. Don't make a botch of it. There'll be hell to pay, but
I'll convince Hopkins that it was the work of a mob, and we'll
search the hills to find your bodies hanging from trees. We won't
find any bodies, naturally, but maybe we'll contrive to find a
mass of ashes where a log hut had been burned to the ground,
and a few hats and belt buckles easy to identify.'

Miller shivered at the implication and stared at Middleton
with painful intensity.

'Middleton, you ain't planning to have us put out of the way?
These men in masks are our friends, not vigilantes you've put
up to this?'

'Don't be a fool!' flared Middleton disgustedly. 'Do you think the gang would stand for anything like that, even if I was imbecile enough to try it? You'll recognize your friends when they come.

'Miller, I want your name at the foot of a confession I've drawn up, implicating somebody as the leader of the Vultures. There's no use trying to deny you and the others are members of the gang. Hopkins knows you are; instead of trying to play innocent, you'll divert suspicion to someone outside the gang. I haven't filled in the name of the leader, but Dick Lennox is as good as anybody. He's a gambler, has few friends, and never would work with us. I'll write his name in your "confession" as chief of the Vultures, and Corcoran will kill him "for resisting arrest," before he has time to prove that it's a lie. Then, before anybody has time to get suspicious, we'll make our last big haul – the raid on the Hopkins and Bisley cache! – and blow! Be ready to jump, when the gang swoops in.

'Miller, put your signature to this paper. Read it first if you want to. I'll fill in the blanks I left for the "chief's" name later. Where's Corcoran?'

'I saw him in the Golden Eagle an hour ago,' growled McNab. 'He's drinkin' like a fish.'

'Damnation!' Middleton's mask slipped a bit despite himself, then he regained his easy control. 'Well, it doesn't matter. We won't need him tonight. Better for him not to be here when the jail break's made. Folks would think it was funny if he didn't kill somebody. I'll drop back later in the night.'

Even a man of steel nerves feels the strain of waiting for a crisis. Corcoran was in this case no exception. Middleton's mind was so occupied in planning, scheming and conniving that he had little time for the strain to corrode his will power. But Corcoran had nothing to occupy his attention until the moment came for the jump.

He began to drink, almost without realizing it. His veins

seemed on fire, his external senses abnormally alert. Like most men of his breed he was high-strung, his nervous system poised on a hair-trigger balance, in spite of his mask of unemotional coolness. He lived on, and for, violent action. Action kept his mind from turning inward; it kept his brain clear and his hand steady; failing action, he fell back on whisky. Liquor artificially stimulated him to that pitch which his temperament required. It was not fear that made his nerves thrum so intolerably. It was the strain of waiting inertly, the realization of the stakes for which they played. Inaction maddened him. Thought of the gold cached in the cave behind John Middleton's cabin made Corcoran's lips dry, set a nerve to pounding maddeningly in his temples.

So he drank, and drank, and drank again, as the long day wore on.

The noise from the bar was a blurred medley in the back room of the Golden Garter. Glory Bland stared uneasily across the table at her companion. Corcoran's blue eyes seemed lit by dancing fires. Tiny beads of perspiration shone on his dark face. His tongue was not thick; he spoke lucidly and without exaggeration; he had not stumbled when he entered. Nevertheless he was drunk, though to what extent the girl did not guess.

'I never saw you this way before, Steve,' she said reproachfully.

'I've never had a hand in a game like this before,' he answered, the wild flame flickering bluely in his eyes. He reached across the table and caught her white wrist with an unconscious strength that made her wince. 'Glory, I'm pullin' out of here tonight. I want you to go with me!'

'You're leaving Wahpeton? *Tonight?*'

'Yes. For good. Go with me! This joint ain't fit for you. I don't know how you got into this game, and I don't give a damn. But you're different from these other dance hall girls. I'm takin' you with me. I'll make a queen out of you! I'll cover you with diamonds!'

She laughed nervously.

'You're drunker than I thought. I know you've been getting a big salary, but –'

'Salary?' His laugh of contempt startled her. 'I'll throw my salary into the street for the beggars to fight over. Once I told that fool Hopkins that I had a gold mine right here in Wahpeton. I told him no lie. I'm *rich!*'

'What do you mean?' She was slightly pale, frightened by his vehemence.

His fingers unconsciously tightened on her wrist and his eyes gleamed with the hard arrogance of possession and desire.

'You're mine, anyway,' he muttered. 'I'll kill any man that looks at you. But you're in love with me. I know it. Any fool could see it. I can trust you. You wouldn't dare betray me. I'll tell you. I wouldn't take you along without tellin' you the truth. Tonight Middleton and I are goin' over the mountains with a million dollars' worth of gold tied on pack mules!'

He did not see the growing light of incredulous horror in her eyes.

'A million in gold! It'd make a devil out of a saint! Middleton thinks he'll kill me when we get away safe, and grab the whole load. He's a fool. It'll be him that dies, when the time comes. I've planned while he planned. I didn't ever intend to split the loot with him. I wouldn't be a thief for less than a million.'

'Middleton—' she choked.

'Yeah! He's chief of the Vultures, and I'm his right-hand man. If it hadn't been for me, the camp would have caught on long ago.'

'But you upheld the law,' she panted, as if clutching at straws. 'You killed murderers – saved McBride from the mob.'

'I killed men who tried to kill me. I shot as square with the camp as I could, without goin' against my own interests. That business of McBride has nothin' to do with it. I'd given him my word. That's all behind us now. Tonight, while the vigilantes and the Vultures kill each other, we'll *vamose*! And you'll go with me!'

With a cry of loathing she wrenched her hand away, and sprang up, her eyes blazing.

'Oh!' It was a cry of bitter disillusionment. 'I thought you were straight – honest! I worshiped you because I thought you were honorable. So many men were dishonest and bestial – I idolized you! And you've just been pretending – playing a part! Betraying the people who trusted you!' The poignant anguish of her enlightenment choked her, then galvanized her with another possibility.

'I suppose you've been pretending with me, too!' she cried wildly. 'If you haven't been straight with the camp, you couldn't have been straight with me, either! You've made a fool of me! Laughed at me and shamed me! And now you boast of it in my teeth!'

'Glory!' He was on his feet, groping for her, stunned and bewildered by her grief and rage. She sprang back from him.

'Don't touch me! Don't look at me! Oh, I hate the very sight of you!'

And turning, with an hysterical sob, she ran from the room. He stood swaying slightly, staring stupidly after her. Then fumbling with his hat, he stalked out, moving like an automaton. His thoughts were a confused maelstrom, whirling until he was giddy. All at once the liquor seethed madly in his brain, dulling his perceptions, even his recollections of what had just passed. He had drunk more than he realized.

Not long after dark had settled over Wahpeton, a low call from the darkness brought Colonel Hopkins to the door of his cabin, gun in hand.

'Who is it?' he demanded suspiciously.

'It's Middleton. Let me in, quick!'

The sheriff entered, and Hopkins, shutting the door, stared at him in surprise. Middleton showed more agitation than the Colonel had ever seen him display. His face was pale and drawn. A great actor was lost to the world when John Middleton took the dark road of outlawry.

'Colonel, I don't know what to say. I've been a blind fool. I feel that the lives of murdered men are hung about my neck for all Eternity! All through my blindness and stupidity!'

'What do you mean, John?' ejaculated Colonel Hopkins.

'Colonel, Miller talked at last. He just finished telling me the whole dirty business. I have his confession, written as he dictated.'

'He named the chief of the Vultures?' exclaimed Hopkins eagerly.

'He did!' answered Middleton grimly, producing a paper and unfolding it. Joel Miller's unmistakable signature sprawled at the bottom. 'Here is the name of the leader, dictated by Miller to me!'

'Good God!' whispered Hopkins. 'Bill McNab!'

'Yes! My deputy! The man I trusted next to Corcoran. What a blind fool I've been. Even when his actions seemed peculiar, even when you voiced your suspicions of him, I could not bring myself to believe it. But it's all clear now. No wonder the gang always knew my plans as soon as I knew them myself! No wonder my deputies – before Corcoran came – were never able to kill or capture any Vultures. No wonder, for instance, that Tom Deal "escaped," before we could question him. That bullet hole in McNab's arm, supposedly made by Deal – Miller told me McNab got that in a quarrel with one of his own gang. It came in handy to help pull the wool over my eyes.

'Colonel Hopkins, I'll turn in my resignation tomorrow. I recommend Corcoran as my successor. I shall be glad to serve as deputy under him.'

'Nonsense, John!' Hopkins laid his hand sympathetically on Middleton's shoulder. 'It's not your fault. You've played a man's part all the way through. Forget that talk about resigning. Wahpeton doesn't need a new sheriff; you just need some new deputies. Just now we've got some planning to do. Where is McNab?'

'At the jail, guarding the prisoners. I couldn't remove him without exciting his suspicion. Of course he doesn't dream that Miller has talked. And I learned something else. They plan a jail-break shortly after midnight.'

'We might have expected that!'

'Yes. A band of masked men will approach the jail, pretend to overpower the guards – yes, Stark and Richardson are Vultures, too – and release the prisoners. Now this is my plan. Take fifty men and conceal them in the trees near the jail. You can plant some on one side, some on the other. Corcoran and I will be with you, of course. When the bandits come, we can kill or capture them all at one swoop. We have the advantage of knowing their plans, without their knowing we know them.'

'That's a good plan, John!' warmly endorsed Hopkins. 'You should have been a general. I'll gather the men at once. Of course, we must use the utmost secrecy.'

'Of course. If we work it right, we'll bag prisoners, deputies and rescuers with one stroke. We'll break the back of the Vultures!'

'John, don't ever talk resignation to me again!' exclaimed Hopkins, grabbing his hat and buckling on his gun-belt. 'A man like you ought to be in the Senate. Go get Corcoran. I'll gather my men and we'll be in our places before midnight. McNab and the others in the jail won't hear a sound.'

'Good! Corcoran and I will join you before the Vultures reach the jail.'

Leaving Hopkins' cabin, Middleton hurried to the bar of the King of Diamonds. As he drank, a rough-looking individual moved casually up beside him. Middleton bent his head over his whisky glass and spoke, hardly moving his lips. None could have heard him a yard away.

'I've just talked to Hopkins. The vigilantes are afraid of a jail break. They're going to take the prisoners out just before daylight and hang them out of hand. That talk about legal proceedings was just a bluff. Get all the boys, go to the jail and get the prisoners out within a half hour after midnight. Wear your masks, but let there be no shooting or yelling. I'll tell McNab our plan's been changed. Go silently. Leave your horses at least a quarter of a mile down the gulch and sneak up to the jail on foot, so you won't make so much noise. Corcoran and I will be hiding in the brush to give you a hand in case anything goes wrong.'

The other man had not looked toward Middleton; he did not look now. Emptying his glass, he strolled deliberately toward the door. No casual onlooker could have known that any words had passed between them.

When Glory Bland ran from the backroom of the Golden Garter, her soul was in an emotional turmoil that almost amounted to insanity. The shock of her brutal disillusionment vied with passionate shame of her own gullibility and an unreasoning anger. Out of this seething cauldron grew a blind desire to hurt the man who had unwittingly hurt her. Smarting vanity had its part, too, for with characteristic and illogical feminine conceit, she believed that he had practised an elaborate deception in order to fool her into falling in love with him – or rather with the man she thought he was. If he was false with men, he must be false with women, too. That thought sent her into hysterical fury, blind to all except a desire for revenge. She was a primitive, elemental young animal, like most of her profession of that age and place; her emotions were powerful and easily stirred, her passions stormy. Love could change quickly to hate.

She reached an instant decision. She would find Hopkins and tell him everything Corcoran had told her! In that instant she desired nothing so much as the ruin of the man she had loved.

She ran down the crowded street, ignoring men who pawed at her and called after her. She hardly saw the people who stared after her. She supposed that Hopkins would be at the jail, helping guard the prisoners, and she directed her steps thither. As she ran up on the porch Bill McNab confronted her with a leer, and laid a hand on her arm, laughing when she jerked away.

'Come to see me, Glory? Or are you lookin' for Corcoran?'

She struck his hand away. His words, and the insinuating guffaws of his companions, were sparks enough to touch off the explosives seething in her.

'You fool! You're being sold out, and don't know it!'

The leer vanished.

'What do you mean?' he snarled.

'I mean that your boss is fixing to skip out with all the gold you thieves have grabbed!' she blurted, heedless of consequences, in her emotional storm, indeed scarcely aware of what she was saying. 'He and Corcoran are going to leave you holding the sack, tonight!'

And not seeing the man she was looking for, she eluded McNab's grasp, jumped down from the porch and darted away in the darkness.

The deputies stared at each other, and the prisoners, having heard everything, began to clamor to be turned out.

'Shut up!' snarled McNab. 'She may be lyin'. Might have had a quarrel with Corcoran and took this fool way to get even with him. We can't afford to take no chances. We've got to be sure we know what we're doin' before we move either way. We can't afford to let you out now, on the chance that she might be lyin'. But we'll give you weapons to defend yourselves.

'Here, take these rifles and hide 'em under the bunks. Pete Daley, you stay here and keep folks shooed away from the jail till we get back. Richardson, you and Stark come with me! We'll have a showdown with Middleton right now!'

When Glory left the jail she headed for Hopkins' cabin. But she had not gone far when a reaction shook her. She was like one waking from a nightmare, or a dope-jag. She was still sickened by the discovery of Corcoran's duplicity in regard to the people of the camp, but she began to apply reason to her suspicions of his motives in regard to herself. She began to realize that she had acted illogically. If Corcoran's attitude toward her was not sincere, he certainly would not have asked her to leave the camp with him. At the expense of her vanity she was forced to admit that his attentions to her had not been necessary in his game of duping the camp. That was something apart; his own private business; it must be so. She had suspected him of trifling with her affections, but she had to admit that she had no proof that he had ever paid the slightest attention to any other woman in Wahpeton. No; whatever his motives or actions in general, his feeling toward her must be sincere and real.

With a shock she remembered her present errand, her reckless words to McNab. Despair seized her, in which she realized that she loved Steve Corcoran in spite of all he might be. Chill fear seized her that McNab and his friends would kill her lover. Her unreasoning fury died out, gave way to frantic terror.

Turning she ran swiftly down the gulch toward Corcoran's cabin. She was hardly aware of it when she passed through the blazing heart of the camp. Lights and bearded faces were like a nightmarish blur, in which nothing was real but the icy terror in her heart.

She did not realize it when the clusters of cabins fell behind her. The patter of her slippered feet in the road terrified her, and the black shadows under the trees seemed pregnant with menace. Ahead of her she saw Corcoran's cabin at last, a light streaming through the open door. She burst in to the office-room, panting – and was confronted by Middleton who wheeled with a gun in his hand.

'What the devil are you doing here?' He spoke without friendliness, though he returned the gun to its scabbard.

'Where's Corcoran?' she panted. Fear took hold of her as she faced the man she now knew was the monster behind the grisly crimes that had made a reign of terror over Wahpeton Gulch. But fear for Corcoran overshadowed her own terror.

'I don't know. I looked for him through the bars a short time ago, and didn't find him. I'm expecting him here any minute. What do you want with him?'

'That's none of your business,' she flared.

'It might be.' He came toward her, and the mask had fallen from his dark, handsome face. It looked wolfish.

'You were a fool to come here. You pry into things that don't concern you. You know too much. You talk too much. Don't think I'm not wise to you! I know more about you than you suspect.'

A chill fear froze her. Her heart seemed to be turning to ice. Middleton was like a stranger to her, a terrible stranger. The mask was off, and the evil spirit of the man was reflected in his dark, sinister face. His eyes burned her like actual coals.

'I didn't pry into secrets,' she whispered with dry lips. 'I didn't ask any questions. I never before suspected you were the chief of the Vultures –'

The expression of his face told her she had made an awful mistake.

'So you know that!' His voice was soft, almost a whisper, but murder stood stark and naked in his flaming eyes. 'I didn't know that. I was talking about something else. Conchita told me it was you who told Corcoran about the plan to lynch McBride. I wouldn't have killed you for that, though it interfered with my plans. But you know too much. After tonight it wouldn't matter. But tonight's not over yet –'

'Oh!' she moaned, staring with dilated eyes as the big pistol slid from its scabbard in a dull gleam of blue steel. She could not move, she could not cry out. She could only cower dumbly until the crash of the shot knocked her to the floor.

As Middleton stood above her, the smoking gun in his hand, he heard a stirring in the room behind him. He quickly upset the long table, so it could hide the body of the girl, and turned, just as the door opened. Corcoran came from the back room, blinking, a gun in his hand. It was evident that he had just awakened from a drunken sleep, but his hands did not shake, his pantherish tread was sure as ever, and his eyes were neither dull nor bloodshot.

Nevertheless Middleton swore.

'Corcoran, are you crazy?'

'You shot?'

'I shot at a snake that crawled across the floor. You must have been mad, to soak up liquor today, of all days!'

'I'm all right,' muttered Corcoran, shoving his gun back in its scabbard.

'Well, come on. I've got the mules in the clump of trees next to my cabin. Nobody will see us load them. Nobody will see us go. We'll go up the ravine beyond my cabin, as we planned. There's nobody watching my cabin tonight. All the Vultures are down in the camp, waiting for the signal to move. I'm hoping none will escape the vigilantes, and that most of the vigilantes themselves are killed in the fight that's sure to come. Come on! We've got thirty mules to load, and that job will take us from now until midnight, at least. We won't pull out until we hear the guns on the other side of the camp.'

'Listen!'

It was footsteps, approaching the cabin almost at a run. Both men wheeled and stood motionless as McNab loomed in the door. He lurched into the room, followed by Richardson and Stark. Instantly the air was supercharged with suspicion, hate, tension. Silence held for a tick of time.

'You fools!' snarled Middleton. 'What are you doing away from the jail?'

'We came to talk to you,' said McNab. 'We've heard that you and Corcoran planned to skip with the gold.'

Never was Middleton's superb self-control more evident. Though the shock of that blunt thunderbolt must have been terrific, he showed no emotion that might not have been showed by any honest man, falsely accused.

'Are you utterly mad?' he ejaculated, not in a rage, but as if amazement had submerged whatever anger he might have felt at the charge.

McNab shifted his great bulk uneasily, not sure of his ground. Corcoran was not looking at him, but at Richardson, in whose cold eyes a lethal glitter was growing. More quickly than Middleton, Corcoran sensed the inevitable struggle in which this situation must culminate.

'I'm just sayin' what we heard. Maybe it's so, maybe it ain't. If it ain't, there's no harm done,' said McNab slowly. 'On the chance that it was so, I sent word for the boys not to wait till midnight. They're goin' to the jail within the next half hour and take Miller and the rest out.'

Another breathless silence followed that statement. Middleton did not bother to reply. His eyes began to smolder. Without moving, he yet seemed to crouch, to gather himself for a spring. He had realized what Corcoran had already sensed; that this situation was not to be passed over by words, that a climax of violence was inevitable.

Richardson knew this; Stark seemed merely puzzled. McNab, if he had any thoughts, concealed the fact.

'Say you *was* intendin' to skip,' he said, 'this might be a good chance, while the boys was takin' Miller and them off up into the hills. I don't know. I ain't accusin' you. I'm just askin' you to clear yourself. You can do it easy. Just come back to the jail with us and help get the boys out.'

Middleton's answer was what Richardson, instinctive man-killer, had sensed it would be. He whipped out a gun in a blur of speed. And even as it cleared leather, Richardson's gun was out. But Corcoran had not taken his eyes off the cold-eyed gunman, and his draw was the quicker by a lightning-flicker. Quick as was Middleton, both the other guns spoke before his, like a double detonation. Corcoran's slug blasted Richardson's brains just in time to spoil his shot at Middleton. But the bullet grazed Middleton so close that it caused him to miss McNab with his first shot.

McNab's gun was out and Stark was a split second behind him. Middleton's second shot and McNab's first crashed almost together, but already Corcoran's guns had sent lead ripping through the giant's flesh. His ball merely flicked Middleton's hair in passing, and the chief's slug smashed full into his brawny breast. Middleton fired again and yet again as the giant was falling. Stark was down, dying on the floor, having pulled trigger blindly as he fell, until the gun was empty.

Middleton stared wildly about him, through the floating blue fog of smoke that veiled the room. In that fleeting instant, as he glimpsed Corcoran's image-like face, he felt that only in such a setting as this did the Texan appear fitted. Like a somber figure of Fate he moved implacably against a background of blood and slaughter.

'God!' gasped Middleton. 'That was the quickest, bloodiest fight I was ever in!' Even as he talked he was jamming cartridges into his empty gun chambers.

'We've got no time to lose now! I don't know how much McNab told the gang of his suspicions. He must not have told them much, or some of them would have come with him. Anyway, their first move will be to liberate the prisoners. I have an idea they'll go through with that just as we planned, even when McNab doesn't return to lead them. They won't come looking for him, or come after us, until they turn Miller and the others loose.

'It just means the fight will come within the half hour instead of at midnight. The vigilantes will be there by that time. They're probably lying in ambush already. Come on! We've got to sling gold on those mules like devils. We may have to leave some of it; we'll know when the fight's started, by the sound of the guns! One thing, nobody will come up here to investigate the shooting. All attention is focused on the jail!'

Corcoran followed him out of the cabin, then turned back with a muttered: 'Left a bottle of whisky in that back room.'

'Well, hurry and get it and come on!' Middleton broke into a run toward his cabin, and Corcoran re-entered the smoke-veiled room. He did not glance at the crumpled bodies which lay on the crimson-stained floor, staring glassily up at him. With a stride he reached the back room, groped in his bunk until he found what he wanted, and then strode again toward the outer door, the bottle in his hand.

The sound of a low moan brought him whirling about, a gun in his left hand. Startled, he stared at the figures on the floor. He knew none of them had moaned; all three were past moaning. Yet his ears had not deceived him.

His narrowed eyes swept the cabin suspiciously, and focused on a thin trickle of crimson that stole from under the upset table as it lay on its side near the wall. None of the corpses lay near it.

He pulled aside the table and halted as if shot through the heart, his breath catching in a convulsive gasp. An instant later he was kneeling beside Glory Bland, cradling her golden head in his arm. His hand, as he brought the whisky bottle to her lips, shook queerly.

Her magnificent eyes lifted toward him, glazed with pain. But by some miracle the delirium faded, and she knew him in her last few moments of life.

'Who did this?' he choked. Her white throat was laced by a tiny trickle of crimson from her lips.

'Middleton –' she whispered. 'Steve, oh, Steve – I tried –' And with the whisper uncompleted she went limp in his arms. Her golden head lolled back; she seemed like a child, a child just fallen asleep. Dazedly he eased her to the floor.

Corcoran's brain was clear of liquor as he left the cabin, but he staggered like a drunken man. The monstrous, incredible thing that had happened left him stunned, hardly able to credit his own senses. It had never occurred to him that Middleton would kill a woman, that any white man would. Corcoran lived by his own code, and it was wild and rough and hard, violent and incongruous, but it included the conviction that womankind was sacred, immune from the violence that attended the lives of men. This code was as much a vital, living element of the life of the Southwestern frontier as was personal honor, and the resentment of insult. Without pompousness, without pretentiousness, without any of the tawdry glitter and sham of a false chivalry, the people of Corcoran's breed practised this code in their daily lives. To Corcoran, as to his people, a woman's life and body were inviolate. It had never occurred to him that that code would, or could be violated, or that there could be any other kind.

Cold rage swept the daze from his mind and left him crammed to the brim with murder. His feelings toward Glory Bland had approached the normal love experienced by the average man as closely as was possible for one of his iron nature. But if she had been a stranger, or even a person he had disliked, he would have killed Middleton for outraging a code he had considered absolute.

He entered Middleton's cabin with the soft stride of a stalking panther. Middleton was bringing bulging buckskin sacks from the cave, heaping them on a table in the main room. He staggered with their weight. Already the table was almost covered.

'Get busy!' he exclaimed. Then he halted short, at the blaze in Corcoran's eyes. The fat sacks spilled from his arms, thudding on the floor.

'You killed Glory Bland!' It was almost a whisper from the Texan's livid lips.

'Yes.' Middleton's voice was even. He did not ask how Corcoran knew, he did not seek to justify himself. He knew the time for argument was past. He did not think of his plans, or of the gold on the table, or that still back there in the cave. A man standing face to face with Eternity sees only the naked elements of life and death.

'*Draw!*' A catamount might have spat the challenge, eyes flaming, teeth flashing.

Middleton's hand was a streak to his gun butt. Even in that flash he knew he was beaten – heard Corcoran's gun roar just as he pulled trigger. He swayed back, falling, and in a blind gust of passion Corcoran emptied both guns into him as he crumpled.

For a long moment that seemed ticking into Eternity the killer stood over his victim, a somber, brooding figure that might have been carved from the iron night of the Fates. Off toward the other end of the camp other guns burst forth suddenly, in salvo after thundering salvo. The fight that was plotted to mask the flight of the Vulture chief had begun. But the figure which stood above the dead man in the lonely cabin did not seem to hear.

Corcoran looked down at his victim, vaguely finding it strange, after all, that all those bloody schemes and terrible ambitions should end like that, in a puddle of oozing blood on a cabin floor. He lifted his head to stare somberly at the bulging sacks on the table. Revulsion gagged him.

A sack had split, spilling a golden stream that glittered evilly in the candle-light. His eyes were no longer blinded by the yellow sheen. For the first time he saw the blood on that gold, it was black with blood; the blood of innocent men; the blood of a woman. The mere thought of touching it nauseated him, made him feel as if the slime that had covered John Middleton's soul would befoul him. Sickly he realized that some of Middleton's guilt was on his own head. He had not pulled the trigger that ripped a woman's life from her body; but he had worked hand-in-glove with the man destined to be her murderer – Corcoran shuddered and a clammy sweat broke out upon his flesh.

Down the gulch the firing had ceased, faint yells came to him, freighted with victory and triumph. Many men must be shouting at once, for the sound to carry so far. He knew what it portended; the Vultures had walked into the trap laid for them by the man they trusted as a leader. Since the firing had ceased, it meant the whole band were either dead or captives. Wahpeton's reign of terror had ended.

But he must stir. There would be prisoners, eager to talk. Their speech would weave a noose about his neck.

He did not glance again at the gold, gleaming there where the honest people of Wahpeton would find it. Striding from the cabin he swung on one of the horses that stood saddled and ready among the trees. The lights of the camp, the roar of the distant voices fell away behind him, and before him lay what wild destiny he could not guess. But the night was full of haunting shadows, and within him grew a strange pain, like a revelation; perhaps it was his soul, at last awakening.

III

High Noon

The Tower of the Elephant

Torches flared murkily on the revels in the Maul, where the thieves of the east held carnival by night. In the Maul they could carouse and roar as they liked, for honest people shunned the quarters, and watchmen, well paid with stained coins, did not interfere with their sport. Along the crooked, unpaved streets with their heaps of refuse and sloppy puddles, drunken roisterers staggered, roaring. Steel glinted in the shadows where wolf preyed on wolf, and from the darkness rose the shrill laughter of women, and the sounds of scufflings and strugglings. Torchlight licked luridly from broken windows and wide-thrown doors, and out of those doors, stale smells of wine and rank sweaty bodies, clamor of drinking-jacks and fists hammered on rough tables, snatches of obscene songs, rushed like a blow in the face.

In one of these dens merriment thundered to the low smoke-stained roof, where rascals gathered in every stage of rags and tatters – furtive cut-purses, leering kidnappers, quick-fingered thieves, swaggering bravoes with their wenches, strident-voiced women clad in tawdry finery. Native rogues were the dominant element – dark-skinned, dark-eyed Zamorians, with daggers at their girdles and guile in their hearts. But there were wolves of half a dozen outland nations there as well. There was a giant Hyperborean renegade, taciturn, dangerous, with a broadsword strapped to his great gaunt frame – for men wore steel openly in the Maul. There was a Shemitish counterfeiter, with his hook

nose and curled blue-black beard. There was a bold-eyed Brythunian wench, sitting on the knee of a tawny-haired Gunderman
– a wandering mercenary soldier, a deserter from some defeated
army. And the fat gross rogue whose bawdy jests were causing
all the shouts of mirth was a professional kidnapper come up
from distant Koth to teach woman-stealing to Zamorians who
were born with more knowledge of the art than he could ever
attain.

This man halted in his description of an intended victim's
charms, and thrust his muzzle into a huge tankard of frothing
ale. Then blowing the foam from his fat lips, he said, 'By Bel,
god of all thieves, I'll show them how to steal wenches: I'll have
her over the Zamorian border before dawn, and there'll be a
caravan waiting to receive her. Three hundred pieces of silver, a
count of Ophir promised me for a sleek young Brythunian of
the better class. It took me weeks, wandering among the border
cities as a beggar, to find one I knew would suit. And is she a
pretty baggage!'

He blew a slobbery kiss in the air.

'I know lords in Shem who would trade the secret of the Elephant Tower for her,' he said, returning to his ale.

A touch on his tunic sleeve made him turn his head, scowling
at the interruption. He saw a tall, strongly made youth standing
beside him. This person was as much out of place in that den as
a gray wolf among mangy rats of the gutters. His cheap tunic
could not conceal the hard, rangy lines of his powerful frame,
the broad heavy shoulders, the massive chest, lean waist, and
heavy arms. His skin was brown from outland suns, his eyes
blue and smoldering; a shock of tousled black hair crowned his
broad forehead. From his girdle hung a sword in a worn leather
scabbard.

The Kothian involuntarily drew back; for the man was not
one of any civilized race he knew.

'You spoke of the Elephant Tower,' said the stranger, speaking Zamorian with an alien accent. 'I've heard much of this tower; what is its secret?'

The fellow's attitude did not seem threatening, and the Kothian's courage was bolstered up by the ale, and the evident approval of his audience. He swelled with self-importance.

'The secret of the Elephant Tower?' he exclaimed. 'Why, any fool knows that Yara the priest dwells there with the great jewel men call the Elephant's Heart, that is the secret of his magic.'

The barbarian digested this for a space.

'I have seen this tower,' he said. 'It is set in a great garden above the level of the city, surrounded by high walls. I have seen no guards. The walls would be easy to climb. Why has not somebody stolen this secret gem?'

The Kothian stared wide-mouthed at the other's simplicity, then burst into a roar of derisive mirth, in which the others joined.

'Harken to this heathen!' he bellowed. 'He would steal the jewel of Yara! – Harken, fellow,' he said, turning portentously to the other, 'I suppose you are some sort of a northern barbarian –'

'I am a Cimmerian,' the outlander answered, in no friendly tone. The reply and the manner of it meant little to the Kothian; of a kingdom that lay far to the south, on the borders of Shem, he knew only vaguely of the northern races.

'Then give ear and learn wisdom, fellow,' said he, pointing his drinking-jack at the discomfited youth. 'Know that in Zamora, and more especially in this city, there are more bold thieves than anywhere else in the world, even Koth. If mortal man could have stolen the gem, be sure it would have been filched long ago. You speak of climbing the walls, but once having climbed, you would quickly wish yourself back again. There are no guards in the gardens at night for a very good reason – that is, no human guards. But in the watch-chamber, in the lower part of the tower, are armed men, and even if you passed those who roam the gardens by night, you must still pass through the soldiers, for the gem is kept somewhere in the tower above.'

'But if a man *could* pass through the gardens,' argued the Cimmerian, 'why could he not come at the gem through the upper part of the tower and thus avoid the soldiers?'

Again the Kothian gaped at him.

'Listen to him!' he shouted jeeringly. 'The barbarian is an eagle who would fly to the jeweled rim of the tower, which is only a hundred and fifty feet above the earth, with rounded sides slicker than polished glass!'

The Cimmerian glared about, embarrassed at the roar of mocking laughter that greeted this remark. He saw no particular humor in it, and was too new to civilization to understand its discourtesies. Civilized men are more discourteous than savages because they know they can be impolite without having their skulls split, as a general thing. He was bewildered and chagrined, and doubtless would have slunk away, abashed, but the Kothian chose to goad him further.

'Come, come!' he shouted. 'Tell these poor fellows, who have only been thieves since before you were spawned, tell them how you would steal the gem!'

'There is always a way, if the desire be coupled with courage,' answered the Cimmerian shortly, nettled.

The Kothian chose to take this as a personal slur. His face grew purple with anger.

'What!' he roared. 'You dare tell us our business, and intimate that we are cowards? Get along; get out of my sight!' And he pushed the Cimmerian violently.

'Will you mock me and then lay hands on me?' grated the barbarian, his quick rage leaping up; and he returned the push with an open-handed blow that knocked his tormenter back against the rude-hewn table. Ale splashed over the jack's lip, and the Kothian roared in fury, dragging at his sword.

'Heathen dog!' he bellowed. 'I'll have your heart for that!'

Steel flashed and the throng surged wildly back out of the way. In their flight they knocked over the single candle and the den was plunged in darkness, broken by the crash of upset benches, drum of flying feet, shouts, oaths of people tumbling over one another, and a single strident yell of agony that cut the din like a knife. When a candle was relighted, most of the guests had gone out by doors and broken windows, and the rest huddled behind stacks of wine-kegs and under tables. The barbarian was gone; the center of the room was deserted except for the gashed body of the Kothian. The Cimmerian, with the unerring instinct of the barbarian, had killed his man in the darkness and confusion.

2

The lurid lights and drunken revelry fell away behind the Cimmerian. He had discarded his torn tunic, and walked through the night naked except for a loin-cloth and his high-strapped sandals. He moved with the supple ease of a great tiger, his steely muscles rippling under his brown skin.

He had entered the part of the city reserved for the temples. On all sides of him they glittered white in the starlight – snowy marble pillars and golden domes and silver arches, shrines of Zamora's myriad strange gods. He did not trouble his head about them; he knew that Zamora's religion, like all things of a civilized, long-settled people, was intricate and complex, and had lost most of the pristine essence in a maze of formulas and rituals. He had squatted for hours in the courtyards of the philosophers, listening to the arguments of theologians and teachers, and come away in a haze of bewilderment, sure of only one thing, and that, that they were all touched in the head.

His gods were simple and understandable; Crom was their

chief, and he lived on a great mountain, whence he sent forth dooms and death. It was useless to call on Crom, because he was a gloomy, savage god, and he hated weaklings. But he gave a man courage at birth, and the will and might to kill his enemies, which, in the Cimmerian's mind, was all any god should be expected to do.

His sandaled feet made no sound on the gleaming pave. No watchmen passed, for even the thieves of the Maul shunned the temples, where strange dooms had been known to fall on violators. Ahead of him he saw, looming against the sky, the Tower of the Elephant. He mused, wondering why it was so named. No one seemed to know. He had never seen an elephant, but he vaguely understood that it was a monstrous animal, with a tail in front as well as behind. This a wandering Shemite had told him, swearing that he had seen such beasts by the thousands in the country of the Hyrkanians; but all men knew what liars were the men of Shem. At any rate, there were no elephants in Zamora.

The shimmering shaft of the tower rose frostily in the stars. In the sunlight it shone so dazzlingly that few could bear its glare, and men said it was built of silver. It was round, a slim perfect cylinder, a hundred and fifty feet in height, and its rim glittered in the starlight with the great jewels which crusted it. The tower stood among the waving exotic trees of a garden raised high above the general level of the city. A high wall enclosed this garden, and outside the wall was a lower level, likewise enclosed by a wall. No lights shone forth; there seemed to be no windows in the tower – at least not above the level of the inner wall. Only the gems high above sparkled frostily in the starlight.

Shrubbery grew thick outside the lower, or outer wall. The Cimmerian crept close and stood beside the barrier, measuring it with his eye. It was high, but he could leap and catch the coping with his fingers. Then it would be child's play to swing himself up and over, and he did not doubt that he could pass the inner wall in the same manner. But he hesitated at the thought of the strange perils which were said to await within. These people were strange and mysterious to him; they were not of his kind – not even of the same blood as the more westerly Brythunians, Nemedians, Kothians and Aquilonians, whose civilized mysteries had awed him in times past. The people of Zamora were very ancient, and, from what he had seen of them, very evil.

He thought of Yara, the high priest, who worked strange dooms from this jeweled tower, and the Cimmerian's hair prickled as he remembered a tale told by a drunken page of the court – how Yara had laughed in the face of a hostile prince, and held up a glowing, evil gem before him, and how rays shot blindingly from that unholy jewel, to envelop the prince, who screamed and fell down, and shrank to a withered blackened lump that changed to a black spider which scampered wildly about the chamber until Yara set his heel upon it.

Yara came not often from his tower of magic, and always to work evil on some man or some nation. The king of Zamora feared him more than he feared death, and kept himself drunk all the time because that fear was more than he could endure sober. Yara was very old – centuries old, men said, and added that he would live for ever because of the magic of his gem, which men called the Heart of the Elephant, for no better reason than they named his hold the Elephant's Tower.

The Cimmerian, engrossed in these thoughts, shrank quickly against the wall. Within the garden some one was passing, who walked with a measured stride. The listener heard the clink of steel. So after all a guard did pace those gardens. The Cimmerian waited, expected to hear him pass again, on the next round, but silence rested over the mysterious gardens.

At last curiosity overcame him. Leaping lightly he grasped the wall and swung himself up to the top with one arm. Lying flat on the broad coping, he looked down into the wide space between the walls. No shrubbery grew near him, though he saw some carefully trimmed bushes near the inner wall. The starlight fell on the even sward and somewhere a fountain tinkled.

The Cimmerian cautiously lowered himself down on the inside and drew his sword, staring about him. He was shaken by the nervousness of the wild at standing thus unprotected in the naked starlight, and he moved lightly around the curve of the wall, hugging its shadow until he was even with the shrubbery he had noticed. Then he ran quickly toward it, crouching low, and almost tripped over a form that lay crumpled near the edges of the bushes.

A quick look to right and left showed him no enemy in sight at least, and he bent close to investigate. His keen eyes, even in the dim starlight, showed him a strongly built man in the silvered armor and crested helmet of the Zamorian royal guard. A shield and a spear lay near him, and it took but an instant's examination to show that he had been strangled. The barbarian glanced about uneasily. He knew that this man must be the guard he had heard pass his hiding-place by the wall. Only a short time had passed, yet in that interval nameless hands had reached out of the dark and choked out the soldier's life.

Straining his eyes in the gloom, he saw a hint of motion through the shrubs near the wall. Thither he glided gripping his sword. He made no more noise than a panther stealing through the night, yet the man he was stalking heard. The Cimmerian had a dim glimpse of a huge bulk close to the wall, felt relief that it was at least human; then the fellow wheeled quickly with a gasp that sounded like panic, made the first motion of a forward plunge, hands clutching, then recoiled as the Cimmerian's blade caught the starlight. For a tense instant neither spoke, standing ready for anything.

'You are no soldier,' hissed the stranger at last. 'You are a thief like myself.'

'And who are you?' asked the Cimmerian in a suspicious whisper.

'Taurus of Nemedia.'

The Cimmerian lowered his sword.

'I've heard of you. Men call you a prince of thieves.'

A low laugh answered him. Taurus was tall as the Cimmerian, and heavier; he was big-bellied and fat, but his every movement betokened a subtle dynamic magnetism, which was reflected in the keen eyes that glinted vitally, even in the starlight. He was barefooted and carried a coil of what looked like a thin, strong rope, knotted at regular intervals.

'Who are you?' he whispered.

'Conan, a Cimmerian,' answered the other. 'I came seeking a way to steal Yara's jewel, that men call the Elephant's Heart.'

Conan sensed the man's great belly shaking in laughter, but it was not derisive.

'By Bel, god of thieves!' hissed Taurus. 'I had thought only myself had courage to attempt *that* poaching. These Zamorians call themselves thieves – bah! Conan, I like your grit. I never shared an adventure with any one, but by Bel, we'll attempt this together if you're willing.'

'Then you are after the gem, too?'

'What else? I've had my plans laid for months, but you, I think, have acted on a sudden impulse, my friend.'

'You killed the soldier?'

'Of course. I slid over the wall when he was on the other side of the garden. I hid in the bushes; he heard me, or thought he heard something. When he came blundering over, it was no trick at all to get behind him and suddenly grip his neck and choke out his fool's life. He was like most men, half blind in the dark. A good thief should have eyes like a cat.'

'You made one mistake,' said Conan.

Taurus' eyes flashed angrily.

'I? I, a mistake? Impossible!'

'You should have dragged the body into the bushes.'

'Said the novice to the master of the art. They will not change the guard until past midnight. Should any come searching for him now, and find his body, they would flee at once to Yara, bellowing the news, and give us time to escape. Were they not to find it, they'd go beating up the bushes and catch us like rats in a trap.'

'You are right,' agreed Conan.

'So. Now attend. We waste time in this cursed discussion. There are no guards in the inner garden – human guards, I mean, though there are sentinels even more deadly. It was their presence which baffled me for so long, but I finally discovered a way to circumvent them.'

'What of the soldiers in the lower part of the tower?'

'Old Yara dwells in the chambers above. By that route we will come – and go, I hope. Never mind asking me how. I have arranged a way. We'll steal down through the top of the tower and strangle old Yara before he can cast any of his accursed spells on us. At least we'll try; it's the chance of being turned into a spider or a toad, against the wealth and power of the world. All good thieves must know how to take risks.'

'I'll go as far as any man,' said Conan, slipping off his sandals.

'Then follow me.' And turning, Taurus leaped up, caught the wall and drew himself up. The man's suppleness was amazing, considering his bulk; he seemed almost to glide up over the edge of the coping. Conan followed him, and lying flat on the broad top, they spoke in wary whispers.

'I see no light,' Conan muttered. The lower part of the tower seemed much like that portion visible from outside the garden – a perfect, gleaming cylinder, with no apparent openings.

'There are cleverly constructed doors and windows,' answered Taurus, 'but they are closed. The soldiers breathe air that comes from above.'

The garden was a vague pool of shadows, where feathery bushes and low spreading trees waved darkly in the starlight. Conan's wary soul felt the aura of waiting menace that brooded over it. He felt the burning glare of unseen eyes, and he caught a subtle scent that made the short hairs on his neck instinctively bristle as a hunting dog bristles at the scent of an ancient enemy.

'Follow me,' whispered Taurus, 'keep behind me, as you value your life.'

Taking what looked like a copper tube from his girdle, the Nemedian dropped lightly to the sward inside the wall. Conan was close behind him, sword ready, but Taurus pushed him back, close to the wall, and showed no inclination to advance, himself. His whole attitude was of tense expectancy, and his gaze, like Conan's, was fixed on the shadowy mass of shrubbery a few yards away. This shrubbery was shaken, although the breeze had died down. Then two great eyes blazed from the waving shadows, and behind them other sparks of fire glinted in the darkness.

'Lions!' muttered Conan.

'Aye. By day they are kept in subterranean caverns below the tower. That's why there are no guards in this garden.'

Conan counted the eyes rapidly.

'Five in sight; maybe more back in the bushes. They'll charge in a moment –'

'Be silent!' hissed Taurus, and he moved out from the wall, cautiously as if treading on razors, lifting the slender tube. Low rumblings rose from the shadows and the blazing eyes moved forward. Conan could sense the great slavering jaws, the tufted tails lashing tawny sides. The air grew tense – the Cimmerian gripped his sword, expecting the charge and the irresistible hurtling of giant bodies. Then Taurus brought the mouth of the tube to his lips and blew powerfully. A long jet of yellowish powder shot from the other end of the tube and billowed out instantly in a thick green-yellow cloud that settled over the shrubbery, blotting out the glaring eyes.

Taurus ran back hastily to the wall. Conan glared without understanding. The thick cloud hid the shrubbery, and from it no sound came.

'What is that mist?' the Cimmerian asked uneasily.

'Death!' hissed the Nemedian. 'If a wind springs up and blows it back upon us, we must flee over the wall. But no, the wind is still, and now it is dissipating. Wait until it vanishes entirely. To breathe it is death.'

Presently only yellowish shreds hung ghostlily in the air; then they were gone, and Taurus motioned his companion forward. They stole toward the bushes, and Conan gasped. Stretched out in the shadows lay five great tawny shapes, the fire of their grim eyes dimmed for ever. A sweetish cloying scent lingered in the atmosphere.

'They died without a sound!' muttered the Cimmerian. 'Taurus, what was that powder?'

'It was made from the black lotus, whose blossoms wave in the lost jungles of Khitai, where only the yellow-skulled priests of Yun dwell. Those blossoms strike dead any who smell of them.'

Conan knelt beside the great forms, assuring himself that they were indeed beyond power of harm. He shook his head; the magic of the exotic lands was mysterious and terrible to the barbarians of the north.

'Why can you not slay the soldiers in the tower in the same way?' he asked.

'Because that was all the powder I possessed. The obtaining of it was a feat which in itself was enough to make me famous among the thieves of the world. I stole it out of a caravan bound for Stygia, and I lifted it, in its cloth-of-gold bag, out of the coils of the great serpent which guarded it, without awaking him. But come, in Bel's name! Are we to waste the night in discussion?'

They glided through the shrubbery to the gleaming foot of

the tower, and there, with a motion enjoining silence, Taurus unwound his knotted cord, on one end of which was a strong steel hook. Conan saw his plan, and asked no questions as the Nemedian gripped the line a short distance below the hook, and began to swing it about his head. Conan laid his ear to the smooth wall and listened, but could hear nothing. Evidently the soldiers within did not suspect the presence of intruders, who had made no more sound than the night wind blowing through the trees. But a strange nervousness was on the barbarian; perhaps it was the lion-smell which was over everything.

Taurus threw the line with a smooth, ripping motion of his mighty arm. The hook curved upward and inward in a peculiar manner, hard to describe, and vanished over the jeweled rim. It apparently caught firmly, for cautious jerking and then hard pulling did not result in any slipping or giving.

'Luck the first cast,' murmured Taurus. 'I –'

It was Conan's savage instinct which made him wheel suddenly; for the death that was upon them made no sound. A fleeting glimpse showed the Cimmerian the giant tawny shape, rearing upright against the stars, towering over him for the death-stroke. No civilized man could have moved half so quickly as the barbarian moved. His sword flashed frostily in the starlight with every ounce of desperate nerve and thew behind it, and man and beast went down together.

Cursing incoherently beneath his breath, Taurus bent above the mass, and saw his companion's limbs move as he strove to drag himself from under the great weight that lay limply upon him. A glance showed the startled Nemedian that the lion was dead, its slanting skull split in half. He laid hold of the carcass, and by his aid, Conan thrust it aside and clambered up, still gripping his dripping sword.

'Are you hurt, man?' gasped Taurus, still bewildered by the stunning swiftness of that touch-and-go episode.

'No, by Crom!' answered the barbarian. 'But that was as close a call as I've had in a life noways tame. Why did not the cursed beast roar as he charged?'

'All things are strange in this garden,' said Taurus. 'The lions strike silently – and so do other deaths. But come – little sound was made in that slaying, but the soldiers might have heard, if they are not asleep or drunk. That beast was in some other part of the garden and escaped the death of the flowers, but surely there are no more. We must climb this cord – little need to ask a Cimmerian if he can.'

'If it will bear my weight,' grunted Conan, cleansing his sword on the grass.

'It will bear thrice my own,' answered Taurus. 'It was woven from the tresses of dead women, which I took from their tombs at midnight, and steeped in the deadly wine of the upas tree, to give it strength. I will go first – then follow me closely.'

The Nemedian gripped the rope and crooking a knee about it, began the ascent; he went up like a cat, belying the apparent clumsiness of his bulk. The Cimmerian followed. The cord swayed and turned on itself, but the climbers were not hindered; both had made more difficult climbs before. The jeweled rim glittered high above them, jutting out from the perpendicular of the wall, so that the cord hung perhaps a foot from the side of the tower – a fact which added greatly to the ease of the ascent.

Up and up they went, silently, the lights of the city spreading out further and further to their sight as they climbed, the stars above them more and more dimmed by the glitter of the jewels along the rim. Now Taurus reached up a hand and gripped the rim itself, pulling himself up and over. Conan paused a moment on the very edge, fascinated by the great frosty jewels whose gleams dazzled his eyes – diamonds, rubies, emeralds, sapphires, turquoises, moonstones, set thick as stars in the shimmering silver. At a distance their different gleams had seemed to merge into a pulsing white glare; but now, at close range, they shimmered with a million rainbow tints and lights, hypnotizing him with their scintillations.

'There is a fabulous fortune here, Taurus,' he whispered; but the Nemedian answered impatiently, 'Come on! If we secure the Heart, these and all other things shall be ours.'

Conan climbed over the sparkling rim. The level of the tower's top was some feet below the gemmed ledge. It was flat, composed of some dark blue substance, set with gold that caught the starlight, so that the whole looked like a wide sapphire flecked with shining gold-dust. Across from the point where they had entered there seemed to be a sort of chamber, built upon the roof. It was of the same silvery material as the walls of the tower, adorned with designs worked in smaller gems; its single door was of gold, its surface cut in scales, and crusted with jewels that gleamed like ice.

Conan cast a glance at the pulsing ocean of lights which spread far below them, then glanced at Taurus. The Nemedian was drawing up his cord and coiling it. He showed Conan where the hook had caught – a fraction of an inch of the point had sunk under a great blazing jewel on the inner side of the rim.

'Luck was with us again,' he muttered. 'One would think that our combined weight would have torn that stone out. Follow me; the real risks of the venture begin now. We are in the serpent's lair, and we know not where he lies hidden.'

Like stalking tigers they crept across the darkly gleaming floor and halted outside the sparkling door. With a deft and cautious hand Taurus tried it. It gave without resistance, and the companions looked in, tensed for anything. Over the Nemedian's shoulder Conan had a glimpse of a glittering chamber, the walls, ceiling and floor of which were crusted with great white jewels which lighted it brightly, and which seemed its only illumination. It seemed empty of life.

'Before we cut off our last retreat,' hissed Taurus, 'go you to the rim and look over on all sides; if you see any soldiers moving in the gardens, or anything suspicious, return and tell me. I will await you within this chamber.'

Conan saw scant reason in this, and a faint suspicion of his companion touched his wary soul, but he did as Taurus requested. As he turned away, the Nemedian slipt inside the door and drew it shut behind him. Conan crept about the rim of the tower, returning to his starting-point without having seen any suspicious movement in the vaguely waving sea of leaves below. He turned toward the door – suddenly from within the chamber there sounded a strangled cry.

The Cimmerian leaped forward, electrified – the gleaming door swung open and Taurus stood framed in the cold blaze behind him. He swayed and his lips parted, but only a dry rattle burst from his throat. Catching at the golden door for support, he lurched out upon the roof, then fell headlong, clutching at his throat. The door swung to behind him.

Conan, crouching like a panther at bay, saw nothing in the room behind the stricken Nemedian, in the brief instant the door was partly open – unless it was not a trick of the light which made it seem as if a shadow darted across the gleaming floor. Nothing followed Taurus out on the roof, and Conan bent above the man.

The Nemedian stared up with dilated, glazing eyes, that somehow held a terrible bewilderment. His hands clawed at his throat, his lips slobbered and gurgled; then suddenly he stiffened, and the astounded Cimmerian knew that he was dead. And he felt that Taurus had died without knowing what manner of death had stricken him. Conan glared bewilderedly at the cryptic golden door. In that empty room, with its glittering jeweled walls, death had come to the prince of thieves as swiftly and mysteriously as he had dealt doom to the lions in the gardens below.

Gingerly the barbarian ran his hands over the man's half-naked body, seeking a wound. But the only marks of violence were between his shoulders, high up near the base of his bull-neck – three small wounds, which looked as if three nails had been driven deep in the flesh and withdrawn. The edges of these wounds were black, and a faint smell as of putrefaction was evident. Poisoned darts? thought Conan – but in that case the missiles should be still in the wounds.

Cautiously he stole toward the golden door, pushed it open, and looked inside. The chamber lay empty, bathed in the cold, pulsing glow of the myriad jewels. In the very center of the ceiling he idly noted a curious design – a black eight-sided pattern, in the center of which four gems glittered with a red flame unlike the white blaze of the other jewels. Across the room there was another door, like the one in which he stood, except that it was not carved in the scale pattern. Was it from that door that death had come? – and having struck down its victim, had it retreated by the same way?

Closing the door behind him, the Cimmerian advanced into the chamber. His bare feet made no sound on the crystal floor. There were no chairs or tables in the chamber, only three or four silken couches, embroidered with gold and worked in strange serpentine designs, and several silver-bound mahogany chests. Some were sealed with heavy golden locks; others lay open, their carven lids thrown back, revealing heaps of jewels in a careless riot of splendor to the Cimmerian's astounded eyes. Conan swore beneath his breath; already he had looked upon more wealth that night than he had ever dreamed existed in all the world, and he grew dizzy thinking of what must be the value of the jewel he sought.

He was in the center of the room now, going stooped forward, head thrust out warily, sword advanced, when again death struck at him soundlessly. A flying shadow that swept across the gleaming floor was his only warning, and his instinctive side-long leap all that saved his life. He had a flashing glimpse of a hairy black horror that swung past him with a clashing of frothing fangs, and something splashed on his bare shoulder that burned like drops of liquid hell-fire. Springing back, sword high, he saw the horror strike the floor, wheel and scuttle toward him with appalling speed – a gigantic black spider, such as men see only in nightmare dreams.

It was as large as a pig, and its eight thick hairy legs drove its ogreish body over the floor at headlong pace; its four evilly gleaming eyes shone with a horrible intelligence, and its fangs dripped venom that Conan knew, from the burning of his shoulder where only a few drops had splashed as the thing struck and missed, was laden with swift death. This was the killer that had dropped from its perch in the middle of the ceiling on a strand of its web, on the neck of the Nemedian. Fools that they were not to have suspected that the upper chambers would be guarded as well as the lower!

These thoughts flashed briefly through Conan's mind as the monster rushed. He leaped high, and it passed beneath him, wheeled and charged back. This time he evaded its rush with a sidewise leap, and struck back like a cat. His sword severed one of the hairy legs, and again he barely saved himself as the monstrosity swerved at him, fangs clicking fiendishly. But the creature did not press the pursuit; turning, it scuttled across the crystal floor and ran up the wall to the ceiling, where it crouched for an instant, glaring down at him with its fiendish red eyes. Then without warning it launched itself through space, trailing a strand of slimy grayish stuff.

Conan stepped back to avoid the hurtling body – then ducked frantically, just in time to escape being snared by the flying web-rope. He saw the monster's intent and sprang toward the door, but it was quicker, and a sticky strand cast across the door made him a prisoner. He dared not try to cut it with his sword; he knew the stuff would cling to the blade, and before he could shake it loose, the fiend would be sinking its fangs into his back.

Then began a desperate game, the wits and quickness of the man matched against the fiendish craft and speed of the giant spider. It no longer scuttled across the floor in a direct charge, or swung its body through the air at him. It raced about the ceiling and the walls, seeking to snare him in the long loops of sticky gray web-strands, which it flung with a devilish accuracy. These strands were thick as ropes, and Conan knew that once they were coiled about him, his desperate strength would not be enough to tear him free before the monster struck.

All over the chamber went on that devil's dance, in utter silence except for the quick breathing of the man, the low scuff of his bare feet on the shining floor, the castanet rattle of the monstrosity's fangs. The gray strands lay in coils on the floor; they were looped along the walls; they overlaid the jewel-chests and silken couches, and hung in dusky festoons from the jeweled ceiling. Conan's steel-trap quickness of eye and muscle had kept him untouched, though the sticky loops had passed him so close they rasped his naked hide. He knew he could not always avoid them; he not only had to watch the strands swinging from the ceiling, but to keep his eye on the floor, lest he trip in the coils that lay there. Sooner or later a gummy loop would writhe about him, python-like, and then, wrapped like a cocoon, he would lie at the monster's mercy.

The spider raced across the chamber floor, the gray rope waving out behind it. Conan leaped high, clearing a couch – with a quick wheel the fiend ran up the wall, and the strand, leaping off the floor like a live thing, whipped about the Cimmerian's ankle. He caught himself on his hands as he fell, jerking frantically at the web which held him like a pliant vise, or the coil of a python. The hairy devil was racing down the wall to complete its capture. Stung to frenzy, Conan caught up a jewel chest and hurled it with all his strength. It was a move the monster was not expecting. Full in the midst of the branching black legs the massive missile struck, smashing against the wall with a muffled sickening crunch. Blood and greenish slime spattered, and the shattered mass fell with the burst gem-chest to the floor. The crushed black body lay among the flaming riot of jewels that spilled over it; the hairy legs moved aimlessly, the dying eyes glittered redly among the twinkling gems.

Conan glared about, but no other horror appeared, and he set himself to working free of the web. The substance clung tenaciously to his ankle and his hands, but at last he was free, and taking up his sword, he picked his way among the gray coils and loops to the inner door. What horrors lay within he did not know. The Cimmerian's blood was up, and since he had come so far, and overcome so much peril, he was determined to go through to the grim finish of the adventure, whatever that might be. And he felt that the jewel he sought was not among the many so carelessly strewn about the gleaming chamber.

Stripping off the loops that fouled the inner door, he found that it, like the other, was not locked. He wondered if the soldiers below were still unaware of his presence. Well, he was high above their heads, and if tales were to be believed, they were used to strange noises in the tower above them – sinister sounds, and screams of agony and horror.

Yara was on his mind, and he was not altogether comfortable as he opened the golden door. But he saw only a flight of silver steps leading down, dimly lighted by what means he could not ascertain. Down these he went silently, gripping his sword. He heard no sound, and came presently to an ivory door, set with blood-stones. He listened, but no sound came from within; only thin wisps of smoke drifted lazily from beneath the door, bearing a curious exotic odor unfamiliar to the Cimmerian. Below him the silver stair wound down to vanish in the dimness, and up that shadowy well no sound floated; he had an eery feeling that he was alone in a tower occupied only by ghosts and phantoms.

3

Cautiously he pressed against the ivory door and it swung silently inward. On the shimmering threshold Conan stared like a wolf in strange surroundings, ready to fight or flee on the instant. He was looking into a large chamber with a domed golden ceiling; the walls were of green jade, the floor of ivory, partly covered by thick rugs. Smoke and exotic scent of incense floated up from a brazier on a golden tripod, and behind it sat an idol on a sort of marble couch. Conan stared aghast; the image had the body of a man, naked, and green in color; but the head was one of nightmare and madness. Too large for the human body, it had no attributes of humanity. Conan stared at the wide flaring ears, the curling proboscis, on either side of which stood white tusks tipped with round golden balls. The eyes were closed, as if in sleep.

This then, was the reason for the name, the Tower of the Elephant, for the head of the thing was much like that of the beasts described by the Shemitish wanderer. This was Yara's god; where then should the gem be, but concealed in the idol, since the stone was called the Elephant's Heart?

As Conan came forward, his eyes fixed on the motionless idol, the eyes of the thing opened suddenly! The Cimmerian froze in his tracks. It was no image – it was a living thing, and he was trapped in its chamber!

That he did not instantly explode in a burst of murderous frenzy is a fact that measures his horror, which paralyzed him where he stood. A civilized man in his position would have sought doubtful refuge in the conclusion that he was insane; it did not occur to the Cimmerian to doubt his senses. He knew he was face to face with a demon of the Elder World, and the realization robbed him of all his faculties except sight.

The trunk of the horror was lifted and quested about, the

topaz eyes stared unseeingly, and Conan knew the monster was blind. With the thought came a thawing of his frozen nerves, and he began to back silently toward the door. But the creature heard. The sensitive trunk stretched toward him, and Conan's horror froze him again when the being spoke, in a strange, stammering voice that never changed its key or timbre. The Cimmerian knew that those jaws were never built or intended for human speech.

'Who is here? Have you come to torture me again, Yara? Will you never be done? Oh, Yag-kosha, is there no end to agony?'

Tears rolled from the sightless eyes and Conan's gaze strayed to the limbs stretched on the marble couch. And he knew the monster would not rise to attack him. He knew the marks of the rack, and the searing brand of the flame, and tough-souled as he was, he stood aghast at the ruined deformities which his reason told him had once been limbs as comely as his own. And suddenly all fear and repulsion went from him, to be replaced by a great pity. What this monster was, Conan could not know, but the evidences of its sufferings were so terrible and pathetic that a strange aching sadness came over the Cimmerian, he knew not why. He only felt that he was looking upon a cosmic tragedy, and he shrank with shame, as if the guilt of a whole race were laid upon him.

'I am not Yara,' he said. 'I am only a thief. I will not harm you.'

'Come near that I may touch you,' the creature faltered, and Conan came near unfearingly, his sword hanging forgotten in his hand. The sensitive trunk came out and groped over his face and shoulders, as a blind man gropes, and its touch was light as a girl's hand.

'You are not of Yara's race of devils,' sighed the creature. 'The clean, lean fierceness of the wastelands marks you. I know your people from of old, whom I knew by another name in the long, long ago when another world lifted its jeweled spires to the stars. There is blood on your fingers.'

'A spider in the chamber above and a lion in the garden,' muttered Conan.

'You have slain a man too, this night,' answered the other. 'And there is death in the tower above. I feel; I know.'

'Aye,' muttered Conan. 'The prince of all thieves lies there dead from the bite of a vermin.'

'So – and so!' the strange inhuman voice rose in a sort of low chant. 'A slaying in the tavern and a slaying on the roof – I know; I feel. And the third will make the magic of which not even Yara dreams – oh, magic of deliverance, green gods of Yag!'

Again tears fell as the tortured body was rocked to and fro in the grip of varied emotions. Conan looked on, bewildered.

Then the convulsions ceased; the soft, sightless eyes were turned toward the Cimmerian, the trunk beckoned.

'Oh man, listen,' said the strange being. 'I am foul and monstrous to you, am I not? Nay, do not answer; I know. But you would seem as strange to me, could I see you. There are many worlds besides this earth, and life takes many shapes. I am neither god nor demon, but flesh and blood like yourself, though the substance differ in part, and the form be cast in different mold.

'I am very old, oh man of the waste countries; long and long ago I came to this planet with others of my world, from the green planet Yag, which circles for ever in the outer fringe of this universe. We swept through space on mighty wings that drove us through the cosmos quicker than light, because we had warred with the kings of Yag and were defeated and outcast. But we could never return, for on earth our wings withered from our shoulders. Here we abode apart from earthly life. We fought the strange and terrible forms of life which then walked the earth, so that we became feared, and were not molested in the dim jungles of the east, where we had our abode.

'We saw men grow from the ape and build the shining cities

of Valusia, Kamelia, Commoria, and their sisters. We saw them reel before the thrusts of the heathen Atlanteans and Picts and Lemurians. We saw the oceans rise and engulf Atlantis and Lemuria, and the isles of the Picts, and the shining cities of civilization. We saw the survivors of Pictdom and Atlantis build their stone age empires, and go down to ruin, locked in bloody wars. We saw the Picts sink into abysmal savagery, the Atlanteans into apedom again. We saw new savages drift southward in conquering waves from the arctic circle to build a new civilization, with new kingdoms called Nemedia, and Koth, and Aquilonia and their sisters. We saw your people rise under a new name from the jungles of the apes that had been Atlanteans. We saw the descendants of the Lemurians who had survived the cataclysm, rise again through savagery and ride westward, as Hyrkanians. And we saw this race of devils, survivors of the ancient civilization that was before Atlantis sank, come once more into culture and power – this accursed kingdom of Zamora.

'All this we saw, neither aiding nor hindering the immutable cosmic law, and one by one we died; for we of Yag are not immortal, though our lives are as the lives of planets and constellations. At last I alone was left, dreaming of old times among the ruined temples of jungle-lost Khitai, worshipped as a god by an ancient yellow-skinned race. Then came Yara, versed in dark knowledge handed down through the days of barbarism, since before Atlantis sank.

'First he sat at my feet and learned wisdom. But he was not satisfied with what I taught him, for it was white magic, and he wished evil lore, to enslave kings and glut a fiendish ambition. I would teach him none of the black secrets I had gained, through no wish of mine, through the eons.

'But his wisdom was deeper than I had guessed; with guile gotten among the dusky tombs of dark Stygia, he trapped me into divulging a secret I had not intended to bare; and turning my own power upon me, he enslaved me. Ah, gods of Yag, my cup has been bitter since that hour!

'He brought me up from the lost jungles of Khitai where the gray apes danced to the pipes of the yellow priests, and offerings of fruit and wine heaped my broken altars. No more was I a god to kindly jungle-folk – I was slave to a devil in human form.'

Again tears stole from the unseeing eyes.

'He pent me in this tower which at his command I built for him in a single night. By fire and rack he mastered me, and by strange unearthly tortures you would not understand. In agony I would long ago have taken my own life, if I could. But he kept me alive – mangled, blinded, and broken – to do his foul bidding. And for three hundred years I have done his bidding, from this marble couch, blackening my soul with cosmic sins, and staining my wisdom with crimes, because I had no other choice. Yet not all my ancient secrets has he wrested from me, and my last gift shall be the sorcery of the Blood and the Jewel.

'For I feel the end of time draw near. You are the hand of Fate. I beg of you, take the gem you will find on yonder altar.'

Conan turned to the gold and ivory altar indicated, and took up a great round jewel, clear as crimson crystal; and he knew that this was the Heart of the Elephant.

'Now for the great magic, the mighty magic, such as earth has not seen before, and shall not see again, through a million million of millenniums. By my life-blood I conjure it, by blood born on the green breast of Yag, dreaming far-poised in the great blue vastness of Space.

'Take your sword, man, and cut out my heart; then squeeze it so that the blood will flow over the red stone. Then go you down these stairs and enter the ebony chamber where Yara sits wrapped in lotus-dreams of evil. Speak his name and he will awaken. Then lay this gem before him, and say, 'Yag-kosha gives you a last gift and a last enchantment.' Then get you from the tower quickly; fear not, your way shall be made clear. The life of man is not the life of Yag, nor is human death the death of Yag. Let me be free of this cage of broken blind flesh, and I will once more be Yogah of Yag, morning-crowned and shining, with wings to fly, and feet to dance, and eyes to see, and hands to break.'

Uncertainly Conan approached, and Yag-kosha, or Yogah, as if sensing his uncertainty, indicated where he should strike. Conan set his teeth and drove the sword deep. Blood streamed over the blade and his hand, and the monster started convulsively, then lay back quite still. Sure that life had fled, at least life as he understood it, Conan set to work on his grisly task and quickly brought forth something that he felt must be the strange being's heart, though it differed curiously from any he had ever seen. Holding the still pulsing organ over the blazing jewel, he pressed it with both hands, and a rain of blood fell on the stone. To his surprise, it did not run off, but soaked into the gem, as water is absorbed by a sponge.

Holding the jewel gingerly, he went out of the fantastic chamber and came upon the silver steps. He did not look back; he instinctively felt that some sort of transmutation was taking place in the body on the marble couch, and he further felt that it was of a sort not to be witnessed by human eyes.

He closed the ivory door behind him and without hesitation descended the silver steps. It did not occur to him to ignore the instructions given him. He halted at an ebony door, in the center of which was a grinning silver skull, and pushed it open. He looked into a chamber of ebony and jet, and saw, on a black silken couch, a tall, spare form reclining. Yara the priest and sorcerer lay before him, his eyes open and dilated with the fumes of the yellow lotus, far-staring, as if fixed on gulfs and nighted abysses beyond human ken.

'Yara!' said Conan, like a judge pronouncing doom. 'Awaken!'

The eyes cleared instantly and became cold and cruel as a vulture's. The tall silken-clad form lifted erect, and towered gauntly above the Cimmerian.

'Dog!' His hiss was like the voice of a cobra. 'What do you here?'

Conan laid the jewel on the great ebony table.

'He who sent this gem bade me say, "Yag-kosha gives a last gift and a last enchantment."'

Yara recoiled, his dark face ashy. The jewel was no longer crystal-clear; its murky depths pulsed and throbbed, and curious smoky waves of changing color passed over its smooth surface. As if drawn hypnotically, Yara bent over the table and gripped the gem in his hands, staring into its shadowed depths, as if it were a magnet to draw the shuddering soul from his body. And as Conan looked, he thought that his eyes must be playing him tricks. For when Yara had risen up from his couch, the priest had seemed gigantically tall; yet now he saw that Yara's head would scarcely come to his shoulder. He blinked, puzzled, and for the first time that night, doubted his own senses. Then with a shock he realized that the priest was shrinking in stature – was growing smaller before his very gaze.

With a detached feeling he watched, as a man might watch a play; immersed in a feeling of overpowering unreality, the Cimmerian was no longer sure of his own identity; he only knew that he was looking upon the external evidences of the unseen play of vast Outer forces, beyond his understanding.

Now Yara was no bigger than a child; now like an infant he sprawled on the table, still grasping the jewel. And now the sorcerer suddenly realized his fate, and he sprang up, releasing the gem. But still he dwindled, and Conan saw a tiny, pigmy figure rushing wildly about the ebony table-top, waving tiny arms and shrieking in a voice that was like the squeak of an insect.

Now he had shrunk until the great jewel towered above him like a hill, and Conan saw him cover his eyes with his hands, as if to shield them from the glare, as he staggered about like a madman. Conan sensed that some unseen magnetic force was pulling Yara to the gem. Thrice he raced wildly about it in a narrowing circle, thrice he strove to turn and run out across the table; then with a scream that echoed faintly in the ears of the watcher, the priest threw up his arms and ran straight toward the blazing globe.

Bending close, Conan saw Yara clamber up the smooth, curving surface, impossibly, like a man climbing a glass mountain. Now the priest stood on the top, still with tossing arms, invoking what grisly names only the gods know. And suddenly he sank into the very heart of the jewel, as a man sinks into a sea, and Conan saw the smoky waves close over his head. Now he saw him in the crimson heart of the jewel, once more crystal-clear, as a man sees a scene far away, tiny with great distance. And into the heart came a green, shining winged figure with the body of a man and the head of an elephant – no longer blind or crippled. Yara threw up his arms and fled as a madman flees, and on his heels came the avenger. Then, like the bursting of a bubble, the great jewel vanished in a rainbow burst of iridescent gleams, and the ebony table-top lay bare and deserted – as bare, Conan somehow knew, as the marble couch in the chamber above, where the body of that strange transcosmic being called Yag-kosha and Yogah had lain.

The Cimmerian turned and fled from the chamber, down the silver stairs. So mazed was he that it did not occur to him to escape from the tower by the way he had entered it. Down that winding, shadowy silver well he ran, and came into a large chamber at the foot of the gleaming stairs. There he halted for an instant; he had come into the room of the soldiers. He saw the glitter of their silver corselets, the sheen of their jeweled sword-hilts. They sat slumped at the banquet board, their dusky plumes waving somberly above their drooping helmeted heads; they lay among their dice and fallen goblets on the wine-stained lapis-lazuli floor. And he knew that they were dead. The promise had been made, the word kept; whether sorcery or magic or the falling shadow of great green wings had stilled the revelry,

Conan could not know, but his way had been made clear. And a silver door stood open, framed in the whiteness of dawn.

Into the waving green gardens came the Cimmerian, and as the dawn wind blew upon him with the cool fragrance of luxuriant growths, he started like a man waking from a dream. He turned back uncertainly, to stare at the cryptic tower he had just left. Was he bewitched and enchanted? Had he dreamed all that had seemed to have passed? As he looked he saw the gleaming tower sway against the crimson dawn, its jewel-crusted rim sparkling in the growing light, and crash into shining shards.

Queen of the Black Coast

1 Conan Joins the Pirates

Believe green buds awaken in the spring,
That autumn paints the leaves with somber fire;
Believe I held my heart inviolate
To lavish on one man my hot desire.

The Song of Bêlit

Hoofs drummed down the street that sloped to the wharfs. The folk that yelled and scattered had only a fleeting glimpse of a mailed figure on a black stallion, a wide scarlet cloak flowing out on the wind. Far up the street came the shout and clatter of pursuit, but the horseman did not look back. He swept out onto the wharfs and jerked the plunging stallion back on its haunches at the very lip of the pier. Seamen gaped up at him, as they stood to the sweep and striped sail of a high-prowed, broad-waisted galley. The master, sturdy and black-bearded, stood in the bows, easing her away from the piles with a boat-hook. He yelled angrily as the horseman sprang from the saddle and with a long leap landed squarely on the mid-deck.

'Who invited you aboard?'

'Get under way!' roared the intruder with a fierce gesture that spattered red drops from his broadsword.

'But we're bound for the coasts of Cush!' expostulated the master.

'Then I'm for Cush! Push off, I tell you!' The other cast a quick glance up the street, along which a squad of horsemen were galloping; far behind them toiled a group of archers, cross-bows on their shoulders.

'Can you pay for your passage?' demanded the master.

'I pay my way with steel!' roared the man in armor, brandishing the great sword that glittered bluely in the sun. 'By Crom, man, if you don't get under way, I'll drench this galley in the blood of its crew!'

The shipmaster was a good judge of men. One glance at the dark scarred face of the swordsman, hardened with passion, and he shouted a quick order, thrusting strongly against the piles. The galley wallowed out into clear water, the oars began to clack rhythmically; then a puff of wind filled the shimmering sail, the light ship heeled to the gust, then took her course like a swan, gathering headway as she skimmed along.

On the wharfs the riders were shaking their swords and shouting threats and commands that the ship put about, and yelling for the bowman to hasten before the craft was out of arbalest range.

'Let them rave,' grinned the swordsman hardly. 'Do you keep her on her course, master steersman.'

The master descended from the small deck between the bows, made his way between the rows of oarsmen, and mounted the mid-deck. The stranger stood there with his back to the mast, eyes narrowed alertly, sword ready. The shipman eyed him steadily, careful not to make any move toward the long knife in his belt. He saw a tall powerfully built figure in a black scale-mail hauberk, burnished greaves and a blue-steel helmet from which jutted bull's horns highly polished. From the mailed shoulders fell the scarlet cloak, blowing in the sea-wind. A broad shagreen belt with a golden buckle held the scabbard of the broadsword he bore. Under the horned helmet a square-cut black mane contrasted with smoldering blue eyes.

'If we must travel together,' said the master, 'we may as well be at peace with each other. My name is Tito, licensed master-shipman of the ports of Argos. I am bound for Cush, to trade beads and silks and sugar and brass-hilted swords to the black kings for ivory, copra, copper ore, slaves and pearls.'

The swordsman glanced back at the rapidly receding docks, where the figures still gesticulated helplessly, evidently having trouble in finding a boat swift enough to overhaul the fast-sailing galley.

'I am Conan, a Cimmerian,' he answered. 'I came into Argos seeking employment, but with no wars forward, there was nothing to which I might turn my hand.'

'Why do the guardsmen pursue you?' asked Tito. 'Not that it's any of my business, but I thought perhaps –'

'I've nothing to conceal,' replied the Cimmerian. 'By Crom, though I've spent considerable time among you civilized peoples, your ways are still beyond my comprehension.

'Well, last night in a tavern, a captain in the king's guard offered violence to the sweetheart of a young soldier, who natur-ally ran him through. But it seems there is some cursed law against killing guardsmen, and the boy and his girl fled away. It was bruited about that I was seen with them, and so today I was haled into court, and a judge asked me where the lad had gone. I replied that since he was a friend of mine, I could not betray him. Then the court waxed wroth, and the judge talked a great deal about my duty to the state, and society, and other things I did not understand, and bade me tell where my friend had flown. By this time I was becoming wrathful myself, for I had explained my position.

'But I choked my ire and held my peace, and the judge squalled that I had shown contempt for the court, and that I should be hurled into a dungeon to rot until I betrayed my friend. So then, seeing they were all mad, I drew my sword and cleft the judge's skull; then I cut my way out of the court, and seeing the high constable's stallion tied near by, I rode for the wharfs, where I thought to find a ship bound for foreign parts.'

'Well,' said Tito hardily, 'the courts have fleeced me too often in suits with rich merchants for me to owe them any love. I'll have questions to answer if I ever anchor in that port again, but I can prove I acted under compulsion. You may as well put up your sword. We're peaceable sailors, and have nothing against you. Besides, it's as well to have a fighting-man like yourself on board. Come up to the poop-deck and we'll have a tankard of ale.'

'Good enough,' readily responded the Cimmerian, sheathing his sword.

The *Argus* was a small sturdy ship, typical of those trading-craft which ply between the ports of Zingara and Argos and the southern coasts, hugging the shoreline and seldom venturing far into the open ocean. It was high of stern, with a tall curving prow; broad in the waist, sloping beautifully to stem and stern. It was guided by the long sweep from the poop, and propulsion was furnished mainly by the broad striped silk sail, aided by a jibsail. The oars were for use in tacking out of creeks and bays, and during calms. There were ten to the side, five fore and five aft of the small mid-deck. The most precious part of the cargo was lashed under this deck, and under the fore-deck. The men slept on deck or between the rowers' benches, protected, in bad weather, by canopies. With twenty men at the oars, three at the sweep, and the shipmaster, the crew was complete.

So the *Argus* pushed steadily southward, with consistently fair weather. The sun beat down from day to day with fiercer heat, and the canopies were run up – striped silken cloths that matched the shimmering sail and the shining goldwork on the prow and along the gunwales.

They sighted the coast of Shem – long rolling meadowlands with the white crowns of the towers of cities in the distance, and horsemen with blue-black beards and hooked noses, who sat their steeds along the shore and eyed the galley with suspicion. She did not put in; there was scant profit in trade with the sons of Shem.

Nor did master Tito pull into the broad bay where the Styx river emptied its gigantic flood into the ocean, and the massive black castles of Khemi loomed over the blue waters. Ships did not put unasked into this port, where dusky sorcerers wove awful spells in the murk of sacrificial smoke mounting eternally from blood-stained altars where naked women screamed, and where Set, the Old Serpent, arch-demon of the Hyborians but god of the Stygians, was said to writhe his shining coils among his worshippers.

Master Tito gave that dreamy glass-floored bay a wide berth, even when a serpent-prowed gondola shot from behind a castellated point of land, and naked dusky women, with great red blossoms in their hair, stood and called to his sailors, and posed and postured brazenly.

Now no more shining towers rose inland. They had passed the southern borders of Stygia and were cruising along the coasts of Cush. The sea and the ways of the sea were neverending mysteries to Conan, whose homeland was among the high hills of the northern uplands. The wanderer was no less of interest to the sturdy seamen, few of whom had ever seen one of his race.

They were characteristic Argosean sailors, short and stockily built. Conan towered above them, and no two of them could match his strength. They were hardy and robust, but his was the endurance and vitality of a wolf, his thews steeled and his nerves whetted by the hardness of his life in the world's wastelands. He was quick to laugh, quick and terrible in his wrath. He was a valiant trencherman, and strong drink was a passion and a weakness with him. Naïve as a child in many ways, unfamiliar with the sophistry of civilization, he was naturally intelligent, jealous of his rights, and dangerous as a hungry tiger. Young in years, he was hardened in warfare and wandering, and his sojourns in many lands were evident in his apparel. His horned helmet was such as was worn by the golden-haired Æsir of Nordheim; his hauberk and greaves were of the finest workmanship of Koth; the fine ring-mail which sheathed his arms and legs was of Nemedia; the blade at his girdle was a great Aquilonian broadsword; and his gorgeous scarlet cloak could have been spun nowhere but in Ophir.

So they beat southward, and master Tito began to look for the high-walled villages of the black people. But they found only smoking ruins on the shore of a bay, littered with naked black bodies. Tito swore.

'I had good trade here, aforetime. This is the work of pirates.'

'And if we meet them?' Conan loosened his great blade in its scabbard.

'Mine is no warship. We run, not fight. Yet if it came to a pinch, we have beaten off reavers before, and might do it again; unless it were Bêlit's *Tigress*.'

'Who is Bêlit?'

'The wildest she-devil unhanged. Unless I read the signs a-wrong, it was her butchers who destroyed that village on the bay. May I some day see her dangling from the yard-arm! She is called the queen of the black coast. She is a Shemite woman, who leads black raiders. They harry the shipping and have sent many a good tradesman to the bottom.'

From under the poop-deck Tito brought out quilted jerkins, steel caps, bows and arrows.

'Little use to resist if we're run down,' he grunted. 'But it rasps the soul to give up life without a struggle.'

It was just at sunrise when the lookout shouted a warning. Around the long point of an island off the starboard bow glided a long lethal shape, a slender serpentine galley, with a raised deck that ran from stem to stern. Forty oars on each side drove her swiftly through the water, and the low rail swarmed with naked blacks that chanted and clashed spears on oval shields. From the mast-head floated a long crimson pennon.

'Bêlit!' yelled Tito, paling. 'Yare! Put her about! Into that creek-mouth! If we can beach her before they run us down, we have a chance to escape with our lives!'

So, veering sharply, the *Argus* ran for the line of surf that boomed along the palm-fringed shore, Tito striding back and forth, exhorting the panting rowers to greater efforts. The master's black beard bristled, his eyes glared.

'Give me a bow,' requested Conan. 'It's not my idea of a manly weapon, but I learned archery among the Hyrkanians, and it will go hard if I can't feather a man or so on yonder deck.'

Standing on the poop, he watched the serpent-like ship skimming lightly over the waters, and landsman though he was, it was evident to him that the *Argus* would never win that race. Already arrows, arching from the pirate's deck, were falling with a hiss into the sea, not twenty paces astern.

'We'd best stand to it,' growled the Cimmerian; 'else we'll all die with shafts in our backs, and not a blow dealt.'

'Bend to it, dogs!' roared Tito with a passionate gesture of his brawny fist. The bearded rowers grunted, heaved at the oars, while their muscles coiled and knotted, and sweat started out on their hides. The timbers of the stout little galley creaked and groaned as the men fairly ripped her through the water. The wind had fallen; the sail hung limp. Nearer crept the inexorable raiders, and they were still a good mile from the surf when one of the steersmen fell gagging across the sweep, a long arrow through his neck. Tito sprang to take his place, and Conan, bracing his feet wide on the heaving poop-deck, lifted his bow. He could see the details of the pirate plainly now. The rowers were protected by a line of raised mantelets along the sides, but the warriors dancing on the narrow deck were in full view. These were painted and plumed, and mostly naked, brandishing spears and spotted shields.

On the raised platform in the bows stood a slim figure whose white skin glistened in dazzling contrast to the glossy ebon hides about it. Bêlit, without a doubt. Conan drew the shaft to his ear – then some whim or qualm stayed his hand and sent the arrow through the body of a tall plumed spearman beside her.

Hand over hand the pirate galley was overhauling the lighter ship. Arrows fell in a rain about the *Argus*, and men cried out. All the steersmen were down, pin-cushioned, and Tito was handling the massive sweep alone, gasping black curses, his braced legs knots of straining thews. Then with a sob he sank down, a long shaft quivering in his sturdy heart. The *Argus* lost headway and rolled in the swell. The men shouted in confusion, and Conan took command in characteristic fashion.

'Up, lads!' he roared, loosing with a vicious twang of cord. 'Grab your steel and give these dogs a few knocks before they cut our throats! Useless to bend your backs any more: they'll board us ere we can row another fifty paces!'

In desperation the sailors abandoned their oars and snatched up their weapons. It was valiant, but useless. They had time for one flight of arrows before the pirate was upon them. With no one at the sweep, the *Argus* rolled broadside, and the steel-beaked prow of the raider crashed into her amidships. Grappling-irons crunched into the side. From the lofty gunwales, the black pirates drove down a volley of shafts that tore through the quilted jackets of the doomed sailor-men, then sprang down spear in hand to complete the slaughter. On the deck of the pirate lay half a dozen bodies, an earnest of Conan's archery.

The fight on the *Argus* was short and bloody. The stocky sailors, no match for the tall barbarians, were cut down to a man. Elsewhere the battle had taken a peculiar turn. Conan, on the high-pitched poop, was on a level with the pirate's deck. As the steel prow slashed into the *Argus*, he braced himself and kept his feet under the shock, casting away his bow. A tall corsair, bounding over the rail, was met in midair by the Cimmerian's great sword, which sheared him cleanly through the torso, so that his body fell one way and his legs another. Then, with a burst of fury that left a heap of mangled corpses along the gunwales, Conan was over the rail and on the deck of the *Tigress*.

In an instant he was the center of a hurricane of stabbing spears and lashing clubs. But he moved in a blinding blur of steel. Spears bent on his armor or swished empty air, and his sword sang its death-song. The fighting-madness of his race was upon him, and with a red mist of unreasoning fury wavering before his blazing eyes, he cleft skulls, smashed breasts, severed limbs, ripped out entrails, and littered the deck like a shambles with a ghastly harvest of brains and blood.

Invulnerable in his armor, his back against the mast, he heaped mangled corpses at his feet until his enemies gave back panting in rage and fear. Then as they lifted their spears to cast them, and he tensed himself to leap and die in the midst of them, a shrill cry froze the lifted arms. They stood like statues, the black giants poised for the spear-casts, the mailed swordsman with his dripping blade.

Bêlit sprang before the blacks, beating down their spears. She turned toward Conan, her bosom heaving, her eyes flashing. Fierce fingers of wonder caught at his heart. She was slender, yet formed like a goddess: at once lithe and voluptuous. Her only garment was a broad silken girdle. Her white ivory limbs and the ivory globes of her breasts drove a beat of fierce passion through the Cimmerian's pulse, even in the panting fury of battle. Her rich black hair, black as a Stygian night, fell in rippling burnished clusters down her supple back. Her dark eyes burned on the Cimmerian.

She was untamed as a desert wind, supple and dangerous as

a she-panther. She came close to him, heedless of his great blade, dripping with blood of her warriors. Her supple thigh brushed against it, so close she came to the tall warrior. Her red lips parted as she stared up into his somber menacing eyes.

'Who are you?' she demanded. 'By Ishtar, I have never seen your like, though I have ranged the sea from the coasts of Zingara to the fires of the ultimate south. Whence come you?'

'From Argos,' he answered shortly, alert for treachery. Let her slim hand move toward the jeweled dagger in her girdle, and a buffet of his open hand would stretch her senseless on the deck. Yet in his heart he did not fear; he had held too many women, civilized or barbaric, in his iron-thewed arms, not to recognize the light that burned in the eyes of this one.

'You are no soft Hyborian!' she exclaimed. 'You are fierce and hard as a gray wolf. Those eyes were never dimmed by city lights; those thews were never softened by life amid marble walls.'

'I am Conan, a Cimmerian,' he answered.

To the people of the exotic climes, the north was a mazy half-mythical realm, peopled with ferocious blue-eyed giants who occasionally descended from their icy fastnesses with torch and sword. Their raids had never taken them as far south as Shem, and this daughter of Shem made no distinction between Æsir, Vanir or Cimmerian. With the unerring instinct of the elemental feminine, she knew she had found her lover, and his race meant naught, save as it invested him with the glamor of far lands.

'And I am Bêlit,' she cried, as one might say, 'I am queen.'

'Look at me, Conan!' She threw wide her arms. 'I am Bêlit, queen of the black coast. Oh, tiger of the North, you are cold as the snowy mountains which bred you. Take me and crush me with your fierce love! Go with me to the ends of the earth and the ends of the sea! I am a queen by fire and steel and slaughter – be thou my king!'

His eyes swept the blood-stained ranks, seeking expressions of wrath or jealousy. He saw none. The fury was gone from the ebon faces. He realized that to these men Bêlit was more than a woman: a goddess whose will was unquestioned. He glanced at the *Argus*, wallowing in the crimson sea-wash, heeling far over, her decks awash, held up by the grappling-irons. He glanced at the blue-fringed shore, at the far green hazes of the ocean, at the vibrant figure which stood before him; and his barbaric soul stirred within him. To quest these shining blue realms with that white-skinned young tiger-cat – to love, laugh, wander and pillage –

'I'll sail with you,' he grunted, shaking the red drops from his blade.

'Ho, N'Yaga!' her voice twanged like a bowstring. 'Fetch herbs and dress your master's wounds! The rest of you bring aboard the plunder and cast off.'

As Conan sat with his back against the poop-rail, while the old shaman attended to the cuts on his hands and limbs, the cargo of the ill-fated *Argus* was quickly shifted aboard the *Tigress* and stored in small cabins below deck. Bodies of the crew and of fallen pirates were cast overboard to the swarming sharks, while wounded blacks were laid in the waist to be bandaged. Then the grappling-irons were cast off, and as the *Argus* sank silently into the blood-flecked waters, the *Tigress* moved off southward to the rhythmic clack of the oars.

As they moved out over the glassy blue deep, Bêlit came to the poop. Her eyes were burning like those of a she-panther in the dark as she tore off her ornaments, her sandals and her silken girdle and cast them at his feet. Rising on tiptoe, arms stretched upward, a quivering line of naked white, she cried to the desperate horde: 'Wolves of the blue sea, behold ye now the dance – the mating-dance of Bêlit, whose fathers were kings of Askalon!'

And she danced, like the spin of a desert whirlwind, like the leaping of a quenchless flame, like the urge of creation and the urge of death. Her white feet spurned the blood-stained deck and dying men forgot death as they gazed frozen at her. Then, as the white stars glimmered through the blue velvet dusk, making her whirling body a blur of ivory fire, with a wild cry she threw herself at Conan's feet, and the blind flood of the Cimmerian's desire swept all else away as he crushed her panting form against the black plates of his corseleted breast.

2   The Black Lotus

In that dead citadel of crumbling stone
Her eyes were snared by that unholy sheen,
And curious madness took me by the throat,
As of a rival lover thrust between.
                                    The Song of Bêlit

The *Tigress* ranged the sea, and the black villages shuddered. Tomtoms beat in the night, with a tale that the she-devil of the sea had found a mate, an iron man whose wrath was as that of a wounded lion. And survivors of butchered Stygian ships named Bêlit with curses, and a white warrior with fierce blue eyes; so the Stygian princes remembered this man long and long, and their memory was a bitter tree which bore crimson fruit in the years to come.

But heedless as a vagrant wind, the *Tigress* cruised the southern coasts, until she anchored at the mouth of a broad sullen river, whose banks were jungle-clouded walls of mystery.

'This is the river Zarkheba, which is Death,' said Bêlit. 'Its waters are poisonous. See how dark and murky they run? Only venomous reptiles live in that river. The black people shun it. Once a Stygian galley, fleeing from me, fled up the river and vanished. I anchored in this very spot, and days later, the galley came floating down the dark waters, its decks blood-stained and deserted. Only one man was on board, and he was mad and died gibbering. The cargo was intact, but the crew had vanished into silence and mystery.

'My lover, I believe there is a city somewhere on that river. I have heard tales of giant towers and walls glimpsed afar off by sailors who dared go part-way up the river. We fear nothing: Conan, let us go and sack that city!'

Conan agreed. He generally agreed to her plans. Hers was the mind that directed their raids, his the arm that carried out her ideas. It mattered little to him where they sailed or whom they fought, so long as they sailed and fought. He found the life good.

Battle and raid had thinned their crew; only some eighty spearmen remained, scarcely enough to work the long galley. But Bêlit would not take the time to make the long cruise southward to the island kingdoms where she recruited her buccaneers. She was afire with eagerness for her latest venture; so the *Tigress* swung into the river mouth, the oarsmen pulling strongly as she breasted the broad current.

They rounded the mysterious bend that shut out the sight of the sea, and sunset found them forging steadily against the sluggish flow, avoiding sand-bars where strange reptiles coiled. Not even a crocodile did they see, nor any four-legged beast or winged bird coming down to the water's edge to drink. On through the blackness that preceded moonrise they drove, between banks that were solid palisades of darkness, whence came mysterious rustlings and stealthy footfalls, and the gleam of grim eyes. And once an inhuman voice was lifted in awful mockery – the cry of an ape, Bêlit said, adding that the souls of evil men were imprisoned in these man-like animals as punishment for past crimes. But Conan doubted, for once, in a gold-barred cage in an Hyrkanian city, he had seen an abysmal sad-eyed beast which men told him was an ape, and there had been about it naught of the demoniac malevolence which vibrated in the shrieking laughter that echoed from the black jungle.

Then the moon rose, a splash of blood, ebony-barred, and the jungle awoke in horrific bedlam to greet it. Roars and howls and yells set the black warriors to trembling, but all this noise, Conan noted, came from farther back in the jungle, as if the beasts no less than men shunned the black waters of Zarkheba.

Rising above the black denseness of the trees and above the waving fronds, the moon silvered the river, and their wake became a rippling scintillation of phosphorescent bubbles that widened like a shining road of bursting jewels. The oars dipped into the shining water and came up sheathed in frosty silver. The plumes on the warrior's head-pieces nodded in the wind, and the gems on sword-hilts and harness sparkled frostily.

The cold light struck icy fire from the jewels in Bêlit's clustered black locks as she stretched her lithe figure on a leopard-skin thrown on the deck. Supported on her elbows, her chin resting on her slim hands, she gazed up into the face of Conan, who lounged beside her, his black mane stirring in the faint breeze. Bêlit's eyes were dark jewels burning in the moonlight.

'Mystery and terror are about us, Conan, and we glide into the realm of horror and death,' she said. 'Are you afraid?'

A shrug of his mailed shoulders was his only answer.

'I am not afraid either,' she said meditatively. 'I was never afraid. I have looked into the naked fangs of Death too often. Conan, do you fear the gods?'

'I would not tread on their shadow,' answered the barbarian conservatively. 'Some gods are strong to harm, others, to aid; at least so say their priests. Mitra of the Hyborians must be a strong god, because his people have builded their cities over the world. But even the Hyborians fear Set. And Bel, god of thieves, is a good god. When I was a thief in Zamora I learned of him.'

'What of your own gods? I have never heard you call on them.'

'Their chief is Crom. He dwells on a great mountain. What

use to call on him? Little he cares if men live or die. Better to be silent than to call his attention to you; he will send you dooms, not fortune! He is grim and loveless, but at birth he breathes power to strive and slay into a man's soul. What else shall men ask of the gods?'

'But what of the worlds beyond the river of death?' she persisted.

'There is no hope here or hereafter in the cult of my people,' answered Conan. 'In this world men struggle and suffer vainly, finding pleasure only in the bright madness of battle; dying, their souls enter a gray misty realm of clouds and icy winds, to wander cheerlessly throughout eternity.'

Bêlit shuddered. 'Life, bad as it is, is better than such a destiny. What do you believe, Conan?'

He shrugged his shoulders. 'I have known many gods. He who denies them is as blind as he who trusts them too deeply. I seek not beyond death. It may be the blackness averred by the Nemedian skeptics, or Crom's realm of ice and cloud, or the snowy plains and vaulted halls of the Nordheimer's Valhalla. I know not, nor do I care. Let me live deep while I live; let me know the rich juices of red meat and stinging wine on my palate, the hot embrace of white arms, the mad exultation of battle when the blue blades flame and crimson, and I am content. Let teachers and priests and philosophers brood over questions of reality and illusion. I know this: if life is illusion, then I am no less an illusion, and being thus, the illusion is real to me. I live, I burn with life, I love, I slay, and am content.'

'But the gods are real,' she said, pursuing her own line of thought. 'And above all are the gods of the Shemites – Ishtar and Ashtoreth and Derketo and Adonis. Bel, too, is Shemitish, for he was born in ancient Shumir, long, long ago, and went forth laughing, with curled beard and impish wise eyes, to steal the gems of the kings of old times.

'There is life beyond death, I know, and I know this, too, Conan of Cimmeria' – she rose lithely to her knees and caught him in a pantherish embrace – 'my love is stronger than any death! I have lain in your arms, panting with the violence of our love; you have held and crushed and conquered me, drawing my soul to your lips with the fierceness of your bruising kisses. My heart is welded to your heart, my soul is part of your soul! Were I still in death and you fighting for life, I would come back from the abyss to aid you – aye, whether my spirit floated with the purple sails on the crystal sea of paradise, or writhed in the molten flames of hell! I am yours, and all the gods and all their eternities shall not sever us!'

A scream rang from the lookout in the bows. Thrusting Bêlit aside, Conan bounded up, his sword a long silver glitter in the moonlight, his hair bristling at what he saw. The black warrior dangled above the deck, supported by what seemed a dark pliant tree trunk arching over the rail. Then he realized that it was a gigantic serpent which had writhed its glistening length up the side of the bow and gripped the luckless warrior in its jaws. Its dripping scales shone leprously in the moonlight as it reared its form high above the deck, while the stricken man screamed and writhed like a mouse in the fangs of a python. Conan rushed into the bows, and swinging his great sword, hewed nearly through the giant trunk, which was thicker than a man's body. Blood drenched the rails as the dying monster swayed far out, still gripping its victim, and sank into the river, coil by coil, lashing the water to bloody foam, in which man and reptile vanished together.

Thereafter Conan kept the lookout watch himself, but no other horror came crawling up from the murky depths, and as dawn whitened over the jungle, he sighted the black fangs of towers jutting up among the trees. He called Bêlit, who slept on the deck, wrapped in his scarlet cloak; and she sprang to his side, eyes blazing. Her lips were parted to call orders to her warriors to take up bow and spears; then her lovely eyes widened.

It was but the ghost of a city on which they looked when they cleared a jutting jungle-clad point and swung in toward the in-curving shore. Weeds and rank river grass grew between the stones of broken piers and shattered paves that had once been streets and spacious plazas and broad courts. From all sides except that toward the river, the jungle crept in, masking fallen columns and crumbling mounds with poisonous green. Here and there buckling towers reeled drunkenly against the morning sky, and broken pillars jutted up among the decaying walls. In the center space a marble pyramid was spired by a slim column, and on its pinnacle sat or squatted something that Conan supposed to be an image until his keen eyes detected life in it.

'It is a great bird,' said one of the warriors, standing in the bows.

'It is a monster bat,' insisted another.

'It is an ape,' said Bêlit.

Just then the creature spread broad wings and flapped off into the jungle.

'A winged ape,' said old N'Yaga uneasily. 'Better we had cut our throats than come to this place. It is haunted.'

Bêlit mocked at his superstitions and ordered the galley run inshore and tied to the crumbling wharfs. She was the first to spring ashore, closely followed by Conan, and after them trooped the ebon-skinned pirates, white plumes waving in the morning wind, spears ready, eyes rolling dubiously at the surrounding jungle.

Over all brooded a silence as sinister as that of a sleeping serpent. Bêlit posed picturesquely among the ruins, the vibrant life in her lithe figure contrasting strangely with the desolation and decay about her. The sun flamed up slowly, sullenly, above the jungle, flooding the towers with a dull gold that left shadows lurking beneath the tottering walls. Bêlit pointed to a slim round tower that reeled on its rotting base. A broad expanse of cracked, grass-grown slabs led up to it, flanked by fallen columns, and before it stood a massive altar. Bêlit went swiftly along the ancient floor and stood before it.

'This was the temple of the old ones,' she said. 'Look – you can see the channels for the blood along the sides of the altar, and the rains of ten thousand years have not washed the dark stains from them. The walls have all fallen away, but this stone block defies time and the elements.'

'But who were these old ones?' demanded Conan.

She spread her slim hands helplessly. 'Not even in legendry is this city mentioned. But look at the handholes at either end of the altar! Priests often conceal their treasures beneath their altars. Four of you lay hold and see if you can lift it.'

She stepped back to make room for them, glancing up at the tower which loomed drunkenly above them. Three of the strongest blacks had gripped the handholds cut into the stone – curiously unsuited to human hands – when Bêlit sprang back with a sharp cry. They froze in their places, and Conan, bending to aid them, wheeled with a startled curse.

'A snake in the grass,' she said, backing away. 'Come and slay it; the rest of you bend your backs to the stone.'

Conan came quickly toward her, another taking his place. As he impatiently scanned the grass for the reptile, the giant blacks braced their feet, grunted and heaved with their huge muscles coiling and straining under their ebon skin. The altar did not come off the ground, but it revolved suddenly on its side. And simultaneously there was a grinding rumble above and the tower came crashing down, covering the four black men with broken masonry.

A cry of horror rose from their comrades. Bêlit's slim fingers dug into Conan's arm-muscles. 'There was no serpent,' she whispered. 'It was but a ruse to call you away. I feared; the old ones guarded their treasure well. Let us clear away the stones.'

With herculean labor they did so, and lifted out the mangled bodies of the four men. And under them, stained with their blood, the pirates found a crypt carved in the solid stone. The altar, hinged curiously with stone rods and sockets on one side, had served as its lid. And at first glance the crypt seemed brimming with liquid fire, catching the early light with a million blazing facets. Undreamable wealth lay before the eyes of the gaping pirates: diamonds, rubies, bloodstones, sapphires, turquoises, moonstones, opals, emeralds, amethysts, unknown gems that shone like the eyes of evil women. The crypt was filled to the brim with bright stones that the morning sun struck into lambent flame.

With a cry Bêlit dropped to her knees among the blood-stained rubble on the brink and thrust her white arms shoulder-deep into that pool of splendor. She withdrew them, clutching something that brought another cry to her lips – a long string of crimson stones that were like clots of frozen blood strung on a thick gold wire. In their glow the golden sunlight changed to bloody haze.

Bêlit's eyes were like a woman's in a trance. The Shemite soul finds a bright drunkenness in riches and material splendor, and the sight of this treasure might have shaken the soul of a sated emperor of Shushan.

'Take up the jewels, dogs!' her voice was shrill with her emotions.

'Look!' A muscular back arm stabbed toward the *Tigress*, and Bêlit wheeled, her crimson lips a-snarl, as if she expected to see a rival corsair sweeping in to despoil her of her plunder. But from the gunwales of the ship a dark shape rose, soaring away over the jungle.

'The devil-ape has been investigating the ship,' muttered the blacks uneasily.

'What matter?' cried Bêlit with a curse, raking back a rebellious lock with an impatient hand. 'Make a litter of spears and mantles to bear these jewels – where the devil are you going?'

'To look to the galley,' grunted Conan. 'That bat-thing might have knocked a hole in the bottom, for all we know.'

He ran swiftly down the cracked wharf and sprang aboard. A moment's swift examination below decks, and he swore heartily, casting a clouded glance in the direction the bat-being had vanished. He returned hastily to Bêlit, superintending the plundering of the crypt. She had looped the necklace about her neck, and on her naked white bosom the red clots glimmered darkly. A huge naked black stood crotch-deep in the jewel-brimming crypt, scooping up great handfuls of splendor to pass them to the eager hands above. Strings of frozen iridescence hung between his dusky fingers; drops of red fire dripped from his hands, piled high with starlight and rainbow. It was as if a black titan stood straddle-legged in the bright pits of hell, his lifted hands full of stars.

'That flying devil has staved in the water-casks,' said Conan. 'If we hadn't been so dazed by these stones we'd have heard the noise. We were fools not to have left a man on guard. We can't drink this river water. I'll take twenty men and search for fresh water in the jungle.'

She looked at him vaguely, in her eyes the blank blaze of her strange passion, her fingers working at the gems on her breast.

'Very well,' she said absently, hardly heeding him. 'I'll get the loot aboard.'

The jungle closed quickly about them, changing the light from gold to gray. From the arching green branches creepers dangled like pythons. The warriors fell into single file, creeping through the primordial twilights like black phantoms following a white ghost.

Underbrush was not so thick as Conan had anticipated. The ground was spongy but not slushy. Away from the river, it sloped gradually upward. Deeper and deeper they plunged into the green waving depths, and still there was no sign of water, either running stream or stagnant pool. Conan halted suddenly, his warriors freezing into basaltic statues. In the tense silence that followed, the Cimmerian shook his head irritably.

'Go ahead,' he grunted to a sub-chief, N'Gora. 'March straight on until you can no longer see me; then stop and wait for me. I believe we're being followed. I heard something.'

The blacks shuffled their feet uneasily, but did as they were told. As they swung onward, Conan stepped quickly behind a great tree, glaring back along the way they had come. From that leafy fastness anything might emerge. Nothing occurred; the faint sounds of the marching spearmen faded in the distance. Conan suddenly realized that the air was impregnated with an alien and exotic scent. Something gently brushed his temple. He turned quickly. From a cluster of green, curiously leafed stalks, great black blossoms nodded at him. One of these had touched him. They seemed to beckon him, to arch their pliant stems toward him. They spread and rustled, though no wind blew.

He recoiled, recognizing the black lotus, whose juice was death, and whose scent brought dream-haunted slumber. But already he felt a subtle lethargy stealing over him. He sought to lift his sword, to hew down the serpentine stalks, but his arm hung lifeless at his side. He opened his mouth to shout to his warriors, but only a faint rattle issued. The next instant, with appalling suddenness, the jungle waved and dimmed out before his eyes; he did not hear the screams that burst out awfully not far away, as his knees collapsed, letting him pitch limply to the earth. Above his prostrate form the great black blossoms nodded in the windless air.

3   The Horror in the Jungle

Was it a dream the nighted lotus brought?
Then curst the dream that bought my sluggish life;
And curst each laggard hour that does not see
Hot blood drip blackly from the crimsoned knife.

The Song of Bêlit

First there was the blackness of an utter void, with the cold winds of cosmic space blowing through it. Then shapes, vague, monstrous and evanescent, rolled in dim panorama through the expanse of nothingness, as if the darkness were taking material form. The winds blew and a vortex formed, a whirling pyramid of roaring blackness. From it grew Shape and Dimension; then suddenly, like clouds dispersing, the darkness rolled away on either hand and a huge city of dark green stone rose on the bank of a wide river, flowing through an illimitable plain. Through this city moved beings of alien configuration.

Cast in the mold of humanity, they were distinctly not men. They were winged and of heroic proportions; not a branch on the mysterious stalk of evolution that culminated in man, but the ripe blossom on an alien tree, separate and apart from that stalk. Aside from their wings, in physical appearance they resembled man only as man in his highest form resembles the great apes. In spiritual, esthetic and intellectual development they were superior to man as man is superior to the gorilla. But when they reared their colossal city, man's primal ancestors had not yet risen from the slime of the primordial seas.

These beings were mortal, as are all things built of flesh and blood. They lived, loved, and died, though the individual span of life was enormous. Then, after uncounted millions of years, the Change began. The vista shimmered and wavered, like a picture thrown on a wind-blown curtain. Over the city and the land the ages flowed as waves flow over a beach, and each wave brought alterations. Somewhere on the planet the magnetic centers were shifting; the great glaciers and ice-fields were withdrawing toward the new poles.

The littoral of the great river altered. Plains turned into swamps that stank with reptilian life. Where fertile meadows had rolled, forests reared up, growing into dank jungles. The changing ages wrought on the inhabitants of the city as well. They did not migrate to fresher lands. Reasons inexplicable to humanity held them to the ancient city and their doom. And as that once rich and mighty land sank deeper and deeper into the black mire of the sunless jungle, so into the chaos of squalling jungle life sank the people of the city. Terrific convulsions shook the earth; the nights were lurid with spouting volcanoes that fringed the dark horizons with red pillars.

After an earthquake that shook down the outer walls and highest towers of the city, and caused the river to run black for days with some lethal substance spewed up from the subterranean depths, a frightful chemical change became apparent in the waters the folk had drunk for millenniums uncountable.

Many died who drank of it; and in those who lived, the drinking wrought change, subtle, gradual and grisly. In adapting themselves to the changing conditions, they had sunk far below their original level. But the lethal waters altered them even more horribly, from generation to more bestial generation. They who had been winged gods became pinioned demons, with all that remained of their ancestors' vast knowledge distorted and perverted and twisted into ghastly paths. As they had risen higher than mankind might dream, so they sank lower than man's maddest nightmares reach. They died fast, by cannibalism, and horrible feuds fought out in the murk of the midnight jungle. And at last among the lichen-grown ruins of their city only a single shape lurked, a stunted abhorrent perversion of nature.

Then for the first time humans appeared: dark-skinned, hawk-faced men in copper and leather harness, bearing bows – the warriors of pre-historic Stygia. There were only fifty of them, and they were haggard and gaunt with starvation and prolonged effort, stained and scratched with jungle-wandering, with blood-crusted bandages that told of fierce fighting. In their minds was a tale of warfare and defeat, and flight before a stronger tribe which drove them ever southward, until they lost themselves in the green ocean of jungle and river.

Exhausted they lay down among the ruins where red blossoms that bloom but once in a century waved in the full moon, and sleep fell upon them. And as they slept, a hideous shape crept red-eyed from the shadows and performed weird and awful rites about and above each sleeper. The moon hung in the shadowy sky, painting the jungle red and black; above the sleepers glimmered the crimson blossoms, like splashes of blood. Then the moon went down and the eyes of the necromancer were red jewels set in the ebony of night.

When dawn spread its white veil over the river, there were no men to be seen: only a hairy winged horror that squatted in the center of a ring of fifty great spotted hyenas that pointed quivering muzzles to the ghastly sky and howled like souls in hell.

Then scene followed scene so swiftly that each tripped over the heels of its predecessor. There was a confusion of movement, a writhing and melting of lights and shadows, against a background of black jungle, green stone ruins, and murky river. Black men came up the river in long boats with skulls grinning on the prows, or stole stooping through the trees, spear in hand. They fled screaming through the dark from red eyes and slavering fangs. Howl of dying men shook the shadows; stealthy feet padded through the gloom, vampire eyes blazed redly. There were grisly feasts beneath the moon, across whose red disk a bat-like shadow incessantly swept.

Then abruptly, etched clearly in contrast to these impressionistic glimpses, around the jungled point in the whitening dawn swept a long galley, thronged with shining ebon figures, and in the bows stood a white-skinned giant in blue steel.

It was at this point that Conan first realized that he was dreaming. Until that instant he had had no consciousness of individual existence. But as he saw himself treading the boards of the *Tigress*, he recognized both the existence and the dream, although he did not awaken.

Even as he wondered, the scene shifted abruptly to a jungle glade where N'Gora and nineteen black spearmen stood, as if awaiting someone. Even as he realized that it was he for whom they waited, a horror swooped down from the skies and their

stolidity was broken by yells of fear. Like men maddened by terror, they threw away their weapons and raced wildly through
the jungle, pressed close by the slavering monstrosity that
flapped its wings above them.

Chaos and confusion followed this vision, during which Conan
feebly struggled to awake. Dimly he seemed to see himself lying
under a nodding cluster of black blossoms, while from the
bushes a hideous shape crept toward him. With a savage effort
he broke the unseen bonds which held him to his dreams, and
started upright.

Bewilderment was in the glare he cast about him. Near him
swayed the dusky lotus, and he hastened to draw away from it.

In the spongy soil near by there was a track as if an animal
had put out a foot, preparatory to emerging from the bushes,
then had withdrawn it. It looked like the spoor of an unbeliev-
ably large hyena.

He yelled for N'Gora. Primordial silence brooded over the jungle, in which his yells sounded brittle and hollow as mockery. He
could not see the sun, but his wilderness-trained instinct told him
the day was near its end. A panic rose in him at the thought that
he had lain senseless for hours. He hastily followed the tracks of
the spearmen, which lay plain in the damp loam before him. They
ran in single file, and he soon emerged into a glade – to stop short,
the skin crawling between his shoulders as he recognized it as the
glade he had seen in his lotus-drugged dream. Shields and spears
lay scattered about as if dropped in headlong flight.

And from the tracks which led out of the glade and deeper
into the fastnesses, Conan knew that the spearmen had fled,
wildly. The footprints overlay one another; they weaved blindly
among the trees. And with startling suddenness the hastening
Cimmerian came out of the jungle onto a hill-like rock which
sloped steeply, to break off abruptly in a sheer precipice forty
feet high. And something crouched on the brink.

At first Conan thought it to be a great black gorilla. Then he saw that it was a giant black man that crouched ape-like, long arms dangling, froth dripping from the loose lips. It was not until, with a sobbing cry, the creature lifted huge hands and rushed toward him, that Conan recognized N'Gora. The black man gave no heed to Conan's shout as he charged, eyes rolled up to display the whites, teeth gleaming, face an inhuman mask.

With his skin crawling with the horror that madness always instils in the sane, Conan passed his sword through the black man's body; then, avoiding the hooked hands that clawed at him as N'Gora sank down, he strode to the edge of the cliff.

For an instant he stood looking down into the jagged rocks below, where lay N'Gora's spearmen, in limp, distorted attitudes that told of crushed limbs and splintered bones. Not one moved. A cloud of huge black flies buzzed loudly above the blood-splashed stones; the ants had already begun to gnaw at the corpses. On the trees about sat birds of prey, and a jackal, looking up and seeing the man on the cliff, slunk furtively away.

For a little space Conan stood motionless. Then he wheeled and ran back the way he had come, flinging himself with reckless haste through the tall grass and bushes, hurdling creepers that sprawled snake-like across his path. His sword swung low in his right hand, and an unaccustomed pallor tinged his dark face.

The silence that reigned in the jungle was not broken. The sun had set and great shadows rushed upward from the slime of the black earth. Through the gigantic shades of lurking death and grim desolation Conan was a speeding glimmer of scarlet and blue steel. No sound in all the solitude was heard except his own quick panting as he burst from the shadows into the dim twilight of the river-shore.

He saw the galley shouldering the rotten wharf, the ruins reeling drunkenly in the gray half-light.

And here and there among the stones were spots of raw

bright color, as if a careless hand had splashed with a crimson brush.

Again Conan looked on death and destruction. Before him lay his spearmen, nor did they rise to salute him. From the jungle-edge to the river-bank, among the rotting pillars and along the broken piers they lay, torn and mangled and half-devoured, chewed travesties of men.

All about the bodies and pieces of bodies were swarms of huge footprints, like those of hyenas.

Conan came silently upon the pier, approaching the galley above whose deck was suspended something that glimmered ivory-white in the faint twilight. Speechless the Cimmerian looked on the Queen of the Black Coast as she hung from the yard-arm of her own galley. Between the yard and her white throat stretched a line of crimson clots that shone like blood in the gray light.

4   The Attack from the Air

The shadows were black around him,
The dripping jaws gaped wide,
Thicker than rain the red drops fell;
But my love was fiercer than Death's black spell,
Nor all the iron walls of hell
Could keep me from his side.

The Song of Bêlit

The jungle was a black colossus that locked the ruin-littered glade in ebon arms. The moon had not risen; the stars were flecks of hot amber in a breathless sky that reeked of death. On the pyramid among the fallen towers sat Conan the Cimmerian like an iron statue, chin propped on massive fists. Out in the black shadows stealthy feet padded and red eyes glimmered. The dead lay as they had fallen. But on the deck of the *Tigress*, on a pyre of broken benches, spear-shafts and leopardskins, lay the Queen of the Black Coast in her last sleep, wrapped in Conan's scarlet cloak. Like a true queen she lay, with her plunder heaped high about her: silks, cloth-of-gold, silver braid, casks of gems and golden coins, silver ingots, jeweled daggers, and teocallis of gold wedges.

But of the plunder of the accursed city, only the sullen waters of Zarkheba could tell, where Conan had thrown it with a heathen curse. Now he sat grimly on the pyramid, waiting for his unseen foes. The black fury in his soul drove out all fear. What shapes would emerge from the blackness he knew not, nor did he care.

He no longer doubted the visions of the black lotus. He understood that while waiting for him in the glade, N'Gora and his comrades had been terror-stricken by the winged monster swooping upon them from the sky, and fleeing in blind panic, had fallen over the cliff; all except their chief, who had somehow escaped their fate, though not madness. Meanwhile, or immediately after, or perhaps before, the destruction of those on the river-bank had been accomplished. Conan did not doubt that the slaughter along the river had been massacre rather than battle. Already unmanned by their superstitious fears, the blacks might well have died without striking a blow in their own defense when attacked by their inhuman foes.

Why he had been spared so long, he did not understand, unless the malign entity which ruled the river meant to keep him alive to torture him with grief and fear. All pointed to a human or superhuman intelligence – the breaking of the water-casks to divide the forces, the driving of the blacks over the cliff, and last and greatest, the grim jest of the crimson necklace knotted like a hangman's noose about Bêlit's white neck.

Having apparently saved the Cimmerian for the choicest victim, and extracted the last ounce of exquisite mental torture, it was likely that the unknown enemy would conclude the drama by sending him after the other victims. No smile bent Conan's grim lips at the thought, but his eyes were lit with iron laughter.

The moon rose, striking fire from the Cimmerian's horned helmet. No call awoke the echoes; yet suddenly the night grew tense and the jungle held its breath. Instinctively Conan loosened the great sword in its sheath. The pyramid on which he rested was four-sided, one – the side toward the jungle – carved in broad steps. In his hand was a Shemite bow, such as Bêlit had taught her pirates to use. A heap of arrows lay at his feet, feathered ends toward him, as he rested on one knee.

Something moved in the blackness under the trees. Etched abruptly in the rising moon, Conan saw a darkly blocked-out head and shoulders, brutish in outline. And now from the shadows dark shapes came silently, swiftly, running low – twenty great spotted hyenas. Their slavering fangs flashed in the moonlight, their eyes blazed as no true beast's eyes ever blazed.

Twenty: then the spears of the pirates had taken toll of the pack, after all. Even as he thought this, Conan drew nock to ear, and at the twang of the string a flame-eyed shadow bounded high and fell writhing. The rest did not falter; on they came, and like a rain of death among them fell the arrows of the Cimmerian, driven with all the force and accuracy of steely thews backed by a hate hot as the slag-heaps of hell.

In his berserk fury he did not miss; the air was filled with feathered destruction. The havoc wrought among the onrushing pack was breath-taking. Less than half of them reached the foot of the pyramid. Others dropped upon the broad steps. Glaring down into the blazing eyes, Conan knew these creatures were not beasts; it was not merely in their unnatural size that he sensed a blasphemous difference. They exuded an aura tangible as the black mist rising from a corpse-littered swamp. By what godless alchemy these beings had been brought into existence, he could not guess; but he knew he faced diabolism blacker than the Well of Skelos.

Springing to his feet, he bent his bow powerfully and drove his last shaft point-blank at a great hairy shape that soared up at his throat. The arrow was a flying beam of moonlight that flashed onward with but a blur in its course, but the were-beast plunged convulsively in midair and crashed headlong, shot through and through.

Then the rest were on him, in a nightmare rush of blazing eyes and dripping fangs. His fiercely driven sword shore the first asunder; then the desperate impact of the others bore him down. He crushed a narrow skull with the pommel of his hilt, feeling the bone splinter and blood and brains gush over his hand; then, dropping the sword, useless at such deadly-close quarters, he caught at the throats of the two horrors which were ripping and tearing at him in silent fury. A foul acrid scent almost stifled him, his own sweat blinded him. Only his mail saved him from being ripped to ribbons in an instant. The next, his naked right hand locked on a hairy throat and tore it open. His left hand, missing the throat of the other beast, caught and broke its foreleg. A short yelp, the only cry in that grim battle, and hideously human-like, burst from the maimed beast. At the sick horror of that cry from a bestial throat, Conan involuntarily relaxed his grip.

One, blood gushing from its torn jugular, lunged at him in a last spasm of ferocity, and fastened its fangs on his throat – to fall back dead, even as Conan felt the tearing agony of its grip.

The other, springing forward on three legs, was slashing at his belly as a wolf slashes, actually rending the links of his mail. Flinging aside the dying beast, Conan grappled the crippled hor-ror and with a muscular effort that brought a groan from his blood-flecked lips, he heaved upright, gripping the struggling, tearing fiend in his arms. An instant he reeled off balance, its fetid breath hot on his nostrils, its jaws snapping at his neck; then he hurled it from him, to crash with bone-splintering force down the marble steps.

As he reeled on wide-braced legs, sobbing for breath, the jungle and the moon swimming bloodily to his sight, the thrash of bat-wings was loud in his ears. Stooping, he groped for his sword, and swaying upright, braced his feet drunkenly and heaved the great blade above his head with both hands, shaking the blood from his eyes as he sought the air above him for his foe.

Instead of attack from the air, the pyramid staggered suddenly and awfully beneath his feet. He heard a rumbling crackle and saw the tall column above him wave like a wand. Stung to galvanized life, he bounded far out; his feet hit a step, half-way down, which rocked beneath him, and his next desperate leap carried him clear. But even as his heels hit the earth, with a shattering crash like a breaking mountain the pyramid crumpled, the column came thundering down in bursting fragments. For a blind cataclysmic instant the sky seemed to rain shards of marble. Then a rubble of shattered stone lay whitely under the moon.

Conan stirred, throwing off the splinters that half covered him. A glancing blow had knocked off his helmet and momentarily stunned him. Across his legs lay a great piece of the column, pinning him down. He was not sure that his legs were unbroken. His black locks were plastered with sweat; blood trickled from the wounds in his throat and hands. He hitched up on one arm, struggling with the debris that prisoned him.

Then something swept down across the stars and struck the sward near him. Twisting about, he saw it – *the winged one!*

With fearful speed it was rushing upon him, and in that instant Conan had only a confused impression of a gigantic man-like shape hurtling along on bowed and stunted legs; of huge hairy arms outstretching misshapen black-nailed paws; of a malformed head, in whose broad face the only features recognizable as such were a pair of blood-red eyes. It was a thing neither man, beast, nor devil, imbued with characteristics subhuman as well as characteristics superhuman.

But Conan had no time for conscious consecutive thought. He threw himself toward his fallen sword, and his clawing fingers missed it by inches. Desperately he grasped the shard which pinned his legs, and the veins swelled in his temples as he strove to thrust it off him. It gave slowly, but he knew that before he could free himself the monster would be upon him, and he knew that those black-taloned hands were death.

The headlong rush of the winged one had not wavered. It towered over the prostrate Cimmerian like a black shadow, arms thrown wide – a glimmer of white flashed between it and its victim.

In one mad instant she was there – a tense white shape, vibrant with love fierce as a she-panther's. The dazed Cimmerian saw between him and the onrushing death, her lithe figure, shimmering like ivory beneath the moon; he saw the blaze of her dark eyes, the thick cluster of her burnished hair; her bosom heaved, her red lips were parted, she cried out sharp and ringing as the ring of steel as she thrust at the winged monster's breast.

'*Bêlit!*' screamed Conan. She flashed a quick glance toward him, and in her dark eyes he saw her love flaming, a naked elemental thing of raw fire and molten lava. Then she was gone, and the Cimmerian saw only the winged fiend which had staggered back in unwonted fear, arms lifted as if to fend off attack. And he knew that Bêlit in truth lay on her pyre on the *Tigress'* deck. In his ears rang her passionate cry: 'Were I still in death and you fighting for life I would come back from the abyss –'

With a terrible cry he heaved upward, hurling the stone aside. The winged one came on again, and Conan sprang to meet it, his veins on fire with madness. The thews started out like cords on his forearms as he swung his great sword, pivoting on his heel with the force of the sweeping arc. Just above the hips it caught the hurtling shape, and the knotted legs fell one way, the torso another as the blade sheared clear through its hairy body.

Conan stood in the moonlit silence, the dripping sword sagging in his hand, staring down at the remnants of his enemy. The red eyes glared up at him with awful life, then glazed and set; the great hands knotted spasmodically and stiffened. And the oldest race in the world was extinct.

Conan lifted his head, mechanically searching for the beast-things that had been its slaves and executioners. None met his gaze. The bodies he saw littering the moon-splashed grass were of men, not beasts: hawk-faced, dark-skinned men, naked, transfixed by arrows or mangled by sword-strokes. And they were crumbling into dust before his eyes.

Why had not the winged master come to the aid of its slaves when he struggled with them? Had it feared to come within reach of fangs that might turn and rend it? Craft and caution had lurked in that misshapen skull, but had not availed in the end.

Turning on his heel, the Cimmerian strode down the rotting wharfs and stepped aboard the galley. A few strokes of his sword cut her adrift, and he went to the sweep-head. The *Tigress* rocked slowly in the sullen water, sliding out sluggishly toward the middle of the river, until the broad current caught her. Conan leaned on the sweep, his somber gaze fixed on the cloak-wrapped shape that lay in state on the pyre the richness of which was equal to the ransom of an empress.

5 The Funeral Pyre

Now we are done with roaming, evermore;
No more the oars, the windy harp's refrain;
Nor crimson pennon frights the dusky shore;
Blue girdle of the world, receive again
Her whom thou gavest me.

The Song of Bêlit

Again dawn tinged the ocean. A redder glow lit the river-mouth. Conan of Cimmeria leaned on his great sword upon the white beach, watching the *Tigress* swinging out on her last voyage. There was no light in his eyes that contemplated the glassy swells. Out of the rolling blue wastes all glory and wonder had gone. A fierce revulsion shook him as he gazed at the green surges that deepened into purple hazes of mystery.

Bêlit had been of the sea; she had lent it splendor and allure. Without her it rolled a barren, dreary and desolate waste from pole to pole. She belonged to the sea; to its everlasting mystery he returned her. He could do no more. For himself, its glittering blue splendor was more repellent than the leafy fronds which rustled and whispered behind him of vast mysterious wilds beyond them, and into which he must plunge.

No hand was at the sweep of the *Tigress*, no oars drove her through the green water. But a clean tanging wind bellied her silken sail, and as a wild swan cleaves the sky to her nest, she sped seaward, flames mounting higher and higher from her deck to lick at the mast and envelop the figure that lay lapped in scarlet on the shining pyre.

So passed the Queen of the Black Coast, and leaning on his red-stained sword, Conan stood silently until the red glow had faded far out in the blue hazes and dawn splashed its rose and gold over the ocean.

A Witch Shall Be Born

1 The Blood-Red Crescent

Taramis, Queen of Khauran, awakened from a dream-haunted slumber to a silence that seemed more like the stillness of nighted catacombs than the normal quiet of a sleeping palace. She lay staring into the darkness, wondering why the candles in their golden candelabra had gone out. A flecking of stars marked a gold-barred casement that lent no illumination to the interior of the chamber. But as Taramis lay there, she became aware of a spot of radiance glowing in the darkness before her. She watched, puzzled. It grew and its intensity deepened as it expanded, a widening disk of lurid light hovering against the dark velvet hangings of the opposite wall. Taramis caught her breath, starting up to a sitting position. A dark object was visible in that circle of light – *a human head*.

In a sudden panic the queen opened her lips to cry out for her maids; then she checked herself. The glow was more lurid, the head more vividly limned. It was a woman's head, small, delicately molded, superbly poised, with a high-piled mass of lustrous black hair. The face grew distinct as she stared – and it was the sight of this face which froze the cry in Taramis' throat. The features were her own! She might have been looking into a mirror which subtly altered her reflection, lending it a tigerish gleam of eye, a vindictive curl of lip.

'Ishtar!' gasped Taramis. 'I am bewitched!'

Appallingly, the apparition spoke, and its voice was like honeyed venom.

'Bewitched? No, sweet sister! Here is no sorcery.'

'Sister?' stammered the bewildered girl. 'I have no sister.'

'You never had a sister?' came the sweet, poisonously mocking voice. 'Never a twin sister whose flesh was as soft as yours to caress or hurt?'

'Why, once I had a sister,' answered Taramis, still convinced that she was in the grip of some sort of nightmare. 'But she died.'

The beautiful face in the disk was convulsed with the aspect of a fury; so hellish became its expression that Taramis, cowering back, half expected to see snaky locks writhe hissing about the ivory brow.

'You lie!' The accusation was spat from between the snarling red lips. 'She did not die! Fool! Oh, enough of this mummery! Look – and let your sight be blasted!'

Light ran suddenly along the hangings like flaming serpents, and incredibly the candles in the golden sticks flared up again. Taramis crouched on her velvet couch, her lithe legs flexed beneath her, staring wide-eyed at the pantherish figure which posed mockingly before her. It was as if she gazed upon another Taramis, identical with herself in every contour of feature and limb, yet animated by an alien and evil personality. The face of this stranger waif reflected the opposite of every characteristic the countenance of the queen denoted. Lust and mystery sparkled in her scintillant eyes, cruelty lurked in the curl of her full red lips. Each movement of her supple body was subtly suggestive. Her coiffure imitated that of the queen's, on her feet were gilded sandals such as Taramis wore in her boudoir. The sleeveless, low-necked silk tunic, girdled at the waist with a cloth-of-gold cincture, was a duplicate of the queen's night-garment.

'Who are you?' gasped Taramis, an icy chill she could not explain creeping along her spine. 'Explain your presence before I call my ladies-in-waiting to summon the guard!'

'Scream until the roof-beams crack,' callously answered the stranger. 'Your sluts will not wake till dawn, though the palace spring into flames about them. Your guardsmen will not hear your squeals; they have been sent out of this wing of the palace.'

'What!' exclaimed Taramis, stiffening with outraged majesty. 'Who dared give my guardsmen such a command?'

'I did, sweet sister,' sneered the other girl. 'A little while ago, before I entered. They thought it was their darling adored queen. Ha! How beautifully I acted the part! With what imperious dignity, softened by womanly sweetness, did I address the great louts who knelt in their armor and plumed helmets!'

Taramis felt as if a stifling net of bewilderment were being drawn about her.

'Who are you?' she cried desperately. 'What madness is this? Why do you come here?'

'Who am I?' There was the spite of a she-cobra's hiss in the soft response. The girl stepped to the edge of the couch, grasped the queen's white shoulders with fierce fingers, and bent to glare full into the startled eyes of Taramis. And under the spell of that hypnotic glare, the queen forgot to resent the unprecedented outrage of violent hands laid on regal flesh.

'Fool!' gritted the girl between her teeth. 'Can you ask? Can you wonder? I am Salome!'

'Salome!' Taramis breathed the word, and the hairs prickled on her scalp as she realized the incredible, numbing truth of the statement. 'I thought you died within the hour of your birth,' she said feebly.

'So thought many,' answered the woman who called herself Salome. 'They carried me into the desert to die, damn them! I, a mewing, puling babe whose life was so young it was scarcely the flicker of a candle. And do you know why they bore me forth to die?'

'I – I have heard the story –' faltered Taramis.

Salome laughed fiercely, and slapped her bosom. The low-necked tunic left the upper parts of her firm breasts bare, and between them there shone a curious mark – a crescent, red as blood.

'The mark of the witch!' cried Taramis, recoiling.

'Aye!' Salome's laughter was dagger-edged with hate. 'The curse of the kings of Khauran! Aye, they tell the tale in the market-places, with wagging beards and rolling eyes, the pious fools! They tell how the first queen of our line had traffic with a fiend of darkness and bore him a daughter who lives in foul legendry to this day. And thereafter in each century a girl baby was born into the Askhaurian dynasty, with a scarlet half-moon between her breasts, that signified her destiny.

'"Every century a witch shall be born." So ran the ancient curse. And so it has come to pass. Some were slain at birth, as they sought to slay me. Some walked the earth as witches, proud daughters of Khauran, with the moon of hell burning upon their ivory bosoms. Each was named Salome. I too am Salome. It was always Salome, the witch. It will always be Salome, the witch, even when the mountains of ice have roared down from the pole and ground the civilizations to ruin, and a new world has risen from the ashes and dust – even then there shall be Salomes to walk the earth, to trap men's hearts by their sorcery, to dance before the kings of the world, and see the heads of the wise men fall at their pleasure.'

'But – but you –' stammered Taramis.

'I?' The scintillant eyes burned like dark fires of mystery. 'They carried me into the desert far from the city, and laid me naked on the hot sand, under the flaming sun. And then they rode away and left me for the jackals and the vultures and the desert wolves.

'But the life in me was stronger than the life in common folk, for it partakes of the essence of the forces that seethe in the black gulfs beyond mortal ken. The hours passed, and the sun

slashed down like the molten flames of hell, but I did not die –
aye, something of that torment I remember, faintly and far
away, as one remembers a dim, formless dream. Then there
were camels, and yellow-skinned men who wore silk robes and
spoke in a weird tongue. Strayed from the caravan road, they
passed close by, and their leader saw me, and recognized the
scarlet crescent on my bosom. He took me up and gave me
life.

'He was a magician from far Khitai, returning to his native
kingdom after a journey to Stygia. He took me with him to purple-
towered Paikang, its minarets rising amid the vine-festooned
jungles of bamboo, and there I grew to womanhood under his
teaching. Age had steeped him deep in black wisdom, not weakened his powers of evil. Many things he taught me –'

She paused, smiling enigmatically, with wicked mystery
gleaming in her dark eyes. Then she tossed her head.

'He drove me from him at last, saying that I was but a common witch in spite of his teachings, and not fit to command the
mighty sorcery he would have taught me. He would have made
me queen of the world and ruled the nations through me, he
said, but I was only a harlot of darkness. But what of it? I could
never endure to seclude myself in a golden tower, and spend the
long hours staring into a crystal globe, mumbling over incanta-
tions written on serpent's skin in the blood of virgins, poring
over musty volumes in forgotten languages.

'He said I was but an earthly sprite, knowing naught of the
deeper gulfs of cosmic sorcery. Well, this world contains all I
desire – power, and pomp, and glittering pageantry, handsome
men and soft women for my paramours and my slaves. He had
told me who I was, of the curse and my heritage. I have returned
to take that to which I have as much right as you. Now it is mine
by right of possession.'

'What do you mean?' Taramis sprang up and faced her sister,
stung out of her bewilderment and fright. 'Do you imagine that

by drugging a few of my maids and tricking a few of my guardsmen you have established a claim to the throne of Khauran? Do
not forget that *I* am queen of Khauran! I shall give you a place
of honor, as my sister, but –'

Salome laughed hatefully.

'How generous of you, dear, sweet sister! But before you
begin putting me in my place – perhaps you will tell me whose
soldiers camp in the plain outside the city walls?'

'They are the Shemitish mercenaries of Constantius, the
Kothic *voivode* of the Free Companies.'

'And what do they in Khauran?' cooed Salome.

Taramis felt that she was being subtly mocked, but she answered
with an assumption of dignity which she scarcely felt.

'Constantius asked permission to pass along the borders of
Khauran on his way to Turan. He himself is hostage for their
good behavior as long as they are within my domains.'

'And Constantius,' pursued Salome. 'Did he not ask your
hand today?'

Taramis shot her a clouded glance of suspicion.

'How did you know that?'

An insolent shrug of the slim naked shoulders was the only
reply.

'You refused, dear sister?'

'Certainly I refused!' exclaimed Taramis angrily. 'Do you, an
Askhaurian princess yourself, suppose that the queen of Khauran could treat such a proposal with anything but disdain? Wed
a bloody-handed adventurer, a man exiled from his own kingdom because of his crimes, and the leader of organized plun-
derers and hired murderers?

'I should never have allowed him to bring his black-bearded
slayers into Khauran. But he is virtually a prisoner in the south
tower, guarded by my soldiers. Tomorrow I shall bid him order
his troops to leave the kingdom. He himself shall be kept captive until they are over the border. Meantime, my soldiers man

the walls of the city, and I have warned him that he will answer for any outrages perpetrated on the villagers or shepherds by his mercenaries.'

'He is confined in the south tower?' asked Salome.

'That is what I said. Why do you ask?'

For answer Salome clapped her hands, and lifting her voice, with a gurgle of cruel mirth in it, called: 'The queen grants you an audience, Falcon!'

A gold-arabesqued door opened and a tall figure entered the chamber, at the sight of which Taramis cried out in amazement and anger.

'Constantius! You dare enter my chamber!'

'As you see, Your Majesty!' He bent his dark, hawk-like head in mock humility.

Constantius, whom men called Falcon, was tall, broad-shouldered, slim-waisted, lithe and strong as pliant steel. He was handsome in an aquiline, ruthless way. His face was burnt dark by the sun, and his hair, which grew far back from his high, narrow forehead, was black as a raven. His dark eyes were penetrating and alert, the hardness of his thin lips not softened by his thin black mustache. His boots were of Kordavan leather, his hose and doublet of plain, dark silk, tarnished with the wear of the camps and the stains of armor rust.

Twisting his mustache, he let his gaze travel up and down the shrinking queen with an effrontery that made her wince.

'By Ishtar, Taramis,' he said silkily, 'I find you more alluring in your night-tunic than in your queenly robes. Truly, this is an auspicious night!'

Fear grew in the queen's dark eyes. She was no fool; she knew that Constantius would never dare this outrage unless he was sure of himself.

'You are mad!' she said. 'If I am in your power in this chamber, you are no less in the power of my subjects, who will rend you to pieces if you touch me. Go at once, if you would live.'

Both laughed mockingly, and Salome made an impatient gesture.

'Enough of this farce; let us on to the next act in the comedy. Listen, dear sister: it was I who sent Constantius here. When I decided to take the throne of Khauran, I cast about for a man to aid me, and chose the Falcon, because of his utter lack of all characteristics men call good.'

'I am overwhelmed, princess,' murmured Constantius sardonically, with a profound bow.

'I sent him to Khauran, and, once his men were camped in the plain outside, and he was in the palace, I entered the city by that small gate in the west wall – the fools guarding it thought it was you returning from some nocturnal adventure –'

'You hell-cat!' Taramis' cheeks flamed and her resentment got the better of her regal reserve.

Salome smiled hardly.

'They were properly surprized and shocked, but admitted me without question. I entered the palace the same way, and gave the order to the surprized guards that sent them marching away, as well as the men who guarded Constantius in the south tower. Then I came here, attending to the ladies-in-waiting on the way.'

Taramis' fingers clenched and she paled.

'Well, what next?' she asked in a shaky voice.

'Listen!' Salome inclined her head. Faintly through the casement there came the clank of marching men in armor; gruff voices shouted in an alien tongue, and cries of alarm mingled with the shouts.

'The people awaken and grow fearful,' said Constantius sardonically. 'You had better go and reassure them, Salome!'

'Call me Taramis,' answered Salome. 'We must become accustomed to it.'

'What have you done?' cried Taramis. 'What have you done?'

'I have gone to the gates and ordered the soldiers to open them,' answered Salome. 'They were astounded, but they obeyed. That is the Falcon's army you hear, marching into the city.'

'You devil!' cried Taramis. 'You have betrayed my people, in my guise! You have made me seem a traitor! Oh, I shall go to them –'

With a cruel laugh Salome caught her wrist and jerked her back. The magnificent suppleness of the queen was helpless against the vindictive strength that steeled Salome's slender limbs.

'You know how to reach the dungeons from the palace, Constantius?' said the witch-girl. 'Good. Take this spitfire and lock her into the strongest cell. The jailers are all sound in drugged sleep. I saw to that. Send a man to cut their throats before they can awaken. None must ever know what has occurred tonight. Thenceforward I am Taramis, and Taramis is a nameless prisoner in an unknown dungeon.'

Constantius smiled with a glint of strong white teeth under his thin mustache.

'Very good; but you would not deny me a little – ah – amusement first?'

'Not I! Tame the scornful hussy as you will.' With a wicked laugh Salome flung her sister into the Kothian's arms, and turned away through the door that opened into the outer corridor.

Fright widened Taramis' lovely eyes, her supple figure rigid and straining against Constantius' embrace. She forgot the men marching in the streets, forgot the outrage to her queenship, in the face of the menace to her womanhood. She forgot all sensations but terror and shame as she faced the complete cynicism of Constantius' burning, mocking eyes, felt his hard arms crushing her writhing body.

Salome, hurrying along the corridor outside, smiled spitefully as a scream of despair and agony rang shuddering through the palace.

2 The Tree of Death

The young soldier's hose and shirt were smeared with dried blood, wet with sweat and gray with dust. Blood oozed from the deep gash in his thigh, from the cuts on his breast and shoulder. Perspiration glistened on his livid face and his fingers were knotted in the cover of the divan on which he lay. Yet his words reflected mental suffering that outweighed physical pain.

'She must be mad!' he repeated again and again, like one still stunned by some monstrous and incredible happening. 'It's like a nightmare! Taramis, whom all Khauran loves, betraying her people to that devil from Koth! Oh, Ishtar, why was I not slain? Better die than live to see our queen turn traitor and harlot!'

'Lie still, Valerius,' begged the girl who was washing and bandaging his wounds with trembling hands. 'Oh, please lie still, darling! You will make your wounds worse. I dared not summon a leech –'

'No,' muttered the wounded youth. 'Constantius' blue-bearded devils will be searching the quarters for wounded Khaurani; they'll hang every man who has wounds to show he fought against them. Oh, Taramis, how could you betray the people who worshiped you?' In his fierce agony he writhed, weeping in rage and shame, and the terrified girl caught him in her arms, straining his tossing head against her bosom, imploring him to be quiet.

'Better death than the black shame that has come upon Khauran this day,' he groaned. 'Did you see it, Ivga?'

'No, Valerius.' Her soft, nimble fingers were again at work, gently cleansing and closing the gaping edges of his raw wounds. 'I was awakened by the noise of fighting in the streets – I looked out a casement and saw the Shemites cutting down people; then presently I heard you calling me faintly from the alley door.'

'I had reached the limits of my strength,' he muttered. 'I fell in the alley and could not rise. I knew they'd find me soon if I lay there – I killed three of the blue-bearded beasts, by Ishtar! They'll never swagger through Khauran's streets, by the gods! The fiends are tearing their hearts in hell!'

The trembling girl crooned soothingly to him, as to a wounded child, and closed his panting lips with her own cool sweet mouth. But the fire that raged in his soul would not allow him to lie silent.

'I was not on the wall when the Shemites entered,' he burst out. 'I was asleep in the barracks, with the others not on duty. It was just before dawn when our captain entered, and his face was pale under his helmet. "The Shemites are in the city," he said. "The queen came to the southern gate and gave orders that they should be admitted. She made the men come down from the walls, where they've been on guard since Constantius entered the kingdom. I don't understand it, and neither does anyone else, but I heard her give the order, and we obeyed as we always do. We are ordered to assemble in the square before the palace. Form ranks outside the barracks and march – leave your arms and armor here. Ishtar knows what this means, but it is the queen's order."

'Well, when we came to the square the Shemites were drawn up on foot opposite the palace, ten thousand of the blue-bearded devils, fully armed, and people's heads were thrust out of every window and door on the square. The streets leading into the square were thronged by bewildered folk. Taramis was standing on the steps of the palace, alone except for Constantius, who stood stroking his mustache like a great lean cat who has just devoured a sparrow. But fifty Shemites with bows in their hands were ranged below them.

'That's where the queen's guard should have been, but they

were drawn up at the foot of the palace stair, as puzzled as we, though they had come fully armed, in spite of the queen's order.

'Taramis spoke to us then, and told us that she had reconsidered the proposal made her by Constantius – why, only yesterday she threw it in his teeth in open court! – and that she had decided to make him her royal consort. She did not explain why she had brought the Shemites into the city so treacherously. But she said that, as Constantius had control of a body of professional fighting-men, the army of Khauran would no longer be needed, and therefore she disbanded it, and ordered us to go quietly to our homes.

'Why, obedience to our queen is second nature to us, but we were struck dumb and found no word to answer. We broke ranks almost before we knew what we were doing, like men in a daze.

'But when the palace guard was ordered to disarm likewise and disband, the captain of the guard, Conan, interrupted. Men said he was off duty the night before, and drunk. But he was wide awake now. He shouted to the guardsmen to stand as they were until they received an order from him – and such is his dominance of his men, that they obeyed in spite of the queen. He strode up to the palace steps and glared at Taramis – and then he roared: "This is not the queen! This isn't Taramis! It's some devil in masquerade!"

'Then hell was to pay! I don't know just what happened. I think a Shemite struck Conan, and Conan killed him. The next instant the square was a battleground. The Shemites fell on the guardsmen, and their spears and arrows struck down many soldiers who had already disbanded.

'Some of us grabbed up such weapons as we could and fought back. We hardly knew what we were fighting for, but it was against Constantius and his devils – not against Taramis, I swear it! Constantius shouted to cut the traitors down. We were not traitors!' Despair and bewilderment shook his voice. The girl murmured pityingly, not understanding it all, but aching in sympathy with her lover's suffering.

'The people did not know which side to take. It was a madhouse of confusion and bewilderment. We who fought didn't have a chance, in no formation, without armor and only half armed. The guards were fully armed and drawn up in a square, but there were only five hundred of them. They took a heavy toll before they were cut down, but there could be only one conclusion to such a battle. And while her people were being slaughtered before her, Taramis stood on the palace steps, with Constantius' arm about her waist, and laughed like a heartless, beautiful fiend! Gods, it's all mad – mad!

'I never saw a man fight as Conan fought. He put his back to the courtyard wall, and before they overpowered him the dead men were strewn in heaps thigh-deep about him. But at last they dragged him down, a hundred against one. When I saw him fall I dragged myself away feeling as if the world had burst under my very fingers. I heard Constantius call to his dogs to take the captain alive – stroking his mustache, with that hateful smile on his lips!'

That smile was on the lips of Constantius at that very moment. He sat his horse among a cluster of his men – thick-bodied Shemites with curled blue-black beards and hooked noses; the low-swinging sun struck glints from their peaked helmets and the silvered scales of their corselets. Nearly a mile behind, the walls and towers of Khauran rose sheer out of the meadowlands.

By the side of the caravan road a heavy cross had been planted, and on this grim tree a man hung, nailed there by iron spikes through his hands and feet. Naked but for a loin-cloth, the man was almost a giant in stature, and his muscles stood out in thick corded ridges on limbs and body, which the sun had long ago burned brown. The perspiration of agony beaded his face and his mighty breast, but from under the tangled black mane that fell over his low, broad forehead, his blue eyes blazed with an unquenched fire. Blood oozed sluggishly from the lacerations in his hands and feet.

Constantius saluted him mockingly.

'I am sorry, captain,' he said, 'that I can not remain to ease your last hours, but I have duties to perform in yonder city – I must not keep our delicious queen waiting!' He laughed softly. 'So I leave you to your own devices – and those beauties!' He pointed meaningly at the black shadows which swept incessantly back and forth, high above.

'Were it not for them, I imagine that a powerful brute like yourself should live on the cross for days. Do not cherish any illusions of rescue because I am leaving you unguarded. I have had it proclaimed that anyone seeking to take your body, living or dead, from the cross, will be flayed alive together with all the members of his family, in the public square. I am so firmly established in Khauran that my order is as good as a regiment of guardsmen. I am leaving no guard, because the vultures will not approach as long as anyone is near, and I do not wish them to feel any constraint. That is also why I brought you so far from the city. These desert vultures approach the walls no closer than this spot.

'And so, brave captain, farewell! I will remember you when, in an hour, Taramis lies in my arms.'

Blood started afresh from the pierced palms as the victim's mallet-like fists clenched convulsively on the spike-heads. Knots and bunches of muscle started out on the massive arms, and Conan bent his head forward and spat savagely at Constantius' face. The *voivode* laughed coolly, wiped the saliva from his gorget and reined his horse about.

'Remember me when the vultures are tearing at your living flesh,' he called mockingly. 'The desert scavengers are a particularly voracious breed. I have seen men hang for hours on a cross, eyeless, earless, and scalpless, before the sharp beaks had eaten their way into his vitals.'

Without a backward glance he rode toward the city, a supple, erect figure, gleaming in his burnished armor, his stolid, bearded henchmen jogging beside him. A faint rising of dust from the worn trail marked their passing.

The man hanging on the cross was the one touch of sentient life in a landscape that seemed desolate and deserted in the late evening. Khauran, less than a mile away, might have been on the other side of the world, and existing in another age.

Shaking the sweat out of his eyes, Conan stared blankly at the familiar terrain. On either side of the city, and beyond it, stretched the fertile meadowlands, with cattle browsing in the distance where fields and vineyards checkered the plain. The western and northern horizons were dotted with villages, miniature in the distance. A lesser distance to the southeast a silvery gleam marked the course of a river, and beyond that river sandy desert began abruptly to stretch away and away beyond the horizon. Conan stared at that expanse of empty waste shimmering tawnily in the late sunlight as a trapped hawk stares at the open sky. A revulsion shook him when he glanced at the gleaming towers of Khauran. The city had betrayed him – trapped him into circumstances that left him hanging to a wooden cross like a hare nailed to a tree.

A red lust for vengeance swept away the thought. Curses ebbed fitfully from the man's lips. All his universe contracted, focused, became incorporated in the four iron spikes that held him from life and freedom. His great muscles quivered, knotting like iron cables. With the sweat starting out on his graying skin, he sought to gain leverage, to tear the nails from the wood. It was useless. They had been driven deep. Then he tried to tear his hands off the spikes, and it was not the knifing, abysmal agony that finally caused him to cease his efforts, but the futility of it. The spike-heads were broad and heavy; he could not drag them through the wounds. A surge of helplessness shook the giant, for the first time in his life. He hung motionless, his head resting on his breast, shutting his eyes against the aching glare of the sun.

A beat of wings caused him to look up, just as a feathered shadow shot down out of the sky. A keen beak, stabbing at his eyes, cut his cheek, and he jerked his head aside, shutting his eyes involuntarily. He shouted, a croaking, desperate shout of menace, and the vultures swerved away and retreated, frightened by the sound. They resumed their wary circling above his head. Blood trickled over Conan's mouth, and he licked his lips involuntarily, spat at the salty taste.

Thirst assailed him savagely. He had drunk deeply of wine the night before, and no water had touched his lips since before the battle in the square, that dawn. And killing was thirsty, salt-sweaty work. He glared at the distant river as a man in hell glares through the opened grille. He thought of gushing freshets of white water he had breasted, laved to the shoulders in liquid jade. He remembered great horns of foaming ale, jacks of sparkling wine gulped carelessly or spilled on the tavern floor. He bit his lip to keep from bellowing in intolerable anguish as a tortured animal bellows.

The sun sank, a lurid ball in a fiery sea of blood. Against a crimson rampart that banded the horizon the towers of the city floated unreal as a dream. The very sky was tinged with blood to his misted glare. He licked his blackened lips and stared with bloodshot eyes at the distant river. It too seemed crimson like blood, and the shadows crawling up from the east seemed black as ebony.

In his dulled ears sounded the louder beat of wings. Lifting his head he watched with the burning glare of a wolf the shadows wheeling above him. He knew that his shouts would frighten them away no longer. One dipped – dipped – lower and lower. Conan drew his head back as far as he could, waiting with terrible patience. The vulture swept in with a swift roar of wings. Its beak flashed down, ripping the skin on Conan's chin as he jerked his head aside; then before the bird could flash away, Conan's head lunged forward on his mighty neck muscles, and his teeth, snapping like those of a wolf, locked on the bare, wattled neck.

Instantly the vulture exploded into squawking, flapping hysteria. Its thrashing wings blinded the man, and its talons ripped his chest. But grimly he hung on, the muscles starting out in lumps on his jaws. And the scavenger's neck-bones crunched between those powerful teeth. With a spasmodic flutter the bird hung limp. Conan let go, spat blood from his mouth. The other vultures, terrified by the fate of their companion, were in full flight to a distant tree, where they perched like black demons in conclave.

Ferocious triumph surged through Conan's numbed brain. Life beat strongly and savagely through his veins. He could still deal death; he still lived. Every twinge of sensation, even of agony, was a negation of death.

'By Mitra!' Either a voice spoke, or he suffered from hallucination. 'In all my life I have never seen such a thing!'

Shaking the sweat and blood from his eyes, Conan saw four horsemen sitting their steeds in the twilight and staring up at him. Three were lean, white-robed hawks, Zuagir tribesmen without a doubt, nomads from beyond the river. The other was dressed like them in a white, girdled *khalat* and a flowing head-dress which, banded about the temples with a triple circlet of braided camel-hair, fell to his shoulders. But he was not a Shemite. The dusk was not so thick, nor Conan's hawk-like sight so clouded, that he could not perceive the man's facial characteristics.

He was as tall as Conan, though not so heavy-limbed. His shoulders were broad and his supple figure was hard as steel and whalebone. A short black beard did not altogether mask the aggressive jut of his lean jaw, and gray eyes cold and piercing as a sword gleamed from the shadow of the *kafieh*. Quieting his restless steed with a quick, sure hand, this man spoke: 'By Mitra, I should know this man!'

'Aye!' It was the guttural accents of a Zuagir. 'It is the Cimmerian who was captain of the queen's guard!'

'She must be casting off all her old favorites,' muttered the rider. 'Who'd have ever thought it of Queen Taramis? I'd rather have had a long, bloody war. It would have given us desert folk a chance to plunder. As it is we've come this close to the walls and found only this nag' – he glanced at a fine gelding led by one of the nomads – 'and this dying dog.'

Conan lifted his bloody head.

'If I could come down from this beam I'd make a dying dog out of you, you Zaporoskan thief!' he rasped through blackened lips.

'Mitra, the knave knows me!' exclaimed the other. 'How, knave, do you know me?'

'There's only one of your breed in these parts,' muttered Conan. 'You are Olgerd Vladislav, the outlaw chief.'

'Aye! and once a hetman of the *kozaki* of the Zaporoskan River, as you have guessed. Would you like to live?'

'Only a fool would ask that question,' panted Conan.

'I am a hard man,' said Olgerd, 'and toughness is the only quality I respect in a man. I shall judge if you are a man, or only a dog after all, fit only to lie here and die.'

'If we cut him down we may be seen from the walls,' objected one of the nomads.

Olgerd shook his head.

'The dusk is too deep. Here, take this ax, Djebal, and cut down the cross at the base.'

'If it falls forward it will crush him,' objected Djebal. 'I can cut it so it will fall backward, but then the shock of the fall may crack his skull and tear loose all his entrails.'

'If he's worthy to ride with me he'll survive it,' answered Olgerd imperturbably. 'If not, then he doesn't deserve to live. Cut!'

The first impact of the battle-ax against the wood and its accompanying vibrations sent lances of agony through Conan's swollen feet and hands. Again and again the blade fell, and each stroke reverberated on his bruised brain, setting his tortured nerves aquiver. But he set his teeth and made no sound. The ax cut through, the cross reeled on its splintered base and toppled backward. Conan made his whole body a solid knot of iron-hard muscle, jammed his head back hard against the wood and held it rigid there. The beam struck the ground heavily and rebounded slightly. The impact tore his wounds and dazed him for an instant. He fought the rushing tide of blackness, sick and dizzy, but realized that the iron muscles that sheathed his vitals had saved him from permanent injury.

And he had made no sound, though blood oozed from his nostrils and his belly-muscles quivered with nausea. With a grunt of approval Djebal bent over him with a pair of pincers used to draw horse-shoe nails, and gripped the head of the spike in Conan's right hand, tearing the skin to get a grip on the deeply embedded head. The pincers were small for that work. Djebal sweated and tugged, swearing and wrestling with the stubborn iron, working it back and forth – in swollen flesh as well as in wood. Blood started, oozing over the Cimmerian's fingers. He lay so still he might have been dead, except for the spasmodic rise and fall of his great chest. The spike gave way, and Djebal held up the blood-stained thing with a grunt of satisfaction, then flung it away and bent over the other.

The process was repeated, and then Djebal turned his attention to Conan's skewered feet. But the Cimmerian, struggling up to a sitting posture, wrenched the pincers from his fingers and sent him staggering backward with a violent shove. Conan's hands were swollen to almost twice their normal size. His fingers felt like misshapen thumbs, and closing his hands was an agony that brought blood streaming from under his grinding teeth. But somehow, clutching the pincers clumsily with both hands, he managed to wrench out first one spike and then the other. They were not driven so deeply into the wood as the others had been.

He rose stiffly and stood upright on his swollen, lacerated feet, swaying drunkenly, the icy sweat dripping from his face and body. Cramps assailed him and he clamped his jaws against the desire to retch.

Olgerd, watching him impersonally, motioned him toward the stolen horse. Conan stumbled toward it, and every step was a stabbing, throbbing hell that flecked his lips with bloody foam. One misshapen, groping hand fell clumsily on the saddle-bow, a bloody foot somehow found the stirrup. Setting his teeth, he swung up, and he almost fainted in midair; but he came down in the saddle – and as he did so, Olgerd struck the horse sharply with his whip. The startled beast reared, and the man in the saddle swayed and slumped like a sack of sand, almost unseated. Conan had wrapped a rein about each hand, holding it in place with a clamping thumb. Drunkenly he exerted the strength of his knotted biceps, wrenching the horse down; it screamed, its jaw almost dislocated.

One of the Shemites lifted a water-flask questioningly.

Olgerd shook his head.

'Let him wait until we get to camp. It's only ten miles. If he's fit to live in the desert he'll live that long without a drink.'

The group rode like swift ghosts toward the river; among them Conan swayed like a drunken man in the saddle, bloodshot eyes glazed, foam drying on his blackened lips.

3   A Letter to Nemedia

The savant Astreas, traveling in the East in his never-tiring search for knowledge, wrote a letter to his friend and fellow-philosopher Alcemides, in his native Nemedia, which constitutes the entire knowledge of the Western nations concerning the events of that period in the East, always a hazy, half-mythical region in the minds of the Western folk.

Astreas wrote, in part: 'You can scarcely conceive, my dear old friend, of the conditions now existing in this tiny kingdom since Queen Taramis admitted Constantius and his mercenaries, an event which I briefly described in my last, hurried letter. Seven months have passed since then, during which time it seems as though the devil himself had been loosed in this unfortunate realm. Taramis seems to have gone quite mad; whereas formerly she was famed for her virtue, justice and tranquillity, she is now notorious for qualities precisely opposite to those just enumerated. Her private life is a scandal – or perhaps "private" is not the correct term, since the queen makes no attempt to conceal the debauchery of her court. She constantly indulges in the most infamous revelries, in which the unfortunate ladies of the court are forced to join, young married women as well as virgins.

'She herself has not bothered to marry her paramour, Constantius, who sits on the throne beside her and reigns as her royal consort, and his officers follow his example, and do not hesitate to debauch any woman they desire, regardless of her rank or station. The wretched kingdom groans under exorbitant taxation, the farms are stripped to the bone, and the merchants go in rags which are all that is left them by the tax-gatherers. Nay, they are lucky if they escape with a whole skin.

'I sense your incredulity, good Alcemides; you will fear that I exaggerate conditions in Khauran. Such conditions would be unthinkable in any of the Western countries, admittedly. But you must realize the vast difference that exists between West and East, especially this part of the East. In the first place, Khauran is a kingdom of no great size, one of the many principalities which at one time formed the eastern part of the empire of

Koth, and which later regained the independence which was theirs at a still earlier age. This part of the world is made up of these tiny realms, diminutive in comparison with the great kingdoms of the West, or the great sultanates of the farther East, but important in their control of the caravan routes, and in the wealth concentrated in them.

'Khauran is the most southeasterly of these principalities, bordering on the very deserts of eastern Shem. The city of Khauran is the only city of any magnitude in the realm, and stands within sight of the river which separates the grasslands from the sandy desert, like a watch-tower to guard the fertile meadows behind it. The land is so rich that it yields three and four crops a year, and the plains north and west of the city are dotted with villages. To one accustomed to the great plantations and stock-farms of the West, it is strange to see these tiny fields and vineyards; yet wealth in grain and fruit pours from them as from a horn of plenty. The villagers are agriculturists, nothing else. Of a mixed, aboriginal race, they are unwarlike, unable to protect themselves, and forbidden the possession of arms. Dependent wholly upon the soldiers of the city for protection, they are helpless under the present conditions. So the savage revolt of the rural sections, which would be a certainty in any Western nation, is here impossible.

'They toil supinely under the iron hand of Constantius, and his black-bearded Shemites ride incessantly through the fields, with whips in their hands, like the slave-drivers of the black serfs who toil in the plantations of southern Zingara.

'Nor do the people of the city fare any better. Their wealth is stripped from them, their fairest daughters taken to glut the insatiable lust of Constantius and his mercenaries. These men are utterly without mercy or compassion, possessed of all the characteristics our armies learned to abhor in our wars against the Shemitish allies of Argos – inhuman cruelty, lust, and wild-beast ferocity. The people of the city are Khauran's ruling caste, predominantly Hyborian, and valorous and war-like. But the treachery of their queen delivered them into the hands of their oppressors. The Shemites are the only armed force in Khauran, and the most hellish punishment is inflicted on any Khauran found possessing weapons. A systematic persecution to destroy the young Khaurani men able to bear arms has been savagely pursued. Many have ruthlessly been slaughtered, others sold as slaves to the Turanians. Thousands have fled the kingdom and either entered the service of other rulers, or become outlaws, lurking in numerous bands along the borders.

'At present there is some possibility of invasion from the desert, which is inhabited by tribes of Shemitish nomads. The mercenaries of Constantius are men from the Shemitish cities of the west, Pelishtim, Anakim, Akkharim, and are ardently hated by the Zuagirs and other wandering tribes. As you know, good Alcemides, the countries of these barbarians are divided into the western meadowlands which stretch to the distant ocean, and in which rise the cities of the town-dwellers, and the eastern deserts, where the lean nomads hold sway; there is incessant warfare between the dwellers of the cities and the dwellers of the desert.

'The Zuagirs have fought with and raided Khauran for centuries, without success, but they resent its conquest by their western kin. It is rumored that their natural antagonism is being fomented by the man who was formerly the captain of the queen's guard, and who, somehow escaping the hate of Constantius, who actually had him upon the cross, fled to the nomads. He is called Conan, and is himself a barbarian, one of those gloomy Cimmerians whose ferocity our soldiers have more than once learned to their bitter cost. It is rumored that he has become the right-hand man of Olgerd Vladislav, the *kozak* adventurer who wandered down from the northern steppes and made himself chief of a band of Zuagirs. There are also rumors that this band has increased vastly in the last few months, and that Olgerd, incited no doubt by this Cimmerian, is even considering a raid on Khauran.

'It can not be anything more than a raid, as the Zuagirs are without siege-machines, or the knowledge of investing a city, and it has been proven repeatedly in the past that the nomads in their loose formation, or rather lack of formation, are no match in hand-to-hand fighting for the well-disciplined, fully-armed warriors of the Shemitish cities. The natives of Khauran would perhaps welcome this conquest, since the nomads could deal with them no more harshly than their present masters, and even total extermination would be preferable to the suffering they have to endure. But they are so cowed and helpless that they could give no aid to the invaders.

'Their plight is most wretched. Taramis, apparently possessed of a demon, stops at nothing. She has abolished the worship of Ishtar, and turned the temple into a shrine of idolatry. She has destroyed the ivory image of the goddess which these eastern Hyborians worship (and which, inferior as it is to the true religion of Mitra which we Western nations recognize, is still superior to the devil-worship of the Shemites) and filled the temple of Ishtar with obscene images of every imaginable sort – gods and goddesses of the night, portrayed in all the salacious and perverse poses and with all the revolting characteristics that a degenerate brain could conceive. Many of these images are to be identified as foul deities of the Shemites, the Turanians, the Vendhyans, and the Khitans, but others are reminiscent of a hideous and half-remembered antiquity, vile shapes forgotten except in the most obscure legends. Where the queen gained the knowledge of them I dare not even hazard a guess.

'She has instituted human sacrifice, and since her mating with Constantius, no less than five hundred men, women and children have been immolated. Some of these have died on the altar she has set up in the temple, herself wielding the sacrificial dagger, but most have met a more horrible doom.

'Taramis has placed some sort of monster in a crypt in the temple. What it is, and whence it came, none knows. But shortly after she had crushed the desperate revolt of her soldiers against Constantius, she spent a night alone in the desecrated temple, alone except for a dozen bound captives, and the shuddering people saw thick, foul-smelling smoke curling up from the dome, heard all night the frenetic chanting of the queen, and the agonized cries of her tortured captives; and toward dawn another voice mingled with these sounds – a strident, inhuman croaking that froze the blood of all who heard.

'In the full dawn Taramis reeled drunkenly from the temple, her eyes blazing with demoniac triumph. The captives were never seen again, nor the croaking voice heard. But there is a room in the temple into which none ever goes but the queen, driving a human sacrifice before her. And this victim is never seen again. All know that in that grim chamber lurks some monster from the black night of ages, which devours the shrieking humans Taramis delivers up to it.

'I can no longer think of her as a mortal woman, but as a rabid she-fiend, crouching in her blood-fouled lair amongst the bones and fragments of her victims, with taloned, crimsoned fingers. That the gods allow her to pursue her awful course unchecked almost shakes my faith in divine justice.

'When I compare her present conduct with her deportment when first I came to Khauran, seven months ago, I am confused with bewilderment, and almost inclined to the belief held by many of the people – that a demon has possessed the body of Taramis. A young soldier, Valerius, had another belief. He believed that a witch had assumed a form identical with that of Khauran's adored ruler. He believed that Taramis had been spirited away in the night, and confined in some dungeon, and that this being ruling in her place was but a female sorcerer. He swore that he would find the real queen, if she still lived, but I greatly fear that he himself has fallen victim to the cruelty of

Constantius. He was implicated in the revolt of the palace guards, escaped and remained in hiding for some time, stubbornly refusing to seek safety abroad, and it was during this time that I encountered him and he told me his beliefs.

'But he has disappeared, as so many have, whose fate one dares not conjecture, and I fear he has been apprehended by the spies of Constantius.

'But I must conclude this letter and slip it out of the city by means of a swift carrier-pigeon, which will carry it to the post whence I purchased it, on the borders of Koth. By rider and camel-train it will eventually come to you. I must haste, before dawn. It is late, and the stars gleam whitely on the gardened roofs of Khauran. A shuddering silence envelops the city, in which I hear the throb of a sullen drum from the distant temple. I doubt not that Taramis is there, concocting more deviltry.'

But the savant was incorrect in his conjecture concerning the whereabouts of the woman he called Taramis. The girl whom the world knew as queen of Khauran stood in a dungeon, lighted only by a flickering torch which played on her features, etching the diabolical cruelty of her beautiful countenance.

On the bare stone floor before her crouched a figure whose nakedness was scarcely covered with tattered rags.

This figure Salome touched contemptuously with the upturned toe of her gilded sandal, and smiled vindictively as her victim shrank away.

'You do not love my caresses, sweet sister?'

Taramis was still beautiful, in spite of her rags and the imprisonment and abuse of seven weary months. She did not reply to her sister's taunts, but bent her head as one grown accustomed to mockery.

This resignation did not please Salome. She bit her red lip, and stood tapping the toe of her shoe against the flags as she frowned down at the passive figure. Salome was clad in the barbaric splendor of a woman of Shushan. Jewels glittered in the torchlight on her gilded sandals, on her gold breast-plates and the slender chains that held them in place. Gold anklets clashed as she moved, jeweled bracelets weighted her bare arms. Her tall coiffure was that of a Shemitish woman, and jade pendants hung from gold hoops in her ears, flashing and sparkling with each impatient movement of her haughty head. A gem-crusted girdle supported a silk skirt so transparent that it was in the nature of a cynical mockery of convention.

Suspended from her shoulders and trailing down her back hung a darkly scarlet cloak, and this was thrown carelessly over the crook of one arm and the bundle that arm supported.

Salome stooped suddenly and with her free hand grasped her sister's disheveled hair and forced back the girl's head to stare into her eyes. Taramis met that tigerish glare without flinching.

'You are not so ready with your tears as formerly, sweet sister,' muttered the witch-girl.

'You shall wring no more tears from me,' answered Taramis. 'Too often you have reveled in the spectacle of the queen of Khauran sobbing for mercy on her knees. I know that you have spared me only to torment me; that is why you have limited your tortures to such torments as neither slay nor permanently disfigure. But I fear you no longer; you have strained out the last vestige of hope, fright and shame from me. Slay me and be done with it, for I have shed my last tear for your enjoyment, you she-devil from hell!'

'You flatter yourself, my dear sister,' purred Salome. 'So far it is only your handsome body that I have caused to suffer, only your pride and self-esteem that I have crushed. You forget that, unlike myself, you are capable of mental torment. I have observed this when I have regaled you with narratives concerning the comedies I have enacted with some of your stupid subjects. But this time I have brought more vivid proof of these farces. Did you know that Krallides, your faithful concilor, had come skulking back from Turan and been captured?'

Taramis turned pale.

'What – what have you done to him?'

For answer Salome drew the mysterious bundle from under her cloak. She shook off the silken swathings and held it up – the head of a young man, the features frozen in a convulsion as if death had come in the midst of inhuman agony.

Taramis cried out as if a blade had pierced her heart.

'Oh, Ishtar! Krallides!'

'Aye! He was seeking to stir up the people against me, poor fool, telling them that Conan spoke the truth when he said I was not Taramis. How would the people rise against the Falcon's Shemites? With sticks and pebbles? Bah! Dogs are eating his headless body in the market-place, and this foul carrion shall be cast into the sewer to rot.

'How, sister!' She paused, smiling down at her victim. 'Have you discovered that you still have unshed tears? Good! I reserved the mental torment for the last. Hereafter I shall show you many such sights as – this!'

Standing there in the torchlight with the severed head in her hand she did not look like anything ever born by a human woman, in spite of her awful beauty. Taramis did not look up. She lay face down on the slimy floor, her slim body shaken in sobs of agony, beating her clenched hands against the stones. Salome sauntered toward the door, her anklets clashing at each step, her ear-pendants winking in the torch-glare.

A few moments later she emerged from a door under a sullen arch that let into a court which in turn opened upon a winding alley. A man standing there turned toward her – a giant Shemite, with somber eyes and shoulders like a bull, his great black beard falling over his mighty, silver-mailed breast.

'She wept?' His rumble was like that of a bull, deep, low-pitched and stormy. He was the general of the mercenaries, one of the few even of Constantius' associates who knew the secret of the queens of Khauran.

'Aye, Khumbanigash. There are whole sections of her sensibilities that I have not touched. When one sense is dulled by continual laceration, I will discover a newer, more poignant pang. – Here, dog!' A trembling, shambling figure in rags, filth and matted hair approached, one of the beggars that slept in the alleys and open courts. Salome tossed the head to him. 'Here, deaf one; cast that in the nearest sewer. – Make the sign with your hands, Khumbanigash. He can not hear.'

The general complied, and the tousled head bobbed, as the man turned painfully away.

'Why do you keep up this farce?' rumbled Khumbanigash. 'You are so firmly established on the throne that nothing can unseat you. What if the Khaurani fools learn the truth? They can do nothing. Proclaim yourself in your true identity! Show them their beloved ex-queen – and cut off her head in the public square!'

'Not yet, good Khumbanigash –'

The arched door slammed on the hard accents of Salome, the stormy reverberations of Khumbanigash. The mute beggar crouched in the courtyard, and there was none to see that the hands which held the severed head were quivering strongly – brown, sinewy hands, strangely incongruous with the bent body and filthy tatters.

'I knew it!' It was a fierce, vibrant whisper, scarcely audible. 'She lives! Oh, Krallides, your martyrdom was not in vain! They have her locked in that dungeon! Oh, Ishtar, if you love true men, aid me now!'

4   Wolves of the Desert

Olgerd Vladislav filled his jeweled goblet with crimson wine from a golden jug and thrust the vessel across the ebony table to Conan the Cimmerian. Olgerd's apparel would have satisfied the vanity of any Zaporoskan hetman.

His *khalat* was of white silk, with pearls sewn on the bosom. Girdled at the waist with a Bakhauriot belt, its skirts were drawn back to reveal his wide silken breeches, tucked into short boots of soft green leather, adorned with gold thread. On his head was a green silk turban, wound about a spired helmet chased with gold. His only weapon was a broad curved Cherkees knife in an ivory sheath girdled high on his left hip, *kozak* fashion. Throwing himself back in his gilded chair with its carven eagles, Olgerd spread his booted legs before him, and gulped down the sparkling wine noisily.

To his splendor the huge Cimmerian opposite him offered a strong contrast, with his square-cut black mane, brown scarred countenance and burning blue eyes. He was clad in black mesh-mail, and the only glitter about him was the broad gold buckle of the belt which supported his sword in its worn leather scabbard.

They were alone in the silk-walled tent, which was hung with gilt-worked tapestries and littered with rich carpets and velvet cushions, the loot of the caravans. From outside came a low, incessant murmur, the sound that always accompanies a great throng of men, in camp or otherwise. An occasional gust of desert wind rattled the palm-leaves.

'Today in the shadow, tomorrow in the sun,' quoth Olgerd, loosening his crimson girdle a trifle and reaching again for the wine-jug. 'That's the way of life. Once I was a hetman on the Zaporoska; now I'm a desert chief. Seven months ago you were hanging on a cross outside Khauran. Now you're lieutenant to the most powerful raider between Turan and the western meadows. You should be thankful to me!'

'For recognizing my usefulness?' Conan laughed and lifted the jug. 'When you allow the elevation of a man, one can be sure that you'll profit by his advancement. I've earned everything I've won, with my blood and sweat.' He glanced at the scars on the insides of his palms. There were scars, too, on his body, scars that had not been there seven months ago.

'You fight like a regiment of devils,' conceded Olgerd. 'But don't get to thinking that you've had anything to do with the recruits who've swarmed in to join us. It was our success at raiding, guided by my wit, that brought them in. These nomads are always looking for a successful leader to follow, and they have more faith in a foreigner than in one of their own race.

'There's no limit to what we may accomplish! We have eleven thousand men now. In another year we may have three times that number. We've contented ourselves, so far, with raids on the Turanian outposts and the city-states to the west. With thirty or forty thousand men we'll raid no longer. We'll invade and conquer and establish ourselves as rulers. I'll be emperor of all Shem yet, and you'll be my vizier, so long as you carry out my orders unquestioningly. In the meantime, I think we'll ride eastward and storm that Turanian outpost at Vezek, where the caravans pay toll.'

Conan shook his head. 'I think not.'

Olgerd glared, his quick temper irritated.

'What do you mean, *you* think not? *I* do the thinking for this army!'

'There are enough men in this band now for my purpose,' answered the Cimmerian. 'I'm sick of waiting. I have a score to settle.'

'Oh!' Olgerd scowled, and gulped wine, then grinned. 'Still thinking of that cross, eh? Well, I like a good hater. But that can wait.'

'You told me once you'd aid me in taking Khauran,' said Conan.

'Yes, but that was before I began to see the full possibilities of our power,' answered Olgerd. 'I was only thinking of the loot in the city. I don't want to waste our strength unprofitably. Khauran is too strong a nut for us to crack now. Maybe in a year –'

'Within the week,' answered Conan, and the *kozak* stared at the certainty in his voice.

'Listen,' said Olgerd, 'even if I were willing to throw away men on such a hare-brained attempt – what could you expect? Do you think these wolves could besiege and take a city like Khauran?'

'There'll be no siege,' answered the Cimmerian. 'I know how to draw Constantius out into the plain.'

'And what then?' cried Olgerd with an oath. 'In the arrow-play our horsemen would have the worst of it, for the armor of the *asshuri* is the better, and when it came to sword strokes their close-marshaled ranks of trained swordsmen would cleave through our loose lines and scatter our men like chaff before the wind.'

'Not if there were three thousand desperate Hyborian horsemen fighting in a solid wedge such as I could teach them,' answered Conan.

'And where would you secure three thousand Hyborians?' asked Olgerd with vast sarcasm. 'Will you conjure them out of the air?'

'I *have* them,' answered the Cimmerian imperturbably. 'Three thousand men of Khauran camp at the oasis of Akrel awaiting my orders.'

'*What?*' Olgerd glared like a startled wolf.

'Aye. Men who had fled from the tyranny of Constantius. Most of them have been living the lives of outlaws in the deserts east of Khauran, and are gaunt and hard and desperate as man-eating tigers. One of them will be a match for any three squat mercenaries. It takes oppression and hardship to stiffen men's guts and put the fire of hell into their thews. They were broken up into small bands; all they needed was a leader. They believed the word I sent them by my riders, and assembled at the oasis and put themselves at my disposal.'

'All this without my knowledge?' A feral light began to gleam in Olgerd's eyes. He hitched at his weapon-girdle.

'It was *I* they wished to follow, not *you*.'

'And what did you tell these outcasts to gain their allegiance?' There was a dangerous ring in Olgerd's voice.

'I told them that I'd use this horde of desert wolves to help them destroy Constantius and give Khauran back into the hands of its citizens.'

'You fool!' whispered Olgerd. 'Do you deem yourself chief already?'

The men were on their feet, facing each other across the ebony board, devil-lights dancing in Olgerd's cold gray eyes, a grim smile on the Cimmerian's hard lips.

'I'll have you torn between four palm-trees,' said the *kozak* calmly.

'Call the men and bid them do it!' challenged Conan. 'See if they obey you!'

Baring his teeth in a snarl, Olgerd lifted his hand – then paused. There was something about the confidence in the Cimmerian's dark face that shook him. His eyes began to burn like those of a wolf.

'You scum of the western hills,' he muttered, 'have you dared seek to undermine my power?'

'I didn't have to,' answered Conan. 'You lied when you said I had nothing to do with bringing in the new recruits. I had everything to do with it. They took your orders, but they fought for me. There is not room for two chiefs of the Zuagirs. They know I am the stronger man. I understand them better than you, and they, me; because I am a barbarian too.'

'And what will they say when you ask them to fight for the Khaurani?' asked Olgerd sardonically.

'They'll follow me. I'll promise them a camel-train of gold from the palace. Khauran will be willing to pay that as a guerdon for getting rid of Constantius. After that, I'll lead them against the Turanians as you have planned. They want loot, and they'd as soon fight Constantius for it as anybody.'

In Olgerd's eyes grew a recognition of defeat. In his red

dreams of empire he had missed what was going on about him. Happenings and events that had seemed meaningless before now flashed into his mind, with their true significance, bringing a realization that Conan spoke no idle boast. The giant black-mailed figure before him was the real chief of the Zuagirs.

'Not if you die!' muttered Olgerd, and his hand flickered toward his hilt. But quick as the stroke of a great cat Conan's arm shot across the table and his fingers locked on Olgerd's forearm. There was a snap of breaking bones, and for a tense instant the scene held: the men facing each other as motionless as images, perspiration starting out on Olgerd's forehead. Conan laughed, never easing his grip on the broken arm.

'Are you fit to live, Olgerd?'

His smile did not alter as the corded muscles rippled in knotting ridges along his forearm and his fingers ground into the *kozak*'s quivering flesh. There was the sound of broken bones grating together and Olgerd's face turned the color of ashes; blood oozed from his lip where his teeth sank, but he uttered no sound.

With a laugh Conan released him and drew back, and the *kozak* swayed, caught the table edge with his good hand to steady himself.

'I give you life, Olgerd, as you gave it to me,' said Conan tranquilly, 'though it was for your own ends that you took me down from the cross. It was a bitter test you gave me then; you couldn't have endured it; neither could anyone, but a western barbarian.

'Take your horse and go. It's tied behind the tent, and food and water are in the saddle-bags. None will see your going, but go quickly. There's no room for a fallen chief on the desert. If the warriors see you, maimed and deposed, they'll never let you leave the camp alive.'

Olgerd did not reply. Slowly, without a word, he turned and stalked across the tent, through the flapped opening. Unspeak-

ing he climbed into the saddle of the great white stallion that
stood tethered there in the shade of a spreading palm-tree; and
unspeaking, with his broken arm thrust in the bosom of his
khalat, he reined the steed about and rode eastward into the
open desert, out of the life of the people of the Zuagir.

Inside the tent Conan emptied the wine-jug and smacked his
lips with relish. Tossing the empty vessel into a corner, he braced
his belt and strode out through the front opening, halting for a
moment to let his gaze sweep over the lines of camel-hair tents
that stretched before him, and the white-robed figures that
moved among them, arguing, singing, mending bridles or whetting tulwars.

He lifted his voice in a thunder that carried to the farthest
confines of the encampment: '*Aie*, you dogs, sharpen your ears
and listen! Gather around here. I have a tale to tell you.'

5   The Voice from the Crystal

In a chamber in a tower near the city wall a group of men
listened attentively to the words of one of their number. They
were young men, but hard and sinewy, with the bearing that
comes only to men rendered desperate by adversity. They
were clad in mail shirts and worn leather; swords hung at
their girdles.

'I knew that Conan spoke the truth when he said it was not
Taramis!' the speaker exclaimed. 'For months I have haunted
the outskirts of the palace, playing the part of a deaf beggar. At
last I learned what I had believed – that our queen was a prisoner in the dungeons that adjoin the palace. I watched my
opportunity and captured a Shemitish jailer – knocked him
senseless as he left the courtyard late one night – dragged him
into a cellar near by and questioned him. Before he died he told
me what I have just told you, and what we have suspected all

along – that the woman ruling Khauran is a witch: Salome. Taramis, he said, is imprisoned in the lowest dungeon.

'This invasion of the Zuagirs gives us the opportunity we sought. What Conan means to do, I can not say. Perhaps he merely wishes vengeance on Constantius. Perhaps he intends sacking the city and destroying it. He is a barbarian and no one can understand their minds.

'But this is what we must do: rescue Taramis while the battle rages! Constantius will march out into the plain to give battle. Even now his men are mounting. He will do this because there is not sufficient food in the city to stand a siege. Conan burst out of the desert so suddenly that there was no time to bring in supplies. And the Cimmerian is equipped for a siege. Scouts have reported that the Zuagirs have siege engines, built, undoubtedly, according to the instructions of Conan, who learned all the arts of war among the Western nations.

'Constantius does not desire a long siege; so he will march with his warriors into the plain, where he expects to scatter Conan's forces at one stroke. He will leave only a few hundred men in the city, and they will be on the walls and in the towers commanding the gates.

'The prison will be left all but unguarded. When we have freed Taramis our next actions will depend upon circumstances. If Conan wins, we must show Taramis to the people and bid them rise – they will! Oh, they will! With their bare hands they are enough to overpower the Shemites left in the city and close the gates against both the mercenaries and the nomads. Neither must get within the walls! Then we will parley with Conan. He was always loyal to Taramis. If he knows the truth, and she appeals to him, I believe he will spare the city. If, which is more probable, Constantius prevails, and Conan is routed, we must steal out of the city with the queen and seek safety in flight.

'Is all clear?'

They replied with one voice.

'Then let us loosen our blades in our scabbards, commend our souls to Ishtar, and start for the prison, for the mercenaries are already marching through the southern gate.'

This was true. The dawnlight glinted on peaked helmets pouring in a steady stream through the broad arch, on the bright housings of the chargers. This would be a battle of horsemen, such as is possible only in the lands of the East. The riders flowed through the gates like a river of steel – somber figures in black and silver mail, with their curled beards and hooked noses, and their inexorable eyes in which glimmered the fatality of their race – the utter lack of doubt or of mercy.

The streets and the walls were lined with throngs of people who watched silently these warriors of an alien race riding forth to defend their native city. There was no sound; dully, expressionless they watched, those gaunt people in shabby garments, their caps in their hands.

In a tower that overlooked the broad street that led to the southern gate, Salome lolled on a velvet couch cynically watching Constantius as he settled his broad sword-belt about his lean hips and drew on his gauntlets. They were alone in the chamber. Outside, the rhythmical clank of harness and shuffle of horses' hoofs welled up through the gold-barred casements.

'Before nightfall,' quoth Constantius, giving a twirl to his thin mustache, 'you'll have some captives to feed to your temple-devil. Does it not grow weary of soft, city-bred flesh? Perhaps it would relish the harder thews of a desert man.'

'Take care you do not fall prey to a fiercer beast than Thaug,' warned the girl. 'Do not forget who it is that leads these desert animals.'

'I am not likely to forget,' he answered. 'That is one reason why I am advancing to meet him. The dog has fought in the West and knows the art of siege. My scouts had some trouble in approaching his columns, for his outriders have eyes like hawks;

but they did get close enough to see the engines he is dragging on ox-cart wheels drawn by camels – catapults, rams, ballistas, mangonels – by Ishtar! he must have had ten thousand men working day and night for a month. Where he got the material for their construction is more than I can understand. Perhaps he has a treaty with the Turanians, and gets supplies from them.

'Anyway, they won't do him any good. I've fought these desert wolves before – an exchange of arrows for awhile, in which the armor of my warriors protects them – then a charge and my squadrons sweep through the loose swarms of the nomads, wheel and sweep back through, scattering them to the four winds. I'll ride back through the south gate before sunset, with hundreds of naked captives staggering at my horse's tail. We'll hold a fête tonight, in the great square. My soldiers delight in flaying their enemies alive – we will have a wholesale skinning, and make these weak-kneed townsfolk watch. As for Conan, it will afford me intense pleasure, if we take him alive, to impale him on the palace steps.'

'Skin as many as you like,' answered Salome indifferently. 'I would like a dress made of human hide. But at least a hundred captives you must give to me – for the altar, and for Thaug.'

'It shall be done,' answered Constantius, with his gauntleted hand brushing back the thin hair from his high bald forehead, burned dark by the sun. 'For victory and the fair honor of Taramis!' he said sardonically, and, taking his vizored helmet under his arm, he lifted a hand in salute, and strode clanking from the chamber. His voice drifted back, harshly lifted in orders to his officers.

Salome leaned back on the couch, yawned, stretched herself like a great supple cat, and called: 'Zang!'

A cat-footed priest, with features like yellowed parchment stretched over a skull, entered noiselessly.

Salome turned to an ivory pedestal on which stood two crystal globes, and taking from it the smaller, she handed the glistening sphere to the priest.

'Ride with Constantius,' she said. 'Give me the news of the battle. Go!'

The skull-faced man bowed low, and hiding the globe under his dark mantle, hurried from the chamber.

Outside in the city there was no sound, except the clank of hoofs and after a while the clang of a closing gate. Salome mounted a wide marble stair that led to the flat, canopied, marble-battlemented roof. She was above all other buildings of the city. The streets were deserted, the great square in front of the palace was empty. In normal times folk shunned the grim temple which rose on the opposite side of that square, but now the town looked like a dead city. Only on the south-ern wall and the roofs that overlooked it was there any sign of life. There the people massed thickly. They made no demon-stration, did not know whether to hope for the victory or defeat of Constantius. Victory meant further misery under his intolerable rule; defeat probably meant the sack of the city and red massacre. No word had come from Conan. They did not know what to expect at his hands. They remembered that he was a barbarian.

The squadrons of the mercenaries were moving out into the plain. In the distance, just this side of the river, other dark masses were moving, barely recognizable as men on horses. Objects dotted the farther bank; Conan had not brought his siege engines across the river, apparently fearing an attack in the midst of the crossing. But he had crossed with his full force of horsemen. The sun rose and struck glints of fire from the dark multitudes. The squadrons from the city broke into a gallop; a deep roar reached the ears of the people on the wall.

The rolling masses merged, intermingled; at that distance it was a tangled confusion in which no details stood out. Charge and countercharge were not to be identified. Clouds of dust rose from the plains, under the stamping hoofs, veiling the action. Through these swirling clouds masses of riders loomed, appearing and disappearing, and spears flashed.

Salome shrugged her shoulders and descended the stair. The palace lay silent. All the slaves were on the wall, gazing vainly southward with the citizens.

She entered the chamber where she had talked with Constantius, and approached the pedestal, noting that the crystal globe was clouded, shot with bloody streaks of crimson. She bent over the ball, swearing under her breath.

'Zang!' she called. 'Zang!'

Mists swirled in the sphere, resolving themselves into billowing dust-clouds through which black figures rushed unrecognizably; steel glinted like lightning in the murk. Then the face of Zang leaped into startling distinctness; it was as if the wide eyes gazed up at Salome. Blood trickled from a gash in the skull-like head, the skin was gray with sweat-runneled dust. The lips parted, writhing; to other ears than Salome's it would have seemed that the face in the crystal contorted silently. But sound to her came as plainly from those ashen lips as if the priest had been in the same room with her, instead of miles away, shouting into the smaller crystal. Only the gods of darkness knew what unseen, magic filaments linked together those shimmering spheres.

'Salome!' shrieked the bloody head. '*Salome!*'

'I hear!' she cried. 'Speak! How goes the battle?'

'Doom is upon us!' screamed the skull-like apparition. 'Khauran is lost! *Aie*, my horse is down and I can not win clear! Men are falling around me! They are dying like flies, in their silvered mail!'

'Stop yammering and tell me what happened!' she cried harshly.

'We rode at the desert-dogs and they came on to meet us!' yowled the priest. 'Arrows flew in clouds between the hosts, and the nomads wavered. Constantius ordered the charge. In even ranks we thundered upon them.

'Then the masses of their horde opened to right and left, and through the cleft rushed three thousand Hyborian horsemen whose presence we had not even suspected. Men of Khauran, mad with hate! Big men in full armor on massive horses! In a solid wedge of steel they smote us like a thunderbolt. They split our ranks asunder before we knew what was upon us, and then the desert-men swarmed on us from either flank.

'They have ripped our ranks apart, broken and scattered us! It is a trick of that devil Conan! The siege engines are false – mere frames of palm trunks and painted silk, that fooled our scouts who saw them from afar. A trick to draw us out to our doom! Our warriors flee! Khumbanigash is down – Conan slew him. I do not see Constantius. The Khaurani rage through our milling masses like blood-mad lions, and the desert-men feather us with arrows. I – ahhh!'

There was a flicker as of lightning, or trenchant steel, a burst of bright blood – then abruptly the image vanished, like a bursting bubble, and Salome was staring into an empty crystal ball that mirrored only her own furious features.

She stood perfectly still for a few moments, erect and staring into space. Then she clapped her hands and another skull-like priest entered, as silent and immobile as the first.

'Constantius is beaten,' she said swiftly. 'We are doomed. Conan will be crashing at our gates within the hour. If he catches me, I have no illusions as to what I can expect. But first I am going to make sure that my cursed sister never ascends the throne again. Follow me! Come what may, we shall give Thaug a feast.'

As she descended the stairs and galleries of the palace, she heard a faint rising echo from the distant walls. The people there had begun to realize that the battle was going against Constantius. Through the dust clouds masses of horsemen were visible, racing toward the city.

Palace and prison were connected by a long closed gallery,

whose vaulted roof rose on gloomy arches. Hurrying along this, the false queen and her slave passed through a heavy door at the other end that let them into the dim-lit recesses of the prison. They had emerged into a wide, arched corridor at a point near where a stone stair descended into the darkness. Salome recoiled suddenly, swearing. In the gloom of the hall lay a motionless form – a Shemitish jailer, his short beard tilted toward the roof as his head hung on a half-severed neck. As panting voices from below reached the girl's ears, she shrank back into the black shadow of an arch, pushing the priest behind her, her hand groping in her girdle.

6 The Vulture's Wings

It was the smoky light of a torch which roused Taramis, queen of Khauran, from the slumber in which she sought forgetfulness. Lifting herself on her hand she raked back her tangled hair and blinked up, expecting to meet the mocking countenance of Salome, malign with new torments. Instead a cry of pity and horror reached her ears.

'Taramis! Oh, my queen!'

The sound was so strange to her ears that she thought she was still dreaming. Behind the torch she could make out figures now, the glint of steel, then five countenances bent toward her, not swarthy and hook-nosed, but lean, aquiline faces, browned by the sun. She crouched in her tatters, staring wildly.

One of the figures sprang forward and fell on one knee before her, arms stretched appealingly toward her.

'Oh, Taramis! Thank Ishtar we have found you! Do you not remember me, Valerius? Once with your own lips you praised me, after the battle of Korveka!'

'Valerius!' she stammered. Suddenly tears welled into her eyes. 'Oh, I dream! It is some magic of Salome's, to torment me!'

'No!' The cry rang with exultation. 'It is your own true vassals come to rescue you! Yet we must hasten. Constantius fights in the plain against Conan, who has brought the Zuagirs across the river, but three hundred Shemites yet hold the city. We slew the jailer and took his keys, and have seen no other guards. But we must be gone. Come!'

The queen's legs gave way, not from weakness but from the reaction. Valerius lifted her like a child, and with the torchbearer hurrying before them, they left the dungeon and went up a slimy stone stair. It seemed to mount endlessly, but presently they emerged into a corridor.

They were passing a dark arch when the torch was suddenly struck out, and the bearer cried out in fierce, brief agony. A burst of blue fire glared in the dark corridor, in which the furious face of Salome was limned momentarily, with a beast-like figure crouching beside her – then the eyes of the watchers were blinded by that blaze.

Valerius tried to stagger along the corridor with the queen; dazedly he heard the sound of murderous blows driven deep in flesh, accompanied by gasps of death and a bestial grunting. Then the queen was torn brutally from his arms, and a savage blow on his helmet dashed him to the floor.

Grimly he crawled to his feet, shaking his head in an effort to rid himself of the blue flame which seemed still to dance devilishly before him. When his blinded sight cleared, he found himself alone in the corridor – alone except for the dead. His four companions lay in their blood, heads and bosoms cleft and gashed. Blinded and dazed in that hell-born glare, they had died without an opportunity of defending themselves. The queen was gone.

With a bitter curse Valerius caught up his sword, tearing his cleft helmet from his head to clatter on the flags; blood ran down his cheek from a cut in his scalp.

Reeling, frantic with indecision, he heard a voice calling his name in desperate urgency: 'Valerius! *Valerius!*'

He staggered in the direction of the voice, and rounded a corner just in time to have his arms filled with a soft, supple figure which flung itself frantically at him.

'Ivga! Are you mad!'

'I had to come!' she sobbed. 'I followed you – hid in an arch of the outer court. A moment ago I saw *her* emerge with a brute who carried a woman in his arms. I knew it was Taramis, and that you had failed! Oh, you are hurt!'

'A scratch!' He put aside her clinging hands. 'Quick, Ivga, tell me which way they went!'

'They fled across the square toward the temple.'

He paled. 'Ishtar! Oh, the fiend! She means to give Taramis to the devil she worships! Quick, Ivga! Run to the south wall where the people watch the battle! Tell them that their real queen has been found – that the impostor has dragged her to the temple! Go!'

Sobbing, the girl sped away, her light sandals pattering on the cobblestones, and Valerius raced across the court, plunged into the street, dashed into the square upon which it debouched, and raced for the great structure that rose on the opposite side.

His flying feet spurned the marble as he darted up the broad stair and through the pillared portico. Evidently their prisoner had given them some trouble. Taramis, sensing the doom intended for her, was fighting against it with all the strength of her splendid young body. Once she had broken away from the brutish priest, only to be dragged down again.

The group was half-way down the broad nave, at the other end of which stood the grim altar and beyond that the great metal door, obscenely carven, through which many had gone, but from which only Salome had ever emerged. Taramis' breath came in panting gasps; her tattered garment had been torn from her in the struggle. She writhed in the grasp of her apish captor like a white, naked nymph in the arms of a satyr. Salome watched cynically, though impatiently, moving toward the carven door, and from the dusk that lurked along the lofty walls the obscene gods and gargoyles leered down, as if imbued with salacious life.

Choking with fury, Valerius rushed down the great hall, sword in hand. At a sharp cry from Salome, the skull-faced priest looked up, then released Taramis, drew a heavy knife, already smeared with blood, and ran at the oncoming Khaurani.

But cutting down men blinded by the devil's-flame loosed by Salome was different from fighting a wiry young Hyborian afire with hate and rage.

Up went the dripping knife, but before it could fall Valerius' keen narrow blade slashed through the air, and the fist that held the knife jumped from its wrist in a shower of blood. Valerius, berserk, slashed again and yet again before the crumpling figure could fall. The blade licked through flesh and bone. The skull-like head fell one way, the half-sundered torso the other.

Valerius whirled on his toes, quick and fierce as a jungle-cat, glaring about for Salome. She must have exhausted her fire-dust in the prison. She was bending over Taramis, grasping her sister's black locks in one hand, in the other lifting a dagger. Then with a fierce cry Valerius' sword was sheathed in her breast with such fury that the point sprang out between her shoulders. With an awful shriek the witch sank down, writhing in convulsions, grasping at the naked blade as it was withdrawn, smoking and dripping. Her eyes were unhuman; with a more than human vitality she clung to the life that ebbed through the wound that split the crimson crescent on her ivory bosom. She groveled on the floor, clawing and biting at the naked stones in her agony.

Sickened at the sight, Valerius stooped and lifted the half-fainting queen. Turning his back on the twisting figure upon the floor, he ran toward the door, stumbling in his haste. He staggered out upon the portico, halted at the head of the steps. The square thronged with people. Some had come at Ivga's incoherent cries; others had deserted the walls in fear of the onsweeping hordes out of the desert, fleeing unreasoningly toward the center of the city. Dumb resignation had vanished. The throng seethed and milled, yelling and screaming. About the road there sounded somewhere the splintering of stone and timbers.

A band of grim Shemites cleft the crowd – the guards of the northern gates, hurrying toward the south gate to reinforce their comrades there. They reined up short at sight of the youth on the steps, holding the limp, naked figure in his arms. The heads of the throng turned toward the temple; the crowd gaped, a new bewilderment added to their swirling confusion.

'Here is your queen!' yelled Valerius, straining to make himself understood above the clamor. The people gave back a bewildered roar. They did not understand, and Valerius sought in vain to lift his voice above their bedlam. The Shemites rode toward the temple steps, beating a way through the crowd with their spears.

Then a new, grisly element introduced itself into the frenzy. Out of the gloom of the temple behind Valerius wavered a slim white figure, laced with crimson. The people screamed; there in the arms of Valerius hung the woman they thought their queen; yet there in the temple door staggered another figure, like a reflection of the other. Their brains reeled. Valerius felt his blood congeal as he stared at the swaying witch-girl. His sword had transfixed her, sundered her heart. She should be dead; by all laws of nature she should be dead. Yet there she swayed, on her feet, clinging horribly to life.

'Thaug!' she screamed, reeling in the doorway. '*Thaug!*' As in answer to that frightful invocation there boomed a thunderous croaking from within the temple, the snapping of wood and metal.

'That is the queen!' roared the captain of the Shemites, lifting his bow. 'Shoot down the man and the other woman!'

But the roar of a roused hunting-pack rose from the people; they had guessed the truth at last, understood Valerius' frenzied appeals, knew that the girl who hung limply in his arms was their true queen. With a soul-shaking yell they surged on the Shemites, tearing and smiting with tooth and nail and naked hands, with the desperation of hard-pent fury loosed at last. Above them Salome swayed and tumbled down the marble stair, dead at last.

Arrows flickered about him as Valerius ran back between the pillars of the portico, shielding the body of the queen with his own. Shooting and slashing ruthlessly the mounted Shemites were holding their own with the maddened crowd. Valerius darted to the temple door – with one foot on the threshold he recoiled, crying out in horror and despair.

Out of the gloom at the other end of the great hall a vast dark form heaved up – came rushing toward him in gigantic frog-like hops. He saw the gleam of great unearthly eyes, the shimmer of fangs or talons. He fell back from the door, and then the whir of a shaft past his ear warned him that death was also behind him. He wheeled desperately. Four or five Shemites had cut their way through the throng and were spurring their horses up the steps, their bows lifted to shoot him down. He sprang behind a pillar, on which the arrows splintered. Taramis had fainted. She hung like a dead woman in his arms.

Before the Shemites could loose again, the doorway was blocked by a gigantic shape. With affrighted yells the mercenaries wheeled and began beating a frantic way through the throng, which crushed back in sudden, galvanized horror, trampling one another in their stampede.

But the monster seemed to be watching Valerius and the girl. Squeezing its vast, unstable bulk through the door, it bounded toward him, as he ran down the steps. He felt it looming behind him, a giant shadowy thing, like a travesty of nature cut out of the heart of night, a black shapelessness in which only the staring eyes and gleaming fangs were distinct.

There came a sudden thunder of hoofs; a rout of Shemites, bloody and battered, streamed across the square from the south, plowing blindly through the packed throng. Behind them swept a horde of horsemen yelling in a familiar tongue, waving red swords – the exiles, returned! With them rode fifty black-bearded desert-riders, and at their head a giant figure in black mail.

'Conan!' shrieked Valerius. *'Conan!'*

The giant yelled a command. Without checking their headlong pace, the desert men lifted their bows, drew and loosed. A cloud of arrows sang across the square, over the seething heads of the multitudes, and sank feather-deep in the black monster. It halted, wavered, reared, a black blot against the marble pillars. Again the sharp cloud sang, and yet again, and the horror collapsed and rolled down the steps, as dead as the witch who had summoned it out of the night of ages.

Conan drew rein beside the portico, leaped off. Valerius had laid the queen on the marble, sinking beside her in utter exhaustion. The people surged about, crowding in. The Cimmerian cursed them back, lifted her dark head, pillowed it against his mailed shoulder.

'By Crom, what is this? The real Taramis! But who is that yonder?'

'The demon who wore her shape,' panted Valerius.

Conan swore heartily. Ripping a cloak from the shoulders of a soldier, he wrapped it about the naked queen. Her long dark lashes quivered on her cheeks; her eyes opened, stared up unbelievingly into the Cimmerian's scarred face.

'Conan!' Her soft fingers caught at him. 'Do I dream? *She* told me you were dead –'

'Scarcely!' He grinned hardly. 'You do not dream. You are queen of Khauran again. I broke Constantius, out there by the river. Most of his dogs never lived to reach the walls, for I gave orders that no prisoners be taken – except Constantius. The city guard closed the gate in our faces, but we burst it in with rams swung from our saddles. I left all my wolves outside, except this fifty. I didn't trust them in here, and these Khaurani lads were enough for the gate guards.'

'It has been a nightmare!' she whimpered. 'Oh, my poor people! You must help me try to repay them for all they have suffered, Conan, henceforth councilor as well as captain!'

Conan laughed, but shook his head. Rising, he set the queen upon her feet, and beckoned to a number of his Khaurani horsemen who had not continued the pursuit of the fleeing Shemites. They sprang from their horses, eager to do the bidding of their new-found queen.

'No, lass, that's over with. I'm chief of the Zuagirs now, and must lead them to plunder the Turanians, as I promised. This lad, Valerius, will make you a better captain than I. I wasn't made to dwell among marble walls, anyway. But I must leave you now, and complete what I've begun. Shemites still live in Khauran.'

As Valerius started to follow Taramis across the square toward the palace, through a lane opened by the wildly cheering multitude, he felt a soft hand slipped timidly into his sinewy fingers and turned to receive the slender body of Ivga in his arms. He crushed her to him and drank her kisses with the gratitude of a weary fighter who has attained rest at last through tribulation and storm.

But not all men seek rest and peace; some are born with the spirit of the storm in their blood, restless harbingers of violence and bloodshed, knowing no other path . . .

The sun was rising. The ancient caravan road was thronged with white-robed horsemen, in a wavering line that stretched from the walls of Khauran to a spot far out in the plain. Conan the Cimmerian sat at the head of that column, near the jagged end of a wooden beam that stuck up out of the ground. Near that stump rose a heavy cross, and on that cross a man hung by spikes through his hands and feet.

'Seven months ago, Constantius,' said Conan, 'it was I who hung there, and you who sat here.'

Constantius did not reply; he licked his gray lips and his eyes were glassy with pain and fear. Muscles writhed like cords along his lean body.

'You are more fit to inflict torture than to endure it,' said Conan tranquilly. 'I hung there on a cross as you are hanging, and I lived, thanks to circumstances and a stamina peculiar to barbarians. But you civilized men are soft; your lives are not nailed to your spines as are ours. Your fortitude consists mainly in inflicting torment, not in enduring it. You will be dead before sundown. And so, Falcon of the desert, I leave you to the companionship of another bird of the desert.'

He gestured toward the vultures whose shadows swept across the sands as they wheeled overhead. From the lips of Constantius came an inhuman cry of despair and horror.

Conan lifted his reins and rode toward the river that shone like silver in the morning sun. Behind him the white-clad riders struck into a trot; the gaze of each, as he passed a certain spot, turned impersonally and with the desert man's lack of compassion, toward the cross and the gaunt figure that hung there, black against the sunrise. Their horses' hoofs beat out a knell in the dust. Lower and lower swept the wings of the hungry vultures.

Red Nails

1 The Skull on the Crag

The woman on the horse reined in her weary steed. It stood with its legs wide-braced, its head drooping, as if it found even the weight of the gold-tassled, red-leather bridle too heavy. The woman drew a booted foot out of the silver stirrup and swung down from the gilt-worked saddle. She made the reins fast to the fork of a sapling, and turned about, hands on her hips, to survey her surroundings.

They were not inviting. Giant trees hemmed in the small pool where her horse had just drunk. Clumps of undergrowth limited the vision that quested under the somber twilight of the lofty arches formed by intertwining branches. The woman shivered with a twitch of her magnificent shoulders, and then cursed.

She was tall, full-bosomed and large-limbed, with compact shoulders. Her whole figure reflected an unusual strength, without detracting from the femininity of her appearance. She was all woman, in spite of her bearing and her garments. The latter were incongruous, in view of her present environs. Instead of a skirt she wore short, wide-legged silk breeches, which ceased a hand's breadth short of her knees, and were upheld by a wide silken sash worn as a girdle. Flaring-topped boots of soft leather came almost to her knees, and a low-necked, wide-collared, wide-sleeved silk shirt completed her costume. On one shapely hip she wore a straight double-edged sword, and on the other a long dirk. Her unruly golden hair, cut square at her shoulders, was confined by a band of crimson satin.

Against the background of somber, primitive forest she posed with an unconscious picturesqueness, bizarre and out of place. She should have been posed against a background of sea-clouds, painted masts and wheeling gulls. There was the color of the sea in her wide eyes. And that was as it should have been, because this was Valeria of the Red Brotherhood, whose deeds are celebrated in song and ballad wherever seafarers gather.

She strove to pierce the sullen green roof of the arched branches and see the sky which presumably lay about it, but presently gave it up with a muttered oath.

Leaving her horse tied she strode off toward the east, glancing back toward the pool from time to time in order to fix her route in her mind. The silence of the forest depressed her. No birds sang in the lofty boughs, nor did any rustling in the bushes indicate the presence of any small animals. For leagues she had traveled in a realm of brooding stillness, broken only by the sounds of her own flight.

She had slaked her thirst at the pool, but she felt the gnawings of hunger and began looking about for some of the fruit on which she had sustained herself since exhausting the food she had brought in her saddle-bags.

Ahead of her, presently, she saw an outcropping of dark, flint-like rock that sloped upward into what looked like a rugged crag rising among the trees. Its summit was lost to view amidst a cloud of encircling leaves. Perhaps its peak rose above the tree-tops, and from it she could see what lay beyond – if, indeed, anything lay beyond but more of this apparently illimitable forest through which she had ridden for so many days.

A narrow ridge formed a natural ramp that led up the steep face of the crag. After she had ascended some fifty feet she came to the belt of leaves that surrounded the rock. The trunks of the trees did not crowd close to the crag, but the ends of their lower branches extended about it, veiling it with their foliage. She groped on in leafy obscurity, not able to see either above or below her; but presently she glimpsed blue sky, and a moment later came out in the clear, hot sunlight and saw the forest roof stretching away under her feet.

She was standing on a broad shelf which was about even with the tree-tops, and from it rose a spire-like jut that was the ultimate peak of the crag she had climbed. But something else caught her attention at the moment. Her foot had struck something in the litter of blown dead leaves which carpeted the shelf. She kicked them aside and looked down on the skeleton of a man. She ran an experienced eye over the bleached frame, but saw no broken bones nor any sign of violence. The man must have died a natural death; though why he should have climbed a tall crag to die she could not imagine.

She scrambled up to the summit of the spire and looked toward the horizons. The forest roof – which looked like a floor from her vantage-point – was just as impenetrable as from below. She could not even see the pool by which she had left her horse. She glanced northward, in the direction from which she had come. She saw only the rolling green ocean stretching away and away, with only a vague blue line in the distance to hint of the hill-range she had crossed days before, to plunge into this leafy waste.

West and east the view was the same; though the blue hill-line was lacking in those directions. But when she turned her eyes southward she stiffened and caught her breath. A mile away in that direction the forest thinned out and ceased abruptly, giving way to a cactus-dotted plain. And in the midst of that plain rose the walls and towers of a city. Valeria swore in amazement. This passed belief. She would not have been surprized to sight human habitations of another sort – the beehive-shaped huts of the black people, or the cliff-dwellings of the mysterious brown race which legends declared inhabited some country of this unexplored region. But it was a startling experience to come upon a walled city here so many long weeks' march from the nearest outposts of any sort of civilization.

Her hands tiring from clinging to the spire-like pinnacle, she let herself down on the shelf, frowning in indecision. She had come far – from the camp of the mercenaries by the border town of Sukhmet amidst the level grasslands, where desperate adventurers of many races guard the Stygian frontier against the raids that come up like a red wave from Darfar. Her flight had been blind, into a country of which she was wholly ignorant. And now she wavered between an urge to ride directly to that city in the plain, and the instinct of caution which prompted her to skirt it widely and continue her solitary flight.

Her thoughts were scattered by the rustling of the leaves below her. She wheeled cat-like, snatched at her sword; and then she froze motionless, staring wide-eyed at the man before her.

He was almost a giant in stature, muscles rippling smoothly under his skin which the sun had burned brown. His garb was similar to hers, except that he wore a broad leather belt instead of a girdle. Broadsword and poniard hung from this belt.

'Conan, the Cimmerian!' ejaculated the woman. 'What are *you* doing on my trail?'

He grinned hardly, and his fierce blue eyes burned with a light any woman could understand as they ran over her magnificent figure, lingering on the swell of her splendid breasts beneath the light shirt, and the clear white flesh displayed between breeches and boot-tops.

'Don't you know?' he laughed. 'Haven't I made my admiration for you plain ever since I first saw you?'

'A stallion could have made it no plainer,' she answered disdainfully. 'But I never expected to encounter you so far from the ale-barrels and meat-pots of Sukhmet. Did you really follow me from Zarallo's camp, or were you whipped forth for a rogue?'

He laughed at her insolence and flexed his mighty biceps.

'You know Zarallo didn't have enough knaves to whip me out of camp,' he grinned. 'Of course I followed you. Lucky thing for you, too, wench! When you knifed that Stygian officer, you forfeited Zarallo's favor and protection, and you outlawed yourself with the Stygians.'

'I know it,' she replied sullenly. 'But what else could I do? You know what my provocation was.'

'Sure,' he agreed. 'If I'd been there, I'd have knifed him myself. But if a woman must live in the war-camps of men, she can expect such things.'

Valeria stamped her booted foot and swore.

'Why won't men let me live a man's life?'

'That's obvious!' Again his eager eyes devoured her. 'But you were wise to run away. The Stygians would have had you skinned. That officer's brother followed you; faster than you thought, I don't doubt. He wasn't far behind you when I caught up with him. His horse was better than yours. He'd have caught you and cut your throat within a few more miles.'

'Well?' she demanded.

'Well what?' He seemed puzzled.

'What of the Stygian?'

'Why, what do you suppose?' he returned impatiently. 'I killed him, of course, and left his carcass for the vultures. That delayed me, though, and I almost lost your trail when you crossed the rocky spurs of the hills. Otherwise I'd have caught up with you long ago.'

'And now you think you'll drag me back to Zarallo's camp?' she sneered.

'Don't talk like a fool,' he grunted. 'Come, girl, don't be such a spitfire. I'm not like that Stygian you knifed, and you know it.'

'A penniless vagabond,' she taunted.

He laughed at her.

'What do you call yourself? You haven't enough money to buy a new seat for your breeches. Your disdain doesn't deceive me. You know I've commanded bigger ships and more men than you ever did in your life. As for being penniless – what rover isn't, most of the time? I've squandered enough gold in the sea-ports of the world to fill a galleon. You know that, too.'

'Where are the fine ships and the bold lads you commanded, now?' she sneered.

'At the bottom of the sea, mostly,' he replied cheerfully. 'The Zingarans sank my last ship off the Shemite shore – that's why I joined Zarallo's Free Companions. But I saw I'd been stung when we marched to the Darfar border. The pay was poor and the wine was sour, and I don't like black women. And that's the only kind that came to our camp at Sukhmet – rings in their noses and their teeth filed – bah! Why did you join Zarallo? Sukhmet's a long way from salt water.'

'Red Ortho wanted to make me his mistress,' she answered sullenly. 'I jumped overboard one night and swam ashore when we were anchored off the Kushite coast. Off Zabhela, it was. There a Shemite trader told me that Zarallo had brought his Free Companies south to guard the Darfar border. No better employment offered. I joined an east-bound caravan and eventually came to Sukhmet.'

'It was madness to plunge southward as you did,' commented Conan, 'but it was wise, too, for Zarallo's patrols never thought to look for you in this direction. Only the brother of the man you killed happened to strike your trail.'

'And now what do you intend doing?' she demanded.

'Turn west,' he answered. 'I've been this far south, but not this far east. Many days' traveling to the west will bring us to the open savannas, where the black tribes graze their cattle. I have friends among them. We'll get to the coast and find a ship. I'm sick of the jungle.'

'Then be on your way,' she advised. 'I have other plans.'

'Don't be a fool!' He showed irritation for the first time. 'You can't keep on wandering through this forest.'

'I can if I choose.'

'But what do you intend doing?'

'That's none of your affair,' she snapped.

'Yes, it is,' he answered calmly. 'Do you think I've followed you this far, to turn around and ride off empty-handed? Be sensible, wench. I'm not going to harm you.'

He stepped toward her, and she sprang back, whipping out her sword.

'Keep back, you barbarian dog! I'll spit you like a roast pig!'

He halted, reluctantly, and demanded: 'Do you want me to take that toy away from you and spank you with it?'

'Words! Nothing but words!' she mocked, lights like the gleam of the sun on blue water dancing in her reckless eyes.

He knew it was the truth. No living man could disarm Valeria of the Brotherhood with his bare hands. He scowled, his sensations a tangle of conflicting emotions. He was angry, yet he was amused and filled with admiration for her spirit. He burned with eagerness to seize that splendid figure and crush it in his iron arms, yet he greatly desired not to hurt the girl. He was torn between a desire to shake her soundly, and a desire to caress her. He knew if he came any nearer her sword would be sheathed in his heart. He had seen Valeria kill too many men in border forays and tavern brawls to have any illusions about her. He knew she was as quick and ferocious as a tigress. He could draw his broadsword and disarm her, beat the blade out of her hand, but the thought of drawing a sword on a woman, even without intent of injury, was extremely repugnant to him.

'Blast your soul, you hussy!' he exclaimed in exasperation. 'I'm going to take off your –'

He started toward her, his angry passion making him reckless, and she poised herself for a deadly thrust. Then came a startling interruption to a scene at once ludicrous and perilous.

'*What's that?*'

It was Valeria who exclaimed, but they both started violently, and Conan wheeled like a cat, his great sword flashing into his hand. Back in the forest had burst forth an appalling medley of screams – the screams of horses in terror and agony. Mingled with their screams there came the snap of splintering bones.

'Lions are slaying the horses!' cried Valeria.

'Lions, nothing!' snorted Conan, his eyes blazing. 'Did you hear a lion roar? Neither did I! Listen at those bones snap – not even a lion could make that much noise killing a horse.'

He hurried down the natural ramp and she followed, their personal feud forgotten in the adventurers' instinct to unite against common peril. The screams had ceased when they worked their way downward through the green veil of leaves that brushed the rock.

'I found your horse tied by the pool back there,' he muttered, treading so noiselessly that she no longer wondered how he had surprized her on the crag. 'I tied mine beside it and followed the tracks of your boots. Watch, now!'

They had emerged from the belt of leaves, and stared down into the lower reaches of the forest. Above them the green roof spread its dusky canopy. Below them the sunlight filtered in just enough to make a jade-tinted twilight. The giant trunks of trees less than a hundred yards away looked dim and ghostly.

'The horses should be beyond that thicket, over there,' whispered Conan, and his voice might have been a breeze moving through the branches. 'Listen!'

Valeria had already heard, and a chill crept through her veins; so she unconsciously laid her white hand on her companion's muscular brown arm. From beyond the thicket came the noisy crunching of bones and the loud rending of flesh, together with the grinding, slobbering sounds of a horrible feast.

'Lions wouldn't make that noise,' whispered Conan. 'Something's eating our horses, but it's not a lion – Crom!'

The noise stopped suddenly, and Conan swore softly. A suddenly risen breeze was blowing from them directly toward the spot where the unseen slayer was hidden.

'Here it comes!' muttered Conan, half lifting his sword.

The thicket was violently agitated, and Valeria clutched Conan's arm hard. Ignorant of jungle-lore, she yet knew that no animal she had ever seen could have shaken the tall brush like that.

'It must be as big as an elephant,' muttered Conan, echoing her thought. 'What the devil –' His voice trailed away in stunned silence.

Through the thicket was thrust a head of nightmare and lunacy. Grinning jaws bared rows of dripping yellow tusks; above the yawning mouth wrinkled a saurian-like snout. Huge eyes, like those of a python a thousand times magnified, stared unwinkingly at the petrified humans clinging to the rock above it. Blood smeared the scaly, flabby lips and dripped from the huge mouth.

The head, bigger than that of a crocodile, was further extended on a long scaled neck on which stood up rows of serrated spikes, and after it, crushing down the briars and saplings, waddled the body of a titan, a gigantic, barrel-bellied torso on absurdly short legs. The whitish belly almost raked the ground, while the serrated back-bone rose higher than Conan could have reached on tiptoe. A long spiked tail, like that of a gargantuan scorpion, trailed out behind.

'Back up the crag, quick!' snapped Conan, thrusting the girl behind him. 'I don't think he can climb, but he can stand on his hind-legs and reach us –'

With a snapping and rending of bushes and saplings the monster came hurtling through the thickets, and they fled up the rock before him like leaves blown before a wind. As Valeria plunged into the leafy screen a backward glance showed her the titan rearing up fearsomely on his massive hinder legs, even as

Conan had predicted. The sight sent panic racing through her. As he reared, the beast seemed more gigantic than ever; his snouted head towered among the trees. Then Conan's iron hand closed on her wrist and she was jerked headlong into the blinding welter of the leaves, and out again into the hot sunshine above, just as the monster fell forward with his front feet on the crag with an impact that made the rock vibrate.

Behind the fugitives the huge head crashed through the twigs, and they looked down for a horrifying instant at the nightmare visage framed among the green leaves, eyes flaming, jaws gaping. Then the giant tusks clashed together futilely, and after that the head was withdrawn, vanishing from their sight as if it had sunk in a pool.

Peering down through broken branches that scraped the rock, they saw it squatting on its haunches at the foot of the crag, staring unblinkingly up at them.

Valeria shuddered.

'How long do you suppose he'll crouch there?'

Conan kicked the skull on the leaf-strewn shelf.

'That fellow must have climbed up here to escape him, or one like him. He must have died of starvation. There are no bones broken. That thing must be a dragon, such as the black people speak of in their legends. If so, it won't leave here until we're both dead.'

Valeria looked at him blankly, her resentment forgotten. She fought down a surging of panic. She had proved her reckless courage a thousand times in wild battles on sea and land, on the blood-slippery decks of burning war-ships, in the storming of walled cities, and on the trampled sandy beaches where the desperate men of the Red Brotherhood bathed their knives in one another's blood in their fights for leadership. But the prospect now confronting her congealed her blood. A cutlas stroke in the heat of battle was nothing; but to sit idle and helpless on a bare rock until she perished of starvation, besieged by a monstrous survival of an elder age – the thought sent panic throbbing through her brain.

'He must leave to eat and drink,' she said helplessly.

'He won't have to go far to do either,' Conan pointed out. 'He's just gorged on horse-meat, and like a real snake, he can go for a long time without eating or drinking again. But he doesn't sleep after eating, like a real snake, it seems. Anyway, he can't climb this crag.'

Conan spoke imperturbably. He was a barbarian, and the terrible patience of the wilderness and its children was as much a part of him as his lusts and rages. He could endure a situation like this with a coolness impossible to a civilized person.

'Can't we get into the trees and get away, traveling like apes through the branches?' she asked desperately.

He shook his head. 'I thought of that. The branches that touch the crag down there are too light. They'd break with our weight. Besides, I have an idea that devil could tear up any tree around here by its roots.'

'Well, are we going to sit here on our rumps until we starve, like that?' she cried furiously, kicking the skull clattering across the ledge. 'I won't do it! I'll go down there and cut his damned head off –'

Conan had seated himself on a rocky projection at the foot of the spire. He looked up with a glint of admiration at her blazing eyes and tense, quivering figure, but, realizing that she was in just the mood for any madness, he let none of his admiration sound in his voice.

'Sit down,' he grunted, catching her by her wrist and pulling her down on his knee. She was too surprised to resist as he took her sword from her hand and shoved it back in its sheath. 'Sit still and calm down. You'd only break your steel on his scales. He'd gobble you up at one gulp, or smash you like an egg with that spiked tail of his. We'll get out of this jam some way, but we shan't do it by getting chewed up and swallowed.'

She made no reply, nor did she seek to repulse his arm from about her waist. She was frightened, and the sensation was new to Valeria of the Red Brotherhood. So she sat on her companion's – or captor's – knee with a docility that would have amazed Zarallo, who had anathematized her as a she-devil out of hell's seraglio.

Conan played idly with her curly yellow locks, seemingly intent only upon his conquest. Neither the skeleton at his feet nor the monster crouching below disturbed his mind or dulled the edge of his interest.

The girl's restless eyes, roving the leaves below them, discovered splashes of color among the green. It was fruit, large, darkly crimson globes suspended from the boughs of a tree whose broad leaves were a peculiarly rich and vivid green. She became aware of both thirst and hunger, though thirst had not assailed her until she knew she could not descend from the crag to find food and water.

'We need not starve,' she said. 'There is fruit we can reach.'

Conan glanced where she pointed.

'If we ate that we wouldn't need the bite of a dragon,' he grunted. 'That's what the black people of Kush call the Apples of Derketa. Derketa is the Queen of the Dead. Drink a little of the juice, or spill it on your flesh, and you'd be dead before you could tumble to the foot of this crag.'

'Oh!'

She lapsed into dismayed silence. There seemed no way out of their predicament, she reflected gloomily. She saw no way of escape, and Conan seemed to be concerned only with her supple waist and curly tresses. If he was trying to formulate a plan of escape he did not show it.

'If you'll take your hands off me long enough to climb up on that peak,' she said presently, 'you'll see something that will surprize you.'

He cast her a questioning glance, then obeyed with a shrug

of his massive shoulders. Clinging to the spire-like pinnacle, he stared out over the forest roof.

He stood a long moment in silence, posed like a bronze statue on the rock.

'It's a walled city, right enough,' he muttered presently. 'Was that where you were going, when you tried to send me off alone to the coast?'

'I saw it before you came. I knew nothing of it when I left Sukhmet.'

'Who'd have thought to find a city here? I don't believe the Stygians ever penetrated this far. Could black people build a city like that? I see no herds on the plain, no signs of cultivation, or people moving about.'

'How could you hope to see all that, at this distance?' she demanded.

He shrugged his shoulders and dropped down on the shelf.

'Well, the folk of the city can't help us just now. And they might not, if they could. The people of the Black Countries are generally hostile to strangers. Probably stick us full of spears –'

He stopped short and stood silent, as if he had forgotten what he was saying, frowning down at the crimson spheres gleaming among the leaves.

'Spears!' he muttered. 'What a blasted fool I am not to have thought of that before! That shows what a pretty woman does to a man's mind.'

'What are you talking about?' she inquired.

Without answering her question, he descended to the belt of leaves and looked down through them. The great brute squatted below, watching the crag with the frightful patience of the reptile folk. So might one of his breed have glared up at their troglodyte ancestors, treed on a high-flung rock, in the dim dawn ages. Conan cursed him without heat, and began cutting branches, reaching out and severing them as far from the end as he could reach. The agitation of the leaves made the monster restless. He rose from his haunches and lashed his hideous tail, snapping off saplings as if they had been toothpicks. Conan watched him warily from the corner of his eye, and just as Valeria believed the dragon was about to hurl himself up the crag again, the Cimmerian drew back and climbed up to the ledge with the branches he had cut. There were three of these, slender shafts about seven feet long, but not larger than his thumb. He had also cut several strands of tough, thin vine.

'Branches too light for spear-hafts, and creepers no thicker than cords,' he remarked, indicating the foliage about the crag. 'It won't hold our weight – but there's strength in union. That's what the Aquilonian renegades used to tell us Cimmerians when they came into the hills to raise an army to invade their own country. But we always fight by clans and tribes.'

'What the devil has that got to do with those sticks?' she demanded.

'You wait and see.'

Gathering the sticks in a compact bundle, he wedged his poniard hilt between them at one end. Then with the vines he bound them together, and when he had completed his task, he had a spear of no small strength, with a sturdy shaft seven feet in length.

'What good will that do?' she demanded. 'You told me that a blade couldn't pierce his scales –'

'He hasn't got scales all over him,' answered Conan. 'There's more than one way of skinning a panther.'

Moving down to the edge of the leaves, he reached the spear up and carefully thrust the blade through one of the Apples of Derketa, drawing aside to avoid the darkly purple drops that dripped from the pierced fruit. Presently he withdrew the blade and showed her the blue steel stained a dull purplish crimson.

'I don't know whether it will do the job or not,' quoth he. 'There's enough poison there to kill an elephant, but – well, we'll see.'

Valeria was close behind him as he let himself down among the leaves. Cautiously holding the poisoned pike away from him, he thrust his head through the branches and addressed the monster.

'What are you waiting down there for, you misbegotten offspring of questionable parents?' was one of his more printable queries. 'Stick your ugly head up here again, you long-necked brute – or do you want me to come down there and kick you loose from your illegitimate spine?'

There was more of it – some of it couched in eloquence that made Valeria stare, in spite of her profane education among the seafarers. And it had its effect on the monster. Just as the incessant yapping of a dog worries and enrages more constitutionally silent animals, so the clamorous voice of a man rouses fear in some bestial bosoms and insane rage in others. Suddenly and with appalling quickness, the mastodonic brute reared up on its mighty hind legs and elongated its neck and body in a furious effort to reach this vociferous pigmy whose clamor was disturbing the primeval silence of its ancient realm.

But Conan had judged his distance with precision. Some five feet below him the mighty head crashed terribly but futilely through the leaves. And as the monstrous mouth gaped like that of a great snake, Conan drove his spear into the red angle of the jaw-bone hinge. He struck downward with all the strength of both arms, driving the long poniard blade to the hilt in flesh, sinew and bone.

Instantly the jaws clashed convulsively together, severing the triple-pieced shaft and almost precipitating Conan from his perch. He would have fallen but for the girl behind him, who caught his sword-belt in a desperate grasp. He clutched at a rocky projection, and grinned his thanks back at her.

Down on the ground the monster was wallowing like a dog with pepper in its eyes. He shook his head from side to side, pawed at it, and opened his mouth repeatedly to its widest extent. Presently he got a huge front foot on the stump of the shaft and managed to tear the blade out. Then he threw up his head, jaws wide and spouting blood, and glared up at the crag with such concentrated and intelligent fury that Valeria trembled and drew her sword. The scales along his back and flanks turned from rusty brown to a dull lurid red. Most horribly the monster's silence was broken. The sounds that issued from his blood-streaming jaws did not sound like anything that could have been produced by an earthly creation.

With harsh, grating roars, the dragon hurled himself at the crag that was the citadel of his enemies. Again and again his mighty head crashed upward through the branches, snapping vainly on empty air. He hurled his full ponderous weight against the rock until it vibrated from base to crest. And rearing upright he gripped it with his front legs like a man and tried to tear it up by the roots, as if it had been a tree.

This exhibition of primordial fury chilled the blood in Valeria's veins, but Conan was too close to the primitive himself to feel anything but a comprehending interest. To the barbarian, no such gulf existed between himself and other men, and the animals, as existed in the conception of Valeria. The monster below them, to Conan, was merely a form of life differing from himself mainly in physical shape. He attributed to it characteristics similar to his own, and saw in its wrath a counterpart of his rages, in its roars and bellowings merely reptilian equivalents to the curses he had bestowed upon it. Feeling a kinship with all wild things, even dragons, it was impossible for him to experience the sick horror which assailed Valeria at the sight of the brute's ferocity.

He sat watching it tranquilly, and pointed out the various changes that were taking place in its voice and actions.

'The poison's taking hold,' he said with conviction.

'I don't believe it.' To Valeria it seemed preposterous to suppose that anything, however lethal, could have any effect on that mountain of muscle and fury.

'There's pain in his voice,' declared Conan. 'First he was merely angry because of the stinging in his jaw. Now he feels the bite of the poison. Look! He's staggering. He'll be blind in a few more minutes. What did I tell you?'

For suddenly the dragon had lurched about and went crashing off through the bushes.

'Is he running away?' inquired Valeria uneasily.

'He's making for the pool!' Conan sprang up, galvanized into swift activity. 'The poison makes him thirsty. Come on! He'll be blind in a few moments, but he can smell his way back to the foot of the crag, and if our scent's here still, he'll sit there until he dies. And others of his kind may come at his cries. Let's go!'

'Down there?' Valeria was aghast.

'Sure! We'll make for the city! They may cut our heads off there, but it's our only chance. We may run into a thousand more dragons on the way, but it's sure death to stay here. If we wait until he dies, we may have a dozen more to deal with. After me, in a hurry!'

He went down the ramp as swiftly as an ape, pausing only to aid his less agile companion, who, until she saw the Cimmerian climb, had fancied herself the equal of any man in the rigging of a ship or on the sheer face of a cliff.

They descended into the gloom below the branches and slid to the ground silently, though Valeria felt as if the pounding of her heart must surely be heard from far away. A noisy gurgling and lapping beyond the dense thicket indicated that the dragon was drinking at the pool.

'As soon as his belly is full he'll be back,' muttered Conan. 'It may take hours for the poison to kill him – if it does at all.'

Somewhere beyond the forest the sun was sinking to the horizon. The forest was a misty twilight place of black shadows and dim vistas. Conan gripped Valeria's wrist and glided away from the foot of the crag. He made less noise than a breeze blowing among the tree-trunks, but Valeria felt as if her soft boots were betraying their flight to all the forest.

'I don't think he can follow a trail,' muttered Conan. 'But if a wind blew our body-scent to him, he could smell us out.'

'Mitra grant that the wind blow not!' Valeria breathed.

Her face was a pallid oval in the gloom. She gripped her sword in her free hand, but the feel of the shagreen-bound hilt inspired only a feeling of helplessness in her.

They were still some distance from the edge of the forest when they heard a snapping and crashing behind them. Valeria bit her lip to check a cry.

'He's on our trail!' she whispered fiercely.

Conan shook his head.

'He didn't smell us at the rock, and he's blundering about through the forest trying to pick up our scent. Come on! It's the city or nothing now! He could tear down any tree we'd climb. If only the wind stays down –'

They stole on until the trees began to thin out ahead of them. Behind them the forest was a black impenetrable ocean of shadows. The ominous crackling still sounded behind them, as the dragon blundered in his erratic course.

'There's the plain ahead,' breathed Valeria. 'A little more and we'll –'

'Crom!' swore Conan.

'Mitra!' whispered Valeria.

Out of the south a wind had sprung up.

It blew over them directly into the black forest behind them. Instantly a horrible roar shook the woods. The aimless snapping and crackling of the bushes changed to a sustained crashing as the dragon came like a hurricane straight toward the spot from which the scent of his enemies was wafted.

'Run!' snarled Conan, his eyes blazing like those of a trapped wolf. 'It's all we can do!'

Sailor's boots are not made for sprinting, and the life of a pirate does not train one for a runner. Within a hundred yards Valeria was panting and reeling in her gait, and behind them the crashing gave way to a rolling thunder as the monster broke out of the thickets and into the more open ground.

Conan's iron arm about the woman's waist half lifted her; her feet scarcely touched the earth as she was borne along at a speed she could never have attained herself. If he could keep out of the beast's way for a bit, perhaps that betraying wind would shift – but the wind held, and a quick glance over his shoulder showed Conan that the monster was almost upon them, coming like a war-galley in front of a hurricane. He thrust Valeria from him with a force that sent her reeling a dozen feet to fall in a crumpled heap at the foot of the nearest tree, and the Cimmerian wheeled in the path of the thundering titan.

Convinced that his death was upon him, the Cimmerian acted according to his instinct, and hurled himself full at the awful face that was bearing down on him. He leaped, slashing like a wildcat, felt his sword cut deep into the scales that sheathed the mighty snout – and then a terrific impact knocked him rolling and tumbling for fifty feet with all the wind and half the life battered out of him.

How the stunned Cimmerian regained his feet, not even he could have ever told. But the only thought that filled his brain was of the woman lying dazed and helpless almost in the path of the hurtling fiend, and before the breath came whistling back into his gullet he was standing over her with his sword in his hand.

She lay where he had thrown her, but she was struggling to a sitting posture. Neither tearing tusks nor trampling feet had touched her. It had been a shoulder or front leg that struck Conan, and the blind monster rushed on, forgetting the victims whose scent it had been following, in the sudden agony of its death throes. Headlong on its course it thundered until its low-hung head crashed into a gigantic tree in its path. The impact tore the tree up by the roots and must have dashed the brains from the misshapen skull. Tree and monster fell together, and the dazed humans saw the branches and leaves shaken by the convulsions of the creature they covered – and then grow quiet.

Conan lifted Valeria to her feet and together they started away at a reeling run. A few moments later they emerged into the still twilight of the treeless plain.

Conan paused an instant and glanced back at the ebon fastness behind them. Not a leaf stirred, nor a bird chirped. It stood as silent as it must have stood before Man was created.

'Come on,' muttered Conan, taking his companion's hand. 'It's touch and go now. If more dragons come out of the woods after us –'

He did not have to finish the sentence.

The city looked very far away across the plain, farther than it had looked from the crag. Valeria's heart hammered until she felt as if it would strangle her. At every step she expected to hear the crashing of the bushes and see another colossal nightmare bearing down upon them. But nothing disturbed the silence of the thickets.

With the first mile between them and the woods, Valeria breathed more easily. Her buoyant self-confidence began to thaw out again. The sun had set and darkness was gathering over the plain, lightened a little by the stars that made stunted ghosts out of the cactus growths.

'No cattle, no plowed fields,' muttered Conan. 'How do these people live?'

'Perhaps the cattle are in pens for the night,' suggested Valeria, 'and the fields and grazing-pastures are on the other side of the city.'

'Maybe,' he grunted. 'I didn't see any from the crag, though.'

The moon came up behind the city, etching walls and towers

blackly in the yellow glow. Valeria shivered. Black against the moon the strange city had a somber, sinister look.

Perhaps something of the same feeling occurred to Conan, for he stopped, glanced about him, and grunted: 'We stop here. No use coming to their gates in the night. They probably wouldn't let us in. Besides, we need rest, and we don't know how they'll receive us. A few hours' sleep will put us in better shape to fight or run.'

He led the way to a bed of cactus which grew in a circle – a phenomenon common to the southern desert. With his sword he chopped an opening, and motioned Valeria to enter.

'We'll be safe from snakes here, anyhow.'

She glanced fearfully back toward the black line that indicated the forest some six miles away.

'Suppose a dragon comes out of the woods?'

'We'll keep watch,' he answered, though he made no suggestion as to what they would do in such an event. He was staring at the city, a few miles away. Not a light shone from spire or tower. A great black mass of mystery, it reared cryptically against the moonlit sky.

'Lie down and sleep. I'll keep the first watch.'

She hesitated, glancing at him uncertainly, but he sat down cross-legged in the opening, facing toward the plain, his sword across his knees, his back to her. Without further comment she lay down on the sand inside the spiky circle.

'Wake me when the moon is at its zenith,' she directed.

He did not reply nor look toward her. Her last impression, as she sank into slumber, was of his muscular figure, immobile as a statue hewn out of bronze, outlined against the low-hanging stars.

2 By the Blaze of the Fire Jewels

Valeria awoke with a start, to the realization that a gray dawn was stealing over the plain.

She sat up, rubbing her eyes. Conan squatted beside the cactus, cutting off the thick pears and dexterously twitching out the spikes.

'You didn't awake me,' she accused. 'You let me sleep all night!'

'You were tired,' he answered. 'Your posterior must have been sore, too, after that long ride. You pirates aren't used to horseback.'

'What about yourself?' she retorted.

'I was a *kozak* before I was a pirate,' he answered. 'They live in the saddle. I snatch naps like a panther watching beside the trail for a deer to come by. My ears keep watch while my eyes sleep.'

And indeed the giant barbarian seemed as much refreshed as if he had slept the whole night on a golden bed. Having removed the thorns, and peeled off the tough skin, he handed the girl a thick juicy cactus leaf.

'Skin your teeth in that pear. It's food and drink to a desert man. I was a chief of the Zuagirs once – desert men who live by plundering the caravans.'

'Is there anything you haven't been?' inquired the girl, half in derision and half in fascination.

'I've never been king of an Hyborian kingdom,' he grinned, taking an enormous mouthful of cactus. 'But I've dreamed of being even that. I may be too, some day. Why shouldn't I?'

She shook her head in wonder at his calm audacity, and fell to devouring her pear. She found it not unpleasing to the palate, and full of cool and thirst-satisfying juice. Finishing his meal, Conan wiped his hands in the sand, rose, ran his fingers through his thick black mane, hitched at his sword-belt and said:

'Well, let's go. If the people in that city are going to cut our throats they may as well do it now, before the heat of the day begins.'

His grim humor was unconscious, but Valeria reflected that it might be prophetic. She too hitched her sword-belt as she rose. Her terrors of the night were past. The roaring dragons of the distant forest were like a dim dream. There was a swagger in her stride as she moved off beside the Cimmerian. Whatever perils lay ahead of them, their foes would be men. And Valeria of the Red Brotherhood had never seen the face of the man she feared.

Conan glanced down at her as she strode along beside him with her swinging stride that matched his own.

'You walk more like a hillman than a sailor,' he said. 'You must be an Aquilonian. The suns of Darfar never burnt your white skin brown. Many a princess would envy you.'

'I am from Aquilonia,' she replied. His compliments no longer irritated her. His evident admiration pleased her. For another man to have kept her watch while she slept would have angered her; she had always fiercely resented any man's attempting to shield or protect her because of her sex. But she found a secret pleasure in the fact that this man had done so. And he had not taken advantage of her fright and the weakness resulting from it. After all, she reflected, her companion was no common man.

The sun rose behind the city, turning the towers to a sinister crimson.

'Black last night against the moon,' grunted Conan, his eyes clouding with the abysmal superstition of the barbarian. 'Blood-red as a threat of blood against the sun this dawn. I do not like this city.'

But they went on, and as they went Conan pointed out the fact that no road ran to the city from the north.

'No cattle have trampled the plain on this side of the city,' said he. 'No plow-share has touched the earth for years, maybe centuries. But look: once this plain was cultivated.'

Valeria saw the ancient irrigation ditches he indicated, half filled in places, and overgrown with cactus. She frowned with perplexity as her eyes swept over the plain that stretched on all sides of the city to the forest edge, which marched in a vast, dim ring. Vision did not extend beyond that ring.

She looked uneasily at the city. No helmets or spear-heads gleamed on battlements, no trumpets sounded, no challenge rang from the towers. A silence as absolute as that of the forest brooded over the walls and minarets.

The sun was high above the eastern horizon when they stood before the great gate in the northern wall, in the shadow of the lofty rampart. Rust flecked the iron bracings of the mighty bronze portal. Spiderwebs glistened thickly on hinge and sill and bolted panel.

'It hasn't been opened for years!' exclaimed Valeria.

'A dead city,' grunted Conan. 'That's why the ditches were broken and the plain untouched.'

'But who built it? Who dwelt here? Where did they go? Why did they abandon it?'

'Who can say? Maybe an exiled clan of Stygians built it. Maybe not. It doesn't look like Stygian architecture. Maybe the people were wiped out by enemies, or a plague exterminated them.'

'In that case their treasures may still be gathering dust and cobwebs in there,' suggested Valeria, the acquisitive instincts of her profession waking in her; prodded, too, by feminine curiosity. 'Can we open the gate? Let's go in and explore a bit.'

Conan eyed the heavy portal dubiously, but placed his massive shoulder against it and thrust with all the power of his muscular calves and thighs. With a rasping screech of rusty hinges the gate moved ponderously inward, and Conan straightened and drew his sword. Valeria stared over his shoulder, and made a sound indicative of surprise.

They were not looking into an open street or court as one would have expected. The opened gate, or door, gave directly into a long, broad hall which ran away and away until its vista grew indistinct in the distance. It was of heroic proportions, and the floor of a curious red stone, cut in square tiles, that seemed to smolder as if with the reflection of flames. The walls were of a shiny green material.

'Jade, or I'm a Shemite!' swore Conan.

'Not in such quantity!' protested Valeria.

'I've looted enough from the Khitan caravans to know what I'm talking about,' he asserted. 'That's jade!'

The vaulted ceiling was of lapis lazuli, adorned with clusters of great green stones that gleamed with a poisonous radiance.

'Green fire-stones,' growled Conan. 'That's what the people of Punt call them. They're supposed to be the petrified eyes of those prehistoric snakes the ancients called Golden Serpents. They glow like a cat's eyes in the dark. At night this hall would be lighted by them, but it would be a hellishly weird illumination. Let's look around. We might find a cache of jewels.'

'Shut the door,' advised Valeria. 'I'd hate to have to outrun a dragon down this hall.'

Conan grinned, and replied: 'I don't believe the dragons ever leave the forest.'

But he complied, and pointed out the broken bolt on the inner side.

'I thought I heard something snap when I shoved against it. That bolt's freshly broken. Rust has eaten nearly through it. If the people ran away, why should it have been bolted on the inside?'

'They undoubtedly left by another door,' suggested Valeria.

She wondered how many centuries had passed since the light of outer day had filtered into that great hall through the open door. Sunlight was finding its way somehow into the hall, and they quickly saw the source. High up in the vaulted ceiling sky-lights were set in slot-like openings – translucent sheets of some crystalline substance. In the splotches of shadow between them, the green jewels winked like the eyes of angry cats. Beneath their feet the dully lurid floor smoldered with changing hues and colors of flame. It was like treading the floors of hell with evil stars blinking overhead.

Three balustraded galleries ran along on each side of the hall, one above the other.

'A four-storied house,' grunted Conan, 'and this hall extends to the roof. It's long as a street. I seem to see a door at the other end.'

Valeria shrugged her white shoulders.

'Your eyes are better than mine, then, though I'm accounted sharp-eyed among the sea-rovers.'

They turned into an open door at random, and traversed a series of empty chambers, floored like the hall, and with walls of the same green jade, or of marble or ivory or chalcedony, adorned with friezes of bronze, gold or silver. In the ceilings the green fire-gems were set, and their light was as ghostly and illu-sive as Conan had predicted. Under the witch-fire glow the intruders moved like specters.

Some of the chambers lacked this illumination, and their doorways showed black as the mouth of the Pit. These Conan and Valeria avoided, keeping always to the lighted chambers.

Cobwebs hung in the corners, but there was no perceptible accumulation of dust on the floor, or on the tables and seats of marble, jade or carnelian which occupied the chambers. Here and there were rugs of that silk known as Khitan which is practi-cally indestructible. Nowhere did they find any windows, or doors opening into streets or courts. Each door merely opened into another chamber or hall.

'Why don't we come to a street?' grumbled Valeria. 'This

place or whatever we're in must be as big as the king of Turan's seraglio.'

'They must not have perished of plague,' said Conan, meditating upon the mystery of the empty city. 'Otherwise we'd find skeletons. Maybe it became haunted, and everybody got up and left. Maybe –'

'Maybe, hell!' broke in Valeria rudely. 'We'll never know. Look at these friezes. They portray men. What race do they belong to?'

Conan scanned them and shook his head.

'I never saw people exactly like them. But there's the smack of the East about them – Vendhya, maybe, or Kosala.'

'Were you a king in Kosala?' she asked, masking her keen curiosity with derision.

'No. But I was a war-chief of the Afghulis who live in the Himelian mountains above the borders of Vendhya. These people favor the Kosalans. But why should Kosalans be building a city this far to west?'

The figures portrayed were those of slender, olive-skinned men and women, with finely chiseled, exotic features. They wore filmy robes and many delicate jeweled ornaments, and were depicted mostly in attitudes of feasting, dancing or lovemaking.

'Easterners, all right,' grunted Conan, 'but from where I don't know. They must have lived a disgustingly peaceful life, though, or they'd have scenes of wars and fights. Let's go up that stair.'

It was an ivory spiral that wound up from the chamber in which they were standing. They mounted three flights and came into a broad chamber on the fourth floor, which seemed to be the highest tier in the building. Skylights in the ceiling illuminated the room, in which light the fire-gems winked pallidly. Glancing through the doors they saw, except on one side, a series of similarly lighted chambers. This other door opened upon a balustraded gallery that overhung a hall much smaller than the one they had recently explored on the lower floor.

'Hell!' Valeria sat down disgustedly on a jade bench. 'The people who deserted this city must have taken all their treasures with them. I'm tired of wandering through these bare rooms at random.'

'All these upper chambers seem to be lighted,' said Conan. 'I wish we could find a window that overlooked the city. Let's have a look through that door over there.'

'You have a look,' advised Valeria. 'I'm going to sit here and rest my feet.'

Conan disappeared through the door opposite that one opening upon the gallery, and Valeria leaned back with her hands clasped behind her head, and thrust her booted legs out in front of her. These silent rooms and halls with their gleaming green clusters of ornaments and burning crimson floors were beginning to depress her. She wished they could find their way out of the maze into which they had wandered and emerge into a street. She wondered idly what furtive, dark feet had glided over those flaming floors in past centuries, how many deeds of cruelty and mystery those winking ceiling-gems had blazed down upon.

It was a faint noise that brought her out of her reflections. She was on her feet with her sword in her hand before she realized what had disturbed her. Conan had not returned, and she knew it was not he that she had heard.

The sound had come from somewhere beyond the door that opened on to the gallery. Soundlessly in her soft leather boots she glided through it, crept across the balcony and peered down between the heavy balustrades.

A man was stealing along the hall.

The sight of a human being in this supposedly deserted city was a startling shock. Crouching down behind the stone balusters, with every nerve tingling, Valeria glared down at the stealthy figure.

The man in no way resembled the figures depicted on the friezes. He was slightly above middle height, very dark, though not negroid. He was naked but for a scanty silk clout that only partly covered his muscular hips, and a leather girdle, a hand's breadth broad, about his lean waist. His long black hair hung in lank strands about his shoulders, giving him a wild appearance. He was gaunt, but knots and cords of muscles stood out on his arms and legs, without that fleshy padding that presents a pleasing symmetry of contour. He was built with an economy that was almost repellent.

Yet it was not so much his physical appearance as his attitude that impressed the woman who watched him. He slunk along, stooped in a semi-crouch, his head turning from side to side. He grasped a wide-tipped blade in his right hand, and she saw it shake with the intensity of the emotion that gripped him. He was afraid, trembling in the grip of some dire terror. When he turned his head she caught the blaze of wild eyes among the lank strands of black hair.

He did not see her. On tiptoe he glided across the hall and vanished through an open door. A moment later she heard a choking cry, and then silence fell again.

Consumed with curiosity, Valeria glided along the gallery until she came to a door above the one through which the man had passed. It opened into another, smaller gallery that encircled a large chamber.

This chamber was on the third floor, and its ceiling was not so high as that of the hall. It was lighted only by the fire-stones, and their weird green glow left the spaces under the balcony in shadows.

Valeria's eyes widened. The man she had seen was still in the chamber.

He lay face down on a dark crimson carpet in the middle of the room. His body was limp, his arms spread wide. His curved sword lay near him.

She wondered why he should lie there so motionless. Then her eyes narrowed as she stared down at the rug on which he lay. Beneath and about him the fabric showed a slightly different color, a deeper, brighter crimson.

Shivering slightly, she crouched down closer behind the balustrade, intently scanning the shadows under the overhanging gallery. They gave up no secret.

Suddenly another figure entered the grim drama. He was a man similar to the first, and he came in by a door opposite that which gave upon the hall.

His eyes glared at the sight of the man on the floor, and he spoke something in a staccato voice that sounded like 'Chicmec!' The other did not move.

The man stepped quickly across the floor, bent, gripped the fallen man's shoulder and turned him over. A choking cry escaped him as the head fell back limply, disclosing a throat that had been severed from ear to ear.

The man let the corpse fall back upon the blood-stained carpet, and sprang to his feet, shaking like a wind-blown leaf. His face was an ashy mask of fear. But with one knee flexed for flight, he froze suddenly, became as immobile as an image, staring across the chamber with dilated eyes.

In the shadows beneath the balcony a ghostly light began to glow and grow, a light that was not part of the fire-stone gleam. Valeria felt her hair stir as she watched it; for, dimly visible in the throbbing radiance, there floated a human skull, and it was from this skull – human yet appallingly misshapen – that the spectral light seemed to emanate. It hung there like a disembodied head, conjured out of night and the shadows, growing more and more distinct; human, and yet not human as she knew humanity.

The man stood motionless, an embodiment of paralyzed horror, staring fixedly at the apparition. The thing moved out from the wall and a grotesque shadow moved with it. Slowly the shadow became visible as a man-like figure whose naked torso and limbs shone whitely, with the hue of bleached bones. The bare skull on its shoulders grinned eyelessly, in the midst of its unholy nimbus, and the man confronting it seemed unable to take his eyes from it. He stood still, his sword dangling from nerveless fingers, on his face the expression of a man bound by the spells of a mesmerist.

Valeria realized that it was not fear alone that paralyzed him. Some hellish quality of that throbbing glow had robbed him of his power to think and act. She herself, safely above the scene, felt the subtle impact of a nameless emanation that was a threat to sanity.

The horror swept toward its victim and he moved at last, but only to drop his sword and sink to his knees, covering his eyes with his hands. Dumbly he awaited the stroke of the blade that now gleamed in the apparition's hand as it reared above him like Death triumphant over mankind.

Valeria acted according to the first impulse of her wayward nature. With one tigerish movement she was over the balustrade and dropping to the floor behind the awful shape. It wheeled at the thud of her soft boots on the floor, but even as it turned, her keen blade lashed down, and a fierce exultation swept her as she felt the edge cleave solid flesh and mortal bone.

The apparition cried out gurglingly and went down, severed through shoulder, breast-bone and spine, and as it fell the burning skull rolled clear, revealing a lank mop of black hair and a dark face twisted in the convulsions of death. Beneath the horrific masquerade there was a human being, a man similar to the one kneeling supinely on the floor.

The latter looked up at the sound of the blow and the cry, and now he glared in wild-eyed amazement at the white-skinned woman who stood over the corpse with a dripping sword in her hand.

He staggered up, yammering as if the sight had almost

unseated his reason. She was amazed to realize that she understood him. He was gibbering in the Stygian tongue, though in a
dialect unfamiliar to her.

'Who are you? Whence come you? What do you in Xuchotl?'
Then rushing on, without waiting for her to reply: 'But you are
a friend – goddess or devil, it makes no difference! You have
slain the Burning Skull! It was but a man beneath it, after all!
We deemed it a demon *they* conjured up out of the catacombs!
Listen!'

He stopped short in his ravings and stiffened, straining his
ears with painful intensity. The girl heard nothing.

'We must hasten!' he whispered. '*They* are west of the Great
Hall! They may be all around us here! They may be creeping
upon us even now!'

He seized her wrist in a convulsive grasp she found hard to
break.

'Whom do you mean by "they"?' she demanded.

He stared at her uncomprehendingly for an instant, as if he
found her ignorance hard to understand.

'They?' he stammered vaguely. 'Why – why, the people of
Xotalanc! The clan of the man you slew. They who dwell by the
eastern gate.'

'You mean to say this city is inhabited?' she exclaimed.

'Aye! Aye!' He was writhing in the impatience of apprehension. 'Come away! Come quick! We must return to Tecuhltli!'

'Where is that?' she demanded.

'The quarter by the western gate!' He had her wrist again
and was pulling her toward the door through which he had first
come. Great beads of perspiration dripped from his dark forehead, and his eyes blazed with terror.

'Wait a minute!' she growled, flinging off his hand. 'Keep
your hands off me, or I'll split your skull. What's all this about?
Who are you? Where would you take me?'

He took a firm grip on himself, casting glances to all sides, and began speaking so fast his words tripped over each other.

'My name is Techotl. I am of Tecuhltli. I and this man who lies with his throat cut came into the Halls of Science to try and ambush some of the Xotalancas. But we became separated and I returned here to find him with his gullet slit. The Burning Skull did it, I know, just as he would have slain me had you not killed him. But perhaps he was not alone. Others may be stealing from Xotalanc! The gods themselves blench at the fate of those they take alive!'

At the thought he shook as with an ague and his dark skin grew ashy. Valeria frowned puzzledly at him. She sensed intelligence behind this rigmarole, but it was meaningless to her.

She turned toward the skull, which still glowed and pulsed on the floor, and was reaching a booted toe tentatively toward it, when the man who called himself Techotl sprang forward with a cry.

'Do not touch it! Do not even look at it! Madness and death lurk in it. The wizards of Xotalanc understand its secret – they found it in the catacombs, where lie the bones of terrible kings who ruled in Xuchotl in the black centuries of the past. To gaze upon it freezes the blood and withers the brain of a man who understands not its mystery. To touch it causes madness and destruction.'

She scowled at him uncertainly. He was not a reassuring figure, with his lean, muscle-knotted frame, and snaky locks. In his eyes, behind the glow of terror, lurked a weird light she had never seen in the eyes of a man wholly sane. Yet he seemed sincere in his protestations.

'Come!' he begged, reaching for her hand, and then recoiling as he remembered her warning. 'You are a stranger. How you came here I do not know, but if you were a goddess or a demon, come to aid Tecuhltli, you would know all the things you have asked me. You must be from beyond the great forest, whence our ancestors came. But you are our friend, or you would not have slain my enemy. Come quickly, before the Xotalancas find us and slay us!'

From his repellent, impassioned face she glanced to the sinister skull, smoldering and glowing on the floor near the dead man. It was like a skull seen in a dream, undeniably human, yet with disturbing distortions and malformations of contour and outline. In life the wearer of that skull must have presented an alien and monstrous aspect. Life? It seemed to possess some sort of life of its own. Its jaws yawned at her and snapped together. Its radiance grew brighter, more vivid, yet the impression of nightmare grew too; it was a dream; all life was a dream – it was Techotl's urgent voice which snapped Valeria back from the dim gulfs whither she was drifting.

'Do not look at the skull! Do not look at the skull!' It was a far cry from across unreckoned voids.

Valeria shook herself like a lion shaking his mane. Her vision cleared. Techotl was chattering: 'In life it housed the awful brain of a king of magicians! It holds still the life and fire of magic drawn from outer spaces!'

With a curse Valeria leaped, lithe as a panther, and the skull crashed to flaming bits under her swinging sword. Somewhere in the room, or in the void, or in the dim reaches of her consciousness, an inhuman voice cried out in pain and rage.

Techotl's hand was plucking at her arm and he was gibbering: 'You have broken it! You have destroyed it! Not all the black arts of Xotalanc can rebuild it! Come away! Come away quickly, now!'

'But I can't go,' she protested. 'I have a friend somewhere near by –'

The flare of his eyes cut her short as he stared past her with an expression grown ghastly. She wheeled just as four men rushed through as many doors, converging on the pair in the center of the chamber.

They were like the others she had seen, the same knotted

muscles bulging on otherwise gaunt limbs, the same lank blue-black hair, the same mad glare in their wide eyes. They were armed and clad like Techotl, but on the breast of each was painted a white skull.

There were no challenges or war-cries. Like blood-mad tigers the men of Xotalanc sprang at the throats of their enemies. Techotl met them with the fury of desperation, ducked the swipe of a wide-headed blade, and grappled with the wielder, and bore him to the floor where they rolled and wrestled in murderous silence.

The other three swarmed on Valeria, their weird eyes red as the eyes of mad dogs.

She killed the first who came within reach before he could strike a blow, her long straight blade splitting his skull even as his own sword lifted for a stroke. She side-stepped a thrust, even as she parried a slash. Her eyes danced and her lips smiled without mercy. Again she was Valeria of the Red Brotherhood, and the hum of her steel was like a bridal song in her ears.

Her sword darted past a blade that sought to parry, and sheathed six inches of its point in a leather-guarded midriff. The man gasped agonizedly and went to his knees, but his tall mate lunged in, in ferocious silence, raining blow on blow so furiously that Valeria had no opportunity to counter. She stepped back coolly, parrying the strokes and watching for her chance to thrust home. He could not long keep up that flailing whirlwind. His arm would tire, his wind would fail; he would weaken, falter, and then her blade would slide smoothly into his heart. A sidelong glance showed her Techotl kneeling on the breast of his antagonist and striving to break the other's hold on his wrist and to drive home a dagger.

Sweat beaded the forehead of the man facing her, and his eyes were like burning coals. Smite as he would, he could not break past nor beat down her guard. His breath came in gusty gulps, his blows began to fall erratically. She stepped back to draw him out – and felt her thighs locked in an iron grip. She had forgotten the wounded man on the floor.

Crouching on his knees, he held her with both arms locked about her legs, and his mate croaked in triumph and began working his way around to come at her from the left side. Valeria wrenched and tore savagely, but in vain. She could free herself of this clinging menace with a downward flick of her sword, but in that instant the curved blade of the tall warrior would crash through her skull. The wounded man began to worry at her bare thigh with his teeth like a wild beast.

She reached down with her left hand and gripped his long hair, forcing his head back so that his white teeth and rolling eyes gleamed up at her. The tall Xotalanc cried out fiercely and leaped in, smiting with all the fury of his arm. Awkwardly she parried the stroke, and it beat the flat of her blade down on her head so that she saw sparks flash before her eyes, and staggered. Up went the sword again, with a low, beast-like cry of triumph – and then a giant form loomed behind the Xotalanc and steel flashed like a jet of blue lightning. The cry of the warrior broke short and he went down like an ox beneath the pole-ax, his brains gushing from his skull that had been split to the throat.

'Conan!' gasped Valeria. In a gust of passion she turned on the Xotalanc whose long hair she still gripped in her left hand. 'Dog of hell!' Her blade swished as it cut the air in an upswinging arc with a blur in the middle, and the headless body slumped down, spurting blood. She hurled the severed head across the room.

'What the devil's going on here?' Conan bestrode the corpse of the man he had killed, broadsword in hand, glaring about him in amazement.

Techotl was rising from the twitching figure of the last Xotalanc, shaking red drops from his dagger. He was bleeding from the stab deep in the thigh. He stared at Conan with dilated eyes.

'What is all this?' Conan demanded again, not yet recovered from the stunning surprize of finding Valeria engaged in a savage battle with these fantastic figures in a city he had thought empty and uninhabited. Returning from an aimless exploration of the upper chambers to find Valeria missing from the room where he had left her, he had followed the sounds of strife that burst on his dumfounded ears.

'Five dead dogs!' exclaimed Techotl, his flaming eyes reflecting a ghastly exultation. 'Five slain! Five crimson nails for the black pillar! The gods of blood be thanked!'

He lifted quivering hands on high, and then, with the face of a fiend, he spat on the corpses and stamped on their faces, dancing in his ghoulish glee. His recent allies eyed him in amazement, and Conan asked, in the Aquilonian tongue: 'Who is this madman?'

Valeria shrugged her shoulders.

'He says his name's Techotl. From his babblings I gather that his people live at one end of this crazy city, and these others at the other end. Maybe we'd better go with him. He seems friendly, and it's easy to see that the other clan isn't.'

Techotl had ceased his dancing and was listening again, his head tilted sidewise, dog-like, triumph struggling with fear in his repellent countenance.

'Come away, now!' he whispered. 'We have done enough! Five dead dogs! My people will welcome you! They will honor you! But come! It is far to Tecuhltli. At any moment the Xotalancs may come on us in numbers too great even for your swords.'

'Lead the way,' grunted Conan.

Techotl instantly mounted a stair leading up to the gallery, beckoning them to follow him, which they did, moving rapidly to keep on his heels. Having reached the gallery, he plunged into a door that opened toward the west, and hurried through chamber after chamber, each lighted by skylights or green fire-jewels.

'What sort of a place can this be?' muttered Valeria under her breath.

'Crom knows!' answered Conan. 'I've seen *his* kind before, though. They live on the shores of Lake Zuad, near the border of Kush. They're a sort of mongrel Stygians, mixed with another race that wandered into Stygia from the east some centuries ago and were absorbed by them. They're called Tlazitlans. I'm willing to bet it wasn't they who built this city, though.'

Techotl's fear did not seem to diminish as they drew away from the chamber where the dead men lay. He kept twisting his head on his shoulder to listen for sounds of pursuit, and stared with burning intensity into every doorway they passed.

Valeria shivered in spite of herself. She feared no man. But the weird floor beneath her feet, the uncanny jewels over her head, dividing the lurking shadows among them, the stealth and terror of their guide, impressed her with a nameless apprehension, a sensation of lurking, inhuman peril.

'They may be between us and Tecuhltli!' he whispered once. 'We must beware lest they be lying in wait!'

'Why don't we get out of this infernal palace, and take to the streets?' demanded Valeria.

'There are no streets in Xuchotl,' he answered. 'No squares nor open courts. The whole city is built like one giant palace under one great roof. The nearest approach to a street is the Great Hall which traverses the city from the north gate to the south gate. The only doors opening into the outer world are the city gates, through which no living man has passed for fifty years.'

'How long have you dwelt here?' asked Conan.

'I was born in the castle of Tecuhltli thirty-five years ago. I have never set foot outside the city. For the love of the gods, let us go silently! These halls may be full of lurking devils. Olmec shall tell you all when we reach Tecuhltli.'

So in silence they glided on with the green fire-stones blinking overhead and the flaming floors smoldering under their feet, and it seemed to Valeria as if they fled through hell, guided by a dark-faced, lank-haired goblin.

Yet it was Conan who halted them as they were crossing an unusually wide chamber. His wilderness-bred ears were keener even than the ears of Techotl, whetted though these were by a lifetime of warfare in those silent corridors.

'You think some of your enemies may be ahead of us, lying in ambush?'

'They prowl through these rooms at all hours,' answered Techotl, 'as do we. The halls and chambers between Tecuhltli and Xotalanc are a disputed region, owned by no man. We call it the Halls of Silence. Why do you ask?'

'Because men are in the chambers ahead of us,' answered Conan. 'I heard steel clink against stone.'

Again a shaking seized Techotl, and he clenched his teeth to keep them from chattering.

'Perhaps they are your friends,' suggested Valeria.

'We dare not chance it,' he panted, and moved with frenzied activity. He turned aside and glided through a doorway on the left which led into a chamber from which an ivory staircase wound down into darkness.

'This leads to an unlighted corridor below us!' he hissed, great beads of perspiration standing out on his brow. 'They may be lurking there, too. It may all be a trick to draw us into it. But we must take the chance that they have laid their ambush in the rooms above. Come swiftly, now!'

Softly as phantoms they descended the stair and came to the mouth of a corridor black as night. They crouched there for a moment, listening, and then melted into it. As they moved along, Valeria's flesh crawled between her shoulders in momentary expectation of a sword-thrust in the dark. But for Conan's iron fingers gripping her arm she had no physical cognizance of her companions. Neither made as much noise as a cat would have made. The darkness was absolute. One hand, outstretched, touched a wall, and occasionally she felt a door under her fingers. The hallway seemed interminable.

Suddenly they were galvanized by a sound behind them. Valeria's flesh crawled anew, for she recognized it as the soft opening of a door. Men had come into the corridor behind them. Even with the thought she stumbled over something that felt like a human skull. It rolled across the floor with an appalling clatter.

'Run!' yelped Techotl, a note of hysteria in his voice, and was away down the corridor like a flying ghost.

Again Valeria felt Conan's hand bearing her up and sweeping her along as they raced after their guide. Conan could see in the dark no better than she, but he possessed a sort of instinct that made his course unerring. Without his support and guidance she would have fallen or stumbled against the wall. Down the corridor they sped, while the swift patter of flying feet drew closer and closer, and then suddenly Techotl panted: 'Here is the stair! After me, quick! Oh, quick!'

His hand came out of the dark and caught Valeria's wrist as she stumbled blindly on the steps. She felt herself half dragged, half lifted up the winding stair, while Conan released her and turned on the steps, his ears and instincts telling him their foes were hard at their backs. *And the sounds were not all those of human feet.*

Something came writhing up the steps, something that slithered and rustled and brought a chill in the air with it. Conan lashed down with his great sword and felt the blade shear through something that might have been flesh and bone, and cut deep into the stair beneath. Something touched his foot that chilled like the touch of frost, and then the darkness beneath him was disturbed by a frightful thrashing and lashing, and a man cried out in agony.

The next moment Conan was racing up the winding staircase, and through a door that stood open at the head.

Valeria and Techotl were already through, and Techotl slammed the door and shot a bolt across it – the first Conan had seen since they left the outer gate.

Then he turned and ran across the well-lighted chamber into which they had come, and as they passed through the farther door, Conan glanced back and saw the door groaning and straining under heavy pressure violently applied from the other side.

Though Techotl did not abate either his speed or his caution, he seemed more confident now. He had the air of a man who has come into familiar territory, within call of friends.

But Conan renewed his terror by asking: 'What was that thing that I fought on the stair?'

'The men of Xotalanc,' answered Techotl, without looking back. 'I told you the halls were full of them.'

'This wasn't a man,' grunted Conan. 'It was something that crawled, and it was as cold as ice to the touch. I think I cut it asunder. It fell back on the men who were following us, and must have killed one of them in its death throes.'

Techotl's head jerked back, his face ashy again. Convulsively he quickened his pace.

'It was the Crawler! A monster *they* have brought out of the catacombs to aid them! What it is, we do not know, but we have found our people hideously slain by it. In Set's name, hasten! If they put it on our trail, it will follow us to the very doors of Tecuhltli!'

'I doubt it,' grunted Conan. 'That was a shrewd cut I dealt it on the stair.'

'Hasten! Hasten!' groaned Techotl.

They ran through a series of green-lit chambers, traversed a broad hall, and halted before a giant bronze door.

Techotl said: 'This is Tecuhltli!'

3   The People of the Feud

Techotl smote on the bronze door with his clenched hand, and then turned sidewise, so that he could watch back along the hall.

'Men have been smitten down before this door, when they thought they were safe,' he said.

'Why don't they open the door?' asked Conan.

'They are looking at us through the Eye,' answered Techotl. 'They are puzzled at the sight of you.' He lifted his voice and called: 'Open the door, Xecelan! It is I, Techotl, with friends from the great world beyond the forest! – They will open,' he assured his allies.

'They'd better do it in a hurry, then,' said Conan grimly. 'I hear something crawling along the floor beyond the hall.'

Techotl went ashy again and attacked the door with his fists, screaming: 'Open, you fools, open! The Crawler is at our heels!'

Even as he beat and shouted, the great bronze door swung noiselessly back, revealing a heavy chain across the entrance, over which spearheads bristled and fierce countenances regarded them intently for an instant. Then the chain was dropped and Techotl grasped the arms of his friends in a nervous frenzy and fairly dragged them over the threshold. A glance over his shoulder just as the door was closing showed Conan the long dim vista of the hall, and dimly framed at the other end an ophidian shape that writhed slowly and painfully into view, flowing in a dull-hued length from a chamber door, its hideous blood-stained head wagging drunkenly. Then the closing door shut off the view.

Inside the square chamber into which they had come heavy bolts were drawn across the door, and the chain locked into place. The door was made to stand the battering of a siege. Four men stood on guard, of the same lank-haired, dark-skinned breed as Techotl, with spears in their hands and swords at their hips. In the wall near the door there was a complicated contrivance of mirrors which Conan guessed was the Eye Techotl had mentioned, so arranged that a narrow, crystal-paned slot in the wall could be looked through from within without being discernible from without. The four guardsmen stared at the strangers with wonder, but asked no question, nor did Techotl vouchsafe any information. He moved with easy confidence now, as if he had shed his cloak of indecision and fear the instant he crossed the threshold.

'Come!' he urged his new-found friends, but Conan glanced toward the door.

'What about those fellows who were following us? Won't they try to storm that door?'

Techotl shook his head.

'They know they cannot break down the Door of the Eagle. They will flee back to Xotalanc, with their crawling fiend. Come! I will take you to the rulers of Tecuhltli.'

One of the four guards opened the door opposite the one by which they had entered, and they passed through into a hallway which, like most of the rooms on that level, was lighted by both the slot-like skylights and the clusters of winking fire-gems. But unlike the other rooms they had traversed, this hall showed evidences of occupation. Velvet tapestries adorned the glossy jade walls, rich rugs were on the crimson floors, and the ivory seats, benches and divans were littered with satin cushions.

The hall ended in an ornate door, before which stood no guard. Without ceremony Techotl thrust the door open and ushered his friends into a broad chamber, where some thirty dark-skinned men and women lounging on satin-covered couches sprang up with exclamations of amazement.

The men, all except one, were of the same type as Techotl, and the women were equally dark and strange-eyed, though not unbeautiful in a weird dark way. They wore sandals, golden breast-plates, and scanty silk skirts supported by gem-crusted girdles, and their black manes, cut square at their naked shoulders, were bound with silver circlets.

On a wide ivory seat on a jade dais sat a man and a woman who differed subtly from the others. He was a giant, with an enormous sweep of breast and the shoulders of a bull. Unlike the others, he was bearded, with a thick, blue-black beard which fell almost to his broad girdle. He wore a robe of purple silk which reflected changing sheens of color with his every movement, and one wide sleeve, drawn back to his elbow, revealed a forearm massive with corded muscles. The band which confined his blue-black locks was set with glittering jewels.

The woman beside him sprang to her feet with a startled exclamation as the strangers entered, and her eyes, passing over Conan, fixed themselves with burning intensity on Valeria. She was tall and lithe, by far the most beautiful woman in the room. She was clad more scantily even than the others; for instead of a skirt she wore merely a broad strip of gilt-worked purple cloth fastened to the middle of her girdle which fell below her knees. Another strip at the back of her girdle completed that part of her costume, which she wore with a cynical indifference. Her breast-plates and the circlet about her temples were adorned with gems. In her eyes alone of all the dark-skinned people there lurked no brooding gleam of madness. She spoke no word after her first exclamation; she stood tensely, her hands clenched, staring at Valeria.

The man on the ivory seat had not risen.

'Prince Olmec,' spoke Techotl, bowing low, with arms outspread and the palms of his hands turned upward, 'I bring allies from the world beyond the forest. In the Chamber of Tezcoti the Burning Skull slew Chicmec, my companion –'

'The Burning Skull!' It was a shuddering whisper of fear from the people of Tecuhltli.

'Aye! Then came I, and found Chicmec lying with his throat cut. Before I could flee, the Burning Skull came upon me, and when I looked upon it my blood became as ice and the marrow of my bones melted. I could neither fight nor run. I could only await the stroke. Then came this white-skinned woman and struck him down with her sword; and lo, it was only a dog of Xotalanc with white paint upon his skin and the living skull of an ancient wizard upon his head! Now that skull lies in many pieces, and the dog who wore it is a dead man!'

An indescribably fierce exultation edged the last sentence, and was echoed in the low, savage exclamations from the crowding listeners.

'But wait!' exclaimed Techotl. 'There is more! While I talked with the woman, four Xotalancas came upon us! One I slew – there is the stab in my thigh to prove how desperate was the fight. Two the woman killed. But we were hard pressed when this man came into the fray and split the skull of the fourth! Aye! Five crimson nails there are to be driven into the pillar of vengeance!'

He pointed at a black column of ebony which stood behind the dais. Hundreds of red dots scarred its polished surface – the bright scarlet heads of heavy copper nails driven into the black wood.

'Five red nails for five Xotalanca lives!' exulted Techotl, and the horrible exultation in the faces of the listeners made them inhuman.

'Who are these people?' asked Olmec, and his voice was like the low, deep rumble of a distant bull. None of the people of Xuchotl spoke loudly. It was as if they had absorbed into their souls the silence of the empty halls and deserted chambers.

'I am Conan, a Cimmerian,' answered the barbarian briefly. 'This woman is Valeria of the Red Brotherhood, an Aquilonian pirate. We are deserters from an army on the Darfar border, far to the north, and are trying to reach the coast.'

The woman on the dais spoke loudly, her words tripping in her haste.

'You can never reach the coast! There is no escape from Xuchotl! You will spend the rest of your lives in this city!'

'What do you mean?' growled Conan, clapping his hand to his hilt and stepping about so as to face both the dais and the rest of the room. 'Are you telling us we're prisoners?'

'She did not mean that,' interposed Olmec. 'We are your friends. We would not restrain you against your will. But I fear other circumstances will make it impossible for you to leave Xuchotl.'

His eyes flickered to Valeria, and he lowered them quickly.

'This woman is Tascela,' he said. 'She is a princess of Tecuhltli. But let food and drink be brought our guests. Doubtless they are hungry, and weary from their long travels.'

He indicated an ivory table, and after an exchange of glances, the adventurers seated themselves. The Cimmerian was suspicious. His fierce blue eyes roved about the chamber, and he kept his sword close to his hand. But an invitation to eat and drink never found him backward. His eyes kept wandering to Tascela, but the princess had eyes only for his white-skinned companion.

Techotl, who had bound a strip of silk about his wounded thigh, placed himself at the table to attend to the wants of his friends, seeming to consider it a privilege and honor to see after their needs. He inspected the food and drink the others brought in gold vessels and dishes, and tasted each before he placed it before his guests. While they ate, Olmec sat in silence on his ivory seat, watching them from under his broad black brows. Tascela sat beside him, chin cupped in her hands and her elbows resting on her knees. Her dark, enigmatic eyes, burning with a mysterious light, never left Valeria's supple figure. Behind her seat a sullen handsome girl waved an ostrich-plume fan with a slow rhythm.

The food was fruit of an exotic kind unfamiliar to the wanderers, but very palatable, and the drink was a light crimson wine that carried a heady tang.

'You have come from afar,' said Olmec at last. 'I have read the books of our fathers. Aquilonia lies beyond the lands of the Stygians and the Shemites, beyond Argos and Zingara; and Cimmeria lies beyond Aquilonia.'

'We have each a roving foot,' answered Conan carelessly.

'How you won through the forest is a wonder to me,' quoth Olmec. 'In bygone days a thousand fighting-men scarcely were able to carve a road through its perils.'

'We encountered a bench-legged monstrosity about the size of a mastodon,' said Conan casually, holding out his wine goblet which Techotl filled with evident pleasure. 'But when we'd killed it we had no further trouble.'

The wine vessel slipped from Techotl's hand to crash on the floor. His dusky skin went ashy. Olmec started to his feet, an image of stunned amazement, and a low gasp of awe or terror breathed up from the others. Some slipped to their knees as if their legs would not support them. Only Tascela seemed not to have heard. Conan glared about him bewilderedly.

'What's the matter? What are you gaping about?'

'You – you slew the dragon-god?'

'God? I killed a dragon. Why not? It was trying to gobble us up.'

'But dragons are immortal!' exclaimed Olmec. 'They slay each other, but no man ever killed a dragon! The thousand fighting-men of our ancestors who fought their way to Xuchotl could not prevail against them! Their swords broke like twigs against their scales!'

'If your ancestors had thought to dip their spears in the poisonous juice of Derketa's Apples,' quoth Conan, with his mouth full, 'and jab them in the eyes or mouth or somewhere like that, they'd have seen that dragons are not more immortal than any other chunk of beef. The carcass lies at the edge of the trees, just within the forest. If you don't believe me, go and look for yourself.'

Olmec shook his head, not in disbelief but in wonder.

'It was because of the dragons that our ancestors took refuge in Xuchotl,' said he. 'They dared not pass through the plain and plunge into the forest beyond. Scores of them were seized and devoured by the monsters before they could reach the city.'

'Then your ancestors didn't build Xuchotl?' asked Valeria.

'It was ancient when they first came into the land. How long it had stood here, not even its degenerate inhabitants knew.'

'Your people came from Lake Zuad?' questioned Conan.

'Aye. More than half a century ago a tribe of the Tlazitlans rebelled against the Stygian king, and, being defeated in battle, fled southward. For many weeks they wandered over grasslands, desert and hills, and at last they came into the great forest, a thousand fighting-men with their women and children.

'It was in the forest that the dragons fell upon them, and tore many to pieces; so the people fled in a frenzy of fear before them, and at last came into the plain and saw the city of Xuchotl in the midst of it.

'They camped before the city, not daring to leave the plain, for the night was made hideous with the noise of the battling monsters throughout the forest. They made war incessantly upon one another. Yet they came not into the plain.

'The people of the city shut their gates and shot arrows at our people from the walls. The Tlazitlans were imprisoned on the plain, as if the ring of the forest had been a great wall; for to venture into the woods would have been madness.

'That night there came secretly to their camp a slave from the city, one of their own blood, who with a band of exploring soldiers had wandered into the forest long before, when he was a young man. The dragons had devoured all his companions, but he had been taken into the city to dwell in servitude. His name was Tolkemec.' A flame lighted the dark eyes at mention of the name, and some of the people muttered obscenely and spat. 'He promised to open the gates to the warriors. He asked only that all captives taken be delivered into his hands.

'At dawn he opened the gates. The warriors swarmed in and the halls of Xuchotl ran red. Only a few hundred folk dwelt there, decaying remnants of a once great race. Tolkemec said they came from the east, long ago, from Old Kosala, when the ancestors of those who now dwell in Kosala came up from the south and drove forth the original inhabitants of the land. They wandered far westward and finally found this forest-girdled plain, inhabited then by a tribe of black people.

'These they enslaved and set to building a city. From the hills to the east they brought jade and marble and lapis lazuli, and gold, silver and copper. Herds of elephants provided them with ivory. When their city was completed, they slew all the black slaves. And their magicians made a terrible magic to guard the city; for by their necromantic arts they re-created the dragons which had once dwelt in this lost land, and whose monstrous bones they found in the forest. Those bones they clothed in flesh and life, and the living beasts walked the earth as they walked it when Time was young. But the wizards wove a spell that kept them in the forest and they came not into the plain.

'So for many centuries the people of Xuchotl dwelt in their city, cultivating the fertile plain, until their wise men learned how to grow fruit within the city – fruit which is not planted in soil, but obtains its nourishment out of the air – and then they let the irrigation ditches run dry, and dwelt more and more in luxurious sloth, until decay seized them. They were a dying race when our ancestors broke through the forest and came into the plain. Their wizards had died, and the people had forgot their ancient necromancy. They could fight neither by sorcery nor the sword.

'Well, our fathers slew the people of Xuchotl, all except a

hundred which were given living into the hands of Tolkemec, who had been their slave; and for many days and nights the halls re-echoed to their screams under the agony of his tortures.

'So the Tlazitlans dwelt here, for a while in peace, ruled by the brothers Tecuhltli and Xotalanc, and by Tolkemec. Tolkemec took a girl of the tribe to wife, and because he had opened the gates, and because he knew many of the arts of the Xuchotlans, he shared the rule of the tribe with the brothers who had led the rebellion and the flight.

'For a few years, then, they dwelt at peace within the city, doing little but eating, drinking and making love, and raising children. There was no necessity to till the plain, for Tolkemec taught them how to cultivate the air-devouring fruits. Besides, the slaying of the Xuchotlans broke the spell that held the dragons in the forest, and they came nightly and bellowed about the gates of the city. The plain ran red with the blood of their eternal warfare, and it was then that –' He bit his tongue in the midst of the sentence, then presently continued, but Valeria and Conan felt that he had checked an admission he had considered unwise.

'Five years they dwelt in peace. Then' – Olmec's eyes rested briefly on the silent woman at his side – 'Xotalanc took a woman to wife, a woman whom both Tecuhltli and old Tolkemec desired. In his madness, Tecuhltli stole her from her husband. Aye, she went willingly enough. Tolkemec, to spite Xotalanc, aided Tecuhltli. Xotalanc demanded that she be given back to him, and the council of the tribe decided that the matter should be left to the woman. She chose to remain with Tecuhltli. In wrath Xotalanc sought to take her back by force, and the retainers of the brothers came to blows in the Great Hall.

'There was much bitterness. Blood was shed on both sides. The quarrel became a feud, the feud an open war. From the welter three factions emerged – Tecuhltli, Xotalanc, and Tolkemec. Already, in the days of peace, they had divided the city between them. Tecuhltli dwelt in the western quarter of the city, Xotalanc in the eastern, and Tolkemec with his family by the southern gate.

'Anger and resentment and jealousy blossomed into bloodshed and rape and murder. Once the sword was drawn there was no turning back; for blood called for blood, and vengeance followed swift on the heels of atrocity. Tecuhltli fought with Xotalanc, and Tolkemec aided first one and then the other, betraying each faction as it fitted his purposes. Tecuhltli and his people withdrew into the quarter of the western gate, where we now sit. Xuchotl is built in the shape of an oval. Tecuhltli, which took its name from its prince, occupies the western end of the oval. The people blocked up all doors connecting the quarter with the rest of the city, except one on each floor, which could be defended easily. They went into the pits below the city and built a wall cutting off the western end of the catacombs, where lie the bodies of the ancient Xuchotlans, and of those Tlazitlans slain in the feud. They dwelt as in a besieged castle, making sorties and forays on their enemies.

'The people of Xotalanc likewise fortified the eastern quarter of the city, and Tolkemec did likewise with the quarter by the southern gate. The central part of the city was left bare and uninhabited. Those empty halls and chambers became a battleground, and a region of brooding terror.

'Tolkemec warred on both clans. He was a fiend in the form of a human, worse than Xotalanc. He knew many secrets of the city he never told the others. From the crypts of the catacombs he plundered the dead of their grisly secrets – secrets of ancient kings and wizards, long forgotten by the degenerate Xuchotlans our ancestors slew. But all his magic did not aid him the night we of Tecuhltli stormed his castle and butchered all his people. Tolkemec we tortured for many days.'

His voice sank to a caressing slur, and a far-away look grew in his eyes, as if he looked back over the years to a scene which caused him intense pleasure.

'Aye, we kept the life in him until he screamed for death as for a bride. At last we took him living from the torture chamber and cast him into a dungeon for the rats to gnaw as he died. From that dungeon, somehow, he managed to escape, and dragged himself into the catacombs. There without doubt he died, for the only way out of the catacombs beneath Tecuhltli is through Tecuhltli, and he never emerged by that way. His bones were never found, and the superstitious among our people swear that his ghost haunts the crypts to this day, wailing among the bones of the dead. Twelve years ago we butchered the people of Tolkemec, but the feud raged on between Tecuhltli and Xotalanc, as it will rage until the last man, the last woman is dead.

'It was fifty years ago that Tecuhltli stole the wife of Xotalanc. Half a century the feud has endured. I was born in it. All in this chamber, except Tascela, were born in it. We expect to die in it.

'We are a dying race, even as those Xuchotlans our ancestors slew. When the feud began there were hundreds in each faction. Now we of Tecuhltli number only these you see before you, and the men who guard the four doors: forty in all. How many Xotalancas there are we do not know, but I doubt if they are much more numerous than we. For fifteen years no children have been born to us, and we have seen none among the Xotalancas.

'We are dying, but before we die we will slay as many of the men of Xotalanc as the gods permit.'

And with his weird eyes blazing, Olmec spoke long of that grisly feud, fought out in silent chambers and dim halls under the blaze of the green fire-jewels, on floors smoldering with the flames of hell and splashed with deeper crimson from severed veins. In that long butchery a whole generation had perished. Xotalanc was dead, long ago, slain in a grim battle on an ivory stair. Tecuhltli was dead, flayed alive by the maddened Xotalancas who had captured him.

Without emotion Olmec told of hideous battles fought in black corridors, of ambushes on twisting stairs, and red butcheries. With a redder, more abysmal gleam in his deep dark eyes he told of men and women flayed alive, mutilated and dismembered, of captives howling under tortures so ghastly that even the barbarous Cimmerian grunted. No wonder Techotl had trembled with the terror of capture. Yet he had gone forth to slay if he could, driven by hate that was stronger than his fear. Olmec spoke further, of dark and mysterious matters, of black magic and wizardry conjured out of the black night of the catacombs, of weird creatures invoked out of darkness for horrible allies. In these things the Xotalancas had the advantage, for it was in the eastern catacombs where lay the bones of the greatest wizards of the ancient Xuchotlans, with their immemorial secrets.

Valeria listened with morbid fascination. The feud had become a terrible elemental power driving the people of Xuchotl inexorably on to doom and extinction. It filled their whole lives. They were born in it, and they expected to die in it. They never left their barricaded castle except to steal forth into the Halls of Silence that lay between the opposing fortresses, to slay and be slain. Sometimes the raiders returned with frantic captives, or with grim tokens of victory in fight. Sometimes they did not return at all, or returned only as severed limbs cast down before the bolted bronze doors. It was a ghastly, unreal nightmare existence these people lived, shut off from the rest of the world, caught together like rabid rats in the same trap, butchering one another through the years, crouching and creeping through the sunless corridors to maim and torture and murder.

While Olmec talked, Valeria felt the blazing eyes of Tascela fixed upon her. The princess seemed not to hear what Olmec was saying. Her expression, as he narrated victories or defeats, did not mirror the wild rage or fiendish exultation that alternated on the faces of the other Tecuhltli. The feud that was an obsession to her clansmen seemed meaningless to her. Valeria found her indifferent callousness more repugnant than Olmec's naked ferocity.

'And we can never leave the city,' said Olmec. 'For fifty years no one has left it except those –' Again he checked himself.

'Even without the peril of the dragons,' he continued, 'we who were born and raised in the city would not dare leave it. We have never set foot outside the walls. We are not accustomed to the open sky and the naked sun. No; we were born in Xuchotl, and in Xuchotl we shall die.'

'Well,' said Conan, 'with your leave we'll take our chances with the dragons. This feud is none of our business. If you'll show us to the west gate we'll be on our way.'

Tascela's hands clenched, and she started to speak, but Olmec interrupted her: 'It is nearly nightfall. If you wander forth into the plain by night, you will certainly fall prey to the dragons.'

'We crossed it last night, and slept in the open without seeing any,' returned Conan.

Tascela smiled mirthlessly. 'You dare not leave Xuchotl!'

Conan glared at her with instinctive antagonism; she was not looking at him, but at the woman opposite him.

'I think they dare,' restorted Olmec. 'But look you, Conan and Valeria, the gods must have sent you to us, to cast victory into the laps of the Tecuhltli! You are professional fighters – why not fight for us? We have wealth in abundance – precious jewels are as common in Xuchotl as cobblestones are in the cities of the world. Some the Xuchotlans brought with them from Kosala. Some, like the firestones, they found in the hills to the east. Aid us to wipe out the Xotalancas, and we will give you all the jewels you can carry.'

'And will you help us destroy the dragons?' asked Valeria. 'With bows and poisoned arrows thirty men could slay all the dragons in the forest.'

'Aye!' replied Olmec promptly. 'We have forgotten the use of the bow, in years of hand-to-hand fighting, but we can learn again.'

'What do you say?' Valeria inquired of Conan.

'We're both penniless vagabonds,' he grinned hardily. 'I'd as soon kill Xotalancas as anybody.'

'Then you agree?' exclaimed Olmec, while Techotl fairly hugged himself with delight.

'Aye. And now suppose you show us chambers where we can sleep, so we can be fresh tomorrow for the beginning of the slaying.'

Olmec nodded, and waved a hand, and Techotl and a woman led the adventurers into a corridor which led through a door off to the left of the jade dais. A glance back showed Valeria Olmec sitting on his throne, chin on knotted fist, staring after them. His eyes burned with a weird flame. Tascela leaned back in her seat, whispering to the sullen-faced maid, Yasala, who leaned over her shoulder, her ear to the princess' moving lips.

The hallway was not so broad as most they had traversed, but it was long. Presently the woman halted, opened a door, and drew aside for Valeria to enter.

'Wait a minute,' growled Conan. 'Where do I sleep?'

Techotl pointed to a chamber across the hallway, but one door farther down. Conan hesitated, and seemed inclined to raise an objection, but Valeria smiled spitefully at him and shut the door in his face. He muttered something uncomplimentary about women in general, and strode off down the corridor after Techotl.

In the ornate chamber where he was to sleep, he glanced up at the slot-like skylights. Some were wide enough to admit the body of a slender man, supposing the glass were broken.

'Why don't the Xotalancas come over the roofs and shatter those skylights?' he asked.

'They cannot be broken,' answered Techotl. 'Besides, the

roofs would be hard to clamber over. They are mostly spires and domes and steep ridges.'

He volunteered more information about the 'castle' of Tecuhltli. Like the rest of the city it contained four stories, or tiers of chambers, with towers jutting up from the roof. Each tier was named; indeed, the people of Xuchotl had a name for each chamber, hall and stair in the city, as people of more normal cities designate streets and quarters. In Tecuhltli the floors were named The Eagle's Tier, The Ape's Tier, The Tiger's Tier and The Serpent's Tier, in the order as enumerated, The Eagle's Tier being the highest, or fourth, floor.

'Who is Tascela?' asked Conan. 'Olmec's wife?'

Techotl shuddered and glanced furtively about him before answering.

'No. She is – Tascela! She was the wife of Xotalanc – the woman Tecuhltli stole, to start the feud.'

'What are you talking about?' demanded Conan. 'That woman is beautiful and young. Are you trying to tell me that she was a wife fifty years ago?'

'Aye! I swear it! She was a full-grown woman when the Tlazitlans journeyed from Lake Zuad. It was because the king of Stygia desired her for a concubine that Xotalanc and his brother rebelled and fled into the wilderness. She is a witch, who possesses the secret of perpetual youth.'

'What's that?' asked Conan.

Techotl shuddered again.

'Ask me not! I dare not speak. It is too grisly, even for Xuchotl!'

And touching his finger to his lips, he glided from the chamber.

4   Scent of Black Lotus

Valeria unbuckled her sword-belt and laid it with the sheathed weapon on the couch where she meant to sleep. She noted that the doors were supplied with bolts, and asked where they led.

'Those lead into adjoining chambers,' answered the woman, indicating the doors on right and left. 'That one' – pointing to a copper-bound door opposite that which opened into the corridor – 'leads to a corridor which runs to a stair that descends into the catacombs. Do not fear; naught can harm you here.'

'Who spoke of fear?' snapped Valeria. 'I just like to know what sort of harbor I'm dropping anchor in. No, I don't want you to sleep at the foot of my couch. I'm not accustomed to being waited on – not by women, anyway. You have my leave to go.'

Alone in the room, the pirate shot the bolts on all the doors, kicked off her boots and stretched luxuriously out on the couch. She imagined Conan similarly situated across the corridor, but her feminine vanity prompted her to visualize him as scowling and muttering with chagrin as he cast himself on his solitary couch, and she grinned with gleeful malice as she prepared herself for slumber.

Outside, night had fallen. In the halls of Xuchotl the green fire-jewels blazed like the eyes of prehistoric cats. Somewhere among the dark towers a night wind moaned like a restless spirit. Through the dim passages stealthy figures began stealing, like disembodied shadows.

Valeria awoke suddenly on her couch. In the dusky emerald glow of the fire-gems she saw a shadowy figure bending over her. For a bemused instant the apparition seemed part of the dream she had been dreaming. She had seemed to lie on the couch in the chamber as she was actually lying, while over her pulsed and throbbed a gigantic black blossom so enormous that it hid the ceiling. Its exotic perfume pervaded her being, inducing a delicious, sensuous languor that was something more and less than sleep. She was sinking into scented billows of insensible bliss, when something touched her face. So supersensitive were her drugged senses, that the light touch was like a dislocating impact, jolting her rudely into full wakefulness. Then it was that she saw, not a gargantuan blossom, but a dark-skinned woman standing above her.

With the realization came anger and instant action. The woman turned lithely, but before she could run Valeria was on her feet and had caught her arm. She fought like a wildcat for an instant, and then subsided as she felt herself crushed by the superior strength of her captor. The pirate wrenched the woman around to face her, caught her chin with her free hand and forced her captive to meet her gaze. It was the sullen Yasala, Tascela's maid.

'What the devil were you doing bending over me? What's that in your hand?'

The woman made no reply, but sought to cast away the object. Valeria twisted her arm around in front of her, and the thing fell to the floor – a great black exotic blossom on a jade-green stem, large as a woman's head, to be sure, but tiny beside the exaggerated vision she had seen.

'The black lotus!' said Valeria between her teeth. 'The blossom whose scent brings deep sleep. You were trying to drug me! If you hadn't accidentally touched my face with the petals, you'd have – why did you do it? What's your game?'

Yasala maintained a sulky silence, and with an oath Valeria whirled her around, forced her to her knees and twisted her arm up behind her back.

'Tell me, or I'll tear your arm out of its socket!'

Yasala squirmed in anguish as her arm was forced excruciatingly up between her shoulder-blades, but a violent shaking of her head was the only answer she made.

'Slut!' Valeria cast her from her to sprawl on the floor. The pirate glared at the prostrate figure with blazing eyes. Fear and the memory of Tascela's burning eyes stirred in her, rousing all her tigerish instincts of self-preservation. These people were decadent; any sort of perversity might be expected to be encountered among them. But Valeria sensed here something that moved behind the scenes, some secret terror fouler than common degeneracy. Fear and revulsion of this weird city swept her. These people were neither sane nor normal; she began to doubt if they were even human. Madness smoldered in the eyes of them all – all except the cruel, cryptic eyes of Tascela, which held secrets and mysteries more abysmal than madness.

She lifted her head and listened intently. The halls of Xuchotl were as silent as if it were in reality a dead city. The green jewels bathed the chamber in a nightmare glow, in which the eyes of the woman on the floor glittered eerily up at her. A thrill of panic throbbed through Valeria, driving the last vestige of mercy from her fierce soul.

'Why did you try to drug me?' she muttered, grasping the woman's black hair, and forcing her head back to glare into her sullen, long-lashed eyes. 'Did Tascela send you?'

No answer. Valeria cursed venomously and slapped the woman first on one cheek and then the other. The blows resounded through the room, but Yasala made no outcry.

'Why don't you scream?' demanded Valeria savagely. 'Do you fear someone will hear you? Whom do you fear? Tascela? Olmec? Conan?'

Yasala made no reply. She crouched, watching her captor with eyes baleful as those of a basilisk. Stubborn silence always fans anger. Valeria turned and tore a handful of cords from a near-by hanging.

'You sulky slut!' she said between her teeth. 'I'm going to strip you stark naked and tie you across that couch and whip you until you tell me what you were doing here, and who sent you!'

Yasala made no verbal protest, nor did she offer any resistance, as Valeria carried out the first part of her threat with a fury that her captive's obstinacy only sharpened. Then for a space there was no sound in the chamber except the whistle and crackle of hard-woven silken cords on naked flesh. Yasala could not move her fast-bound hands or feet. Her body writhed and quivered under the chastisement, her head swayed from side to side in rhythm with the blows. Her teeth were sunk into her lower lip and a trickle of blood began as the punishment continued. But she did not cry out.

The pliant cords made no great sound as they encountered the quivering body of the captive; only a sharp crackling snap, but each cord left a red streak across Yasala's dark flesh. Valeria inflicted the punishment with all the strength of her war-hardened arm, with all the mercilessness acquired during a life where pain and torment were daily happenings, and with all the cynical ingenuity which only a woman displays toward a woman. Yasala suffered more, physically and mentally, than she would have suffered under a lash wielded by a man, however strong.

It was the application of this feminine cynicism which at last tamed Yasala.

A low whimper escaped from her lips, and Valeria paused, arm lifted, and raked back a damp yellow lock. 'Well, are you going to talk?' she demanded. 'I can keep this up all night, if necessary!'

'Mercy!' whispered the woman. 'I will tell.'

Valeria cut the cords from her wrists and ankles, and pulled her to her feet. Yasala sank down on the couch, half reclining on one bare hip, supporting herself on her arm, and writhing at the contact of her smarting flesh with the couch. She was trembling in every limb.

'Wine!' she begged, dry-lipped, indicating with a quivering

hand a gold vessel on an ivory table. 'Let me drink. I am weak with pain. Then I will tell you all.'

Valeria picked up the vessel, and Yasala rose unsteadily to receive it. She took it, raised it toward her lips – then dashed the contents full into the Aquilonian's face. Valeria reeled backward, shaking and clawing the stinging liquid out of her eyes. Through a smarting mist she saw Yasala dart across the room, fling back a bolt, throw open the copper-bound door and run down the hall. The pirate was after her instantly, sword out and murder in her heart.

But Yasala had the start, and she ran with the nervous agility of a woman who has just been whipped to the point of hysterical frenzy. She rounded a corner in the corridor, yards ahead of Valeria, and when the pirate turned it, she saw only an empty hall, and at the other end a door that gaped blackly. A damp moldy scent reeked up from it, and Valeria shivered. That must be the door that led to the catacombs. Yasala had taken refuge among the dead.

Valeria advanced to the door and looked down a flight of stone steps that vanished quickly into utter blackness. Evidently it was a shaft that led straight to the pits below the city, without opening upon any of the lower floors. She shivered slightly at the thought of the thousands of corpses lying in their stone crypts down there, wrapped in their moldering cloths. She had no intention of groping her way down those stone steps. Yasala doubtless knew every turn and twist of the subterranean tunnels.

She was turning back, baffled and furious, when a sobbing cry welled up from the blackness. It seemed to come from a great depth, but human words were faintly distinguishable, and the voice was that of a woman. 'Oh, help! Help, in Set's name! Ahhh!' It trailed away, and Valeria thought she caught the echo of a ghostly tittering.

Valeria felt her skin crawl. What had happened to Yasala

down there in the thick blackness? There was no doubt that it had been she who had cried out. But what peril could have befallen her? Was a Xotalanca lurking down there? Olmec had assured them that the catacombs below Tecuhltli were walled off from the rest, too securely for their enemies to break through. Besides, that tittering had not sounded like a human being at all.

Valeria hurried back down the corridor, not stopping to close the door that opened on the stair. Regaining her chamber, she closed the door and shot the bolt behind her. She pulled on her boots and buckled her sword-belt about her. She was determined to make her way to Conan's room and urge him, if he still lived, to join her in an attempt to fight their way out of that city of devils.

But even as she reached the door that opened into the corridor, a long-drawn scream of agony rang through the halls, followed by the stamp of running feet and the loud clangor of swords.

5   Twenty Red Nails

Two warriors lounged in the guardroom on the floor known as the Tier of the Eagle. Their attitude was casual, though habitually alert. An attack on the great bronze door from without was always a possibility, but for many years no such assault had been attempted on either side.

'The strangers are strong allies,' said one. 'Olmec will move against the enemy tomorrow, I believe.'

He spoke as a soldier in a war might have spoken. In the miniature world of Xuchotl each handful of feudists was an army, and the empty halls between the castles was the country over which they campaigned.

The other meditated for a space.

'Suppose with their aid we destroy Xotalanc,' he said. 'What then, Xatmec?'

'Why,' returned Xatmec, 'we will drive red nails for them all. The captives we will burn and flay and quarter.'

'But afterward?' pursued the other. 'After we have slain them all? Will it not seem strange, to have no foes to fight? All my life I have fought and hated the Xotalancas. With the feud ended, what is left?'

Xatmec shrugged his shoulders. His thoughts had never gone beyond the destruction of their foes. They could not go beyond that.

Suddenly both men stiffened at a noise outside the door.

'To the door, Xatmec!' hissed the last speaker. 'I shall look through the Eye –'

Xatmec, sword in hand, leaned against the bronze door, straining his ear to hear through the metal. His mate looked into the mirror. He started convulsively. Men were clustered thickly outside the door; grim, dark-faced men with swords gripped in their teeth – *and their fingers thrust into their ears*. One who wore a feathered head-dress had a set of pipes which he set to his lips, and even as the Tecuhltli started to shout a warning, the pipes began to skirl.

The cry died in the guard's throat as the thin, weird piping penetrated the metal door and smote on his ears. Xatmec leaned frozen against the door, as if paralyzed in that position. His face was that of a wooden image, his expression one of horrified listening. The other guard, farther removed from the source of the sound, yet sensed the horror of what was taking place, the grisly threat that lay in that demoniac fifing. He felt the weird strains plucking like unseen fingers at the tissues of his brain, filling him with alien emotions and impulses of madness. But with a soul-tearing effort he broke the spell, and shrieked a warning in a voice he did not recognize as his own.

But even as he cried out, the music changed to an unbearable shrilling that was like a knife in the ear-drums. Xatmec screamed in sudden agony, and all the sanity went out of his face like a flame blown out in a wind. Like a madman he ripped loose the chain, tore open the door and rushed out into the hall, sword lifted before his mate could stop him. A dozen blades struck him down, and over his mangled body the Xotalancas surged into the guardroom, with a long-drawn, blood-mad yell that sent the unwonted echoes reverberating.

His brain reeling from the shock of it all, the remaining guard leaped to meet them with goring spear. The horror of the sorcery he had just witnessed was submerged in the stunning realization that the enemy were in Tecuhltli. And as his spearhead ripped through a dark-skinned belly he knew no more, for a swinging sword crushed his skull, even as wild-eyed warriors came pouring in from the chambers behind the guardroom.

It was the yelling of men and the clanging of steel that brought Conan bounding from his couch, wide awake and broadsword in hand. In an instant he had reached the door and flung it open, and was glaring out into the corridor just as Techotl rushed up it, eyes blazing madly.

'The Xotalancas!' he screamed, in a voice hardly human. *'They are within the door!'*

Conan ran down the corridor, even as Valeria emerged from her chamber.

'What the devil is it?' she called.

'Techotl says the Xotalancas are in,' he answered hurriedly. 'That racket sounds like it.'

With the Tecuhltli on their heels they burst into the throne-room and were confronted by a scene beyond the most frantic dream of blood and fury. Twenty men and women, their black hair streaming, and the white skulls gleaming on their breasts, were locked in combat with the people of Tecuhltli. The women on both sides fought as madly as the men, and already the room and the hall beyond were strewn with corpses.

Olmec, naked but for a breech-clout, was fighting before his throne, and as the adventurers entered, Tascela ran from an inner chamber with a sword in her hand.

Xatmec and his mate were dead, so there was none to tell the Tecuhltli how their foes had found their way into their citadel. Nor was there any to say what had prompted that mad attempt. But the losses of the Xotalancas had been greater, their position more desperate, than the Tecuhltli had known. The maiming of their scaly ally, the destruction of the Burning Skull, and the news, gasped by a dying man, that mysterious white-skin allies had joined their enemies, had driven them to the frenzy of desperation and the wild determination to die dealing death to their ancient foes.

The Tecuhltli, recovering from the first stunning shock of the surprize that had swept them back into the throneroom and littered the floor with their corpses, fought back with an equally desperate fury, while the door-guards from the lower floors came racing to hurl themselves into the fray. It was the death-fight of rabid wolves, blind, panting, merciless. Back and forth it surged, from door to dais, blades whickering and striking into flesh, blood spurting, feet stamping the crimson floor where redder pools were forming. Ivory tables crashed over, seats were splintered, velvet hangings torn down were stained red. It was the bloody climax of a bloody half-century, and every man there sensed it.

But the conclusion was inevitable. The Tecuhltli outnumbered the invaders almost two to one, and they were heartened by that fact and by the entrance into the mêlée of their light-skinned allies.

These crashed into the fray with the devastating effect of a hurricane plowing through a grove of saplings. In sheer strength no three Tlazitlans were a match for Conan, and in spite of his weight he was quicker on his feet than any of them. He moved through the whirling, eddying mass with the surety and destructiveness of a gray wolf amidst a pack of alley curs, and he strode over a wake of crumpled figures.

Valeria fought beside him, her lips smiling and her eyes blazing. She was stronger than the average man, and far quicker and more ferocious. Her sword was like a living thing in her hand. Where Conan beat down opposition by the sheer weight and power of his blows, breaking spears, splitting skulls and cleaving bosoms to the breastbone, Valeria brought into action a finesse of sword-play that dazzled and bewildered her antagonists before it slew them. Again and again a warrior, heaving high his heavy blade, found her point in his jugular before he could strike. Conan, towering above the field, strode through the welter smiting right and left, but Valeria moved like an illusive phantom, constantly shifting, and thrusting and slashing as she shifted. Swords missed her again and again as the wielders flailed the empty air and died with her point in their hearts or throats, and her mocking laughter in their ears.

Neither sex nor condition was considered by the maddened combatants. The five women of the Xotalancas were down with their throats cut before Conan and Valeria entered the fray, and when a man or woman went down under the stamping feet, there was always a knife ready for the helpless throat, or a sandaled foot eager to crush the prostrate skull.

From wall to wall, from door to door rolled the waves of combat, spilling over into adjoining chambers. And presently only Tecuhltli and their white-skinned allies stood upright in the great throneroom. The survivors stared bleakly and blankly at each other, like survivors after Judgment Day or the destruction of the world. On legs wide-braced, hands gripping notched and dripping swords, blood trickling down their arms, they stared at one another across the mangled corpses of friends and foes. They had no breath left to shout, but a bestial mad howling rose from their lips. It was not a human cry of triumph. It was the howling of a rabid wolf-pack stalking among the bodies of its victims.

Conan caught Valeria's arm and turned her about.

'You've got a stab in the calf of your leg,' he growled.

She glanced down, for the first time aware of a stinging in the muscles of her leg. Some dying man on the floor had fleshed his dagger with his last effort.

'You look like a butcher yourself,' she laughed.

He shook a red shower from his hands.

'Not mine. Oh, a scratch here and there. Nothing to bother about. But that calf ought to be bandaged.'

Olmec came through the litter, looking like a ghoul with his naked massive shoulders splashed with blood, and his black beard dabbled in crimson. His eyes were red, like the reflection of flame on black water.

'We have won!' he croaked dazedly. 'The feud is ended! The dogs of Xotalanc lie dead! Oh, for a captive to flay alive! Yet it is good to look upon their dead faces. Twenty dead dogs! Twenty red nails for the black column!'

'You'd best see to your wounded,' grunted Conan, turning away from him. 'Here, girl, let me see that leg.'

'Wait a minute!' she shook him off impatiently. The fire of fighting still burned brightly in her soul. 'How do we know these are all of them? These might have come on a raid of their own.'

'They would not split the clan on a foray like this,' said Olmec, shaking his head, and regaining some of his ordinary intelligence. Without his purple robe the man seemed less like a prince than some repellent beast of prey. 'I will stake my head upon it that we have slain them all. There were less of them than I dreamed, and they must have been desperate. But how came they in Tecuhltli?'

Tascela came forward, wiping her sword on her naked thigh, and holding in her other hand an object she had taken from the body of the feathered leader of the Xotalancas.

'The pipes of madness,' she said. 'A warrior tells me that

Xatmec opened the door to the Xotalancas and was cut down as they stormed into the guardroom. This warrior came to the guardroom from the inner hall just in time to see it happen and to hear the last of a weird strain of music which froze his very soul. Tolkemec used to talk of these pipes, which the Xuchotlans swore were hidden somewhere in the catacombs with the bones of the ancient wizard who used them in his lifetime. Somehow the dogs of Xotalanc found them and learned their secret.'

'Somebody ought to go to Xotalanc and see if any remain alive,' said Conan. 'I'll go if somebody will guide me.'

Olmec glanced at the remnants of his people. There were only twenty left alive, and of these several lay groaning on the floor. Tascela was the only one of the Tecuhltli who had escaped without a wound. The princess was untouched, though she had fought as savagely as any.

'Who will go with Conan to Xotalanc?' asked Olmec.

Techotl limped forward. The wound in his thigh had started bleeding afresh, and he had another gash across his ribs.

'I will go!'

'No, you won't,' vetoed Conan. 'And you're not going either, Valeria. In a little while that leg will be getting stiff.'

'I will go,' volunteered a warrior, who was knotting a bandage about a slashed forearm.

'Very well, Yanath. Go with the Cimmerian. And you, too, Topal.' Olmec indicated another man whose injuries were slight. 'But first aid us to lift the badly wounded on these couches where we may bandage their hurts.'

This was done quickly. As they stooped to pick up a woman who had been stunned by a war-club, Olmec's beard brushed Topal's ear. Conan thought the prince muttered something to the warrior, but he could not be sure. A few moments later he was leading his companions down the hall.

Conan glanced back as he went out the door, at that shambles where the dead lay on the smoldering floor, blood-stained dark limbs knotted in attitudes of fierce muscular effort, dark faces frozen in masks of hate, glassy eyes glaring up at the green fire-jewels which bathed the ghastly scene in a dusky emerald witch-light. Among the dead the living moved aimlessly, like people moving in a trance. Conan heard Olmec call a woman and direct her to bandage Valeria's leg. The pirate followed the woman into an adjoining chamber, already beginning to limp slightly.

Warily the two Tecuhltli led Conan along the hall beyond the bronze door, and through chamber after chamber shimmering in the green fire. They saw no one, heard no sound. After they crossed the Great Hall which bisected the city from north to south, their caution was increased by the realization of their nearness to enemy territory. But chambers and halls lay empty to their wary gaze, and they came at last along a broad dim hall-way and halted before a bronze door similar to the Eagle Door of Tecuhltli. Gingerly they tried it, and it opened silently under their fingers. Awed, they stared into the green-lit chambers beyond. For fifty years no Tecuhltli had entered those halls save as a prisoner going to a hideous doom. To go to Xotalanc had been the ultimate horror that could befall a man of the western castle. The terror of it had stalked through their dreams since earliest childhood. To Yanath and Topal that bronze door was like the portal of hell.

They cringed back, unreasoning horror in their eyes, and Conan pushed past them and strode into Xotalanc.

Timidly they followed him. As each man set foot over the threshold he stared and glared wildly about him. But only their quick, hurried breathing disturbed the silence.

They had come into a square guardroom, like that behind the Eagle Door of Tecuhltli, and, similarly, a hall ran away from it to a broad chamber that was a counterpart of Olmec's throne-room.

Conan glanced down the hall with its rugs and divans and

hangings, and stood listening intently. He heard no noise, and the rooms had an empty feel. He did not believe there were any Xotalancas left alive in Xuchotl.

'Come on,' he muttered, and started down the hall.

He had not gone far when he was aware that only Yanath was following him. He wheeled back to see Topal standing in an attitude of horror, one arm out as if to fend off some threatening peril, his distended eyes fixed with hypnotic intensity on something protruding from behind a divan.

'What the devil?' Then Conan saw what Topal was staring at, and he felt a faint twitching of the skin between his giant shoulders. A monstrous head protruded from behind the divan, a reptilian head, broad as the head of a crocodile, with down-curving fangs that projected over the lower jaw. But there was an unnatural limpness about the thing, and the hideous eyes were glazed.

Conan peered behind the couch. It was a great serpent which lay there limp in death, but such a serpent as he had never seen in his wanderings. The reek and chill of the deep black earth were about it, and its color was an indeterminable hue which changed with each new angle from which he surveyed it. A great wound in the neck showed what had caused its death.

'It is the Crawler!' whispered Yanath.

'It's the thing I slashed on the stair,' grunted Conan. 'After it trailed us to the Eagle Door, it dragged itself here to die. How could the Xotalancas control such a brute?'

The Tecuhltli shivered and shook their heads.

'They brought it up from the black tunnels *below* the catacombs. They discovered secrets unknown to Tecuhltli.'

'Well, it's dead, and if they'd had any more of them, they'd have brought them along when they came to Tecuhltli. Come on.'

They crowded close at his heels as he strode down the hall and thrust on the silver-worked door at the other end.

'If we don't find anybody on this floor,' he said, 'we'll descend into the lower floors. We'll explore Xotalanc from the roof to the catacombs. If Xotalanc is like Tecuhltli, all the rooms and halls in this tier will be lighted – what the devil!'

They had come into the broad throne-chamber, so similar to that one in Tecuhltli. There were the same jade dais and ivory seat, the same divans, rugs and hangings on the walls. No black, red-scarred column stood behind the throne-dais, but evidences of the grim feud were not lacking.

Ranged along the wall behind the dais were rows of glass-covered shelves. And on those shelves hundreds of human heads, perfectly preserved, stared at the startled watchers with emotionless eyes, as they had stared for only the gods knew how many months and years.

Topal muttered a curse, but Yanath stood silent, the mad light growing in his wide eyes. Conan frowned, knowing that Tlazitlan sanity was hung on a hair-trigger.

Suddenly Yanath pointed to the ghastly relics with a twitching finger.

'There is my brother's head!' he murmured. 'And there is my father's younger brother! And there beyond them is my sister's eldest son!'

Suddenly he began to weep, dry-eyed, with harsh, loud sobs that shook his frame. He did not take his eyes from the heads. His sobs grew shriller, changed to frightful, high-pitched laughter, and that in turn became an unbearable screaming. Yanath was stark mad.

Conan laid a hand on his shoulder, and as if the touch had released all the frenzy in his soul, Yanath screamed and whirled, striking at the Cimmerian with his sword. Conan parried the blow, and Topal tried to catch Yanath's arm. But the madman avoided him and with froth flying from his lips, he drove his sword deep into Topal's body. Topal sank down with a groan, and Yanath whirled for an instant like a crazy dervish; then he ran at the shelves and began hacking at the glass with his sword, screeching blasphemously.

Conan sprang at him from behind, trying to catch him unaware and disarm him, but the madman wheeled and lunged at him, screaming like a lost soul. Realizing that the warrior was hopelessly insane, the Cimmerian side-stepped, and as the maniac went past, he swung a cut that severed the shoulder-bone and breast, and dropped the man dead beside his dying victim.

Conan bent over Topal, seeing that the man was at his last gasp. It was useless to seek to stanch the blood gushing from the horrible wound.

'You're done for, Topal,' grunted Conan. 'Any word you want to send to your people?'

'Bend closer,' gasped Topal, and Conan complied – and an instant later caught the man's wrist as Topal struck at his breast with a dagger.

'Crom!' swore Conan. 'Are you mad, too?'

'Olmec ordered it!' gasped the dying man. 'I know not why. As we lifted the wounded upon the couches he whispered to me, bidding me to slay you as we returned to Tecuhltli –' And with the name of his clan on his lips, Topal died.

Conan scowled down at him in puzzlement. This whole affair had an aspect of lunacy. Was Olmec mad, too? Were all the Tecuhltli madder than he had realized? With a shrug of his shoulders he strode down the hall and out of the bronze door, leaving the dead Tecuhltli lying before the staring dead eyes of their kinsmen's heads.

Conan needed no guide back through the labyrinth they had traversed. His primitive instinct of direction led him unerringly along the route they had come. He traversed it as warily as he had before, his sword in his hand, and his eyes fiercely searching each shadowed nook and corner; for it was his former allies he feared now, not the ghosts of the slain Xotalancas.

He had crossed the Great Hall and entered the chambers beyond when he heard something moving ahead of him – something which gasped and panted, and moved with a strange, floundering, scrambling noise. A moment later Conan saw a man crawling over the flaming floor toward him – a man whose progress left a broad bloody smear on the smoldering surface. It was Techotl and his eyes were already glazing; from a deep gash in his breast blood gushed steadily between the fingers of his clutching hand. With the other he clawed and hitched himself along.

'Conan,' he cried chokingly, 'Conan! Olmec has taken the yellow-haired woman!'

'So that's why he told Topal to kill me!' murmured Conan, dropping to his knee beside the man, who his experienced eye told him was dying. 'Olmec isn't so mad as I thought.'

Techotl's groping fingers plucked at Conan's arm. In the cold, loveless and altogether hideous life of the Tecuhltli his admiration and affection for the invaders from the outer world formed a warm, human oasis, constituted a tie that connected him with a more natural humanity that was totally lacking in his fellows, whose only emotions were hate, lust and the urge of sadistic cruelty.

'I sought to oppose him,' gurgled Techotl, blood bubbling frothily to his lips. 'But he struck me down. He thought he had slain me, but I crawled away. Ah, Set, how far I have crawled in my own blood! Beware, Conan! Olmec may have set an ambush for your return! Slay Olmec! He is a beast. Take Valeria and flee! Fear not to traverse the forest. Olmec and Tascela lied about the dragons. They slew each other years ago, all save the strongest. For a dozen years there has been only one dragon. If you have slain him, there is naught in the forest to harm you. He was the god Olmec worshipped; and Olmec fed human sacrifices to him, the very old and the very young, bound and hurled from the wall. Hasten! Olmec has taken Valeria to the Chamber of the –'

His head slumped down and he was dead before it came to rest on the floor.

Conan sprang up, his eyes like live coals. So that was Olmec's game, having first used the strangers to destroy his foes! He should have known that something of the sort would be going on in that black-bearded degenerate's mind.

The Cimmerian started toward Tecuhltli with reckless speed. Rapidly he reckoned the numbers of his former allies. Only twenty-one, counting Olmec, had survived that fiendish battle in the throneroom. Three had died since, which left seventeen enemies with which to reckon. In his rage Conan felt capable of accounting for the whole clan single-handed.

But the innate craft of the wilderness rose to guide his berserk rage. He remembered Techotl's warning of an ambush. It was quite probable that the prince would make such provisions, on the chance that Topal might have failed to carry out his order. Olmec would be expecting him to return by the same route he had followed in going to Xotalanc.

Conan glanced up at a skylight under which he was passing and caught the blurred glimmer of stars. They had not yet begun to pale for dawn. The events of the night had been crowded into a comparatively short space of time.

He turned aside from his direct course and descended a winding staircase to the floor below. He did not know where the door was to be found that let into the castle on that level, but he knew he could find it. How he was to force the locks he did not know; he believed that the doors of Tecuhltli would all be locked and bolted, if for no other reason than the habits of half a century. But there was nothing else but to attempt it.

Sword in hand, he hurried noiselessly on through a maze of green-lit or shadowy rooms and halls. He knew he must be near Tecuhltli, when a sound brought him up short. He recognized it for what it was – a human being trying to cry out through a stifling gag. It came from somewhere ahead of him, and to the left.

In those deathly-still chambers a small sound carried a long way.

Conan turned aside and went seeking after the sound, which continued to be repeated. Presently he was glaring through a doorway upon a weird scene. In the room into which he was looking a low rack-like frame of iron lay on the floor, and a giant figure was bound prostrate upon it. His head rested on a bed of iron spikes, which were already crimson-pointed with blood where they had pierced his scalp. A peculiar harness-like contrivance was fastened about his head, though in such a manner that the leather band did not protect his scalp from the spikes. This harness was connected by a slender chain to the mechanism that upheld a huge iron ball which was suspended above the captive's hairy breast. As long as the man could force himself to remain motionless the iron ball hung in its place. But when the pain of the iron points caused him to lift his head, the ball lurched downward a few inches. Presently his aching neck muscles would no longer support his head in its unnatural position and it would fall back on the spikes again. It was obvious that eventually the ball would crush him to a pulp, slowly and inexorably. The victim was gagged, and above the gag his great black ox-eyes rolled wildly toward the man in the doorway, who stood in silent amazement. The man on the rack was Olmec, prince of Tecuhltli.

6   The Eyes of Tascela

'Why did you bring me into this chamber to bandage my legs?' demanded Valeria. 'Couldn't you have done it just as well in the throneroom?'

She sat on a couch with her wounded leg extended upon it, and the Tecuhltli woman had just bound it with silk bandages. Valeria's red-stained sword lay on the couch beside her.

She frowned as she spoke. The woman had done her task silently and efficiently, but Valeria liked neither the lingering, caressing touch of her slim fingers nor the expression in her eyes.

'They have taken the rest of the wounded into the other chambers,' answered the woman in the soft speech of the Tecuhltli women, which somehow did not suggest either softness or gentleness in the speakers. A little while before, Valeria had seen this same woman stab a Xotalanca woman through the breast and stamp the eyeballs out of a wounded Xotalanca man.

'They will be carrying the corpses of the dead down into the catacombs,' she added, 'lest the ghosts escape into the chambers and dwell there.'

'Do you believe in ghosts?' asked Valeria.

'I know the ghost of Tolkemec dwells in the catacombs,' she answered with a shiver. 'Once I saw it, as I crouched in a crypt among the bones of a dead queen. It passed by in the form of an ancient man with flowing white beard and locks, and luminous eyes that blazed in the darkness. It was Tolkemec; I saw him living when I was a child and he was being tortured.'

Her voice sank to a fearful whisper: 'Olmec laughs, but I *know* Tolkemec's ghost dwells in the catacombs! They say it is rats which gnaw the flesh from the bones of the newly dead – but ghosts eat flesh. Who knows but that –'

She glanced up quickly as a shadow fell across the couch. Valeria looked up to see Olmec gazing down at her. The prince had cleansed his hands, torso and beard of the blood that had splashed them; but he had not donned his robe, and his great dark-skinned hairless body and limbs renewed the impression of strength bestial in its nature. His deep black eyes burned with a more elemental light, and there was the suggestion of a twitching in the fingers that tugged at his thick blue-black beard.

He stared fixedly at the woman, and she rose and glided from

524 *Heroes in the Wind: From Kull to Conan*

the chamber. As she passed through the door she cast a look over her shoulder at Valeria, a glance full of cynical derision and obscene mockery.

'She has done a clumsy job,' criticized the prince, coming to the divan and bending over the bandage. 'Let me see –'

With a quickness amazing in one of his bulk he snatched her sword and threw it across the chamber. His next move was to catch her in his giant arms.

Quick and unexpected as the move was, she almost matched it; for even as he grabbed her, her dirk was in her hand and she stabbed murderously at his throat. More by luck than skill he caught her wrist, and then began a savage wrestling-match. She fought him with fists, feet, knees, teeth and nails, with all the strength of her magnificent body and all the knowledge of hand-to-hand fighting she had acquired in her years of roving and fighting on sea and land. It availed her nothing against his brute strength. She lost her dirk in the first moment of contact, and thereafter found herself powerless to inflict any appreciable pain on her giant attacker.

The blaze in his weird black eyes did not alter, and their expression filled her with fury, fanned by the sardonic smile that seemed carved upon his bearded lips. Those eyes and that smile contained all the cruel cynicism that seethes below the surface of a sophisticated and degenerate race, and for the first time in her life Valeria experienced fear of a man. It was like struggling against some huge elemental force; his iron arms thwarted her efforts with an ease that sent panic racing through her limbs. He seemed impervious to any pain she could inflict. Only once, when she sank her white teeth savagely into his wrist so that the blood started, did he react. And that was to buffet her brutally upon the side of the head with his open hand, so that stars flashed before her eyes and her head rolled on her shoulders.

Her shirt had been torn open in the struggle, and with cynical cruelty he rasped his thick beard across her bare breasts, bringing the blood to suffuse the fair skin, and fetching a cry of pain and outraged fury from her. Her convulsive resistance was useless; she was crushed down on a couch, disarmed and panting, her eyes blazing up at him like the eyes of a trapped tigress.

A moment later he was hurrying from the chamber, carrying her in his arms. She made no resistance, but the smoldering of her eyes showed that she was unconquered in spirit, at least. She had not cried out. She knew that Conan was not within call, and it did not occur to her that any in Tecuhltli would oppose their prince. But she noticed that Olmec went stealthily, with his head on one side as if listening for sounds of pursuit, and he did not return to the throne chamber. He carried her through a door that stood opposite that through which he had entered, crossed another room and began stealing down a hall. As she became convinced that he feared some opposition to the abduction, she threw back her head and screamed at the top of her lusty voice.

She was rewarded by a slap that half stunned her, and Olmec quickened his pace to a shambling run.

But her cry had been echoed, and twisting her head about, Valeria, through the tears and stars that partly blinded her, saw Techotl limping after them.

Olmec turned with a snarl, shifting the woman to an uncomfortable and certainly undignified position under one huge arm, where he held her writhing and kicking vainly, like a child.

'Olmec!' protested Techotl. 'You cannot be such a dog as to do this thing! She is Conan's woman! She helped us slay the Xotalancas, and –'

Without a word Olmec balled his free hand into a huge fist and stretched the wounded warrior senseless at his feet. Stooping, and hindered not at all by the struggles and imprecations of his captive, he drew Techotl's sword from its sheath and stabbed the warrior in the breast. Then casting aside the weapon he fled on along the corridor. He did not see a woman's dark face peer cautiously after him from behind a hanging. It vanished, and presently Techotl groaned and stirred, rose dazedly and staggered drunkenly away, calling Conan's name.

Olmec hurried on down the corridor, and descended a winding ivory staircase. He crossed several corridors and halted at last in a broad chamber whose doors were veiled with heavy tapestries, with one exception – a heavy bronze door similar to the Door of the Eagle on the upper floor.

He was moved to rumble, pointing to it: 'That is one of the outer doors of Tecuhltli. For the first time in fifty years it is unguarded. We need not guard it now, for Xotalanc is no more.'

'Thanks to Conan and me, you bloody rogue!' sneered Valeria, trembling with fury and the shame of physical coercion. 'You treacherous dog! Conan will cut your throat for this!'

Olmec did not bother to voice his belief that Conan's own gullet had already been severed according to his whispered command. He was too utterly cynical to be at all interested in her thoughts or opinions. His flame-lit eyes devoured her, dwelling burningly on the generous expanses of clear white flesh exposed where her shirt and breeches had been torn in the struggle.

'Forget Conan,' he said thickly. 'Olmec is lord of Xuchotl. Xotalanc is no more. There will be no more fighting. We shall spend our lives in drinking and love-making. First let us drink!'

He seated himself on an ivory table and pulled her down on his knees, like a dark-skinned satyr with a white nymph in his arms. Ignoring her un-nymphlike profanity, he held her helpless with one great arm about her waist while the other reached across the table and secured a vessel of wine.

'Drink!' he commanded, forcing it to her lips, as she writhed her head away.

The liquor slopped over, stinging her lips, splashing down on her naked breasts.

'Your guest does not like your wine, Olmec,' spoke a cool, sardonic voice.

Olmec stiffened; fear grew in his flaming eyes. Slowly he swung his great head about and stared at Tascela who posed negligently in the curtained doorway, one hand on her smooth hip. Valeria twisted herself about in his iron grip, and when she met the burning eyes of Tascela, a chill tingled along her supple spine. New experiences were flooding Valeria's proud soul that night. Recently she had learned to fear a man; now she knew what it was to fear a woman.

Olmec sat motionless, a gray pallor growing under his swarthy skin. Tascela brought her other hand from behind her and displayed a small gold vessel.

'I feared she would not like your wine, Olmec,' purred the princess, 'so I brought some of mine, some I brought with me long ago from the shores of Lake Zuad – do you understand, Olmec?'

Beads of sweat stood out suddenly on Olmec's brow. His muscles relaxed, and Valeria broke away and put the table between them. But though reason told her to dart from the room, some fascination she could not understand held her rigid, watching the scene.

Tascela came toward the seated prince with a swaying, undulating walk that was mockery in itself. Her voice was soft, slurringly caressing, but her eyes gleamed. Her slim fingers stroked his beard lightly.

'You are selfish, Olmec,' she crooned, smiling. 'You would keep our handsome guest to yourself, though you knew I wished to entertain her. You are much at fault, Olmec!'

The mask dropped for an instant; her eyes flashed, her face was contorted and with an appalling show of strength her hand locked convulsively in his beard and tore out a great handful. This evidence of unnatural strength was no more terrifying than the momentary baring of the hellish fury that raged under her bland exterior.

Olmec lurched up with a roar, and stood swaying like a bear, his mighty hands clenching and unclenching.

'Slut!' His booming voice filled the room. 'Witch! She-devil! Tecuhltli should have slain you fifty years ago! Begone! I have endured too much from you! This white-skinned wench is mine! Get hence before I slay you!'

The princess laughed and dashed the blood-stained strands into his face. Her laughter was less merciful than the ring of flint on steel.

'Once you spoke otherwise, Olmec,' she taunted. 'Once, in your youth, you spoke words of love. Aye, you were my lover once, years ago, and because you loved me, you slept in my arms beneath the enchanted lotus – and thereby put into my hands the chains that enslaved you. You know you cannot withstand me. You know I have but to gaze into your eyes, with the mystic power a priest of Stygia taught me, long ago, and you are powerless. You remember the night beneath the black lotus that waved above us, stirred by no worldly breeze; you scent again the unearthly perfumes that stole and rose like a cloud about you to enslave you. You cannot fight against me. You are my slave as you were that night – as you shall be so long as you shall live, Olmec of Xuchotl!'

Her voice had sunk to a murmur like the rippling of a stream running through starlit darkness. She leaned close to the prince and spread her long tapering fingers upon his giant breast. His eyes glazed, his great hands fell limply to his sides.

With a smile of cruel malice, Tascela lifted the vessel and placed it to his lips.

'Drink!'

Mechanically the prince obeyed. And instantly the glaze passed from his eyes and they were flooded with fury, comprehension and an awful fear. His mouth gaped, but no sound issued. For an instant he reeled on buckling knees, and then fell in a sodden heap on the floor.

His fall jolted Valeria out of her paralysis. She turned and sprang toward the door, but with a movement that would have shamed a leaping panther, Tascela was before her. Valeria struck at her with her clenched fist, and all the power of her supple body behind the blow. It would have stretched a man senseless on the floor. But with a lithe twist of her torso, Tascela avoided the blow and caught the pirate's wrist. The next instant Valeria's left hand was imprisoned, and holding her wrists together with one hand, Tascela calmly bound them with a cord she drew from her girdle. Valeria thought she had tasted the ultimate in humiliation already that night, but her shame at being manhandled by Olmec was nothing to the sensations that now shook her supple frame. Valeria had always been inclined to despise the other members of her sex; and it was overwhelming to encounter another woman who could handle her like a child. She scarcely resisted at all when Tascela forced her into a chair and drawing her bound wrists down between her knees, fastened them to the chair.

Casually stepping over Olmec, Tascela walked to the bronze door and shot the bolt and threw it open, revealing a hallway without.

'Opening upon this hall,' she remarked, speaking to her feminine captive for the first time, 'there is a chamber which in old times was used as a torture room. When we retired into Tecuhltli, we brought most of the apparatus with us, but there was one piece too heavy to move. It is still in working order. I think it will be quite convenient now.'

An understanding flame of terror rose in Olmec's eyes. Tascela strode back to him, bent and gripped him by the hair.

'He is only paralyzed temporarily,' she remarked conversationally. 'He can hear, think, and feel – aye, he can feel very well indeed!'

With which sinister observation she started toward the door, dragging the giant bulk with an ease that made the pirate's eyes dilate. She passed into the hall and moved down it without hesitation, presently disappearing with her captive into a chamber that opened into it, and whence shortly thereafter issued the clank of iron.

Valeria swore softly and tugged vainly, with her legs braced against the chair. The cords that confined her were apparently unbreakable.

Tascela presently returned alone; behind her a muffled groaning issued from the chamber. She closed the door but did not bolt it. Tascela was beyond the grip of habit, as she was beyond the touch of other human instincts and emotions.

Valeria sat dumbly, watching the woman in whose slim hands, the pirate realized, her destiny now rested.

Tascela grasped her yellow locks and forced back her head, looking impersonally down into her face. But the glitter in her dark eyes was not impersonal.

'I have chosen you for a great honor,' she said. 'You shall restore the youth of Tascela. Oh, you stare at that! My appearance is that of youth, but through my veins creeps the sluggish chill of approaching age, as I have felt it a thousand times before. I am old, so old I do not remember my childhood. But I was a girl once, and a priest of Stygia loved me, and gave me the secret of immortality and youth everlasting. He died, then – some said by poison. But I dwelt in my palace by the shores of Lake Zuad and the passing years touched me not. So at last a king of Stygia desired me, and my people rebelled and brought me to this land. Olmec called me a princess. I am not of royal blood. I am greater than a princess. I am Tascela, whose youth your own glorious youth shall restore.'

Valeria's tongue clove to the roof of her mouth. She sensed here a mystery darker than the degeneracy she had anticipated.

The taller woman unbound the Aquilonian's wrists and pulled her to her feet. It was not fear of the dominant strength that lurked in the princess' limbs that made Valeria a helpless, quivering captive in her hands. It was the burning, hypnotic, terrible eyes of Tascela.

7   He Comes from the Dark

'Well, I'm a Kushite!'

Conan glared down at the man on the iron rack.

'What the devil are *you* doing on that thing?'

Incoherent sounds issued from behind the gag and Conan bent and tore it away, evoking a bellow of fear from the captive; for his action caused the iron ball to lurch down until it nearly touched the broad breast.

'Be careful, for Set's sake!' begged Olmec.

'What for?' demanded Conan. 'Do you think I care what happens to you? I only wish I had time to stay here and watch that chunk of iron grind your guts out. But I'm in a hurry. Where's Valeria?'

'Loose me!' urged Olmec. 'I will tell you all!'

'Tell me first.'

'Never!' The prince's heavy jaws set stubbornly.

'All right.' Conan seated himself on a near-by bench. 'I'll find her myself, after you've been reduced to a jelly. I believe I can speed up that process by twisting my sword-point around in your ear,' he added, extending the weapon experimentally.

'Wait!' Words came in a rush from the captive's ashy lips. 'Tascela took her from me. I've never been anything but a puppet in Tascela's hands.'

'Tascela?' snorted Conan, and spat. 'Why, the filthy –'

'No, no!' panted Olmec. 'It's worse than you think. Tascela is old – centuries old. She renews her life and her youth by the sacrifice of beautiful young women. That's one thing that has reduced the clan to its present state. She will draw the essence of Valeria's life into her own body, and bloom with fresh vigor and beauty.'

'Are the doors locked?' asked Conan, thumbing his sword edge.

'Aye! But I know a way to get into Tecuhltli. Only Tascela and I know, and she thinks me helpless and you slain. Free me and I swear I will help you rescue Valeria. Without my help you cannot win into Techultli; for even if you tortured me into revealing the secret, you couldn't work it. Let me go, and we will steal on Tascela and kill her before she can work magic – before she can fix her eyes on us. A knife thrown from behind will do the work. I should have killed her thus long ago, but I feared that without her to aid us the Xotalancas would overcome us. She needed my help, too; that's the only reason she let me live this long. Now neither needs the other, and one must die. I swear that when we have slain the witch, you and Valeria shall go free without harm. My people will obey me when Tascela is dead.'

Conan stooped and cut the ropes that held the prince, and Olmec slid cautiously from under the great ball and rose, shaking his head like a bull and muttering imprecations as he fingered his lacerated scalp. Standing shoulder to shoulder the two men presented a formidable picture of primitive power. Olmec was as tall as Conan, and heavier; but there was something repellent about the Tlazitlan, something abysmal and monstrous that contrasted unfavorably with the clean-cut, compact hardness of the Cimmerian. Conan had discarded the remnants of his tattered, blood-soaked shirt, and stood with his remarkable muscular development impressively revealed. His great shoulders were as broad as those of Olmec, and more cleanly outlined, and his huge breast arched with a more impressive sweep to a hard waist that lacked the paunchy thickness of Olmec's midsection. He might have been an image of primal strength cut out of bronze. Olmec was darker, but not from the burning of the sun. If Conan was a figure out of the dawn of Time, Olmec was a shambling, somber shape from the darkness of Time's pre-dawn.

'Lead on,' demanded Conan. 'And keep ahead of me. I don't trust you any farther than I can throw a bull by the tail.'

Olmec turned and stalked on ahead of him, one hand twitching slightly as it plucked at his matted beard.

Olmec did not lead Conan back to the bronze door, which the prince naturally supposed Tascela had locked, but to a certain chamber on the border of Tecuhltli.

'This secret has been guarded for half a century,' he said. 'Not even our own clan knew of it, and the Xotalancas never learned. Tecuhltli himself built this secret entrance, afterward slaying the slaves who did the work; for he feared that he might find himself locked out of his own kingdom some day because of the spite of Tascela, whose passion for him soon changed to hate. But she discovered the secret, and barred the hidden door against him one day as he fled back from an unsuccessful raid, and the Xotalancas took him and flayed him. But once, spying upon her, I saw her enter Tecuhltli by this route, and so learned the secret.'

He pressed upon a gold ornament in the wall, and a panel swung inward, disclosing an ivory stair leading upward.

'This stair is built within the wall,' said Olmec. 'It leads up to a tower upon the roof, and thence other stairs wind down to the various chambers. Hasten!'

'After you, comrade!' retorted Conan satirically, swaying his broadsword as he spoke, and Olmec shrugged his shoulders and stepped onto the staircase. Conan instantly followed him, and the door shut behind them. Far above a cluster of fire-jewels made the staircase a well of dusky dragon-light.

They mounted until Conan estimated that they were above the level of the fourth floor, and then came out into a cylindrical tower, in the domed roof of which was set the bunch of fire-jewels that lighted the stair. Through gold-barred windows, set with unbreakable crystal panes, the first windows he had seen in

Xuchotl, Conan got a glimpse of high ridges, domes and more towers, looming darkly against the stars. He was looking across the roofs of Xuchotl.

Olmec did not look through the windows. He hurried down one of the several stairs that wound down from the tower, and when they had descended a few feet, this stair changed into a narrow corridor that wound tortuously on for some distance. It ceased at a steep flight of steps leading downward. There Olmec paused.

Up from below, muffled, but unmistakable, welled a woman's scream, edged with fright, fury and shame. And Conan recognized Valeria's voice.

In the swift rage roused by that cry, and the amazement of wondering what peril could wring such a shriek from Valeria's reckless lips, Conan forgot Olmec. He pushed past the prince and started down the stair. Awakening instinct brought him about again, just as Olmec struck with his great mallet-like fist. The blow, fierce and silent, was aimed at the base of Conan's brain. But the Cimmerian wheeled in time to receive the buffet on the side of his neck instead. The impact would have snapped the vertebræ of a lesser man. As it was, Conan swayed backward, but even as he reeled he dropped his sword, useless at such close quarters, and grasped Olmec's extended arm, dragging the prince with him as he fell. Headlong they went down the steps together, in a revolving whirl of limbs and heads and bodies. And as they went Conan's iron fingers found and locked in Olmec's bull-throat.

The barbarian's neck and shoulder felt numb from the sledge-like impact of Olmec's huge fist, which had carried all the strength of the massive forearm, thick triceps and great shoulder. But this did not affect his ferocity to any appreciable extent. Like a bulldog he hung on grimly, shaken and battered and beaten against the steps as they rolled, until at last they struck an ivory panel-door at the bottom with such an impact that they splintered it its full length and crashed through its ruins. But Olmec was already dead, for those iron fingers had crushed out his life and broken his neck as they fell.

Conan rose, shaking the splinters from his great shoulder, blinking blood and dust out of his eyes.

He was in the great throneroom. There were fifteen people in that room besides himself. The first person he saw was Valeria. A curious black altar stood before the throne-dais. Ranged about it, seven black candles in golden candlesticks sent up oozing spirals of thick green smoke, disturbingly scented. These spirals united in a cloud near the ceiling, forming a smoky arch above the altar. On that altar lay Valeria, stark naked, her white flesh gleaming in shocking contrast to the glistening ebon stone. She was not bound. She lay at full length, her arms stretched out above her head to their fullest extent. At the head of the altar knelt a young man, holding her wrists firmly. A young woman knelt at the other end of the altar, grasping her ankles. Between them she could neither rise nor move.

Eleven men and women of Tecuhltli knelt dumbly in a semi-circle, watching the scene with hot, lustful eyes.

On the ivory throne-seat Tascela lolled. Bronze bowls of incense rolled their spirals about her; the wisps of smoke curled about her naked limbs like caressing fingers. She could not sit still; she squirmed and shifted about with sensuous abandon, as if finding pleasure in the contact of the smooth ivory with her sleek flesh.

The crash of the door as it broke beneath the impact of the hurtling bodies caused no change in the scene. The kneeling men and women merely glanced incuriously at the corpse of their prince and at the man who rose from the ruins of the door, then swung their eyes greedily back to the writhing white shape on the black altar. Tascela looked insolently at him, and sprawled back on her seat, laughing mockingly.

'Slut!' Conan saw red. His hands clenched into iron hammers

as he started for her. With his first step something clanged loudly and steel bit savagely into his leg. He stumbled and almost fell, checked in his headlong stride. The jaws of an iron trap had closed on his leg, with teeth that sank deep and held. Only the ridged muscles of his calf saved the bone from being splintered. The accursed thing had sprung out of the smoldering floor without warning. He saw the slots now, in the floor where the jaws had lain, perfectly camouflaged.

'Fool!' laughed Tascela. 'Did you think I would not guard against your possible return? Every door in this chamber is guarded by such traps. Stand there and watch now, while I fulfill the destiny of your handsome friend! Then I will decide your own.'

Conan's hand instinctively sought his belt, only to encounter an empty scabbard. His sword was on the stair behind him. His poniard was lying back in the forest, where the dragon had torn it from his jaw. The steel teeth in his leg were like burning coals, but the pain was not as savage as the fury that seethed in his soul. He was trapped, like a wolf. If he had had his sword he would have hewn off his leg and crawled across the floor to slay Tascela. Valeria's eyes rolled toward him with mute appeal, and his own helplessness sent red waves of madness surging through his brain.

Dropping on the knee of his free leg, he strove to get his fingers between the jaws of the trap, to tear them apart by sheer strength. Blood started from beneath his finger nails, but the jaws fitted close about his leg in a circle whose segments jointed perfectly, contracted until there was no space between his mangled flesh and the fanged iron. The sight of Valeria's naked body added flame to the fire of his rage.

Tascela ignored him. Rising languidly from her seat she swept the ranks of her subjects with a searching glance, and asked: 'Where are Xamec, Zlanath and Tachic?'

'They did not return from the catacombs, princess,' answered a man. 'Like the rest of us, they bore the bodies of the slain into the crypts, but they have not returned. Perhaps the ghost of Tolkemec took them.'

'Be silent, fool!' she ordered harshly. 'The ghost is a myth.'

She came down from her dais, playing with a thin gold-hilted dagger. Her eyes burned like nothing on the hither side of hell. She paused beside the altar and spoke in the tense stillness.

'Your life shall make me young, white woman!' she said. 'I shall lean upon your bosom and place my lips over yours, and slowly – ah, slowly! – sink this blade through your heart, so that your life, fleeing your stiffening body, shall enter mine, making me bloom again with youth and with life everlasting!'

Slowly, like a serpent arching toward its victim, she bent down through the writhing smoke, closer and closer over the now motionless woman who stared up into her glowing dark eyes – eyes that grew larger and deeper, blazing like black moons in the swirling smoke.

The kneeling people gripped their hands and held their breath, tense for the bloody climax, and the only sound was Conan's fierce panting as he strove to tear his leg from the trap.

All eyes were glued on the altar and the white figure there; the crash of a thunderbolt could hardly have broken the spell, yet it was only a low cry that shattered the fixity of the scene and brought all whirling about – a low cry, yet one to make the hair stand up stiffly on the scalp. They looked, and they saw.

Framed in the door to the left of the dais stood a nightmare figure. It was a man, with a tangle of white hair and a matted white beard that fell over his breast. Rags only partly covered his gaunt frame, revealing half-naked limbs strangely unnatural in appearance. The skin was not like that of a normal human. There was a suggestion of *scaliness* about it, as if the owner had dwelt long under conditions almost antithetical to those conditions under which human life ordinarily thrives. And there was nothing at all human about the eyes that blazed from the tangle of white hair. They were great gleaming disks that stared unwinkingly, luminous, whitish, and without a hint of normal emotion or sanity. The mouth gaped, but no coherent words issued – only a high-pitched tittering.

'Tolkemec!' whispered Tascela, livid, while the others crouched in speechless horror. 'No myth, then, no ghost! Set! You have dwelt for twelve years in darkness! Twelve years among the bones of the dead! What grisly food did you find? What mad travesty of life did you live, in the stark blackness of that eternal night? I see now why Xamec and Zlanath and Tachic did not return from the catacombs – and never will return. But why have you waited so long to strike? Were you seeking something, in the pits? Some secret weapon you knew was hidden there? And have you found it at last?'

That hideous tittering was Tolkemec's only reply, as he bounded into the room with a long leap that carried him over the secret trap before the door – by chance, or by some faint recollection of the ways of Xuchotl. He was not mad, as a man is mad. He had dwelt apart from humanity so long that he was no longer human. Only an unbroken thread of memory embodied in hate and the urge for vengeance had connected him with the humanity from which he had been cut off, and held him lurking near the people he hated. Only that thin string had kept him from racing and prancing off for ever into the black corridors and realms of the subterranean world he had discovered, long ago.

'You sought something hidden!' whispered Tascela, cringing back. 'And you have found it! You remember the feud! After all these years of blackness, you remember!'

For in the lean hand of Tolkemec now waved a curious jade-hued wand, on the end of which glowed a knob of crimson shaped like a pomegranate. She sprang aside as he thrust it out like a spear, and a beam of crimson fire lanced from the pomegranate. It missed

Tascela, but the woman holding Valeria's ankles was in the way. It smote between her shoulders. There was a sharp crackling sound and the ray of fire flashed from her bosom and struck the black altar, with a snapping of blue sparks. The woman toppled side-wise, shriveling and withering like a mummy even as she fell.

Valeria rolled from the altar on the other side, and started for the opposite wall on all fours. For hell had burst loose in the throneroom of dead Olmec.

The man who had held Valeria's hands was the next to die. He turned to run, but before he had taken half a dozen steps, Tolkemec, with an agility appalling in such a frame, bounded around to a position that placed the man between him and the altar. Again the red fire-beam flashed and the Tecuhltli rolled lifeless to the floor, as the beam completed its course with a burst of blue sparks against the altar.

Then began slaughter. Screaming insanely the people rushed about the chamber, caroming from one another, stumbling and falling. And among them Tolkemec capered and pranced, deal-ing death. They could not escape by the doors; for apparently the metal of the portals served like the metal-veined stone altar to complete the circuit for whatever hellish power flashed like thunderbolts from the witch-wand the ancient waved in his hand. When he caught a man or a woman between him and a door or the altar, that one died instantly. He chose no special victim. He took them as they came, with his rags flapping about his wildly gyrating limbs, and the gusty echoes of his tittering sweeping the room above the screams. And bodies fell like fall-ing leaves about the altar and at the doors. One warrior in des-peration rushed at him, lifting a dagger, only to fall before he could strike. But the rest were like crazed cattle, with no thought for resistance, and no chance of escape.

The last Tecuhltli except Tascela had fallen when the princess reached the Cimmerian and the girl who had taken refuge beside him. Tascela bent and touched the floor, pressing a design upon it. Instantly the iron jaws released the bleeding limb and sank back into the floor.

'Slay him if you can!' she panted, and pressed a heavy knife into his hand. 'I have no magic to withstand him!'

With a grunt he sprang before the women, not heeding his lacerated leg in the heat of the fighting-lust. Tolkemec was coming toward him, his weird eyes ablaze, but he hesitated at the gleam of the knife in Conan's hand. Then began a grim game, as Tolkemec sought to circle about Conan and get the barbarian between him and the altar or a metal door, while Conan sought to avoid this and drive home his knife. The women watched tensely, holding their breath.

There was no sound except the rustle and scrape of quick-shifting feet. Tolkemec pranced and capered no more. He realized that grimmer game confronted him than the people who had died screaming and fleeing. In the elemental blaze of the barbarian's eyes he read an intent deadly as his own. Back and forth they weaved, and when one moved the other moved as if invisible threads bound them together. But all the time Conan was getting closer and closer to his enemy. Already the coiled muscles of his thighs were beginning to flex for a spring, when Valeria cried out. For a fleeting instant a bronze door was in line with Conan's moving body. The red line leaped, searing Conan's flank as he twisted aside, and even as he shifted he hurled the knife. Old Tolkemec went down, truly slain at last, the hilt vibrating on his breast.

Tascela sprang – not toward Conan, but toward the wand where it shimmered like a live thing on the floor. But as she leaped, so did Valeria, with a dagger snatched from a dead man, and the blade, driven with all the power of the pirate's muscles, impaled the princess of Tecuhltli so that the point stood out between her breasts. Tascela screamed once and fell dead, and Valeria spurned the body with her heel as it fell.

'I had to do that much, for my own self-respect!' panted Valeria, facing Conan across the limp corpse.

'Well, this cleans up the feud,' he grunted. 'It's been a hell of a night! Where did these people keep their food? I'm hungry.'

'You need a bandage on that leg.' Valeria ripped a length of silk from a hanging and knotted it about her waist, then tore off some smaller strips which she bound efficiently about the barbarian's lacerated limb.

'I can walk on it,' he assured her. 'Let's begone. It's dawn, outside this infernal city. I've had enough of Xuchotl. It's well the breed exterminated itself. I don't want any of their accursed jewels. They might be haunted.'

'There is enough clean loot in the world for you and me,' she said, straightening to stand tall and splendid before him.

The old blaze came back in his eyes, and this time she did not resist as he caught her fiercely in his arms.

'It's a long way to the coast,' she said presently, withdrawing her lips from his.

'What matter?' he laughed. 'There's nothing we can't conquer. We'll have our feet on a ship's deck before the Stygians open their ports for the trading season. And then we'll show the world what plundering means!'

Contemporary ... Provocative ... Outrageous ...
Prophetic ... Groundbreaking ... Funny ... Disturbing ...
Different ... Moving ... Revolutionary ... Inspiring ...
Subversive ... Life-changing ...

What makes a modern classic?

At Penguin Classics our mission has always been to make the best
books ever written available to everyone. And that also means
constantly redefining and refreshing exactly what makes a 'classic'.
That's where Modern Classics come in. Since 1961 they have been an
organic, ever-growing and ever-evolving list of books from the last
hundred (or so) years that we believe will continue to be read over and
over again.

They could be books that have inspired political dissent, such as
Animal Farm. Some, like *Lolita* or *A Clockwork Orange*, may have
caused shock and outrage. Many have led to great films, from *In Cold
Blood* to *One Flew Over the Cuckoo's Nest*. They have broken down
barriers – whether social, sexual, or, in the case of *Ulysses*, the
boundaries of language itself. And they might – like *Goldfinger* or
Scoop – just be pure classic escapism. Whatever the reason, Penguin
Modern Classics continue to inspire, entertain and enlighten millions
of readers everywhere.

'No publisher has had more influence on reading habits than Penguin'
Independent

'Penguins provided a crash course in world literature'
Guardian

The best books ever written

PENGUIN 🐧 CLASSICS

SINCE 1946

Find out more at www.penguinclassics.com